GRACE

L.G. WRIGHT

Copyright

For Mrs Jones, who believed.
And for the one who made me believe.

PROLOGUE

London, March 1953

As ever, she is punctual, he is late. He comes to the door barefooted, sock in hand.

"For Christ's sake, Daniel. It's practically noon. How are you still not dressed?"

She stops at the sight of his self-deprecating grin and the sight in his eyes of her frumpy, maternal side reflected back at her. Her half-huff is softened by a rueful half-quirk of her mouth and, shaking her head, she squeezes past him in the narrow hallway. Behind her, she can feel him craning round the door jamb to get a glimpse of the battered Ford parked on the street.

"No Michael?"

"I do listen to you, you know."

"Really?"

"It has been known."

"When?"

"Alright, so I listened to you this time."

A small victory won, Daniel strolls through the cluttered flat to the kitchen, whistling tunelessly. `

"Time for a cuppa?" he offers conciliatorily.

"We shouldn't waste time. There's no knowing what state the roads will be in."

"On your head be it," he raises his voice to be heard over the clatter of mugs and spoons. "You know I'm not worth talking to unless I've had at least one cup before we go."

She doesn't bother to respond but picks her way across the decaying grey-green carpet to the ugly, threadbare velour sofa. It is strewn with papers, variously covered in Daniel's distinctive but indecipherable scrawl, numerous crossings out and several surprisingly complex diagrams.

"What are you working on?"

"Hmm?" Daniel's head reappears around the door to the kitchen. "Oh, that. Ignore it. It won't come to anything. Just throw it on the floor if you're looking for somewhere to sit down. And," turning back to the kitchen, "before you start, don't. I'm won't be in the mood for another lecture about wasted talent, the need to settle down, my general lack of direction or any of your other favourite subjects until after at least my second cup of tea, OK?"

She can't resist his grin. "OK." She perches on the edge of the sofa and gives in to the thought uppermost in her mind. "So, do you know what it's about?"

Daniel sets two steaming mugs down on the rickety-looking coffee table. "Dad's call? I have no idea."

"Don't you think it's a bit melodramatic, a call out of the blue, demanding to see us? Not like him at all."

"Isn't it? What do they say? Still waters run deep," he teases.

"Oh, please, now you're being melodramatic. Maybe you get it from him." Silence. She can hear him chewing his nails in the background. She tries again. "You have to admit, it's not like him."

To her tuned eye, Daniel's half-shrug speaks of an unwillingness to engage more than a lack of insight. "No, it's not. He didn't have anything to say all that time we were growing up. I can't imagine what he would have to say now."

"Is that what he said to you? That there's something he has to say to us?"

"Not in so many words but that's the impression I was left with. But you know me, I can never recall a conversation properly."

"From the conversation I had with him I just thought he wanted to talk about his will or something."

"No." His sister gives a snort of exasperation. "Oh, that blasted man! How many times have we sat with him in that miserable little room struggling to make conversation and never once did he try to talk to us. And why does he have to be so mysterious? I can't believe he's got anything to say that can't just be said by phone."

"Well, we'll know soon enough."

"Daniel the peacemaker, at it again." He can hear the wry smile softening her sarcasm. "Anyway, we'd better get going," in her best school-ma'am tones. "Wouldn't want to be late for dear old Dad, would we?" Sober suddenly. "I hope it's nothing serious. At his age, you know..."

"Darling, he's fifty-seven. He's hardly ready for the glue factory yet."

"I know but he's not been the same since Mum died."

"Don't worry."

"Easier said than done."

"Yes, but if it's good news you'll have worried unnecessarily and if it's bad we'll just deal with it the way we've always dealt with everything. You and me, kid, it'll be fine."

"Less of the kid, little brother." But his calm confidence reassured her. "Ready?"

"As I'll ever be."

* * * * * * *

The wooden door has warped in the winter wet. These vast old Georgian houses are almost getting too much to maintain. Daniel pushes aside Rebecca's hand to grasp the key in the Yale lock and she moves back against the black-painted twisted iron railings at the top of the wide stone steps to give him room. He turns his left shoulder into the central panel between the two cut-glass panes and heaves his weight inwards against the wood. It gives way with a groan, a clatter of the brass door knocker and a scattering of black gloss paint chips onto the sisal doormat and black-and-white chequered marble tiles in the hallway. Daniel eases the door back to admit them both, but both hesitate on the threshold, reluctant to enter.

"Ladies first," extending a mock-courteous arm.

Narrowing her eyes at him in mock-thanks, she draws a deep breath and steps into the entrance hall.

Something is different. It isn't something she can put her finger on. At face value, the place looks the same as ever. Dark oak panelled doors to the drawing room on the left at the front, the library behind, dining room opposite, the kitchen and staff quarters at the back beyond the stairs and, to the right, her father's study. It is the same dark place it has become in her mind in the years since her mother's death, old-fashioned, poorly lit, cold, oppressive. Except it isn't cold. Instinctively, she crosses the wide hall floor, pulling off one glove and resting her hand on the Victorian-style radiator.

"He's got the central heating on," her bemusement carries through her whisper to Daniel as he uses his back to shove the door until he hears the lock click into place. He quirks an eyebrow in wry amusement. "But he never has the heating on," she defends.

As she turns to survey the hallway for other signs of change, a sudden echo catches her. Their younger selves chasing between the rooms that lead off from the entrance hall, hands hanging onto ornate architrave as they swing to change directions in a rush to catch or escape the other. Never when he was here, of course.

All the doors stand slightly ajar, giving no indication of where he is to be found.

"Dad?" she calls. "It's us."

"It was hardly going to be anyone else," comes the muffled, rusty grumble from behind the study door.

She grits her teeth at Daniel and pushes into the room. After the darkness of the wide hallway, she feels blinded in the small bright room and hesitates to allow her eyes to adjust. The heavy damask curtains in the bay window, usually fully drawn, are thrown back as far as they will go and every light in the room is lit, as is the fire in the grate.

Another change. In her memory, this room is his dark sanctuary, a small, hidden escape from the noise and life of the rest of the house, curtains carefully over-lapped to block any chink of light, dimly lit by the shaded table lamp on a dark-wood occasional table tucked against the wall between the fireplace and the brace of winged leather chairs flanking the hearth. In the darkness, the familiar smells were almost overpowering: tobacco, whisky and books. The musty, dusty smell of hundreds and hundreds of old hardback books, jacketless, dented at the corners and mottle-paged. The scent that would always be most redolent of their father.

Daniel catches Rebecca's hesitation and nudges her forward to allow him to cross to the window. He stands for a moment, taking in the view from the front of the house. The stately iron palings running down either side of the wide steps and casting along the boundary of the double-fronted Georgian terrace house, shielding the street from the drop to the basement. The wide road that runs onto the more exclusive square next to their street, choked at the edges now with nose-to-tail parked cars but which he can remember alive with perambulators, nurse-maids, children and long-skirted ladies. The exclusive central garden, secreted behind a mirroring barrier of more palings, overwhelmed in places, now as then, by glossy-leaved viburnums and laurels. His haven, his heaven. A child's haunt and hideaway.

"Thank you for coming." The sudden interruption sweeps twenty years away. The voice, perhaps through lack of use, seems rough. Daniel turns back towards the fireplace to see his father now leaning round the wing of the chair, supporting his weight on one arm. The long fingers of his right hand are tapping unconsciously on the round-headed brass tacks that both held and ornamented the dark

5

blue leather, index finger to little finger, little finger to index finger, left to right, right to left. A nervous twitch never observed before.

"Right," asserts Rebecca, "I'll see if Annie can rustle up some tea, shall I?"

She waits just long enough for the slight nod of permission – such an old instinct – before crossing back into the hall and turning to the kitchen.

Three steps takes Daniel across the width of the small square room and he hesitates on the opposite side of the fireplace from his father, resting his hand on the back of the other chair, briefly drawing on the advantage of his standing position. Then his father dips his chin, nodding Daniel into the chair, and the transitory advantage dissipates as he takes his seat and looks across into the old man's level blue gaze.

"It was good of you to come at short notice."

"You're welcome, Dad."

"We'll wait for your sister before we start."

Silence, then. Though not. The heavy tick, tick, tick of the old ormolu mantel clock marks the moments and the distant hum of traffic infiltrates through the ill-fitting wooden window frames.

If called upon to encapsulate his father in one word, that word would be, and always had been, silence. Mostly heavy silences at the dinner table or alone in his study in the evening, even in the midst of long-ago Christmas revelries with Daniel's voluble maternal family.

But, he realises now, there was background music to those silences. Literally, sometimes, in terms of the sounds of jazz music on the record player when he retreated into his study after work, but also the gentle crackle and sputter of the fire as he read in the evenings, the flick of a turned page and this interminable clock.

As Daniel lets his eyes drift around the room, he remembers the feeling of displacement it has always occasioned in him. For years, he attributed it to believing himself an intruder in this space, so clearly his father's inner sanctum, just as he believed he and Rebecca

6

were intruders in his life, children born to a man not meant to be a father. Now, he sees the room with eyes made unfamiliar by the distance of time and he has an uneasy sense that it was the room that was displaced, that it had somehow been constrained, squashed and compacted into a space too small for its original dimensions. The large leather chairs and the ornate clock are disproportionate to the mean grate and cast iron surround, a once-grand, now-threadbare Persian rug occupies too much of the floor space, the lamps teeter on occasional tables too small to provide proper support.

Of course, the sensation is heightened by the books. The bookshelves fit – the only objects that seem to have been tailored to the room – but they are ranged on every wall, floor to ceiling, functional, plain shelves that waste no space with decoration or embellishment. And the books overflow, numerous volumes stacked horizontally on top of otherwise neatly ordered lines, the only sign of disorder in a world regimented and controlled in every other respect.

Rebecca reappears in the doorway, the silver tray of their childhood teas filled with the paraphernalia of a modern-day tea break: three mugs with floating tea bags, a half-used silver top milk bottle and a depleted bag of Silver Spoon granulated sugar, complete with sterling silver spoons poking out of the top. Not that it matters. Those old routines belonged to their mother, never their father.

Daniel rises to clear a pile of books from the coffee table before the threadbare sofa squeezed behind the door. As Rebecca settles the tray and sets about straining the tea bags, pouring the milk and passing out the mugs, he sinks down onto the sofa and turns his eyes on his father. This tall, lean, spare man, little diminished by age except in the gun-metal grey of his hair; Daniel knows how paper-thin are his own defences against this distant, forbidding parent. Only through distance and detachment does he gain the strength to break free from the shadow of this most formative of relationships.

Rebecca perches on the edge of the sofa next to him, protectively wrapping her hands around her mug of tea like a shield. They glance at one another, at a loss how to break the silence. Reprobate children again, awaiting their disciplining.

Their father's chair is facing slightly away from them towards the fire and he seems lost in thought as he stares at the flame. Then he raises his head and turns to look across his shoulder towards where they sit. Acknowledging them but not attempting to meet their eyes. There is a strange tension in his face but, just for a second, the shadow of a smile plays at the corner of his mouth and Daniel catches the flame of something he can't identify burn in those cool eyes.

Silence but for the tick, tick, tick. He gives a slight nod. More a decision than an interaction.

"You must be wondering why I wanted you to come. There's something I need you to know and now is the right time. I'll tell you and then I'll explain. You'll have questions and I'll answer them if I can. And then we'll be done."

A pause. A roughly drawn breath.

"I need to tell you that the woman you thought of as your mother wasn't."

PART I - ENGLAND

Chapter One

London, December 1919

I met your mother at Christmas in 1919. She was the most striking woman I'd ever seen and her confidence, her self-possession took my breath away. We were survivors.
I had demobbed in March. A year after the war was nominally done, we were still looking for ways to rebuild the world we had shattered. I found two rocks to hold onto. First, your grandfather. Then, through him, your mother.

They were late and it was making Jack anxious. He hovered tensely at the door to their rooms, hat in hand, great coat folded neatly across his arm. Not his from France. A practical but insensitive gift from his parents that had become painfully welcome in the bitter winter currently gripping London. He glanced down at the small second-hand leather suitcase waiting on the floor at his feet for the umpteenth time, in case it might irrationally have disappeared in the thirty seconds since he last checked. He imagined he saw a speck of dirt on his shiny shoes and, licking his finger, bent down to clean away the flaw, carefully brushing his fingertips across the worn leather than had taken hours to make respectable.

As he straightened up, the bathroom door was suddenly flung open and Alfie emerged, cheerfully whistling as he used the towel flung across his shoulder to brush away the remnants of his shaving cream. His shirt was half-buttoned, the tails half-hanging out of his trousers as he heaved his braces over his shoulders.

"Jackie boy, you ready already? God, man, we've got ages yet."

With deliberation, he withdrew his father's fob watch from his waistcoat pocket and flicked open the face to show his roommate the immutable facts. "Alfie, it's gone three. If we don't leave now, we'll miss the train. I don't know about you but I can't afford to be late."

11

"Lad, you worry too much. We'll get there in plenty of time, you'll see."

Jack closed his eyes and fought to control his pulse as he half-listened to the sounds of Alfie readying himself, whistling, almost under his breath, and tapping his foot to keep time with whatever song was running through his brain. Jack could hear the throb, throb of his own pulse in his ears and fought to suppress the mounting anxiety he felt building in his brain. The room was bitterly cold, the air rapidly chilled since the paltry morning fire in the grate had petered out. He could hear the dominant roar of the cars in the road and, more distantly, men shouting across the street to each other. His wool coat was heavy, rough to the touch, and his starched white collar, still too large since his return from France, chafed the side of his neck whenever he moved.

He closed his eyes and tried to focus on his breaths, a long inhale, hold, exhale; inhale, hold, exhale; inhale, hold, exhale. Fill the chest with air, every glorious, unwarranted, unsought breath a reminder that life is good and death is to be evaded at all costs. A reminder of the ecstasy of tasting English air again, with the bitter tang of salty sea-spray at one with the salt-tears stinging his eyes. A reminder of that bitter taste stinging the back of his throat, his nostrils, his eyes, the same that stole the last breaths of so many others, so many friends.

Enough.

Jack forced his eyes open and, wearily, shrugged his coat over his ill-fitting suit, wrapping it around his shrunken frame to force out the chill. He sank into one of the worn armchairs, defeated, to wait.

* * * * * * *

Liverpool Street station was alive with people and Jack and Alfie were immediately engulfed in the pre-Christmas crowds as they leapt from the back of the tram and into the throng. They forced their way through the obstacle course of porters, suitcases, chattering parents, squalling children, grey-frocked nannies either cajoling or dictatorial, and bought two return tickets to Cambridge using, of course, Jack's money.

The platform was thick with smoke. The third-class carriages were equally choked with still-hatted men, bonneted women and their offspring, huddled together on the rough seats to keep the increasing winter chill at bay. As Jack hesitated the whistle suddenly blew from behind him on the platform and, with a rough hand on his back, Alfie shoved him into the mêlée. They found the last unoccupied seats and, while Alfie settled himself into the midst of a family on one side of the carriage and immediately launched into conversation with the father, Jack squeezed himself into a corner seat across the aisle and turned to stare out of the window.

The shortest day having just passed, darkness had already descended outside the station. The weak winter sun was no competition for the glowering snow clouds that had been hovering all day, which now started to shed their burden into the grime of north London. With his body folded into itself and half-turned towards the window, just in case anyone needed to be further discouraged from talking to him, Jack stared determinedly out at the gradually changing landscape. Industrial buildings, looming, faceless, soulless. Interminable terraced rows running at diagonals to the track, some windows ablaze with light, others carefully shuttered against the elements. Then, open farmland, flat, barren, barely visible now in the gloom, interrupted by lights from the occasional farmhouse or village in the distance. Gradually, Jack felt his mind release and the tension ease in his muscles. He closed his eyes and feigned sleep.

* * * * * * *

At Cambridge, Alfie shook him awake and he rose, cold and stiff, to lift his small case down from the overhead rack.

Snow was softly falling again as their cab turned off the country lanes and onto a gravelled driveway bound in on both sides by dense shrubbery. Jack could feel the tension return and leant forward, both anxious and intrigued, to gain a first glimpse of their employer's country home. The disappointingly short drive ended with a sudden swing to the right into a blaze of lights and a hubbub of people and noise. In the seconds before their cab pulled up behind another, he absorbed the impression of a vast two-storey house, Georgian in style, flat-fronted but for the grand porticoed entrance squarely positioned at the centre of the frontispiece. The tall windows along the ground floor cast brilliant light onto the driveway, the substantial circular pond and statue to their right and the dozen cars and as many carriages ranged in front of the entrance to disgorge their occupants into the night.

George Samuels, standing at the entrance, had done a good job of turning himself physically into the archetype of a country squire. He may, once and probably very briefly, have been a handsome man, with a thick head of dark hair and a laughing temperament to make up for what he lacked in height. Now in his fifties, while the hair remained, albeit more salt-and-pepper than jet, good living had left him portly, florid and prone to gout, which was the only time his good humour failed him. His substantial frame was illuminated from the grand entrance hall behind him, which was visible through double doors held open by uniformed footmen. He had set his stage to match his physique.

"He never said the party would be this big, did he?" Alfie huffed as they joined the queue of guests.

Jack shook his head, casting off the dread that was threatening to settle over him. "Would it have mattered if he'd told us?" he asked softly, under his breath. "Neither of us can live up to this anyway."

"Perhaps he guessed how we'd feel and didn't want us to worry?"

Jack looked at Alfie with surprise. "I think that's the most generous thing I've ever heard you say about him."

Alfie shrugged. "I'm not stupid. I may talk big but I know what a good thing we're onto with him. He's a decent governor, probably because he started where we are."

"Why do you insist on using dockside language, Alfie? Everyone knows you're from Epping."

Alfie winked salaciously. "Anything to get the girls. Anyhow, you've got to respect what the old man's achieved and how he still treats all of us. How many bosses do you know who'd invite the likes of us to his house, let alone for Christmas?"

No argument there. Jack was still having trouble accepting that they were standing in the middle of the countryside, preparing to spend Christmas with the man who owned Richmond Bank.

Jack glanced up to see a young woman appear from the entrance hall. She slipped her arm through one of the guest's and drew her into the warmth and light of the house. The husband turned to follow, jovially shaking Mr Samuels' hand as he did so.

"Of course, of course," cried Mr Samuels. "Get on into the warmth. I'll see you shortly." Then, turning the full blaze on his attention onto them and reaching out to shake first Jack's hand and then Alfie's, "Lads, lads!" he cried. "You made it! I'm delighted. Come on in, welcome, welcome."

"Mr Samuels, we're so grateful for your kind invitation," Jack started.

"Not at all, my boy. Just delighted you could make it. Christmas will be so much the merrier with you fellas around. John, my boy, you must meet my daughter." Turning towards the entrance hall, "Sarah, Sarah!" he called. "Where are you, lass?"

The woman ahead of them paused long enough to excuse herself from the couple she had just ushered in and to turn them in

15

the direction of the ballroom, although the volume of chatter, laughter and music left no doubt where the party had gathered. She smiled them through and turned back to meet her father's new guests.

"Good girl," beamed Mr Samuels. "Now come and meet the lads I was telling you about. John, this is Sarah, my eldest and my right-hand woman when it comes to running this place."

Jack held out his hand, hesitant and embarrassed as she placed hers into his, uncertain whether to shake it or kiss it. He met her eyes, soft brown but somehow challenging, and found instant reassurance. His hesitant smile found a confident answering one on her lips and he nodded his head in acknowledgement.

"You're most welcome, Mr Westerham," she enjoined. "Mr Edmonds, too," holding out a hand to draw Alfie to her. "I hope your journey wasn't too arduous?"

"Not at all," Jack hastened to reassure. "I was just saying to your father how grateful we are to you for inviting us. It's very generous of you."

She smiled. "We're a small household and I always enjoy Christmas with more people around us. Fortunately, my father's a gregarious man." She turned away to beckon a uniformed footman hovering in a corner. "James will take your bags up to your rooms and let's get you into the warm."

She drew them into the imposing hall, its marble floor hosting an imposing dark-wood staircase kitted out in a deep red carpet and sweeping from the centre.

Jack shook his head to try to clear the sense of unreality. It was everything one might assume a grand country estate should be. Panelled walls, plush carpeting, the obligatory ancestral oils adorning the walls of the hall and the galleried landing where the staircase split at the top to lead to the east and west wings of the house. Imposing, opulent and fake. The sort of house acquired and adorned to meet the craving of new money for what could never be bought from old money: heritage.

But, as he hesitated at the foot of the stair and turned to look back across the hall, Jack realised none of that mattered. While the money had built the shell, the people had turned this house into a home. The laughter from the ballroom was ringing through to the hall and echoed by the jovial greetings of his host, still standing in his open doorway to clasp the hands of friends, neighbours and colleagues alike and draw them in, where his eldest daughter waited to collect them with gentle courtesy from her father's hands and transport them into the warmth of their home. For the first time since he returned from hell, Jack felt the faintest stir of a memory of some emotion long buried, long forgotten.

* * * * * * *

The double-height room was ablaze with light and colour, and alive with music, chatter and laughter. It dazzled as the flickering wall lights sparkled off the central chandelier and onto the multitude of diamonds and other gems augmenting the ears, necks and hands of the women whirling around the room. In formal black-and-white, the men offset the jewel-like colours of the silks, satins and chiffons adorning the young women they held in their arms. While they two-stepped energetically around the central dance floor, their more soberly-clad matriarchs played their part, admiring and gossiping from the fringes in blacks, greys and deep sapphire blues.

The room was packed; there had to be almost three hundred people. The dancers were so many that the couples could barely turn without colliding. Jack couldn't believe they could even hear the music, drowned out by the incessant talk: high-pitched and chattering from the gaggles of mothers; low-pitched, gruff and increasingly aggressive from the fathers, husbands and those bachelors wanting to retain their status, gathered in patches around the room and encircled by a haze of cigar and cigarette smoke.

George Samuels took up a suitably statesmanlike position with his back to an enormous stone hearth halfway down the long wall, opposite the high windows that overlooked the drive. The roaring fire had drawn many of the guests to bask in its heat, the men supplementing it with the internal warmth of George's single malt. Mr Samuels caught Jack's eye and waved him and Alfie across to his group, where glasses were quickly pushed into their hands and Mr Samuels effected the introductions.

"John, my boy, come and meet my neighbours. Gents, this is Mr John Westerham, works for me at the bank, got a bright future ahead of him. And his friend, Mr Edmonds."

"Alfie, please. A pleasure to meet you."

"John, Alfred, this is Richard Soames, owns half of Cambridgeshire, or," with an elbow in the ribs, "he did until he kindly sold me this little patch for Richmond House. His sons," working his way around the group, "Richard, the elder, and Edward, who's just down from Trinity. David Stevenson, my lawyer, and Simon Stevenson, his brother and my land agent. And this is their cousin, Peter Fellowes. Peter's father is over in New York at the moment looking at some opportunities for me while Peter holds the reins of the estate over on the Norfolk side of us."

Jack was suddenly distracted by a sudden burst of laughter from the dance floor to his left and a flash of long blonde hair flying loose as a slight-framed girl flew past, whirling in the arms of a man clearly entranced by his partner. In the next second, another blonde flash whipped past, no less elegantly and with apparent equal determination at delight, though her equally-wrapt partner was clearly lacking in the dancing skills being enjoyed by her sister.

Alfie appeared at his elbow. "The Samuels angels," he hazarded. "I'm off to try my luck."

"Alfie," Jack warned, a stilling hand on his shoulder.

"You heard the old man, Jack. Here's Jack, the wonder boy and his sidekick. I can't rely on him to make my fortune, my lad, so you can't blame me for trying to make it for myself." He shook off Jack's hand and, straightening his back, pulled down his dinner jacket and ostentatiously adjusted his tie.

Sarah's eyes met Jack's for a fleeting second. The contrast was extreme. Jack could only assume that George Samuels' younger daughters took after their mother. Their slight frames and almost white-blonde hair gave them an ethereal quality. Their three-quarter length, sheath-like satin dresses in silver and pale green flowed like water across their slender, youthful figures. Bands of matching material across their brows bound peacock feathers to their heads that nodded and danced as they paraded around the room.

Sarah's rich brown hair was piled high, adorned with diamonds. Her burgundy silk gown offset the mahogany shine of her hair and complemented the raised colour in her cheeks. Her dance partner, a tall, dark-haired and solid-looking man, moved her cautiously across the floor, navigating his way between the flights of fancy that flitted across his path. As they crossed in front of Jack, Sarah's face was turned slightly away from her partner's and her eyes determinedly met his again as she passed him.

The string quartet at the far end of the room drew the dance to a close with a flourish and the dancers broke into polite applause before a buzz of conversation as they exchanged partners.

"Sarah, darling," Mr Samuels' voice boomed across the dance floor to where his daughter was introducing her partner to a shy-looking young woman hovering at the edge of the room where her strident mother was volubly engaged in telling her counterparts about a recent encounter with the Prince of Wales.

Sarah smiled as the young woman lifted enchanted eyes to meet the gaze of the suddenly diffident man, and pressed his arm absently as she turned and crossed back to her father's set. Mr Samuels reached out his hand for hers and drew her into his circle. "Sarah, darling, Peter hasn't danced all evening and refuses to dance with anyone but you. Do put him out of his misery."

Peter Fellowes was looking all the more miserable at his host's explanation but Sarah's warm smile swept away his embarrassment. "I'd be delighted, Father. Mr Fellowes, the pleasure is all mine," taking his hand and leading him towards the dancers. Passing Jack, she paused. Speaking low so that he had to bend to hear her, she murmured, "Happy as I am to indulge my father this time, Mr Westerham, perhaps you might indulge me for the next dance?" and then she was away before he'd even had time to respond.

"John, my boy," Mr Samuels was at his elbow, turning him round towards the men's discussion and his back towards the dancers as Jack tried to gather his thoughts, "we were just debating this new League of Nations. What do you make of the notion? Our resident cynic, Soames, swears it'll never be anything but a talking shop. Isn't that right, Soames?"

"I don't see how it can be anything but," opined Soames, in the most dead-pan voice Jack had ever heard. "It has no powers, no jurisdiction, and only what authority the members imbue it with. It can hardly be expected to succeed that way."

"But what happens without it?" interjected his younger son. "We can't live through another war like that one. The war to end all wars, they're calling it. But it won't be unless we can stop the behind-the-scenes machinations of countries like Germany."

"Much you know about it, Edward," the elder Soames son scoffed. "You've been able to watch from the sidelines while the rest of us were up to our armpits in mud in a Flanders field."

"I'd have been there with you if I could, you know that," Edward rejoined, the anguished enthusiasm of the young and naïve plain in his voice. "I'd have shown the Bosch a thing or two, given half a chance. I can't help being born too late."

Jack dropped his eyes, desperately wanting to disengage himself from the conversation. Why did conversation turn back to the war so frequently? Didn't they want to forget? Didn't they want to move on?

"Well I, for one, was delighted you couldn't go," Soames responded gruffly, clapping his younger son on the shoulder. "Your mother could barely stand the knowledge that one of you was across the Channel. Given half a chance, she'd have been in there herself, sorting it all out. Besides, we had plenty to be getting on with here. It wasn't easy managing without a generation of young men for almost five years."

"Enough war talk, boys," Mr Samuels broke in. At a quick gesture to the hovering footman, crystal glasses clinked and flashed in the firelight as empty tumblers were replaced with new. Raising his glass and, with a sweep, encompassing the loose circle of men around the fire, "Let's drink to peace."

"To peace," came the muttered, mumbled responses. Jack threw back his glass and swallowed hard. The fiery whisky licked flames all down his throat, making him cough once, hard, then settled into gently smouldering embers in his stomach. At a slight nod from Mr Samuels, Jack found Hesketh, the butler, discretely refilling his glass with a slightly larger measure than before. He met Mr Samuels' eyes with a grim nod.

"Still," the younger Soames, it seemed, couldn't let it go, "we have to have something to believe in now and the League of Nations gives us hope of a sustainable peace."

"Good God, Papa, not more war talk?" An angel materialised at Jack's side, a shimmer of white and silver that made the warming blaze of the fire seem suddenly brash and over-powering, though her slightly whining tone struck him as strangely at odds with her other-worldliness. "This is a party and we want our guests to enjoy themselves. Though," frowning in the general direction of the band, "had I known what you planned in the way of musical entertainment, I'd have dragged something more entertaining back with us from London."

The bulky man on self-appointed protection duty beside the angel stopped glowering at the mention of the war. "Were you talking about the war? Got drafted in June '17, almost as soon as Congress made it official. Spent almost six months in some God-forsaken corner of France before being invalided out. What were you fellows up to?"

The angel rolled her eyes then introduced her companion as "Frederick Williams the second of Chicago". "He's in banking, like you, Papa."

"Are you now? George Samuels," reaching out to have his hand engulfed in a bear-like paw and finding he had to crane his neck to meet the man's gaze.

"You have a beautiful daughter, Mr Samuels."

George Samuels smiled. "Indeed, I'm blessed with no fewer than three, Mr Williams. Charlotte's the middle one."

Mr Samuels had barely completed the introductions around the group before Edward Soames leapt in. "How were you injured, Mr Williams?" The eagerness of youth overflowed. Jack recognised the desperate need to feel part of that shared history but, coming from the other side of the equation, he couldn't empathise with it.

"Hah!" There was a bear of a laugh to go with the paws. "Thank the Lord I managed to dodge all the German bullets and shells but the damn French winter did for me. Got pneumonia in February '18 and shipped over to 'good old Blighty' to recover." The English emphasis sounded strange on an American tongue.

"And did you see much action?"

"Oh, yes, enough. Plenty of sitting around waiting too. Endless smoking, games of poker. Anything to pass the time. What about you fellows? You must have seen action."

Jack felt his instinctive barriers go up as the full glare of the group was turned on him.

"You try to forget..." he deflected.

"What trophies did you bring back?"

Jack's head shot up at that. He found himself staring across into blue eyes that were warmer, more humane than he'd expected. "Trophies?"

"War wounds. You know."

A slight shake of his head. He desperately wished he could stop this conversation. "I was invalided out twice. A bullet the first time. Shrapnel in my leg the second." He deliberately damped down the temptation to rub his hand down his thigh, which was throbbing in sympathy. It was still healing and he should have been using a cane but pride prevented him. "Though the physical wounds are barely the half of it." He glanced up to find his host watching him carefully. "But tonight's really not the night for all that. The war's over. It's time we all moved on."

"Well said, Mr Westerham." He hadn't noticed that Sarah had reappeared at his side. Fellowes was already re-ensconced in his position between the fire and one of the Stevenson brothers.

"Miss Samuels, forgive me. I hadn't realised the dance had ended."

"I willingly forgive if you will indulge me with that promised dance?"

He bowed, formally, and, as she put her hand into his, she laughed and he felt an alien glow of warmth. His head came up and he caught his breath as Sarah turned to lead him onto the dance floor. Keeping her hand in his, he slid his other onto her waist and their eyes met. For a second, their gaze held then they caught the rhythm if not the notes of the band and were swept up into the strains of a Viennese waltz.

"Thank you for saving me," he muttered.

Sarah leaned back slightly to scrutinise him more closely. "What is it about Americans, do you suppose, that makes them so keen to compare scars? As if there were merit in levels of pain endured."

23

"You speak as if your experience extends beyond Mr Williams."

"You'd think it would make me more tolerant of the species, too, but I find certain traits quite consistent. There were several Americans among the men I nursed. We did what we could for our wounded coming back from France and Belgium. Those we helped went home or back to the front. Those we couldn't we at least tried to comfort."

Colours flashed past him in a blur. He watched Sarah's face flush with colour as they turned across the floor. Her eyes seemed to glow as they wheeled around, constantly flitting across the room from him to the dancers to her father and their other guests. Ever the hostess. He was watching her so closely he caught the split second when her eyes narrowed, though from calculation or consternation, he couldn't tell.

Instinctively, he asked "What is it?" then instantly regretted the question, knowing it to be an intrusion beyond the accepted bounds of their limited relationship.

Her eyes snapped back to meet his. "You're very observant, Mr Westerham," she replied with a tilt of the head. "I shall have to watch myself."

"Forgive me, I didn't mean to pry but I couldn't help myself. Your face gave you away."

"You're the first person ever to have thought so, Mr Westerham."

"Won't you call me Jack?" Her deep brown eyes held his.

"Perhaps," with a slight upturn at one corner of her generous mouth, "when I know you better. Though I notice my father calls you John."

Jack smiled. "He considers my formal name more appropriate for work. I'm still getting used to it. I haven't been called John since I left home at eighteen."

"You went to work?"

"No, to war."

"How early did you enlist?"

"August 1914." Abrupt, his voice rough.

"Ah, I see I am now the one intruding, Mr Westerham. I apologise." Though her eyes challenged.

Glancing away to give himself a moment to regain his composure, Jack caught sight of Alfie, entwined with one of the angels. She was laughing up at him, a brittle but intoxicating sound. The sort that swells a man's ego at being the source of it. A siren sound.

Jack found Sarah following his gaze and he nodded with understanding. "That's what you were frowning about."

"I have no reason to be suspicious of your friend, Mr Westerham, but I know my sisters so I hope you will understand my concern. I fear that is one match we should discourage tonight. But, for a moment, I wish to indulge myself. Tell me a little about yourself."

"I'll happily oblige." Attempting to play the gallant. To see if he could remember how. "Tell me what you would like to know."

"Let's start on safe territory. How do you find working for my father?"

"What makes you think that territory is safe?"

"One must start somewhere," she smiled. "Since it would be both rude and insensitive of me to launch into interrogating your familial background, your life's loves or your war record, I must begin somewhere and your work at least gives us common ground through my father. Though now I'm wondering, what makes that territory unsafe?"

Jack hesitated, fearful of her conclusions but drawn to share something of himself with her. "I owe a debt of gratitude to your father for taking me on when he did. Many had already given up on me before him and, without him, I might well be in very different place today."

Sarah nodded slowly. "It is gratifying to hear he has been both able and willing to help. What you should know, though, is that my father is a generous man but he's no fool. If he helped you, it will have been as much to his ends as to yours. He's quick to recognise potential and I can only assume he saw something in you that made him think you a good bet."

"He has passed his generous spirit onto you, I see," Jack surmised. "For that, I thank you both."

At that moment, the music slowed and the band drew the waltz to a close. They broke apart and Sarah curtsied neatly in response to Jack's stilted bow. Tilting her head to one side, she looked up to meet his eyes.

"Will you tell me more?" she asked, holding his gaze.

Jack smiled. "It would be ungentlemanly to deny so beautiful a lady."

She pulled back, her expression disapproving. "Mr Westerham, please don't flatter me. I value honesty far above flattery. That way, I know where I stand."

He appraised her in silence for a second then replied solemnly: "You've already ascertained that my friend Alfie, there, is the one more qualified to flatter than I, Miss Samuels. I lack his silver tongue and smooth words so I hope you will believe me when I tell you that, tonight, you are truly enchanting. And I commit that I shall always tell you the truth."

Sarah nodded twice. "Thank you, Mr Westerham. Let's hope the enchantment doesn't blind you to the truth. And now, if you will forgive me, I must rescue your friend from my sister."

* * * * * * *

Jack lay still for some time, his head still buzzing from lack of sleep as much as from last night's alcohol. He kept wondering at George Samuels' motivation for inviting Alfie and he to be part of this family occasion but his head was not clear enough to fathom it out and his dry mouth soon drove him in search of water. With the help of a young maid, startled to see any of the guests up so early, he found himself in the morning room, where the floor-to-ceiling drapes had been thrown back to allow the weak winter light to filter into the room. The snow had finally ceased to fall and, through the French windows, Jack could see a world blanketed in white silence. The sky was a brilliant blue and the sun dazzled the crystalline, unblemished snow. It reflected off the intricately designed silk wallpaper to throw more light over the floral and pastel soft furnishings. It was a very feminine room, compounded by the copies of *The Tatler* and *Vogue* scattered across the coffee table between the sofas and the unfinished cross-stitch hoop discarded on the arm of one of the chairs.

"Well," George Samuels suddenly appeared in the doorway, "I wasn't expecting anyone else to be up so early. I imagine we shan't see most of the ladies until late morning at least."

"Good morning, Sir." Jack crossed the room to shake his employer's extended hand.

"Morning, John. Sleep well?"

"Indeed, thank you, Sir. I've just asked for a quick cup of tea to set me up for the day."

"Excellent. And enough with the "Sir". Here, at least. I hope you enjoyed yourself last night? Stay up late?"

"I retired just after two. I think Alfie was still going strong at that point."

"Hmm, no doubt. Seems to me he's got the constitution of an ox that one, at least when it comes to having a good time. Well, make yourself comfortable. Still plenty of time before we have to dress for breakfast."

Jack suddenly felt over-dressed with Mr Samuels wearing a navy blue silk dressing gown under which his pyjamas and monogrammed velour slippers were visible.

27

"Thank you again for inviting me..." he started awkwardly but stopped as Mr Samuels held up a hand.

"Think nothing of it. I'm sure Sarah will already have told you we're delighted to have you here. I'm glad Edmonds was able to come with you too, helps to balance out such a female-dominated household."

"Are you expecting many today, Sir?"

"We had a dozen here overnight, Peter Fellowes as well as you and Edmonds, plus some of the girls' friends from London. David and Simon Stevenson will be back for dinner, both confirmed bachelors so I feel an obligation to give their lives a bit of sparkle. I expect we'll see Richard Soames and at least one his sons tonight, assuming the weather's still fit for them to drive over."

George Samuels crossed to the grate where a fire had already been lit and poked about in the coals to encourage the sulky blaze to ignite. Resting his hand against the mantle and casting a look back over his shoulder, he asked, "I'm curious, John. What would you have been doing had you not been here?"

Jack perched on the edge of the sofa.

"Probably dinner with our landlady. She's on her own now, just one young daughter. Her husband was lost at Passchendaele so she lets out the top floor of her place to give herself an income."

Mr Samuels nodded, still staring into the fire.

"And your parents?"

Jack rose abruptly and shoved his hands deep into the pockets of his trousers. He had deliberately avoided answering questions at work about his family, fearful of how he might be measured. The war had given him a different standing and he was enjoying the comparative anonymity born of a status that related only to his own actions.

He felt George Samuels turn to watch him, knowing he was reading resistance in his stiff back. He heard the older man pat

28

absently at the pockets of his dressing gown then retrieve his pipe and tobacco.

"My parents are good people, Mr Samuels," his back still turned to the older man. "Gentlemen farmers back through the generations at our place down in Devon. It's not a substantial business and we've never been a wealthy family, at least not in living memory, but they do alright. My brother's still there and his wife. They were childhood sweethearts. Their first is due in April. My brother will take over the farm when my father passes on."

"Your brother's older than you?"

"No, four years younger, thank God. It meant he missed all but the end of the war."

"How is it he gets the farm, if you don't mind my asking?"

"I told them I didn't want it, I couldn't be part of it any longer. For eighteen years that world was my life. My brother's too. Ed couldn't wait to get back there after his unit demobbed in January."

"But not you."

"No." A pause. "I didn't feel the same when I came back."

Mr Samuels carefully crossed the room to stand by the frozen man staring unseeing out at the frozen world. "I shan't pretend to understand, Jack." He stared out at the smooth snow. "But I shall be grateful to my dying day that God never blessed me with a son I had to send to war."

They stood shoulder to shoulder – or, more accurately, shoulder to head as Jack outstripped his employer – for a long time, staring out of the windows.

"Are you much of a walker, John?"

Jack creased his brow, bemused by the sudden change of subject.

"Sir?"

"It seems my eldest daughter has taken a shine to you." Jack frowned, unable to follow Mr Samuels' train of thought or to know how to respond. "Never could resist the snow. She's been a substitute mother to those flyaways for so long that the romantic in her is deeply buried but there's something about the snow that's always brought out her better side. I think you might go and join her, John."

The older man turned away, giving Jack no chance to refuse.

* * * * * * *

The world was less silent than he'd been expecting. With the sun now creeping over the horizon, the trees were alive with the sound of blackbirds, swooping from their vantage point down to harvest the golden-yellow berries on the firethorn trained up the front of the house.

In places, the snow had drifted up to a foot deep but only a few inches lay across the drive, criss-crossed with footprints and the tracks of car and carriage wheels where guests had departed during the small hours of the morning. There was a sharp bite in the winter air. What better way to clear his head, not only of the previous night's after-effects but also of that conversation?

Since he'd come home, it seemed that people wanted to talk about nothing but the war. Such a contrast. When he'd been home during his recuperation, it was the one topic of conversation everyone avoided. As if he were home for an amicable family visit, not to recover from his shattered leg nor to heal the shrapnel wounds that lacerated the left side of his body, from shoulder to hip. His leg gave an involuntary twinge and he strode faster down the drive, denying the pain.

"Mr Westerham."

Jack started. He had been so intent on driving away the memories and their legacy, he missed Sarah.

"Forgive me, I was miles away," he defended.

She smiled that strange half-quirk of hers that already felt familiar. "I'd hazard somewhere in a French field." Her voice was light but her gaze was penetrating.

30

Jack shoved his hands deep into his coat pockets, defensively. "You're almost right. Actually, it was a Devon farmhouse but it was a French field that had taken me there."

"Your family?" she hazarded.

"I was wondering," he admitted, "why it is that everyone is now so keen to talk about the war, now it's over, when everyone avoided the topic while it was going on. At least, in my experience."

Sarah met his gaze. "I know what you mean, though I suspect for rather different reasons. While my father and I would frequently discuss it, my sisters showed no interest in my work." She smiled indulgently. "In some ways, I am grateful that their lives were so little touched by that level of destruction and brutality. It leaves its mark, even on those of us otherwise unscarred." She squared her shoulders and stared down the line of hedges. "I'm walking part of the perimeter of the estate. Would you care to join me, Mr Westerham?"

He fell in beside her and they crossed the width of the drive to rejoin the boundary hedge.

"Where in Devon does your family live?"

"It's a small place, quiet. Barely a hamlet, these days, now so many families have moved away to Exeter or Bristol, or even London."

"Tell me about your family."

"We're farmers by heritage. The farm's been in the family for generations but it used to be much wealthier than it is now. Too many ancestors who mismanaged or were lazy or lacked ideas. Add to that poor harvests and newly landed gentry desperate to buy acres and you get a history that diminishes from local landowner to proud but impoverished gentleman farmer with a living that can barely sustain one generation, let alone two."

He stopped. Sarah stared ahead, as if deliberately avoiding his gaze, knowing that he had shared more than he intended.

"You don't plan to return to the farm?"

"No, it's not for me anymore. Edward – my brother – is so much better suited to the life and he and his wife work well with our parents. They'll raise a family there, start the next generation of farming Westerhams. The cycle continues, regardless."

"And for you?"

They crossed the other end of the horseshoe-shaped driveway and headed through a gap in the shrubbery into open fields, bound now by a low dry-stone wall.

"Your father has been very good to me. I'm glad of an opportunity to follow a different path."

"What is it you do for my father?"

"I joined the bank in April after we demobbed in March. He took on half-a-dozen men from the regiment who had no other profession to which to return, including Alfie and I. Initially, I was clerking, managing account records and learning the basics of banking. Alfie's stayed as a clerk but, recently, I've been working in the clearing house or supervising the floor. I aim to learn as your father did, from the ground up."

Sarah laughed lightly. "Ah, Mr Westerham, don't be too taken in by my father's 'poor boy made good' stories. He had a little more help than you might hear."

"Please, Miss Samuels, don't shatter my illusions. Your father teaches me to aspire in a way I would never have thought possible six months ago."

"How old are you, Mr Westerham?" Sarah's penetrating gaze was turned full upon his face and he felt disarmed.

"I shall be twenty-four in January."

Sarah nodded, with a smile. "Plenty of time to progress, then. And I'm sure my father will be very supportive. I'm glad the war left us some good men."

Jack felt his face drain as unbidden memories, so long suppressed, flooded to the surface. Images forever imprinted in his mind. Darkness, always darkness, even during what should have been daylight hours. The smell of wet earth, cigarette smoke, sodden leather, rotting flesh, bitter, retching gas clouds. The sight of shattered limbs, disconnected limbs, flesh gouged and slashed by barbed wire, red, red blood black in the darkness. He turned away from Sarah, stumbling against the wall. He closed his eyes, sought control. A sheen of sweat drenched his face, chilling his skin.

Sarah paused beside him, leaning back against the wall to face away from him. She didn't speak.

"The war took the best of us." He dropped his hands to the surface of the wall to prop himself up and blindly stared out across the fields. "We must make do with what remains."

Sarah had half-turned her head towards him as he spoke. Now she looked away again. "Are you talking of friends lost or of yourself?"

Desperate for a distraction to fight the reaction, Jack fumbled in his jacket pocket for cigarettes. The delay in searching, extracting, lighting and deeply inhaling gave him the precious seconds he needed to deflect her. The hand holding the cigarette shook slightly.

"You're very direct," he posed, exhaling smoke and misty breath into the chill air. He turned round to face the same direction as she, leaning back against the stone. He shoved the cigarettes back into his pocket and left his hand there, striving for nonchalance.

The walls had gone up. He knew she could see it.

"I spent the first eighteen months of the war in Paddington, nursing at St Mary's. I won't say it was easy. The hours were long and a lot of the wounds we saw were horrific. But I've been sister and mother to Charlotte and Rose since I was young and there was little that touched me in the physical wounds we tended. We patched them up, we cheered their souls and we sent them back to die. Most were with us for such a brief period, we had no time to become attached.

"In the late winter of 1916, one of the doctors approached me with the idea of establishing a convalescent home, here at Richmond

House. We were close enough to London to make it an easy journey from the main hospitals but we're isolated enough to offer peace and calm. I'm sure the facilities and prospect of some financial support from my father were uppermost in his mind but he did also request that I become part of the staff. Of course, I took the opportunity and left my sisters in London to return here.

"The convalescent home was for soldiers with mental rather than physical problems. I thought myself equipped to take on most nursing tasks until then. Any blind affiliation I had felt to the cause till that point, I lost within weeks." She turned to look at him. "It wasn't the screaming. It wasn't the terror in their eyes or even the inconsolable tears that did it for me. It was the silence. The ones who stayed rigidly unspeaking. Their greatest fear was letting go. You could see it in their eyes: they knew they would lose themselves."

The cigarette hung, forgotten, between his fingers. Sarah reached across with a smiled "May I?" and took the cigarette from him. She held it naturally, like a man, not with the affectation of her sisters he had witnessed the night before. She took two deep drags and returned it to him. He flicked the ash away.

She nodded in the general direction of the house. "We should make our way back. My guests may be rising soon." Jack was happy to oblige.

"And now?" Jack started as they retraced their steps. "I mean, what are you doing now?"

"The last of our soldiers returned home in the autumn, since when I've been putting the house to rights and supporting my father's entertaining efforts. In truth, I'm looking for my next project. I fear I don't have the temperament for a more leisurely life."

"Something that might take you back to London, perhaps?" His pulse seemed to pause for her answer.

"Perhaps. I do love the life here but I prefer the activity and variety of London. As do my sisters," she remarked, "though for rather different reasons."

"How do they fill their days?"

A half-laugh under her breath. "Not so much days, Mr Westerham, as nights. From my experience, they often return home in the early hours or later, so I can frequently go from one end of the day to the other before I see them. They lead uncomplicated lives, their only pursuit the latest fashion, music or entertainment."

"You envy them?"

Sarah laughed, a sound so free and without bitterness that Jack was startled.

"Oh, Mr Westerham, in so many ways, yes, but I'd still never want their lifestyle. They are young and beautiful, frivolous, self-centred and gregarious. Everywhere they go they are admired and adored. Their lives are easy but so meaningless. They will go through life always supported and cosseted. Their greatest vexations can be cured with a stamp of the foot or a pout of the lip because there will always be someone to handle every difficult situation for them. For now, it's my father and I. Next, it will be their husbands, who as long as they are superficial as my sisters, will have glorious lives. All that, I can appreciate from a distance without wanting – or resenting – any of it."

She was slightly ahead of him, his injured leg starting to hold him back now they had walked far. It gave him the opportunity to asses her, covertly. She was tall for a woman, taller than her father. She lacked her sisters' fashionable willowy figures but, even wrapped up in a grey winter coat, her height made her appear slender. A thick fur collar hugged her jawline; her felt hat matched its sable tones. The hem of her coat brushed the surface of the snow drifts.

Jack caught himself wondering why she wasn't married and stopped short. He must keep reminding himself that this was Mr Samuels' daughter and, therefore, none of his business. He felt he had fallen into a trap, she was putting him at his ease in a most unexpected way.

Sarah turned at his abrupt stop, a question in her eyes. Jack sought a distraction.

"Sorry, a twinge in my knee. It'll clear in a minute."

"My father keeps a beautiful old stick in the coat cupboard in the hall. It might help."

Her tone was full of understanding, absent sympathy, but he couldn't help resenting it. He needed to prove to himself that life could be normal again, to deny the war's attempt to have a long-lasting grip on him. Physically, at least. He knew it was a futile denial but it had helped, until now. But he sensed that, with Sarah, there would be none of the judgment he so feared.

Resuming their walk back to the house, Sarah matched her pace to his and they trudged in silence, enjoying the continued chattering of the birds and the crunch of the crisp snow beneath their boots.

* * * * * * *

Emerging from his room, changed into a suit, he noticed Alfie backing out of a room at the far end of the corridor, cautiously drawing the door closed, apparently to avoid the click as it shut. Alfie spotted his friend as he straightened up and glanced down the hallway. With a smirk and a finger to his lips, he silenced Jack's startled question and loped down the carpet in bare feet.

"Don't say it, old boy," he chided in a furtive whisper and with a distasteful wink. "I'm off to freshen up. Catch you downstairs in a bit."

* * * * * * *

Breakfast was a disparate affair. Sarah played hostess in the absence of her father, who disappeared into his study with Peter Fellowes. Work, it seemed, had no reason to stop for Christmas Day. Frederick Williams was tackling an unimaginably sized English breakfast when Jack arrived in the breakfast room and Alfie eventually emerged half-an-hour later to demolish a pile of sausage, black pudding, bacon, eggs and mushrooms at least a large as Williams'.

Just before ten o'clock, Sarah and her father re-appeared to invite their guests to join them at the local church for the morning service. No-one took up the invitation. Williams and Alfie muttered their excuses. Jack was torn. He wanted so much to conform, to comply. He wanted desperately to be accepted by his employer and his daughter but they were asking of him the one thing he couldn't bring himself to do. The wounds were still too raw, the healing scars all too frequently ripped open again. He couldn't forgive God for the war and he wouldn't bring himself to walk into God's house. Sarah's eyes met his, enquiring. He thought she could read the conflict in him. He hoped she understood. He broke he gaze and stared deliberately at the tablecloth.

Without any ladies present to entertain him, Alfie rapidly reached his boredom threshold and challenged Williams to a game of billiards to pass the time before dinner. Jack hung around briefly as a spectator until it became apparent that neither player had any skill that warranted watching and, unimpressed, he wandered through to the morning room. As the morning's initial brilliant blue sky had submitted to threatening grey clouds, the room had lost its brilliancy and he resorted to one of a pair of wide, low armchairs that straddled the hearth, picked up a book left on a nearby table and soon found himself immersed.

When his attention was roused by Sarah, he discovered he'd lost all track of time. She had changed, he noticed. A soft satin gown in moss green.

"You enjoy Mr Maugham's writings, Mr Westerham?"

Jack turned the book to study its cover. "I read *Of Human Bondage* during my convalescence in '16. I wasn't hugely taken with it but I'm prepared to give him the benefit of the doubt."

Sarah nodded. "I'm only half-way through, though, so I'll wait to see how it turns out."

"I had no idea it was yours." Jack started, dropping the book back onto the table, embarrassed.

"Please, don't worry. I'm glad you're enjoying it. We have plenty more contemporary novels in the library, if you'd like more reading matter."

Jack gave a non-committal nod with his muttered thanks, knowing she was just being polite. He cast around for a subject, finding himself keen to keep her there with him for a moment longer.

"How was the service?"

Sarah smiled and Jack felt his stomach tighten.

"The church is 12th century and would benefit from either some more efficient heating or some work to address the areas where the drafts come in. I wouldn't mind but Reverend Marshall is not, unfortunately, able to compensate for the failings of the building with a sermon sufficiently inspiring to help us forget our physical circumstances."

As she spoke, Sarah put her hands out to warm them at the fire but her head was turned so that she could watch him over her shoulder. Jack felt compelled to explain why he hadn't joined them for the service. "I'm sorry I couldn't go with you," he started. His voice trailed off; he didn't know what to say anyway.

Sarah rested one hand on the mantelpiece and leaned in to reposition the logs with the poker.

"Please, Mr Westerham, don't feel you have to. If nursing here taught me one thing, it's that our reactions to religion are both complex and intensely personal."

"I wish I could it explain it to you. I think I'm not ready to forgive the things I've seen."

Sarah settled herself into the chair on the opposite side of the fire. "That's explanation enough. Why don't you finish my book? We have plenty of time yet before our Christmas feast will be ready."

It almost sounded like a dismissal but Jack was grateful. There was no need to continue the conversation but she was still there with him. He took up the book again as Sarah started to flick through a magazine, noticing absently that the click-click of billiard balls was becoming muffled beneath the sound of bluster and laughter – both masculine and feminine – in the room next door. The sisters had emerged at last, it seemed.

At two o'clock, as the marble clock on the mantelpiece chimed its elaborate tune, Sarah discarded the latest magazine she had been leafing through and disappeared. Jack returned to his book. As he finally closed it, Sarah reappeared, accompanied by a servant with a vast silver tray conveying a bewildering variety of drinks.

"A cocktail before dinner, Mr Westerham?" she offered. Then, seeing his hesitation, "Or, perhaps, a whisky? My fashionable sisters insist on the cocktails but my father's a whisky man through and through. It's only his desire to indulge them that overcomes his reluctance to accept such American ways," she laughed.

Jack accepted a crystal tumbler and followed Sarah through to the billiards room where the servant worked around a large gaggle of people in one corner of the room, half-hidden by a haze of cigarette smoke. Girls in an array of sumptuous materials were lounging in chairs, gazing adoringly at equally adoring, equally well-attired men in dinner jackets. Alfie leaned sideways against the billiard table, turned towards one of Sarah's sisters who had perched on the billiard table and rucked up the skirt of her dress so that it hung across her knees, legs crossed to show off her slim ankles and elegant heels. Williams towered over them all, his stance slightly stilted in their midst, clearly keen to be part of the group but not quite at ease with their frivolity.

There were voices outside the room – Jack recognised Mr Samuels' affable tones – and the sister rapidly propelled herself off the billiard table and across the room to slip her arm through Williams'. She was gazing adoringly at him as George Samuels entered the room, followed by Peter Fellowes and the two Stevenson brothers.

"Are we all here, Sarah?" Mr Samuels cut through the chatter as he retrieved whisky glasses from the tray and furnished Fellowes and the Stevensons with one each. "Marvellous. In which case," raising his glass, "happy Christmas, everyone."

Over the noise of the collective response and clinking of glasses, Mr Samuels invited everyone through to the dining room. Jack noticed Sarah slip one arm through her father's and, with the other, draw Peter Fellowes to her, her softly spoken, "Merry Christmas, Peter," met with a hesitant but warm smile as they led the party out of the billiard room, across the hall and through the library on the opposite corner. Jack had barely a moment to take in the grandeur of the dark room – the impression of wall-to-wall shelving, groups of comfortable chairs, thick rugs and a cluster of silver-framed family photographs – before they disappeared into the brilliantly lit dining room, sparkling with the reflection of fire- and candle-light on crystal, glass and silverware. The full-length brocade curtains were already drawn against the darkening winter afternoon.

Mr Samuels – or perhaps Sarah, Jack conjectured – had carefully positioned the guests around the table. George Samuels took the head, Sarah the opposite end, with Peter Fellowes on her left, David Stevenson on her right. Mr Samuels' other daughters sat one on each side of him, with Simon Stevenson and Williams alongside them. Clearly, Mr Samuels had decided he was rather taken with his fellow banker. Jack was surprised to see Alfie taking the position next to Williams, having expected him to be opposite Jack and next to David Stevenson. A slight frown on Sarah's face suggested he was not mistaken but her expression quickly cleared as Charlotte's and Rose's friends – two men, two girls – repositioned themselves around the table, apparently unaware of the change to the arrangements.

As the courses progressed, the table soon split into three discussions. After briefly engaging with his daughters and their friends, Mr Samuels lapsed into quiet conversation with Simon

Stevenson, which, from the snippets Jack caught amid lapses in the general chatter, seemed to revolve around estate business. Mr Samuels' daughters and their friends accepted Alfie into their banter and, as the wine flowed, Jack started to notice Alfie's voice more and more. He turned to see him leaning across Williams, apparently telling a joke to Rose and Charlotte. The table erupted in loud laughter, which engulfed Williams and the sisters' friends opposite.

That left Sarah to draw out Peter Fellowes, David Stevenson and Jack. Naturally, the discussion turned to local topics: news of shared acquaintances, local farmers struggling with a lack of sufficient manpower, births, marriages and deaths. The vicar's daughter who, after years as her widower father's housekeeper, was finally moving to Edinburgh to marry a young professor with whom she had been corresponding ever since he spent a brief summer with them eight years previously. The Whitmores, whose sons had both been lost in the war and who were contemplating selling some or all of their acreage, no longer able to manage the land they had farmed for fifty years. The young couple who had recently taken over the Post Office, he without the use of his left arm as the result of an injury sustained, people assumed, in the war. The festering disagreement between the village schoolmaster and the church organist, which had flared up again at the Advent carol service but which was of such long standing that no-one could recall what had started it initially.

Unable to contribute to the discussion, Jack watched Sarah as she absorbed and shared this local news. The disconcerted frown that he could read more in a narrowing of her eyes than in the lines of her face. The genuine pleasure he saw in the upturn of her mouth when it was allied to a drop of her chin and a downturn of her eyes. The slightest shake of her head too ambiguous to call.

To Jack, Sarah glowed. The angelic blonde of her sisters' hair he had so admired the previous night looked brash and flat in this light, their high-pitched voices were harsh, their laughter grating.

Sarah's hair shone as the candlelight picked up tones of russet and bronze in her rich, deep darkness, hanging loose today and brushing her shoulders. The emerald and diamond choker at her throat glittered and sparkled, reflecting into her eyes. Sarah's lower, softer tone drew the men to her, leaning in to hear her better, to share her thoughts and emotions. With barely a sign to the staff, barely a moment's distraction from the conversation, she was in complete control of the dinner, perfectly judging the moment to clear one course, to initiate another.

When, finally, George Samuels pushed back his chair and, with a replete huff, settled his hands on his distended stomach, Jack looked up with surprise; he had almost forgotten the rest of the guests were there.

"Well, I shall suffer for that tonight," Mr Samuels laughed, "but it will have been worth it." His guests smiled indulgently. "Gentleman," he smiled broadly round the table, patting his gut absently, "shall we retire to the library for port and a cigar?"

"Oh, papa," interjected Charlotte. "You're so old-fashioned! I'm sure the gentlemen would far sooner join us in the drawing room for cocktails and dancing."

Mr Samuels laughed and patted his daughter's hand. "I'm sure, my love. Why don't you and your young friends take the drawing room and I'll retire to the library with anyone else whose old bones feel more inclined to lounging than dancing?"

Charlotte and Rose leapt to their feet so rapidly that the servants hovering at the edge of the room hardly had time to rush forward to pull back their chairs. Each grabbed a gentleman's hand and they were almost dancing already as they hurried out of the room. With a quick backwards glance at Jack, Alfie rapidly followed them, with Williams on his heels.

George Samuels smiled indulgently and led his remaining guests back through to the library, which the servants had transformed the room into a haven of warmth and light. Lamps were lit on small tables all around the room, casting pools of soft light. A fire was well-established in a large stone hearth on the wall opposite the windows that overlooked the park at the front of the house.

Mr Samuels marshalled the servants to gather enough chairs from around the room to set by the fire then settled himself in a leather-covered, hooded chair set close to the blaze. Sarah joined him and the way that Fellowes and the Stevensons took up their positions in the circle of chairs suddenly made Jack feel as if he were intruding on a regular party. He hesitated on the edge of the group until Sarah caught his gaze and, with a subtle movement of her hand and eyes, invited him to join her.

One of the servants worked round the group with a box of cigars and one of cigarettes, another with the port. The sound of jazz suddenly flared up from the drawing room and Jack caught the distant scraping of furniture being moved around. Mr Samuels, Fellowes and the Stevensons immediately lapsed into a conversation about next year's crops. Sarah poured them each a small glass of port and Jack forced himself to relax back into the sofa, savouring the deep, smoky, warming flavour. Gradually, the room softened into a haze of cigar smoke.

After a while, Williams strolled back in, pulled up a chair and accepted a cigar.

"Have you had enough of the dancing, Mr Williams?" Sarah enquired.

"I fear my dancing style is a little too old-fashioned for your sisters," Williams joked. His skin appeared to redden slightly, Jack thought, though it was hard to tell in the low light. Jack wondered how Alfie was getting on.

"Never mind the dancing, Mr Williams," Mr Samuels interjected, "tell us about the news from the United States. How's the banking industry faring?"

Williams leaned back in his chair and brought one ankle to rest on his knee. It was a pose Jack would never have expected of a gentleman but it spoke to him of a deep well of confidence that would no doubt be allied to strong personal opinions.

"If those fools in Washington could leave well alone, we'd be doing just fine. Plenty of opportunities to invest in right now, there's so much building going on and new industry growing up all the time, all of them looking for financing."

"The new skyscrapers are a view to behold, I believe," Peter Fellowes suggested.

"You've never seen anything like it," Williams promoted proudly. "Like a new Constantinople, they're saying, in its grandeur and awe."

"I'm not sure such a thing would work well in London, though," Samuels contradicted. "I'd hate to see our historic architecture replaced."

"The benefit of being a young nation," one of the Stevenson brothers interjected. "That and the amount of wealth that's flowing around America now."

"For which our Government is immensely grateful," Sarah smiled at Williams.

"Perhaps if they could finalise these reparation payments from Germany we could get on with paying them back sooner rather than later." Stevenson again.

"Then we had better hope for a change of government in France," Jack inserted. All eyes turned on him for an explanation. "They hate the Germans. How can they be rational about the reparations or the territorial settlement? They were humiliated. You can understand why they want to inflict as much pain in revenge as they can. I can't see Clemenceau leading us to a sensible solution."

"But surely it's right that he should be looking to cripple Germany?" Fellowes suggested. "We can't afford her to be the aggressor again and France is always the one most as risk."

"They'd get to a solution much faster if they set the reparations at a level Germany could stomach," Samuels observed, sucking contemplatively on his pipe.

"The trouble is," Jack responded, "the French and British need to see Germany punished but too much punishment and the German people will rebel. Not against their own leaders but against the other nations."

"Hence the need for the League of Nations." David Stevenson this time. The lawyer. He saw dissent in Jack's expression and raised his eyebrows. "You disagree, Westerham?"

Jack shook his head, not wanting to cause a row. "It's a very worthy notion," he placated.

"But?"

He relented. "But I can't help wonder..." he paused. "How can a body that's predicated on the full co-operation of all the parties can be expected to resolve an issue that arises because not all the parties wish to co-operate?"

George Samuels burst out laughing and clapped his hands. "Well said, that man!"

"Then, if we can't rely on the politicians, we'd better hope the businessmen can make a better fist of things," Williams rejoined and turned the conversation moved back to the opportunities to invest, both in America and in Europe, now the war was over.

Just as the fire burned down, Rose appeared to demand her father preside over the present-giving, hauling him out of his chair in response to his feigned reluctance and insisting the rest follow them through to the library.

A huge fir tree dominated one corner of the room, wrapped around with red ribbons and glittering baubles. The estate men took what appeared to be a regular position in a huddle by the fireplace, Mr Samuels at the centre as usual, and the group was augmented by the timely arrival of Richard Soames and his sons, the younger of whom quickly took up a position at the gramophone and started flicking through the music selection. Sofas and chairs had been pushed back to create a dance area in the middle of the room, where the carpet had been rolled up and was now lying again the far wall. Four couples were dancing. Alfie, Jack noticed, had attached himself Charlotte.

Having settled himself, Mr Samuels clapped his hands for attention and the dancing and music stopped. "Now, everyone," he boomed, "time for presents."

Charlotte and Rose squealed – there was no other word for it – and hopped up and down together, clapping their hands like children. The party took their seats on the rearranged furniture, some perching on the arms of chairs and sofas where insufficient seats were available.

"Sarah, my girl, help me pass these out," Mr Samuels called. She obliged, embellishing each delivery with a word, a touch or a kiss, depending on the familiarity of the relationship.

Jack received his unexpected gift from her with a smile, uncertain how to accept graciously, particularly when he had nothing with which to respond, but the open warmth in Sarah's expression went some way to putting him at his ease. He watched as the others tore into their gifts, particularly the sisters who each had a pile of presents to work through and abandoned the pleasure of opening the gift for the exultation of knowing they now possessed beautiful new fur-lined leather gloves, glittering jewelled bracelets and exquisitely finished satin dancing shoes. Seeing the rest finishing their unwrapping, Jack slowly unfurled the ribbon tying his gift and slid his finger under the paper. A long, narrow black box emerged and revealed a beautifully crafted black and silver fountain pen on a bed of soft white velvet. He looked up to catch Mr Samuels' eye to thank him but found him turning over the pages of a book with Richard Soames senior. He suddenly realised Sarah was watching him with a gentle curve to her mouth and an emotion he couldn't name caught in his throat.

46

Suddenly, there was a call for music again and the dancers reassembled, Alfie capturing Charlotte Samuels again, much to Williams' distaste to judge by a side glance that Jack caught. The evening dissolved into laughter, bursts of lively music and flashes of glorious colour as the girls whirled around the makeshift dance floor, applauded and encouraged by men of all ages, under the thoughtful, indulgent gaze of Sarah Samuels and the distant, watchful eyes of an outsider.

Chapter Two

London, January 1920

That Christmas Day is one I shall never forget, not only for being the first I spent with Sarah but also for the warmth and welcome I experienced. After the long years of war, it was the first time I felt as if I could return to something approximating a normal life. Alfie and I returned to London on Boxing Day and by Saturday morning I was back at work. I had no expectation of seeing Sarah Samuels again. I had taken George Samuels' invitation for a piece of Christmas charity and expected nothing further. I expected to go back to my normal life, contentedly working and occasionally sharing an evening out with Alfie.

It was cold in the bathroom. The hot water in the tub had rapidly cooled, forcing Jack out of his quiet contemplation sooner than he wished. He so rarely had time to himself, time to think. He had declined to accompany his landlady on her usual Sunday morning stroll to give himself time. Alfie, after another drunken night in town, was stentoriously sleeping the morning away.

The tiled floor was absorbing any remaining warmth from Jack's feet as he stood over the sink, badger's brush and soap dish in hand, half his face lathered.

He was at a loss. Everything had changed. He felt himself to be at an impasse, unsure whether – or even how – to go back, utterly convinced that finding the way to carry on was not yet in his grasp. Niggling at the back of his mind was the question, why had Mr Samuels invited them to share his Christmas with him?

It was a wonderful Christmas. It wasn't just the wealth, the splendour, the opulence, though he wouldn't deny the effect of that. It was the warmth, the generosity, the genuine affection both within the Samuels family and with their closest, most trusted friends. The joy with which they approached life. The simultaneous lack of pomposity and yet respect for tradition. He felt himself – knew himself – to be an outsider looking in, a rare moment of privilege, and yet he had been welcomed and made to feel comfortable.

So, everything had changed. In two short days that he had no right to expect to see replicated.

Jack stared at his face in the still-misty mirror. The detached, distant expression in those blue eyes disconcerted him, slightly. The man looking back at him was unfamiliar, dislocated. The farmer had been replaced by the soldier. Now the soldier was what? A clerk? He had quickly discovered that he needed more than the simple routine he had initially craved. A banker?

As he drew his razor through the foam on his left cheek, he contemplated re-growing his moustache. His first act as a newly demobbed civilian had been to find a barber and have it shaved off. Others in the unit had decamped to The Bull around the corner for a swift pint before heading off to find their wives, mothers and sweethearts. When he joined them, there was a split second of stunned silence before the ribbing began. He had grown the 'tache at the beginning of the war to hide his youth. He was already drawing a line under what they had shared, leaving them behind with a new face for a new era. He didn't miss it, so why was he thinking of changing again?

He had to acknowledge he at least needed a haircut. He hadn't noticed how much it had grown but couldn't remember when he had last had it cut. Used to keeping it closely cropped during the War, the better to manage the lice, he'd forgotten its tendency to start curling at the ends when it grew too long. He rang his fingers through the thick thatch, absently noting the patches of grey down each side seemed to be spreading, and resolved on a visit to the barber.

* * * * * * *

"Happy New Year, Mr Westerham."

In the suspended moments between hearing her soft voice and turning to meet her warm brown eyes, Jack was infinitely grateful he had had the time to visit the barber on Tuesday.

"Miss Samuels. Happy New Year to you, too. I hope you enjoyed the rest of the festive season?"

"Very much, thank you. We stayed on at Richmond House through the New Year but my sisters and I returned to London this morning to join my father in preparing for celebrations with some of his banking colleagues this weekend. Family comes first but business is always a close second with my father. And you, how did you enjoy yourself?"

"I shared a very pleasant dinner with my landlady and her daughter at the café in Crystal Palace, then we climbed the hill to watch the fireworks over the city. You can see as far as Hampstead from there. I'm not up to Alfie's style of celebrating, I fear."

"Nor I my sisters'," Sarah Samuels concurred. "I retreated soon after midnight but Charlotte and Rose were still entertaining their friends when the maids rose to clear the fireplaces the following morning." Her eyes drifted across to the young clerk hovering hesitantly behind Jack's shoulder. "Forgive me, Mr Westerham, I see I've interrupted you. I shall allow you to get on." Holding out her leather-gloved hand, "It was a pleasure to see you again."

Jack shook her hand, finding it a firm grip. "You too, Miss Samuels." Then, as she turned to go, "And, thank you, again, for such a wonderful Christmas."

She nodded a smile and turned to cross the marble floor to the cashiers' desks. The hem of her dress, a soft blue satin just long enough to show beneath the hem of her three-quarter length turquoise coat, was just short enough to show off a pair of neat ankles, accentuated by an elegant pair of heels in a co-ordinating shade of blue that almost matched her hat and gloves. Amid the dark grey and brown clerks' suits and the rich black frock coats of the managers, she was like a flash of sun-filled sky. Mr Kelly, the cashiers' manager, was already hovering to open the door to admit her behind the counter. A quiet word and a smile before she passed on and through the frosted glass door that would take her upstairs to the offices and her father's daily domain.

Jack finally remembered the clerk hovering nervously by his side once Sarah Samuels had disappeared from sight and turned to face him, determined to get to the root cause of George Duncan's persistent tardiness.

* * * * * * *

He felt rather than saw the moment Sarah Samuels returned to the bank floor. For a moment, he thought it was his own heightened awareness that alerted him, feeling his pulse suddenly pick up its rhythm, but he realised it was the rustle of whispering and nudges among the clutter of clerks hovering in the shadows near him.

An agony of hesitation as Sarah and Mr Samuels paused to exchange greetings with an older woman dressed head to toe in black and bonneted in a rather old-fashioned style. Then, as the woman returned to her transaction, Mr Samuels caught Jack's eye and beckoned him across to meet them. Jack felt every clerk's gaze branded into his back as he hurried over.

"Afternoon, John," Mr Samuels greeted him. "Sarah has expressed an interest in visiting the Clearing House. Would you take care of that, please?"

Even before he had finished speaking, Mr Samuels' attention was being demanded by another customer on the other side of the room, so Jack quickly nodded his assent as Mr Westerham, with an absent-minded pat of his daughter's arm, hurried away with a muttered "I must just..."

"The Clearing House, Miss Samuels?" Jack asked with a raised eyebrow.

51

"You say it as if I were asking to be escorted to a bawdy house, Mr Westerham."

Jack laughed, his heart lightening. "It's certainly an unusual request for a lady. An equally unusual experience for the clerks of the Clearing House."

"In three years, Mr Westerham, I shall be old enough to vote. Surely if we've progressed far enough to allow women to influence the political process, we've progressed far enough for us to be accepted into the Clearing House?"

Jack acknowledged the point. "Then I would be delighted, Miss Samuels. I normally leave for the Clearing House at half-past four. Would that suit you?"

"That would ideal. I have some errands to complete ahead of tonight's dinner so I shall return in a few hours. Until then, Mr Westerham," and she took her leave.

* * * * * * *

It was raining hard by the time Sarah returned and Jack held a large umbrella over her as they hurried the four hundred yards from Richmond Bank's headquarters to the London Bankers' Clearing House in Post Office Court, just off King William Street. What weak light there had been that day had long since disappeared behind the thunder clouds. The pavement and road shone slickly with water and Jack angled his back towards the road to take the brunt of the spray from passing cars.

It was nearing a quarter to five as he held open the heavy iron-embossed oak door for her and the hubbub of the daily climax was already well underway. Sarah declined to take a seat so they squeezed themselves against the wall near the three desks that had the Richmond Bank name set onto the wall above them. The large room was a mêlée of clerks from the major London banks, scurrying around to drop off cheques in the open boxes beside the banks' desks, and the banks' designated Clearing House clerks rapidly recording the transaction and tallying their impact against their running total.

As they watched and he talked through the process, a suspicion soon lodged in his mind that this circumstance had been engineered for some reason other than Sarah's education. As to be expected, many eyes were drawn in their direction but it seemed Sarah met them with slight nods of acknowledgement, as of meeting with long-established acquaintances. He stopped talking as the process neared its five o'clock climax and observed her instead.

"You have visited the Clearing House before." He tried to make it a question, to keep the accusation out of his voice, but did not succeed. Her amused smile confirmed his suspicion. She made him feel a fool. "Then…"

"I thought I might invite you to join me for tea, Mr Westerham," pulling at her gloves as if to straighten them, then suddenly glancing up and meeting his gaze directly. Evidently, she read the anger he would not voice for her expression suddenly shifted. "You do not think I meant to embarrass you?" she challenged. "I only sought an opportunity." He found he could not turn his eyes from hers at the implication of her words and it was left to her to take the lead. "Why don't I find us a table at the café on King William Street and you can join me there when you're ready?" The challenge in her eyes softened.

"I should be glad to join you there shortly," he conceded as he suppressed his anger. Catching sight of one of the Metropolitan Bank clerks, he took the excuse to break away from her, handing her the umbrella as he turned his back to hide his confusion.

* * * * * * *

The rain was thundering down as he emerged into street. Rivers of rainwater were now streaming off the crest of the road in the direction of Gracechurch Street. The winter darkness had augmented the heavy clouds overhead, poorly alleviated by the gas lamps. At the other end of the street he could see a pair of lamp-lighters making their way towards him, faint flickers in the driving rain. He ran fast across the road, dodging the cars and the crush of bicycle-mounted clerks starting for home.

The café was welcome light and brightness after the deluge outside. He found Sarah in the far corner, the small, round, white-clothed table already adorned with a china tea-set and a three-tiered cake stand sparsely laid with sandwiches and cakes. Shaking off his hat and coat, he was suddenly conscious of his well-worn brown suit next to Sarah's immaculately tailored dress, her perfectly fitted gloves, laid as a neat pair on the corner of the table, and her stylish hat, pinned at a slight angle over her warm, glossy hair, neatly coiffed into curves resting on her shoulders.

He was forcefully reminded of the distance between them. She was at home with tea at the Ritz or the Savoy, not this down-at-heel café with threads pulled on its tablecloths, the colours worn on its china from over-washing, the walls in need of a lick of paint, a distinct chill in the air from the inadequate heating system.

His self-consciousness made him hesitant, even after Sarah's smile had invited him to sit.

"So," she broached, "will you now tell me what you were discussing with the Metropolitan boys or," with a glint of laughter at her lips tempering the steel of her voice, "do I need to warn my father about you conspiring with the competition?"

Jack sat back in his chair, the better to observe her but also feeling in need of a little distance, unsure how his actions would be perceived. Sarah offered him a sandwich, which he took, the better to displace her attention.

"George Duncan, the clerk I was speaking with this morning when you arrived?" Sarah nodded her recognition. "He's been with Richmond for a couple of years, joined us straight out of school, I

54

believe. From what I've seen of him, he's been doing well and is usually diligent in his work. There have been a few instances of tardiness recently, though, and I wanted to find out what might be behind them."

"That's what you were discussing this morning?"

Jack bowed his head in acknowledgement. "It seems his mother is unwell, has been since before Christmas, and the family is struggling to cope with the day-to-day operations of the home while she convalesces."

"Which has made George late?"

"Yes. Specifically, taking his younger brothers and his sister's children to school in the morning. I promised him I would find a way to help, somehow. Fortunately, one of Metropolitan's Clearing House clerks lives in the same neighbourhood as George. His wife, I suspect, walks past George's house on her way to the school so I asked if she might be willing to collect the Duncan children. Richard agreed to speak with her."

"That's a kind thought," Sarah reflected.

Jack shrugged off her words, reaching for his tea cup as a deflection. "It's little enough. It tackles the symptom not the cause, though, so I'm not sure how effective it might prove."

"Is there a more substantial problem to tackle?" Sarah probed.

"Perhaps. It seems George's mother has been ill for some time and the family are struggling to make up for her lost wage. I wonder whether she is receiving the support she should from her Friendly Society. It wouldn't be the first time."

Sarah's eyes narrowed.

"I'll look into it," she promised, closing the subject.

He contemplated her for a moment, considering whether her recent directness gave him permission to be equally direct. "In spite of your..." he reached for the right word, "misdirection," a raise of an eyebrow at that, "today, you do take quite an interest in your father's business."

"I do," she acknowledged.

"Few women would."

"You will, I hope, acknowledge that I am not like most women." A challenge and a hint of a promise. She sat back, like he, and contemplated him. "I feel it's important for me to understand my father's business if I'm to be anything more than a well-attired prop when he's entertaining colleagues and clients. I had started learning before my time and attention were diverted by the war and now I'd like to resume my education."

"He relies on you frequently?"

"I'm happy to oblige. Besides, one can hardly complain at having the opportunity to dine at the best restaurants in London. Although, personally, I prefer entertaining at home, however formally."

"Where is home?" Jack was starting to feel as if he were intruding but curiosity was overcoming his reluctance. He needed to know more about this unusual woman, so calm, so intelligent, so self-possessed.

"Belgravia. Where else?" Sarah's tone came close to irony and he raised his eyebrows. "My father puts little store by possessions but he certainly understands the importance of perception." Jack frowned that he did not follow her line of thought. "Our clients, Mr Westerham, are some of this country's wealthiest individuals. They value the confidence of knowing that their banker is part of their world, territorially at least."

"Territorially?"

"Banking is a strange world," Sarah reflected. "You only have to delve into my father's upbringing to understand we are clearly upper middle class by birth and yet banking enables us to straddle the classes. If we were handling any other product for them, I'm sure we would be considered part of the mercantile class and, therefore, clearly below their notice but, somehow, because it's their money we handle, we're tinged with respectability. Certainly we'll never be accepted as part of the landed gentry's set but they seem to tolerate us on the right occasions."

Jack absorbed her meaning, absent-mindedly running his hand across his five o'clock shadow. "I wonder how long it will last?" he mused. "The status quo, I mean."

"Are you a Bolshevik, Mr Westerham?"

"God, no." Sarah laughed at the shock on his face and Jack dropped his hand to the table, staring hard at his knuckles. A stiff silence descended until Sarah stretched across the table and covered his clenched hand with hers. Her hand was warm, the nails short but tidy, unpainted, the fingers short, capable and unadorned. His hand tingled beneath hers.

"Forgive me, Mr Westerham. I shouldn't have laughed. Believe me, I wasn't laughing at your politics. It was your passion that stirred me. You've been so careful with your views so far, your fervency caught me by surprise." A squeeze of his hand caused Jack to look up and meet her gaze. Her eyes were warm; his stomach lurched. "Please," with a dip of her head and a slight lean towards him. "Forgive me."

Jack looked away again. "It's nothing," he muttered.

Sarah withdrew her hand but Jack knew she was still watching him intently. "Please, Mr Westerham, don't do that," she insisted. Jack met her gaze with a frown. "Don't be polite with me. I spend much of my life being polite with people, never saying what I mean, never taking offence when they fail to show the same consideration. I would so like someone to be honest with me. To tell me truly how they are feeling, what they are thinking."

"But, with your family...?"

"Certainly, with my father, though even there I feel I am occasionally playing a part, the dutiful daughter and his hostess for business dinners. A woman sufficiently intelligent and well-educated to warrant tolerating at their table. And, of course, I am

57

always surrogate mother to my flighty sisters so they have no interest in seeing me for myself."

Jack's couldn't keep the roughness from his voice as he asked, "Why with me, then?"

She sat back, her eyes averted briefly, her head tilted to one side as she considered the question. "I'm not sure why. I think, I feel, that we think alike. I'm not saying we have the same views but I feel I understand you and that you could understand me. Do you know what I mean?" Her eyes returned to meet his and he nodded. "Am I forgiven, then?"

"If you will overlook my being too sensitive," he bargained.

Sarah smiled. "Agreed. So, now, will you please share with what you meant, about the status quo?"

Jack picked at the last sandwich on his plate, instantly uncertain again. "It may be fanciful but I feel change may be coming. It may have to." He drew a deep breath and broached the subject he shied away from with everyone else. "In France, all our officers were drawn from the ruling class. They stood for honour and courage, they unquestioningly accepted everything Command threw at us. At least, they didn't question it in front of us. We lost so many of them, those young sons of the nobility."

"We lost of lot of working men, too," Sarah pointed out.

"Yes, we did. Far too many. But, you see, there was never a shortage of men like me, particularly after conscription. We're cannon-fodder, always have been, because we're numerous enough for it not to matter. But after a while you could see the effect we were having on what is quite a small group of families. They've lost a whole generation of sons. How does the ruling class continue after that? That sort of devastation changes things. You can see it throughout history. Like the Black Death in the fourteenth century. Almost half of the population was wiped out and lasting social upheaval followed within a generation. Indeed, almost revolution at points."

Sarah's expression was bemused. "You enjoy history, Mr Westerham?"

"Is that so surprising?" he challenged.

"It's unexpected."

"Because I'm a bank clerk?" he bristled.

"Because so few of the men of my acquaintance are avid readers of anything other than *The Times*."

Jack was stung, shamed for assuming she was judging him. He knew it said more about his defensiveness of his upbringing than about how she had treated him during their acquaintance so far.

"And, besides," Sarah smiled, "you're not a bank clerk, are you?"

Jack laughed, releasing his tension. "No, I suppose I'm not. It makes me wonder what I am, though."

"What do you mean?"

Jack chose to deflect the question with the one that had been burning at him for weeks now. "Of all the people who work at the bank, why did your father invite Alfie and I to join you for Christmas? Don't think me ungrateful," he qualified. "It was a generous gesture and very much appreciated by both of us. I would like to understand, though."

Her head was tilted to one side. "Why do you think it was?"

"Honestly, I'm at a loss. I understand – and applaud – his philanthropy but I cannot fathom how he selects the beneficiaries."

"Nothing my father does is by accident, Mr Westerham, and his motives are rarely purely philanthropic. He always has one eye open to opportunities, be they investments, clients or people. It's how he's built such a successful business from the small, parochial bank he inherited from his father."

"How is that relevant to us?"

"I think he's looking for capable people to bring through the ranks. The 'ruling class', as you describe them, aren't the only ones who lost important people in the war and Father needs to rebuild.

With him, though, it's never just about work and he would have wanted to see you in a social setting."

"It was a test?"

"If you want to see it in those terms, yes. I prefer to think of it as getting to know you better."

Jack didn't know whether to feel flattered or insulted. "Did I pass?" he joked, with rather more bitterness in his tone than he had intended.

"I know I thoroughly enjoyed your being one of the party," she soothed. "Selfishly, it made for a more entertaining Christmas than I might otherwise have expected. You will already have seen I have no interest in being part of my sisters' entertainments, which leaves me with my father's estate colleagues for company. However worthy and dear they may be, however much I value their friendship to my father, we share little in common."

"You're being kind," Jack surmised.

"I asked you to be honest with me, Mr Westerham," Sarah responded. "I hope you trust I am honest with you."

"It would mean a lot to me if you were."

"Then we're agreed," she smiled, holding out her hand to shake his across the remains of their afternoon tea. "Now, I must make a move or I shan't have enough time to dress for dinner and I can't risk scandalising tonight's guests."

"Of course," Jack turned round in his chair to attract the waitress's attention.

Sarah put her hand on his forearm. "Don't worry, Mr Westerham, I've already paid for tea."

"But..."

She broke into his protest with a squeeze of his arm. "It was my invitation, John."

Jack's breath shortened at the sound of his name – however formal – on her breath. He couldn't feel the warmth of her hand through the thick material of his suit jacket but the pressure was spurring his pulse to a different pace. He tipped his head in acceptance of her offer.

They rose together and Jack helped Sarah into her peacock-blue coat, enjoying the texture of the soft material between his fingers. He folded his own coat across the arm she had held, glancing towards the glass frontage to ascertain that the deluge had recently moved away. As they exited onto the pavement, still black and glossy with rain but lit now by the soft glow of the gas lamps, a Silver Ghost pulled up from further down the street with a soft hush of wet tyres.

"My father's driver," Sarah explained. Jack regarded her, questioningly, and she explained with a soft curve touching her lips, "I preferred to walk to the Clearing House with you so I sent him on ahead."

More of this afternoon had been planned than he knew, Jack surmised, and Sarah's slightly amused expression seemed to reinforce his conclusion. Not that it mattered, he decided.

Before the driver could jump out, Jack opened the door of the beautifully polished, burgundy-coloured car and offered Sarah his hand as she climbed in. She settled herself on the pale leather seat, pulling her fur collar around her cheeks against the chill of the night air.

"Thank you for today, John," she murmured.

"It was my pleasure," he responded.

"I wonder if I might impose on you for one more thing?" she asked. Then, to his silent assent, "My sister, Charlotte has, I believe, spent a considerable amount of time with Mr Edmonds since Christmas. I'm concerned they may not be a good influence upon each other."

"You put it generously," Jack suggested.

"Not at all. I know my sister, all too well."

"What are you asking of me?"

She paused before replying. "Only to be alert to the situation, to keep an eye open from your side. Nothing more. For now."

"It seems sensible for both their sake's," Jack agreed. As Sarah sat back in her seat and pulled a rug across to wrap over her knees, Jack quipped, "Do I take it Alfie didn't pass the test, then?"

Sarah looked up to meet his gaze. "Mr Edmonds was only ever invited to put you at your ease, John. Surely you realise that?"

* * * * * * *

She had to be the most self-assured, self-contained woman he had ever met, Jack concluded, tucked in the corner at the back of the bus, rattling its way towards Crystal Palace. Self-conscious of his background, his lack of position, he wondered why he didn't feel intimidated by Sarah or want to keep his opinions as closely guarded as he did with everyone else. Here he was, opening up to her, disputing with her, challenging her even. He hardly recognised himself.

The rain was falling again. A young mother squeezed into the seat next to him, dumping bags full of shopping around her feet before hauling up her toddler to balance him on her knee. Jack retreated as far against the window as he could, craving space and peace. He stared out of the window but could discern little more than the broad shapes of cars and houses in the street outside.

Was Sarah pursuing him? If so, to what end? Surely not romantically. Quite aside from her own personal merits, she was George Samuels' daughter and could expect to marry very well. Professionally, then? Perhaps he was still being tested. But, no, she had asked for his honesty, to put aside the politeness that he used to keep people at a distance and ignorant of his thoughts.

He mulled over how he felt about what she had told him. His instinctive reaction had been to resent being tested without his knowledge but, sitting here in the peaceful anonymity of the homeward commute, he started to unpick this emotion. It had made him vulnerable. This wasn't the sort of job interview he had undertaken when originally applying to join Richmond Bank, when he had been able to prepare, to put on an appropriate face. This approach stripped his veneer, judged him on his personality, views and intellect. It left no hiding place. He had to acknowledge the effectiveness of Mr Samuels' approach. Jack might have worked for him for years without George Samuels being any the wiser about him as a person. He had cut through the façade with an act of kindness and generosity, exposing Jack in return for giving him a glimpse his own private world.

Jack laid his emotions aside and asked himself how, then, he felt about the thought that he was being considered for something else at the bank. He admitted to some trepidation but also a stirring of animation. He wasn't what he would call ambitious. He knew enough of himself to understand he wasn't after power for its own sake but he took pride in his work and knew he had more to contribute than he had been able to thus far. Of course, he was flattered that Mr Samuels had noticed him and thought well of him. As ever, though, those instincts warred with an acute awareness of his position in life. Of family dignity lost over the decades until the latest generation was suffocated by the pride of a long-established, long-respected family without the resources to maintain the standards expected of it. He was born into an old family with nothing to recommend it but past glories. A family that pretended to a standard of education it could no longer afford to acquire, that steadfastly refused to vacate a house it could ill afford to maintain, that cared more for the opinion of the neighbourhood than for their personal comfort.

Enough. He had left that behind. In the war, he had been able to shrug off that legacy. There was a world of opportunity open to capable men now and he had the aptitude and attitude to succeed. He could make of his life whatever he wished.

Which brought him squarely back to Sarah. Considerate, considered, elegant, self-assured Sarah. He went back to staring out through the raindrops on the bus window.

* * * * * * *

Lights blazed from the window of The Old Tun on the opposite side of Church Road in Crystal Palace from Jack's bus stop. It was still early and, not feeling hungry after his tea with Sarah, he had no imperative to return home promptly. He waited for the bus to pull away then ran across the road and through the swing doors, glazed with Victorian stained glass.

The pub was busy, noisy and smoky but Jack knew where to find Alfie. He wove through the crowds to find him amid his usual group of fellow drinkers by the fire, most of them hunched on stools over small circular wooden tables already cluttered with empty and half-empty pint glasses. Alfie was standing on the edge of the group, huddled in conversation with a dark-coated man, his hat pulled down over his eyes, whispering into Alfie's ear. Jack caught a flash of notes changing hands then, with a quick handshake and a tug of his hat brim that pulled it even further down over his eyes, the man took his leave, brusquely shoving past Jack.

Alfie looked up as he pocketed the cash and, catching sight of Jack, shouted an order for a pint to an ageing and slovenly barmaid. Jack opened his cigarette case as he approached, offered it to Alfie, took one himself and lit a match. Cupping his hands around the flame, he offered it to Alfie first. By the time he had lit his own and taken a deep drag, Alfie was reaching round him to collect Jack's pint from the bar.

"Changed your mind about coming out on the tiles tonight?" Alfie quipped. Jack shook his head, knowing Alfie had no expectation of him accepting the offer. "No arrangements to meet up with your fancy woman later, then?"

Jack frowned. "What are you talking about?"

"George's eldest, of course. I heard you were entertaining her with a tour of Clearing this afternoon."

Jack ignored him and took a deep draught of his pint. There was no malice in the question. It was just Alfie reminding him how well informed he was about all the comings and goings at the bank – and everywhere else, for that matter.

"I've got a book to finish tonight before it goes back to the library tomorrow."

"Don't know how you stand the excitement, Jack boy."

Jack laughed. "Make me jealous, then. What's on your agenda tonight? I take it you're not settling in here for the duration?" He took in the rabble of working men with a sweep of the pint in his hand.

"This bunch of losers? Not me. I'm heading up in the world. Dinner at Roberto's then off to a club in Soho. With mutual acquaintances of ours."

Jack sobered suddenly, remembering Sarah's warning. "You mean Charlotte and Rose?"

"Charlotte at least. Rose has other plans, I believe. Someone in another set is planning to introduce her to the infamous Duff Cooper. Seems we're just not good enough for Rosie these days."

"Charlotte's not going with Rose?"

"No, she's a sensible girl. Knows which side her bread's buttered, if you know what I mean. Seems more interested in slumming it than going up in the world," Alfie laughed.

"By which you mean, you?"

"I can't help it if the girl's got good taste, can I?"

"She seemed terribly young to me," Jack reflected, "when we saw her at Christmas. I hope you know what you're doing."

Alfie snorted. "Not such a little innocent, that one, believe me. Definitely not keeping her knees together until she's got a ring on her finger." He burst into a laugh at the fastidious expression on

Jack's face. "Oh, come on, Staff. You weren't so priggish when we were in France and looking for a little entertainment."

Jack stared down at his pint. "France was France," he defended. "We're back in London now and trying to get back to a normal life."

"Not me," Alfie dismissed. "Billy was right. Life's too short."

Jack gave Alfie a hard stare. "Billy's dead."

Alfie shrugged. "At least he made the most of what time he had. Don't think I'm going to suffocate by living the way you do. And when an opportunity like Charlie presents itself, don't think I'm going to turn her down."

"You can't seriously expect something to come out of it? They live in a different world from us. We're not supposed to be part of that world."

"Man, you take life far too seriously," Alfie clapped his hand on Jack's shoulder. "I'm not looking for marriage, Jackie boy. I'm looking to have a damn good time with a girl who's rich enough to buy me champagne all night and treat me to a slap-up meal. And if I get some at the end of the night, so much the better. I'm not the one taking the risk here."

Jack raised his hands in surrender. "Alright, Alfie. I get it. Tell me any time you like to keep my nose out but I worry about you."

Alfie squared his shoulders, straightening up so he could look Jack in the eye. "Keep your nose out, Staff Sergeant," he laughed and started to turn away until Jack put his hand on his shoulder.

"Alfie, take it from me, you're not the only one who keeps abreast of what's going on. I'm not saying don't. I probably should but I know you won't listen. So I'm just saying, be careful."

Alfie grinned recklessly. "Always am, old fella. Always am. Now, it's your round, I believe."

Chapter Three

London, 24 January 1920

*I wasn't altogether unhappy about Alfie's stepping out with
Charlotte. However tenuous, it gave me a sense of a link to
Sarah, a hope that it might lead to my seeing her again.
In my mind, I knew that to be a futile wish but I lived in hope.
Life settled back into its appropriate routine for a few weeks.
Then, my birthday arrived and, thanks to Alfie's continuing
dalliance, I saw Sarah again.*

He had not seen her for some weeks but she had rarely been far
from his mind. He found himself hoping she might turn up at the
bank, starting suddenly whenever a woman of her height came
through the bank doors, mistaking her for women he caught sight of
in the street with dark hair dressed in a shoulder-length style.

Even his usual diligent focus at work was slipping. Thankfully,
Saturday morning at the bank was always busy and gave his mind
little time to drift. All the City and businessmen too occupied to
attend during the week would squeeze into Richmond Bank's brief
weekend business hours. Jack was even more grateful for the
distraction in that it gave him little time to dwell on it being his
birthday or to worry about the planned evening entertainment to
which Alfie's badgering had forced him to agree.

As the central clock ticked inexorably towards one o'clock,
Jack and George Duncan were hovering in the shadows, watching
for late signals from the client managers. George was shifting his
weight awkwardly from foot to foot and frequently glancing across
to the clock.

"George," Jack ordered under his breath, "stand still. You're
not giving the customers a good impression. What's bothering you?"

George stared down at his shoes. "I've been wanting to ask you something all morning, Mr Westerham. Only I don't want to impose and I'm worried you'll feel obliged and I don't want to put you to any obligation after everything you've already done for us..."

Jack raised his hand to stem the flow. "George, whatever you want to ask me, just ask."

George coughed and shuffled again. "Well, you see, Mr Westerham...the thing is, I was wondering, that is, my mam was wondering, would you take lunch with us today? At home, I mean. As a thank you for everything you did for us. Things are so much better and we're all very grateful. So we'd like to invite you to have lunch with us today. If you'd like to. It being your birthday and everything, I didn't know if you'd already have plans, you see," he finished in a rush and drew and exhaled a deep breath.

Jack smiled, perplexed. "George, that's very kind but it's really not necessary."

George's face crumpled. "Oh, no, of course. We just thought..."

Jack put his hand on George's shoulder. "George, what I mean is there shouldn't be a sense of obligation here. I really didn't do that much to help. I'm delighted to hear things are better but I don't feel you owe me anything."

The concentration showed in George's face as a frown. "But what you and Miss Samuels did made such a difference.

"Sarah? After Sarah visited?"

"I don't know her Christian name but it was Mr Samuels' eldest, the elegant one who comes up the bank from time to time. Mam was a bit worried about letting her in, of course, but the house wasn't in such a bad state and she needed to see for herself how Mam was doing and to talk to Dad about how the Friendlies were helping us. She said she'd heard other examples of them backing out when people needed them most and said she'd take up our case for us." Jack let the boy run on, his mind running too. "You wouldn't believe the difference those medicines made to Mam once we'd got the money for them. Six weeks she'd had that cough. So bad she couldn't get out of bed most days. And barely a week after she's started taking them she's back on her feet and ruling the roost again. You see for yourself how well she's looking now. She'll be back at work in another week or so, the doctor reckons."

* * * * * * *

Mrs Duncan's substantial roast lunch and suet pudding had a soporific effect on Jack. He dozed his way back to Crystal Palace, miraculously nodding himself awake just in time to change buses. Having pushed to the back of his mind his inevitable feeling of fraudulence, he had settled himself into thoroughly enjoying lunch with the Duncans. It was a long time since he had last had a proper family lunch, bound around by multiple family members crowded around a small dining table.

As he dozed, Jack's mind was mulling over the news of Sarah's involvement in resolving George Duncan's domestic issues. He hadn't seen her since their visit to the café. There had been no sign of her at work so how had she become involved in the Duncans' situation? Did she not want him to know?

Jack cursed under his breath as he suddenly realised he had missed his bus stop. He jumped up and squeezed past the conductor to the steps at the back. As the bus slowed to turn a corner, he leapt off and ran to the pavement.

The sun had set and, with it, the mild warmth had leeched out of the day. Still distracted, Jack turned up his coat collar and wandered slowly back along the High Street, continuing to mull over the situation. He made a virtue of having the extra time to think, though it hardly helped resolve anything. By the time he turned into his street, it was approaching six o'clock and the street had lapsed into contented suburban quiet.

Unlocking the front door, Jack caught the strains of music from Mrs Jones' sitting room. Shedding his coat, scarf, hat and gloves, he

69

quietly mounted the two flights of stairs to his and Alfie's shared rooms. Their lodgings supplemented the meagre income of Mrs Jones' war pension and her clerical role at the offices of the local newspaper and it seemed ideal to Jack and Alfie when they were searching for shared rooms after they demobbed. A bedroom each, a small but adequate bathroom and a shared space as a sitting room. Most nights, they took dinner with Mrs Jones and her quiet, gaunt teenage daughter, Lucy. At least, Jack took dinner with them. More often than not, Alfie was out for the evening, either at The Old Tun or, more recently, dining, drinking and dancing with the Samuels daughters' crowd.

Not that Jack was complaining. Alfie's frequent absences gave him the sense that the rooms were practically his own. As it was, the only significant feature of the sitting room – other than the threadbare chairs they had picked up second-hand – was the piles of books stacked against the wall by the fireplace.

It was Jack's one indulgence. The shared rent for the rooms was quite affordable since his promotion to a supervisory role and Jack rarely spent money dining out. Rationally, he knew it made more sense to use the local library than to buy for himself but the library's selection was rather too narrow for his tastes.

He was at his least restrained when selecting books. He read widely on any subject or from any author that caught his attention, fiction and non-fiction, classics, biographies and modern novels, English, American and French. Unable to obtain sufficient books from home during the war, he had taken to borrowing from the locals in France, painstakingly enhancing his schoolboy French with a translation dictionary and, where necessary, explanations from one of commanding officers. Having developed the skill, he maintained it with a smattering of French novels among his other consumptions.

With any luck, he might be able to slip away from the pub sooner rather than later and return for a few hours' quiet reading. He was sure Alfie would barely notice his absence.

As he turned on the landing that housed his landlady's and her daughter's bedrooms and put his foot on the first step of the second flight of stairs up to their rooms, Jack stopped. The music was coming from upstairs, not from Mrs Jones' rooms. And laughter. Female laughter followed by a clink of glasses. Jack grimaced and forced himself to climb the stairs.

A shaft of light beamed onto the landing from where their sitting room door was ajar. Music, light and warmth spilled into the darkness where he hovered, uncertain whether to interrupt. As he eased the door open, an embracing couple swept past him in a contrasting blur of rich black and shimmering silver. Drops flew at him from the champagne glass in the lady's hand, hooked over Alfie's shoulder, and caught Jack in the face. The room was ablaze with light, including from an unnecessarily large fire in their tiny grate.

Oblivious to his entrance, Alfie and Charlotte continued to whirl around the tiny room, somehow keeping up with the frenetic rhythm of the jazz music, which Jack realised was coming from a gramophone precariously balanced on a pile of his books in the corner. As they swept past him, Jack realised they weren't the only ones in the room. In one corner, an uncomfortable-looking Frederick Williams was slumped back in an armchair for which he was far too large, his substantial fist closed clumsily around a fragile champagne flute. His eyes sullenly followed the couple round the room; or, more accurately, sullenly followed Charlotte's face as she spun round and round in Alfie's arms, her eyes sparkling, her face flushed, her mouth laughing. Perched on the edge of a matching chair in the other corner, her body turned towards the fire and, seemingly, deliberately away from her sister's exhibition, Rose Samuels was staring blackly into the blaze.

As the couple completed another circuit of the room and returned to where he hovered at the entrance, Alfie noticed Jack and brought the dance to a sudden halt.

71

"Jack, my boy," he shouted over the music, "you're late. Where've you been all this time? We've had to start the party without you," he explained, drawing Charlotte's hand up to kiss it with a look in his eyes that made her giggle. "Never mind," he interrupted as Jack opened his mouth to answer him. "Just hurry up and get changed. We're going to miss the first act if we don't get a wriggle on." He turned back to take Charlotte in his arms again.

Jack crossed the room to lift the needle from the gramophone. The interrupted last note seemed to echo on in the sudden silence. He turned back to Alfie, who was now nuzzling into Charlotte's neck.

"Alfie," he said quietly, commanding his room-mate's attention. Alfie looked up, distractedly. Jack tipped his head in the direction of his bedroom door and led the way across the room. His bedroom was blissfully cool and dark after the sitting room. Jack closed the door softly behind them.

"Alfie," he said quietly, keeping his voice low. "What's going on?"

Alfie clapped Jack's arm. "What do you think, you fool? We're celebrating your birthday. Like I promised."

Jack closed his eyes at the image of his peaceful evening slipping away. "I thought we were having a quiet drink at the pub."

"Change of plans, old boy," Alfie laughed. "Charlotte got tickets to some play in town so we're all going there and then heading to a little place in Chelsea she knows for a spot of dinner and dancing. Jump to it, Jackie boy." Alfie clapped his hands. "We haven't got a moment to waste. And put on your best." Alfie pulled open the door then turned back. "Thankfully we've got old man Samuels' car coming so we don't have to worry about local transport." The jazz music restarted as Alfie closed the door behind him.

* * * * * * *

Resigned to making the most of the evening, Jack smartened himself up and returned to the sitting room where dancing had given way to solid drinking. There were two empty champagne bottles lying on the floor by the gramophone and Williams was replenishing their glasses from a third. All four of them were now standing around the fireplace, Alfie's arm casually draped around Charlotte's shoulders. Jack took in the immaculate cut of Williams' suit and the girls' glamorous, if somewhat impractical, dresses and realised how shabby he and Alfie must look by comparison.

Straightening his shoulders, Jack crossed the room to greet the rest of the party and apologise for his abrupt behaviour earlier. Williams looked almost relieved to see him and Rose greeted him warmly with an apology for their unexpected presence. Charlotte spared him a brief glance before returning her attentions to Alfie, worming her way back under his arm and linking hers around his waist.

"Ready at last, Jackie?" Alfie smirked. "Right, girls, get those down your necks. It's past time we were making tracks."

Rose and Williams deposited their half-drunk glasses on the mantelpiece. Alfie and Charlotte raced to down theirs and, laughing, headed for the door. Jack paused to damp down the over-loaded fire and fit the guard in place. By the time he reached the front door, the other four were already seated in the back of two cars, one of which Jack recognised. In spite of himself, Jack's breath quickened in hope before his stomach dropped as he accepted Sarah wasn't among them; rationally, though, he was thankful that she hadn't seen how he and Alfie lived.

The chauffeur held the door as Jack clambered in and settled himself opposite Alfie and Rose. There was blessedly little conversation as the car wound through Camberwell, crossed the river at Blackfriars Bridge and headed towards Strand. On Haymarket, the chauffeur slid in behind Williams' car and came round to open the car door. The street was noisy and busy, full of people floodlit in red

73

and gold by the theatre's billboard lights. Jack jumped out and held out his hand to help Rose onto the busy street, using his body as a barrier to prevent her being jostled by the crowd. She smiled gratefully and drew her fur around her shoulders with a shiver.

Alfie and Jack checked their coats and hats at the cloakroom while the girls hesitated in the middle of the foyer, apparently looking around for the ticket office. Williams, with his height advantage, soon spotted what they were looking for and pointed them in the right direction. As they headed over to collect their tickets, Jack suddenly realised someone was waiting for them, someone he had unreasonably but desperately hoped to see. Nerves twisted his guts as he smoothed back his hair.

Engulfed by her sisters claiming their tickets and programmes from her, it was some moments before Sarah could acknowledge Jack. She looked so elegant in a long dove-grey silk dress with elbow-length matching gloves. Her rich, dark hair was piled high on her head, exposing a lace-like diamond choker that ran the length of her neck. Matching earrings hung from her ears, swinging slightly as she moved her head. She wore hardly any make-up, in contrast with her ethereal sisters.

As she turned – at long last, it seemed to Jack – to greet him, he caught a glimpse of a sudden flush in her cheeks, though her eyes said she was as calm and together as ever.

"Hello, John," holding her hand out to him, which he automatically took in both his, subconsciously drawing the two of them closer together.

"It's good to see you again, Miss Samuels," he said, softly.

She nodded. "You too. Many happy returns of the day."

Jack snorted. "It seems I've done a very poor job of keeping it as quiet as I would have liked."

"I'm afraid that may be my fault," Sarah admitted, with the grace to look a little sheepish. "After you told me at Christmas that you would soon be celebrating a birthday, I took the liberty of checking it at the bank. I may have mentioned it to a couple of people." Her eyes suddenly met his. "Forgive me'?"

Taken aback, Jack lost his breath at the intensity of her expression.

The theatre bell rang suddenly and Sarah glanced around at the thinning crowd. "It seems we've lost our companions," she remarked, sliding her hand into the crook of Jack's arm. "Perhaps we should join them?"

It was all Jack could do to stop himself placing his hand over hers to hold it there. His skin tingled, even through the thickness of his evening jacket. Sarah lifted the train of her evening dress with her other hand, a small evening bag dangling from her wrist. Jack caught the fragrance of her perfume, warm, subtle and soft. He noticed that her hair was pinned with the same diamond clip she had been wearing at Richmond House at Christmas.

Slowly following the rest of the crowd up the tight, twisting staircase, they emerged into a small but opulent theatre, dazzled by the quantity of gold leaf on the ceiling, cornicing and pillars, which served to offset the mass of satin and diamonds on display. Sarah spotted her sisters and led them to their seats at the end of the row at the front of the circle. Almost immediately, the lights dimmed and the stage curtain was raised.

In the darkness, Jack felt, somehow, even more intensely aware of Sarah, sitting composedly next to him in the narrow seats, her hands neatly folded in her lap. He fixed his eyes on the stage, forcing himself to be still, but his mind span and he found it impossible to follow the thread of the Wilde comedy. To judge by the raucous laughter coming from Alfie and Charlotte, and the more muted version from Rose and even Williams, he was sure the play was entertaining. There was no corresponding laughter from Sarah, though, but he didn't dare turn to see if she was smiling. Her hands, he realised, were not as still as he had supposed, as she kept folding and refolding them, easing the gloves at the tips then crossing her fingers to pull the material tight again. Her knee was close to his and, as she shifted in her seat, unexpectedly came to rest against his leg. He held so still, resisting the instinct to move his leg away to give her more room, waiting for her to re-adjust her position away from him. She didn't. His mind buzzed.

The interval came suddenly with warm applause rippling throughout the theatre as the curtain came down. Sarah's eyes met his for a split second before she was distracted by Charlotte and Alfie climbing past them in search of refreshments.

Sitting back down after letting them through, Sarah turned slightly towards him in her chair, resting her hands on the arm between them, just brushing his sleeve.

"How was your birthday, John?" she asked. Her tone was quiet, intimate.

Distracted by her eyes, Jack struggled for a moment to recall how he had spent the day but, eventually, memories of George Duncan and his family cleared through the fog.

"I had a most enjoyable lunch with a colleague," he remarked, innocently.

"Indeed?"

"Yes. The eternally grateful George Duncan and Mr and Mrs Duncan insisted on giving me lunch as a thank you for the lengths to which I'd gone to help them in their predicament."

"Oh." The quiet sound was muffled by Sarah dropping her head.

"I felt a terrible fraud for taking the credit for something I haven't done," Jack confessed, picking absently at a thread in his cuff.

Sarah settled her hands back in her lap. "I apologise," she said, earnestly. "I would have told you if I'd seen you. There was no deception intended."

Jack relented. "I never thought there was. But, please, help me understand what happened. I didn't want to ask the Duncans, of course."

"I didn't really do that much," Sarah started. "After we had tea, I checked the details we hold on George at the bank and paid a visit to find out what the problem was at home. Poor Mrs Duncan was in a terrible state. I'm afraid I rather imposed on her by insisting on seeing her though she was so sick."

"I'm glad you did. I can assure you, she was looking much better today."

"That's a relief. You were right about the Friendly Society. They were dragging their heels in helping with their medical bills so Mrs Duncan didn't have access to the medicines she needed. I ensured our family doctor visited her immediately and then put Mr Andrews from the bank on the case to work with Mr Duncan to sort out the issue."

"That's incredibly kind of you. But I still don't understand how I got the credit for so much?"

"When I visited, I didn't want George to worry that the bank was checking up on him so I told them I was there are your behest, that you had specifically asked me to help them out."

Jack leant forward, his head still turned towards her. "I'm sorry you don't get to enjoy their gratitude directly. I can tell you, they are immensely thankful to you for your generosity and consideration. I am too. George is a good worker and a good lad. He and his family deserve the best."

"I was only following your lead," Sarah replied. "I wouldn't have known anything of their predicament had you not been trying to fix it yourself when I saw you last."

"Regardless," Jack insisted, gruffly, "thank you for your kindness. On George's behalf," he added, "and mine."

Sarah put her hand on his. "You're welcome." She held his gaze, her brown eyes as warm as the soft silk that touched his skin.

She seemed about to speak again but they were interrupted by the return of the refreshment-laden Alfie and Charlotte who started distributing ice-creams among their small party.

"Ice creams, Alfie?" Jack laughed. "In the depths of winter?"

"Charlotte tells me it's obligatory, old man," Alfie retorted, "so get it down your gullet and stop complaining. Don't you know it's your job to indulge everyone else on your birthday?"

Jack gave a forced laughed and settled back in his chair, still very conscious of Sarah sitting next to him and disappointed that the moment with her had passed.

* * * * * * *

The second act couldn't have passed quickly enough for Jack so, naturally, it seemed interminably slow. He quickly caught up the plot once he recalled he had read the play some years back and tried, unsuccessfully, to lose himself in the entertainment. He was relieved when the couples were finally reconciled and the apparent natural order of things was restored.

He slipped away from the crowd as the applause continued and managed to be one of the first in the queue to collect their belongings from the cloakroom. As Sarah and the rest of the party emerged from the stairs, he distributed various coats, hats and cloaks to the others, retaining Sarah's stole so that he could hold it out for her. She smiled her thanks over her shoulder as he stood behind her to drape the fur around her neck. His hands hovered; he was sorely tempted to run them over her shoulders, to feel the lines of her bones through the soft, sleek material. Sarah's head was still turned towards him, her face in profile, her breathing shallow, her body still, waiting. As Jack dropped his hands and took a step backwards, she forced a smile of thanks and, turning away, led the party out onto the pavement, searching out the car. They were ahead of the crowds and their driver managed to locate them quickly, pulling out of a bank of cars waiting further up Haymarket, waiting for their employers to disgorge onto the street. The soft hush of the tyres as their two cars pulled up in front of them made Jack realise it had been raining while they were in the theatre but now the night was clear and cold.

Sarah gave the driver the name of an hotel in Chelsea before settling herself into the corner seat at the back. The conversation was much less stilted leaving the theatre than arriving, with the younger Samuels sisters and Alfie happily regaling their quiet audience with a reprise of some of the funnier parts of the play. Gradually, the volume of traffic thinned and the street lights became a little less glaring until the car hushed to a halt in front of the glass doors of the hotel.

They hurried through the double doors, dodging the rain, which had restarted with avengeance. Sarah and her sisters disappeared in the direction of the powder-room and the men headed towards the bar where they were welcomed by the soft sound of piano music filtering through from the dance floor at the far end and the gentle hum of diners from the restaurant next door.

Alfie drew up a stool at the bar and, propping himself up on his elbows, immediately ordered champagne. Williams supplemented the order with a curt demand for scotch. Jack leant back against the highly polished bar and surveyed the scene. It was a new hotel, fitted out in a modern geometric style with monochrome walls offset with enormous mirrors in bold shapes. The thick carpet around the bar was an impractical combination of off-white and circular patterns in various tones of brown and cream. It was a startling but pleasing contrast with the gaudy opulence of the theatre. Couples and small groups were gathered around carefully positioned tables that, though the place was remarkably busy, gave an impression of both space and intimacy. Sheer fabrics adorned the full-length windows of the high-ceilinged room instead of the usual heavy brocades and were clearly more for adornment than practicality as none had been drawn against the night. The brilliant lights, electric but with candles to

79

enhance the ambience, multiplied as reflections in the darkened windows, creating a dizzying sense of an even more extensive room. The bar opened onto a dance floor at the far end where Jack could dimly make out the form of couples swaying slowly to a bittersweet melody from the piano. Another set of glass double-doors gave onto the dining room, where candlelight seemed the predominant light source, enclosing each table in an intimate cocoon of light and dark.

Sarah appeared in the doorway from the foyer, slightly detached from her two sisters whose heads were close together as they shared a whispered conversation. Jack and Williams immediately stood up but Alfie leaned casually back against the bar, waving a half-empty glass in the direction of their companions.

"Drinks, ladies?" he offered, handing around glasses as the barman filled more.

Though she came round to stand next to Alfie, there was something in Charlotte's manner that suggested to Jack she was now being slightly more circumspect towards Alfie in Sarah's presence. Accepting a glass from his room-mate, he concluded that was no bad thing.

The maître d' arrived to usher them to their table, the only unoccupied one in the extensive dining room. A hovering waiter collected their glasses on a large silver salver and, preceding them to their table, returned their glasses to each of them as they took their seats. The way the staff were deferring to Sarah, Jack concluded she was either a frequent diner here or the table reservation must have been her doing. He started to wonder how much of a hand she had had in the plans for the evening.

Sarah ordered another bottle of champagne and a refill of Williams' tumbler as the waiter distributed out-size menus to them, fan-shape to mirror the outline of the styling decorating the bar and walls. The sommelier appeared almost instantly, unwrapping the foil on a bottle of vintage champagne. A waiter appeared alongside him to replace their existing glasses with fresh ones and he filled their glasses.

Sarah raised her glass and toasted John. "To John," as everyone else raised their glasses. "Many happy returns for today and may you have many more."

John acknowledged each of them, noting absently how Alfie's and Charlotte's attention was less than focused on him before returning to Sarah, her gaze holding his as she tipped her glass towards him with a smile then sipped the crystal dry champagne. Jack drained half his glass in one go, his eyes still fixed on Sarah's.

The sudden sound of a chair being pushed back on the dark wood floor broke Jack's concentration and he looked up to see Rose glaring at Charlotte, whose hand was entwined in Alfie's. Charlotte was still starting at Alfie but his gaze had been distracted by her sister, her slender frame rigid with tension and, Jack guessed, anger. Rose snatched up Williams' hand and, turning her back on her sister, demanded "Dance with me, Freddie." Williams just had time to put down his whisky tumbler before she was pulling him to his feet and dragging him in the direction of the dance floor.

"Rosie," Sarah called after her. "Don't you want to order first?"

Rose broke her stride briefly, throwing back over her shoulder "Just order me the sole," then, as her upbringing broke through, slowing and turning back properly though she continued to walk backwards as, almost in spite of herself, she glanced at her companion then added to her order, "and better make it a steak for Freddie."

Williams gave Sarah a slightly rueful shrug of the shoulders, though to judge by the grin on his face he was evidently enjoying the attention. His eyes strayed briefly to Charlotte, who, Jack noticed, had broken away from Alfie's embrace and had a slight vertical frown line between her brows. She had leant forward as if to call something to Williams but seemed to think better of it as Alfie covered her hand with his. She glanced down as she twined her fingers into his.

"Shall we?" suggested Alfie with a nod towards the departing couple.

"Come on, then," Charlotte responded, not waiting for Alfie to pull out her chair for her but leaping to her feet and following her sister at a pace.

"And what am I ordering for you two?" Sarah commented, drily.

"Steak for me too, please," Alfie responded, holding Charlotte back briefly with a short tug on her hand and a meaningful look.

"I don't want anything," Charlotte snapped at Alfie, impatient to get after Rose.

"Charlotte..." Sarah started, her tone containing a warning.

Her sister stopped abruptly and she spun back on her heel towards Sarah. "Alright, order me a Manhattan, if they know how to make one."

"You need to eat," Sarah called after her but elicited no further response.

With a slight sigh, Sarah turned back to Jack to apologise. "I'm afraid my sisters seem to have lost their manners and I seem to have lost my authority with them."

"You shouldn't be apologising for them," Jack cautioned. "They're both old enough to take responsibility for themselves."

"That's true," Sarah acknowledged, "but it doesn't make me feel any the less responsible for them."

Jack played with the ornate stem of his champagne glass. "Do you think you will always feel that way?"

He could feel Sarah studying him though his gaze was fixed on his glass.

"I don't know," she admitted, her tone thoughtful. "Perhaps. Or perhaps it'll stop once I have children of my own and someone else to worry about."

Jack thought about that for a moment. "You think you need to have someone of whom you need to take care," he suggested.

"Probably," dropping her gaze to the menu and starting to turn the pages deliberately. "Whether it's in my nature or just by virtue of the fact that I've always done it, I couldn't say. Certainly the instinct is a strong one."

Jack stared at the far end of the room where Alfie was enthusiastically whirling Charlotte around the dance floor and Williams was more cautiously manoeuvring Rose.

Shortly, the waiter reappeared and, after Jack had requested the lamb shank, Sarah ordered for the rest of them, including a fish dish for Charlotte, and discussed the selection of both a red and a white wine with the sommelier.

The tempo from the dance floor picked up, where the pianist, joined by a bass player and a clarinettist, was now picking out a jazz tune. Couples from the tables around them who had completed their meals peeled away and headed into the slightly darker area at the far end of the room to join the dancing couples.

Jack turned back to Sarah, an unspoken enquiry in his eyes. "Maybe later," she suggested, following his train of thought. "First, I'd like to give you your birthday present."

"But, you shouldn't..." Jack started, startled by the idea of Sarah selecting a present for him, unsure how he should respond.

"It's nothing big," she reassured him, touching her hand briefly to his forearm. "Just something I thought you would like," as she handed over a small parcel.

Jack stared at the elegantly wrapped package uncertainly. It was the only present he had received for his birthday and the thought choked his throat. He weighed the gift in one hand before ripping through the paper.

"I know you have already read it," Sarah was saying as he turned it over, "but I also know you like to collect books and I thought you should have this one in your library."

Jack shook his head, trying to clear the buzzing in his ears. It was an elegant, leather-bound copy of *The Moon and Sixpence*, and, as he opened the cover, he discovered a signature on the fly-leaf.

"It's signed by the author?" he glanced up, disbelieving.

Sarah smiled broadly. "One of the benefits of having good connections," she admitted, then her smiled appeared to falter slightly. "You do like it, don't you? You never did tell me what you thought of the book."

Jack gave a warm smile, wanting to reassure her. "Regardless of what I think of the book, this is a gift I shall always treasure."

Sarah folded her hands together. "I'm glad. I know it's not much but I wanted to give you something."

"It's more than you can know," Jack muttered. Sarah looked at him, quizzically. Jack drew a breath and looked up at the tables around them, at the dance floor, at the bar next door. Anywhere to avoid looking directly at Sarah. "It's the first time I've celebrated my birthday since before the war," he admitted.

Sarah frowned. "Before the war?"

Jack shrugged. "There didn't seem to me to be much point celebrating in France."

"I don't understand," Sarah pressed. "I would have thought celebrating a birthday would be, somehow, I don't know...life-affirming? Amid all that turmoil. And death."

Jack sat back in his chair and thought about that for a moment. "I'm sure it was, for most people. There were plenty of occasions when I helped others celebrate, both on the front line and when we were resting."

"But not for you," she prompted.

"That first year," Jack explained, "I was in training and we all still thought it would be over so fast. We were so optimistic, so confident. I thought, I won't celebrate my birthday here, I'll wait until we're back home and I can be with my family again. They sent me a parcel, you know," he mused, remembering suddenly. "Homemade cake, tea, tobacco. The works. I gave it away."

"Ignoring your birthday became your way of coping?"

Jack shrugged. "After that first time, I couldn't bring myself to celebrate any of the subsequent birthdays. Not even when I was in England, recuperating after I was invalided out the second time."

"You're still waiting to make up for that first missed birthday," Sarah observed.

"I guess I am," Jack acknowledged.

Sarah raised her glass. "To many more birthdays," she toasted. Jack smiled and touched his glass to hers in response. Sarah drained her glass and Jack reached across for the bottle to refill it but she shook her head. "Honestly, John, I think we could go for something a bit stronger. How about a glass of whisky before our meals arrive?"

Jack signalled to the hovering waiter and ordered a single malt for each of them. When the waiter brought the drinks, Jack clinked his glass against Sarah's, his eyes on hers as she put the glass to her mouth. He caught the ghost of a smile as she watched him watching her, pausing momentarily with her glass to her lips before tipping back the tumbler and downing the measure in one go. Jack hesitated a second before following her lead. Sarah laughed and beckoned to the waiter, ordering a refill.

"So," she mused, "you never did tell me what you thought of the book?"

Jack batted it back. "You first. You were reading it before me, after all."

Sarah leaned forwards, resting her forearms on the table. "I think Charles Strickland is one of the most obnoxious characters in English literature."

Jack laughed. "You don't pull your punches, do you?"

"You disagree?" Sarah responded, bemused. "The way he abandons his wife, treats his saviour and friend, the malicious enjoyment he takes in stealing away Stroeve's wife. How could you think anything else?"

"I think it is difficult to know what it takes out of someone to produce great art, nor whether there needs to be something odd for a person to be outstanding in their field. To me, the irony is that Maugham creates great art by writing a story that exposes it. It made me question what I am prepared to tolerate for the sake of having something beautiful or stirring to look upon, or something extraordinary to hear, for the sake of having art to stir my soul when I am incapable of creating it for myself. I think he takes Strickland to the extreme, lacking in subtlety, to make us question what we are prepared to tolerate."

Sarah raised her eyebrows. "You've thought deeply about it," she observed. "But did you enjoy it?"

"No," he laughed. "Charles Strickland is one of the most obnoxious characters in English literature."

Sarah burst out laughing, just as a waiter appeared at her elbow to serve their dinners and Jack looked up to see the rest of their party making their way back to the table. He was surprised to see Charlotte was being escorted by Williams. Her hand was on his sleeve, her body turned towards his, and he was looking down at her with a broad smile on his face, responding to her continuous chatter. Rose and Alfie were ahead of them and, to look at them, Jack would have concluded this was how they had started out. Rose was dancing along at Alfie's side as he told her a joke, apparently oblivious to Charlotte's flirtation with Williams. Alfie gallantly held out Rose's chair for her and, instead of returning to his previous place next to Charlotte, took Williams' seat, forcing the other couple to reposition themselves. Alfie twisted in his seat, turning his back towards Charlotte, the better to focus on Rose.

Jack frowned and turned to see Sarah's reaction. Her face seemed to mirror his bemusement and she raised an eyebrow at him.

He gave a slight shrug of his shoulders and turned his attention to his lamb.

Rose was neglecting her food in favour of continuing to distract Alfie. She had taken over his steak, pushing her own meal to one side, and was cutting it into small pieces as Alfie leaned towards her and whispered in her ear. She laughed and speared a piece of steak on her fork, offering to feed it to Alfie. Glancing across at Jack and Sarah, Alfie apparently caught a disapproving gaze as he took the fork from Rose and turned himself back to face the table. Rose, catching his change in attitude and discerning the reason for it, also adjusted her position and pulled her own plate back in front of her. She leaned sideways to push her shoulder conspiratorially against Alfie's and he glanced across at her and winked.

On the other side of Alfie, Charlotte was tucking into the meal she hadn't ordered. At least she had the good grace to glance up at Sarah and smile her thanks for the food. The cocktail order, it seemed, had been forgotten.

"Great steak," Williams observed. "Almost as good as I can get back home."

"High praise, Mr Williams," Sarah retorted. "Though I suspect the Scottish farmers would beg to differ. How's the lamb, John?"

Jack nodded, swallowing his mouthful. "It's wonderful, thank you. The best lamb I've had all day."

Sarah laughed. "Meaning your pork shoulder at lunchtime was better?"

"How did you know what we ate?" Jack asked, astounded. Sarah refused to answer, shaking her head with laughter in her eyes. "Well, it's hard to beat a good home-cooked meal, isn't it?" Jack retorted.

"Sure is," Williams observed, with a surprising amount of feeling.

"You poor thing," Charlotte patted his arm. "Are hotel living and fine dining starting to pall? Why don't you come to us for dinner? Mrs Hesketh would be delighted to feed you."

"How long is it since you last went home, Mr Williams?" Sarah enquired. "Or saw your family?"

"Freddie's sister is coming over next month," Rose interjected, leaning across Alfie, keen to demand her share of the attention. "Isn't she, Freddie?"

"Sure is, little one," Williams affirmed. "Her first trip to England and I'm happy you ladies will take her under your wing."

"We would be delighted to see you both for dinner at Lyall Street," Sarah offered.

"And we'll take you to all the best spots in the West End," Charlotte promised.

"Alfie must come too, then," Rose pouted at him. "He knows all the most exciting new places, don't you, Alfie?" leaning into him again with her hand on his.

Alfie swelled visibly. "I certainly do, sweetheart. No one knows London like me. The best restaurants, clubs and bars, just ask Alfie."

"That's settled then," Charlotte interjected. "As soon as Isabella arrives, we'll show her the sights."

"You might want to include some of the cultural high points as well," Sarah proposed. "I'm sure Miss Williams will want to see the National Gallery, St Paul's and Westminster Abbey as well."

Williams nodded enthusiastically. "Thank you, Miss Samuels, that's a grand suggestion. Isabella will be with us for at least a month so I'm sure we'll have plenty of time."

"Tell me about her?" Charlotte begged, turning herself towards Williams to cut Rose and Alfie out of the conversation. In the darkness it was hard to be sure but Jack strongly suspected Williams blushed with pleasure at the attention.

Jack leant towards Sarah, his voice low. "What's going on here?"

Sarah met his eyes then glanced back towards her sisters, both of whom were now paying close attention to their own companions. Charlotte and Williams were leaning forward, resting their arms on the table. Alfie had sat back in his chair and stretched his arm across the back of Rose's, encouraging her to turn in her chair to face him, almost tucking herself underneath his shoulder in the process.

"I can explain what's happening with my sisters," Sarah responded, meeting his gaze again, "but I'd appreciate your insight into Mr Edmonds."

"Believe me," Jack replied, "Alfie is very straightforward. He's just looking for a good time, with whoever can give him it."

Sarah's eyes narrowed. "That's it? He doesn't expect anything more? He's not looking for marriage?"

"In this company?" Jack denied. "Absolutely not. We're not fools, Miss Samuels. Either of us."

Sarah frowned. "I wish you wouldn't group the two of you together that way. Don't you see how different you are from Mr Edmonds?" with a quick glance in Alfie's direction.

Jack shook his head. "We're not that different, he and I."

"I disagree. You're an intelligent, thoughtful, educated man. They are not terms I would apply to Mr Edmonds."

"Educated? What do you know about my education?" Jack demanded, stung.

Sarah tipped her head to one side and contemplated him. "That's a sore point for you. I'm sorry, I didn't mean to intrude. But I know about the scholarship you gave up to go to war."

Jack shrugged it off. "There's no point thinking about 'What if?'. Perhaps I'm better off with my books instead. And," with a glance back at Alfie, "perhaps you do him a disservice," though there was little conviction in his voice. Sarah's expression showed him her scepticism. "Regardless, I can't believe Alfie's looking for marriage here."

"I accept your insight," Sarah conceded.

"So," he prompted, "your sisters?"

Sarah pursed her lips and glanced from one to the other. "They are, I fear, very competitive with each other, always have been. Underneath, Charlotte is looking for a husband but she has a rebellious streak that causes conflict within her. Intellectually, she wants to be a modern, liberated woman. Emotionally, she loves the attention of a man, wants the security and comfort of a good home and craves the status of being well married."

"You're a tough critic," Jack observed.

"I like to think I see things clearly," Sarah retorted.

Jack held up his hand. "I didn't mean it as a criticism. I just meant, nothing escapes you."

"I like to think not," Sarah relented, her offence swiftly disappearing. She returned to contemplating her sisters. "They are both so young. There are five years between myself and Charlotte, another thirteen months with Rose. It's Rose's second season, Charlotte's third. Charlotte has already seen several of her compatriots marry and, with so many men lost in the war, part of her is starting to fret. Unnecessarily in my view," she commented, "but Charlotte and Rose have both always been more obsessed by marriage than I."

"Why, then," Jack interjected, "is she spending time with Alfie?"

"That's the rebel in her," she explained. "Mr Edmonds represents an exciting, largely forbidden world. He's carefree and lacking in inhibitions. He's less careful of his behaviour than the other men of her acquaintance and she finds that dangerously attractive."

Jack nodded. "So, what's happening tonight?"

"Charlotte's no fool. She knows Mr Williams is a very good prospect for her. He's clearly interested in her, which naturally recommends him to her, and he's outside the normal sphere, being American, which appeals to her contrarian side. He's wealthy, possibly more wealthy than my father, so could easily maintain her lifestyle. When Rose started flirting with Mr Williams, Charlotte feared he might switch his attentions away from her so made a move to reassert her position."

Charlotte's head was close together with Williams', their voices had dropped to a whisper. In contrast, Alfie was still lounging back in his chair, enjoying the increasing attention he was getting from Rose.

"Where does Rose sit in all of this?"

Sarah grimaced. "Rose is infinitely more straightforward than her sister. She's besotted with Mr Edmonds and is determined to make him in love with her. The most strategic play she has made so far is to dance with Mr Williams to make Charlotte fear her position."

"Are you concerned about any of this?" Jack couldn't resist asking.

"Rose, no," she responded with a shrug. "It's a three-month infatuation and she will soon find someone else on whom to fix her attentions. Hopefully someone young and innocent enough to fall for her charms and marry her quickly. She will blossom when she finds herself in a settled world in which she has her own status. For now, she's too busy trying to compete with her more glamorous sister."

"And Charlotte?"

"She could do a lot worse than to marry Mr Williams," Sarah posed. "He's a strong man, confident and more experienced than she. She needs someone to lead her but someone who can also expand her horizons. There's an explorer's spirit in my sister that needs to be satisfied. She would do well to marry someone from outside her set who can open a new world to her."

"At least we know one thing in all this?" Jack commented drily.

"Which is?"

"Alfie will come out of this unscathed."

"No risk of him falling in love?" Sarah tested.

Jack shook his head. "No risk whatsoever. Alfie has an innate resilience drawn from very shallow emotional attachments. It was an invaluable armour for him in France. We lost so many of our men but Alfie was always the first to recover and pulled the rest of us out of the darkness."

"That's why you keep him around?"

"Perhaps," Jack considered. "I sometimes fear I think too much for my own good. Alfie's very good at distracting me. He makes me notice the rest of the world again."

They fell silent as Sarah considered Jack's assessment of himself and Jack summoned up the courage to ask the question that naturally followed their line of conversation. He coughed slightly to clear his throat.

"What about you? Sarah," hesitantly.

She contemplated him for a moment, resting her hand on his wrist. A glint appeared in her eye. "I, John? There's only one thing I want," with a glance to the far end of the room where the earlier trio of musicians had now expanded into a small band. "I want to dance."

Jack's heart jumped to a faster beat and he stood up to pull out Sarah's chair for her. She held out her hand as she rose and he took it in his, feeling the warmth of her skin through the thin satin gloves. She led the way between the tables, most of them now deserted by their occupants who had migrated to the dance floor.

The lighting was more subdued there and the floor was crowded with couples. Sarah found a way through to a space in the middle. Jack eased his arm around her waist, hesitantly drawing her to him. Her face was almost level with his, turned slightly away to look over his shoulder, her arm resting against his. His cheek brushed against her hair, a soft caress. The deep throb of the bass set a gentle rhythm and they moved slowly together, barely travelling across the floor.

Jack's breathing was shallow, hardly daring to draw breath. Turning his head slightly, he noticed Charlotte and Williams had joined them for the dance but Alfie and Rose had disappeared.

"Thank you for tonight."

"It was my pleasure," she smiled. "Hopefully we can start to make up for the lost years." She seemed to be considering him for a moment. "My father would like me to make a request, John," she started. There was a surprising hesitance in her voice that made Jack frown. "We're hosting our annual partners' dinner at the house at the end of the month. My father would like you to join us."

"Then I would be delighted to accept."

"You will need formal dress." Hesitant again. "My father..." She stopped and glanced towards Charlotte and Williams. She drew a breath. "My father is more than willing to pay for a new suit, should you need one."

Jack tensed and he knew she would feel it, that close to his body. He schooled his face into a blank expression, suppressing the instinctive pride that he swelled within him. "Thank you, Miss Samuels," he responded formally. "I am more than able to acquire a new suit for myself."

Sarah closed her eyes for a moment and sighed. "I'm sorry," she admitted. "I knew how you would feel. Please understand, my father means no slight. We feel we are imposing on you and that, as such, it is unfair to expect you to incur the cost."

"Are you still testing me?" Jack's jaw was rigid.

"What? No! Please, John," her eyes concerned now. "It was never a test. You're part of the future as we see it, my father and I. We want you to have a chance and that means involving you in things like this. Please understand."

Jack could feel Alfie's eyes on him from across the dance floor. He forced his shoulders to relax.

"You're very kind to include me and I'll be delighted to attend but I will take care of the suit for myself. I'm sure I'll get good use out of it at some point. Perhaps for Alfie's wedding," he forced himself to joke, relenting now and wanting to lighten the atmosphere his reaction had created. Sarah smiled and Jack's anger flooded away. "I'm sorry," he apologised, "I'm being so ungrateful. Especially after such a wonderful evening."

Sarah leaned back slightly to look into his face, holding his hand more tightly to balance herself and causing her legs to brush against his.

"Do you mind?" she murmured. He raised one eyebrow. "About Alfie and my sisters, I mean," with a slight movement of her eyes towards their empty table. "He's your friend and they are both using him for their own ends."

Jack gave a slight shake of his head. "Alfie knows how to look after himself," he muttered. "I did enough worrying about him in France and eventually worked out he has a knack for sorting things out for himself. Whatever happens, Alfie will be fine."

Sarah gave a tight smile. "I'm glad. I would hate to see you hurt by all this."

"You're very kind to me," Jack responded. They had almost stopped moving around the dance floor, swaying gently now to the music. "Why is that?" he whispered.

Sarah held his gaze. "Perhaps my sisters aren't the only ones looking for love," she whispered back. For a split second, Jack was sure the world stopped moving. His eyes were held by Sarah's, her warm brown eyes a deep liquid black in the subdued lighting. Unquestioning, he pulled her closer, closing the slight gap between them until he could feel the warmth of her body against his and rested his cheek against her smooth hair. Her hand tightened on his and he turned his arm inwards to draw her hand against his chest. She splayed her fingers on the lapel of his jacket, softly stroking the material. As he closed his eyes, she turned her face against his and he felt her soft lips fleetingly touch his cheek.

94

Chapter Four

The world around me started changing after that. At the bank, I was finding myself drawn into meetings with the management and even Mr Andrews had taken to saying 'good morning' to me. I was on almost constant alert, ever watchful for Sarah.

A letter was waiting for him on the hall table.

Jack stared at the heavy cream envelope lying on the dark-stained oak cupboard. He never received post. In fact, he had walked past this one twice, first when he returned from work and ran upstairs to change, second when he came down from his rooms to join Mrs Jones and Lucy. It was only as he rose to retire for the night, carrying their empty cocoa mugs through to the kitchen, that Mrs Jones drew his attention to it.

Even in the dimly lit darkness, he could tell the paper was of a good quality. The writing he didn't recognise. Black ink, sloping forward, looping. Confident, careful and precise, he thought. Somehow, he didn't need to see the return address written on the back to know it came from Sarah.

He picked it up. It wasn't thick. Only one sheet of paper inside.

He turned the envelope over and saw the address in Lyall Street, confirming his suspicion, his hope. Finally, he ran his finger under the seal and opened it.

It was dated that morning.

Dear Mr Westerham

I have taken the liberty of making you an appointment at three o'clock on this coming Saturday with my father's tailor. If you can forgive my clumsy attempt to offer our financial support, I hope you will accept this service instead. Mr Goldman is a tailoring marvel and would be delighted to provide a suit for you. However, as he has assured me, like any true artist his work demands time and he will need three weeks to deliver his masterpiece, hence my intervention on your behalf. I hope you do not object. Mr Goldman's establishment is at Highfield Avenue in Golders Green.

Yours,

Sarah Samuels.

Jack slowly walked up the stairs, re-reading the letter. Their rooms were quiet – Alfie was dining out, again – and he sank into the armchair nearest the fire to read the letter a third time by the light of the flickering flames. He sat back, thinking, the letter resting face down on his knee. Mulling over each word in his mind, trying to glean her intent.

Her offer to pay no longer stung, though even now his pride would not allow him to accept. He could distance himself enough to appreciate its intent without resenting its implication. It was an expensive gesture on his part to refuse her offer but not unaffordable. He still had most of his demob pay in the bank and had been carefully saving a portion every month since taking the job at Richmond's a year ago. It was an indulgence. He had little use for formal attire, the way his life was currently. Yet he knew he had little choice but to comply and he was grateful that she had thought ahead while he had buried his head in the sand.

For a long time, he stared into the fire, the letter resting face down on his knee, a cigarette slowing burning between his fingers, and gave in to thinking about Sarah. The house settled into silence as Lucy retreated to her bedroom. Mrs Jones would, by now, be dozing over her darning in her chair in the kitchen, her great black cat curled on the crocheted rug across her knees. Outside, the darkness deepened and the flickering flames cast long shadows across the floorboards of Jack's sitting room.

He understood his own motivations well.

He was twenty-four years old. At his age, his parents had been married for five years, borne two healthy sons and lost another, stillborn. They had worked from dawn until dusk, every day of the year, shouldering the burden of a dilapidated, rambling house alongside Jack's grandparents while still supporting the ageing previous generation. The few habitable rooms of the house had been filled with the dutiful tolerance of three generations determinedly maintaining their legacy for the new generation, for Jack and his brother. And here was Ed, repeating the same rhythms with his wife, Annie. His childhood sweetheart, not yet twenty-one and her first child expected at Easter.

Jack knew he should envy it but he didn't. He suspected now he may never have been cut out for that life but, regardless, the war had ensured he wouldn't go back to it. His life had fragmented. The time before, not uncomfortable but unchallenging. Then the black, brutal confusion that was the war. Memories to be forgotten, ignored, suppressed, endured. And after. Now. Independence. Solitude. Silence. Peace. And, if he was honest with himself, detachment. Around him, people to be treated with consideration, courtesy, a kindness born of that brutality. But none who touched the empty space within him. None who saw the hard wall of trampled emotion built around that void. None who saw beyond the surface or suspected the vacuum trapped beneath.

Except, perhaps, Sarah. That acute, considering stare of hers. When she sat with her head tilted slightly to one side, resting her chin on her thumb, the side of her forefinger tapping unconsciously against her lips, the slight narrowing of her dark eyes and the faint vertical line between her brows revealing her frowning contemplation. He worried she thought she saw more than the surface of him.

Intellectually, she interested him, certainly intrigued him. He envied her apparent comfort in any environment, her ease with people, her ability to reach out to and connect with everyone from the bank's partners to its lowliest clerk.

The disparity in their financial circumstances was considerable but their dispositions were not so very different. An interest in books, in knowledge, had survived a mediocre education. Their healthy respect for the preoccupations of their countryside communities left them without a burning wish to be immersed in them. A tendency to view the world from the outside helped them understand the motivations and foibles of others.

But her motivations were an enigma to him.

"Perhaps my sisters aren't the only ones looking for love," she had said. But she wasn't flighty like her sisters. She didn't give in to emotional fancies. She was a practical, intelligent, confident woman and she had no need of marriage. He knew that. It wasn't only that George Samuels was extraordinarily successful. She was a wealthy woman in her own right thanks to her well-born mother and a substantial trust inherited when she turned twenty-five. Even if she should choose to marry, there was a plethora of suitable opportunities around her, in London or in Cambridgeshire. What could he possibly offer her? He felt paralysed. To progress he feared would seem presumptuous, inappropriate.

Picking up the signed Somerset Maugham and turning it over in his hand, he caught the faintest trace of her perfume and an intense physical reaction swept through him. For an instant, he remembered the pressure of her hand against his jacket as they danced, her soft hair against his cheek, the brief brush of her lips.

He threw the book on the floor and stood up, turning his back to the fire as he heard the pressure of footsteps on the stairs. The light from the landing was blocked briefly as Alfie's silhouette appeared in the doorway, his head turned back towards the person behind him, his muttered words eliciting a soft female laugh. As he straightened up and moved into the room, he caught sight of Jack.

"Still up, Staff?" Alfie's tone was jovial, slightly mocking but there was an edge behind it. "Thought you'd have retired long since, it being a school night."

Jack looked beyond Alfie to where Charlotte was hovering behind his shoulder, her head down. Jack raised an eyebrow at Alfie, who jerked his head in the direction of Jack's bedroom door and raised his eyebrows in return. Jack frowned, a slight shake of his head his silent reproof but he bent to pick up the book he'd discarded and crossed the room.

"You're right," he conceded, opening the door to his room. "Good night, Alfie."

He could just make out Alfie's grin as he closed the door behind him. In the darkness of his room, broken only by the moonlight cast between the undrawn curtains, he swiftly undressed and clambered beneath the blankets. In the silence that ensued, he heard the muffled click of the door to Alfie's room closing.

* * * * * * *

He had written his response to the invitation before he left the following morning and dropped it in the post box en route to work. He wondered, briefly, whether to attempt to pass the response via the bank but something held him back, some qualm about keeping the bank and his personal time separate, however much Sarah was mixing them.

He approached Saturday with inevitable trepidation. The weather – a brilliant blue sky and sharp but chill sunshine – was conspiring to put him in a good mood, which only made him regret that he wasn't in the frame of mind to enjoy it. There was only one answer to that and he promised himself some time, however brief, in Charing Cross Road before he fulfilled his appointment in Golders Green.

As soon as he pushed open the glass door of Donaldson & Sons' Second-Hand Books Store, a reassuring calm settled over him. It was the smell, he decided. That dusty, musty scent of long-stationary books, of damp-mottled pages and tatty dust-jackets. There was a timelessness about the smell that conveyed a sense of a world standing still or, at least, standing apart.

Of course, he lost track of time and found himself cutting it fine for the journey across town. Paying for his latest choices as quickly as possible, he left the shop and broke into a run, heading towards the bus stop at the far end of Charing Cross Road. The weak winter sun had given way to a light drizzle while he was in the shop and he pulled his collar up around his jawline, tucking his parcel under one arm to protect it from the worst of the rain. Head down, he ran straight past Williams emerging from Foyle's and was only brought up short by the loud bark of his name in a trans-Atlantic tongue.

"Westerham! Hold up." Williams held his bear-sized hand out to greet him. "Where are you off to in such a hurry?"

"I can't stop," Jack stalled, catching his breath. "I'm late for an appointment at the tailor's. I've got to catch that bus," nodding in the direction of the bus trundling up the road behind him.

"Where are you off to?" Williams interjected.

"Golders Green."

"Well, never mind the bus, then," Williams dismissed. "I'll get you there. The car's just round the corner."

"That's very kind," Jack started to refuse.

"I insist," raising his hand to silence the objection he could see building in Jack. "Besides, it'll give me a chance to show off my new automobile. Come on."

With Williams determinedly striding down the road, Jack felt he had no alternative but to follow. He broke into long strides to catch him up as he disappeared into a side street.

A shining red Bugatti roadster, long and low slung, was parked outside one of the town houses, blocking much of the narrow road. Jack could see why Williams was wanting to show off.

"There's my baby," he practically crooned. "Just had her shipped over from Europe. Had enough of being driven around by everyone else and thought it was time to show you English what a proper car looks like," he laughed, releasing the brake and shooting the car forward. Pedestrians crossing the street scattered rapidly and Jack, unable to watch as Williams wove through the parked cars, turned to questioning Williams about the car.

"She's got twenty-five brake horse power and will do seventy-five miles an hour, top whack. Montague Andrews is racing her at Brooklands this year and I'd put money of him being in with a shot. Chrysler and Mercedes have got nothing to compare to this."

"I didn't know they were re-opening Brooklands," Jack mused.

"Yep, just as soon as they finish the track repairs. Criminal what the War Office did to the place, running those planes across it. It's more about flying than racing these days. Still, perhaps it'll be better than ever. Here's hoping."

"You know your cars," Jack reflected.

"Anything to do with engineering," Williams confirmed. "Back home, I was forever tinkering. Anything I could lay my hands on, any car or plane that I could get someone to take me to see. The old man almost despaired of me going into the family business. Swore I was going to end up a grease monkey somewhere."

Jack contemplated the man before him. Immaculately dressed in fashionable Oxford bags and with carefully slicked hair, he could nevertheless imagine this well-built man with his large, capable hands and his aura of underlying strength would be just as at home clad in overalls and splattered in oil. Williams reminded him of Sarah: that innate confidence and comfort in their own skin that would put them at home in almost any circumstance.

"You weren't tempted, then?"

Williams snorted and turned to glance at Jack, even as he spun them round a tight corner. "A man can dream," he laughed, accelerating hard, "but he also has to live up to reality, doesn't he? I'm my father's only son. There was never anyone else for him to leave the business to so there was never any question of me doing anything else. Besides, how else would I have met the beautiful Charlotte? What about you, then?" with a quick glance across at Jack. "You're not in the family business?"

Jack stared hard ahead, immediately defensive. "Not necessary in my case," slipping into Williams' more clipped conversation style. "My brother was better suited, freeing me up for other things."

"Banking, you mean?"

"The war," Jack commented drily.

"How much younger is he, your brother?" Williams probed. In half of his brain, Jack started sifting around for a subject to distract Williams but the man was relentless. "Did he see any action?"

"Just under a year," Jack admitted after several seconds of silence. In so many ways, knowing his little brother was out in the field as well was much harder than coping with the day-to-day turmoil of his own life. It opened a raw wound of fear, an emotion Jack had done without for years by then. "He was conscripted in July '17, sent into Belgium in November. Thankfully, he didn't see a lot of action. Mostly tedium and lack of supplies were the worst he faced."

Williams shrugged off Jack's falsely nonchalant tone, realising he needed to change the subject. "And now you've finished your first year at Richmond's, what do you make of the banking industry?"

"Old-fashioned, stilted and pre-occupied with its own self-importance."

Williams barked a laugh, slapping his hand against the steering wheel. "You don't pull your punches, do you, Westerham? Why don't you say what you really think?"

Jack smiled. "I might get fired if I did that."

"No worries on that score," Williams conjectured. "Not with you and Miss Samuels so close."

Jack stared hard at the road ahead of them, noticing the pedestrians had thinned out now that they were nearing Golders Green. When Williams' continued silence forced him to look up, he deflected the conversation. "When is your sister arriving?"

* * * * * * *

In the end and thanks to Williams' capable if somewhat breath-taking driving, they were barely three minutes late when they drew up outside Mr Goldman's establishment, a substantial place spread across four shop fronts and, according to the gilded lettering on the windows, combining a haberdasher's with a bespoke tailoring service.

"Hello, Mr Westerham," Sarah greeted him with a smile, holding out her hand to shake Jack's. "Thank you for accepting my invitation. And Mr Williams," reaching out to the tall American squeezing into the small reception area behind Jack. "A pleasure to see you again."

"You too," Williams returned, giving a mock bow over her hand. "I hope I got Mr Westerham here in time?" his eyes already sliding past Sarah to where Charlotte was hovering in the shop behind her.

"That was very kind of you to give him a lift. I hope it didn't take you out of your way?"

"Not at all. Perhaps Charlie might help me shop for a welcome gift for Isabella while Jack's getting kitted out?"

Charlotte looked more than a little unhappy at finding herself in Jack's company again, so much so that she completely ignored Williams' invitation and grabbed at Sarah's arm, pulling her away with a hissed "I want a word with you".

Sarah resisted, giving her sister a hard stare. "Let me introduce Mr Westerham to Mr Goldman first, Charlotte." Charlotte turned on her heel and stalked towards the other end of the shop. Sarah watched her go with a slight frown before shaking her head and turning to smile at Jack.

"John," reaching out with one hand to drawn him forward to the counter. "Allow me to introduce Mr Goldman." Turning to the wiry-framed tailor, "Mr Goldman, this is Mr Westerham, one of my father's associates, as I explained. He needs evening dress for our usual dinner at the end of next month. I was hoping you would be able to apply your considerable talents to help him."

Sarah was almost flirting with the older man, resting her hand on the arm of his immaculate morning suit as he came out from behind the counter to stand before Jack. He felt uncomfortable under the direct and intense scrutiny of the tailor's narrowed eyes, running up and down his ready-made lounge suit and, Jack was certain, finding it wanting. To such an educated eye, his clothes, shoes and hat must scream his status in society. The tailor, with his oiled silver hair, black jacket and striped trousers with their blade-sharp creases and perfect drape to a pair of highly polished shoes, must be wondering why this shabby man in front of him would ever be in need of an evening suit.

Then, suddenly, the little man's face broke into a brilliant smile. He clapped his hands together, once, then held out his hand to Jack.

"Leonard Goldman at your service, Sir. It is a pleasure to meet any friend of Mr Samuels'," he cracked another smile. "Especially one with such a good canvas on which to work."

Jack frowned in bemusement at Sarah, who smiled reassurance at him.

"Mr Goldman is an artist, John," she explained, tucking her hand into the crook of Mr Goldman's elbow, who turned the rays of his smile upon her. "My father rates none as highly as he, not even amongst all of Jermyn Street and Saville Row."

"Tchk," Mr Goldman's tongue clicked his disdain. "None can match my eye for cut or my attention to detail, my dear. I must say," he remarked, his hand still grasping Jack's and earnestly meeting his eye, "what a pleasure it is to see a young man investing in a quality dress suit these days. So many young men coming back from the war seem to have forgotten the importance of clothes and," with an obvious tut in the direction of Williams, "seem to be embracing informality. Little good will come of it, believe me." Jack almost burst out laughing that the old tailor could find fault in Williams' clearly expensive attire. He controlled his expression as the tailor drew him behind the counter. "Come, come. Leave your hat and coat and come through to my fitting room."

Jack handed his winter attire to the nearest assistant and started to follow the little man through the door to one side of the counter but was brought up short by the tailor stopping suddenly.

"No, no, Miss Samuels," grasping Sarah's hand with both his own as she made to follow him into the fitting room. "It simply won't do. No lady has ever entered the inner sanctum. I must ask you to take a seat for a moment."

"Mr Goldman," Sarah laughed, "surely…"

"No, no, Miss Samuels." The little tailor fixed her with his stare. "Never."

Sarah stifled her smile, glancing at Jack with a shrug and stepping aside to allow him to pass through.

"Mr Goldman," she called after them. Jack carried on into the inner sanctum as the tailor hurried back to attend her. "I hope," Jack could just distinguish her words in her lowered tone, "you will allow me to be involved in the process of selecting the cut and materials. Please," her tone became more insistent at the slight murmur of objection from the tailor, "it would mean a lot to me."

Mr Goldman demurred and shuffled, slightly hunched, into the fitting room.

105

Some minutes later they re-emerged, Jack having been measured, re-measured, turned and pulled. As the tailor and his assistant started to pull bolts of cloth and patterns books out of drawers and off the shelves, Jack wandered back to the main area of the shop, shrugging back into his jacket. He caught sight of Sarah, sitting with Charlotte in the far corner, Williams standing over them. They appeared to be in intense conversation. Or, at least, Sarah's lower mutterings appeared intense from the way she was leaning toward Charlotte, her hand resting on the corner of Charlotte's chair. In contrast, her sister's attitude appeared defensive and her expression was stubborn, her body turned away from Sarah and refusing to meet her gaze.

With Sarah's back turned towards Jack, Charlotte noticed him first and her eyes flared with distaste and anger. She cut into Sarah's conversation abruptly, turning to her face until it was only inches from hers and staring hard at her.

"I don't care what you say," Charlotte's raised voice rang clear across the shop. "He's not our class and you're just giving him ideas above his station."

"Sweetheart," Williams interjected, leaning over her, "what Sarah wants is her own business."

"Freddie," she countermanded, "you're making yourself ridiculous. There could never be anything between them."

"Oh, Charlie, darling, I never knew you had such old-fashioned standards," Williams teased. "Why, my father married the boss's daughter and they've all done very well out of it. Perhaps it's your quaint English ways but that's really not how the world works any more."

"Don't scoff, Freddie," Charlotte snapped. "You know nothing about how things work here in England."

"I may not know England," he retorted, "but I know people and I know how your sister feels about this fella," meeting Sarah's gaze.

Charlotte leapt to her feet and her eyes raked Jack up and down. "How could she? He's just an employee," she spat and flounced away, throwing the shop door open and slamming it behind her. The window frames shuddered. As she turned to watch her sister leave, Sarah's expression, frozen in anger at Charlotte's words, transformed as she realised Jack was in the room. She followed his gaze to where he was watching Charlotte jump into the passenger seat of Williams' car and fold her arms in temper. Williams straightened and slowly crossed the room. He stopped before Jack and clapped his big hand briefly on his shoulder.

"Don't mind her," he advised, his tone low. "The prejudices of a young, indulged girl, however attractive," with a wry grin, "are not representative of those among us who value you as a person, not as a heritage." He clapped Jack's shoulder once more and left the shop. Jack heard the engine of the car fire up and the squeal of the tyres in complaint as Williams pulled away too fast.

As Sarah approached him, Jack could see in her face she was fighting her mortification and her anger. He knew he needed to shrug it off, for her sake, for the sake of both of them. If he ever expected something to come from this – and he increasingly believed that was, at least, Sarah's intent – then he would also have to be prepared to face more of this. He felt the slow burn of anger in the pit of his stomach and steeled his nerve around it to suppress the part of him that agreed with Charlotte's assessment.

He held up his hand as Sarah reached him, forestalling her apology.

"She's wrong about one thing," pleased that his voice betrayed none of his anger or his fear. Sarah looked at him quizzically. "While my employment may suggest a certain 'station', your class background and mine are not so very different at heart. My country thought my life good enough to risk giving it up for the defence of the world you and she enjoy. As such, I will not allow Miss Samuels or anyone else to define my 'station' in life. Only I will do that."

He stopped, his heart racing and his breath coming short and shallow. Sarah stepped closer until she was almost against him, her hand resting on his arm and meeting him eye to eye. "Bravo," she whispered and leaned in to brush his cheek with her lips. "Bravo."

* * * * * * *

If Mr Goldman and his assistant had heard the commotion, they showed no sign and Jack silently applauded their professionalism. Mr Goldman hovered in the background until he caught Sarah's attention then drew her back to the counter and engaged her in reviewing the cut and material he was proposing for Jack's suit. Jack followed and stood silently by, little involved in the process until he was asked to shed his coat and try various different styles of jacket. His self-consciousness returned as he was stood before a cheval mirror, surrounded by Sarah, Mr Goldman and two tailor's assistants, scrutinising him, turning him, buttoning and unbuttoning the jackets, straightening the collars, tugging the tails. He submitted in silence to trying four different styles before Sarah, reading his expression, declared herself happy with the second one he had tried and called a halt to his discomfort.

She quickly selected three different materials from the samples placed on the counter and, calling for the bolts of cloth to be laid before her, pulled off her dark leather gloves, laying them on the counter.

Standing behind her, Jack was absorbed by watching her hands running over and over the fabric, stroking the nap, rubbing it between her fingers to gauge its thickness. Her nails, cut short, emphasised her square, capable hands. Jack lost all track of what she was saying. He knew she was talking to Mr Goldman, her voice soft, her tone amused, but Jack couldn't focus, couldn't hear her words. Her hands continued to play with the fabric, turning it over, smoothing it back into place, tapping it as she emphasised a point. He stood stock still, absorbed by the idea of those hands reaching out to him in the darkness, finding him.

He broke out of his reverie as the assistants started to heave the lengths of cloth off the counter and return them to the shelves. He realised the decisions had been made during his temporary mental absence. He knew he should object to her taking the decisions for him but he had such little inclination to do so that he let it go.

He also noticed that Sarah's tone had changed, suddenly becoming somewhat harder, more determined. She was refusing to meet his gaze, keeping her eyes fixed on the small tailor and with her body turned slightly away from him now, almost defensively. "If you would be good enough to charge that to my father's account."

Jack started forward. "What? No…"

She met his gaze now, the determination in her voice clearly evident in her eyes as she held up her hand. "No, John," she forestalled him. She raised her chin.

Anger swept through Jack, swiftly followed by a simultaneous sense of frustration and futility. He knew he had been manipulated because he could tell so well where this was going. Catching hold of her elbow, he drew Sarah towards the window, away from the counter.

"Sarah," even as he prepared to dispute with her, he acknowledged to himself how right it felt now to be calling her by her Christian name. He wondered when he had slipped from the formal to the informal and what it meant. "I won't let you pay for that suit." There were so many arguments he could make about his pride, about people taking him as they found him but he knew full well none would actually cut any ice with Sarah. She would smooth away his concerns, dismiss his fears and get her way. Better to get to the crux of the issue, knowing, even as he did so, where it would inevitably lead. It was a ridiculous dance around his pride and her determination.

She narrowed her eyes at him, carefully preparing her answer. He dropped his hand from her elbow but stayed standing close to her, so close he could hear her breathing change tempo.

"Let us understand each other," she murmured, trying to keep her voice steady but speaking so low he had to lean towards her to catch her words. "I mean for the partners at the bank to accept you as one of their own. My father's intent is the same. These are old-fashioned men whose sense of worth is wrapped up in their visible status, which is represented as much by their dress as by their oak-panelled offices and bowing subordinates." She placed her hand on his upper arm and ran her hand down the sleeve, and he knew she could feel the rigidity of the muscles in his forearm. Her skin touched his clenched hand, burning him. She looked up at him through dark lashes and he knew he had lost. "Do this for me," she whispered. "Do it for us."

* * * * * * *

The room at Lyall Street was already full when Mr Hesketh held the door open for Jack and ushered him in. It was stuffy, smoky too, with the haze emanating from a group hovering around the chairs grouped by the fireplace.

As Jack immediately caught sight of Sarah, he had the pleasure of watching her unobserved for a few seconds. She was wearing an exquisitely styled gown, silhouetting her shapely figure in dark green silk, her hands and forearms enveloped in dark satin gloves. Her hair was beautifully dressed too, drawn up from her shoulders and back from her face, adorned with feathers and emeralds. She gave nothing to the modern fashions but she looked classically, timelessly elegant.

He also enjoyed her noticing his arrival and the evident satisfaction that flashed across her face before she could calm her features into what she considered an appropriate expression. She took her eyes off him only long enough to rest her hand lightly on

110

her father's forearm, nodding him in Jack's direction. Mr Samuels deposited his whisky glass on the mantel and, squeezing one man's shoulder as his passed, crossed the floor to greet Jack, his hand outstretched.

"John, my boy," with encouraging warmth in his voice, Samuels captured Jack's hand in both his own. "You scrub up well, now, don't you?" he remarked, clear amusement in his eyes at Jack's new suit.

Jack lifted his shoulders ever so slightly, as if trying to shrug off his discomfort. "Miss Samuels has very good taste in clothes," he deflected, adding "as do you in tailors."

Samuels barked a laugh, releasing one of his hands from Jack's to grasp Jack's upper arm. "Never forget those who've been with you at the bottom, John," he advised. "I may not be exclusively Mr Goldblum's customer any more but I certainly put enough custom his way to keep him happy. Now," turning to face the rest of the room alongside Jack, "let's introduce you to those who have arrived so far. We're a small group tonight. Just us, two of the girls and the bank's six partners, plus two wives. It appears," he explained as he drew Jack into the group, "that banking is not well-suited to those seeking matrimony. Isn't that right, Mr Marsh?"

It also, to Jack's eyes, appeared to attract a very specific type of person. To a man, the four arrivals so far were of the same low stature and expansive frame as Mr Samuels, an impression reinforced by their uniform of evening dress, carefully controlled hair and bushy collection of facial hair in the varying forms of sideburns, bristling moustaches or, in one case, the two crashing together in a silvery wave across his cheeks.

Mr Marsh – Jack chose to distinguish him by the above average smattering of grey in his slicked back hair and over-powering smell of pomade – looked up obligingly as Samuels steered them alongside.

"What's that, Mr Samuels?" His voice was strangely at odds with his stature, light, high, almost effeminate.

"I was saying," Samuels repeated, "that banking seems to be a particularly attractive profession for either confirmed bachelors or widowers, to judge by our party tonight."

Mr Marsh scanned around the room as if he had never observed this for himself previously. "So it would seem, Mr Samuels," he rejoined, "so it would seem. Of course," dropping his voice to a confiding tone, "there's more than one of us would wish it otherwise, were Miss Samuels ever to consider relinquishing her surname," with an intent stare in Sarah's direction.

Samuels suppressed a smile beneath his moustache, drawing Jack forward. "Mr Marsh, you remember John Westerham from the clerks department. Mr Marsh," turning back to Jack to explain, "is our newest partner, having joined the bank – what is it now, Mr Marsh, 13 years? – yes, 13 years ago."

Jack shook the other man's hand. "Is Miss Samuels holding out on you, Sir?" he couldn't resist asking.

Mr Marsh gave him a quick wink. "I'm sure Miss Samuels is holding out for the right man, Mr Westerham. Sadly, she didn't find him among the partners so she must needs look elsewhere, I am sure." Withdrawing his hand and placing it solemnly over his heart. "I'm not sure how I shall bear the disappointment but a man must struggle along somehow. Though, as a widower myself, perhaps I shouldn't be so greedy as to believe I can twice marry well."

"Well said, Adam," Samuels clapped him on the back. "Now I must introduce John to everyone else, if you will excuse us for a moment."

Samuels drew Jack into the midst of the small crowd around the fire, apparently accidentally bringing him to stand alongside Sarah, who welcomed him with a brief smile. As Jack was introduced to all four partners already present, Sarah passed him a whisky then left his side briefly to welcome four further guests, the other two partners and their wives, who arrived together. Jack recognised one as Mr William Morton, senior partner at the bank. The other, by a process of elimination, had to be Mr Wise. The two wives were female incarnations of their husbands: Mrs Wise short and stout, Mrs Morton tall, sharp-featured and wiry.

Mr Morton, Jack observed, seemed intent on holding himself somewhat aloof from the group, his wife hovering just behind his right shoulder. Mr and Mrs Wise were quickly absorbed into the party, warmly shaking hands and exchanging kisses with the other partners but Mr Morton's brief nod to Mr Acre across the group caused the other man rapidly to rethink his apparent intention of stepping forward to greet him, dropping his eyes and falling back into the safety of the wider group. The rest paid the older partner no heed, picking up their conversation from where it had faltered at the new arrivals. Looking up, Jack was startled to find Mr Morton's eyes on him, appraising him but with no small amount of disdain poorly hidden in the set of his mouth. He looked away rapidly only to find Sarah's enquiring gaze on him and her eyes flicking suddenly across to Mr Morton.

Just as they finished their drinks and Hesketh announced dinner, Williams and Charlotte arrived in the room, the latter looking a little flustered. It earned them a sharp look from Sarah as she and Samuels marshalled their guests and led them back across the hall through to the dining room. Jack hung back from the group to greet Williams and acknowledge Charlotte, who met his eyes with a tremulous half-smile.

Dinner was an occasion intended to impress. Samuels hovered at the door, directing each of them to their designated chair. The dining table, a substantial mahogany affair covered in a heavy white cloth and set in a pool of light in the middle a dark, heavily panelled room, was set with the best silverware, crystal and crockery, every bit as opulent as had been Christmas as Richmond House. Six courses ensued, in every way belying the continuing shortages from the war and the hard winter, from the tender grouse to the succulent steak and alcohol- and sugar-rich trifle for dessert. Seated to Mr Samuels' left at the centre of the table, Jack enjoyed an uninterrupted view of Sarah, carefully managing Mr Wise and his nervous-looking wife to her right and the jovial, amorous Mr Marsh to her left. As the dessert was cleared and replaced with impossibly copious quantities of cheese, the conversation inevitably turned to bank business. Catching the tail end of a discussion as other conversation drifted away, Jack realised Williams was gnawing away at a theme he had heard him expound before.

"But there's only one way to come out of this and that's to invest."

"What's that, Mr Williams?" Samuels inserted the rest of the table into the discussion.

"I was saying, Mr Samuels," slowing his naturally quick tones to be heard better around the group, "that both our governments need to be investing right now, particularly in infrastructure, to pull us out of the doldrums we're both suffering. We need to get our industries working again but our governments need to be backing private investment with money of their own in the big projects we require to support the entrepreneurs."

"There are no two ways about it," Mr Wise interjected mournfully. "We are not coming out of the war well. The papers are reporting ever higher unemployment and the discontent from last December looks like it's spreading."

Tuts and clicks around the table suggested most recognised the problem but had little to offer in the way of solutions.

"And what do we do about all the young women?" Mrs Wise proposed, speaking directly at her husband though loud enough to take in the whole table. "They have no interest in returning to their usual duties now they have had to be useful for the last few years."

"'Had to be useful'," Mr Morton scorned, staring intently at his lean fingers carefully turning the twisted stem of his wine glass. "Are you suggesting being a wife, mother and housekeeper is not a useful preoccupation for a woman now?" He brought his gaze up suddenly and stared intently as the unfortunate target of his disdain. Mrs Wise blushed and sank back in her seat.

Charlotte leant forward, intent on taking up the baton. "Mr Morton, you know full well that's not what she meant," she chided him, confidently drawing his attention away from the other woman. "It's a very reasonable question. A lot of the young women of my acquaintance don't see why they should give up their jobs now just because the men are back from the war. They were doing the jobs just as capably as the men so why shouldn't they continue to do so?"

"Oh but, my dear, what about our poor heroes?" Mr Marsh posed. "They've given us so much. We owe them a living when they are ready to work again." He rested his hand on Sarah's as he spoke, patting it absently like an affectionate old uncle. Sarah stilled the flicker of a smile that Jack glimpsed playing around her mouth.

"Then what must the women do?" Charlotte had the bit between her teeth. "Return to paying visits and embroidering their afternoons away? This is the 1920s. It's time we were allowed to spread our wings," she insisted.

"Fine words, Miss Samuels," Mr Morton rejoined. "And what is it we are keeping you from doing, exactly?" Stung, the colour drained from Charlotte's cheeks and her eyes flicked to Sarah for reassurance.

"We're not debating to what Charlotte would like to turn her talents," Sarah leapt to her sister's defence but her tone was calm, rational, "but the right of women to continue to work. Clearly, we must support our men and enable them to return to as normal a life as possible, but must that be to the exclusion of our women?" She looked around the table, naturally drawing others to her side. "Our girls have discovered they have more to contribute. Surely we should encourage that?"

"And what would you do, Miss Samuels?" Mr Morton was now leaning forward, his face cold but his tone underlined with contempt. "Have the men claim this absurd new unemployment benefit? We all know where that will end. With the lazy masses scrounging off hard-working, decent people, that's where. With unemployment pay, there's no incentive whatsoever for them to get out of their slums and back to work."

Jack sat up in his chair, straightening his back, but hesitated to speak.

"Mr Morton," Sarah was saying, "the men I have come across, including many in our employ at the bank, are almost exclusively proud and independent men, entirely reluctant to rely on government support except in the most dire circumstance." Her eyes met Jack's, briefly. "These men were good enough for us to conscript, good enough to fight our war for us, without question. Why are they not, then, good enough for us to help when they have no other option available to them?"

"You're confusing the issue with emotion," Mr Morton dismissed, turning his face away from Sarah. Sitting next to Mr Samuels, he failed to discern the expression that flashed across his host's face. "This is economics, pure and simple," he addressed the partners at the right-hand end of the table. "You give a man something for nothing, why should he change his behaviour?"

There were murmurs from the partners, though whether of agreement or dissent, Jack could not discern.

"The trouble with economics," Sarah responded tartly, "is that it singularly fails to take account of the individual's response and treats us all as if we were like-thinking automata."

"The masses might as well be," half-joked Mr Wall, seated to the right of Mrs Morton. He half-glanced at Mr Morton as if looking for approval, though he found none.

"What I find so sad," Mr Marsh's musing tone was clearly intended to change the direction of the conversation, "is how many of our great families have been devastated by the war. Why, only yesterday the Dowager Countess departed the adjoining square for her country estate, with no intention of returning. I understand her London home is now to be put on the market."

Mr Samuels confirmed Mr Marsh's news. "Both the Earl and his two younger brothers were lost during the war," he affirmed. "The family has been shattered. The Countess is now left with a babe in arms as the heir to the estate and two grieving widows to support. Thank goodness she's of such a determined disposition herself or I don't know how she would cope."

Williams settled back in his chair, glass in hand, resting his other arm along the back of Charlotte's chair next to him. "Look on the bright side," he proposed, with more than a trace of humour in his voice, "at least it's an opportunity for men of talent to progress," with a wink and a slight tip of his glass in Jack's direction.

Mr Morton's face, already flushed from the endless stream of wine and port served with dinner, seemed to take on a deeper hue. "It's a Machiavellian man indeed who considers the tragic loss of a generation of our finest men 'an opportunity', Williams," he growled.

Williams' face took on an expression of innocence. "How so, Mr Morton? Is there no benefit to be had from overcoming centuries of in-breeding and all the inherent weaknesses therein to allow vigorous, intelligent men from the middle classes to come through, bringing with them innovation, fresh thinking and a determination to succeed?"

Belatedly realising Williams was intending to get a rise out of him, Mr Morton steeled his face and stared intently at the younger man. "Mr Williams," he started, dismissively. "As an American, you might be forgiven for undervaluing the heritage of generations of well educated, well brought-up families. Your ignorance, however, does not excuse your prejudice. Until you have something worthwhile to contribute, you would be well advised to listen and learn, and to save forming your opinions until you have had the benefit of being in our country a little longer."

If he had intended to belittle Williams into silence, he was both disappointed and instantly shocked as Williams burst out laughing, applauding his sparring partner.

Sarah exchanged glances with her father and, pushing back her chair, took the opportunity to rise from the table. "On that note," she invited the other ladies, "shall we retire to the drawing room and leave the gentlemen to their debates over their cigars?" As she circled the table, she paused between her father and Jack. Leaning down to kiss her father's cheek, she rested her hand on Jack's shoulder, squeezing it briefly as she moved away. He looked up but she turned away without looking at him, one hand drawing up the heavy hem of her dress, which rustled as she left the room. Jack watched her leave.

As the door closed behind the ladies, there was much scraping of chairs and heaving of sighs as the over-filled gentlemen settled themselves more comfortably in their seats and eased the waistbands of their trousers. Silence descended for a moment as Hesketh appeared with a box of cigars and proceeded round the table, trimming and lighting for each man who partook. Williams shook his head at the proffered cigar box, reaching into his breast pocket to withdraw a silver cigarette case. Catching Jack's eye, he leaned across the table to offer the contents, which Jack accepted gratefully.

Mr Samuels eased back his chair, drawing on his cigar and exhaling a cloud of smoke. "You really must try these one day, John," he advised. "There's nothing like it after a substantial meal."

"I'm afraid the new generation seems to have abandoned them in favour of cigarettes," Marsh observed. "Yet another sign of our declining standards, I'm sure," he proposed with a laugh.

"It's no joke, Marsh," Mr Morton, it seemed, was intent upon maintaining his argumentative mood. "Our way of life is under threat. Just look at what's been happening in Russia."

118

"Come now, William," Samuels cautioned in a deceptively easy tone. "One can hardly compare the Bolshevik revolution and the murder of the Tsar and his family to the gradual rebalancing we are seeing in this country."

Mr Morton puffed himself up at the casual use of his Christian name. "Perhaps you should worry rather more about this 'gradual rebalancing' as you put it," his tone now haughty. "After all, how many of our clients' families have been diminished through the war? From where will your next customers come?"

"Our customers, surely, William?" Samuels admonished, lightly. "Your family's bank may have been subsumed into Richmond but you are as much part of the business as anyone here. Unless you disagree?" An edge of reprimand had stolen into Samuels' voice. Mr Morton sank back in his chair. He posed his elbows on the arms of the chair, steepled his fingers and glowered sullenly across the table.

Samuels reached across for the decanter of port and poured a glass each for himself and Mr Morton before passing it to Jack.

"What's your view, then, John?" he asked carefully. "You've been quiet thus far but I know you will have a view."

Jack sat forward in his seat, allowing his hands to hang between his knees, thinking carefully about his response. "I think," he started, hesitantly, "we can spend a lot of time talking about what's gone before or we can face the circumstances before us. The economy has been left in a poor state by the cost of the war, there is a swathe of young men who would naturally have been our leaders who aren't coming back and even more who need to return to work that has been done very ably in their absence. This war has shifted our axis and we have to recognise and adapt to the fact that our world is turning differently now."

"What high-browed nonsense," Mr Morton muttered from the other side of Mr Samuels. Jack ignored him, warming to his subject.

"In many ways, Mr Williams is right. I know it seems counter-intuitive when we are already carrying so much debt but the government does need to invest because it will create jobs and create more wealth in the wider community."

Mr Norcliffe leaned forward from his position at the far end of the table to cut himself a substantial slice of stilton. "Surely we should be focusing on reducing our debt, stabilising the country's financial position?" he suggested.

"I don't believe our financial position is as bad as the press would have us believe," Jack responded. "Before the war, we were one of the world's leading exporters. The Empire is a huge market for us and we're highly productive. Our balance of payments can be healthier now the war isn't disrupting trade so much. The government should be investing in making us as strong an exporter as we can be."

"I agree," Mr Acre interjected. "What we need is the right infrastructure to support growth. Look what the rail network did for the country in the old Queen's day."

"But there isn't the money," Mr Norcliffe objected, in a less-than-convinced tone.

"Of course there is," Samuels stepped in. "Who wouldn't take Government bonds right now?" he asked, glancing around the table.

"I wouldn't," muttered Mr Morton, sullenly. Mr Samuels turned in his chair to look enquiringly at the older man. Mr Morton rolled his eyes and tapped the ash from his cigar. "We're facing rampant inflation, mass unemployment and a bleeding-heart Government intent of paying every man to sit around doing nothing all day. Are you going to cuddle that port all night, Acre?" he demanded suddenly, grabbing the decanter from his neighbour.

"Now you're just being argumentative," Mr Samuels surmised. "Government bonds have always been the bedrock of this business, the solid foundation that has given us the flexibility to take greater risk in other areas."

"Jack's right," Williams inserted himself into the conversation. "Right now we need to be putting in the road and rail network to support growth, and we need to be investing in companies willing to take risks, including in America."

"But it's more than that," Jack suggested, accepting another cigarette from Williams across the table.

"Meaning what, John?" Samuels encouraged him.

Jack drew a lungful of smoke before he spoke again. "Housing," he replied, exhaling. "A significant minority of the people in this country live in appalling conditions. A significant majority haven't got enough housing to go around. We end up with over-crowded conditions that benefit neither the individuals nor the economy."

"I have never heard such a load of liberal clap-trap in my life," Mr Morton was galvanised back into life. "What exactly is this little upstart doing here, Samuels?" Mr Morton practically spat as he spoke, such was the disdain in his voice. "What gives him the right to a place at your table? He's a minion, and not even a longstanding one at that. He arrived at the bank a matter of months ago. What exactly qualifies him to tell people who have worked in this industry for decades how to do our jobs."

The atmosphere in the room changed at an instant, shock freezing the expressions on the other partners around the table and a rush of blood flooding Mr Samuels' cheeks. He was about to interject when Jack leaned round him to address Mr Morton directly. "What exactly is it you object to, Mr Morton?" he posed. "The thought that investing in our people can be beneficial to the country at large? We already know that if you create a quality of life for people, they will be more productive. Cadbury and Rowntree proved that in the last century."

Mr Morton drew his chair in towards the table. "You honestly think giving people houses and unemployment benefit is going to improve this country's economy? You're living in cloud cuckoo land, boy," he scorned, bringing his fist down on the table for emphasis, causing the cutlery to jump and Mr Acre's port glass to tip over. Mr Marsh and Mr Norcliffe threw their napkins at him to stop the stain seeping through to the mahogany table beneath but managed to knock one of the candles over in the process, which spattered out but threw its pool of wax across the tablecloth.

Jack wasn't prepared to concede. As so often ahead of battle in the war, he found himself instilled with a calmness, a cool determination, just as the rest around him found the adrenalin flooding their blood and raising their tempers. His head was so clear it was as if he had not drunk a drop of alcohol all evening.

"Mr Morton," his voice cool, clear. "What we're talking about is government and private investment in an industry that will benefit our manufacturing industries and create profitable business for the housing companies. Plus support demand for extensions to our road and rail networks, encouraging further investment in infrastructure. That's what puts money in the pockets of our workers. It creates employment and makes unemployment benefit a necessary evil of the past. And at the same time families currently living in squalid, over-crowded, unhygienic conditions will have the opportunity to live to a standard that would still be significantly below the one you take for granted every day of the week."

He stopped speaking and drew a breath, staring at his adversary who had sunk back in his chair again but was trying to stare the younger man down. He raised his eyebrows to encourage Mr Morton's response but was interrupted as Williams burst out with a laughing "Bravo, Jack!" and a sharp applause. Mr Samuels indulged a slight smile on the half of his face visible to Jack, who also noticed the other partners in his line of sight were nodding in agreement.

"Right, then, John," Mr Samuels responded, sitting forward in his chair to block the adversaries' view of each other. "So what does this mean for Richmond Bank? What would you have us do?"

Jack sat back, leaning slightly towards Mr Samuels. "It only works if the building companies are confident there's enough demand for the houses being built. They will be looking for capital themselves so there's an opportunity there but they will need to see that we are prepared to offer mortgages to a wider group of people than previously. It will also need Government commitment to provide the road and rail connections to the areas being developed by the builders. It's a long game. There's no quick return to be won here but it's a sustainable, self-fulfilling business if we can only build confidence in the right areas."

Samuels nodded. "All of that is achievable," he reflected. "Gentlemen, I think we have an additional topic for discussion at Monday's Board meeting, don't you?" The muffled responses from around the table were supportive but seemed to contain amusement as much as agreement. "Excellent," Samuels closed the discussion. "In that case, I propose we join the ladies in the drawing room, shall we?"

As Jack rose from his chair, Williams came round the table and clapped him hard on the shoulder, keeping his arm there to guide them out of the room. Jack noticed Mr Samuels drawing Mr Morton to one side, waiting for the rest of his guests to vacate the room.

"Nice job, Jackie boy," Williams was congratulating him in a rather too-loud voice. "Nice job. Morton has had that coming for a long time but none of the others has the backbone and Samuels is intent on playing the peacemaker."

"It wasn't about Mr Morton," Jack insisted.

"I know that," Williams responded. "But that doesn't mean it wasn't a beneficial side-effect, now does it?"

Opening the drawing room door, he led Jack through. The room had been rearranged in their absence, with a larger group of sofas and chairs now lined up, regimentally, either side of the fireplace, and more lights lit around the room. The two sisters were seated together on one of the sofas, opposite Mrs Morton and Mrs Wise.

The paraphernalia of coffee was ranged between them but conversation seemed to have stalled and both Charlotte and Sarah shot them grateful glances at their arrival. Williams naturally made his way over to take the seat next to Charlotte; at a gesture, Jack more cautiously took the seat beside Sarah.

"Mary." The bark of command came from Mr Morton, silhouetted in the doorway to the hall. "It's time we returned home," he ordered.

Sarah looked up and seemed to assess the situation rapidly. She rose calmly, smoothing down her skirts, as the narrow woman opposite rose to take her leave. "I'm sorry to see you leave so early," she commiserated.

Mrs Wise took her leave at the same time as she and her husband were sharing a car home with the Mortons. Mrs Morton's thanks to her host were somewhat miserly, in Jack's view, as the three women crossed back to join Mr Morton at the doorway. Mr Morton's frigid half-bow spoke volumes before he spun on his heel and clipped across the hall, his wife trailing dutifully in his wake.

By the time Sarah returned, Norcliffe, Marsh and Acre had settled themselves in the drawing room and Mr Samuels followed his daughter into the room, conversing with her quietly under his breath. Sarah's eyes sought Jack's as her father filled her in on the post-dinner discussions and a slight smile played about her lips. Hesketh appeared behind them at the door with a tray of fresh coffee and they parted to allow him through.

Charlotte took the opportunity of the coffee arriving to vacate her seat, drawing Williams after her, and to disappear to the far corner of the room, ostensibly to choose records to play on the gramophone. Sarah suggested "something soothing" as she crossed the room to resume her seat next to Jack. Taking up the hostess position again, she provided coffee to each of the men without needing to ask how each chose to take it, until she got to Jack.

"Just cream, please," he requested.

"Most men seem to need theirs sweetened," Sarah observed. "Not you?"

"I got used to drinking it without in the trenches. Of necessity," Jack admitted. "However bad it tastes, I've never been able to go back since."

"Mr Westerham," Jack's attention was drawn by Mr Norcliffe. He had grown increasingly withdrawn during the debate over the dinner table but edged forward on his seat now, playing absently with the cuff buttons of his jacket. "How much do you stand by what you said just now?"

Jack frowned. "Why would you assume I didn't mean every word I said?" he posed, accepting his coffee from Sarah.

Mr Norcliffe looked down at his cuff and started to tease a stray thread back into place. "Very few people say exactly what they mean in the heat of debate," he noted, somewhat casually to Jack's mind.

Jack considered for a moment. "I know it's not fashionable to consider the condition of the worker in business today," he reflected. "But the men who are striking today aren't anti-capitalists. We're not facing a Russian revolution. What they're asking for is a fair opportunity to feed, clothe and educate their children, to put a decent roof over their heads, to buy their wives nice dresses. What they're getting is squeezed from every direction. A lack of employment opportunities. A squeeze on their pay. Costs that are sky-rocketing. They're in the worst of all worlds and they feel their leaders, whether commercial or political, are doing nothing for them. Add to that a strong sense of injustice that they risked their physical and mental well-being or even their lives to maintain this world they live in and you get frustrated, angry men misrepresented by the newspapers as radicals or revolutionaries in order to diminish the value of their arguments."

"Are you sure you're in the right business, Mr Westerham," laughed Mr Marsh. "With rhetoric like that, surely you should be looking for a seat in Parliament?"

The other partners laughed but Sarah, who had gone very still during Jack's impassioned speech, looked at him with that intense, speculative, assessing expression of hers, with only the hint of an upturn to the corners of her mouth to reassure Jack that he hadn't gone too far.

He stared down at his hands, cradling his tumbler of whisky. His hands were cold against the crystal. "If my convictions make me over-passionate, forgive me," he proposed. "But don't mistake my views as liberal rhetoric. From a commercial perspective, I fundamentally believe a worker will give more when not distracted by the conditions of his home or worried about the health of his family. Or, to argue the converse, I've seen first-hand how the distractions of home impaired the confidence, focus and determination of my fellow soldiers at the front."

"You have real-life examples?" Mr Norcliffe encouraged, leaning forward again.

"Too many to enumerate. Husbands worrying over impoverished wives, sons fretting for ailing parents, fathers fearing for sick children. All of them too distracted by their concerns to prepare themselves mentally for what lay ahead. You need not just believe me," Jack surmised, conscious suddenly that every eye in the room was trained on him and desperately wanting to deflect the attention. "I'm sure Williams can tell the same story?"

"Not I, brother," Williams admitted cheerfully, pouring himself a slug of whisky from the decanters on the sideboard and, with a gesture at Jack, offering him the same. "We came to the battle too late for me to see much action directly, though I thoroughly enjoyed putting my engineering skills to good use elsewhere." He rested his hand on the back of the chair taken by Charlotte. "But I buy everything you're saying about investing in housing. I see a great opportunity to make money at all stages in the game, from the investors to the builders to the buyers to the Government. If you're looking for support," directing the question now towards Mr

126

Samuels, standing by the mantelpiece, "I'm sure my father would be happy to stand behind you."

"That's very kind," Mr Samuels remarked, accepting a whisky from Hesketh who had come forward with a frown of disapproval to take over the whisky distribution from Williams, "but if the Board considers this a worthwhile area on which to focus we have the resources to pursue it ourselves, wouldn't you say, gentlemen?" There were nods of agreement among the remaining partners. "Besides," with a sip from his glass and a secretive smile, "I have other things in mind for you and your father."

"Sounds promising," Williams rejoined with a similar smile. Charlotte, who had been surprisingly quiet all night and was watching the interplay between Williams and her father with an intrigued expression, took the lapse in conversation to demand a dance from Williams who, with a shrug of feigned resignation, allowed himself to be dragged into the corner where the gramophone had lapsed temporarily into silence.

"Ah, what it is to be young and in love," mused Mr Marsh. "Shouldn't you two young things be joining them?" with a playfully innocent glance at Jack and Sarah. She raised an eyebrow at him in amusement, clearly knowing he was not about to dance before this audience. Jack shook his head with a wry smile and drained by glass. "Forgive me," he reflected, rising to his feet and giving Sarah an awkward half-bow, "but I must be heading home. Gentlemen," shaking hands with each of the partners in turn, "it has been a pleasure to meet you properly. Thank you for making me feel welcome tonight."

"Young man," Mr Norcliffe commented, "it has been a pleasure getting to know you a little better. I can see we must find out how we can make the most of you at the bank," with a nod towards Mr Samuels. "You have a brain that should be taxed rather harder than I suspect is the case with your current role."

"I couldn't agree more," Mr Samuels concurred, holding his hand out to Jack. "We'll see what we can do about that when we see you at the bank on Monday, John."

"Thank you, Sir," Jack gratefully shook the older man's hand. "For everything," he added quietly. Mr Samuels nodded and Jack turned to leave.

"I'll see you out," Sarah suggested, appearing at his side to lead the way back into the hall. As they left the room, Jack could sense a certain amount of movement among the partners and a buzz of conversation spring up around the four grouped on the sofas, joined now by Mr Samuels. Sarah discretely closed the door behind them.

"How are you planning to get home, John?" she posed.

"I'll see whether the buses are still running," he chanced, with a frown at the time showing on his pocket watch and secretly doubting his likelihood of success. Still, a long walk home might be the right outcome if it could clear his head a little.

"Nonsense," Sarah asserted. "Hesketh, could you order the car for Mr Westerham, please? He's returning to Crystal Palace. Byrne knows the way." Jack didn't catch Hesketh's expression as he turned away, which he thought was just as well. Left alone in the hall, Sarah took Jack's hand in one of hers and ran her other down the lapels of his jacket, pulling him slightly closer to her.

"You made a strong impression tonight," she murmured to him.

He narrowed his eyes, assessing her words. "'A strong impression'," he mirrored. "But does that necessarily mean it was a good one?"

"To those who matter, yes," her expression was amused. "You could never make a strong impression and please everyone here. Your audience was too diverse."

"Another test, Sarah?" he suggested, his breathing slightly shallow at her closeness, her hand flattened against his chest.

"Not for me," she smiled, raising her chin to meet his gaze. "I've long since learnt what I needed to. But we have to step carefully and that includes carrying the right opinions along the way."

"I need to be allowed some degree of independence," he warned, softening his voice to take the edge out of his words.

Her hand wound its way around the back of his neck, causing the hairs in his nape to stand on end. "Not from me, I hope," she whispered, drawing his head down until his mouth met hers.

Chapter Five

London, March 1920

*Over the next month, I would see Sarah at least three or four times
a week, dining with her family or some of the bank partners,
sharing a box at the theatre, drinking and dancing with Charlotte
and Williams at fashionable West End bars. She introduced me to a
world I had neither known nor expected to know. Then Isabella
burst into our world.*

Isabella Williams arrived in a flurry of furs, instantly
glamorising a world they had all considered fairly glamorous until
that point but causing them rapidly to adjust that perception and
understand it was lit in shadowy shades of grey.

"Darling," was, within minutes, recognisable as Isabella's
favourite term and one which Jack initially suspected was intended
to overcome an inability or unwillingness to commit people's names
to memory but eventually came to accept was just Isabella's effusive
adoration of everyone she met. "Darling, they told me it was cold so
I packed practically my entire winter wardrobe but, heavens, it's
practically summer here compared to New York and home."

Home was Chicago, though it transpired she spent little time
there. In fact, it seemed unlikely that Isabella had any kind of
permanent base as it appeared she was constantly trotting between
New York, Boston, Chicago and California.

It was dark outside and not a little cold as a deep fog, damp and
chill, had settled over London that evening. Spring still seemed a
long way off. They were gathered in the hall of Lyall Street, Jack
standing with Sarah, shedding his coat and hat having arrived at just
the moment Williams' sister swept through the grand entrance,
Williams trailing in her wake with Charlotte on his arm, his head
close to hers.

"Darling, you must be Sarah! Freddie and Charlie have told me so much about you already," Isabella held out a gloved hand, pulling back the wide furred cuff of her coat to enable her tiny hand to emerge.

"Miss Williams, it is a pleasure to meet you." To Jack's now-trained ear, Sarah's greeting was a little formal but also a little amused. "Am I to assume that 'Charlie' is my sister, Charlotte?" meeting her sister's defiant gaze with a smile.

"I think it's charming," Charlotte defended. "I think I shall have everyone call me 'Charlie' from now on."

"You mean they don't already?" Isabella's immaculately lip-sticked mouth was pursed into a perfect 'oh'. "But, darling, it seems so natural. So you."

Charlotte gave her sister a satisfied expression as Isabella started to unwind herself from her heavy, full-length coat. Hesketh appeared silently at her side to relieve her of the garment but if he had hoped to make a quiet exit he was to be disappointed. "Oh, how darling! A proper English butler. And what is your name?"

Hesketh gave Sarah a bemused look, who raised her eyebrows in resignation. "I am Hesketh, Miss. Butler to Mr and the Misses Samuels."

"Mr Hesketh, it is a pleasure to meet a genuine English butler," holding out her hand to him.

"Please, Miss, just Hesketh," he retorted, with a stiff bow over the extended hand.

"Oh," her hands flew to her mouth as she looked from one to another of them, "how silly of me. I've been trying so hard to remember who should be Mr and who shouldn't. Look at me," clapping her hands to her chest in a way that drew everyone's attention to her, "anyone would think I'm practically just off the boat. But, of course, I am, aren't I, Freddie!" Peals of light laughter announced her delight at her own joke.

She broke off just as suddenly as she had started, turning to Sarah with an exclamation. "In that case, I'm sure I should have called you Miss Samuels," holding out her hand again for a more formal introduction, "but I do hope," drawing herself closer to Sarah and covering their joined right hands with her left one, "you will call me Issie. Won't you, please?"

Sarah smiled, any formality swept away in the face of Isabella's attention. "I would be delighted," she responded.

"After all," drawing them even closer together and lowering her voice, "we're practically family, aren't we?" with a meaningful look towards Williams who was helping Charlotte out of her coat and scarf.

Sarah looked up at the pair of them with no small amount of satisfaction in her expression. "That would please me very greatly," she rejoined.

"So you must be Mr Westerham." Suddenly the blazing beacon of Isabella's lighthouse attention swung across to Jack and he felt startled, finding himself staring into the largest eyes he had ever seen, brilliant blue in colour. A deep, powerful blue, with an intensity that made everyone else fade into the background. Jack found his hand enveloping the most fragile fingers he had ever held but with a grip almost as strong as her brother's. Standing before her now, he suddenly realised how he dwarfed this petite creature. He hadn't expected that. Her bone structure was like a miniature version of her brother's, the same square chin, the same broad shoulders but softened, feminised. Her dark hair, so dark as to be almost black but glossy like a raven's wing, was short and bobbed, a careful curl caressing her jawbone. She wore more make-up than he was used to but it was deftly used, enhancing her sensuous mouth, framing her sparkling eyes.

She was watching him, her head tilted to one side, scrutinising him intently. "I see what Charlie means," she mused. "You are dark, aren't you? But she's wrong about you being intimidating. You're far too handsome for that."

Jack was at a total loss how to respond appropriately to her strange assessment, his eyes flicking across to catch Charlotte rapidly turning her eyes away from him, her cheeks flushed. Thankfully, Sarah rescued them both, inviting Isabella through to the drawing room for drinks.

The three ladies led the way, Isabella slipping her arm through Charlotte's, her head leaning in to catch her audience's attention. Williams gave Jack a rueful smile and shrugged his shoulders. "You'll get used to her, all of you. I know she can come across as a bit superficial but she's got a heart of gold that one. That is," he corrected himself, "until she's crossed. She can be your fiercest ally or your most formidable enemy."

Jack snorted. "I'll bear that in mind," he confirmed. Isabella flopped onto one of the sofas, declaring herself "absolutely pooped".

"I never imagined sailing could be so draining, Charlie darling," she explained. "I fully expected I would be able to relax for the journey. I'm so in need of recuperating after our latest jaunt but I hardly had a moment to myself. Captain Jefferson – can you imagine, Freddie darling," interrupting herself and gesticulating to attract her brother's attention, "a direct descendant of Thomas Jefferson himself, no less! Anyway, Captain Jefferson just insisted that I join their table every night and he was such a charming man I would have felt terrible disappointing him. He did have some charming guests," turning her butterfly attention back to her new confidante, Charlotte, "so it was hardly a chore. Mr Henry Mills Nesfield was my absolute favourite. What a sweetheart of a man. Some sort of wheat magnate, I believe. He seems to own half of the Great Plains. He lost his wife recently and seems to have lost his way in the process. I felt I had to keep his spirits up, which seemed so ready to flag otherwise. Though," dropping her voice as if sharing a confidence though she was still audible to everyone in the room,

"Lady Hutchinson, I'm sorry to say, didn't seem to take to me at all. I can't imagine what I could have done to upset her. And yet her two sons were so delightful to me. I would have danced all night if they had had their way!"

Isabella paused for breath long enough to accept a large glass of whisky from her brother. She sat up straight on the front edge of the sofa, carefully crossing her slender legs, revealing beneath the fringing on the hem of her dress an elegant, tiny pair of ankles, encased in high-grade silk stockings and slim straps to her heeled shoes, perfectly colour matched to the sea green of her satin dress.

"So what's the plan for tonight, brother mine?" she posed, carefully curling her hair back behind her ear. "I'm so desperate to see the sights of London."

"What did I tell you?" Williams appealed to Charlotte.

"What? What have I done now?" Isabella demanded. "Have I made another faux pas? I'm sure I shall be afraid to say anything for fear of putting a step wrong here."

"It's nothing, Issie, darling," Charlotte consoled her, quickly slipping into her new friend's mannerisms. "It was just that I thought you might be too tired after your journey to want to go out tonight but Freddie insisted you would be up for anything."

"Oh, darling, that's terrible kind of you to be so concerned for me," clasping Charlotte's hand in both hers. "But don't you find life's just too short to be wasting a moment of it sitting at home? I'm sure I shall have enough time for that when I'm old and married so I must make the most of my chances while I'm young and free. You do see, don't you?"

Charlotte nodded in vigorous agreement. "That's just what I've been telling Sarah all these years," she affirmed. She leapt to her feet and rang the bell. Hesketh almost instantly appeared and Charlotte gave him rapid instructions to postpone their planned dinner and to call ahead to The Asprey to let them know to expect their party within the hour. Sarah frowned her displeasure at the abruptness of her sister's commands to Hesketh but her glower seemed to go ignored.

"I must go and change," Charlotte insisted, turning her attention back to the small group. "I feel positively dowdy next to your glamorous dress," she informed Isabella. "Just give me fifteen minutes and I'll see what I can find that will come up to scratch."

"Don't rush on my account, darling," Isabella insisted. "A girl must be allowed enough time to look her very best. And I'm sure Freddie and Mr Westerham can keep me entertained," with a nod in Sarah's direction, "if you wanted time to change too, Miss Samuels."

Sarah looked up in surprise then glanced at her dress. It was more than suitable for dining at home, an elegant black velvet affair with wide sleeves that draped almost like a cloak. She touched her hair, the first self-conscious gesture Jack had ever seen her perform, and rose from her chair. "Perhaps a few minutes to smarten up," she agreed, with a slight grimace at Jack as she left. Jack faintly caught the sound of her apologising to Hesketh in the hallway for her sister's behaviour.

"Now, Mr Westerham," rising from her position on the opposite sofa and inserting herself between Jack and her brother, "tell me everything about you. I've heard heaps about Charlie and Sarah and Rosie but Freddie's very mysterious about you."

"Is that right?" Jack smiled. "I am, of course, at your disposal and will tell you anything you wish to know."

"Wonderful," she clapped her hands together. "So far, I know you work at the bank, Miss Samuel is very fond of you and Charlotte needs to be educated about her uptight, old-fashioned views."

"Issie…" Williams warned in rough tones. She tapped him on the knee to silence him. He rose and walked over to the drinks tray.

"I also know you are more than averagely intelligent, not inclined to share your views unless forced and very reticent about discussing how you feel about Miss Samuels."

Jack, his eyebrow quirked in a question, looked across Isabella to Williams, who gave him a shrug of chagrin. "Isabella has always been more than averagely blunt," he quipped.

"Hush, Freddie," Isabella ordered. "Do you have a cigarette, Mr Westerham?" She drew one out of his offered case and leant forward to accept his light. She scrutinised Jack for a long moment through a haze of smoke, playing the immaculately manicured, red-painted nails of her little finger and thumb against each other while balancing the cigarette between her first two fingers. In anyone else, the posture would have looked affected but she carried it off with style. "So, Mr Westerham, so far, so little. Tell me, then, have you and Miss Samuels discussed marriage?"

"Issie, really, you go too far," exclaimed Williams. Isabella just stared at Jack.

"No, we haven't," Jack replied, his voice level, his tone neutral. She was making him feel defensive but he wasn't about to reveal it.

"But you have considered it?" she probed.

"I can hardly speak for Miss Samuels," Jack reasoned. Isabella dismissed the comment with a flick of cigarette ash into the ashtray and a quirk of her left eyebrow. "As for myself, I have known Sarah since December. You will find me quick to make up my mind about people but I compensate for that by being much slower to act."

Isabella frowned and gnawed contemplatively at her bottom lip, painted to match her nails. It was a strangely erotic mannerism, drawing the eyes to the full, bruised skin, emphasising the impossible whiteness of her small, square teeth.

"She's a well-turned out woman," Isabella remarked, pointedly.

"She is," Jack concurred.

"Intelligent and very astute," she continued, watching him closely. "Business-wise."

"Undoubtedly."

"She clearly has flawless taste in men." Jack smiled but refused to respond. "And I do like a woman who knows her own mind," she remarked. "A woman who knows where she's going. Don't you, Mr Westerham?"

"In the current company, how could I possibly think otherwise?" Jack deflected.

Isabella leant forward, placing her hand on Jack's knee. "You are playing with me, Mr Westerham," she observed.

"It takes two to tango, Miss Williams," Jack threw back at her with a smile. She burst out laughing.

"Oh, Mr Westerham, I can see you and I are going to get along famously!" she pealed. "Miss Samuels may have to watch out. I might yet set my cap at you myself, Mr Westerham, if you're not careful. So, please, do call me Issie." Jack smiled his affirmation.

"Does that mean the interrogation is over?" Williams interrupted. "Because I think Jack's earned himself a drink," handing a glass over the back of the sofa to where Jack was sitting.

"Oh, I shall let Mr Westerham off the hook for now," Isabella asserted. "But," leaning towards him and dropping her voice to effect a menacing tone, "don't think I won't get my way with you," she warned. Then, sitting back and crossing her legs, "So have you and my brother revolutionised the staid world of British banking, yet?"

Jack frowned at Williams for clarification. "I've been updating Issie on various discussions here," Williams elucidated. "She's very close to my father and maintains a keen interest in our industry, on both sides of the pond."

"What do you think about Richmond Bank investing in America, Mr Westerham?" she proposed.

Jack swirled his whisky around in the bottom of the tumbler. It was the first he had heard of it but it was no sooner said than other fragments started to piece themselves together. He rolled it around in his mind. Was that why Williams was here? All this time he had taken it that Williams was a rich, charming playboy squandering his time beneath the pretence of learning about the British banking industry. Clearly, there was more to it than he had discerned. Was that why Charlotte...? "It's an interesting opportunity," he observed neutrally.

"Oh, Jack, it's so much more than that!" Isabella retorted. "I may call you Jack, mayn't I?" Her wide blue eyes met his, disarming him entirely. Long black lashes framed that simultaneously innocent yet oh-so-knowledgeable expression, a perfectly curled frame almost individually enhanced, lash by lash.

"You may," Jack concurred, wondering for a second if he would ever refuse this woman anything.

She crushed the stub of her half-smoked cigarette in the ashtray and requested another, which Jack instantly supplied, trying not to wonder how low his supply was getting. He struck a match and held it out to her. She cupped her hands around his to bring the light forward to her, even as she leant towards him. She ignited the cigarette, balancing it in the corner of her mouth and leaning forward to blow out the match, holding onto his hand the whole time. The flame shook slightly before she extinguished it. She held his eyes for a split second before leaning back and drawing deeply on the cigarette.

"This could be the making of both our banks," she returned to her subject so abruptly that, for a moment, Jack was lost.

"It could," Jack responded cautiously. He sensed Williams hovering behind them and was deliberately avoiding his gaze in the hope that he could play along long enough to find out what Isabella already knew.

"The way I see it," she continued, "you bring the trust they associate with a British bank, we bring the opportunities and the route in. It resolves a conundrum for both of us. US companies and investors need to know they're working with a bank they can trust, which Richmond's history gives us, but in their parochialism they also want to work with a US bank. What better, then, than to combine our strengths to make both of us stronger?"

"In a market where everyone is crying out for capital before the bandwagon of growth gets away from them," Jack observed wryly.

"Pre-cise-ly!" Isabella enunciated, missing his sarcasm.

"When did your father and Mr Samuels first meet, then?" Jack enquired casually.

"Almost two years ago now, I think," she speculated. "Yes, that must be right, isn't it, Freddie?" They both looked up to find Williams watching them carefully. There was an enquiry in his eyes as he met Jack's gaze and something stirred in Jack's gut, a warning. There was, then, more to this than he realised.

Williams raised his head at the noise of ladies' shoes on the tiled hall floor and the soft tones of women's voices. "It sounds as if Charlotte and Sarah are ready," he observed. "Time to make a move?"

Isabella leapt to her feet and danced across the floor. "Time to party!" she announced.

* * * * * * *

The Asprey was heaving. As they broke through from the chill night into the hotel, they hit a wall of heat and noise, the combined muddle of hundreds of over-heating bodies and a cacophony from two competing bands, one in the bar, one by the dance floor in the restaurant. The crowd at the bar was already three-deep and parties of people were huddled together between there and the maître d's desk, awaiting their turn. Williams pushed to the front and announced their party with great effect as they were immediately swept through the crowds and into the restaurant.

"Cocktails! Thank the Lord you Brits haven't decided to try Prohibition." Isabella pronounced as they took their seats in the heart of the crush around a small circular table, covered in a pink tablecloth and festooned with pink flowers and pink candles. "I'm inspired by the décor," she laughed at the waiter, "so I'll have a Pink Lady," but, on hearing it wasn't on the menu, leapt to her feet and ordered the waiter to take her to the head bartender. She disappeared back into the throng.

"You will get used to her," Williams assured them all. "I know I'm biased but nearly everyone takes to her sooner or later."

Charlotte rested her hand over Williams' on the table. "Darling, I think she's adorable. So like you in so many ways."

Williams choked on the glass of whisky he had deftly stolen from a passing waiter's tray. Jack could see the poor man apologising to the rowdy table he was serving for having fallen short with the order. Jack slapped him between the shoulders as Williams spluttered his objection to Charlotte's analysis. Thankfully, their waiter arrived with menus and, shortly thereafter, Isabella returned with a flustered waiter in tow carrying a silver tray and five cocktail glasses on one hand, cautiously navigating the crowds.

"Pink Ladies all round!" Isabella announced, then paused, her hands on her hips, frowning at the table. "No, this will never do," she reflected. "Freddie, you need to move round. I'm not having you and Jack sitting next to each other all night and talking about boring bank business. Charlie, darling, would you mind shifting round one seat, there's a love? There," positioning herself between Jack and Williams and opposite Charlotte and Sarah, "that's so much better. Now, where was I? Oh yes, Pink Ladies all round!" signalling to the waiter to deposit a glass with each person.

"I am not drinking one of your girly concoctions," Williams refused with a growl. "I'll be sticking to a man's drink, thank you very much," signalling to the waiter to bring him a fresh glass and one for Jack. "Trust me, Jackie, you'll be wanting one of these in a second." Sarah discretely attracted the waiter's attention and ordered a whisky for herself too.

Jack contemplated the cloudy pink liquid, sniffed at it and took a sip. The bitterness of the gin was all but masked by a sickly sweetness. Jack shuddered theatrically and Williams burst out laughing. "I warned you," he crowed. "Here, Charlotte, you have mine. I'm sure you'll enjoy it more than I."

"Shall we order?" Sarah suggested, seeming to want to get some sort of control back over the evening.

"What a good idea," Isabella concurred. "What would you recommend?" leaning back in her chair to talk to the waiter. Thankfully, his recommendations of the steak and the plaice suited everyone around the table in some shape or form. "Right!" announced Isabella, clapping her hands together as soon as the orders were placed. "How about a dance before dinner? There's no better way to work up an appetite."

"Look, Issie," Charlotte hissed, clasping her new friend's forearm. "Look who's just come in the door. It's Annabella Winter, the actress. Wasn't she on Broadway last year?"

Isabella spun in her seat, craning her neck above the crowds. "Oh, Bella, you mean? She was. It was such a divine performance. I must go and say 'hello'."

"You can't just introduce yourself, Issie," Charlotte's voice betrayed her dismay at her new friend's potential faux pas.

"Don't worry, darling, we're old friends," a flap of the hand dismissing Charlotte's concerns. "In fact, why don't you come and meet her?" She slipped her arm through Charlotte's as they rose. "Do excuse us for a moment, Sarah, won't you?" she excused herself and departed with a laughing "don't miss us too much, boys" thrown back over her shoulder at Jack and Williams, who had risen as they left the table. Her brother rolled his eyes at Jack in mock despair.

As the whiskies arrived, Williams picked up the conversation that had been interrupted earlier, explaining to Sarah that Isabella had let the cat out of the bag about the US plan. "So, now you know," he asked Jack, "what do you think?"

Jack shrugged. "What do I know so far? That you and Mr Samuels are planning some sort of – what, a joint venture? A new investment in the US?"

"Let's call it that for now," Williams submitted.

Jack rolled his glass between his hands, thinking. "It seems very plausible on the surface," he reflected. "It would mean a change in profile for Richmond," with a glance at Sarah, who was watching him closely, "but that's not inconsistent with how Mr Samuels has run your grandfather's bank since he took it over altogether." Williams waited, knowing there was more to come. Jack went back to contemplating his whisky, swirling the golden liquid in the bottom of the glass. He frowned. "Knowing Richmond Bank as I do, I can see what's in it for Mr Samuels but what's in it for your bank?"

"It's too big a venture for us to go it alone," Williams commented, "if we really want to take this seriously and go after the chance big style, which I believe we should. The opportunity is vast and will favour those brave enough to stake it big and take a big chunk of the market."

Jack nodded, accepting the explanation. "OK, so you would benefit from more capital behind you and Mr Samuels would benefit from another market in which to put his not insignificant capital to work." He went back to rolling his glass between the palms of his hand, thinking hard. "But," he hesitated, frowning, "I'm missing something, aren't I? There's more to it than that?"

Williams studied his fingernails. "We have a bit of a reputational issue to overcome," he admitted, looking away at where Isabella and Charlotte were chatting to the actress, not meeting Jack's eye. "Some less-than-sound investments we made during the war. We were too ambitious, over-stretched ourselves."

"You didn't tell me that," Sarah cautioned in a low voice. Williams shrugged one shoulder, embarrassment clear on his face. Sarah folded her arms and sat back in her chair.

"So," Jack summarised, "you're wanting Richmond Bank's reputation for solidity, respectability to front the business, supported by your father's connections to find the right opportunities?"

"That's about the sum of it," he acknowledged.

Sarah rested her hand on his. "So, what do you think of it? From Richmond's perspective? Should we do it?"

Jack prevaricated. "I'd need to see the projections in detail."

"Understood," Sarah accepted. "But, in principle, it's something you would support, subject to seeing the business case?"

"The principles are right," Jack agreed. "Richmond has a well-established position in London and the provinces, it's a trusted bank and, as a result, has a lot of capital behind it. The priority has to remain investing in Britain because it's the most straightforward way for the bank to make money but if Mr Samuels wants to take more of a risk with some of his capital and to invest abroad, pairing up with Williams' family seems a sensible way to go about it."

"Good," said Sarah, with a quick nod towards Williams. "Now, the girls are on their way back so shall we change the subject?" she suggested. Her face froze as she caught sight of another group across the dining room. Jack noticed her expression as he and Williams stood again to welcome Charlotte and Isabella back to the table and he followed her gaze until he saw Alfie, lounging back in a chair, his arm around the back of a girl's chair, casually running his hand up and down her upper back. It took him another few seconds to realise the girl was Rose. He met Sarah's enquiring gaze and shook his head. He had no idea Alfie had moved on from one sister to another.

Charlotte immediately started to chastise Williams. "You never told me you knew movie stars, Freddie!" she accused. "Issie says you've met loads of them." She flopped into her chair with a sulky expression on her face.

"Sweetheart," Williams brushed the idea away with a wave of his hand, which he then casually ran over her carefully styled hair, toying with the turquoise feathers projecting from the left-hand side of her head. "When you're in the room, why on earth would I be thinking about any of them?"

"Smooth," Jack muttered under his breath. Isabella caught the sound and winked at him.

"So, Mr Westerham, are you going to give me that dance now?" she enquired. Catching Sarah's eye, she added, "if Miss Samuels doesn't mind if I borrow you for a minute." Jack didn't see Sarah's response but he sensed her reach across to retrieve her whisky and had a strange feeling he had been dismissed. Isabella's hand reached out for his and pulled him to his feet, ignoring his half-protest.

"I can hardly dance with my brother, now can I, Jack?" she reasoned, weaving her way through the closely packed tables in the direction of the band. "So you will have to do."

"I'm so flattered," Jack commented drily.

"I don't go in for unnecessary flattery," Isabella noted, accepting the hand Jack held out and resting her other hand on his shoulder. "Not when I'm dealing with my intellectual equal. I prefer honesty. It's so much easier to know where one stands, don't you think?"

Jack laughed. "I'm surprised you accept anyone as your intellectual equal," he retorted, secretly pleased with her assessment of him. "Besides, how do you know if I am?"

She narrowed her eyes, peering at him through those brilliant blue eyes, which had darkened in the low-lit room. "Like you, Mr Westerham, you will find me quick to make up my mind about people. I suspect the only difference is that I act on my assessment rather faster than you."

Jack narrowed his eyes in return, mimicking her expression. "Decide in haste, repent at leisure," he advised in a half-mocking tone.

Isabella smiled, bringing her face closer to his. "I think you'll find, Mr Westerham," she advised, slightly breathlessly, though Jack

144

suspected she could turn on that sensuality whenever she wanted, "that the phrase is 'marry in haste, repent at leisure'."

"Even better advice," Jack acknowledged.

She laughed, a huskier version of that he had heard earlier. "No danger there, then," she confirmed.

"You have a man in mind already?" he surmised. Her hand slipped slightly in his and he grasped it tighter.

"Jack, darling," she joked, "You surely don't expect me to tell you all my secrets in one night, now do you?" Her eyes were asking him not to pursue that thought so he dropped it. "At least, not until I've had several more drinks," skirting them close to the edge of the dance floor and swiping a full champagne flute from a passing waiter's tray.

"You're as bad as your brother," Jack chided. "In fact, I think you must be a bad influence on him."

"But of course I am," she acknowledged. "Don't you know the younger child always gets away with so much more than the older?"

Jack contemplated her. "I suspect what you get away with has very little to do with age," he reflected, "and everything to do with charm. I suspect you have been twisting men around your little finger since you were five years old."

"Darling," she purred, "I started so much sooner than that." Jack laughed but, as he did so, caught sight of Sarah at their table. She was turned around slightly in her chair, facing away from the table and towards the dance floor. She was watching them. From this distance, her expression was inscrutable but her body language showed discomfort.

As the music came to an end, Jack stepped back from Isabella and gave her a formal bow, dropping her hand. As she led the way back to the table, Jack realised their numbers had expanded while they were away. Rose had taken Jack's seat next to Sarah and Alfie was ranged alongside in his usual pose, lounging backwards with his arm across the back of Rose's chair. As Jack walked past them, he noticed Alfie's hand absently caressing Rose's back.

He signalled a waiter for two chairs and settled Isabella next to her brother before positioning his own chair next to Sarah. She met his eyes with a slight smile. Finding another attractive woman at the table, Alfie immediately swung round to introduce himself. Isabella naturally went back into flirtation mode, the flattering, girly mask Jack was coming to suspect she used to present an appealing, unthreatening version of herself.

Rose was chattering away to Sarah and Alfie was into full charm mode with Isabella but Jack noticed that Charlotte and Williams had gone both silent and very still. Williams' hand on his lap was clenched into a fist and his back was rigid. Charlotte seemed to be having trouble lifting her eyes from her lap until she gradually became aware of Williams' discomfort. She covered the fist with her two hands, running them over his fingers and wrist. Finally he broke his stare away from Alfie and, meeting her pleading gaze, instantly relaxed.

"Dance with me, Freddie," she appealed in a low voice. Williams looked back across the table to where Isabella and Alfie were now engaged in an intense flirtation. He seemed to hesitate. Jack guessed he was unwilling to leave Isabella in Alfie's clutches but he knew as well as Williams she was more than capable of looking after herself. Charlotte hesitated and her second plea came out as barely a whisper. "Please."

Williams shook himself out of his mood and, giving her a broad, reassuring grin, stood, bowed ostentatiously and held out his hand to lift her out of her chair. They disappeared into the throng.

Jack glanced at Sarah who, like Williams, was watching Alfie closely. Thankfully, Alfie and Isabella also soon disappeared in the direction of the dance floor, leaving Sarah free to start grilling her sister.

"I ran into him a couple of weeks ago at a club," Rose explained. "I was out with the girls and they were bored because there were too few men to entertain them. Alfie recognised me and came across to say 'hello'. He's very charming and entertaining. Pretty soon all the girls were hanging on his every word."

Sarah's eyes narrowed in displeasure. "So that's why he's here with you tonight?"

"Oh, Sarah, he's not here with me," Rose declaimed in some embarrassment. "Daisy invited him."

"Don't be naïve, Rose," Sarah advised. "He's a very experienced man." Without looking at him, she rested her hand on Jack's knee. He put his hand on hers to reassure her. He wasn't about to take offence at anything she said about Alfie.

"I wish you wouldn't treat me as the baby sister!" Rose objected, pushing back her chair forcefully and rising to her feet. Anger flushed her cheeks. It seemed to come from nowhere which made Jack suspect it had been simmering under the surface for a while. Her hands, grasping the back of the chair, were trembling and her mouth was set hard. She stared in the direction of the dance floor, where her sister could be seen to be smiling up at her dance partner. She was hesitating over something, clearly warring with herself in her own mind. Determination seemed to steal across her brow, the set of her eyes. She looked straight at Sarah and said, calmly, coldly almost, "I'm not nearly as naïve as Charlotte". She finished her pronouncement with the slightest of nods then immediately turned on her heel and stalked off back to her friends' table.

Sarah frowned, shocked by the force of her sister's pronouncement. Her hand on Jack's knee tightened slightly. She tilted her head towards him so that he was in her range of vision but she wasn't looking at him directly. "What do you suppose she meant by that?" she murmured.

Jack expelled the breath he hadn't even realised he had been holding. Did she really not know? Thoughts fled through his mind.

Should he lie to her? Could he lie to her? Did she want to know? Could she take knowing? What would it change? How would she react? What would it do to Williams, whom he had come to consider a personal friend?

Within a fraction of a second, though, he had dismissed all doubts. For the sake of their still-fledgling relationship and by reason of who he was and what he felt for her, he was not going to lie to her, however hard the truth.

"I believe she's intimating that she knows Charlotte has slept with Alfie in the past." He kept his voice as low and as level as he could. Now Sarah met his gaze, shock written in her expression. She looked away, marshalling her thoughts. He was getting to know her expressions so well now. Appal, disgust, anger and, finally, realisation flitted across her face. She shifted in her seat and turned to face him, resting her knees against his leg as if for reassurance.

"When did it stop?" Her tone of voice matched his.

"A few weeks ago, I think."

She nodded, assimilating the information. She glanced over her shoulder at the offending sister. "She's not only naïve but also stupid, then." She judged before turning her gaze back on Jack. "You didn't tell me." It wasn't an accusation but Jack knew she was testing him. He wasn't about to apologise for his action – or inaction – but he was prepared to explain himself.

"They are both adults," he reminded her gently. "However much we might want to protect, we also have to allow them to make their own choices. I warned Alfie, after our conversation at the tea shop, but what decisions they make after that are up to them."

She nodded again and looked away. She was obviously not inclined to be angry with him. Wanting to reassure her, he took both her hands in his. "Sarah," the command in his voice brought her eyes back to his. "I will never lie to you," he pledged. "However hard the truth, I know how strong you are and I will tell you what you ask of me."

"But you may sometimes omit to tell me the truth," she vocalised his implication. His eyes confirmed her assessment. The set of her mouth said she accepted his distinction. "John, you are probably the most moral man I have ever known. Occasionally, it seems, our moral codes may not be aligned but I trust you will do the right thing, as you see it. That's all I can ask."

She leaned forward and kissed his cheek, sealing the agreement. Jack raised her hand and planted a hard kiss on her palm, holding her hand there. She splayed her fingers against the rough skin of his cheek, caressing his cheekbone with her fingertips. She brought her face close to his. "I trust you," she whispered.

Chapter Six

London, March 1920

Isabella instantly became an integral part of our group. Every time I arrived at Lyall Street, Isabella and Williams were already there. She dazzled us. Charlotte was half in love with her and half with Williams. She brought glamour and sparkle to our seemingly dull work, intent on enjoying herself in London, where she had temporarily broken free from the shackles of home. She sought all manner of entertainments and, in the process, entertained us. Though, occasionally, she would go too far.

"What do you want from life, Jack?"

Jack sensed Sarah tense next to him.

"Health, happiness and enough money to get by," was his glib response to Isabella's probing, his barriers going up. Ever since Isabella had arrived, it seemed she had been trying to draw him out. As if his natural reticence to talk about himself were somehow a particular challenge to her. "Isn't that what everyone wants?" He glanced around the table in the hope of drawing others into the conversation and displacing Isabella's attention onto someone else.

"That's not enough for me." Charlotte, thankfully, took up the baton.

Williams grinned at her, catching her hand and drawing it through the crook of his arm.

They were walking through St James's Park in the fading light of a crisp Saturday afternoon. It was the first good weather of the year, daffodils tentatively extending their green-flushed yellow trumpets. They had met Jack after his half-day at the bank to encourage him out for lunch and a walk.

"So what would be enough for you, sweetness?" Williams teased.

"I want to travel," Charlotte announced grandly, her eyes taking on a distant expression as she gazed beyond the constraints of her existing horizons. "I want to see New York and Los Angeles. I want to see the pyramids, the ruins of Pompeii and Michelangelo's statue of David. I want to be dressed by the best New York fashion houses and to dazzle everyone with my daring taste when I walk into a room. I want to party through the night with Hollywood stars then swim naked in the Pacific ocean as the sun comes up."

In short, Jack surmised, she wanted to be Issie. Williams snorted and she playfully slapped his forearm. He caught her hand and gallantly kissed it. "Whatever you want can be yours," he pledged.

There was carefully disguised pleasure in Sarah's expression as she met Jack's glance. She wove her hand around his elbow, rubbing her hand against the rough fabric of his greatcoat.

"What about children?" Isabella was like a dog with a bone. Jack suspected the unaddressed question was thrown in his direction but Charlotte flushed a deep scarlet, turning her face away from the group. He felt a strange sense of protectiveness come over him and leapt to answer the question in an effort to distract Isabella, who was watching Charlotte's reaction rather too closely.

"Everyone wants children, don't they?" He was prevaricating again.

Isabella turned her attention back to him, evidently more interested in her original target than the new one she sensed was developing.

"Not everyone," she disagreed. She had a strong argumentative streak, Jack had learned, though he suspected that, much of the time, she disagreed to have a debate rather than to expound her own contrary views. "Who would bring a child into the world at this time?" she mused, plucking at the catkins of a willow bowing over their path and scrunching them in her hand. "A world shattered by war, shackled by high unemployment and scarred by deprivation."

"On that basis, Issie," Sarah reflected, "the human race would never procreate again."

Isabella laughed. "Perhaps that's no bad thing," she cried, whirling around, her arms opened wide and setting the tassels of her fringed dress dancing. "Given what a terrible job we're making of it so far." Her raised voice drew the disapproving attention of a pinch-faced elderly couple on the park bench by the railings.

"Issie," Williams interjected, "stop being so argumentative."

"Who says I don't mean it?" she pouted. "Why shouldn't I? I'm sure this world would be a much better place without men to fight over petty pieces of land under the guise of grandiose differences of principle."

"But what you're arguing doesn't make sense anyway. It would only be the upper classes who stopped having children based on philosophical grounds." Williams could be as argumentative as his sister when he chose. "The working classes would happily keep on popping out families of ten or a dozen and where would that leave us in thirty years? Within a generation you'd have no educated leaders left and then we'd all go to rack and ruin."

Isabella feigned horror at that. "Freddie, you've clearly been spending too much time in England. Have you lost all your American principles? Have you been brainwashed by the creed of the upper classes? I'm ashamed of you. Besides," she started her argument again, "in the circumstances you describe, clearly the education currently reserved to the elite would be available to the middle class and you'd find a whole new echelon of capable leaders emerging from the proletariat instead of the aristocracy."

"Enough!" Williams' natural good humour declared defeat. "Can we please get back to talking some sense?"

They rounded the end of the lake and paused for a moment on the arched bridge, Charlotte leaning forward over the railings to stare into the depths below. Sarah rested her back against the parapet, facing towards the slowly setting sun.

Isabella hovered between the sisters, leaning forward like Charlotte ostensibly to watch what she was watching but, Jack suspected, more interested in the expression on her friend's face. Finding her friend unwilling to engage with her, Isabella reverted to Jack for entertainment, requesting a cigarette, which he presented and then offered to the others before lighting up his own.

"I must say," she preened the curls emerging from beneath her cloche hat as she pondered Jack, her head tilted to one side, the cigarette balanced between two fingers, her arm waving in the arm, "your friend Mr Edmonds is most charming, Jack." If Charlotte was detached before, her attitude was frozen at this pronouncement. She stared icily into the middle distance.

Jack saw it would fall to him to catch the thread of Isabella's conversation. He drew on his cigarette and blew the smoke down towards his boots. "Alfie? I didn't realise you had seen him again," he observed, neutrally.

"Oh, yes, darling. We ran into him last night, didn't we, Charlie?" with a tip of her head towards her silent friend. "At the Carlton, where we went for drinks after you left us after dinner."

Jack nodded to acknowledge her statement but sensed his contribution to the other side of the conversation wasn't really required. He waited for whatever it was Isabella was working up to.

"He's a tremendously good dancer," Isabella observed, apparently to no one in particular. "It's always good to have a good dancer in one's party, especially now we have such a dearth of attractive young men to entertain us."

Williams growled. "Issie, that's not very sensitive," he warned.

"Darling, I'm hardly criticising," Isabella protested, putting on her best impression of wounded feelings. "I know we all fervently wish those darling men were back amongst us again. I was just reflecting how hard it is to find a decent dancing partner these days."

"As long as he stays just a dancing partner," Williams' voice had a rough edge to it as he warned his sister.

Her eyes widened in apparent shock. "What are you suggesting, brother mine?" she declaimed. "You know me better than that," she insisted, her hand resting on Williams' shoulder. "Don't you?"

Williams relented with an embarrassed shrug of his shoulder. Isabella drew on the cigarette again and allowed her eyes to drift across to Jack, watching the interplay between them. "We can all flirt a bit," she justified, holding Jack's gaze. "But it doesn't mean we ignore our obligations at the end of the day." Her eyes seemed to be asking Jack to corroborate her view. "I mean," drawing herself upright and squaring her shoulders, "I know my position as my father's daughter and there's no way I would let him down." For the first time, Jack felt he was seeing beyond her myriad masks to the true heart of Isabella Williams.

"No one's doubting it, sweetheart," Williams reassured her, his voice still with a rough edge. He put his arm round her shoulders and squeezed her to him. Isabella hit playfully at his chest and shoved him away with a laugh, straightening her fur collar where his embrace had rucked it up. She gave Williams a mean glare and danced away from him, turning around in a way that enabled her to take in the expressions and preoccupations of the rest of the group. Finding Charlotte still determinedly staring out over the river, she alighted on Sarah, drawing her eyebrows together in an intense query.

"And you, Miss Samuels?" she probed. "What sort of family would you like?"

Her unexpected return to their previous topic of conversation threw all of them. Sarah's eyes narrowed as she seemed to ponder for a long moment. Not, Jack guessed, to know the answer in her mind but, rather, to decide how to frame her response to Isabella. Ever sensible of how her comments could be misread or manipulated by her companion, she was proving increasingly cautious with her answers to Isabella.

"I adore children," Sarah said simply, with rather more emotion in her voice than Jack had expected. Her eyes met his briefly then moved away to stare into the distance in a gesture strangely redolent of her sister's. "It's the strongest instinct I have ever known," she reflected. "I think I've had it ever since I was young. Maybe it came from losing my own mother so early."

Jack noticed Charlotte was watching her sister now, questions in her eyes. "Perhaps that's why you've always been so maternal towards us," she suggested, shrugging her cloak more tightly around her.

Sarah shrugged. "I don't think I could help myself," a self-deprecating amusement softening her voice.

"Well," Isabella reinserted herself into a discussion that was becoming rather too sentimental for her preference, "I for one plan to churn out no more than an heir and a spare before I get back to putting myself first. And," she pronounced, "I shall ensure I have a bevy of nurses and governesses so that I never have to do more than give the little darlings a goodnight kiss before I head out for dinner and dancing."

"Issie, darling," Williams warned, heavily mimicking his sister's preferred endearment, "have you ever wondered what might happen should someone take you seriously?"

Isabella put on a hurt expression, her hand raised to her throat in feigned shock. "Freddie, darling," her mock dismay making her voice tantalisingly breathy, "you stab me with your words."

Williams burst out laughing and levered himself off the bridge. "My sweet sister," gathering her in his arms and planting a kiss on her hair, "you know I adore you. We all adore you," he pronounced, looking to Jack for reassurance. Jack smiled and offered his arm to Sarah, who took it willingly as they headed down the far side of the bridge and back towards Piccadilly. Williams offered an arm each to his sister and to Charlotte, and followed them.

* * * * * * *

From their walk, it was inevitable that they would end up at The Ritz for early evening drinks but his hopes of dinner there and a relatively quiet night were soon frustrated as Isabella insisted on moving across town to a considerably more down-at-heel restaurant on the other side of the theatre district.

"Issie, when are you going to tell us what you've got planned?" Williams demanded as they took their seats in a dark and crowded dining room. He, Jack and Sarah had been covering for an unusually withdrawn Charlotte all evening. However much Isabella tried to draw her out, to tease her, to provoke her, Charlotte has remained monosyllabic at best, silent at worst.

"I told you," Isabella insisted, "it's a surprise." Her eyes met Jack's and a shiver of distaste crawled over his skin. When he shook himself, Sarah looked at him in concern and placed her hand on his knee with a question in her eyes. He shook his head at her, unable to articulate the sense of someone having walked over his grave.

It was the noise and excitement at a table in the opposite corner of the room that first alerted them. It caught Isabella's attention first and her smile of satisfaction distracted the rest of them. Charlotte turned in her seat to get a better view.

A small, dark-haired woman was standing over the people at the table, her hand on the shoulder of the man next to her, his upturned face showing bemusement and not a little discomfort. His fellow diners, though, seemed much intrigued and amused by the woman's words, the ladies' faces in particular betraying their dark delight.

"That's Elsie Batsford." Isabella's tone suggested the name should hold meaning for all of them but Jack found Williams' and Sarah's faces as blank as his.

"The medium?" Charlotte's tone spoke disbelief and not a little awe.

156

Isabella nodded. "I found out she's attends dinner here once a week. She goes from table to table, communicating what the dead are telling her."

Jack went rigid and Sarah seemed to sense it. She looked up at him enquiringly. He shook his head, once, hard. She frowned her confusion but whatever she was about to respond was interrupted by Isabella leaping to her feet and crossing the floor with surprising haste to attract Mrs Batsford's attention. It was the work of a moment to charm the medium into changing her route around the room and join their party, Isabella towering over the diminutive and shrunken frame as she supported the woman across the room to their table.

"Please, Mrs Batsford, won't you take a seat?" Isabella encouraged. Close to, the woman was evidently much older and more frail than had been apparent across the room, and the knuckled fists on which she leaned her weight against the table were twisted and swollen with arthritis.

"I shall not," she discouraged, her voice much stronger than her frame.

"Let me introduce…" Isabella started but was cut down by the woman.

"No names, no details," she insisted. Her black lace shawl slipped from her shoulders as she raised her hand to prevent Isabella. Instinctively, Jack, sitting next to her, caught it before it hit the floor. She fumbled as she reached to take it from him so he stood in order to drape it around her shoulders. As he sat back down, she placed one of those wizened hands on the back of his. Her hands were ice cold, the skin papery dry. The nails, too long, caught at his fingers and made his flesh crawl.

"Your scepticism is irrelevant," she looked him in the face with a warning. "Whether you want to believe it or not, they will speak and be heard if they will it." She raised her head and turned her eyes from one to the other of the group. "I need silence while I listen," she ordered. "No one must speak until I do." She closed her eyes and

157

Jack felt her lean against the table again. Was it his imagination or did the buzz of conversation around the room seem to diminish?

He deliberately looked away from her, away from all of them, staring at the far wall. He tried to empty his mind, turning his thoughts inwards, closing himself off from his environment. It was a technique he had learnt in France. As the silence continued, his mind started to drift. He started thinking about his impending visit to his family in Devon, including the newest member, Edward's newborn son, Charlie. The Easter bank holiday weekend was coming up and this was the first opportunity for him to go home since he had demobbed. Or, at least, the first of which he had chosen to take advantage. He felt ambiguous about returning, torn between an innate longing for his home and an inescapable sense of fracture, of never truly being part of that world again.

"There are many here tonight who would speak." The harshness of the voice, the suddenness of her words broke through his constructed silence. "But there is one who demands to be heard. He's showing me terrible places, scenes of blood and pain and despair. France, he says. But that's not where he died." Jack went rigid. "He's showing me a warmer place. Italy. Mountains lit with sun and lush with summer grass. That's where he died, he says. That's where he lost his life."

The claw-like hand suddenly grasped Jack's hand again and he couldn't help but look up. The woman's face, eyes opened now, turned slowly around the members of the group, from Isabella to Williams, Charlotte, Sarah and, finally, Jack. The glassy eyes stared straight into his, clear, cold, hard, and, yet, somehow distant, almost unseeing. "He speaks to you. He says you know this place and you know what happened here." The eyes suddenly lost their distance and blazed into his. "He says you must forgive and forget. He says you carry a burden that is not yours. He says it was his fault."

Jack's mouth had gone dry and he felt as if all the blood had rushed to his face, leaving his hands and feet feeling chilled. His muscles, rigid in denial, were painfully tight, his hands clenched on the table. He was dimly aware of Sarah turning in her seat and covering his other hand with hers. She moved as if in slow-motion. He could feel the cool satin of her gloves warm against his cold skin, the careful pressure calling his attention to her. He could hear her breathing, slow and deep, and realised it must be because he was holding his own breath. His eyes were fixed, unseeing, on the medium's eyes where he could make out her mouth, still moving though he no longer heard her words, drowned out by the pounding blood in his ears.

Somehow, a slight movement across the table caught his eye and he turned to meet Isabella's gaze. Her hand was raised to her mouth. Kid gloves, still too new to have developed their full suppleness. Three buttons decorating the cuff in a matching grey shade. The fur cuff of her evening coat slightly pulled back, revealing a narrow stretch of skin. A wrist so slender he could see the bones of her arms through the skin. Her face was flushed. From the warmth of the room or from something else? He could not tell. A strand of hair had escaped – been artfully placed? – beneath her cloche hat and twisted just below her left ear.

But her eyes. Her eyes were wide with shock and, he thought, not a little fear. He wondered abstractedly how appalling the expression on his own face must be to have generated such a one on hers. He wondered if his visage was betraying the fury boiling in his blood. A detached part of his brain started to wonder how he might yet contain his anger and continue to present a rationale, controlled face to the world. He must not lose control. He must never lose that control. The floodgates held back too much pain to risk even the slightest weakness in their defences.

It was as if the world had slowed to a fraction of its normal pace. He could hear his own heartbeat thumping now in his ears and feel the flush of anger gradually creep across his face from his neck to his crown. He continued to hold his breath, tightening his fists, and forced the rage rising in his gullet to retreat. The red mist that was threatening to cover his eyes, blocking from him all view of the room, started to recede. He concentrated hard on his heartbeat and, gradually, felt it slow, the blood draining from his face, leaving him feeling chilled but in control.

He realised Sarah was still clasping his hand. He faced her and, as gently as he could force himself to be, removed her hand from his. He rose slowly from his seat, refusing to turn his eyes towards Isabella again, though he knew, instinctively, her gaze was trained on him. He looked down into the eyes of the medium and found challenge and determination staring back into his.

Against every instinct to run, he forced himself to walk steadily from the room, knowing every tread was watched by the rest of the diners and determined he would reveal none of his fear. Eventually, he gained the front door and the blessed release of the bitingly cold night air. He walked down the road to stand directly below the solitary gas light, reaching for his cigarettes and matches. He stared at his hands for a moment, surprised to find they weren't shaking. Drawing a deep draught, he steeled himself for the appearance of the others.

He knew Isabella had deliberately brought them there. To get a reaction out of him? Maybe. She seemed to have been trying that for some weeks so it was entirely possible. Those details, though. Where had they come from? He knew there was only one plausible answer but he didn't want to think that Alfie would have behaved that way towards him. Not with their shared history.

The door opened and Williams appeared, Charlotte just behind him, exclaiming to Isabella, "Issie, where did you find that woman?"

"She's just someone a friend recommended," Isabella demurred, her eyes on Jack.

"Well, she's amazing," Charlotte opined. "We must come again."

"I think once is more than enough," Sarah remarked, drily.

"But, Sarah, she was amazing," Charlotte repeated, "I've heard so much about what frauds these people can be but that was so real. Didn't you think so?"

"Charlie, darling," Williams inserted himself between Charlotte and Jack, taking her arm and drawing her down the street back to the main road, "it was just a show, a performance."

"Don't be so silly, Freddie," Charlotte denied. "Of course it wasn't."

Williams laughed, but it was forced mirth, calculated to start breaking the tension that was hovering around and between them. "Honestly, Charlotte, if I'd known you were this susceptible I would have taken you in hand long ago. None of it was genuine. Was it, Issie?" with a glance thrown over his shoulder towards his sister, hovering behind him. Jack was still standing rigidly under the lamp. Sarah was next to him now, her hand resting on his arm. His body was turned away from Isabella, blocking his face from her. "Isabella," Williams' tone was harsh. He took a step to the side to stop her sheltering behind him. "Tell him," pointing at Jack. "Tell him it was all a show. Tell him how you primed her. He deserves to know." Jack had never seen him angry with his sister.

"Darling, you're taking it far too seriously," Isabella started, flapping at Williams with one hand. "It was just a joke. But...," defensive now, "she knew more than I gave her," she insisted.

"What I don't understand," Sarah interjected, "is why you did it at all? What did you think you were doing?"

"I only did it to see how he would react," Isabella was ready to attack to defend now, colour clearly staining her cheeks, even in the weak lamplight. She took a step nearer to Jack, narrowing the gap between them. "You're so damn calm, all the time," she accused, staring into his face. "How can you stand it? It's not normal. It's not natural."

She was almost shouting into Jack's face by now and Sarah, seeing a flash of anger on Jack's face, stepped in, putting her hand on Isabella's arm. "I don't think it's for us to say what is normal, Isabella," she cautioned. "Not for those who have seen what we haven't."

Jack broke his stare at Isabella to look at Sarah. "You think I'm not normal?" his voice sounded strain, his tone not a little bewildered.

Sarah's eyes narrowed. "That's not what I said," she murmured.

"Issie, time to go. You've done enough damage for one day and you can apologise to Jack tomorrow." Jack heard Williams drawing his sister away, leaving Sarah and he alone in the street.

Jack turned away from Sarah, lighting another cigarette to cover his emotions for a moment. Now his hand shook slightly and the flame of the match danced. He blew it out. "What did you mean then?" His voice was low, forced calmness.

Sarah took the cigarette from him and drew on it, considering her words as ever, then handed it back to him as she exhaled. "We've never discussed it so I know next to nothing about what you've been through," she observed. "I can't pretend to empathise, however much I might sympathise. What I do know is that I've seen the many different ways in which men have dealt with their experiences, those who have coped and those who have been broken by them instead."

Jack felt cold suddenly. The sweat that had broken out on him earlier had left him chilled outwardly as well as inwardly. He pulled his gloves from his pocket, the cigarette hanging from his lips. "What's your diagnosis then, doctor?" He was unable to inject enough humour into his tone to hide the bitterness.

Sarah looked at him, seeking out his eyes though he was trying to avoid looking at her. "Do you really want to do this here?" she posed, quietly. "I'm practically frozen and it's getting late. If you can stand it, I would very much like you to tell me about what it was like for you in the war but not here." She gave a reassuring smile. "Let's go back to Lyall Street and talk this through there. Shall we?"

Jack considered for a moment, torn between the need to be with her and the ancient instinct to avoid taking the lid off that particular box. He shook his head. "I can't face anyone else tonight," he reflected.

Sarah contemplated him. "Then walk me home. We can talk at the same time." She threaded her hand into his elbow, settling the matter; without thought, he bent his arm to accommodate her and, straightening, turned his back on the dingy street.

By the time they had retraced their steps and found their way back to Shaftesbury Avenue, the street was almost deserted. It was still early but the theatre-goers were already ensconced in their seats, their cars and drivers tucked into nearby side streets and their related taverns. Jack's repaired shoes tapped on the cobbles as they crossed Haymarket back into Piccadilly.

"You think I'm suppressing my war experiences," Jack mused as they walked. Sarah stayed silent. He gave a slight laugh, harsh in the quiet. "How I wish that were true. There's much I remember that I wish I didn't." With more clarity, more detail than he could bear, sometimes, too. He turned his head away briefly, forcing all-too-vivid images from his mind. "I've never talked to anyone about my experiences," he admitted after a moment's silence.

"Not your family?" Sarah frowned.

"Least of all."

When it appeared he wasn't going to elucidate, Sarah prompted him. "How so?"

He sighed. "Like many, the first time I was home on leave, I made the mistake of going home. I'd been wanting for weeks to see them. For most of us, it was initially what kept us going, the thought that life was going on as usual, that what we were doing was worth something to protect the world we loved."

"But?"

"But no one knew how to treat me or even how to talk to me. My experiences changed me, I knew that, but I hadn't expected them to change those around me. Or, at least, how those closest behaved towards me. Looking back, I think they didn't know how to react. They wouldn't ask me anything about how it was in France. They read the newspaper reports, they watched the newsreels, but they couldn't talk to me."

"Did you want to talk to them at that stage?"

"Honestly, I don't know," he admitted. "The reality was so different from everything they were being told. Perhaps they didn't want to know the truth. Perhaps I couldn't bring myself to open their eyes. It was hardest with my little brother, Ed, who was just desperate to get over there himself. Thank God he wasn't old enough until it was too late."

"Meaning?" Sarah pushed.

"Thankfully, by the time he had come of age, signed up and been trained, the war was all but done."

"When did you enlist?" Jack looked at Sarah warily. "What is it?" she probed.

He took a deep breath. "Sarah, I think I'm not ready to discuss this in detail with you. With anyone," he amended.

Sarah thought for a moment. "Why don't you just fill in the background for me, for now? Do you think you can do that?" Jack gave the slightest of shrugs, knowing he couldn't say no to her but still resistant. "So, you enlisted in Devon?"

"Yes, almost as soon as war was declared," he admitted, then gave a slight laugh of wry self-amusement. "I heard Mrs Pankhurst speak at a rally in Plymouth in August '18. She was advocating young men signing up."

"Mrs Pankhurst?" Sarah smiled. Jack's answering smile showed chagrin. "I wouldn't have pegged you as a suffragist."

"I was dragged there by Bella Carter. She's the daughter of the neighbouring farmer. We grew up together. She was desperate to hear Mrs Pankhurst preach so I drove her over there in her father's car. There was a recruiting station outside the hall. Dozens of us signed up then and there. We were actually fearful the war would end before we reached the trenches. We dreaded having to sit silently by, listening to the war tales of those who got there before us." He gave a bitter laugh. "Hindsight is a terrible thing, isn't it?"

"Where were you deployed?"

"We became the 8th Battalion of the Devonshires. We completed our training the following May and were attached to the 25th Brigade in August '15 in France. They told us stories," he reflected, "the men who were already there. Tales of when they landed in Le Havre nine months before, how they had been met with such a delirium of noise, of cheers and ships' whistles. There was no such welcome for us. Just freight trains we were packed into and rushed to the front."

"What were conditions like when you got there?" Sarah persisted in dragging information out of him.

"The losses had already been so severe they were desperate for every new man they could get their hands on. It was difficult, in some ways, because the Brigade had already covered itself in glory in '14, and we all felt the weight of expectation. Though it made it easier for the youngest ones, giving them something to fix their minds on. Some of them were so young, lads really, who should never have enlisted. Worse still, some were boys who had been working for the local and county councils and had been 'released' from their jobs so they could sign up. At least I had chosen my path."

"They would have been called up sooner or later," Sarah consoled.

"Yes," Jack acknowledged, "but how different might it have been for them if they hadn't reached the trenches until a year later?"

"You must have been young yourself," Sarah reflected.

"I turned nineteen the January before we departed so I was by no means the youngest. Nor the most naïve. One sees plenty of death and blood in farming," he commented drily.

They were passing opposite The Ritz hotel and could hear jazz music playing, drifting out from a club on Dover Street. Nearing the corner, they almost cannoned into some dance girl, exploding out of the club doors and falling down the steps into the street. She collapsed against Jack, laughing uncontrollably and grabbing onto his coat collar to stop herself falling in a heap on the pavement. "Oh my!" she exclaimed. "Aren't you a peach. Fancy a dance, darling?"

Jack helped her to her feet, steadying her as much as possible with one hand. "I think we should find you a taxi," he observed. "I'm guessing you've had enough for one night."

Her face seemed to crumple in disappointment. "But the night's only just begun," she protested with a pout of her painted lips. At that moment, another party-goer, a man in white tie, burst through the doors. "Daisy," he cried. "You can't leave me yet!"

The young lady pouted at Jack and smacked his hand away. "You see, peaches?" she slurred. "Just getting started." She took the young man's hand and staggered back up the steps into the blazing lights.

Jack smiled ruefully at Sarah and offered her his arm again. They continued their walk down Piccadilly.

"Just think," Sarah commented drily, "we fought a World War to give them the right to drink themselves into a stupor."

Jack shrugged. "We did what we had to," he stated flatly. "What we make of what remains is now up to all of us."

Sarah frowned. "You're surprisingly philosophical."

"It's easier than being angry," he agreed. "I have enough anger to last me a lifetime. I fear I have little room to add any more to my count so I choose not to do so for someone so trivial and, ultimately, harmless."

They walked in silence for a while towards Belgrave Square as Sarah absorbed his words. As they turned the corner into Lyall Street, she returned to their interrupted discussion.

"Were you in France throughout the war?"

166

He shook his head. "In '17 they selected us to move to Italy. The resistance needed support so they sent us first to the mountains and then onto the River Piave. We were there until the end."

"I've always imagined Italy is so very beautiful," Sarah sounded wistful. "I should like to see it some day."

"For us," Jack recalled, "it was like another world. Especially after the floods of Passchendaele. But, for all that, I have no real fix in my mind of the beauty of the place. I sense it, I have a vague awareness of it, but it seemed so unreal, the warmth, the greenness, after years of mud."

Sarah brought her other hand to rest on his forearm. "Perhaps we shall see it together," she supposed.

Jack looked down into her face. "I should value that very much," he responded softly, his voice made deep by his emotion.

"Thank you for sharing even this little with me, John," Sarah reciprocated. "I appreciate the effort and your trust in me." Before he could respond, she continued. "If you would indulge me once more, tomorrow I have a visit to make and I would welcome you keeping me company."

They came to a halt at the steps before Sarah's house. Jack frowned. "Will you tell me where? I have had enough of surprise visits for now after tonight."

Sarah relented. "I'm going to visit a recuperation hospital in Paddington. It's a small place, no grand affair, but I want to see what's possible to determine whether there is a way in which I may be of help."

Everything in Jack rebelled against the idea. Beyond Alfie, he had studiously avoided anything that continued to remind him of the war, including the Victory Parade and the Great Silence the year before.

"I don't think that would be wise," he evaded.

Sarah put her head on one side, contemplating his face in the gaslight. "I think it's time, though," she mused, her tone firm though quiet. "Isn't it?"

Jack closed his eyes, breathing deeply. Perhaps it was. He kept his eyes closed, even as he felt her hand on his cold cheek, her other resting on his arm as she leaned forward and pressed her lips to his. She came down from her tiptoe position as he opened his eyes and looked into her dark gaze.

"Even so," he demurred.

* * * * * * *

The large windows of the substantial Victorian brick building housing the sanatorium were starting to steam up. Not that it made much difference to the view: it had been raining, hard and incessantly, since daybreak and the constant rivulets of water on the panes had long since blurred any sight of the inadequate courtyard garden outside.

The room was painfully overheated, the cast iron radiators surprisingly efficient, in contrast with the ice block that was the corridor beyond, which, somehow, managed to maintain a temperature below that outside.

Jack's greatcoat was beginning to steam slightly but he still felt unable to shed his protective outer layer. He sat, legs crossed, arms folded, against the wall nearest the door, surveying the scene but far from ready to engage in it.

Visiting hour. What an appalling concept. A solitary hour once a day, perhaps even once a week in some people's circumstances, in which to recapture a facsimile of life before the war. After years apart, shattered families were trying to carry on a normal life with their husband, son, brother, father, in a single, unnatural hour. As unnatural for the families as for their damaged loved ones. Starting with those offensive signs outside, "Quiet for the wounded", the layer of sand distributed on the cobbles to muffle the horses' hooves and that absurd name plate proclaiming their welcome to 'The Grove'. As if there were anything sylvan about this forbidding Victorian monstrosity.

The inevitable stench of bleached hygiene had greeted them. Sarah, already well-known to the staff, was warmly greeted by a staff nurse and the resident psychiatrist, a gangly chap, receding hairline, small oblong spectacles, a chin set back from the upper jaw, a narrow pinstripe suit that had obviously been made for him and yet contrived to look some sizes too large for his spare, elongated frame. Jack acknowledged the introduction, shook the man's hand then promptly contrived to allow the man's name to slip from his memory.

He led them down the arctic corridor to the heavy double doors that gave onto the main recreation room. Small panes at eye level gave the intruders a glimpse of their targets before entering. They seemed instinctively to have congregated on the far side of the room around the tall windows, whether to take advantage of the weak light filtering into the room or desperate to be as close to a possible escape route as possible, Jack couldn't say.

As they entered the room, the official started pointing out patients to Sarah and reporting on their progress, as if they were so many rats in an experiment. Jack detached himself from the group as they started to parade around the room and deposited himself in a distant sanctuary.

Thank God for Sarah, he reflected, who was successfully softening the brutality of the professionals with a word here, a hand held or a shoulder squeezed there, counteracting the inhumanity of the doctor and his sidekick pronouncing prognoses and clinically delineating relapses while lauding it over these shattered souls.

There were some obvious injuries here. Men with bandaged eyes, sadly vacant jacket sleeves or trouser legs, wheelchairs in abundance. But there were more with subtler signs of damage. The one who couldn't meet his sweetheart's eyes, even as she caressed the hand lying unmoving between hers and sought his gaze. Another loudly ranting at a man of about his age, a brother perhaps.

At least they had visitors. Jack estimated fewer than a third had external company this Sunday afternoon. Several of those without had gravitated together but many more sat alone.

Jack sank further into his coat, pulling the collar up around his chin and resting his shoulder against a radiator.

"Do you mind if I join you?" The voice interrupting Jack's contemplation was deep, gruff almost, with the clipped tones inculcated on the playing fields of Eton or Harrow. The face, though, was less precisely clipped. The hair had been allowed to grow rather too long, curling now above the collar of a good quality but well-worn suit. What might once have been an impressive, bristling moustache seemed to have run to grass and now presented as a bushy but unkempt beard covering a substantial portion of the face. There were traces, though, of the man he had once been in the deep laughter lines engraved around a pair of blue eyes, perhaps originally sharp but, now, somewhat dimmed by…what? Pain? Anger? Resignation? There was, though, in this man's bearing still that which instinctively identified to Jack an officer and that same instinct propelled him out of his seat, straightening his coat as he did so. He very nearly saluted.

Standing face-to-face with the man, eye to eye, he recognised rather more steel in those eyes than he had first observed. There was respect, too, and perhaps a little amusement at Jack's response, reinforced by the slightest quirk of the thin lips, just visible through the forest of facial hair. He recognised Jack with a quick nod and an invitation to retake his seat. He pulled up another chair and positioned himself alongside Jack, taking in the scene presented by the inmates and their guests.

"You're visiting with Miss Samuels." A statement, not a question. He must have watched them arrive.

"You're familiar with her?" Jack responded, feeling his way.

170

"I couldn't claim familiarity but I have had the pleasure of meeting her on a previous visit." Sarah chose that moment to glance across at Jack, which caused Jack's companion to scrutinise him with some interest.

"Is it a friend or a family member you're visiting today?" Jack enquired. The short, sudden laugh in response was almost a bark.

"I'm not visiting, my boy, I'm part of the asylum." He seemed somewhat pleased by Jack's error.

Jack frowned. "Sarah, Miss Samuels," he corrected himself, so used now to the informal address, "described this place as a sanatorium, not an asylum."

His companion gave a brittle smile. "Don't worry, you wouldn't class us as clinically insane," he reassured, "though," leaning nearer to Jack and lowering his voice, "I wouldn't like to class us as entirely not either. If you know what I mean." Jack smiled conspiratorially. The man held out his hand. "Stephen Thomasson," he introduced himself.

Jack shook his hand, a firm, confident grip, no signs of weakness. "Jack Westerham," he reciprocated. "I was half expecting you to give me your rank as well," he observed.

Stephen shrugged. "All done with that for now. Hopefully for good."

"Hopefully?"

"I've done my share between South Africa and Europe," Stephen reflected. "I'm hoping I'll be too old by the time we're foolish enough to get embroiled in another war."

"I thought this was supposed to be 'the war to end all wars'?" Jack suggested, drily.

"Hah! That would assume a fundamental change in human nature, not just a temporary rebalancing of political power. There's a reason they're also calling it the First World War."

"Please God not," Jack prayed, slumping back against his chair and pushing his hands into the pockets of his greatcoat.

"Amen to that," Stephen concurred.

Jack scrutinised his companion, chewing over something he had said. "You fought in the Boer War as well?" he noted.

"Now there was a proper war," Stephen reminisced. "When it was all about daring cavalry charges across the plains, glorious red jackets showing us off for miles around and the superiority of our munitions and artillery to blow the buggers to smithereens," throwing his hands up to mimic his words. "None of this wallowing in mud for months on end, quietly dying of the tedium before foolhardily parading across a worthless strip of no-man's land in dismal khaki only to be gunned to pieces by two men behind a machine gun. Where's the courage in blasting out hundreds of rounds a minute against a disheartened shamble of conscripted soldiers? Where's the glory in a war that's more about technology than the raw guts of men? Give me the Boers over the Hun any day of the week." His oratory seemed directed as some invisible audience, more than Jack. He stopped, his face suffused with colour beneath his otherwise heavily tanned skin.

Jack folded his arms across his chest. "In my opinion," keeping his voice calm and low, "there is infinitely more courage in the man who goes over the top knowing there's been no aerial bombardment to clear his way, that he'll cross yards of mud littered with the rotting corpses of his compatriots, that he faces an enemy equipped with a gun capable of taking down him and all his battalion in a matter of seconds. That, should he even make it that far, he will have to cut his way through rolls and rolls of barbed wire to gain access to a fully manned German line with, if he's lucky, a handful of his team to help him storm the trench. All to gain a few hundred yards of some other man's country which, in all likelihood, will be back in the enemy's hands within weeks. All the while, the parading generals sit comfortably back at base issuing idiotic orders in total ignorance of the conditions on the ground or the equipment of the men, surrounded by their chauffeurs, their many-course meals and their warm, dry beds. That thousands of our boys not only tolerated these conditions but actively embraced them with a minimum of fuss or rebellion is nothing short of miraculous and is undoubtedly the most courageous behaviour I have ever had the privilege to witness." Jack stopped, his breathing quick and shallow.

"Bravo!" proclaimed his companion, clapped his hands. "Well said, that man!" Nearly all the eyes in the room turned towards them, including Sarah's, and Jack rose with embarrassment, rapidly crossing the floor to join her.

"You met the Major," the nameless suit observed as Jack drew nearer. "He was recognised for capturing a German trench at the third Battle of the Somme, you know."

Jack glanced back at Stephen. "Why is he here?"

"Shell-shock, like many of them. Saw his own son gunned down on no-man's land. Shouldn't have been anywhere near each other but the boy strayed miles from his unit, disorientated in the smoke. The Major went to pieces after that. Keeps harking back to the old campaigns, holding onto the glory of the old wars to prevent himself facing up to the realities of this one."

"What's his treatment, Dr Payne?" Sarah enquired.

"Rest and quiet is about all we can do for him. He flatly refuses to discuss his experiences so we make his day as stable and secure as possible and we are there to comfort and protect him when the terrors arrive in the night." The level of compassion behind the clinically delivered words surprised Jack and he looked at the doctor with renewed interest.

"Do the nightmares stop?" he probed. "Eventually?"

The doctor frowned at him. "They have been known to, with plenty of rest and..." His voice trailed off as yelling suddenly broke out in the far corner of the room. One of the patients, a dressing gown over his clothes, was on his feet at one of the tables, screaming unrelentingly and pulling at what little hair was left on his head. His wife, a thin-faced, tired-looking woman, had clutched their young daughter to her and was trying to cover the child's ears. Orderlies and nurses from across the room ran to restrain the man and to encourage the woman to withdraw to another room. As the noise gradually abated, the man now in restraints and being marched out and down the corridor, Sarah turned to Jack and invited him to meet some of the men who were otherwise without visitors.

She introduced him to several of the men over the next forty minutes or so. A 22-year-old lad from the Cotswolds who, like Jack, had a farming background. His lungs were weak from pneumonia and his breathe came short after only a couple of minutes' conversation.

Two men in their thirties, cousins who had grown up together, were both being treated for shell-shock. As one recovered, the other relapsed and then the process reversed itself. The older of the two was lucid today and explained the situation to them, sitting next to his cousin at a table, his hand constantly resting on the other's fist as he stared, blankly, across the room.

A Newcastle miner kept picking at his nails throughout their conversation, explaining how he could never get his hands clean, either from the coal or from the mud of France, permanently embedded under his nails. His hands were torn to shreds, the nails bitten almost to the quick. At one point, Sarah took both his hands in hers and stared directly into his eyes, explaining to him that he was safe now, he was home. For moments, his hands stilled but, as soon as they rose from the table, the man fell to picking at his fingers once more.

Jack shook the left hand of a middle aged man who had lost his right arm as far as his elbow, shattered by a mortar that killed three of his friends, sheltering in a crater in no-man's land up to their thighs in freezing water and surrounded by rats running over the ever-increasing number of corpses generated in that latest push.

At the end of visiting hour, a loud bell sounded and, instantly, there was much shuffling of chairs as the relatives stood to go. Some,

174

it seemed, couldn't get out of there soon enough. For others, it was a lingering farewell of tears and kisses, promises of another visit next week.

The place was forlorn without the buzz of visitors. Men left sitting individually at tables naturally started to congregate together, making up foursomes for a game of cards or sharing around a packet of cigarettes. Sarah absented herself to say good-bye to the staff.

The Major, Jack noticed, had stayed exactly where he had left him, practically in the same pose, hands resting on knees, legs straight, shoulders back. He crossed the room and held out his hand.

"It was a pleasure to meet you, Major," Jack offered.

The older man smiled slyly. "Even though I made your blood boil, boy?" he wheezed. "However good you are at presenting a calm exterior."

"Even so," Jack concurred.

The Major rose, brushing down his suit, patting the pockets meaningfully as if searching for a packet of cigarettes. Jack retrieved his and offered them, lighting one for the Major then, apparently absently, leaving them on the nearest table.

"I'll be out of here one day," the Major exhaled. "Once I can stop the damn shakes."

"And where will you go?" Jack enquired, lightly.

"My daughter's, I should think. She married a military man, fool that she is, and lives out in Berkshire with their two little ones. He's out in Greece or Turkey or some Godforsaken place, helping with the clean-up, apparently. I might be able to help them out." His eyes drifted away. "Soon."

Jack nodded towards the end of the room where Sarah had reappeared. "My escort has arrived," he commented. "Time for me to depart."

"Well, off you go, my boy. It'll never do to keep a lady waiting. Don't they teach you anything in the Army these days?"

175

Jack smiled and then, hesitating only slightly, drew himself to attention and saluted the Major. He held the pose until the Major, somewhat stiffly, reflected his motions and returned the salute. They shook hands and Jack turned to go, stopped, turned back. "I'll come and visit you, if I may, Sir?" he proposed.

The Major nodded. "You know where to find me, boy."

* * * * * * *

The café just around the corner from the hospital was evidently the place to which families gravitated for a pick-me-up after the visit. Jack recognised several of the faces as he escorted Sarah to a table and ordered tea and muffins for them both.

"Thank you for coming with me," Sarah started as a waitress laid out their cups and saucers, tea pot, matching hot water pot, sugar bowl and milk jug.

"I'm glad you asked me," Jack acknowledged.

Sarah nodded. "I can imagine it wasn't easy for you but I hope it wasn't too painful either."

Jack shook his head. "I won't say I'm happy to be forced to confront all this again but I concede I've been avoiding it too."

"In that case, perhaps you'll tell me now, who was the man the medium talked of?" Sarah asked nonchalantly, raising her cup of tea and taking a sip to soften the directness of her question. She kept her eyes on the table.

Jack didn't insult her intelligence by pretending not to know to what she referred. "Why does it matter?"

"I'm curious why Alfie furnished Isabella with that particular story." She had reached the same conclusion as he, then.

"What makes you think it came from Alfie?" he deflected.

Sarah shrugged. "Obviously it wasn't genuine so it was just a question of Isabella's information source. She had already remarked earlier in the day that she had seen him quite recently. Perhaps I'm more ready than you to believe him capable of such a malicious action."

"I'm obviously learning," Jack admitted, "since the thought did go through my head."

"But you don't want to accept it?" Sarah tested.

Jack offered her a toasted muffin, butter pooling on the plate, then helped himself as a temporary distraction. "We've been through a lot together," he explained, simply. "While Alfie's always had a proclivity for practical jokes, I had hoped he would stop before talking about Billy."

"His name was Billy?"

Jack sighed and folded his hands. "I met Alfie and Billy at the same time. When we arrived at the front, we were stationed together, immediately posted to man the Support Trench before relieving the men in the Fire Trench. There was real tension that first night as we expected a push from the other side at any time. We got to know each other well in a short space of time. Alfie was a reservist having served eight years in the regular army. He'd spent three years in the reserves but was easily the most experienced of the men. By contrast, Billy was the baby. He'd lied his way through a pair of less-than-scrupulous recruiters. He wasn't far short of his eighteenth birthday but it was enough to make us feel protective of him. And after he narrowly escaped a sniper's bullet having forgotten to duck as he passed a gap in the sandbags, he became something of a lucky mascot too. By some miracle, the three of us made it out of France together, albeit with each of us carted off to the Clearing Hospital at least once."

"I visited one in Thiepval," Sarah mused.

Jack was glad of any slight deviation from his topic, however much he knew it to be only a temporary reprieve. "What took you there?" he responded.

"I'd been nursing at St Mary's for a little over a year by then and was talking to Father about how to use Richmond House. The matron was transferring and suggested I go with her to help set up a new team intended to improve triage for potential amputees. I'd seen so much as St Mary's that I wanted to understand better from where all these men were coming, under what conditions they were operating. I felt I could hardly understand shell-shock without any exposure to the field of war." Jack's face must have betrayed some measure of his shock. "You find that odd?" she conjectured.

Jack shook his head as if to cast off his thoughts. "Remarkable," he disagreed, "and extraordinarily compassionate. Though none the less foolhardy – or brave –for that."

Sarah shrugged. "Perhaps it was all of those. I rarely feel the need to question or analyse my actions that way. I suspect that's the result of my upbringing. It felt the right thing to do so I did it."

"What do you feel you learnt?"

"There were plenty of practical lessons gained from understanding for myself the treatment the soldiers had received. At an emotional level, I think I started to appreciate the sense of isolation I'd witnessed in some of the men. From having been tightly embraced by a small unit, often friends or even family from home, the wounded became anonymous, disconnected men, treated as individual wounds rather than people, labelled, tagged and bagged like so much luggage and shipped from trench to Aid Post to Dressing Station to Clearing Station to, if they were lucky, England. The most humane contact might be the Chaplain but so many of the men had abandoned God by then that the only use the Chaplains seemed to be was in informing the men's families about their loved ones. So many of the men who passed through my hands seemed shut down, disconnected from the world. Putting myself in their shoes, however briefly, I could start to see why."

Jack stared at Sarah, reminded yet again of what a remarkable woman she was. For once slightly embarrassed by his scrutiny, Sarah shrugged again and turned to top up their tea. Then she touched his hand with one finger to jolt him out of his contemplation. "Will you tell me how you were injured?" she suggested.

"I was shot the first time then caught by shrapnel the second."

"How did it happen?"

Jack resigned himself to the fact that she was going to keep pushing for information and decided to start volunteering what details he could. He took a deep draught of tea and pushed his half-eaten muffin to one side.

"The first time was at Loos," he started. We arrived in the August and the battle started at the end of September. In truth, I was lucky to get away with an injury. It wasn't war, it was slaughter."

His words were emotional but, abstractedly, Jack noticed how unemotional was his tone of voice. The defence mechanisms were firmly in place, even as his brain was telling him he needed to share some of himself, some of his history with this woman, that she was asking him not so much to know the truth as to anchor those tenuous threads that seemed to float between them, wanting to bind them more closely to one another. He dragged up a visual memory of the day, the better to spark an emotional reaction too but it was no good. It had taken years of closing down his emotions, his reactions, one by one, to enable him to come through the other side of the war without his mind fragmenting, without his soul disappearing into the dark void where so many of the men in that hospital had vanished. All he could do was share the facts; perhaps the rest might come in time.

"We'd spent the nights before," he resumed, "carrying cylinders of chlorine through the communication trenches to the front. We were exhausted so they didn't send us out on the first day but so few men came back that we had to be pressed into action on the second day.

"We must have made quite a sight. Columns of a thousand men in each, waves of us walking across maybe a mile of land, straight towards the machine guns. There had been no bombardment beforehand, nothing to clear the wire, the trenches or the gun positions. We were walking over the corpses of the push from the

179

day before. So many dead that no one had had the chance to clear them, let alone bury them.

"I took a bullet in my right hip. I never saw it coming, just felt this flare of white heat burst in my skin and heard it grind into the bone. My leg went from under me and I went down on one side. Alfie was just behind me. Somehow, in all that paraphernalia, he hauled me up, threw my arm over his shoulder and dragged me back to the trench."

He stopped and stared across the café, watching a young mother dab he handkerchief with her tongue and wipe the crumbs of a Victoria sponge from her son's mouth. She smiled at him in a distracted way as he tried to evade her, playing all the while with a chess piece he was rolling over and over on the tablecloth.

"I, for one, am just glad you're alive." Sarah's voice seemed to be reaching out to him from some distance away. He tried to focus on her. He noticed the mottling in the pheasant feathers in her dark brown hat, the plush velvet of her coat collar, the luminescent gleam of pearls at her ears. The faint flecks of gold in the deep, liquid brown of her eyes. The upturn to one corner of her month where it caused a deeper line to be drawn in the curve of her skin and the slightest dimpling in her cheek. Now the flicker of a pursing of those lips; impatience, amusement or frustration? He looked into her eyes to find out and realised she was waiting for his response.

He shrugged. He couldn't help it. It was, simultaneously, a warding off of some latent superstition, a deflection of her attentiveness and a defensive shirking of her concern. He knew it was the wrong thing to do, that he should acknowledge and welcome her sentiment, but it was beyond him. He was so tightly wired into barricading his defences, he had left no chink, no gap for her to infiltrate.

Yet she persisted and he was silently grateful for her determination.

"What, then, happened to your knee?" she asked, softening her voice, making it clear she would push but not demand.

"That was in Italy," Jack began but he stopped again. He started turning the sugar bowl round and round on the table.

"You don't want to talk about that?" Sarah surmised. Jack shook his head. "And I'm guessing it had something to do with Billy." His silence confirmed it for her. "OK, enough probing for one day, then. Why don't you tell me what you think about the sanatorium, instead?"

"Why are you looking at it? Are you thinking of helping out?"

"Not as such, no. Their motives are good but their execution is poor. I've been involved for a little over a year and have tried to influence their thinking, to suggest alternative approaches. As you can see, they're not interested my input so much as my funds. So, I'm thinking about starting my own recuperation centre. It's the only way I can find to do it my way." Jack smiled and couldn't resist reaching his hand across the table to touch her hand briefly. "You find that amusing?" Sarah's tone was curious, not defensive.

"No, Sarah. It's just how frequently you remind me what a remarkable woman you are," he reflected. "Would that I had your self-belief. I feel I could achieve so much more."

Sarah tilted her head to one side, scrutinising him with a contemplative expression on her face. "You don't think it's just about my wealth, then? That I can get things done by throwing money at it?"

"Why would you think that?" Jack was surprised. "I suspect you've never thrown money at anything in your life. You're not your sisters," he remarked, lowering his voice. "You know what it is to be responsible and that with your kind of privilege comes responsibility."

Sarah looked pleased. Strange. Not happy. Not flattered. Pleased. The expression was quickly hidden as she turned her attention to pouring them more tea but Jack was sure he had read it correctly.

"So," Sarah probed. "Will you tell me know what you think of The Grove?"

"Why don't you tell me what you're planning and I'll add my comments as you go?"

"Mr Westerham," she teased, "you are the most impossible man to pin down. Why is that?" she mused, serious suddenly. She didn't wait for an answer, though. "What I've got in mind is something smaller and more personal. It strikes me that these institutions just reinforce the sense of disconnection and isolation these men are experiencing. If we want to change how their minds react, we have to change their environment first."

"Specifically?" He wondered how much she understood. If only she did. It would make it easier to talk to her about his experiences. In time.

"Personal rooms instead of wards. Communal areas that mimic a sitting room or dining room at home. Open house for visitors so they can come and go at times to suit them, not restricted to specific visiting times. A facility for family members to stay at certain times so they can spend more time with their loved ones."

"They need exercise too, something to get them physically fit again," Jack contributed.

"Of course. What else?"

"They have nothing to do all day, no sense of purpose or valued contribution. They've come from an environment where every second of their day was regimented and now they're left to their own devices at a time when they have no mental or physical resources to fall back on."

"They need to work," Sarah proposed.

"Either inside the facility or, perhaps, in time, outside," Jack concurred. "Where were you thinking of setting it up? Richmond House?"

Sarah looked at him a bit sharply. "What makes you say that?"

Jack was taken aback by her tone. "I didn't mean anything. I mean, I know it's your family home."

"But?"

He hesitated. "It's a good environment and there must be plenty of work for the men on the estate. It would keep the house staff occupied too, when the family wasn't there."

"Which we are but rarely," Sarah completed his implication. Jack shrugged. "At least, at the moment."

Jack stayed silent, wondering at her intent, but it seemed she was not inclined to expand on her comment.

The café was emptying, the sky starting to darken on the other side of the large window at the front.

"I should get home," Sarah commented, staring out of the window. Jack got the strange sense she was avoiding his gaze. "Father has Mr and Mrs Marsh coming for dinner." Jack rose and held out Sarah's chair for her. "I do appreciate your insight," she assured him as he helped her into her coat. She covered his hand with hers where it rested on her shoulder, her head turned towards him over her shoulder. "I'm going to miss you," she murmured.

"I'll only be gone five days," he reassured her, his face close to hers.

Sarah nodded. "We've seen so much of each other," she reflected. "I've become used to having you around. But," pulling herself away and turning towards the door, "it's good that you're going to see your family. You've been away a long time."

He held the café door open for her. The chauffeur, efficient as ever, was waiting down the street. He started up the engine and slowly rolled down the street to where they were waiting. "I wish I could say I was looking forward to it," Jack admitted.

"Your first chance to see your new nephew," she prompted, resting her hand on his coat.

"Maybe that bit," Jack conceded. "I don't feel part of the family any more but I think they neither realise that nor understand how I feel."

Sarah ran her hand down Jack's arm then wound her fingers into his. "Give them a chance," she advised softly. "I'm glad to have been the recipient of the company denied your family. I know what they're missing out on. Just let them get to know you again."

"Do you know how good for me you are?" Jack reflected softly, tightening his grip on her hand. The next week stretched ahead of him without the prospect of her company. They had been spending a lot of time together and he had to acknowledge he would miss her.

"We're good for each other," Sarah corrected. "I'll see you when you get back." She smiled. "Hurry back."

Chapter Seven

Devon, April 1920

It was my first trip back to Devon in more than a year. I couldn't even claim to have been a regular correspondent with my family, my mother having maintained a steadfast flow of news in spite of the absence of responses from me. I approached the journey back, then, with some trepidation.

By the time the train pulled into Westerham station, it was late afternoon and Jack was thoroughly sick of his own company. While he had initially relished the peace of a surprisingly quiet Penzance Express train, the lack of diversion in his almost-empty carriage had begun to pall long before he disembarked at Plymouth North Road to join the local service to Newton Abbot.

Falling back on his own reserves was usually a pleasure, particularly with a small library of new books at his disposal like that squeezed into his luggage but, instead, his mind had wandered and he found himself dwelling overly on the one subject of which he was hoping to clear his mind: Sarah.

He needed distance to help him become again the rational, considered man he prided himself on being. While he wouldn't describe himself as having been swept away, her determination to ignore his deeply ingrained prejudices of upbringing and wealth had left him feeling out of his depth, borne on a tide that was keeping him afloat but without the security of a sure footing or, he suspected, sufficient strength to fight against the ebb and flow.

He was one of several people disembarking at the station and the sudden flurry of activity – of porters rushing up with carts to unload variously sized suitcases and trunks, of women embracing, children shouting and men impatiently trying to usher them along – meant Jack almost missed his father waiting hear the exit, half-hidden by a wrought iron pillar. It was only as he was passing through the doors that some instinct caused him to glance back, to give the shadow in the corner a second look.

"Almost didn't recognise you, Jackie." The slow Devon drawl was instantly familiar but, otherwise, Jack was shocked by his father's appearance. He seemed to have shrunk to a much-diminished form of the man Jack held in his memory, his childhood hero, the stern, unemotional but solid, reliable, stalwart man of his youth. This man had clearly shrunk within his own clothes, his collar hanging loosely at the neck. The shock was quickly subsumed by guilt, the one emotion he had effectively suppressed for the last months, no, years. His father was ill and he had known nothing about it.

He held out his hand – his father was never one for more effusive displays of affection – and gripped the large paw offered to him, unavoidably noting the liver spots on the skin and the prominence of the bones beneath the thinning flesh. How could this be happening? His father was only in his late fifties. Far too young to look this way.

"Hello, Dad." He aimed to keep his voice steady, not to betray the emotions running through him. "How are you?"

"As you see, lad," he shrugged off the attention. "Time's catching up with me. Let's not worry about that now. Time's a-wasting and your mother will have tea on the go by now so we shouldn't be late." He held out his hand to take Jack's suitcase from him. Of course, his instinct was to refuse but he knew the depth of pride that welled in his father and handed over his burden without a word. "I hope you don't mind the truck," his father raised his voice as Jack made to climb into the passenger seat and he hoisted the luggage into the back. "Your mother wouldn't be happy if I spoiled your best suit."

Jack didn't answer. There was nothing to be gained from explaining that, far from being his best suit, this was one he no longer considered fit for work but kept for walking and more relaxed occasions.

"It belongs to Mac," Albert Westerham elucidated, nodding at the truck when Jack's raised eyebrows showed he wasn't following the thread of the conversation. "Bought it last year almost new from some fool who thought he'd try his hand at farming, spent a fortune on the latest equipment then threw in the towel in less than nine months. No staying power, some people. This one hankered after some sort of idyllic country life. Trying to escape his memories, your mother says he was. Soon went running back to Blackburn or Bolton or wherever it was he came from."

"How is everyone, Dad?" Jack cut across the soliloquy at his first convenient moment.

"Never better, Jackie boy," and a smile of such sunlit radiance crossed his father's face that Jack was taken aback for the second time in as many minutes. "The little 'un is an absolute charmer. Got your mother and everyone dancing to his tune already."

"Is Ed a very proud father?" Jack surprised himself with the wistful tone in his voice. He had never considered himself paternal but he had to admit to the slightest twinge of jealousy at his younger brother's apparently perfect family life. Only for a second, though, before his pragmatic side resurfaced and he considered how difficult life must still be at the Manor, scraping a less than affluent living out of working all the daylight hours available and, in all likelihood, seeing very little of the newborn.

"It'll be the making of him, for sure," his father predicted. "He's settling into our way of life at last. No more gallivanting after you, scarching for who knows what who knows where." Jack suspected his father was not as oblivious as he portrayed to the criticism of Jack implicit in his statement. "The young lass did well to wait for him until he got that wanderlust out of his mind. She's brought him back down to earth and the laddie has rooted him firmly back in the soil. Where he should be."

Before, Jack would have let the comment pass unchallenged. The greatest unspoken disagreements had created a vast chasm between them in the past, resentment on the one hand of an implicit rejection of a way of life, guilt and frustration on the other at a lack of understanding of a different outlook and drive. It was a chasm of silence that neither knew how to bridge. In the end, Jack had walked away instead.

"What's that say about me, Dad?" he challenged, keeping his voice steady.

Albert stretched his hand out against the wheel. "Why should it say anything about you?" he responded, slightly belligerently, Jack thought. Jack stared out of the window to his left, turning his face away. He didn't pursue the issue. "Anyway," Albert resumed, "he's been doing a grand job of the Manor. Expanded into strawberry growing, can you believe? And the lass has settled in well, helping your mother with all the chores around the place, right up until her due date. And she was up and helping with the daffodils less than a week after."

"And Gramma?"

Albert grunted. "Don't get much out of her these days. Long as the fire's stoked and she's got her tea or milk, she makes no fuss. Can't imagine she's that comfortable, seeing how gnarled her hands are now. Still, no use complaining, is there?"

"Any more problems with the house during the winter?" Jack was beginning to feel like the grand inquisitor, firing questions at his father one after another, but he didn't know how else to keep the conversation going. He feared his father's possible questions about his own life, feared exposing how distant and unfamiliar his world was now. Feared even more a sudden and uncomfortable silence between them.

"We've had to close the eastern wing." There was real sadness in the admission. "Roof started leaking in February. Haven't had a moment to spare to fix it. To be honest, we're better off without it.

Eddie and Annie moved into your old room and Gramma is in the little snug off the kitchen. Does much better in there with the heat of the range all year. We can keep an ear out for the nipper too with them closer to us."

"I'll take a look at it while I'm here, shall I?" Jack suggested.

"No need for that," Albert insisted, stiffly. "The boy and I are quite capable. Though," with a slight concession, "glad to hear you're prepared to roll your sleeves up while you're here," he commented, slightly acerbically. "Your mother had some fool notion that you're on holiday and shouldn't do anything but sit around. Told her there's never been room for anyone sitting around in this place but she's having none of it. Got all of us messing up our routines for today so's we can all be there for high tea. High tea! I ask you. When has tea been anything more than a quick brew and a slab of cake on the run before getting back outside 'fore the light's gone."

He tutted loudly then suddenly slammed on the brakes, forcing Jack to brace himself against the dashboard.

"Teach me to talk so much," Albert muttered. "Almost missed the turn." He heaved the wheel to the left and gingerly eased the bonnet past the hedge at the side of the turning. In the gathering darkness, Jack hadn't even recognised the lane to the Manor. His previously unsettled feeling gave way to a stronger anxiety. He was nervous.

There were lights blazing in the downstairs windows on either side of the door as they neared the bottom of the lane. The Manor was, originally, a very handsome Elizabethan brick-and-timber construction, a distant property of a many-propertied lord who spent most of his time in far grander surroundings somewhere in Norfolk. During periods of wealth, it had been extended and reshaped with little thought for the aesthetics of the place and much for the comfort of the inhabitants. The gradual but consistent decline of the family's fortunes over the last century, however, had seen increasing dilapidation not only in the house but also in the Manor's

189

outbuildings. Many had been pulled down for want of funds to repair them or need to use them as the farm's annual output gradually declined too.

The lights made for a most welcoming sight as they emerged out of the darkness cast by the high hedges flanking them in the lane. Even before they had drawn up at the front the house, the old oak door had opened – sticking slightly as it always did – and Maud Westerham appeared, smoothing down the front of her Sunday best dress and patting her hair absently to check it was still in place. Jack's anxiety left him in an instant, subsumed by a tenderness and warmth. His mother was as nervous as he.

As soon as the truck had come to a halt, Jack leapt from the cab and ran the short distance to where she stood waiting. Without a second thought, he gathered his mother in his arms and lifted her off her feet, whirling her round until the skirts of her gingham dress billowed in the soft evening air. She burst out laughing, a wonderfully joyous and light-hearted sound right in Jack's ear and he grasped her tighter, laughing too. She thumped a hand on his shoulder as he squeezed her, demanding to be set back on her feet. The moment he did as he was bid, she went back to straightening her dress and hair again but there was new colour in her cheeks and the moisture in her eyes caught the light from the hallway and sparkled for an instant.

She appraised him in silence for a few seconds, his suit getting a silent nod of approval. "You've grown, Jack," she observed, her voice a painfully familiar soft, low sound. Jack shook his head and bent down to kiss her cheek.

"Sorry, Mum," he commented, "but I stopped growing when I was seventeen. I think you've shrunk."

She smacked him playfully on the arm.

"Are you two coming in?" Albert demanded, carrying Jack's bag through the door. "You're letting all the cold air in. And why in God's name have you got all the lights on, woman?" His voice waned as he disappeared down the corridor. "We're not made of candles, you know."

Maud smiled shyly at Jack. He offered his hand and she took it gratefully, seemingly pleased to be able to hold onto any part of him to stop him disappearing again.

She led the way through to the kitchen at the far end of the flagstone corridor, reminding him to duck his head at the low portal though he'd been doing that since he hit his first growth spurt at the age of thirteen. The early spring chill in the air had vanished the instant Jack had shut the front door behind him and the heated air only intensified as they approached the kitchen where the range was fired up for the night and the cast iron kettle was just coming to the boil on the plate. Albert squeezed past him as he entered, presumably returning to extinguish the oil lamps Maud had lit in the hall and drawing room to welcome him.

Everything was instantly familiar. The battered, scrubbed oak table in the middle of the room, the range at the far end with the oak dresser displaying their rarely used hand-me-down best china. The coats and boots tucked in the corner behind the door, drying out and warming up in the room's overheated atmosphere. Even the old cat commanding the room from the vantage point of one of the two kitchen chairs placed on either side of the range and turned toward it to absorb its warmth. Jack's grandmother – his father's mother – was dozing in the other chair, her head rolling forward slightly then starting back up as she tried to keep awake a little longer. Maud touched her shoulder lightly as she passed, grabbing the heat pad with the other to lift the kettle and transfer its contents into the oversize earthenware teapot that stood ready.

Jack knelt in front of his grandmother, gently taking her worn hands in his.

"Hello, Gramma," he said softly, looking up into watery eyes so diluted of their blue colour as to be almost white. She released one hand from his and placed it against his cheek, just resting it there, no longer able to straighten her arthritis-riddled joints. "About time you came home," she pronounced, her voice as dry and withered as her hands. Jack sensed his mother half-turn to look at them.

"I know, Gramma," he conceded, softly. "I know."

She seemed satisfied and placed her hands back in her lap, drawing up the rug across her knees, which Jack helped to tuck in. She laid her head back and closed her eyes.

The sound of feet running down the stairs had Jack standing again. Unfamiliar footsteps, which must mean it was Annie.

"Jack!" she launched herself straight into his arms. "We were beginning to think you were never coming home."

"Your hair!" he exclaimed, holding her at arm's length. "What have you done?" She fell away from him, self-consciously putting her hand up to her short, bobbed hair.

"It's much more practical since Charlie arrived," she defended, her voice adopting the slightly sullen tone Jack knew so well from their childhood. Her chin came up. "And it's the latest fashion. I thought you'd know all about these things, living in the Big Smoke," she challenged.

Jack laughed. "Sweetheart, you look amazing," he reassured. "Easily the equal of any of those girls in London. But you know how much I loved your long hair."

She pushed her hand against his chest and shoved him backwards. "Smooth as ever," she teased. "Though you lost the right to call me 'sweetheart' years ago and I don't think your brother would approve. Particularly since you didn't make it back for the wedding."

"I'm sorry I missed it," Jack's contrition was tempered by humour, "but if you will have a shotgun wedding when half of us are stationed overseas, what's a man supposed to do?"

"It was not a shotgun wedding," Annie was indignant. She always had been so easy to tease, right from their earliest days, playing with the other neighbourhood children.

The kitchen door slammed suddenly on a blast of cold air. "You're here for two minutes and already you're flirting with my wife." Edward crossed the kitchen and pulled Annie into his arms, planting a firm kiss on her lips. She laughed, breathlessly. "Oh well, at least it means you're still attractive after the baby," he teased, earning himself a playful slap on his chest and a pout. He put his arm over her shoulders, a little proprietorially, and turned them around to face Jack, holding out his hand. "Welcome home, brother," he offered.

Jack shook the hand gratefully, smiling slightly. "It's good to see you, Ed," he murmured.

"Right, now everyone's here, let's eat," Maud ushered them to the table, laden with sandwiches, cakes and biscuits. Maud was welcoming home the prodigal son.

* * * * * *

Jack woke to silence.

He lay still for a long time, disorientated by an environment so familiar and yet alien. His own boyhood furniture but moved into a different room, crammed into a space too small for it. The quality of the light streaming through the inadequately thin curtains. The clean, fresh smell of the air. So redolent of an unquestioning, undemanding youth. So unreal now, untenable almost.

The longer he lay there, the more he became aware of his surroundings. The scratchy texture of the blankets, tickling his skin through the worn cotton of the sheet. The motes of dust dancing in the sun where it broke through the curtains. The mustiness of the unused but freshly cleaned room, the swept floorboards, the beaten rug, threadbare in places from decades, perhaps, of use. The sudden gust of wind whistling down the chimney and rattling in the grate. The distant shout of a man's voice, sounding like a greeting though too distant to distinguish words. The clunk of metal pales being

193

carried by someone across the yard, kicking up a sudden cacophony of barking from the farm dogs. There was no sound of anyone moving about the house but still it creaked and wheezed, its timbers settling into a new position as the sun warmed its skeleton and eased its ancient joints.

He noticed a mug of tea on the small chest of drawers beside his bed. Long since cold and now with a heavy layer of skin on top. How strange the tea had tasted last night. Not just the local water, so much softer than the chalk-filled water in London, but that strange, forgotten flavour of goat's milk instead of the cow's milk, farmed in places just like this and shipped into the City for the likes of him. It reminded how long it had taken to get used to the flavour when he first moved away and how here he was in reverse.

He watched the rays of the sun, framed by the panes of the mullioned window, slowly travel across half of the far wall. He promised himself he would get up as soon as the sun touched the side of the wardrobe but he lacked the energy to enforce his promise and let it drift across the whole of one door before he finally levered himself out of the bed and padded across to the bathroom.

He felt reluctant to relinquish his solitude, knowing that the second he showed his face he would have little or no time to himself until he closed his bedroom door on them again at the end of the day. He shaved slowly, frequently distracted by his thoughts between strokes, and dressed with equal leisure, struggling to find clothes that would fit in with those around him. In the end, he opted for a worn pair of trousers and a collarless shirt, but he felt half-dressed against his brother's and father's additional uniform of waistcoat, neckerchief and cap. Perhaps he could borrow from them while he was here.

After some minutes of reacquainting himself with the books on his bookshelf, reminiscing with a smile, he realised he had moved from reluctance to avoidance and put the book he was scanning resolutely back on the shelf. As he made his way downstairs to the kitchen, he started to notice tell-tale details to which he had been oblivious the night before. The wind whistling down the corridor from the eastern side of the house, presumably from where the roof was exposed. The holes developing in the stair carpet from the same feet treading the same path too often. The chips and scratches in the white painted woodwork on either side of the stair treads. The cracked stone in the middle of the hallway's flagged floor. The black smoke trails on the walls above the oil lamps. He couldn't fault the place for cleanliness – his mother was nothing if not house-proud – but there was no escaping the fact that it was increasingly down-at-heel. As he reached the bottom stair, the padding of paws announced the arrival of Sheba, the matriarch of the farm dogs but now too riddled with arthritis to work. He put out his hand and allowed her to sniff his scent, noticing one eye was now entirely cloudy and the other seemed to be heading in the same direction. Satisfied he was no threat, however strange he may now be, she turned tail and led him through to the kitchen.

Gramma was dozing by the range again, her half-empty mug of milk balanced precariously on her lap and threatening to tip over at any moment. Jack rescued it from her just as the back door opened and his mother came through. He signed to her not to break the silence. When a smile of joy spread slowly across her face, he couldn't resist crossing the room and giving her another hug. His mother was a tiny woman, dwarfed by husband and sons alike, and she broke into laughter as Jack's hug lifted her feet off the floor.

"Put me down, you fool," she demanded in a loud whisper. "You'll spill the milk."

Jack did as he was bid and Maud moved past him with a slight squeeze of his arm as she did so.

"Though I don't know why we're whispering," she observed, still in a half-hushed tone. "She's as deaf as a post and nothing short of an earthquake would wake her after breakfast. Talking of which,

195

what would you like? It's getting late but you've still got time enough before dinner."

She decanted the pail of milk into jugs and deposited them in the pantry then set about making Jack his breakfast.

"I thought I'd take a look at the roof later," Jack suggested, taking a seat at the kitchen table.

"You shouldn't feel you're expected to work while you're here," Maud warned him.

Jack shrugged. "I can't sit around all day while everyone else is working. I could do with something more suitable to wear, though," indicating his attire.

"We'll find some of Eddie's," Maud promised. "Though I have to say I prefer you in your suit. It's nice to see at least one member of the family properly dressed. I trust I can show you off in your best suit at church on Sunday?"

Jack smiled his reluctance. "I'll go if Dad does," he bargained, knowing full well hell would freeze over before his father would set foot in a church. "Besides, it's not my best suit." Maud placed a plate of bacon, egg and sausages in front of him and sat down opposite him at the table. He explained about the trip to the tailor and his formal dinner suit as he ate.

"She sounds like an interesting woman," she noted lightly, a slight smile in her voice. Jack gave her a look and she raised her hands in mock surrender. "I'm not prying," she defended.

"I do want to tell you about her, Mum," Jack admitted. "I want to talk about her. And I will, while I'm here. But I also need some time to clear my mind."

"You always did over-think things, sweetheart," Maud said, patting his hand as she rose and turned to the sink to clean the dishes. As she did so, the sound of a baby's cries suddenly broke through the stillness. Jack looked up, shock written across his face. Maud smiled again. "Time to meet your nephew?" He nodded, strangely overwhelmed and unable to speak, and pushed away his half-eaten breakfast.

Maud wiped her hands on the tea towel and led the way upstairs to Jack's old room. The curtains were drawn against the morning light and were doing a much more effective job than those in Jack's room. He could make out the shapes of the furniture in the darkness but little else. Maud, though, made her way unfalteringly to the cot in the corner from where the cacophony continued. She leant over the side and ran her hand over the baby's back, soothing him with her hands and with crooned nonsense. As his cries eased, she leant across to the window and pulled aside one of the curtains, casting a shaft of sunlight over the crib. She beckoned Jack over from where he was hovering uncertainly in the doorway, drumming his fingers on the doorframe.

"Come on, Jack," she urged as he continued to hesitate. "Meet your nephew." Jack crossed the room but he stood behind his mother, leaning over her shoulder to view the baby. She turned him over onto his back, running her hands over his downy hair. "Blonde," she murmured. "Just like both of you when you were born. Charlie," she raised her voice slightly, rubbing his rounded belly, "this is your Uncle Jack. He's the brains of the family and, when you're ready, he'll teach you everything you want to know. Assuming he's around," she observed with a warning tone. "Say 'hello', Jack. Stop hovering there like you're afraid of something so tiny and helpless."

"I can't imagine there is anything more terrifying than having something so tiny and so helpless that it is completely reliant on you," Jack remarked drily. "I'm not sure I do a good job of looking after myself, sometimes."

Maud smiled. "Thankfully, Mother Nature takes over and she doesn't leave you enough time to worry about it," she reflected.

Hesitatingly, Jack stretched out a hand and ran one of his fingers over Charlie's tiny hand. The little fingers flexed in reaction and Jack did it again.

"I envy him, Mum," he admitted in a low voice.

"Charlie?"

He shook his head. "Ed," he clarified. "Watching him last night, he's so content, with Annie and now with Charlie."

"Are you worried you won't find that?" There she went, always getting to the heart of the issue.

"I don't think I'm cut out to be content. At least, not like Ed is."

Maud shook her head at him. "Nor shall you be with that attitude. But why should you be any less able than the rest of us?" she challenged. Jack stared, unseeing, at Charlie, absently holding the tiny hand. He felt his mother squeeze his arm. "Stay here with him," she suggested. "Being around a baby for any amount of time always makes things simpler. Come down when you're ready."

* * * * * *

When Jack appeared in the kitchen again some time later, he was dressed for work having raided his brother's wardrobe. Maud nodded in approval. "You'll find your brother outside with the ladder. Just be careful both of you."

Jack stepped out into the bright late morning sunlight and stopped, both to allow his eyes to adjust and to absorb some of the warmth into his skin. He turned back the cuffs of his shirt, slowing scanning the yard. He could hear the faint sounds of his father singing, as he was wont to do when preoccupied with some repetitive task or other. The expectant cows – Devon Rubies – had been brought down to the field adjoining the farmhouse, for calving. The grass was growing thick and lush, which was just as well because it appeared they were down to the last of the hay in the barn opposite. Spring seemed to be much more advanced down here than in London, so much warmer and wetter than the capital. The cherry blossoms in the orchard at the end of the informal garden were almost fully out and many of the daffodils had all but gone over.

"How was the crop this year?" Jack asked, nodding at the daffodils to Ed who had just appeared around the side of the house, along with a wooden ladder under one arm.

"Best yet," Ed responded cheerfully. "Annie's down there this morning picking the last of them. Nice mature bulbs now and they seem to have benefitted from the harsh winter. Guess it made sales better too since everyone seemed desperate in town for a splash of Devon sunshine. Right," he redirected Jack's attention, "let's get this sorted while Dad's out of the picture. I've been avoiding this 'til now. Can't risk him up a ladder now that he's getting weaker."

He positioned the ladder at the far end of the stone house and rapidly scaled it. Jack followed more cautiously, aware suddenly of the toll a year of office work had had on the strength of his muscles. He edged gingerly onto the roof and braced himself on the gable end to climb up to the pitch. Ed was already inspecting the damaged area where, Jack guessed, one of the winter storms had lifted the decaying tiles and exposed the timbering beneath.

"Right," Ed called to him, "looks like some felt and a dozen new tiles should do the trick. I'll run down for what we need and pass it across." He disappeared back down the ladder and into one of the outbuildings. Jack braced his back against the gable wall and took a moment to survey the world.

He missed this. Desperately. It was what had made the deployment to Italy so poignant, the reminiscence of Devon. After three long years of France's apocalyptic landscape, the lush verdure of the Italian mountains had stirred an almost physical sickness for the beauty and safety of his childhood home.

But, much as he felt emotionally drawn to the place and much as he could appreciate its aesthetic appeal, he could no more contemplate returning here than he could never seeing Sarah again.

That thought brought him up with a jolt. He hadn't realised he had allowed himself to become so entwined, emotionally. But there it was, the same sickness to his stomach as he had experienced in

Italy now resurfaced at the incomprehensible thought of his life without Sarah.

"Here we go," Ed broke into his thoughts.

"I'll go over," Jack volunteered, "you bring me what we need."

"Still taking charge, big brother?" Ed teased. Jack 'hmphed' at him and shuffled his way across to the damaged area.

* * * * * * *

It took them barely a couple of hours to complete and Maud was waiting at the foot of the ladder when they descended.

"All set, Mum," Jack reassured. "You'll be able to use the east rooms again now."

"No, lad, we should have given up using those rooms years ago," she reflected, wiping flour from her hands. "We've been much better off since we stopped trying to heat that side of the house. Oh, it needed doing," she contradicted Jack as he opened his mouth to ask why they had just spent the last two hours on repairs. "We can't let the place go to rack and ruin but we have to be sensible. We don't need the space and we were only creating more work for ourselves. Much better this way." Her voice had a jarring note to it, a false gaiety, and Jack read a wistfulness – sadness, even – in her eyes that belied her tone. "Anyway, if you're done, your dinner's ready, so go and wash up while I call your Dad."

As if he needed reminding of his less-than-fit state, Jack's leg muscles protested as he climbed the stairs for a quick wash in the bathroom. By the time he reappeared, Gramma, Annie and Ed were at the table and Albert was vigorously scrubbing his hands and exposed forearms at the kitchen sink, ignoring his wife's glowering expression. Almost thirty years married and she still hadn't been able to break him of the habit.

The tantalising smell of meat pudding greeted Jack, instantly setting his mouth watering and his stomach growling, albeit he had eaten a larger breakfast than he was used to only hours before. How strange to be eating his main meal at lunchtime again. And how strange that such a long-held habit with which he had grown up should become unfamiliar so fast.

"Got that roof sorted, then?" Albert observed, his tone somehow implying some dissatisfaction.

"All set, Dad," Ed confirmed cheerfully, piling his plate up with potatoes and spring greens.

"And we've picked the last of the daffodils this morning," Annie interjected before Albert could come back with a complaint. "They'll be on the train to London tonight."

"Dad said you're looking at new ideas for the farm, Ed?" Jack encouraged, equally aware that Albert was scowling at his sons and trying to redirect the conversation.

"Strawberries," Ed mumbled, his mouth full of suet crust. Jack raised an eyebrow at him, inviting him to elucidate. Ed held up his hand to make him wait, swallowed and gulped down half a pint of milk. "We planted a crop last autumn on the upper slope of the spinney field. The aspect and the drainage are ideal. And it's the same principle as the daffs – whoever gets first to market gets the best price. We don't have to produce volumes, just quality."

"We found a new variety," Annie explained. "Royal Sovereign. It's the earliest we could find so we may even beat the other local growers."

"It's an ideal intermediary crop," Ed took up the baton again. "Tides us over until the main harvests."

"And it's perfect work for the girls in the village," Annie reinforced, "and the older ladies who can't help with the heavier work now."

"Enough!" Jack threw up his hands in mock surrender. "I get it, it's a brilliant idea." He watched Ed and Annie exchanged satisfied glances. "But you do know you don't have to convince me, don't you?" he suggested earnestly. "It's your business, you should do whatever you think is right."

"Washing your hands of us, are you?" Albert's surly mood had deepened as they jabbered on, preventing him from voicing his frustration at being excluded from the work on the roof. Jack frowned and hesitated before answering.

"The farm will always mean a lot to me," he assured Albert. "But I've made my choice and my life is taking me elsewhere. So I have to respect the decisions you make on what to do here." Ed looked gratified but he seemed only to have fuelled Albert's anger.

"Too good for us now, is that it?" he challenged. "Too far above us to get your hands dirty?"

"Enough, Albert!" Maud commanded sharply. "We've been through this before. There's no point re-treading old ground."

Albert stared at his wife hard, clearly resenting her intervention, but he knew better than to argue. He pushed away his plate, threw back his chair and stormed out into the yard, slamming the kitchen door so hard it rattled on its hinges.

* * * * * * *

Knowing his father would take some time to cool off, Jack made himself scarce after dinner. Maud and Gramma had taken to the chairs before the stove to sleep off their meal, Annie had gone upstairs to see to Charlie and Ed had headed over to a neighbouring farm to check out the state of their boundary hedges. Surprisingly sleepy himself but determined not to succumb to the temptation to be indolent, Jack elected to walk the mile or so back into Westerham.

There was, seemingly for the first time in months, real warmth in the air as Jack regained the main road from their lane and headed along the well-worn, rough road, and he soon shed his jacket and rolled up the cuffs of his shirt sleeves.

In spite of their arguments at home, he felt an unfamiliar sense of peace, of ease, steal over him. The cares and responsibilities he carried with him in London seemed diminished here, amid the warm air, burgeoning growth of crop, hillside and hedgerow alike, auditorially adorned by the unfailingly cheerful sound of birdsong.

His initial steady pace soon started to falter as the sun's warming rays seeped into his skin and the hopeful, rejuvenating beauty of his native landscape distracted his senses. Slowly, his ever chattering mind stilled and he stopped his circular internal arguments about Sarah, stopped fretting about what was expected of him by everyone around him, stopped considering how Alfie and all those other remnants of men might be helped, stopped worrying about how his presence here was upsetting the equilibrium of his family's life.

Stopped. And, for a long moment, knew his first peace in years.

* * * * * * *

"Annie's lying down," Maud explained, putting a steaming mug of freshly made tea down in front of Jack at the kitchen table. "She's been trying to do too much too soon and the young lad was fretful all afternoon too."

The soft light of early evening was settling around them and the house was starting its usual creaking as the warmth of the day seeped out of its old bones. Maud refuelled the range while a saucepan of milk warmed for Gramma. Jack drank his tea, enjoying the stillness of the warm dusk, the chatter of birds filtering through the stable door, the top half slightly ajar to counter the stuffiness of the burning logs.

"Time you told me what's happening with Dad?" he suggested, dropping his voice so as not to be overheard by Gramma. Maud glanced at her mother-in-law anxiously but the old woman seemed to be sleeping soundly.

"He was diagnosed three months ago with farmer's lung. It did for old Tom and it looks like it's going to take Albert too." His mother's tone was surprisingly dispassionate but Jack could see the tension in the lines around her eyes and mouth, deepening perceptibly even in the gathering gloom. "The doctor says there's nothing they can do except make him comfortable when the time comes."

"How long?" Jack's voice was rough.

Maud shrugged. "You've seen this before. You know as well as I do it can take months or years. You've seen the state of him already, though. Much more of this and he'll be able to fit into his wedding suit again." She looked at Jack suddenly. "You will come back again, won't you? When the time gets near? Edward and Annie are wonderful to me but…they're not you, Jack."

Jack held her gaze steadily. "I won't lie to you, Mum," he warned. "I can't make you a promise but I will do everything in my power to be here." Strange to think how, in the past, he would have made the promise, blindly and unthinking. Promises made and broken in war, though, had taught him a hard lesson.

Maud appeared to be about to respond but Gramma stirred at that moment and she changed her mind. She rose to pour Gramma's warm milk into a large mug and helped wrap the old woman's hands around it, the warmth easing her gnarled joints.

"You'll be coming to church with us in the morning," Maud stated, placing a plate of tea bread between herself and Jack as she sat down again. Never a particularly devout family, they had always adhered to the major Christian festivals.

"I'm sorry, Mum, but I won't," Jack responded, quietly but with a hint of determination in his voice. She scrutinised him for a long moment before deliberately dropping her eyes to her mug.

"I would have thought you would want to give thanks to the Lord for bringing you safely through the war," she challenged, a hint of rebuke in her tone.

Jack reached across the table and took her hand in his.

"There was no God with us in France," he stated firmly. "Men left Him behind. There was no other way for us to do what we did to each other."

The bleakness in his eyes shocked her. He had let his guard down and, suddenly, she was aware of a fraction of what he was hiding behind it. She saw it and it appalled and frightened her. Her own son, her first born. What had he had to do during those years?

"You've never told us…" she started but stumbled, not knowing how to ask him.

"You never asked," he explained softly. "But you're not the only ones," he reflected. "I think most of those we left behind couldn't face knowing. It's as if you were maintaining our way of life for us even as we were fighting to protect yours for you. But all the time, the things we were being asked to do meant we would never be the same people again and we couldn't go back to living the lives we had left to uphold in the first place."

Maud's eyes filled with tears and she covered her mouth. Jack felt a wave of pain at her distress but his defences were already shutting him down. He could not risk feeling her pity for him for fear that he might start to pity himself. That road let to the pit of despair he had seen in the faces of those men at the hospital. He drained his mug and pushed back his chair. "I'll go and find Dad and Ed," he covered his emotions and left the kitchen without another glance at his mother.

After the stifling heat of the kitchen, the cool evening air was a welcome relief. The sky was still clear, a fading blue to the west, dark already in the east. There were lights in the cow byre so Jack headed in that direction.

"Ed," he called, approaching the door.

"In here," came the muffled reply.

In the dark, the smell of the damp cowshed was almost overpowering. The floor had been swept through after milking and the slurry sloshed into one corner of the yard for dealing with in the daylight. The stone floor and the open doors at either end where the cows entered and exited meant that, while it was bitterly cold outside, it was somehow several degrees cooler in the barn. He walked past the milking stalls to the wider stalls at the far end where they stored hay and feed. He found his father holding an oil lamp over Ed who was on his knees beside a prone cow, cautiously feeling his way around her distended hind quarters. He caught sight of Jack.

"Bring another lamp over," he ordered. "Can't see a damn thing down here now the light's gone." He continued to run his hands over the cow, the occasional prod eliciting a grunt of protest and a sudden raising of her head. The huge eyes were wide with distress.

"Bess looks to be ready to calve," Ed explained.

Jack squatted down beside his brother, running a hand over the cow's flank. "How can I help?" he offered. Ed looked at him questioningly.

"Sure you're up to it?" he questioned.

Jack's pride rankled. "I may have been away a while but I think I can still remember what I've spent years of my life doing," he retorted, belatedly realising he was being teased. "I'll tell Mum to put some water on to boil," he recovered, turning back towards the house.

"Better make that some soup as well," Ed suggested. "Going to be some while yet and it's a mite chilly out here tonight."

* * * * * * *

As Maud poured some leek and potato soup into bowls, she glanced anxiously at Jack.

"Will you keep an eye on your father for me?" she pleaded. "He'll be thinking he can carry on doing this just the way he always has but he's not strong enough any more. If it goes on too long, you'll need to tell him to go off to bed."

Jack laughed humourlessly. "There's not a chance in Hell of him listening to me," he observed.

206

Maud gave him a sharp look. "There's no need for language like that at the best of times," she reprimanded him. "Even less so on the night of Mary's vigil."

Jack frowned at her but she was looking out of the window at the lights in the yard.

"I can imagine Golgotha was a tad warmer," he sought to lighten the mood but Maud was having none of it.

"Get that soup out to them before it starts cooling, then," she instructed, hardily.

Albert and Ed had made themselves comfortable on a couple of wooden crates by the time Jack returned. He handed them their soup then crouched down beside Bess, drawing up some straw to keep her warm in her prone position.

"We should take shifts," Ed proposed, blowing on his soup to cool it. "I'll take the first shift with Jack then you can take over from one of us in a couple of hours, Dad."

"Best I take over from you, then," Albert answered. "We'll need one or other of us here throughout. Can't imagine Jack's had much recent experience of calving."

The jibe, second time around, had worn even thinner. Jack ignored it, in part because he suspected Albert was rather more serious in it than Ed had been.

They ate their supper in silence, listening to Bess's sporadic grunts and occasional attempts to shift her position.

After a couple of hours, Albert eased his legs out and rose, his joint creaking painfully. Jack could hear the breath in his lungs was becoming raspy, aggravated, he suspected, by the cold and the dust-filled air from the quantities of straw packed around and beneath the cow. Albert's breath was short and shallow as he paced around the shed, apparently using the excuse of stretching out the stiffness in his legs to cover his efforts to catch his breath.

"Why don't you go inside to warm up for a couple of hours?" Jack proposed. "We'll keep an eye out there."

Albert stopped stamping around the yard and folded his hands across his chest. "She's my cow," he refused stubbornly. "I'll stay and see this through like I always do, thank you."

Ed glanced at Jack. "I'll give you a shout when she gets close," he promised. "We'll need at least one of us with hands warm enough to be workable by then."

Jack saw an exchange of looks between father and son, and was surprised to see a nod of acceptance from his father.

"Two hours," he conceded, checking his fob watch and winding it for good measure. They could heart him muttering under his breath as he stamped his way back to the house.

Jack took his father's seat next to Ed and tucked his hands under his arms, next to his chest, to keep warm. The temperature had dropped again and mist was appearing as they breathed.

"Mum likened this to Mary's vigil the night before Christ's resurrection," Jack shared with Ed.

Ed humphed. "She's been spending too much time at that Methodist church," he scorned. "Apparently she started going more often when we were away. Annie told me," he explained to Jack's enquiring expression. "Fell out with the biddies at St Stephen's over something or other and took up with the Methodists instead."

"She's not said much about it to me," Jack reflected.

"Me neither," Ed admitted. "Just as well. Had enough of that from my Captain in France. Kept filling the boys with superstitious nonsense and grandiose ideas about how God was on our side."

Jack looked at Ed curiously but the light had now completely faded from the day and the oil lamps casting harsh lines on his brother's face distorted his expression. He did notice, though, how much older his brother now appeared, as if the light had taken away Jack's recollection of Ed's boyish face and the night was now revealing to him the man beneath.

"You don't think what we did was right?" Jack queried, his voice low to take any sound of judgment out of it.

Ed let his hands swing between his knees, eyes ahead, watching the straining cow.

"I don't have any qualms on that score," he dismissed. "What we were fighting for was right and I'd go back tomorrow to fight again if needs be. But it was all those chaplains and the others, the religious ones, trying to make out God was with us and supporting our cause. That's what I couldn't stomach."

"Why?" Jack blew on his hands to warm the tips where they were turning numb. He agreed with his brother, on that point at least, but he wanted to understand Ed's view on it.

"God wasn't behind the war," Ed's fervour was evident in the warmth of his tone. "As far as I can make out, it was all about who wanted what power and what pieces of land." He stared hard at Jack, daring him to disagree.

"The first German I killed – the first man I ever killed," Jack amended, "was in a German trench in Loos. Three of us had made it through the line. The trench had been abandoned, I guessed, less than a minute before so we headed down the line to find them. As we came round the corner, there was a lad tucked in the bend, his back against the trench wall, his knees in front of him and his pistol balanced on his knees, gripped in both hands. I automatically dropped to my knees to make a smaller target and I heard my two fellows fall back behind me, out of sight. In the second that I took aim, I could see his mouth moving and I caught the words he was muttering to himself. Strange, isn't it," Jack reflected, starting out of his contemplative posture and glancing across at Ed, "how many of their words sound like ours. Gott. Vater. I didn't know the words at the time but even then I could tell he was praying."

"You shot him?" Ed's voice was hushed.

Jack nodded. "He got off a shot at the same second as I did but he was shaking so much the bullet just embedded in the wall next to me. It happened so fast I didn't even see the light go out of his eyes. One second he was alive, the next he had gone. After that," he concluded, "I figured God didn't have much to do with it when both sides were talking to the same one." Even to his own ears, the narrative sounded horribly dispassionate.

Ed's voice, by contrast, had taken on that awed, hero-worshipping tone Jack knew so well from their youth. "How many did you kill, Jack?"

Jack shook his head vigorously. "We're not going there, Ed," he ordered. "There's no glory in taking another man's life."

"No glory?" Ed practically spluttered with outrage. "How can you say that? How many medals did they give you?"

"I don't know and I don't care," Jack retorted. Of course he did know but he couldn't find it in his soul to take any pleasure or pride in them.

Ed frowned, bemused. "Don't you think we did the right thing, Jackie?" He almost sounded bewildered, as if he needed Jack's reassurance they had made the right choices.

"You and I, Ed," Jack consoled him, contemplating his hands as he threaded and unthreaded his fingers, clenching them together. "Yes, we did the right thing. Those at the top, those who started the whole thing and those who sent millions of men to their deaths. They will have to search their own souls to answer that."

"I don't understand you, Jackie." Ed's voice was still concerned. "You were one of the first to sign up and you went back time and again without ever arguing or questioning in the way I saw so many other men do. How can you have done that if you doubted the cause?"

Jack stood up abruptly and shoved his hands into his trouser pockets. He stood in the doorway, still watching Bess, the air from her nostrils condensing as she breathed hard.

"It stopped being about 'the cause' after that first imbecilic battle in the dust and heat of France. When I saw men walking to their deaths, to be slaughtered by men who, after three hours of just gunning down man after man after man, were so sick of the death

210

they dealt that day that they allowed the survivors to walk unchecked across no-man's land to collect our wounded. From that moment, it was no longer about the cause for me. It was only ever about the men."

He stopped abruptly, aware his heart was pounding hard beneath his ribs and the familiar shortness of breath was warning him he needed to take control again. He turned and stared out into the night.

In the darkness, deepening as the oil lamps burned low, he heard rather than saw Ed move and felt his brother come and stand beside him at the open door. Ed held out a cigarette to him. Jack took it gratefully, hoping his brother couldn't see the slight tremor in his hand as he did so. He accepted a light and they smoked without speaking, staring out at the midnight blue sky, now clear and sparkling with stars, all the brighter for not being outshone with only the sliver of a new moon visible. As Jack finished his cigarette, Ed disappeared into the house without saying a word, returning a couple of minutes later with two mugs of steaming tea.

"So, who's this woman you're seeing?" Ed, it appeared, was ready to change the subject but his choice of alternative took Jack by surprise. Already on the defensive, Jack gave him a warning look. "What? You'll tell me about the war but you won't tell me who you're courting?"

Jack sighed, covering his eyes with his hand. "It's complicated."

Ed snorted. "What's so complicated? She's not married, is she?" Jack gave him a dismissive look. "OK, not married. Then, what?" He waited but Jack stayed silent, drinking his tea. "At least tell me her name." Ed could be very persistent.

"Sarah," Jack retorted shortly.

"Just Sarah?"

"Just Sarah?" Jack confirmed.

"Is she pretty?"

Jack prayed this wasn't going to go on for too long. "I don't think that's the word I'd use," he reflected. "Striking, perhaps."

"Gracious," Ed quipped. "I'm not sure Annie would want me describing her that way."

"Thankfully, Sarah's not that conventional about those things," Jack replied.

"How long have you known her?"

"Since Christmas."

"How did you meet?"

"Through work."

"She works at the bank?" Jack made a non-committal noise. "You've got to give me something, Jackie boy," Ed pleaded. "Mum sent me on a fishing expedition and she'll be sorely disappointed if I go back with nothing." Jack had to smile at that. He might have known his mother was behind this. "What's she like?" Ed probed, sensing a chink in Jack's armour. "What do you like best about her?" So much for getting her off his mind, Jack surrendered.

"I like her determination," he admitted, his tone contemplative. "Anything she fixes in her mind you know she's going to make happen. And the confidence that goes with that, her self-belief. I like that she seems to understand me and to be accepting of who I am without judging me. I like that she seems to see things in me that others don't, that I don't always see in myself, even. I like that she makes me want to be more than I am to live up to her expectations. I like that she encourages me to be a better version of myself." He stopped and feigned interest in his empty mug of tea to cover his embarrassment at how forthright he had been.

Ed gave a low whistle. "Sounds like you like this girl a lot," he commented. "What are you planning to do about it?"

Jack leaned back against the door frame and stared up at the stars. He'd forgotten how massive the night sky was, having grown used to the glimpses he got in London. So much he'd grown used to so quickly. "I told you…" he started.

"It's complicated," Ed parroted. "Have you ever thought it's you who makes things complicated, Jackie boy? Uh oh," Ed jerked upright, jolted out of his complacent teasing by a sudden noise from Bess. "Sounds like the calf's on the way. Best run and wake Dad while I get started."

* * * * * * *

It took Jack a good hour and a brisk walk around the farm the following morning to shake the groggy feeling from last night's vigil. The calf, surprisingly robust for the earliness of the birth, had made her appearance just before midnight. With his father's arrival, Jack had soon felt like a spare part but it was so long since he had last experienced this that he stayed throughout, keeping out of the way while trying to hold up enough light for his father and brother to see their work. As soon as mother and calf were settled, they had headed back to the kitchen for a hot cup of tea. Jack felt elated by the experience but for Alfred and Ed this was not only normal and prosaic but also part of a lengthy ongoing birthing period. So while Jack was in the mood to talk and reflect, he soon found himself abandoned by the rest of the family heading off to catch as much sleep as they could.

Retrieving his father's whisky, Jack had settled himself in front of the range in Gramma's chair, accepting one of the cats onto his lap as welcome company in his solitude. He smoked a series of cigarettes, absorbing the peace from the quiet of the house and the night. The room gradually cooled around him but his feline hot water bottle and the banked down range kept him warm.

He had surprised himself by talking to Ed so easily about the war. Somehow, it did come more comfortably with people he knew to have shared the experience, in whatever form it took for them. Somehow, there was a natural acceptance that, whatever they had experienced, whatever they felt as a result, it was accepted and not

213

to be criticised or questioned. That was the problem with talking to civilians. Too many questions. Too many attempts to understand, to share in an experience that, in reality, was too alien to be communicated, let alone comprehended by an outsider.

In the silence, it was perhaps inevitable he started to think about the men he had known who were now no more than memories, names on graves – here or overseas – or on war memorials, their shattered bodies somewhere in the mud of Flanders, lost. He tried not to think of the circumstances in which they died but, instead, to draw up memories of them at rest or at leisure. Smoking, drinking, whoring, playing cards, writing to loved ones, reading or re-reading those precious messages from home.

Unavoidably, though, his mind returned to those last moments. The mindless wait at the base of the ladders before going over the top, boots caked in wet clay, ears deafened by days of futile shelling, blood pumping so fast through his veins that he felt quite light-headed, which gave the whole experience that other-worldly, unreal aspect. The shock of the Private who fell dead at his feet, his life ended in the blink of an eye by the pinpoint accuracy of a German sniper. Worse, the men who didn't die so quickly, whose horrific wounds, guts torn open, limbs shattered and ripped, were beyond imagining but who still took long minutes to die. That man in the mud at Passchendaele. He stopped, shut his mind down at that unbearable image. He closed his eyes, leant his head back against the chair and forcibly emptied his mind of every last thought. And that last thought was of Sarah.

* * * * * * *

He woke, stiff and cold, in the early hours of the morning. The light was grey, unbroken by lamp or fire light, and the first sounds of the dawn were audible even through the closed windows. Opening the back door, he could see the imminent dawn was thinning the darkness behind the house, silhouetting the surrounding hills and the trees in the copse. One of the dogs, disturbed by his movements, padded lightly across from the barns and sniffed at his extended hand. Jack ruffled its head and crossed the cobbled courtyard to the byre. Mother and daughter were both standing in their stall, their warm breath creating clouds of mist in the chill morning air. As the calf moved to suckle, Jack rested his hand on the cow's head, distractedly stroking the soft velvet of her ears. He didn't know how long he stood there, his mind as quiet as the day as he absorbed the soft sounds of life emerging around him. Slowly, the sun rose and its dilute rays flowed over the courtyard and up the wall of the house. Knowing the family would soon be stirring and not in the frame of mind for conversation, Jack finally stirred himself and, treading quietly, made his way up to his room, closing the door behind him.

* * * * * *

With Maud at church this Easter morning, Annie had been left in charge of breakfast. Unfortunately, Charlie took up his demand for nourishment just as she set the eggs to fry alongside the bacon in the pan.

"Leave it with me," Jack ordered blearily, rubbing his hand over his eyes to force himself to wake up after his brief sleep.

"You look awful," Annie pronounced as she handed over to him. "You'll never get yourself a decent woman looking like that."

"Just as well I plan on being a confirmed bachelor, then," he retorted as she squeezed past and headed for the stairs.

"Christ," Ed declared, stamping the mud from his boots as he entered through the back door. "Don't tell me you're cooking. And I was really looking forward to my breakfast today."

"Not to worry," Jack assured him. "I've had plenty of experience over a brazier in France. This can't be that different. So

215

make the tea," indicating the pot just coming to the boil, "otherwise I'll eat all of this myself."

With his innate ability to arrive just in time for a meal, Albert appeared in the doorway as Jack was sharing the contents of the frying pan across the plates Annie had put to warm. He looked more pale than Jack had ever seen him, almost ashen, and his breath seemed to be coming with difficulty. He propped himself up with one hand on the door jamb for a moment, breathing hard. Jack watched him briefly then busied himself with the tea and toast to give his father space. When he looked up again, there was more colour in his father's face and he had straightened up. He acknowledged Jack with a nod, washed his hands at the kitchen sink as usual then settled in his place at the head of the table, just as if Maud were there.

"Calf looks healthy enough," Ed observed, eliciting only a grunted acknowledgement from Albert. A quick glance at each other and the two brothers joined him at the table, eating in silence. By the time Annie reappeared, Albert and Ed had disappeared back to their work and Jack was preparing to head out for a walk to clear the fog from his brain.

"All settled?" he asked of Charlie.

She nodded. "If you're going out, don't forget to be back by noon." He raised his eyebrows in question. "Maud will be back from church by then and she'll be expecting everyone here this afternoon. It's Easter Sunday, a day of rest," she explained to Jack's continuing bemusement. "That's why everyone's rushing to get the work done while she's out."

* * * * * * *

Not only a day of rest but also a day to be on their best behaviour, it seemed. On returning from his walk, his lungs refreshed and his throat sore from the crisp air and his mind cleared by the exertion, Jack was ordered by his father to don his best suit before Maud got back.

"I don't remember all this fuss when we were young," he reflected to Ed as they made their way upstairs to get changed.

"That's because she was too busy to be this strict," Ed retorted. "She's had too much time to think while we were away and now she's making up for it."

"I don't ask much of you," was Maud's explanation over lunch, "so it can't be too much to want a little observance of the Lord's sacrifice once a year, now can it?" The mutterings from Albert suggested otherwise but were quickly stifled. "I've never known a family complain about being forced not to work for half a day," Maud remarked. "Surely there's something you can all find to do with your time."

No one could miss the glance exchanged by Ed and Annie, who flushed a flattering shade of pink. "Well, Dad will probably fall asleep while pretending to read," Ed joked to cover their embarrassment.

"A day of rest should mean just that," Albert enforced and proved true to his word by retiring to the drawing room as soon as dinner was finished, sitting by the window to enjoy the warming rays of the afternoon sun. Gramma decided she would join him in there and leaned heavily on Jack as he helped her across the hallway and into the rarely used but well-furnished room. Having settled her in an armchair, wrapped a blanket around her knees and stoked the fire to keep her warm, he browsed the bookshelves for some minutes, reacquainting himself with old favourites before finally resorting to his childhood copy of Great Expectations to while away a few hours.

Maud was at the sink working her way through the washing up. Of Annie and Ed, there was no sign. He picked up a tea towel and started to work through the pile of plates and pans Maud had been accumulating on the draining board. He watched her soap-covered hands as she washed and rinsed the plates, noticing how her knuckles were starting to swell, looking more like Gramma's hands than he had seen before.

"Dad feels the cold now," he observed, thinking of that illness-shrunken frame and the pleasure in the older man's face as he absorbed the warmth of the sunshine.

"He does," Maud agreed, somewhat curtly. "But I don't want to talk about him, I want to talk about you."

"Mum..." Jack started, a warning note in his voice. She turned to fix him with one of her determined looks and Jack smiled though, inwardly, he gave a resigned sigh.

"Sarah," Maud ordered. "Tell me about her."

Jack knew better than to argue. "What would you like to know?"

Maud gave him the look. "You know I'm not on a fact-finding mission," she chastised. "I want to form an impression of her and of what's happening between you."

"I wish I knew," Jack rejoined. "I thought coming here would clear my mind and help me understand better."

"It hasn't."

"It's just making me doubt more. My world – her world – is so far removed from the life I've always known here. I know I've been away a long time but I can't be that different from the person who grew up here. I fear there's a person she thinks I am but that reality won't live up to her expectations."

Maud frowned. "Who is she, that her life is so different from ours?"

Jack closed his eyes briefly then looked directly at Maud. "Sarah is Sarah Samuels. She's Mr Samuels' eldest daughter. The boss' daughter."

Maud held his gaze for a long moment. "Am I supposed to be shocked?" she asked him at last.

"Aren't you?" he frowned.

"She could have been landed gentry and I still wouldn't have been," Maud scorned.

"But, of all people, Mum, you have such a respect for position and tradition."

"Maybe I also have more respect for our position here than you do," she retorted. "Are you and she so very different in terms of your backgrounds?" Jack, knowing he had used the same argument himself, stayed silent. "Your family, whatever our straightened circumstances, is still the leading family in the neighbourhood. We have the heritage, the manor house, the local village named after the family, the…"

"Don't bring up the title, Mum," Jack groaned. "It's an absurd and meaningless anachronism."

Maud relented and moved on. "Directly or indirectly, we provide employment for more than a third of the families living here and most of the others are living in properties originally built and owned by this family."

"That's just history," Jack countered. "How pointless is that heritage when we can only afford to keep half of this house heated?"

"We're not talking about us," Maud disputed. "We're talking about you, who you are and where you came from. You have a long and respected lineage. You have an education. Maybe not as good as the one I would have wanted for you but it's nothing of which you could be ashamed. And you have a brain. No," she ordered, putting an index finger firmly on Jack's hand as he was about to disagree with her, "you don't get a scholarship in Cambridge unless they think you can do justice to that level of education. You are one of the brightest people I know and I've never met anyone with your appetite for knowledge."

"Even saying I accept all that," Jack relented, "I'm still just a glorified clerk at a bank and she's the daughter of the man who owns the bank at which I work. Our prospects are leagues apart."

Maud folded her arms across her chest. Evidently, she was settling in for a long debate. "That matters to Sarah, then," she mused.

"No, but..."Jack started. Maud raised an eyebrow at him. "Perhaps it should," he enforced.

"Why?" Maud was watching him a little too closely.

"What I can offer her on a clerk's salary? I can't match the lifestyle she's enjoying."

"Firstly," Maud countered, "you're not a clerk so don't go putting yourself down for rhetorical purposes. Secondly," holding up her hand to forestall Jack's interruption, "I can't imagine for one minute you would stay in your current position if Mr Samuels accepted your marriage."

"Marriage?" Jack countered. "Who's talking about marriage?"

"Oh, Jack, don't treat me like an idiot," Maud cautioned. "We wouldn't be having this conversation if you weren't thinking this was serious."

Jack pushed back his chair and turned his back on his mother to stare out at the beautiful countryside, basking in spring sunshine. He thrust his hands into his pockets.

He heard his mother move behind him and half-expected her to cross over to him but, instead, he caught the sounds of her putting water on to boil and spooning tea from the battered old caddy into the tea pot. The air was so still, he caught the distant sounds of his father's slumbering snufflings and the sudden squeal of Annie's laughter from upstairs. The sun had warmed the air where he stood, making the dust dance and catching it, sparkles in the shaft of light. A pair of blackbirds started a cacophony in the hedgerow, presumably to ward off some unseen prowling cat with its sights set on their nest. Jack's mind drifted as he stood there for a long moment. He thought about the night he had met Sarah, her striking looks contrasting with the flighty, ethereal beauty of her sisters. About the quiet concern in her eyes as she talked to the patients at the hospital.

About her determination to help him make the most of himself, bordering on pushiness but, he knew, well-intentioned. And he understood now. He would never lead their relationship, too conscious of the disparities in their positions in society, their financial status. Sarah had seen that in him from the start and had been finding ways to take the initiative, to reach out to him beyond what divided them. She had never accepted those differences but had seen him for who he was, so much more than a background or a set of circumstances. Only his pride was what really stood in the way.

"I love her, Mum." Jack turned back to face Maud. "She's the most remarkable woman I have ever known. She's compassionate, determined, considerate. She carries her responsibilities so lightly yet I have never known anyone take their commitments more seriously. In so many ways, her life has never been her own and yet she has forged her own path and has such a strong sense of what she stands for and what she wants to achieve. Never once has she made me feel inferior for my position or status. In fact, I think she sees something in me that I don't yet fully understand for myself." Maud gave a slow smile and, passing a mug of tea back across the table, invited him to sit back down. "She's so beautiful, Mum," taking the opposite chair and wrapping his lean fingers around the mug for reassurance as much as for warmth. "I mean," he corrected himself, "she's not conventionally beautiful and she will always be outshone by her two sisters but, to me, she has an inner warmth, heart, that you can see in her eyes and it makes her beautiful. People are drawn to her. They trust her, instinctively. I would trust her with my life."

Maud's smile had broadened as he talked and there were tears in her eyes as he stopped. She reached a hand across the table and held his tightly. "I always wanted this for you," she murmured. "And I was so fearful you had shut yourself off from it. I never worried about Ed," pulling a handkerchief from her sleeve to clear her eyes. "He was so easy-going, his problem was going to be falling in love too often. But you were always such a serious lad. Right from your earliest years, I felt you were headed for something other than the life we lead here. And I felt you would need someone special to go through life at your side. It sounds like you've found her."

"But what can I do about it?" Jack questioned roughly. "Whatever I feel, there's no escaping the fact that, in so many ways, I am beneath her in life. I have no right even to think about marriage with her."

Maud straightened in her chair. "It didn't do your father and I any harm, love," she observed. Jack frowned. He hadn't even thought about the parallels with his parents' relationship. "Just think about it," Maud urged. "A successful marriage isn't about status. It's about two people wanting the same things in life and working together towards them."

All well and good in theory, Jack thought, but he couldn't for a moment see himself proposing marriage to Sarah Samuels.

Chapter Eight

Devon, Easter Monday, 1920

*I had the clarity I had sought, though not in the way I had
expected. Not that I felt it was likely to change anything in the
near future. Though life has a way of taking you in
unexpected directions.*

Standing at the back door, mug of tea in hand and the sun
warming his face, Jack was shocked by the wave of home sickness
that suddenly swept over him, so violent and intense that he almost
felt nauseous.

The prospect of a long train journey back to London followed
by four days' work before he could spend time with Sarah again
certainly wasn't helping. Yet, it was more than that. He felt divided.
As if he were somehow two different people, playing two different
roles in two very different places. He felt more relaxed here in Devon
than he had for a long time. Here, there was no struggle to be more
than he was, no striving to better himself. It was easy,
uncomplicated. Hard physical work, certainly, and gruelling days,
but no self-doubt, no questioning, no fear about whether he fitted in.
Never, though, would it be enough for him and, for that reason,
ironically, he did not fit in. He needed that sense of direction and
purpose, that tension that meant he was rarely at his ease, that drive
to be more and to do more. Here, his brain would stagnate and he
would end up resentful of this peaceful but narrow world. There, he
would doubt and he would fear but he could take more pleasure and
pride from his achievements for facing and overcoming those
hurdles. Perhaps he would never fit, a man always on the periphery,
on the outside looking in. Sooner that, he acknowledged, than putting
a cap on his potential at such a young age.

The ancient tom cat broke Jack's contemplation, wrapping himself around Jack's legs in farewell before hobbling off in the direction of the hedgerow to find a sun-bathed patch to which to retire.

Jack's suitcase stood packed and ready in the hallway, Albert was over at Mac's borrowing the truck to take him back to the station. He felt a pair of arms come around his waist and turned to embrace Maud, who rested her cheek on his chest. He held her tightly, feeling the slight tremors in her petite frame as she fought back tears. He rested his cheek against her hair.

"I'll be back when I can," he promised. He felt her nod in acknowledgement. "And you'll let me know how Dad's getting along? Or if I can help in any way?" Another nod.

"And I'll be expecting to meet Sarah soon, shall I?" Maud hazarded, a teasing note masking her underlying intent.

"Perhaps," Jack smiled. "If the time is right."

"I hope she's good enough for you," Maud said forcefully, pushing away from him, determinedly dry-eyed. She met Jack's eyes steadily, in control of herself again. "I don't care if she's as rich as Croesus, she had better deserve my son."

Jack quickly kissed her cheek to hide how choked he was by her words, said farewell to Gramma and took his case out to the front of the house where Albert was just pulling up. Throwing his case in the back, he jumped in the front and nodded to Albert to make a quick getaway. He couldn't resist, though, looking back at Maud, alone in the doorway, as they pulled away and he left his childhood home again.

* * * * * * *

At Jack's request, they made a brief detour to the war memorial in Westerham. The wind had picked up slightly as he stood there, hat in hand, reading the names of his fallen fellows. He knew most of the names though he would have been hard-pressed to put a face to some. He had been the first to go and so not served with many of them directly but he still felt a comradeship born of shared endurance and suffering. He wished he could pray, felt he should out of respect for their sacrifice, but the words wouldn't come. He bowed his head in silence, remembering what it had been like for them. He hoped they might build a better world now but he doubted it.

* * * * * * *

He was early for the train but Albert didn't wait – had, in fact, barely stopped long enough for Jack to jump out and retrieve his bag before he pulled away with nothing but a casual wave. Jack knew he was avoiding an emotional farewell, both of them inevitably wondering whether they would see each other again, but his ability to rationalise it didn't prevent the sense of rejection that stabbed at him.

Tucked in a corner seat of an otherwise empty carriage, for some minutes he watched the familiar landscape of his childhood slip away. That restlessness that had consumed him on the journey down, he noticed, had evaporated and he found himself settled enough, for the first time in days, to relish the prospect of time to read the books he had brought with him but not even opened until now.

Was he any clearer in his mind as a result of his time away? Perhaps. If he was honest, he had already known himself to be in love with Sarah but this was the first time he had openly acknowledged it. With his acute awareness of their relative positions, he knew in himself the acknowledgement changed nothing in his intentions. It was for Sarah to dictate their future direction because Jack did not consider himself to be in a position to do so. Many men, he knew, would have no such qualms in the face of Sarah's evident interest but he was no such man. He loved her, he could see himself wanting to spend his future days with her, but there was no way for him to decide whether or not that became a reality.

Settled in his own mind, he reflected back over his brief sojourn in Devon. Not 'at home', he suddenly thought, startled by the idea that Devon was no longer home in his mind. When had that happened? Throughout his time in France and then Italy, that old manor house was always where his mind drifted when people around him spoke of home. It was everything that was natural, simple and right in his life. Had London, then, subsumed that position? He thought not, struggling to associate his cramped rooms with that innate sense of comfort and well-being. He shouldn't be surprise to discover himself, in effect, homeless. After all, that sense of detachment and isolation had become more familiar to him, more comfortable, than his own family. Falling back into some of those old habits and behaviours with his parents and brother had only served to emphasise to him how very different was the man he now was from the boy he was then.

Would he ever have that sense of comfort and familiarity with Sarah? Emotionally, he hoped so. Rationally, he thought it possible. In so many ways, they already thought alike: shared values, shared priorities frequently showed in their perspectives on everything from her sisters to the management of that hospital. He had not found that kindred sense before, not in family, friend or lover. How rare it was, he could only guess. Based on his observation of those around him, he sensed it was not commonplace. Were it just the two of them, it would be simpler, without the sisters' judgement, the bank's partners' hostility. Though, thinking about it, many had been quite accepting. Williams, for instance, who had welcomed Jack as an equal from the first and treated him as a friend. Some of the partners, too, had been more open and courteous than Jack felt he had a right to expect. Was he, then, allowing the distorted opinions of a minority to influence his own perceptions disproportionately?

He stared out of the carriage window for a while, mulling over these ideas. Eventually, he took up one of the books at random and pushed the thoughts from his mind with the distractions of another time, another place.

* * * * * * *

By the time he had fought his way through the crowds at Paddington station and struggled across town with his bag on public transport on a surprisingly mild April evening, he was bone-weary, aching in muscle and mind, and impossibly tetchy.

Feeling the need to clear his head before having to engage with Mrs Jones, Lucy or Alfie, he deliberately got off the bus two stops early, even though it meant having to carry his case back up the hill to Crystal Palace. Traffic, both pedestrian and mechanical, was considerably quieter here and the late afternoon sun warmed his coatless shoulders, easing his tension.

He felt, in some ways, a sense of homecoming as he closed the gate behind him on the path to the front door. At least it offered the solitude and calm that was so vital to his sense of well-being. Mrs Jones, he concluded from the sense of stillness standing in the hallway, must be at her Monday night whist club, which meant Lucy was either reading in her room or at the pictures with friends. With any luck, Alfie might also be out socialising, giving Jack a few more precious hours of quiet reading time this evening before facing the prospect of returning to work tomorrow and the more positive prospect of perhaps seeing Sarah.

He was rapidly disabused of his hope, though, catching the sound of raised voices as he climbed the stairs to the top floor.

He had never seen Sarah so distressed. The sight shocked him to the core and he reacted instinctively, dropping his bag by the door and taking her in his arms, catching a fleeting glance of her face, tight-eyed and drained of colour, suddenly crumple in evident relief at the sight of him. She was trembling so hard he pulled her closer,

227

his hand against the back of her head, stroking her hair in comfort as she shook with sudden tears.

"Thank God," she heard him whisper, her voice choked. "Help me, Jack."

Jack stared over at Alfie, sunk back in one of the threadbare chairs by the fireplace, thrown by the fact she had – for the first time as far as he could tell – called him Jack, not John.

He frowned a question at Alfie and was surprised to get a shifty expression in response. He concluded something must be seriously wrong.

"Alfie," he prompted, putting as much severity into his tone as he could while trying not to pre-judge – or misjudge – the situation. "Don't you think you had better tell me what's going on?"

Alfie raised his hands defensively. "It's nothing to do with me..." he started.

Sarah instantly turned on him. "How dare you?" she cried, considerable strain evident in her voice as well as in the taut lines around her eyes. "Does nothing touch you, then? Do you take responsibility for none of your actions?"

Alfie's response was to sink even further back into his chair – though from where Jack was standing that hardly seemed plausible – and to turn his face away from Sarah, staring stubbornly at the blank wall.

Jack put his hands on Sarah's upper arms and held her far enough away from him to be able to read her face.

"Tell me," he urged quietly, his eyes searching out hers.

"Charlotte's missing," she admitted, her voice breaking on the second word as if she could barely stand to admit it.

"Since when?" Jack probed.

"This afternoon. We had an argument and she went up to her room. I went to find her a couple of hours later to clear the air but she had disappeared. I don't know how she got out without me seeing," bewilderment filling her voice. "I was in the drawing room the whole time. I would have heard."

Jack frowned. "Surely she's out with Williams or one of her friends?" he suggested.

Sarah shook her head, covering her mouth with her hand as tears started into her eyes again. "She's so upset. She's not thinking clearly. I shouldn't have said...what I said," she finished, hesitatingly.

Jack was struggling to put the pieces together. "Was the argument that bad?" he attempted, sensing that she was holding back from him the nature of the argument and not wanting to ask directly. When Sarah started visibly shaking, unable to speak, he pulled her back into his arms, his mind racing through the possibilities. He stared hard at Alfie, who was trying to avoid looking at the pair of them.

"What does this have to do with Alfie?" Jack asked slowly, starting to put the pieces together, then redirected the question at his friend. "Why is Sarah here, Alfie?"

Alfie rose and shoved his hands deep into his trouser pockets, hunching his shoulders defensively. Seeing he wasn't going to get an answer, Jack pushed again, a warning tone making his voice louder, harsher. "Alfie."

"I told her," Alfie gesticulated at Sarah. "It's nothing to do with me. Why should I know where her damn sister is? I haven't seen her in weeks."

Anger and disdain flared in Sarah's face as she pulled away from Jack and went to stand directly in front of Alfie. "Where else would she have gone?" she demanded. "Who else could she have turned to in this?"

"She tried to turn to you," Alfie attacked. "Much good that did her."

Sarah's face, suddenly suffused with colour, instantly paled again. "You have seen her," she accused. "What did you do? Where did you send her?"

Jack intervened. "Alfie, what exactly does this have to do with you?" he probed again.

"I told you," Alfie dismissed his assertion with a wave of his hand. "Absolutely nothing."

"How dare you?" Sarah cried. "This have everything to do with you. How can you deny it?"

"You have no proof," Alfie shouted into Sarah's face. "How do you know this isn't someone else's fault?"

Sarah slapped his face so hard he staggered back against the mantelpiece, holding his jaw.

"Because there hasn't been anyone else," she spat at him, somehow managing to drop her voice even in her rage.

Jack stared at the pair of them, staring each other down in fury, as the pieces slotted together.

"Charlotte's pregnant," he concluded. Sarah nodded, still staring at Alfie though more, Jack suspected, because she was unable to meet his own gaze instead.

"And it's your...friend's...responsibility." Sarah's words dripped contempt like venom.

Jack didn't have to look at Alfie for confirmation. He knew enough of the history and enough of Alfie's face to know she spoke the truth.

"Where is it you think she's gone?"

Sarah was still starting at Alfie, her hands balled into fists. Jack had to reach out and pull her towards him to break her attention. Instantly she looked into his face, the anger seemed to flood out of her, replaced, he thought, with guilt and despair.

"To get rid of it," she whispered. "I'm so afraid for her."

"If you'd been a bit more sympathetic she wouldn't have needed to," Alfie, still stinging from the blow, seemed to feel a need to lash out himself.

Jack stared at him coldly. "You have seen her, then?" he assessed, drawing Alfie's eyes to him. Perhaps it was the condemnation that Alfie read in his eyes but Jack caught a flicker of remorse in his face as he nodded.

"She arrived here a couple of hours ago. She was so distraught, I couldn't make much sense of what she was saying. Then she demanded to know where she could find Emily Thomas." Jack and Alfie exchanged a look of understanding. Emily, the wife of one of Alfie's friends, had sought out an abortion after falling pregnant from an affair while her husband was away working.

"Did you tell her?" Jack pushed.

Alfie shook his head. "No need," he elucidated. "I could tell her who Emily had seen."

"You sent her where?" This was like torture, having to drag every detail out of him.

"Edward Black's sister."

Jack gritted his teeth. He could feel his anger at Alfie building, fuel on top of the smouldering fire of old resentments and disputes long backed down from for the sake of their friendship. For Sarah's sake, suddenly so quiet and subdued at his side, he knew this was not the moment to lose control.

"The address, Alfie," he demanded, his hand closing around Sarah's.

* * * * * * *

Thankfully, Sarah had dismissed the chauffeur after he dropped her at Jack's house. They might yet stand a chance of discretion, then, when they found Charlotte. It did mean, though, that they were hampered by a slow progress across London on a series of buses and trams.

Jack kept Sarah held tightly at his side, his arm around her shoulders. He was shocked by how fragile she seemed, how emotional, how disturbed. He was used to her self-reliance, her calm self-assurance, particularly in the face of her sibling-children. He had instinctively known she would defend her sisters, protective in her maternal instincts, but he had never conceived she had such a passionate temper. Nor such contempt, transparent in her dark eyes as she stared at Alfie.

Sarah's face, washed out by the subdued light of the gas lamps as they changed transport for the third time, now onto a bus to take them into Hackney, was frighteningly pale. Her jaw was set, the lines around her eyes tight with anxiety. Jack suspected she was trying to keep herself in check. He wanted to lift the burden from her, knowing himself capable of carrying it for the both of them. He knew enough of himself to understand he not only coped well with difficult situations but was invariably the best suited to take charge. He had never felt more in control in their relationship.

Checking his watch as they left the bus, he realised they had been travelling for almost an hour. It was not fully dark, oppressed by a heavily clouded sky. It had been raining for most of their journey. They left the bus at the main road. Jack had got them this far but, unfamiliar with the area, he had to stop other pedestrians twice before he got adequate directions to Queen Victoria Terrace.

The back-to-back street was even more depressing and run-down than Jack had feared. Keeping Sarah close with his arm around her waist, they picked their way among rubbish, discarded broken furniture, piles of timber off-cuts. The street was empty, everyone driven indoors by the rain. The air was somehow thicker here, choked with soot from the open fires in the houses, compounded by the factory whose chimneys were just visible against the skyline a few streets away.

They lost moments searching for house number 138. Few had gone to the expense of numbering their properties. Jack stood in front of Sarah as he hammered on the front door, abstractedly noticing the peeling paint and warped wood as he waited for the sound of movement behind the door. Not hearing anything, he thumped hard several times.

"Mrs Woods," he yelled, his face close to the door. "Open this door."

He heard footsteps in the hall and could make out a dark shape behind the glass. "Mrs Woods," he demanded. "I need you to open this door. We're looking for Charlotte."

Long seconds passed. He looked at Sarah. Now they were here, her eyes were shadowed with the fear of what they might find. Finally, the door opened a fraction. "If you want that time-wasting slut, you'll find her in the back yard." It was a woman's voice but, in the darkness, they could make out little of her face. Jack took a step forward and tried to push against the opening but she was quicker than he and slammed it shut. He heard the lock turn.

"Round the back," the voice was muffled now behind the carrier of the door. "I'll leave the gate open."

Jack took Sarah's hand and led her back down the street, catching her as she stumbled in the darkness.

If the street had been poorly lit, this alley way at the back between two rows of houses was damn near unnavigable. Jack went first, still firmly holding Sarah's hand but trying to find a safe passage through. Counting the gates in the brick walls was the only thing that gave him any sense of location. As they neared where he took number 138 to be, he could just make out a lighter shade of grey in the elongated boundary and prayed silently they had found the right place.

The gate was propped ajar with a shovel, its handle broken. Jack forced it all the way back to enable both of them to see into the yard. It stank of rotting vegetables and the unmistakable stench of blood. Jack knew that smell so well and hoped that Sarah didn't.

His eyes had adjusted somewhat in the alley way but he still had to stand for several seconds trying to discern shapes in the darkness, unrelieved by any light from the forbidding wall of the house at the back. He could make out a coal scuttle and indistinct shapes of boxes.

Standing in the silent darkness, hearing Sarah's ragged breath – from anxiety or exertion, he didn't know – he caught the slightest sound from the far corner, behind the gate. A sound like a stifled whimper.

Crossing the cramped space, he crouched down to the huddled figure, having to feel as much as see his way. As his hand touched hers, he felt her flinch, an uncontrollable, instinctive reaction of self-preservation. What concerned him more was that her hands were ice cold and her clothes – and hair, as he made out her shape and position with his hands – were soaked through. She was not so much shivering with cold as shaking bodily with ague-like tremors of one both emotionally and physically drained.

"Charlotte," he said softly. She turned her head towards the wall as if trying to hide her eyes from him. "We're here to take you home," he told her firmly but quietly. Ignoring the slight shake of her head, he gathered her up in his arms and, easing backwards, forced himself to stand. Adjusting her position to keep her secure, he felt Sarah's hand on his arm, briefly, then he led the way out of the yard and back down the alley way, Sarah following.

He carried her as far as the main road where lamp light and a nearby bench afforded them the opportunity to assess Charlotte's condition. Her eyes were so wide and dark in the weak light that Jack, for a moment, feared for her mind. She was incoherent, staring but somehow unseeing, unable to focus on him. She reeked of alcohol, whether ingested or used as a steriliser, Jack could only guess. All colour had drained from her skin and she continued to shake uncontrollably.

Sarah sat on the other side of her, chaffing those chilled hands in a vain attempt to instil both warmth and recognition back into her.

"We have to get her home as fast as we can," Jack urged. "She's soaked through and looks already to have caught a chill." Even as he spoke he was shrugging off his greatcoat and wrapping it around Charlotte's shoulders. "She's going to need a warm bath, a doctor and rest, as soon as possible."

"How?" Sarah whispered, distressed. "The car has gone and it'll take forever to go back the route we came."

"I'll go and hail a cab." Jack pushed to his feet.

"But we need to be discrete," Sarah cautioned. "They can't know where we live or what's happened."

In Jack's mind, given Charlotte's condition there were more immediate concerns for her health than for her reputation but he pushed that thought away.

"We'll get dropped off a distance away. I'm sure we can give the impression she's had too much to drink." Sarah nodded her acquiescence. "I'll be as quick as I can," he assured her, his heart going out to her as she tried to stay determined and in control.

In the end, the wet night and the less-than-salubrious neighbourhood meant it took him a lot longer than he expected to flag down a taxi on the main road. By the time they pulled up, he was relieved to see Charlotte sitting more upright than before, albeit she was leaning for warmth and support against Sarah, who had her arm around Charlotte's shoulders.

He jumped out of the taxi and, pulling Charlotte's arm around his shoulder, almost bodily lifted her into the back of the cab. Seating himself in the corner, he pulled her towards him and wrapped both his arms around her, holding her against his chest for warmth. In only his suit, he was none too warm himself but it was better than nothing, particularly when, he realised with concern, her shaking was showing no sign of abating. Sarah took the opposite end of the seat. Rubbing her arms to chafe some warmth back into Charlotte's body, she rested her hand briefly on Jack's. His eyes met hers and he read there her relief and gratitude.

In a little over half-an-hour they were back in Belgravia. Jack stopped the taxi two streets away and paid off the driver. Putting his shoulder under Charlotte's arm, he slowly walked her down the street, Sarah close on the other side.

She let them into Lyall Street as quietly as possible, hoping not to disturb the servants. The lights, though, were still on in the drawing room and the sound of the door closing behind them drew Mr Samuels out of his light doze.

"Sarah," he called from the other room. "Is that you?"

She looked at Jack in despair, at a loss to explain their situation and clearly wanting to keep the truth from her father. Mr Samuels appeared in the doorway. "Sarah?" He caught sight of Charlotte, practically collapsing between the two of them. "Charlotte?" His voice broke on his instant parental fear and Jack knew he needed to stay in control a while longer.

"It's alright, Sir," he reassured the older man. "Charlotte's come down with a chill. We just need to get her out of these wet things and warmed up as quickly as possible."

He motioned to Sarah to start taking Charlotte upstairs before Mr Samuels could gather his wits. Sarah started to move but Charlotte, without Jack as a prop, almost collapsed on the floor. Cursing under his breath, he pulled her into his arms again and carried her up the stairs.

Sarah directed him to Charlotte's room, Mr Samuels following. Jack propped Charlotte up on the bed and eased her out of his coat.

"Sir, I think you had better send for a doctor," he prompted his employer, finding Charlotte's skin was starting to burn with fever.

Sarah looked at him aghast, paralysed by the thought of their family physician having to attend to Charlotte's underlying condition. "Dr Streets is away," she leapt in. "He's visiting his daughter in Brighton this week." God, she could lie well, Jack thought. "I'll see if Dr Jones can come instead, from The Grove."

Mr Samuels, standing in the doorway to Charlotte's room, was looking dazed but he suddenly recovered himself. "Give me the details," he ordered Sarah. "I'll get James to fetch him personally." Sarah told him the address and he disappeared back downstairs.

Sarah headed into Charlotte's bathroom and he heard the sound of water running into the bath. When she returned, her skin was ashen but she had a steely look on her face.

"John," she ordered. "I need you to fetch me a bottle of gin from the drawing room." She crossed the room and started to peel away the sodden layers of Charlotte's clothes.

"Gin?" Jack echoed, bemused.

Sarah refused to meet his gaze. "While you were fetching the cab, Charlotte told me that she didn't go through with it. The guilt and the pain made her stop that butcher. But it looks like it's already gone too far," indicating a dark stain of dried blood on Charlotte's skirts. She straightened up and looked Jack directly in the eye. "I'm going to finish what Charlotte and nature have already started," her voice low but steady, her face set with determination.

"You can't be serious," Jack started.

"I will do whatever I must to make this right for her," she challenged. "An extra hot bath and a quantity of gin may be all it takes to sort this out." She was staring hard at him. Jack couldn't tell if she was pleading with him not to defy her or begging him to understand. He just stared. Nothing he had seen had prepared him for this. Sarah looked away first but only to help Charlotte to her feet and lead her to the bathroom. "The gin, John," she called back over her shoulder.

* * * * * * *

237

He felt uncomfortable sitting in the drawing room, not knowing whether he was expected to wait or to leave. He told himself he wasn't leaving until he knew Charlotte was safe.

Tempted though he was to start on the whisky after he had taken the gin up to Sarah, he decided to stay sober, suspecting he needed a clear head to work through this. He felt complicit in what Sarah was doing, for not preventing it, indeed arguably for aiding her by complying with Sarah's request for alcohol.

He didn't know where Mr Samuels had gone after he had put out orders for the doctor. Sarah, he was sure, would not have allowed him to be nearby for the examination. The doctor had arrived almost an hour-and-a-half after they had returned. He had already been upstairs for forty minutes. For the first twenty of those, Jack had anxiously paced the room, walking from door to fireplace, fireplace to windows, windows to door. Eventually, though, he had forced himself to sit, forced patience, forced acceptance of an outcome over which he had no influence.

Slowly, the tension of the events and the length of the day took hold and tiredness overwhelmed him. He rested his head back against the chair, trying and failing to keep his eyes open.

It was the sound of the front door closing, quiet in itself but loud in the silence, that stirred him. He opened his eyes to find Sarah hesitating in the doorway. He rose as she approached but didn't go to her. She paused to pour them both a large measure of whisky and crossed to hand it to him but kept her distance. They both knew their relationship had changed and were wary of taking the first step that would define its new status.

Not quite meeting his eyes, she took a seat on the sofa opposite and Jack settled back in his chair, waiting for her to speak.

"She's sleeping," Sarah finally broke the silence. "The doctor gave her a sedative. He says the hot bath dealt with the worst of it but we'll know over the next twenty-four hours how much the chill has taken hold. I sent Father to bed once he knew she was comfortable." She stopped and took a large draught of her drink. Jack waited, unable to ask the question. She started at the amber liquid in the glass, swirling it round and round. "The...other matter resolved itself," she stated, baldly, perhaps defiantly. "That woman had done enough damage to make it unstoppable. It was already done before the doctor arrived."

Jack looked away, unable to look at the woman he loved. He stared at the fire, which needed to be either stoked up or banked down. He should leave shortly.

"It's because Williams proposed."

The statement, quietly delivered, was so surprising that Jack couldn't help but look at Sarah again. She met his eyes this time. "She had suspected for a while but tried to pretend nothing was wrong. Then Williams proposed to her yesterday and she decided she had to do something about it."

"It was Alfie, then." Jack's voice sounded rusty from the strain.

"Williams, it seems, is too much of a gentleman. I hope we can continue to rely on that instinct."

Jack frowned. "She intends to marry him?"

Sarah crossed her legs and stared hard at Jack. "I intend that she will marry him," she asserted. "And that she will be happy with him."

Jack didn't flinch. "That means you won't be telling him the truth," he observed.

"No need." Sarah's voice was still so calm. "The matter is resolved. She's had a lucky escape after getting herself into a stupid position. I don't see the need to punish her more than she is doing herself."

Jack thought about the tall American, wondering how he would feel in his friend's position. Because he did consider Williams a friend now, not just an acquaintance. He didn't deceive himself that Williams was deeply in love with Charlotte. As far as he could discern, he had made himself a good choice: a wife who was pleasant to look upon, engaging to be with and who would be a perfect hostess to entertain his business partners. Theirs could be an amicable and happy marriage, should both come to it with the right expectations: mutual affection, support in good times and bad, and a healthy environment for children.

"I just hope," Sarah murmured, almost to herself, "that this hasn't done any lasting damage. An heir will be very important to Williams."

It never ceased to surprise Jack how much they thought alike.

Jack drained the whisky and stood up. "I'm glad Charlotte is safe," he commented, the warmth in his voice betraying the words he wasn't prepared to say. He started to cross the room but Sarah's voice stopped him.

"Don't leave." It was somewhere between a plea and an order.

He turned back and she rose, walking cautiously towards him and stopping only a matter of inches away, within touching distance. He could smell the faintest traces of her perfume, surely applied many hours earlier. He looked down into her face and saw the strains of the day etched there.

"I have shocked you to-day," she murmured, clenching her hands together in an uncharacteristically nervous manner. "Appalled you, perhaps?" He didn't allow his face to react to her words. This close to her, he was in danger of his physical and emotional reactions to her overwhelming his rational ones. "I'm sorry if that's the case," her voice hushed. "But I won't apologise for defending my family. I will do whatever it takes to make my family happily. It seems that's how I'm made."

"Whatever it takes," Jack iterated, holding her gaze.

Sarah took a step towards him, coming so close that they were practically touching.

"I will be sorry," she continued, "if this changes what is happening between us. I missed you terribly while you were away. It reinforced for me what I thought I already knew: that you are a very important part of my life. And," hearing his sharp intake of breath, she placed her hands on his chest, closing the gap between them, "what I saw in you tonight is the man I've been wanting to find for so long. I'm a strong, independent woman and I need a man who can deal with that. But I also need a man who can be strong when I can't be. I want someone who will stand by my side in everything I want to do in my life. John, if you don't understand why I have done what I have today, I hope you will at least find it in your heart to sympathise and, if you can, to forgive. Because I don't want to lose you."

Jack drew a ragged breath, not realising he'd been holding his breath since she had touched him. Whatever else this woman was, she was honest with him.

He took her face in his hands, the blood pumping in his veins. Forcing himself to be gentle, he stroked her cheek with his thumb, staring into her eyes. "Sarah," he whispered, then captured her mouth with his, kissing her long and hard. He felt her sink against him and her arms move around to hold him tight against her. He mirrored her movements, shifting his weight in an effort to get even closer to her. After long moments, he broke away from her mouth, holding her face far enough from his to read her eyes.

"I love you, Sarah," he said harshly, his breathing uneven. "For better or worse, it seems that's how I'm made."

Chapter Nine

London, Summer 1920

After that, change came quickly that summer.

"I'll be gone by the time you get back."

Jack stopped buttoning the waistcoat of his morning suit and looked at Alfie in the mirror over the fireplace in their rooms.

"Going somewhere?" He bent his head to concentrate on the buttons again.

"I'm leaving, Jackie." Alfie sounded nonchalant but Jack wasn't buying it. "I'm starting a new job on Monday at Richmond's Yorkshire office. I'm catching the midday train. There's a car coming for me shortly to pick up my bags."

Jack turned slowly, letting his hands hang down at his sides. "When was this decided?" He was getting suspicious but kept his voice low not to betray himself.

"It came up several weeks ago. I interviewed for the position Thursday of last week and confirmation came through on Monday." Alfie had still not raised his head. Having plucked a thread free from the seat cushion, he was winding it round the forefinger of his left hand.

"You didn't think to mention it before now?"

Alfie shrugged. "I'm telling you now. Mrs Jones knows. I've paid her a month's rent in lieu of notice so she won't go short. She told me she doesn't need the money now anyway so she won't be looking for another lodger." Finally, Alfie looked up at Jack. "Seems you've got the place to yourself," he remarked. "I'm sure you'll enjoy the lack of disruption."

"And you didn't think to mention it before now?" Jack shook his head, trying to clear it. "You're seriously telling me you're going?" he challenged. "Just like that? Five years and it's 'so long, Jack, see you sometime'?"

Alfie stood and dusted down his trousers.

"Seems to me you've been leaving me behind for a while," he quipped, lifting Jack's morning coat from where it was hanging out of the way. He held it out by the collar for Jack to put on. "Time you were leaving," he chivvied. "You wouldn't want to be late for the wedding of the year."

Jack turned around and slid his arms into the coat. Alfie hoisted it over his shoulders and set the collar straight. Jack turned back to face him but Alfie made a show of picking fluff off the coat and sorting out the collar to avoid looking at him.

"You're sure this is what you want?" he pressed Alfie, frowning.

Alfie laughed at him. "We both know why this is happening. But what could be better? More money, fresh air and a whole new bevy of young ladies to entertain. Sounds more like a holiday than work to me."

Jack had always known when Alfie was lying. He wondered sometimes why he bothered but, for some reason, they both fostered the pretence. He took a step back, pulling the bottom of his jacket to straighten it.

"How do I look?" he asked, trying to find a neutral subject.

"Like you'll fit right in," Alfie taunted.

Jack held out his hand. "Have a safe journey. Let me know that you arrived safely."

Alfie shook his hand briefly. "You're not responsible for me any more, Jackie," he warned, heading towards his bedroom. "Not that you ever were," he reflected, pausing on the threshold. "But I'll look after myself from this point forwards." He disappeared into his bedroom and closed the door on their friendship.

* * * * * * *

St Margaret's Church, Westminster. Chosen chapel of the rich and famous and, ever since the announcement of their engagement had hit the newsstands, properly written up in The Times, the only place Charlotte would contemplate marrying her betrothed. It wasn't every day the 'enchanting' daughter of a well-connected British financier (Mr Samuels' status as a banker clearly wasn't sufficient for the discerning readers of *The Times*) married the 'wealthy and debonair' only son of 'one of America's greatest banking dynasties'.

On this glorious July day, set fair according to meteorologists and social commentators alike, no shadow was cast from the dark days at the beginning of April.

For three days, Charlotte had seen no one but Sarah, her father, her maid and the doctor. As far as anyone was concerned, she had contracted a chill from being caught in the rainstorm and, having seen off the fever within twenty-four hours, was recovering her strength.

The first person she saw after emerging from her sanctuary was Williams. If he had been anxiously awaiting an answer to his proposal, he was swiftly put out of his misery by her expeditious acceptance. Jack, as was becoming usual, was sitting in the drawing room with Sarah at the point the happy couple came in to break the news and detected only a slight wariness in Charlotte's acceptance of his warm congratulations. For a few days after the families had been informed, Charlotte was somewhat subdued, showing less enthusiasm for the preparation of the announcement than Williams and Isabella. The arrival of the first messages of congratulation, however, soon encouraged her to abandon her reticence and give herself up to the pleasure of preparing for a wedding scheduled for only three months hence. Mr Samuels, who had initially baulked at the unseemliness of such a short engagement, had been prevailed upon by Charlotte's enthusiasm and, more practically, Sarah's behind-the-scenes manipulation, to give permission for the nuptials to proceed in July. The impatience of youth proved an endless topic of discussion at the next partners' dinner, though Jack knew the timing had more to do with the planned venture between Richmond Bank and Williams' father. Williams was due to move to New York in September to lead the investment bank and he had made it conditional on getting to spend time with his bride before they moved.

Given his experience of Williams and Isabella, Jack found their parents to be everything he expected. Frederick Williams Senior was a slightly shorter, less broad version of his son, balding now and starting to run to paunch but still fundamentally athletic and hearty. In Susanna Williams he discovered a more content, settled version of Isabella, the same slightness of frame and sharpness of bone structure, the same lightness of spirit and teasing sense of humour but tempered by an awareness of her status and responsibilities, and how her appearance and behaviours reflected on her husband. Around her parents, Isabella became Isabella, not Issie, a less flighty, quieter, slightly subdued version of herself. Jack saw, now, how her arrival in London some months before must have seemed like a temporary release from reality into a world where Issie had been a more extreme version of her natural personality traits. Part of Jack missed Issie but he liked and respected Isabella more.

The two families met over a getting-to-know-you dinner hosted by Mr Samuels at Lyall Street. Charlotte, having spent the afternoon with them at their suite at The Ritz, arrived with her soon-to-be new family, her cheeks flushed with evident pleasure at what must have been a successful afternoon. For a moment, Jack wondered how he would be introduced to them, having no formal status in the family, but it seemed either Williams or Charlotte had already explained the position as he was introduced purely as Mr Westerham. He hoped Williams had been the one responsible for the explanation. Charlotte, he feared, had too many reasons not to give an unbiased perspective.

Now, the families were filling the pews at the front of the church. With every row filled and every guest extravagant in their top hats and flamboyant hats and dresses, the place looked packed. The impression was enhanced by the fact that every nook and cranny was draped in flowers. The scent of the lilies was not only overpowering but liable to spark an epidemic of hayfever. Even outside Jack had had to fight his way through a small crowd, the like of which seemed to gather for a glimpse of any society wedding, whether they had heard of the participants or not.

He stood at the back of the church for some moments, catching his breath and taking in the view. Williams was pacing at the front, his best man – a fellow Harvard oarsman – occasionally slapping his back in a jovial fashion that would do little for Williams' evident nerves. Not that he had any doubts on this milestone day, Jack knew. Even when he proposed he had experienced no fear that Charlotte would do anything other than accept. The frenetic activity of the last few days and weeks, though, was enough to instil some level of anxiety into even the most sanguine of men.

As he watched Williams pace out the short space from the aisle to the south door for the umpteenth time, the crowds parted briefly and Jack saw Sarah.

Since that fateful day in April, their courtship had subtly but significantly changed. Nothing had been said to make expectations on either side more concrete and Jack was still adamant any decision to change the status of their relationship would be Sarah's alone, but he felt they were, if not quite on an equal footing, certainly less unequal than before. He also felt his eyes had, once and forever, been opened to who Sarah was. What was liberating was the recognition that this knowledge made no difference. He felt he had seen the worst of Sarah and, while he could not say he loved her the more for it, he did at least love her in the full knowledge of what she was capable. She, on the other hand, seemed to see that night as some sort of test that he had passed. His reward was a deeper trust than before and shared confidences, whether her views on an acquaintance or her knowledge of Samuels' latest business plans. Indeed, she had gone further, not only sharing information with him but also seeking his insight.

So when he caught sight of her talking to Mr and Mrs Morton in the third row and she excused herself to make her way to the back of the church to join him, holding her hand out to claim his, in his heart he felt pride and there was no doubting her proprietorial attitude as she stood alongside him to survey the gathered throng and slipped her hand into the crook of his arm.

Jack, for his part, couldn't take his eyes off her. Her beautiful, shining chestnut hair was tied back beneath a wide-brimmed hat in a soft, pale grey colour that matched her full-length, sheath-like silk dress. Dove grey satin gloves finished above the elbow and she wore a long string of pearls, wrapped once around her throat like a choker and then allowed to fall between her breasts. It was the most fashionable outfit Jack had ever seen her wear. She was simply, subtly dressed, under-stated elegance, and she looked exquisite.

Sarah, realising he was both entranced and unable to articulate his reaction, gave him a slight side glance and ran one gloved hand over his. Leaning close to his ear, she whispered, "You look rather wonderful too, Mr Westerham."

He was about to speak when a sudden noise at the west door sent all the ushers scurrying into their positions. Sarah smiled at Jack and led him to their pew at the front.

Barely thirty minutes later and Williams and Charlotte emerged blinking into the brilliant midday sunlight, man and wife.

From Westminster, it was a pleasant ride down to Claridges for the wedding breakfast but the sheer volume of chauffeur-driven Rolls Royces departing the church and then arriving en masse at the hotel conspired to make them almost an hour late for luncheon. Still, the free-flowing champagne kept most of the guests happily entertained, particularly the American contingent who were making the most of their temporary liberation from Prohibition.

Sarah had been commandeered to assist in greeting the guests alongside her father, sister, new brother-in-law and his parents. Jack had been surprised by the warmth of Charlotte's kiss of greeting as he made his way down the line. It was as close as she had ever come to thanking him for his help in April.

"Top up?" Isabella appeared at Jack's side with a half-full bottle of champagne snaffled from one of the waiters. Jack held out his glass. "Experience tells one to be self-reliant at these things. I can't take the risk of waiting hours for a refill."

Jack smiled and watched Sarah greet first Mr Norcliffe, dashing in a hand-embroidered red waistcoat, and then David and Simon Stevenson from the Cambridgeshire estate, both looking somewhat uncomfortable with their surroundings. Jack reflected quite how far he had come since he first met them more than half-a-year ago.

"She looks quite beautiful, doesn't she?" Isabella enjoined, following Jack's gaze.

"I've never seen her looking more beautiful," Jack agreed, feeling the slightest edge of jealousy as Peter Fellowes greeted her rather too warmly for his liking.

"I meant Charlotte," Isabella teased, her lips quirked in amusement. Jack looked down at her, a smile playing in his own eyes.

"I know you did," he acknowledged.

Isabella narrowed her eyes at him in that flirtatious way she had. "You're getting more confident by the day, Mr Westerham," she mused, pouting ever so slightly at him. "I must say it's quite an attractive trait."

Jack hid his smile and went back to watching Sarah. Isabella refilled her glass again.

"Isn't it time you did something about it?" she challenged, falling into her old habit of wanting to spark a reaction in Jack.

"You can talk," he replied lazily, sipping his drink then almost spilling it as Isabella smacked his arm in a fit of pique.

"That was ungentlemanly," she criticised, her pout becoming more pronounced. Jack caught the genuine hurt in her eyes.

"Forgive me," he soothed.

Isabella's flash of anger evaporated as a secretive grin started to spread over her lips. "Besides," she murmured, leaning against Jack's arm the better to whisper into his ear, "there may be news on that front sooner than you think. So," leaning back on her heels and raising her voice, "if you want to do something about it, you'd better think of this as your last chance."

She was putting on a show, Jack suspected, and realised why when, a moment later, Sarah slipped her arm though his. She smiled a dismissal at Isabella who, laughing, went off in search of someone else with whom to flirt.

"All done?" Jack asked, collecting a glass for Sarah from a passing waiter.

"For now, thankfully."

Jack released her hand from his arm and carefully slipped it around her waist, turning her slightly towards him.

"I meant to say earlier," he murmured, his mouth close to her ear, "that I have never seen you looking more beautiful. But you literally took my breath away."

Sarah closed her eyes for a moment, resting her head against his. "Thank you," she whispered. "I needed that." He frowned his lack of understanding. "Charlotte's being a bit off with me today."

"Why?"

"I am the keeper of her secrets," she sighed, "but that also means I am a constant reminder of that which she wishes to forget. To-day is not a day for her to be reminded."

Jack kissed her forehead. "You are more forgiving than I," he judged.

Sarah smiled. "We both know that isn't true," she replied.

* * * * * * *

Sometime after luncheon, after several speeches and toasts, Jack found himself sitting alone at the top table with George Samuels, smoking cigars and drinking the smoothest single malt he had ever tasted. Samuels' eyes never left Charlotte, dancing with her new husband, laughing with her guests. Jack's eyes, by contrast, never left Sarah, who was making a slow progress around the room, a smile, a greeting and a personal word for every one of their guests, whether friends of the bride or of the groom. He watched in awed admiration as she raised a smile from the taciturn retired naval veteran, a distant cousin of Williams' father, with whom Jack had tried and failed to hold a conversation earlier.

Mr Samuels, who was surprisingly coherent given the amount of alcohol Jack knew him to have consumed, started watching him watching Sarah. He drew on his cigar, puffing the smoke at the ceiling.

"How much longer so you intend to keep my daughter waiting, John?"

Jack forced his gaze away from Sarah to her father. "Sir?" He frowned.

Samuels leaned forward, stabbing with his cigar for emphasis. "Look, I can understand why you might have chosen to wait once these two stole a march on you but there's nothing to make you wait any longer, is there? She's not getting any younger, after all." Jack turned in his chair to look directly at his employer. "I mean," Mr Samuels corrected himself, "she's in her prime but no woman likes to be upstaged by her younger sister. I know she puts on a sophisticated and business-like front but, underneath, she's still a young girl dreaming of her moment in the spotlight."

Jack could almost have laughed at George Samuels' absurd description of his eldest daughter had not the subject matter been so interesting to him. "Sir," feeling his way as casually as he could, "you don't see any impediment? Nothing that would stand in the way?"

"Nothing as far as I can see," Samuels dismissed. "Except maybe your pride. Or possibly hers. Either way, that's the worst reason I've ever heard. Of course," waving his empty glass at a nearby waiter, "it would mean some changes. We'd need to find you a new position at the bank. We can't have you still working the floor. And somewhere for the two of you to live. Unless," brightening at an idea that had apparently just occurred to him, "you move into Lyall Street. It could prove very beneficial to have both of you close at hand. Not least with Sarah still needing to come back often to host dinners for me. And with Charlotte leaving."

Jack's pulse had picked up its pace, adrenaline flooding his system and a sense of fearful anticipation beginning to flutter in his gut.

"I loved her mother very much," Samuel's tone turned maudlin. "Her time with us was tragically short. It gave me an appreciation for not wasting time. Or worrying about what other people think."

He looked Jack directly in the eyes and he realised with a jolt that Mr Samuels was a lot more sober than he was giving him credit for. He stared across at Sarah for a long moment than took a deep breath. "Are you giving me your permission, Sir?" he asked, cautiously.

Samuels laughed, hard. "John, my boy," he counselled, "if you think it's my permission you need, maybe you're not the man for her after all. Though," wiping a tear away from his eye, "I'm not sure I have much say in that either." He held out his hand and Jack took it in his. "Let's just say I'm giving you my blessing, my boy," putting his other hand on Jack's shoulder. "The rest is up to you."

"Sir," Jack felt he really must clear the way before he could feel free to proceed. "Doesn't it bother you at all? That I have no money, no status. That Sarah could marry someone with much better

251

prospects than I? Are you sure I'm not just after her for her money – or yours?"

"First," Mr Samuels caveated, sounding more sober by the minute, "I consider neither myself nor my daughter to be that poor a judge of character," with a steely look of criticism in his eye. "Second," leaning back in his chair now and waving down yet another refill for his glass, "I'm only three generations away from a coal-mining Yorkshireman, and I mean he dug the stuff out of the seam with his own hands, not that he owned the mine. As I see it," he counselled, "prospects aren't something you're born with, they're what comes to men with the right brains and aptitude to see opportunities and the attitude to do something about them. On that basis, I think you've got more prospects than most, particularly with me behind you. Third, that woman," nodding towards Sarah, who was being led onto the dance floor by Williams' best man, "has always known her mind, ever since she came to me at the age of eight and told me she intended to be chairman of the bank so that I could retire and spend more time at home with my family. She told me what was in her mind in January and, thankfully, I have no reason to argue with her decision. Unless you intend to tell me otherwise?"

Jack smothered a smile and shook his head. "I'm learning not to argue with her either," he concurred, now properly distracted by the sight of Williams' best man leaning close to Sarah to whisper in her ear. Jack rose. "Excuse me, Sir," he said, distractedly. "I think there's somewhere I need to be."

Samuels clapped his hands together. "Go to it, my boy," he proclaimed.

Jack quickly caught Sarah's eye as he weaved between the dancers to reach them. She seemed torn between amusement at the expression on his face and relief that she was about to be released from her heavy-footed partner. The man was clearly disappointed by his dismissal but gave way graciously and went off in search of a bridesmaid.

252

Jack took Sarah in his arms without commenting but Sarah couldn't resist.

"I don't think I've ever seen you so proprietorial," she observed, straight-faced.

"It's bad enough the Yanks have stolen one English rose today," Jack remarked. "I didn't think we should risk them taking a second."

"You fear I was about to be swept off my feet by the prospect of a merry-go-round of social occasions in New York, Martha's Vineyard and the south of France?"

"I give you far too much credit to think such trivialities would have overtaken your natural sympathy for your home country or your antipathy for the meaningless social whirl. However," seeing the light of laughter in her eyes, "I can't speak for the risk to your rational side being overwhelmed by an entirely natural physical reaction to a wealthy, tanned and athletic young Harvard graduate who seems to have all the women here falling at his feet."

Sarah pressed her lips together to suppress a smile. "Not all of the women," she corrected, her eyes dark, staring deeply into his.

"Why are we even talking of him?" Jack asked, holding her gaze.

She tilted her head, narrowing her eyes quizzically. "What would you prefer to talk about, John?" she provoked. When he didn't answer, her smile deepened. She leaned into him, resting her cheek against his. "How about what you and my father were discussing," she murmured.

Jack's arm around her waist tightened, holding her close to him. "What do you know about what we were discussing?" His voice was rough with emotion.

"You should know my father and I have no secrets from each other," she warned.

"That's good to know," Jack acknowledged. "But I really don't want to talk about him either."

Sarah leaned back against his arm to look into his face. "We're in danger of running out of topics if you keep dismissing them," she murmured. "Why don't you tell me what you would like to talk about?"

"What I want to talk about, I don't want to discuss here." In an instant, she caught the serious edge to his mood.

"Then let's find somewhere less busy," she suggested, her voice soft. Taking his hand, she led him away from the mêlée. Thankfully, the bar outside the dining room was almost empty with only a waiter clearing the tables.

Sarah found them a quiet corner. Turning, she made to release Jack's hand. "No," he objected. "Don't. I need you close to me," he admitted, drawing her to him again.

"I'm here," she affirmed, placing her hand on his chest, waiting.

"I wish I could say I had planned this, I wish we had somewhere more romantic, more fitting."

"John, you know me well enough to know it's not about where you are or how you do it, it's about what you say and whether you mean it."

Jack took her face in his hands. "And you," he murmured, "know me well enough to know I mean it."

"Enough riddles, John." Her breathing was shallow and her face slightly flushed.

"Enough riddles," he agreed. "Sarah, you know I love you. I can't quite believe I am allowed to but, however much we should be wrong for each other on paper, I have never experienced something that feels so right. I love your determination, your single-mindedness and your confidence. I love how you take care of everyone around you. And I want to be the one who gets to take care of you. I may not always be the best person to do it but I can promise you no one would ever try harder." He stopped, his heart beating hard.

Sarah's smile encouraged him. "John, I love you too but I think there's supposed to be a question in there somewhere."

"I was coming to that," he teased, bringing his face close to hers, their mouths almost touching. "Sarah Elizabeth Samuels, I promise to love, honour and protect you to the best of my abilities. Will you marry me?"

"About time," Sarah whispered. "Yes," she promised and pulled his mouth down to meet hers.

* * * * * * *

Charlotte had set the precedent for short engagements in the Samuels family. Sarah, for all her more conservative tendencies, was more than inclined to follow suit. In the end, Charlotte and Williams only just made it back from their extended honeymoon in France and Italy for Charlotte to be Sarah's matron of honour in September.

Neither bride nor groom was tempted by the opulence and scale exhibited at the Williams' wedding, much to Charlotte's apparent distaste but, Jack knew, to her secret pleasure too.

By choosing the chapel on the Richmond House estate, they succeeded in both avoiding a direct comparison of the weddings in the society columns and in restricting the guest list to those who really mattered to the couple.

The one sadness of the day for Jack was that his father was not well enough to make the lengthy journey to Cambridgeshire. He and Sarah had travelled to Exeter for the August bank holiday and Albert and Maud had journeyed up by train to have lunch with them. Jack wasn't proud of the fact that he had engineered a meeting that didn't involve taking Sarah to the Manor but he was truly ashamed when he realised the effort even that short train journey had cost his father. So it was Maud and Ed who represented Jack's side of the family, Annie having stayed in Devon to manage the sick and ancient element, as well as the rapidly growing babe-in-arms.

Not even Alfie was there. Jack had written with his news and re-written when he had received no reply. Having resorted to a telegram still without success, he capitulated and resigned himself to Alfie's evident wish to stay out of reach. Thankfully, that did at least avoid the conflict of whether to ask Alfie or Ed to stand up with him as his best man and Ed was enthusiastic in his responsibilities, delighted as he was to wear a formal wedding suit. He had still been in uniform for his own wedding.

Jack was quietly pleased to have one unusual guest on his side for the day. Having taken to dropping in on Major Thomasson whenever Sarah was visiting The Grove, he had unexpectedly formed a warm – if sometimes cantankerous – friendship with the veteran. Conversation between them was often rare but they both took enjoyment from and solace in the companionable silence of their games of backgammon, draughts or chess. The Major's wedding gift to the couple – a Mahjong set – was soon appropriated by the Major himself with the promise to have it waiting for Jack in London upon his return from honeymoon.

Dinner the night before the wedding came, in some ways, to mean as much to Jack as the day itself. He had insisted, in the face of teasing opposition from Sarah, on staying, with Ed, in the Red Lion pub in the nearest village rather than taking up Mr Samuels' offer of hospitality. He did accept the offer on behalf of his mother who, after several hours on a variety of trains, was delighted to settle into the most comfortable and best equipped house she had ever stayed in.

A wet August presaged an Indian summer, Rose had promised the couple when Charlotte had been contentedly threatening them with monsoon conditions for their wedding day. To judge by the unseasonably warm conditions that Jack and Ed were enjoying on their evening stroll from the pub to Richmond House, it looked like Rose would be proved right.

Inevitably, Jack's mind went back to his first arrival at Richmond House, barely nine months ago. He could hardly credit how much his life had changed. Immediately after the announcement of their engagement in July, Mr Samuels had taken Jack away from the front-of-house operations at the bank and started him on the first of what he intended to be a series of assignments with one of the partners, Mr Acre. He described it to Jack as an accelerated apprenticeship, an education in the strategy and operations of the bank achieved in months instead of the years that it had taken Mr Samuels to work his way up.

"The difference being," Mr Samuels assured him when Jack's natural reticence caused him to baulk at the proposal, "that a bright lad like you needn't waste as much time as I did having to learn from my mistakes."

The dinner was a small affair, a more intimate version of that Christmas celebration. Richard Soames and his younger son Edward were there, together with the Stevenson brothers and Peter Fellowes. Only the younger Richard Soames was missing, away in Bristol working on a transaction. Williams and Charlotte were looking tanned and healthy after several weeks' travel in sunnier climes. In fact, Charlotte seemed a more contented version of herself, less demanding of attention, happy just to be at her husband's side. He, thankfully, was happily playing the role of doting newly-wed, giving her all the attention and apparent affection she could crave. It helped, perhaps, that Isabella had returned to the US, summoned back to be attentive to her intended, whose eyes had finally started to stray in the months-long absence of his beloved. Wedding bells were not expected to be too far behind for Isabella either, if she played her part as expected.

By the time they had eaten their way through quail, halibut, partridge and an indescribable though delicious and spectacular meringue, cream and raspberry confection, Jack was surprised any of the ladies was able to move for their traditional retreat into the drawing room. He was, however, grateful that he could, at last, ease back in his chair and release one of his waistcoat buttons. Much more of this and he was in danger of generating a stature to compete with

Mr Samuels'. Now he understood the years of effort that had done into developing that rotund figure.

The cigars went round with the port and the gentlemen relaxed into a comfortable smoke-embued stupor.

It meant much to Jack that he had been welcomed into this close-knit and conservative group once his status in relation to Sarah had been clarified. The slightly stilted conversation of Christmas time had gone. Talk flowed easily around the table of the business of the estate, which came so naturally to Jack and Ed as well. However different the scale, common ground was soon found in the day-to-day challenges of taking a living from the land. They found themselves so at ease that Sarah came in search of them, wondering why they hadn't adjourned to the drawing room for coffee.

Realising the lateness of the hour, Jack and Ed prepared to depart. The Stevensons dropped Jack and Ed part way along the road back to the pub and they made the rest of the way, none too soberly, in the not-quite-darkness of a late summer night.

* * * * * * *

Looking back, years later, Jack found he could recall only intermittent moments of much of his wedding day, most of it being a blur of faces, well-wishers, friends, family.

How dark it was standing in the small bathroom, squinting at himself in the mirror as he tried to see to shave in the dim light from the tiny window overhung by the eaves of the thatched roof. Outside the open window, the sunlight had that warm autumnal quality of harvest time, heavy with the dust of the crops and warm with late summer's residual heat, even that early in the morning. There was a chatter of sparrows somewhere in the hedge below the window and the smell of frying bacon drifting up from the kitchen. Mrs Payne insisted on feeding her guests well before they departed.

He remembered Ed's expression – disbelief mingled with delight – when the car drew up to take them to Richmond House, making him realise afresh how extraordinary was this new life on which he was embarking, more privileged than he would ever had imagined. A moment's doubt passed through him, wondering at his ability to live up to the world he was entering. Only a moment. Not because he was any more confident now than before but because, that day he proposed to Sarah, he made himself a promise that he would never let her down. Whether he could live up to it or not was irrelevant. He would spend his life trying.

Maud's perfume, fresh and floral, which enveloped him as she enfolded him in her arms, her skin warm from where she had been standing in the sun on the doorstep of Richmond House, waiting for them to arrive. The shimmer of tears in her eyes as she took their arms to walk the short distance to the church down a gravel path, crunching beneath their feet.

The tones of the organ, solemn and peaceful, drifting out to reach them as they neared the church. The warmth of the old yellow stone, basking in the midday sunlight, and the sweet, cloying scent of the climbing rose tumbling over the apex of the dark oak porch, tight peach-coloured buds melting through to blown blooms, paled almost to cream.

The calm, cool sanctuary of the church, tiled floor and old plastered walls, timeless, shaded, silent. The sudden peace of the organist finishing his practice, his final notes reverberating around the almost empty space.

Long moments of standing alone before the altar, settling his mind, his eyes on the carved wooden crucifix on the white painted eastern wall of the church, behind the altar. The tiniest details of the carving, the exquisitely produced expression of pain on Christ's face, the intricately carved thorns of his crown. The unexpected sense of solitude, isolation almost, that stole over him, even as he was aware of the church filling up behind him.

The creeping sadness, suppressed too late, that Alfie should be missing this day, his only link to those wartime experiences, seemingly so unreal at this safe distance, physical and temporal.

Then the moment when everything on the periphery fell away, the sounds, the smells, the cool air, the soft shafts of sunlight. When all the self-consciousness of being on display ebbed away, lost in the haze that was the now-blurred world around him. The moment everything that mattered came sharply into focus, clear and fresh and simple. Staring into those impossibly deep brown eyes, holding her warm hand and feeling his own shake as he pledged to have and to hold her, for better, for worse, for richer, for poorer, in sickness and in health, to love and to cherish until Death came to part them.

The prayers too. Kneeling beside her, husband and wife now, borne out by the simple gold band on her finger. The sonorous tones of the preacher. "Give them, oh Lord, wisdom and devotion… Grant that their wills may be so knit together… Give them grace, when they hurt each other, to recognise and acknowledge their fault, and to seek each other's forgiveness and yours."

* * * * * *

What started as a mercifully small and intimate affair seemed to swell at various stages during the course of the day. From, Jack estimated, thirty of their closest friends and family in the church, it was already twice that by the time they sat down to a seven-course luncheon at Richmond House. By late afternoon, with more guests arriving both from the local area and from further afield as the rest were spilling out onto the lawns to enjoy the temporary reprieve from the threatened autumn, Jack was sure the party was well over a hundred people and that he knew fewer than a fifth of them.

Not that it mattered. Sarah knew all of them, it seemed, and was more than happy to introduce them proudly to her new husband, her hand in his or her arm in the crook of his elbow. For once, it felt as if she couldn't bear to be too far away from him.

The sun shone, the champagne flowed and the hum and buzz of conversation and laughter rose and fell over the crescendo and diminuendo of the string quartet providing a musical backdrop to their celebration. Luncheon had taken so long that they left the cutting of the cake until just before dusk started to settle, the heat seeping out of the day and shawls appearing on the shoulders of the less hardy ladies.

One of the maids completed the task of dividing the cake into equal parts and distributing it among their guests and Mrs Hesketh very deliberately removed the top layer out of harm's way 'for the christening'.

Sarah was starting to look tired, though immensely happy, more happy at this event than Jack had thought likely. He wondered if perhaps Mr Samuels' comments last July hadn't been so wide of the mark.

He leant forward, brushing his lips on her forehead. "Can we now decently depart?" he muttered, running his arm over her shoulder to pull her close. She gave the slightest shiver of pleasure.

"Yes, please," she affirmed, her eyes alight.

"Is there any chance we might slip away unnoticed?" Jack's hope was answered with a mock pursing of the lips and a raised eyebrow. "Why don't you start without me, then, while I check our bags have been loaded?"

Sarah reluctantly released him. "Don't think you can get away with it that easily," she warned, teasingly.

Jack found Hesketh and requested the car be brought round to the front. He chose to wait for it rather than face more meaningless small-talk with anonymous people. He wasn't alone for long, though, as Maud slid her hand over his arm, smiling wordlessly at him. They watched the light dim and the first star appear against the deepening backdrop of the evening sky.

"You do like her, don't you?" Maud's opinion of Sarah meant a lot to him.

"That's at least the third time you've asked me that, Jack," Maud smiled "and my answer remains the same as before. As long as she makes you happy, I like her."

"That's no answer, Mum," he complained.

"But it's the only one you should need, son. It doesn't matter what anyone else thinks in this. Nothing matters but what you two mean to each other." She looked into the distance for a moment, remembering. "When your father and I got married, I had plenty of people around to tell me it was a mistake, that I would come to regret being so headstrong. But never once, not even in the darkest days we've faced, have I regretted it. I knew he was the right man for me and no one could tell me otherwise."

Jack snorted. "It seems I'm destined to be surrounded by single-minded women," he joked.

Maud patted him on the arm. "It's the best thing for you," she responded tartly, "did you but know it."

"So you do like her?" Jack pushed.

Maud relented with a laugh. "What's not to like? She's smart, elegant, determined. And she has excellent taste in men."

Impulsively, Jack hugged her then went to check the luggage in the car.

* * * * * * *

In the end, it took them almost an hour to get away. By the time Sarah was satisfied no one of import had been neglected, it was fully dark and the crowd gathered on the driveway beneath a night sky dazzling with stars. The lights of every room at the front of the house were ablaze to cast a glow over them, augmented by the cars' headlamps and the servants' torches. Arm-in-arm, the guests had paired off, husbands and wives reminiscing about their own special days now this one was drawing to a close. The air had cooled and the strains of Bach had given way to the tinnier tones of American jazz, blasting out from the gramophone Rose had set up in the library.

Jack and Sarah had exchanged their formal wear for more relaxed travelling attire for the journey. Offering her his arm, they made their exit through an impromptu phalanx of guests and staff, waving to them and crying their best wishes. Quick hugs for her sisters were followed by a longer one for her father who, there was no doubting this time, was clearly the worse for some bottles' worth of champagne. Jack kissed Maud quickly – she had already done her crying and wasn't about to indulge too much emotion in so public a forum – then shook both Ed's hand and Mr Samuels'.

"Make her happy, my boy," George Samuels ordered him, clapping him on the arm, "and there'll be a home here waiting for both of you on your return."

Jack nodded his acknowledgement, not trusting himself to speak. He held the door open for Sarah and handed her into the car. Following her in, he tucked himself in the far corner as she sat forward on the seat, waving farewell. The car started with a judder and they turned down the drive to the sound of cheers and cries of best wishes.

With their backs to the crowd now, Jack pulled Sarah back in the seat, his arm around her shoulders the better to tuck her against him. She turned her head towards him and he realised her eyelashes were wet.

"You've already made me happy, Mr Westerham," she whispered, trailing her fingers down his cheek in a way that sent a shock of reaction shooting through him.

One handed, he pulled her face towards him. "I haven't even started," he promised in a harsh whisper, "Mrs Westerham," and claimed her mouth in a long, turmoil-creating kiss.

* * * * * * *

263

A week in Cornwall was nothing like long enough. By the time their train pulled back into Paddington, Jack was thoroughly resentful of Williams' and Charlotte's miniature Grand Tour and would have given his eye teeth for just one more day alone with Sarah without responsibilities, without having to suit anyone but themselves.

If asked, he would be hard-pressed to delineate for anyone how they had passed their days. As uncharacteristic as it was for either of them, they had, as if by mutual consent, fallen into enjoying unstructured, plan-free days. They had walked, they had visited local sights but it had all been without strain or expectation on either side. It was as if they were both seeking to postpone what they knew their new life together would soon be – dutiful, regimented and not their own – and that they sought to store memories of a time when, however briefly, life was about nothing but the two of them.

Even upon returning to Lyall Place on the Saturday afternoon, they found themselves faced with a welcoming party for dinner, involving not only the family but also Mr and Mrs Morton, Mr and Mrs Wise and Mr Acre. By the Sunday lunchtime – luncheon with Mr Wall, Mr Northcliffe and Mr Marsh – their first week had been mapped out with a series of dinners and visits to friends, acquaintances and even prestigious clients of the bank.

For Sarah, this non-stop entertaining was not so unusual but for Jack, used to having his evenings and much of his weekends to himself to read, it was, at times, difficult to endure. It also took him a while to adjust to how close Sarah was to her father. In the absence of his wife, Sarah seemed to have fulfilled some of the vacant roles, both personal, with frequent discussions about Charlotte and Rose, and business-related, as his confidante and sounding board in his plans for the bank. On the latter, Jack was also increasingly involved but, he felt, as an apprentice not an equal.

It wasn't necessarily a trait he valued in himself, but there was no escaping the fact that he needed periods of solitude in his life to be able to cope with the day-to-day demands of his position. For he had discovered that a 'position' was what he now had, whether he liked it or not. He had stopped being Jack Westerham and become instead George Samuels' protégé, Sarah Samuels' husband, Richmond Bank's newest and youngest manager. Long days of early mornings and late nights – as, for now, he was still insisting on working a full day at the bank, indeed was often working longer hours than previously, reluctant to give anyone an excuse to accuse him of getting his position through his marriage and determined to prove himself worthy of the trust and confidence placed in him – inevitably took their toll.

For some weeks, Sarah observed him with concern but without comment. In time, though, Jack discerned she had started to adjust their schedule, arranging for herself and Mr Samuels to dine out with old friends a couple of nights a week, leaving Jack alone in the house. The first couple of instances of this freedom were so unexpected that Jack was temporarily at a loss how to use his time. Swiftly, though, this became his reading time and the small study on the ground floor at the front of the house became his personal space, a library and sanctuary.

The one area where his newly wealthy status sat easily with him was in being able to indulge his passion for books and the study, lacking in sufficient shelf space, was soon reminiscent of his rooms at Mrs Jones', piles of books propped against the wall and beside his fireside chair, positioned not only for warmth but also to take advantage of the view of the front door in order that he might be ready to welcome Sarah when she returned from dinner.

The area he found sat with him least well was the servants. Being waited on, having his meals prepared, his clothes pressed, being driven to and from the bank was no great chore, admittedly, but the proximity of the personal servants – Ellerby, Sarah's maid, and James, his manservant – was disconcerting. The fact that James was as unused to this as he alleviated that somewhat, the comfort of the blind leading the blind, but he was under the tutelage of Mr Samuels' man, Mr Milton, and keen to prove himself worthy of having been given the opportunity to progress beyond the status of footman. Jack made every effort to get to know the lad, an eighteen-year-old who had been in service since he turned fourteen, having grown up in the East End and only escaped a life of factory labour thanks to his aunt, Mrs Richards, the housekeeper, whose recommendation had brought him into the Samuels household. James, as a result, had a strong sense of his position instilled in him and resisted Jack's attempts to ask questions about him, answering only what he must to avoid the appearance of rudeness. Jack persisted, trying to engage him on topics as varied as politics, football and the latest society scandals, without success, and eventually surrendered to James' fixed notions of their relationship.

Ellerby proved even more difficult. It was bad enough that Jack could not get into the habit of talking to his wife while Ellerby was in the room, helping her dress or dressing her hair. What made it worse was that Ellerby was evidently all too aware of Jack's previous status and condemned him as unworthy of her mistress' attention. Sarah noted the poisonous looks Ellerby shot at him and her habit of blanking him when he attempted to engage her in conversation, but she had long since accepted that there was no point castigating her and no question of dismissing her so the behaviour was ignored and even tolerated with gentle amusement. Not that it bothered Jack that her opinion of him should be so low but it was strange to be sharing the house with a force verging on malevolent.

Their rooms were also grander than Jack expected. Sarah had sequestered rooms on a separate floor of the six-storey house from the main family apartments and ordered their redecoration, without Jack's knowledge, before the wedding. As newlyweds, there was no question in their minds but that they would share a bedroom, much as Ellerby, used to a different generation, had frowned her disapproval. They did, though, have separate bathrooms and dressing rooms, and another room had been allocated for an as-yet-undefined purpose. In Ellerby's mind, it was intended for Jack's bedroom once the couple came to their senses and accepted the long-held sense of separate rooms. In Sarah's it was a nursery.

Ever since that day in St James's Park, Jack had been aware that children would be an integral part of Sarah's future. Whenever he watched her with the offspring of the hospital patients during visiting hour, he was impressed by how natural she was with them, how much at ease regardless of age or temperament. He was also keenly aware of the way her eyes followed young mothers with their babes and the distant, distracted look on her face. They had never discussed it but there was an implicit expectation that they would be expanding their family sooner rather than later.

Inevitably, then, it was pain he saw in her eyes at Christmas when Charlotte, surrounded by Williams and her in-laws, announced that she would be expecting the arrival of their first child the following May.

He should have seen it coming. Ever since they had arrived at Richmond House the day before Christmas Eve, he had discerned a proprietorial quality to Williams' behaviour, the hand in the small of her back as he escorted her to dinner, the conspiratorial whispers in her ear that made her giggle childishly. He had mistaken it for newly-wed romance, to which he had also attributed Charlotte's blushes.

Of course, they saved the news for Christmas night, with a maximum audience now that the estate team – the Stevenson brothers and Peter Fellowes – and Richard Soames and his sons had joined the party, tempted into straying from their homes by the mildness of the weather and the incomparability of George Soames' cellar.

He recognised and comprehended the disappointment he read in Sarah's expression. What he didn't expect was the unmistakable flash of anger her caught as, having congratulated the couple with a hug and a kiss, she turned away and discretely excused herself from the party.

Leaving a few minutes after Sarah's departure, he also slipped out of the room, leaving Samuels, Rose, her new beau and the rest clustered around Charlotte whilst Williams looked on with indulgent pride.

For some moments, Jack stood in the middle of the entrance hall, listening for sounds to give him an indication of where Sarah had gone. The air was noticeably colder here and smelt strongly of the pine and resin from the enormous tree in the corner, awkwardly positioned, thanks to Rose's directions, in front of the green baize door to the servants' quarters. Aside from the hum of excited voices drifting through from the drawing room, the house was silent and all the downstairs rooms either had their doors closed or lay in darkness.

Jack took the stairs slowly, his damaged leg aching from the chill. They had not enjoyed the same level of privacy here at Richmond House that they had been able to claim at Lyall Street and were sharing rooms on the same corridor as Charlotte and Williams.

His and Sarah's room was in darkness, deepened by the drawn heavy drapes, but an instinct told Jack she was there. Knowing better than to turn on the light, he waited at the door for his eyes to adjust until he could make out the still upright form in the opposite corner. As he crossed the room, something crunched beneath his shoes.

"I broke the crystal bowl."

Sarah's calm explanation belied the evident violence behind the action. As he reached her, he realised she had both her arms wrapped around herself as if she was trying to hold herself in. Her face, as far as he could make out, was calm and dry-eyed. Was the anger lanced or only suppressed?

He stood in front of her and looked at her without saying a word until, eventually, reluctantly, she met his eyes. The pain he read there told him what he needed to know and he reached out and pulled her into his embrace, her arms still folded. She held herself rigidly, refusing to give into the emotions that had evidently flashed for a moment before he arrived. She shook her head in wordless refusal as he stroked her hair and touched his mouth to her cheek, and he felt her shake with resistance as he drew her head to his shoulder and muttered soft nothing words of reassurance until, finally, she broke her arms apart and pushed him backwards.

"Don't, John!" she exclaimed, a stricken expression on her face. He had allowed himself to be forced to step back but he immediately came at her again, raising his hand, palm upwards, to place it against her cheek, his thumb softly stroking the skin. "Don't do this," Sarah warned though her eyes pleaded.

"Tell me," he ordered, his voice soft and low. She shook her head in mute refusal. He took a step closer, his hand still on her cheek, feeling her lean into him ever so slightly, and placed his other hand on her waist. "Tell me," he encouraged.

"I can't," she denied, despairing.

"You can," he contradicted.

"If I do, I'll either hate her or I'll hate myself."

Jack placed his other hand on her cheek, holding her face. "As long as you don't hate me," he suggested.

"But what if you hate me?" she whispered.

"Never," he promised softly.

Her face sagged in resignation. "Why her?" she whispered. "After everything she's done and everything I've done for her, why her?" Jack lowered his hands to her shoulders but stayed close, waiting. "How does she deserve it?" Sarah's tone was tortured. "All my life I've known I wanted to be a mother and I always expected to be married and with children long before Rose or Charlotte."

Jack frowned, running through the ramifications of what she was saying to try to understand her anguish. "It will happen soon enough for us," he promised gently. Sarah shook her head, biting her lip against the anger Jack could see building in her eyes. "It will," he reinforced, grasping her shoulders harder to emphasise his point.

"You don't understand," Sarah negated, her hands balling into fists.

Jack let his hands fall, giving up on the cajoling and sensing he would need to force through this confrontation. He folded his arms. "Enlighten me," he ordered, hardening his voice.

Sarah made to push past him. "If you're as sharp as you think you are, you work it out," she condemned.

Jack already had a pretty good idea but he knew this needed to be out in the open, at least between the two of them. He put out an arm to stop her walking past him. "I need to hear it from you."

"How can you not get it?" Sarah cried, turning to face him even as he stayed side on towards her, only his face turned in her direction. "Everything I've worked for, everything I've helped build up and everything I do from this point forward, all of it could be for nothing!"

"Why, Sarah?" Jack insisted. "Tell me why."

Gesticulating towards the door, she spat, "Because if she has a boy all of it goes to him!"

Jack turned towards her now. "And she doesn't deserve to win," he finished for her.

Hearing him articulate the thoughts in her head and knowing how much he must despise her for them, as she despised herself, Sarah's face drained of colour.

"Don't hate me," she implored, her voice breaking. There was no question of hating her. Jack knew all too well the grip in which Sarah was held by her pride in her heritage and her passion for the family business.

"I love you, Sarah," he said roughly, putting his arms around her. "How could I hate you for anything," he told her in her ear, "let alone for something that's so fundamental to what makes you who you are?"

Sarah sagged against him, her face in her hands as she sought to hide her shame and guilt. Jack eased her back far enough to pull her hands away and replace them with his own, feeling dampness of tears on her cheeks. He kissed her once, hard. "I love you, Sarah Westerham," he repeated forcefully.

She responded instinctively to his kiss, pulling his head down to repeat it and pushing her body against his. When he broke away, he looked into her face and saw the anger replaced with desire. He captured her mouth again. She was breathless when the kiss ended.

"You already knew, didn't you?" she surmised, holding his gaze. He didn't need to answer. "I should be happy for her," she criticised.

"Once you've got used to the idea," Jack observed, "you'll be relieved that she's not suffered any long-term effects from what happened." Sarah started to object but he continued with a smile before she could interrupt. "And you'll be happy for her once she gives birth to a girl."

Sarah smiled. "It worries me sometimes," she reflected, "that you should know me so well. I fear you're far too observant. Remind me never to try to keep something from you."

Jack felt warmth flood through his body as her hands started to work loose the buttons of his waistcoat. "We've probably already been missed," he warned, not stopping her.

Her hands hesitated. "You had better lock the door then," she ordered, tilting her head to invite another kiss.

PART II - NEW YORK

Chapter Ten

New York, May 1921

It was a testament to Sarah's unfailing devotion to her family that she put aside her own feelings and gave herself up to helping Charlotte prepare for the arrival. Twice in the coming months she undertook the Atlantic crossing to spend several weeks in New York with her sister. She had for support not Ellerby but a new, younger lady's maid brought down from Richmond House, Ellerby having pleaded a terror of sea-crossings, engendered, no doubt, from cinematic news footage of the demise of Titanic and Lusitania.

Jack missed her more than he had expected, finding it hard to slip back into his soon-forgotten bachelor routines. He discovered the pleasures of Mr Samuels' club where his father-in-law had introduced him as a member, not only the almost academic environment of the well-stocked library but also the robust debates over dinner with an eclectic group of men drawn from finance, commerce and politics. With his extensive reading standing him in good stead, he was gaining a reputation as a provocative but methodical debater, an old principle liberal ready to challenge the excessive enthusiasms of the free marketeers.

Sarah's frequent letters proved not only a lifeline for them in those absences but also a revelation. At a distance that obviated embarrassment or vulnerability, both discovered a willingness to share more of themselves than they might have done in their day-to-day exchanges, which had so easily fallen into the routine narrative of the day's experiences. In the pages that passed between them, they found the space they needed to explore each other's ideas, thoughts and reflections, to question and challenge the other's suppositions, to articulate emotions they would both have struggled to express in person.

Jack particularly welcomed her honesty about the situation with Charlotte, that she trusted him enough to express candidly the feelings of which she was least proud but that were perhaps an inevitable consequence of the sisters' unusual relationship. Whether the difficulties that were a feature of Charlotte's pregnancy were entirely genuine or, at least in part, a manifestation of her need to be the centre of attention, Jack could not discern. Whichever, the pregnancy was proving challenging for all those involved. An extended period of morning sickness gave way to a listlessness and periodic migraines that left Charlotte little inclined to do anything but rest on the day bed she had had moved to the morning room, yet simultaneously tetchy with boredom and demanding of entertainment. The small group of friends she had started to cultivate since arriving in New York soon melted away, all too interested in their own lives to be willing participants in Charlotte's own dramas. That left Isabella – herself full of excuses as much as she could to be away from the house – and Sarah. Of Williams, Sarah said, they saw a decreasing amount as the pregnancy progressed, which only served to feed Charlotte's paranoid jealousy, compounded by a downward spiral of self-esteem as the lack of exercise also caused her to gain weight.

A stranger to New York, nevertheless Sarah undertook all the planning and preparations for the birth of Charlotte's child, the hiring of a midwife and a nursemaid, and furnishing and decoration of the nursery on the fifth storey of their townhouse, an elegant brownstone in the Upper West Side, sufficiently distant from its parents rooms that the child might not disturb them in the night.

Sarah stayed throughout February, discovering the delights and challenges of a level of snowfall entirely unknown in her experience previously, then returned to London briefly in March before travelling again to New York at the end of the month. For the second year in succession, they were unable to celebrate her birthday together and Charlotte was none too interested in marking the occasion either, falling as it did on the anniversary of the day she had disappeared in London.

Sarah's letters to Jack became the outlet for her anger and frustration that enabled her to remain the calm, reliable and unflustered support her sister both needed and expected.

* * * * * * *

As they neared the end of April and Jack started to intuit from Sarah's letters that Charlotte was unlikely to release her sister from her duties now that she was so far gone, he broached with Mr Samuels the idea of a short trip to New York to visit his wife.

They were sitting in the library at the club after an exceptional steak dinner, settling their digestion with the remains of a bottle of full-bodied red wine. To Jack's slight surprise and considerable satisfaction, Mr Samuels not only consented to the idea but augmented it.

"It would be just the thing," Samuels contemplated, padding down the tobacco in his pipe while sucking abstractedly on the stem.

"Sir?" Jack prompted.

"I've been thinking," Mr Samuels started then stopped for several seconds as he lit the tobacco. "I've been thinking for a while that we could do with having someone on the ground in New York. To represent our interests in the new venture, you understand. I feel," he elucidated, exhaling a cloud of smoke, "very much the junior partner. What with young Williams running things day-to-day and Williams Senior so nearby, on the ground as it were, to steer the ship."

"Are you concerned the business is not progressing as expected?" Jack probed. He, like Mr Samuels, had seen the monthly reports submitted by Williams and his team, and been impressed by the initial results.

"No, no," Samuels flapped a hand in denial. "Nothing like that, lad. Still," he reflected, "it's a significant amount of our capital at risk, more of a proportion of our business than in Williams' case, and I feel a responsibility to be diligent. This is beyond our usual sphere of business and we should be close to the decisions, both to protect ourselves and, if we can, to learn from our American cousins."

Jack hid a smile having heard Mr Samuels' rather more strident views before on the topic of business standards 'across the pond'.

"You have something in mind?" Jack suggested.

"I think you have just presented a viable option," Mr Samuels observed. "I was concerned about sending one of the partners, who I fear may be resented by young Williams as an intruder, diminishing our access and insight. You, however, we may present to him as needing to learn all aspects of the business and, hence, no threat. Williams trusts you as a friend and, it seems to me, would be much more open with you about the business. Moreover, I am sure you will assess the venture with clear eyes, unblinded by the inevitable prejudice built from doing the same thing the same way for three decades together."

"For how long were you thinking?" Jack was intrigued by the opportunity to work in this newest part of the empire.

"How long 'til the boy arrives?" Mr Samuels was insistent his first grandchild was going to be a boy, much to Sarah's mingled chagrin and amusement, having been assured by the midwife that the way Charlotte was carrying meant it was certain to be a girl.

"A month, Sarah says."

"In that case, why don't we plan for you're being there for up to three months? Knowing my daughter, she will be needing Sarah as much after the event as before. There's nothing you can't leave behind here?" Jack shook his head. "That's settled, then. I'll telegraph the Williamses in the morning and we'll get you over there as soon as we can get you a berth."

Much settled in mind now, it seemed, Mr Samuels eased back in his chair and, setting his pipe in the corner of his mouth, returned to his earlier perusal of the evening paper. Jack took up his latest read, the economic theories of Adam Smith, but found himself strangely unable to concentrate, distracted by the thought of seeing his wife again.

* * * * * * *

Eleven days later, with the distractedness hardly diminished in the intervening period, he finally found himself walking down the gangway of the ship and, for the first time, onto US soil. In fact, he reflected, he had never been abroad before except when he was deployed and he relished discovering another country with both the time and the resources at his disposal to explore it.

The leisurely Atlantic crossing had, itself, been an experience. A naturally solitary man, he had initially been uncomfortable being in such intimate proximity with strangers, the ship lacking privacy beyond his own berth which, being too small for real comfort, had lost its attractions within the first twenty-four hours. Emerging somewhat reluctantly into the communal areas, the dining room, the library and the garden room, he nevertheless found himself pleasantly engaged with a number of couples and small family groups, most of whom made the journey relatively frequently and were delighted to acquaint a first-time traveller with the joys of ocean travel. By the time they disembarked, he had received two invitations to visit the west coast and one promise of dinner within the next two weeks.

He was utterly unprepared for the wave of deep satisfaction that flooded through him at the sight of Sarah waiting in the arrivals hall after he stepped off the ferry from Ellis Island. The constant company on the ship had proved a useful distraction from thinking about her but now he was forcefully reminded how much he had missed her.

Yet, the moment he stood in front of her, an inexplicable awkwardness overcame him. Perhaps it was the awareness of the frankness they had shared in their letters. Perhaps it was the natural shyness of a newly-wed couple after a parting and before they had found again the shared familiarities that reinforce their relationship. Either way, he found himself wishing to reach out to her but absolutely unable to act on the impulse.

Moreover, he feared Sarah would not have welcomed a public demonstration, a fear reinforced when she didn't reach out to him either but only smiled and said, "Hello, John."

"Sarah," he responded, hoping she would hear in the roughness of his voice and slight urgency of his tone everything he found himself unable to express. Her smile suggested she did.

"The car is waiting for us," she nodded towards the exit then led the way.

A large red car, so ostentatious it had to belong to Williams, was parked in the prime position at the front of the building. A small man, silver-haired and uniformed, cap in hand, tossed his cigarette in the gutter as they approached.

"Welcome to New York, Sir," he greeted Jack, relieving him of his suitcases.

"Your trunk with the rest of your things arrived yesterday," Sarah informed him, climbing into the back of the car.

Jack settled in the corner seat beside her. "You look well," he ventured, admiring her unfamiliar peacock blue coat.

Sarah glanced behind her to ensure the driver was still busy loading the cases then leaned across, pulled Jack towards her by his coat lapels and kissed him for long seconds. "I'm glad to see you," she assured him with feeling.

Jack kissed her again quickly. "I've missed you," he said simply, lightly touching her cheek. Her smile widened. She sat back as the driver took his seat but she threaded her hand into Jack's and left it there for the journey.

* * * * * * *

He had never seen anything like New York. London was beautiful with its centuries of different architecture. Paris was elegant, a period frozen in time. Manhattan was awe-inspiring, an icon to an age of rebirth, redevelopment and new technology. He couldn't take his eyes off the skyscrapers, impossible to imagine, only slightly less difficult to comprehend in reality. What struck Jack was how busy the streets were and how enclosed he felt, particularly by those towering new skyscrapers. As they headed up town, the volume of cars, buses, bikes, trams and pedestrians felt to be beyond anything he had seen in London. Sam, the driver, seemed intent on giving Jack the guided tour of his home town through the Village and the terrible poverty of the immigrant-dominated Hell's Kitchen, along the western perimeter of Central Park and into the Upper West Side. The views of Central Park gave some relief but how different from those wide open spaces of London's parks where the eye was drawn for longer distances. Here, even the park felt like a captured and contained environment.

As they headed out of the city, though, he relaxed more, finding a sense of familiarity in the wider, tree-lined boulevards out of town. The brownstones of the Upper West Side were heavier, darker than the cream-painted Georgian town houses of Belgravia but solid and pleasingly proportioned.

The house in front of which they finally drew up was one such brownstone, a steep flight of steps running up to the colonnaded and porticoed entrance of the five-storey brick building. In many ways, it mimicked those older London properties, a regiment of windows in perfect lines delineating carefully proportioned rooms. Jack liked it instantly.

A tiny maid, incongruous in almost exactly the same uniform such a position would require in London but with her frizzy black hair forcibly contained under a mob cap, greeted them, opening both the tall doors to ease their entrance. Used to the wide, grandiose entrances of both Richmond House and Lyall Street, this was an interesting contrast. A narrow hall, oak floored not marble, just wide enough to shed one's hat and coat, which the maid stored in a cupboard hidden in the panelling. Visible beyond was a wide open area seemingly running the width of the relatively narrow house, furnished as a sitting area with fireplaces at both ends. It, in turn, let onto a bright, sun-flooded room, visible through French doors to either side of a partition wall and, from this distance, apparently filled with hot house plants. Rugs covered the floor in places, breaking and warming the expanse of oak. Paintings were carefully displayed on the walls; not heritage portraits like those in England but landscapes of, at a guess, Italy and France, some of areas unfamiliar to Jack that he presumed were other parts of America, and portraits of ordinary people at work or at rest, not stilted, unnatural sittings. He had never experienced a place feel so instantly welcoming and comfortable.

"Charlotte will be upstairs at this time of day," Sarah informed him, removing her gloves. "We must see if she's up as she will expect to see you."

Jack didn't reply that it would be the first time Charlotte had shown any interest in seeing him. Sarah led them up the staircase tucked around the corner from the hallway. Like everything else he had seen so far, it was of more domestic proportions than that to which Sarah must be used but it appealed to him for that very reason.

The first floor appeared to be split into just two rooms, the dining room and a drawing room, both of which ran from the front to the back of the house.

Following Sarah into the drawing room, he was surprised to find the drapes already drawn against the gently fading spring light and only a couple of lamps lit to counter the gloom. As a result, it took several seconds for him to realise that the prostrate form on the chaise longue was his heavily pregnant sister-in-law and that there was a second figure in the room, perched rigidly upright and seated far forward on a low chair positioned perpendicular to where Charlotte's head was resting

Sarah went forward to meet the old woman who, standing to be kissed on her cheek, was barely five foot tall and engulfed in the voluminous skirts of an older generation.

"Aunt Millie," Sarah greeted her, "it's so kind of you to keep Charlotte company." From where he stood, Jack caught a grimace on Charlotte's face that told him she didn't share Sarah's polite enthusiasm. "May I introduce my husband, John Westerham?" turning to encourage him to step forward.

"About time, young man." The voice was papery but the tone commanding. "I was beginning to fear you to be a figment of Mrs Westerham's imagination." She held out her hand to shake his and Jack half-expected to be rapped over the knuckles by the edge of a closed fan, such was the impression of a matriarch from another era.

"Aunt Millie is Mr Williams Senior's maternal aunt," Sarah explained. Which, Jack calculated quickly, must put her somewhere in her seventies or even eighties and explained why the papery quality extended beyond her voice to the skin of both the hand he held and the heavily lined face he beheld.

"It's a pleasure to meet you," he responded politely. "Unfortunately for me, while I would infinitely prefer to be attendant on my wife as you suggest, my father-in-law has commanded my presence elsewhere until now." Strange to find himself lapsing so naturally into mimicry of her antiquated language style.

"Alas, the demands of commerce," Aunt Millie bemoaned, finally releasing his hand.

"Perhaps now you're here, you might remind my husband that he too needs to be more attentive to his wife."

Charlotte, who was evidently now too substantial to make unnecessary moves such as rising to greet a guest, interjected from her prone position.

"Hello, sister," Jack greeted her smoothly, bending over to kiss her cheek, knowing the familiarity of both the greeting and the gesture would tease her. He was surprised, then, to see a softness, almost of relief, on her face as he rose. "You're looking well," he complimented her, stretching the truth with an instinctive sympathy in reaction to her obvious unhappiness. In reality, she was looking, as he had expected from Sarah's letters, rather too pasty, more rounded of face than before and distinctly uncomfortable. To his further surprise, she caught his hand as he made to step back.

"Please, Jack," she begged. "When you see Freddie, you will tell him he should be home with me more, won't you?"

"I'm sure he would be here if he could." Jack sought to reassure her. "I can imagine the new venture is consuming a lot of time at this early stage."

"But I'm about to have his first child," Charlotte complained. "How could anything be more important to him than that?" Her voice sounded strained, almost verging on hysteria, and she leaned forward from the chair, putting her weight on his arm.

Jack glanced across at Sarah. This was obviously a well-rehearsed subject. "I'll raise it when I see him," he assured her, covering her hand with his own.

Relief flooded Charlotte's face and she sank back into the chair, covering her eyes with one hand.

"I'll ring for tea," Sarah murmured.

"Not for me, Mrs Samuels." The matriarch started to pack up her carpetbag, which Jack hadn't spotted on the floor. Embroidery paraphernalia disappeared into the capacious bag, together with two volumes and her reading spectacles. "Perhaps you could call me a carriage instead?"

Sarah gave instructions for tea and for the car to be brought round then escorted the little old woman downstairs.

"Peace at last!" Charlotte opined as the door closed, raising her hand from her eyes. "Why that woman sees the need to inflict her presence on me day after day. I don't need a babysitter every moment of the day."

Jack pulled up a chair. "Sarah tells me you have had a difficult time," he sympathised, sensing the self-absorbed side of Charlotte was to the fore and in need of reassurance.

"Oh, Jack," she cried. "No one understands how difficult these months have been. Uprooted from everything I know and love, transplanted into this most alien of environments only to find myself alone and facing the most traumatic event of a woman's life. It was unbearable until Sarah arrived."

"Had you no time to make friends here?" Jack suggested gently.

"Hah!" Charlotte disdained. "Some friends. After only a fortnight of morning sickness to abandon me to the tedium and loneliness. Even Issie barely visits twice a week now."

"And Aunt Millie makes for poor company?" Jack guessed.

"The worst," she concurred. "Sitting there for hours at a time telling me how fortunate I am and how grateful I should be to have a husband as wonderful as her great-nephew. Who is, himself, never here and who, I might add, is a mite fortunate in his choice of spouse as well!"

Colour was staining Charlotte's cheeks now but Jack was concerned it spoke more to a disordered mind than to any physical abnormality.

"I'm glad Sarah has been able to make the situation more tolerable for you," he reflected, seeking to ease her temper.

"It's the least she could do for her sister," came the sullen response.

Jack felt anger flare at her ingratitude but sought to curb his own temper. "You must be looking forward to the arrival of the child," he suggested. "Your father's certainly impatient to meet his first grandchild."

The expression that crossed Charlotte's face as she stared at her distended stomach, touching it tentatively with her fingertips as if it

285

were something alien and separate from herself, was fear. "I'm terrified, Jack," she admitted in a whisper and he saw in her eyes the raw emotion that her selfishness and impatience had masked. He leant forward and took her hand in both his. She looked at him directly. "I'm terrified of the pain I can't now avoid. I'm terrified that I will be a bad mother and the thing will hate me." Tears were falling down her pale face and choking her throat. "But most of the all," sobbing, "I'm terrified it will be deformed in some way. As a punishment for what I did before."

Jack did the only thing his instincts were telling him to do. He knelt on the floor beside her chair and opened his arms. With a sob, she fell into his embrace and cried and cried against his shoulder. In her distress, she didn't hear the drawing room door open but Jack saw Sarah enter. He prayed she could read the expression on his face. To his relief, she observed the situation for a moment, met his eyes and nodded once, silently leaving the room and closing the door.

* * * * * * *

An exhausted Charlotte retreated to her bedroom after she had cried herself into quietness. Sarah, not saying a word, met her as she emerged from the drawing room and supported her slow progress up the stairs.

Left for a moment, Jack set about lighting the rest of the lamps in the drawing room and rang for the servant to re-order the delayed tea. It arrived just as Sarah returned.

"I've been fearing that for a while," she noted, taking a seat and busying herself with the tea. "Though," looking thoughtfully at Jack, "I was hardly expecting you would bear the brunt of it."

Jack took the seat opposite, wishing he could, instead, take his wife in his arms. "I think I was a convenient substitute for Williams," he observed, rubbing his eyes against the tiredness that was starting to infiltrate. "She doesn't look at all well," accepting the cup Sarah offered him.

"She's had a difficult time," she agreed. "Prolonged sickness then headaches."

"She was complaining that her friends hadn't been very supportive." Jack felt the need to share some of the conversation with Sarah, who grimaced.

"She had developed some superficial friendships when she first arrived but they didn't outlast the first few weeks of sickness and Charlotte's inevitable self-pity." Ever clear-sighted, even where her family was concerned.

"And Isabella?"

"She visits – as she knows she must – two or three times a week. It can be trying when the topic of conversation is narrowed to Charlotte's condition, though. Isabella sought to entertain her for a while with stories from society but that only served to make Charlotte more regretful of what she was missing." Sarah's tone was wry and Jack saw clearly what she had herself endured, so far from her own familiar surroundings and the causes and business that otherwise filled her days and enlivened her quick brain. Encouraged by tenderness for this remarkable woman, he rose from his seat and took the one on the sofa next to her. Putting his arm around her shoulder, he leaned back and she settled against him, her head soft against his shoulder. He kissed her forehead and she turned in towards him, laying her hand against his chest.

"I'm so glad you're here," she murmured.

"I'm only sorry I left it so long," he concurred, leaning his cheek on her hair.

They rested together in silence for some minutes, soothed by the steady tick of the clock on the mantelpiece and the occasional sound of doors opening and closing as the servants went about their business. Jack's eyes drifted around the room, taking in the elaborate Persian rug before the hearth, the ornate French-style gilt clock, seemingly too large for the mantelpiece, the heavy brocade drapes, the European-style hunting pictures grouped on the far wall.

"Was this Williams' house before he married Charlotte?" he asked, perplexed by the incongruity of the style and what he knew of his friend's passion for modernity.

He felt rather than saw Sarah's shake of the head. "It's Aunt Millie's house. The rest of the family live in not inconsiderable splendour on the Upper East Side but Aunt Millie was adamant the newly-weds would prefer to live at a distance that gave them some privacy. She volunteered to vacate this house, which her husband owned until he died five or so years ago. Now, she lives with Mr and Mrs Williams in their mansion, claiming she is too old and frail to live alone any longer. And Charlotte and Williams get this place."

"That's very generous of her."

Sarah smiled. "You wouldn't think so to listen to Charlotte. She's convinced Aunt Millie has been trying to get out of this house for years and that they were a convenient excuse to pass on 'this carbuncle'. Charlotte's friends all live in the Upper East Side," she elucidated.

"The Upper West Side isn't fashionable enough?" Jack guessed and Sarah nodded. "And tell me what's been happening with Williams," he prompted. He was disappointed when Sarah drew away from him, sitting forward in her seat and studying her hands. He sat up too. "What is it?" he pressed.

Sarah glanced at him then away again. "He's just not been here as much as Charlotte would have wished," she justified. "I'm sure he's very busy at work."

Jack frowned. "But you suspect there's more to it than that," he suggested.

"I'm trying not to," she defended. "I know he's your friend…"

"And Charlotte's my wife's sister," Jack interrupted.

"More importantly," Sarah responded, "he's the lead partner in the joint venture and there's more than a marriage at risk here."

288

"Is there something you know or do you suspect?" Jack clarified.

"Suspicions only," she admitted.

Jack nodded, twice. "Then leave it with me and I'll find a way to tackle him," he committed. Reassured, Sarah nodded her agreement. "Now," easing her back in the seat, "come back here where we were comfortable."

She sank back against him, threading her fingers through his. "I've been so glad of Rachel while I've been here," she admitted. "I know it sounds strange but she and you are the only people who have stopped me feeling alone in this."

"I know nothing about her," Jack observed.

"She's quiet, capable and attentive. What else is there to know?" Her tone was, somehow, defensive.

"From where did she come? I know Ellerby picked her as her replacement but I didn't even meet her when you came back in March."

"Ellerby was still with me then so Rachel went back to Richmond House."

He shifted his position slightly to see Sarah's face more clearly. "What aren't you telling me?" he probed. "You're being evasive."

She met his gaze straight on. "Perhaps protective rather than evasive," she qualified. He waited for her to explain. "There's some confusion among the servants about Rachel's personal circumstances," she started. "That she had originally been trained as a lady's maid was understood, as was the fact that a bad marriage had taken her away from service. How she had come to be working in Richmond House's kitchens was less certain. Ellerby claimed she had been widowed and Mrs Hesketh asserts she escaped her abusive husband one night with the help of a women's refuge charity in the East End of London. Whatever the truth, Ellerby takes the credit for elevating her from drudgery to the heights of lady's maid."

"Which story do you favour?" Jack asked, wondering where this was going.

"Does it matter?" she challenged. The way she held his gaze steadily intrigued him.

"To me? Not a whit. It sounds like she's had a tough life and deserves better."

"In that case," almost a smile appearing at the corner of her mouth, "neither is entirely true. It's not an accident she appeared at Richmond House. I sent her. She came to The Grove looking for work when I was there with Dr Alexander one day. He couldn't help her and was about to dismiss her when I noticed the bruise on her cheekbone she kept covered with her hair. Once I'd noticed that, I realised her hands were trembling. She was hiding it well but I could tell she was desperate. I walked out with her, gave her the fare to get to Richmond House and told her to ask for Mrs Richards. I rang ahead and gave her instructions to find her some work. I had no idea about her hidden skills so Ellerby may rightly claim the credit for that."

"Are you happy with her as your lady's maid?"

Sarah considered. "She's discrete, quiet and deferential. And she has the advantage of being younger than me so hopefully I shan't have to break in a new maid again for a long time to come."

Jack was relieved to hear some lightness in her voice. "I thought Ellerby took responsibility for the training?"

"What? And have Rachel pick up all the bad habits I've been trying to wean her off for the last five years?" She looked away, studying her hands, serious suddenly. "There's something about Rachel," she noted, thoughtfully. "I can't say specifically what it is. Maybe it's the way she listens." She shook her head, unable to pinpoint what she meant. "It may have something to do with her eyes."

"Why is it you call her by her Christian name like that?" Jack noticed the inconsistency.

"It's not actually her name," Sarah admitted, her expression a little wary. "She did leave her husband and she's terrified that he will come looking for her. So I gave her a new name as well as a new home."

Jack smiled tenderly. "You see what I mean about you taking care of everyone else?"

"I don't deny it," Sarah accepted, "but I'm not about to change either. At least," she acknowledged, "I now have someone who can do the same for me."

She smiled at him and tucked sideways against him. Jack reached into the breast pocket of his coat to withdraw a small, wrapped box.

"Better late than never," he murmured, handing it to her. "Happy birthday, Sarah."

She pressed her lips together in a half-smothered smile and, leaning across, kissed his cheek.

"You are a wonderful husband," she reflected.

"You don't know what it is yet," he caveated.

Unwrapping her gift, she ran her finger over the delicate filigree working of the small silver brooch. "It's lovely, John. Thank you."

"It may not be much," he apologised, "but I paid for it with my own hard-earned money."

She stroked his cheek. "You are a proud man, John," she noted. "And I am proud and thankful that you are my husband."

"In that case," he breathed, bringing his mouth temptingly close to hers, "after almost a month apart I would be grateful if you could show me to my wife's bedroom."

* * * * * * *

He saw for himself later what his wife had been struggling to explain about Rachel. It was her eyes that struck him the most. He found himself looking back at her, time and again, drawn to those strange eyes but then looking away again, embarrassed almost, as soon as she looked at him, feeling his eyes on her.

She had clear grey eyes, the clearest, brightest eyes Jack had ever seen. Framed by dark lashes and circled with a dark line around the irises, they seemed inexorably to draw his attention. It was the closest he had ever come to understanding the term 'mesmerising'.

His second impression was of a calm inner stillness, as if, somewhere at the centre of her, the turmoil and trial of the world suddenly just stopped. It was the most curious sensation; when she looked at him, everything peripheral fell away.

He would, after that first meeting for instance, have struggled to describe her. If pushed, he might have guessed that she was at or below the mean height, young but of indeterminate age, and dark haired, but none of it could he have described with conviction.

Suddenly aware that he had forgotten his manners when introduced, he held out his hand to shake hers. The grip was good, not dainty like so many women's, but he could feel the slenderness off her frame in those narrow bones.

"I've heard a lot about you," he tried to temper the peculiar formality that had overcome him with friendly words. He was overly conscious of Sarah standing nearby. "I hope you will be happy with us."

She bobbed a curtsey and he found himself hating the formality between them. There was nothing in her manner to suggest subversion of the normal servant relationship but there was that within her that naturally encouraged a greater familiarity or, at least, less formality than usual. Never entirely comfortable with treating the servants as his inferiors, he was more aware of it now than ever before.

"You see what I mean?" Sarah explained under her breath as Rachel turned and left the room.

Jack gave a non-committal response, realising as he did so that Rachel hadn't spoken a word during their introduction.

* * * * * * *

There is a very different quality to a scream of pain from a scream of terror. Of the latter, Jack had experienced more than his share, both during the war and since with the memories Alfie had carried with him.

It was that experience that instantly defined for him the piercing scream that ripped him from his sleep. Long hours of travelling and an unfamiliar, darkened room, though, left him otherwise disorientated and it took the sound of Sarah's voice and her words to bring him to a sense of the situation.

"It's Charlotte."

Throwing on the lights, Sarah was already halfway through the door, wrapping her dressing gown around her as she went. Jack quickly followed her lead.

Another scream rent the air as they hurried down the corridor. Lights now appeared at the other end of the house as the servants also descended from their attic space.

"Fetch the doctor," Jack ordered the first of them as Sarah disappeared into Charlotte's room. He hesitated only a moment before entering too.

In the low light of a single lamp, he could make out Charlotte on the bed, doubled up in pain, or bent over as far as her pregnancy would allow. She appeared to be straining, the chords on her neck standing out unnaturally and her sweat-soaked hair sticking to her face.

"Get it out! Get it out!" she screamed as Sarah crossed to the other side of the bed.

"Hush," Sarah soothed, grasping one of Charlotte's hands and, with gentle pressure on her shoulder, easing her back against the pillows. "You're having contractions so the baby is on its way but this may take some time and you need to save your strength." Some of the wildness seemed to go out of Charlotte's eyes. "Jack," Sarah called his attention, her voice steady and low, "would you fetch me some towels and a damp flannel from the bathroom, please?" As he obeyed her instructions, he could hear Sarah crooning soothing nothings to her sister, easing her distress.

Returning with her requests, he saw the blood-stained sheets that Sarah sought to cover and placed one of the towels over it as she took the damp flannel and wiped Charlotte's brow.

"Rachel," Sarah called, knowing her maid would be nearby. "A bowl of iced water, please," she instructed. "And tell Madison to show the doctor and Mrs Wilson up as soon as they arrive. The doctor's wife is the midwife," she explained to the look of enquiry on Jack's face.

"Where's Freddie?" Charlotte's voice was as weak as her face was pale. Jack couldn't imagine how she would have the strength to see this through. Wide-eyed, she sought out Jack's gaze. "Please, Jack, bring him to me."

"We'll send Madison to fetch him," Sarah assured her.

"No! I want Jack to go," Charlotte pleaded. "Please, Jack, please fetch him to me."

Jack looked to Sarah for confirmation. "If he's not here, he'll be at his club on East 67th Street. Get Madison to wake Sam to take you there."

"I'll wait until I know the doctor has arrived," Jack caveated.

"No!" Charlotte demanded, a flash of pain across her face. "I can't wait that long."

"By the time Sam is ready, Dr Wilson will already be here," Sarah reassured them. "He only lives two blocks away. Go, John," she nodded his dismissal. The soothing sounds started again as Jack took his leave.

* * * * * * *

Williams wasn't at the club. Having explained his mission, the manager, who in himself was certain he had seen Williams depart earlier that night, nevertheless undertook a thorough search of the facility to confirm the fact while Jack waited impatiently in the lobby. At a loss on how to proceed, he retreated to the car and explained his problem to Sam, the chauffeur. In a flicker of Sam's otherwise placid expression, he thought he saw a way forward.

"Sam," he encouraged, "if you have any idea where Mr Williams might be, it is imperative that you take me there." Another flicker of a dilemma behind those dark eyes. "I will be discrete," he assured him, "wherever he may be. Right now, his wife needs him and he has a responsibility to be there. Sam." He saw in his eyes when the decision was made. In silence, the chauffeur started the car and turned them northwards.

They drove the deserted streets for almost twenty minutes. Jack had no idea where they were going but it was easy to recognise the gradually deteriorating quality of the housing as they progressed. Eventually, they pulled up in front of a weathered clapboard house, its front garden littered with rubbish. Thankfully, there were at least lights on in the house.

Sam turned around in his seat. "Let me deal with this, Sir," he asked. Jack considered for a moment then nodded his consent. He watched him knock on the door and be readily admitted inside.

Uneasily, he glanced around as he waited for Sam to reappear. The neighbourhood showed more signs of activity at this late hour than had theirs. From a distance, the strains of jazz music filtered through the warm night air, otherwise alive with the buzz of insects. Down the street, in the flickering light of a gas lamp – evidently electrification was only partial for this side of the city – two men were scrapping inelegantly, wild punches frequently failing to connect with their targets, while a third looked on. Another argument was audible through the open upstairs window of the house across the street. Even the street cats decided to join in with screeches that set Jack's teeth on edge. He tapped his watch impatiently, feeling the minutes drain slowly away. He had no idea how badly Charlotte was faring but he didn't want to risk being absent for longer than was absolutely necessary.

Finally, he heard a door open and Sam reappeared, followed in short order by Williams, still buttoning his coat. To judge by his attire, he had at least started the evening at the club.

It was his shaken expression as he clambered into the back of the car that stopped Jack's natural retort about his absence.

"How is she, Westerham?" he asked, a tremor in his voice.

"I can't say," Jack informed him. "The doctor hadn't arrived by the time we left to fetch you."

"There must be something you can tell me?" Williams implored.

Jack hesitated only a moment. "She's bleeding and she appears to have gone into labour at least two weeks early. Beyond that, you will have to wait until we hear the doctor's verdict." Williams sank back into the corner of the car seat and stared morosely out of the window.

The return journey seemed, mercifully, quicker than the outbound search and they were soon back in the familiar environs of the Upper West Side. A block away from the house, Williams suddenly stirred himself and broke the silence.

"Don't judge me too harshly," he suggested, still staring out of the window. "It hasn't been the easiest of times for either of us." As Jack stayed silent, his friend turned to look at him. "Westerham?" he prompted.

Jack finally looked at him as Sam stopped the car before the house. "I try not to judge," he affirmed. "None of us is really in a position to judge another. But I will say, Williams: my actions wold not have been yours in these circumstances."

Grim-faced, Williams acknowledged his words. "I hope, my friend, you never find the truth of your view tested."

Together, they climbed the steps of the house and let themselves into the hall. The doctor was collecting his hat and coat, ready to depart, as they arrived.

"About time, Williams," he chided at the sight of the absent father-to-be. "Straight upstairs, your wife is still asking for you and I doubt will settle until she's had a chance to curse your sorry soul." Williams, with one departing look at Jack, did as instructed, taking the stairs two at a time. The doctor held out his hand. "You must be Mr Westerham. Dr Wilson," he introduced himself.

"How is Mrs Williams, doctor?" Jack enquired.

"She'll be fine," he predicted confidently. "All the better for knowing her husband has now arrived to fret and pace the next several hours of labour. She's early," to Jack's questioning expression, "but she's young and the child seems strong. We'll be some hours yet so I've left my wife with her for now. I'll return in a few hours unless I'm needed before but she's in good hands."

He pushed his hat on his headed and made for the door. Without turning, he called, "Remember that when it's your turn, Mr Westerham," and disappeared out into the night.

* * * * * * *

Jack found Sarah hovering outside Charlotte's bedroom door.

"I thought I'd give them a moment," she explained, nodding at the closed door. "I won't interrupt unless I hear breaking china."

Jack kissed her forehead and gave her a hug. "You look tired," he observed. It was just gone two in the morning.

"No time for that," she denied. "We've a way to go yet. You took longer than I expected. He wasn't at the club?"

Jack shook his head. "Don't ask," he warned.

"Don't tell," Sarah returned.

The door of the room opened and Williams emerged, looking relieved but not yet reassured. Sarah disappeared back into the room and shut the door.

"You look like you need a drink," Jack observed drily.

"I thought I'd had enough earlier tonight," Williams' tone was self-critical. "Now I'm not so sure."

Together, they descended to the first floor and, drawing large measures of bourbon for each of them and taking the decanter with them over to the sofas, they settled in for the long haul.

"Welcome to New York, Jack," Williams toasted him ironically.

"The doctor seemed confident," Jack sought to reassure but Williams seemed to be in the mood for self-flagellation.

"It would be a fitting punishment for me if something went wrong. Though hardly fair on Charlotte or the child," he corrected himself.

"What happened to you two? You've been married less than a year." If they were going to keep each other company for the next few hours, Jack wasn't going to skirt around the issue.

"It was the pregnancy." Williams downed his drink and poured himself another. "When we came back after last Christmas, the sickness hit her. The doctor said he'd never seen anything like it. She spent so much time being sick she could barely leave the house. She lost a lot of weight very fast and the doctor got her worrying about what that might do to the child. She seemed so fretful that something could be wrong with the baby. She spent all her time either in tears or concocting every-more-appalling potential problems. As soon as she could eat again, she started over-eating to compensate for what she'd lost. Issie told me how obsessive she became, talking about nothing else with her friends, chasing away anyone who arrived with the slightest sniffle. Then the migraines started and she's been living in near-darkness for the last couple of months. Thank God Sarah's been here."

"Where were you in all this?" Jack had heard the excuses but he wasn't about to let his friend off the hook.

Williams looked askance at him then stared into his drink. "At first, I was just so busy with the bank I didn't notice what was happening. Most of it I got from Issie and Sarah a few weeks back when they took me to task."

"At first?"

His discomfort increased. "I challenge any man alive not to have let work become the excuse," he defended. "It was easier not to be here, to leave it to Issie and Sarah. Woman's work, you know?"

Jack tried to keep his expression neutral. Condemning his friend wasn't going to help.

"And tonight?" He drained his own glass and held it out for Williams to refill it.

Now he had the good grace to look ashamed. "Just some woman I met outside the club. God!" he exclaimed, pushing his fingers through his hair, "I don't know whether it's worse that I don't know who she is or not. If it had been a friend of Charlotte's, would it have been more or less of a betrayal?"

Jack leaned his head back against the chair. "I think the more pertinent question," he mused, staring at the intricately carved ceiling, "is what you plan to do now."

Williams pushed to his feet and went to stand in front of the window, throwing back the curtains to stare down at the empty street. "If anything were to happen to either of them, I'd blame myself." He pushed his hands deep into his trouser pockets. "'For better, for worse'. I fell at the first hurdle, didn't I?" Jack didn't reply. "Let's hope I've been given a second chance. Maybe it'll be better for all of us after this."

"I assume you aren't going to tell her?"

Williams gave a hollow laugh. "Right now all she thinks is I'm an absent husband. I'm not about to disabuse her of that."

Jack's eyes started to close. He blinked them open but it was hard to avoid the length of the day catching up with him.

"Why don't you tell me about the bank?" he suggested, hoping to find a way both to keep Williams' mind off things and to keep his own awake.

Williams continued to stare out at the street, considering. "We're making better progress than I expected at this stage," he at length reflected. "At least," crossing his arms, "we've had no shortage of demand for the capital we want to lend. We can afford to be selective."

"What industries?"

"Mainly manufacturing, cars, construction, particularly here in New York and in Chicago. It's electricity that interests me, though." Jack invited him to elucidate. He refilled their glasses and settled down opposite Jack, one ankle resting on the other knee in that confidence-bordering-on-arrogance pose that Jack would always associate with him. "There are swathes of the country, particularly the South, that are still not electrified. Sooner or later it'll have to be done but it needs scale to make it work. The kind of local and regional generators we're used to here. A couple of companies are looking for capital to expand." He shook the ice in the bottom of his glass. "In fact, what they're really after is investors, someone willing to share some of the risk." Feigned nonchalance. He knew, then, that what he proposed was counter to the explicit instructions of Richmond Bank.

"That's unlikely to find favour with the Board," Jack caveated.

"The old man's open-minded," Williams shrugged. Another calculatedly indifferent gesture. "Maybe you and I could just run the numbers, while you're here?" Jack stayed silent. "It's where the big money's to be made." Williams' tone was becoming less distant. "And it's a proven business model, tried and tested on both the east and west coasts."

"Let's see," Jack conceded. There was no harm in scanning the numbers.

Williams knew when to seed an idea and when to press his advantage. He let the subject fall.

"Married life seems to be suiting you," Williams reflected, running his eyes over Jack's new suit and shoes. "You look more the ideal son-in-law every day."

"We won't think about what that makes you, then," Jack retorted, stung by Williams' unsubtle reference to his wardrobe having been enhanced by Samuels money.

"Hey, I'm not criticising," Williams held up his hands in defence. "Just observing, is all. But you are looking well on it, Jack. You must really love her."

"You don't, then?" Jack challenged, his pride still stinging.

Again, that nonchalant shrug. "Perhaps I did in the beginning. When life together was entertaining and Charlotte was only interested in having fun. She had an appetite for adventure. I thought she would fit in well around here. Who knows, perhaps that will all come back once the baby's born and we can hand it off to the nurse and the nanny. What about you to?" taking a great gulp of his drink. "No signs yet?"

"It'll happen when it's meant to," Jack reassured himself. "We've enough in our lives to be grateful for a few months of just the two of us."

"How long are you staying?"

Jack's tired brain was starting to slow down. He failed to stifle a yawn. "Two, three months. We'll see."

"Checking up on me for the old man?" Williams smiled but there was also an edge in his voice.

Jack mirrored Williams' nonchalant shrug. "We'll see," he reiterated.

Williams heaved a deep sigh and rested his head back. "I suppose it wouldn't look good if I took myself off to bed?" Jack didn't answer so Williams looked up to catch his expression. "Thought not. Oh well, get comfy, Jackie. My mother was thirty-two hours in labour with me." Jack closed his eyes. Somehow, that didn't surprise him.

* * * * * * *

Daylight was flooding through where Williams had left the curtains askew when Sarah came to wake them both just after seven o'clock.

"The doctor's returned," she explained. "And Charlotte's asking for you," with a nod to Williams, who hauled himself to his feet and headed back upstairs.

Sarah sank onto the sofa next to Jack, tucked into his side. "Don't let me sleep too long," she warned, resting her head on his shoulder and closing her eyes.

* * * * * * *

It was a long day. Isabella arrived late morning but went away again as soon as she heard what was in progress. The two men, at a loose end, wandered aimlessly around the drawing room, unable to settle to anything, constantly listening for significant sounds from upstairs. Meals were served at the correct hours but no one had much of an appetite. The servants seemed to be trying to make themselves more invisible than usual.

At five o'clock, just as the maid was leaving the drawing room with the mainly-untouched tea things, they caught what could have been the sound of a baby's cry. Williams started to his feet, uncertain in a way Jack had never seen in him before, but sat down again at a signal from Jack. "Sarah will fetch us when they're ready," he advised.

Twenty long minutes later, Sarah appeared and gave Williams the nod. As he disappeared, she walked into Jack's embrace. "It's a girl," she whispered. He hugged her hard.

"How is Charlotte doing?"

"Exhausted but very proud of herself. Will you come and see the child?" Jack could tell she was anxious to be nearby again.

Charlotte was propped against the pillows, washed, changed and looking very content with the babe in her arms and Williams standing over both of them, seemingly afraid to get too close. She looked up as Jack and Sarah entered, smiling widely.

"We're arguing about a name," she explained. "I want Rebecca but Freddie thinks we should name her after Aunt Millie as we're in her house." The sullen expression that came over Charlotte's face clearly showed what she thought of that idea. She glanced at Williams, apparently for approval as he nodded slightly. "There's one thing we are agreed on, though," a little shyly in her glance at Jack. "We'd like you to be the baby's godparents. Both of you. And Issie, as well."

Sarah's smile was as broad as Charlotte's as she approached the bed. "We're honoured. May I hold my goddaughter for a moment?" Charlotte looked reluctant but she could hardly refuse the woman who had stood by her throughout. The reluctance quickly disappeared, though, as Williams sat on the side of the bed and took her hand. He certainly knew how to play his part.

Sarah settled the child in the crook of her arm, turning her back on her sister. Jack approached but, seeing how absorbed she was, just watched her stroke the child's downy cheek and plant a surreptitious kiss on her forehead. Jack discretely checked the parents weren't watching and stood between them and Sarah to shield her. She teased her little finger into the fat little hand, seeing the tiny fingers flex and grasp. A slight movement at the open door caused him to look up and he saw Rachel there, half-hidden by the door jamb, her eyes on Sarah. Even at this distance, he could read the protectiveness in her expression. It was only the return of the nursemaid and the midwife that interrupted them and it was with a longing look that she relinquished the child.

That evening, in hindsight, was a haven of peace. They spent the evening together, neither woman standing to be too far from the babe, and neither man wishing to be too far from his wife. It was only Sarah's muffled plea, "When will it happen for us?" as Jack held her in bed that night that marred the sense of tranquillity that had settled over them.

* * * * * * *

The following morning, the problems started. Charlotte awoke with a fever and with joints aching so much she cried out in pain every time she moved. The nursemaid isolated the child who, starved of maternal attention, became increasingly fractious until, mid-afternoon, Sarah violated the embargo and stepped in to take charge. In the arms of her aunt, the babe swiftly grew calm and Sarah stayed near to maintain the welcome peace.

In the silence, Charlotte slept for long hours, exhausted and ailing. Visitors who appeared, including Williams' parents and sister, were given brief access to the new arrival before being handed back to Jack and Williams' inadequate hosting skills. Both were relieved to have the excuse of returning to work on the following day to re-establish some normalcy in their lives.

By the time Charlotte was strong enough to leave her bedroom, five days had elapsed since the birth and the natural maternal bond has been stretched almost to breaking point. Worst, the fever had affected Charlotte's ability to lactate. The tenuous link snapped.

Depression was an almost inevitable consequence, with Charlotte blaming herself, then blaming Williams. This became a downward spiral as her emotional outbursts and sudden changes of mood drove Williams into working longer hours in the office and Charlotte blamed her altered appearance for failing to attract her husband while cursing him for failing to support her. Her moods were reflected in the child's response, who naturally sought another source of comfort and found it in her aunt and the nursemaid.

Conscious that her closeness to the child – still nameless a month later – was exacerbating the situation, Sarah tried to regulate the time she spent in the nursery but the siren call was too great for

305

her maternal instincts and the nursemaid was too grateful for the support.

Jack saw all this in the brief periods he spent at the house, in between long days at the office, keen to learn everything he could in the time available and to provide valuable insight in his reports back to Mr Samuels. He worried for Charlotte's health, for her marriage and for the child's stability. He worried more for the day when Sarah would be turned away from her niece and forced to confront the reality of her childless life once again.

* * * * * * *

The parting, when it came, was more brutal than even his worst expectations. In the end, the visit had been curtailed to two months, ostensibly because Mr Samuels needed Jack and Sarah back in London but in reality because Jack had shared an edited version of his concerns with his father-in-law and they had, together, engineered the separation.

Their trunks had already been sent to the docks for loading onto the liner. As the family came together for a farewell dinner, Jack felt as if they were closing ranks around Charlotte and Williams, all hoping a new, normal routine could be established once the interlopers had been removed and Charlotte forced onto a stable path.

It was a small farewell dinner with Williams' parents and Isabella also in attendance. Her fiancé was absent, attending a family affair of his own. Isabella had achieved what was expected of her upon her return from England. The chosen gentleman's wavering attentions were soon fixed firmly back on her and the engagement announcement had not been long in coming. The gentleman in question looked, to Jack's eyes, unprepossessing, of average height and with an already receding hairline, but his family was of the oldest and wealthiest Connecticut stock and well-endowed with attractive properties in all the right parts of New York and the Capitol. Isabella, though lacking the lineage, was of the right background to fit with the young man's political ambitions while being able to hold her own in the equally political world of Wendell's extensive family. The old-fashioned standards of the family had dictated at least a twelve-month engagement for the couple, though, and as Isabella insisted on at least a spring wedding if not a summer one, they were still a year away from that occasion.

What Jack knew was that this man would not make Isabella happy. He lacked both the wit and the joie de vivre that typified Issie in his mind and noted the more formal, straight-laced front she assumed in his presence. Knowing her, though, he was confident she would still find ways to make herself happy.

Charlotte, by contrast, was increasingly resting her own happiness in her husband and Williams was not up to the task.

Conversation over dinner flowed as freely as the wine. The Williams family were entertaining company, full of anecdotes about friends and acquaintances. Isabella's new status had clearly not prevented her being out in society at least as much as before. Charlotte, her erstwhile partygoer-in-arms, had, Jack recalled, been out for dinner only twice since the birth of the baby, both times to the Williams' Upper East Side mansion, which only served to underline her resentment at her perceived inferior accommodation.

At the news that the older Williams would shortly be vacating the New York house to return to Chicago for some months, Charlotte saw her opportunity.

"It won't be for long, maybe a few months," Mr Williams explained. "I don't know about you, Jack, but it seems Fred's got things under control here?" Jack agreed. "I've been neglecting the Chicago end of things too long in favour of this new business but I must get back now. There's no knowing what they've been up to in my absence." He laughed. Frederick Williams the second had a tight hold of the tiller. There was no question but that he knew exactly what was going on in any part of his extensive business empire on any day of the week.

"We'll be back after the summer," Susannah Williams reassured them. "Certainly in time to view the autumn collections," reaching across to squeeze Isabella's hand.

"Issie isn't going with you?" Charlotte's voice had a tremor of desperation, faced with the unpalatable prospect of losing both Sarah and Isabella.

"No, no," Mrs Williams assured her. "Isabella will be staying with the Dexter Whites. Lucille has promised to take her under her wing so she and Wendell don't have to be parted." She smiled indulgently at her daughter, who returned the smile with her best look of unquestioning compliance.

"You don't want to stay in the house, Issie?" Charlotte seemed never to have cottoned onto the fact that Isabella was only ever "Issie" in her parents' absence. She also could not understand anyone wanting to leave such an attractive home, particularly for the more distant and somewhat isolated, if grand, Dexter White property.

Isabella shook her head. "We always shut up the house at this time of year. There's no point still running such a large property just for me."

Charlotte sat forward in her seat. "Aunt Millie isn't staying?"

"We couldn't leave her here," Mrs Williams lightly chided. "I know she seems as tough as old boots but she's more frail that she lets on. She'll come to Chicago with us."

"Why don't we go and stay with Issie, then?" Charlotte looked to her husband to help build her case. "You could stay where you are, then," appealing to Isabella. "It's so much more convenient for the city and you'd like the company of people your own age, wouldn't you? It won't be half as much fun stuck out in the sticks with the Dexter Whites."

Isabella looked at her friend with sympathy. "If you're worried that we won't see each other," she proposed, "I promise I'll be here as often as I can, Charlotte."

"That's not it at all," Charlotte dismissed. "Wouldn't you sooner stay in your own home?"

"I don't mind," Isabella looked to reassure her mother that the view Charlotte was expressing was not her own. "It's an ideal opportunity for me to get to know my future family. After all, I shall be living there after the wedding."

"It would suit us well enough, wouldn't it, Freddie?" Charlotte tried another tack. "It would be nice to have a bit more space and we could keep an eye on the house for your parents."

Freddie laughed. "Don't worry, I think old Mason has been doing that well enough all these years. I'm sure he can manage without our help. And we're much better placed here for getting to and from the office."

"You always have to think of yourself first." Charlotte, thwarted, turned sullen. Her muttered comment was painfully audible and Williams, at the head of the table opposite her, turned red.

"I don't know about you, Susannah," Williams Senior addressed his wife opposite him, "but some of my happiest memories are from our first house together. You remember? That lovely little place on Berwyn Street. An old brick house barely half the size of this one."

His wife supported his attempt to change the direction of the conversation. "With no running water and kitchen staff who hadn't a clue how to construct a menu," she recalled with a smile. "Then Freddie arrived and we haven't known a day's peace since," she teased her son, who smiled gratefully at her.

"She might have told me that before I married him," Charlotte muttered, sunk back in her chair. Fortunately, she was quiet enough this time for only Sarah and Jack to hear her. Seeking to calm her sister, Sarah covered her hand with her own, injecting a gentle warning tone into her voice when she cautioned, "Charlotte."

"No!" Charlotte threw off her sister's hand, shouting her rejection. "You know nothing of what I'm going through, Sarah, so stay out of it."

Sarah went as white as Williams had gone red and sat back in her chair, her rigid spine telling Jack the pain she was holding in.

"Charlotte." Williams' warning tone, a mirror of Sarah's but more commanding and harsh, caught Charlotte short. She stared hard at him but the outburst had stopped and she too sat back in her chair, her lips pursed.

Timing being what it is, the unfortunate nursemaid chose that moment to enter the dining room. The stony silence she encountered made the words she was about to speak die on her lips until Williams, seeing her discomfort, urged her to speak.

"I'm sorry, Sir," she started uncertainly. "I didn't mean to interrupt. It's just," hesitantly, looking from Sarah to Charlotte and back again, "Baby won't settle. She's been fractious for hours and I was wondering," hesitating again and then taking her courage in her hands and asking for the person she really wanted to help, "I was wondering if Mrs Westerham might spare a moment."

Sarah was half out of her seat already, placing her folded napkin on the table, when Charlotte shouted her objection. "No!" She pushed back her chair, glaring at her sister. "She's my daughter, I should be the one to go."

Sarah stood by the dining table. "Charlotte, Mary's only thinking that she doesn't want to break up the party and take you away from your guests. I don't mind stepping out for a moment."

Charlotte, half-way across the room, turned back. "I bet you don't," she hissed. "You've been taking every opportunity you can get to try to come between me and my daughter."

Williams rose to his feet and took his wife's arm. "Charlotte, we're very grateful to Sarah for all her support over the last months," he reminded her.

"I don't see why we should be," she snapped at him. "She's only done it for her own purposes."

Williams frowned, shaking his head. "Charlotte, I think you're distraught. You've had a long day, why don't you go and lie down? I'm sure our guests will understand."

"You're defending her!" Charlotte accused, aghast. "She's trying to steal my daughter from me and you're defending her!"

Sarah couldn't help but step forward, stung by her sister's accusation. "Charlotte, you can't possibly think that," she corrected her.

Charlotte wrested her arm from her husband's firm grip and strode back to confront her sister.

"Yes I can," she disputed. "You've been trying to do that ever since she was born. You could have left all the work to the nursemaid. She's paid to do it, after all. But, no, you had to interfere. You had to take over when I was sick and couldn't be there. And now you're leaving and I'll have to pick up the pieces of a baby who only stops crying when her aunt holds her. How is that supposed to have helped me? How is that supposed to make me feel?"

"Charlotte," Sarah reasoned, "you're making no sense."

"No? Well, how about this? You did it because you're jealous. You're jealous of my life. You've always been jealous of Rose and me for being the pretty ones, the ones who get all the attention. And I know how desperately you want a child. You can't have one of your own so you think you can supplant me with mine."

If Sarah's face had been white before, her skin was almost translucent now, shock showing in her widened, staring eyes.

Jack and Williams were taking no more. They moved simultaneously, Jack to stand beside his wife, Williams to grab Charlotte's arm and physically march her from the room. He closed the dining room door but they could still hear him order Charlotte to take responsibility and to deal with the child herself.

Sarah wouldn't look at Jack. He tried to place a hand on her arm but she shook him off, not violently but determinedly. He could almost visibly see her building the emotional and mental walls around the pain she was experiencing, steeling herself against the sympathy and, frankly, suspicions of those around her. She knew the eyes of Fred and Susannah Williams, and Isabella, were on her and she needed to present a calm, unemotional face to them.

Williams' return to the room had them all turning their eyes in his direction.

"Sarah, I can't apologise enough," he started but Sarah's raised hand stilled him.

"There's no need, Freddie," she assured him, her voice almost steady. "She's not herself. I know she didn't mean it."

"Still," he reiterated, "there's no excuse for such ingratitude. I don't know how we would have coped without you here these months."

Sarah looked at him directly. "Let's hope I haven't ended up making things worse," she commented and retook her seat at the table.

* * * * * * *

There was no sign of Charlotte at breakfast the following morning or when they were ready to depart. Dinner the night before had, unsurprisingly, broken up shortly after Charlotte's outburst. Susannah Williams had hugged Sarah with genuine affection and extended an open invitation to both of them to visit them in Chicago. She almost succeeded in breaking Sarah's brittle emotional shell but a visible effort on her part and Sarah was in control again.

Alone together, Jack had hoped she would relent at last but, if anything, Sarah had steeled herself even further, apparently fearful

312

of Jack's ability to break her shield and force the release of more emotion than she knew how to deal with.

He saw, too, the effort it cost her not to visit her niece for a farewell. She ordered the car to be brought round as soon as was reasonable after the silent, stilted breakfast they shared with Williams. He said his farewell, briefly but with genuine affection, gratitude and sympathy before departing for work.

The silence of the house was driving them out, the determined absence of Charlotte compounded by the evident discomfort of the few servants they saw.

They arrived on the dockside early but were allowed to board and escorted to their cabin, a stateroom, rather more opulent than the single cabin Jack had endured on his outbound journey. Rachel left them to seek out her own accommodation and to sort their luggage.

Silence descended between them with Jack's attempts at conversation consistently rebuffed. They noted without comment the gradually increasing volume of chatter as more people joined the ship and crowds gathered on the dockside to see them off. As the blasts finally announced their departure, Jack suggested they go up on deck. The side of the ship being crowded with people they walked aft and stood side-by-side but untouching, looking east towards home.

Jack tentatively put his arm around his wife's waist but she moved away from him and he let his hand fall by his side.

"I can't, John," she spoke steadily. "Not yet. It hurts too much and I can't afford to let it out."

He looked at her, her face apparently calm.

"She will come to her senses," he assured her, "and realise she was in the wrong."

Sarah looked down at her hands, twisting her wedding ring round and round. "I don't mean Charlotte," she confessed. "There's more than a little truth in what she said but she shouldn't have said it. I know Charlotte. She will apologise soon and she will forget it."

She stared out at the River Hudson as they pulled away from Manhattan.

"You mean the child," Jack surmised.

She nodded. "Rebecca," she concurred, a slight smile at the corner of her mouth as she remembered. Jack raised his eyebrows in question when she glanced at him. "They couldn't agree," she explained, "but Mary and I couldn't bear to keep calling her Baby. It seemed so uncaring. We thought Charlotte would win the argument in the end. So we called her Rebecca."

* * * * * * *

Except she wasn't. The news arrived barely a week after they had returned to Lyall Street. The apology from Charlotte – grudging at best and, Jack suspected, under some duress from her husband – came with the news that Susanna Millicent Williams, Millie to her family and to the delight of her namesake, was to be christened the following Sunday, just in time to involve the senior Williams parents before they departed for Chicago. Millie's London-based godparents had been supplanted by a cousin and her husband. Jack watched without comment as Sarah shut away that betrayal in the furthest, darkest part of her heart then ordered an extravagant display of flowers to be sent to Charlotte and hand-picked a delicately engraved silver bracelet for her niece.

Chapter Eleven

London, 1921

*We returned to London and soon settled into a new routine, though
I knew something had fundamentally changed for Sarah.*

At first, Jack worried about the frenetic activity of Sarah's life.
To his mind, she was distracting herself from the sadness at the heart
of her until it could become, somehow, an empty space within her, a
dark void waiting to be filled with all the maternal love she could
hold.

In time, he came to respect her determination not to allow it to
dominate her life. After the pain of her experience in New York,
though, he noticed she studiously avoided situations that would bring
her into daily contact with children, in spite of the number of
charitable organisations who approached her.

The bank and the convalescent home became her saviour. Most
days she travelled to the bank with Jack and Samuels, spending a
couple of hours with the partners or with clients before heading out
to the hospital, appointments or fundraising events.

They started the search for a suitable building for the
convalescent home Sarah was intent on creating. The more time she
and Jack spent at The Grove, the more they were convinced an
alternative approach would benefit these men more. In the year since
his first visit, Jack had grown familiar with many of the patients, their
common experiences helping Jack to build trust with many of them.
What disappointed him was how many of the faces remained familiar
more than a year later, highlighting the lack of progress the doctors
were making. He came to understand the hospital's purpose was not
to resolve but to contain the situation. It was when he realised these
men – some as young as twenty-one – would be there until they died
that he became the driving force behind the project.

His vision remained as it had when they discussed it in the café the previous Easter but Sarah was reluctant to consider using the Richmond House estate. So they spent fruitless hours visiting one site after another, trying to envisage their shared hopes being achieved in an abandoned Victorian workhouse, a pocket of north London where derelict houses were due to be demolished or a widowed woman's unwieldy inherited mansion.

"What they need," Jack argued, "is open space, clean air and work. Something to give them a purpose and something to rebuild their physical strength. The rest will follow."

"It will take one of us to be involved every day," Sarah disputed. "If we set up in Cambridgeshire, we will never see each other. I don't believe either of us wants that."

He couldn't disagree with her there. Having remained childless, he found they were somehow more reliant on each other in their relationship than they observed in others. It was helped, certainly, by the fact that they also worked together, both on bank business and on the project, but while children became the focus for the wives in other marriages and the husbands returned to some of their bachelor ways, absorbed by work and dining frequently at their clubs to avoid the tedium of domesticity, that diversion of paths had never arisen for the two of them.

It was Christmas before they both accepted the rightness of the Richmond House estate for the project and resolved to find a way to make it viable.

Neither of them had returned to America since their painful departure in April, though Jack had stayed close to the business and Sarah had sustained a correspondence with both Isabella and Susanna Williams as a means of staying in touch with the family's progress.

In fact, Jack had long since taken primary responsibility for Richmond Bank's involvement in the New York business, vetting the proposals Williams put forward. He had advocated to the partners

Williams' idea of taking a shareholding in certain opportunities in addition to lending capital and he received tentative backing. His cautious approach had led him to support only a handful of Williams' proposals so far and, though it was early days, the business was prospering.

Nothing, though, would have induced him to return to New York when Mr Samuels proposed visits to see his granddaughter, first in the summer and then again at Christmas. In this, he and Sarah knew they were in accord without needing to broach the matter with each other. It wasn't just the deterioration in the sisters' relationship. It was the aching breach of the short relationship with her niece and the weeks of unspoken pain that Jack was keen not to replicate. Sarah, self-preserving, knew better than to consider it either.

So it ended up that Jack and Sarah hosted a diminished party at Richmond House for Christmas that year, with Mr Samuels absent for the first time since he had acquired the estate, choosing instead to celebrate with Charlotte and his seven-month-old granddaughter in New York. Rose, too, was absent. She had made, to Sarah's mind, a most suitable engagement during the summer to the second son of a baronet. Jack thought him innocuous enough, uninspired by his narrow-minded, unchallenging, establishment views but he seemed genuinely to care for Rose and solicitous for her welfare. He was an attaché in the India Office and faced being transferred to the subcontinent at some point but, as this did not seem to faze Rose, Jack had to assume it might yet be a match characterised by more than the absence of failure.

Taking advantage of her father's absence, Rose had chosen to spend Christmas at the fiancé's family estate in Warwickshire.

Others of the usual group were also absent. The younger Richard Soames was en route to South Africa to view an investment in an estate and Simon Stevenson was recuperating in the south of France after a bout of his recurrent malaria, contracted some years ago on a trip to Egypt.

317

It was, then, a more subdued party who found themselves easing back in their armchairs before the drawing room fire, finishing the turn-of-the-century port from Mr Samuels' cellar as they lit cigars and accepted Sarah's offer to replenish their drained glasses.

"Here's to a better year in 1922," Peter Fellowes toasted.

"Just be grateful the strikes have died down for now," Richard Soames chided. "Always be thankful for small mercies."

"Anyone would think employment was in endless supply," countered David Stevenson, "the way they're behaving."

"I miss the time before the war," Soames reminisced nostalgically to a collective groan. "I do. Then, men were grateful for what work they could get and servants didn't get above themselves and start thinking they'd be better off working in some business or other in the cities. You wouldn't believe the trouble I've had replacing a footman."

"The same here with the outside staff," Sarah concurred. "I'd heard stories of estates struggling with fewer staff wanting to return after the war but I thought we'd escaped the worst of it. Not any longer."

"I blame the women," Fellowes challenged. "Present company excepted," with a nod at Sarah. "First they wanted to keep the men's jobs after the war, now they're encouraging the men to expect more."

"Perhaps the men should expect more," Jack mused. "After everything we put them through."

"I don't think anyone would disagree with the principle," Stevenson returned, "but the practice is becoming a problem. We've lost maybe two dozen lads from the local farming families, tenants and landowners just in this neighbourhood. If those who did return don't want to do the work, how is it going to get done?"

"How short-handed are you?" Jack's tone was non-committal but his mind was already putting pieces together.

318

"On Home Farm? Simon says he'll be after at least a score extra hands late spring," his brother explained.

"Hard labouring or indoor work?" Jack could feel Sarah's eyes on him but if she wanted to stop this she would have to speak up for herself.

David Stevenson looked to Richard Soames for guidance in the absence of his land agent brother.

"I'd guess a mix of both," Soames conjectured. "It'll be the animals as well as the fields. I could do with some help myself, actually. It's not just a Home Farm problem. Why, do you have anyone in mind?"

"Perhaps a few people," Jack spoke cautiously. "Men back from the war who have struggled to settle back into their old routines. Sarah and I," finally he risked a glance at his wife and was relieved to see her expression betrayed as much amusement at his manoeuvring as exasperation, "we've been supporting a hospital in Paddington for ex-servicemen. We're not entirely supportive of their methods and would like to set up a recovery centre."

"Recovery?" Stevenson's tone was doubtful already. "What type of wounds are we talking about?"

"Some physical," Sarah interjected. "Mostly disorders of the mind. Nothing that requires protecting them or those around them," she caveated quickly, seeing objections arise in the faces of those around her. "More the sort that needs support, understanding and time to heal."

"And good, honest labour," Jack added. "Something they can take pride in, that can re-establish a normal routine in their lives."

"You're thinking they could help with the farm work?" Richard Soames was always going to be a natural ally in this, his gratitude for the safety of his sons evident to all.

"It would need a variety of work to reflect their different physical capabilities," Jack submitted.

"Who are you proposing would take care of them, treat them?" Stevenson, the lawyer, was going to be the voice of reason in this.

"I've identified a doctor who can lead the effort," Sarah noted, "and he has some colleagues who would help him build a team. We've looked at a lot of sites in and around London but we've not found a suitable one yet. John advocates bringing them out here to give them good physical, outdoor labour as part of their recovery," she concluded, generously conceding Jack's side of the argument.

"He's right too," Soames concurred. "There's nothing like physical activity for taking a man's mind off what's worrying him."

"But where are you going to put them?" Peter Fellowes interrupted. "Surely not in Richmond House?"

Jack held back from answering. This was where his dispute with Sarah always fell down. While he had little feeling for the house and could look on it dispassionately as a poor use of space, he could also respect those who saw it as a family home.

It was Edward Soames who finally broke the silence. "How many men are you talking about?"

Sarah looked at the young man, sitting slightly aside from the men of his father's generation.

"At most, twenty," she told him. "Fewer in the first instance. But with their families able to visit and to stay, too, so we would need guest accommodation as well as the main facilities and the communal areas." As the lad didn't respond, indeed seemed to lapse back into silently teasing a puzzle apart in his mind, she encouraged him further. "What were you thinking, Edward?"

He shook his head slightly as if dismissing his own thoughts. "I was just thinking about the stable block," he suggested hesitantly. "Not the new one but the old one on the other side of the Dutch barns. Richard and I played in there when we were boys. It's mostly a shell but it's pretty solid. Perhaps it could be brought back into use. But I can't imagine it would accommodate that many."

"No but it's a start," Sarah mused. "It wouldn't be too difficult to convert it and there's plenty of space around to extend the buildings."

"Who would be here to oversee it?" the pragmatist again.

Sarah glanced at Jack. A decision seemed to form behind her eyes. "I would." A slight nod to Jack confirmed it. His vision had become hers too.

"It will take some months to do the work." Edward Soames again. "I would like to help, if you would permit me?" he volunteered to Sarah who smiled her support.

"About time you did some real work," Soames words were critical but his tone was proud. "Perhaps you can put that expensive education to some practical use at last."

* * * * * * *

"What changed your mind?"

The party had broken up around midnight as their guests, a little unsteadily, made their diverse ways home.

Sarah massaged cream into her hands, sitting at her dressing table and, in the mirror, watching Rachel put away her evening clothes.

"It was over lunch today. Looking round the table and realising what a small party we made." Her eyes flickered from watching him to studying her own reflection. "This isn't a home any more. We're all moving on, starting new stages in our lives. Rose will be married before the next year is out. Father will be spending more time in London because his girls aren't here anymore. It seems a shame to let this place lie empty and stale." What was more telling was what she didn't say: that they wouldn't be re-peopling the house with a new generation any time soon. Jack stopped trying to remove his cufflinks and came to stand behind her, resting his hands on her shoulders. She leaned back against him.

"I've been thinking, though." She met his eyes in the mirror. "It seems a shame to waste yet more months waiting for the facilities to be built." She left the comment open for Jack to follow her thought process.

"You're thinking we should use Richmond House in the meantime?" As he said "we", it made him realise, suddenly, how much he liked being an equal partner with her in this project. That wouldn't be easy to maintain once she was on the ground and he was stuck at the bank in London.

"It might be useful to build up gradually," she concurred. "The staff will be needed to support the facility, at least for the first couple of years. It would be no bad thing to get them used to supporting a larger household again before we get operational."

"The doctor?"

She nodded. "And a couple of the more able patients. They could help shape the facility, input their ideas as well as support the building work."

Jack sat down on the corner of the bed, his mind turning over the idea. Sarah turned on the seat and took his hands in hers.

"What are you thinking?" frowning at his frown.

"I was thinking Major Thomasson would be the best man to help."

"He's none too strong," Sarah caveated.

"But he has a first-rate mind and organisational skills," Jack argued. He met Sarah's gaze. "More than that," he admitted. "He needs to get out of that place. I believe he's a prime candidate for benefitting from what we want to do."

"The Major it is, then," Sarah accepted. She looked at him hard then glanced across at Rachel who, instinctively meeting her glance, discretely departed the room. "There's something else," Sarah surmised.

Jack held his hand against her cheek, stroking her cheekbone with his thumb. She leant into the caress. "I had hoped to have you

322

to myself a while longer before our work took us apart," he confessed.

Sarah leant towards him. "You could always give up the bank and come and work here with me?" she suggested, knowing he wouldn't even as she said it. He didn't even have to shake his head. "Or," resting her hands on his shoulders, "you'll just to visit every spare moment you have."

He leant forward suddenly and lifted her up, pulling her onto his lap so that her face was above his and running his hand into her hair.

"Or," he said throatily, "we could just make the most of what time we have," pulling her head down until her mouth met his.

* * * * * * *

The early spring of 1922 brought high winds blowing across parts of England, uprooting trees and casting down slates from many roofs. Mrs Hesketh, in superstitious tones, decried them as the winds of change blowing through their lives. In retrospect, Jack found it hard to disagree with her assessment.

It started with the sudden news of the death of his father. While his condition hadn't visibly worsened, it appeared to have taken its toll on his heart, which gave out while he was dozing in his chair one cold March night. Jack and Sarah travelled to Devon for the funeral. He planned on staying several days to help his mother and brother but soon found he was only getting in the way. Their adjustments, made some time since to compensate for his father's progressive weakening, meant the end, when it came, was a quiet, almost undisruptive passing. He returned to London only a day after Sarah.

The changes continued with Sarah moving to Richmond House, swiftly followed by the Major, full of promises to keep an eye on her for Jack. For the first couple of months, that proved unnecessary as fundraising for the centre brought Sarah back to London for at least

323

a couple of days a week and Jack would travel to Cambridgeshire with her on a Friday, using the time to assess the rapidly increasing number of proposals that were arriving from Williams every week. He started to wonder whether Williams wasn't proposing to take a stake in every company that he approved for a loan. There was no doubting that the investments, on paper at least, were generating a far greater return than they could achieve from the interest on the debts. Assessing the first year of performance, the partners had agreed to double their initial capital injection in reflection of a similar investment made by Williams' father. It seemed everyone in America was starting to take on debt to fund their new lifestyles – radios, refrigerators, air conditioning, cars – and more and more businesses were looking for the capital to start up or to expand to meet the increases in consumer demand.

Technology had arrived at Richmond House and Lyall Place too. Sarah had installed a telephone now that she was going to be away for some of the week. It was one of Jack's daily pleasures to be able to speak to her, however briefly, though there was part of him that regretted the loss of the long, thoughtful letters they had shared during her time in America.

"You're frowning." Sarah's voice broke his concentration. "And you've been staring at the same proposal for the last fifteen minutes."

"My mind was elsewhere," he excused himself, rubbing his hand over his eyes. The paperwork from Williams was spread over the spare seats in their first-class compartment. The one in front of him perplexed him. Eighty per cent. of the proposal was solid but a small, recent acquisition looked out of kilter with the rest of the company activities. He could see no rationale for the divergence from building materials into electricity generation and yet it was for this that the company sought most of its investment. The rest of the business looked sound but something felt wrong about this part.

Dismissing the problem for now, he put the proposal on top of the pile and started to tidy them away as they pulled into Cambridge station.

The car was waiting for them on the station forecourt and they were soon running through sunlit Cambridgeshire countryside, daffodils lining the verges and adding to an overall sense that spring was breaking through.

"I thought I would take a break for the week of my birthday," Sarah proposed. "Come and spend as much time as possible in London with you."

"Not that I'm against the idea but weren't you just saying how much you have to do here?" Jack queried. He noticed how she was absent-mindedly pulling the fingers of her gloves, drawing them back on again then pulling the fingers again. There was more to this than she was saying. He took one of her hands in his and kissed the palm. "I can think of nothing I would like more," he assured her. "Where shall we go to celebrate your birthday?"

The smile she gave him only increased the sensation that there was something she wasn't telling him. "Actually, I'd like a quiet birthday this year. Just the two of us, just dinner."

Jack accepted her request without comment, certain that she would tell him when she was ready.

The Major appeared in the hall as soon as they arrived. Sarah submitted graciously to his kiss on her cheek and disappeared into the morning room, which was now doubling up as her study and the site office, to catch up on her correspondence.

Jack shook his friend's hand, noting how much stronger he was looking already, in the few short weeks since his move out of London.

"Come and see the progress," Stephen encouraged him, ignoring in his enthusiasm the fact that Jack had only just walked through the door. He was happy to indulge him, though, and they walked the short distance to the site.

It was barely mid-morning but the place was alive with labourers carrying bricks, unloading timbers and mixing mortar. Dinner with the partners had kept Jack in town the previous weekend and he was surprised by the amount of progress in the two weeks since his last visit.

Edward Soames caught sight of the two of them and hurried across. Shaking hands, Jack congratulated him on how fast the project was coming together.

"There's something very satisfying in seeing it take form," Edward admitted. "Of course, the building work in the quickest stage but at least it's starting to look like proper accommodation."

He offered to show Jack around, highlighting the communal areas – a dining room, drawing room, a library – the treatment rooms and the first of the bedrooms to be constructed in the old stables roof space. Alongside, the foundations of the family accommodation wing had been laid and the first courses of bricks had now reached the level of the sills of the ground floor windows.

As the Major and Jack wandered back from the site, enjoying a leisurely stroll in the slight warmth of the March sun, Jack observed to his friend how much healthier he looked.

"Who wouldn't be?" the Major challenged. "Good lodgings, outstanding fare courtesy of Mrs Hesketh and that little lot to keep me busy." Jack didn't ask how he was faring otherwise. He knew from Sarah their nights were already less frequently disturbed by nightmares from either the Major or the two other men who had also taken up early residence. "No," the Major continued, "I'm not the one you should be concerned with now."

Jack frowned. "Meaning?"

"It's that lovely wife you need to keep an eye on," the Major schooled him. "Twice this week she's been sick and she's been looking green around the gills for nigh on three weeks now."

Jack avoided the Major's gaze and excused himself as they arrived back at the house. So much for being the observant one.

Sarah was bent over her desk, writing furiously as Jack arrived in the morning room. He perched on the arm of the sofa closest to her desk as he waited for her to finish, sniffing at the odd aroma in the room, which he identified as emanating from the cup and saucer on her desk.

"It's ginger tea," she explained without stopping as Jack picked up the cup to examine it. "Ellerby wrote to recommend it."

"It smells foul," Jack analysed.

"Maybe," finally putting down her pen and turning towards him, "but apparently it does wonders for the digestion."

"I wouldn't put it past her to be feeding you something to keep you away from me," Jack teased.

Sarah leant across and smacked his knee playfully. As she made to straighten up, Jack caught her wrist and held her there, her face, close to his, looking up at him in surprise.

"Is there anything else you want to tell me?" he murmured quietly.

He was so close to her that he could see her pupils dilate suddenly in shock. There was an internal struggle in her mind before, a few seconds later, she shook her head.

"I can't," she whispered, something akin to fear showing in her face. "If it's not... If something... I can't be certain," she finished lamely. "I can't until I know."

After everything, Jack understood her hesitation. He kissed her cheek and released her, leaving the room to go in search of his paperwork.

She may now allow herself to be certain but when Sarah leapt out of bed at seven o'clock the following morning and fled to the bathroom, Jack had no doubts.

* * * * * * *

She was right to be worried.

Jack arrived back at Lyall Street late on the Tuesday evening two weeks later to find Sarah unexpectedly present.

The second he saw her, sitting in the drawing room, a book on her lap, he knew something was wrong. On the surface, everything appeared normal but there was a tightness around her eyes and a slight stiltedness in how she held herself as he bent down to kiss her cheek. He wouldn't say she flinched away from him exactly but only because she was holding herself rigidly enough to prevent that instinctive reaction.

"This is a nice surprise," Jack greeted her, keeping his tone light. "Had I known I would have abandoned Mr and Mrs Reynard immediately."

"Best you didn't," Sarah rejoined. "You may be all that's standing between them taking their business to Westminster Bank."

"Have you eaten?"

Sarah nodded. "Dinner with Father. Rose was out again tonight." She surprised him by rising and preparing to leave the room. "It's been a long day. I'm going to retire. I just wanted to see you first."

He allowed her to get as far as the door before he called her name. "I'm glad to see you," he told her. She hesitated and he saw her wrap her arms around herself in that odd, protective gesture of hers.

"Aren't you wondering why I'm here?" she asked, her voice tense.

He watched her carefully. "I thought you would tell me when you were ready." Seeing her hesitate, he offered her a drink as an enticement to return to the room. Not waiting for her answer, he poured two measures of whisky and held out one of the glasses to her. He was careful not to let his fingers brush against hers as she took the glass. He sensed she was holding herself together and physical contact might shatter her control. He took a seat on one of the sofas, leaving her the choice of sitting with him or opposite him:

she did neither, crossing instead to the mantelpiece, straightening the ornaments and family photos.

"I have an appointment tomorrow morning in Harley Street." She didn't look at him as she spoke. "Originally, I made it to find out if there was a reason I couldn't conceive. Then I thought it wasn't necessary. But now…" She stopped, turning a miniature carved wooden eagle over and over in her hands. "If I was… If I did…" The words wouldn't come. "I'm not any more." Jack started to rise, intent on reaching out to her. "Don't," she commanded, one hand out both to ward him off and to instruct him to sit again. "It doesn't matter. But I had neglected to cancel the appointment so I thought I might as well keep it."

This must, Jack calculated, have happened within the last day, two at most. At the weekend, she had been fine. More than fine. It was as if she had an inner knowledge, a secret, that was giving her an internal warmth and light.

He cursed the fact that he hadn't been nearby. She had already shut down, encased the pain in a steel shell as her way of coping with it. It stood between them, a vacuum between her experiences and his understanding.

He had seen how effectively she controlled her emotions on leaving New York. Then, he had seen how it affected her as well as how she dealt with it and understood what she had been through and how it would colour her future experiences and reactions. Now, his absence meant he lacked that insight and she had closed the emotions away from both of them.

"I'm going to bed." Sarah's slow movements spoke of a soul-deep weariness. To be verging this close to despair, she must have allowed herself to hope more than she had led him to believe. She couldn't even look at him as she left the room. He didn't reach out to her.

Alone in the silent house and wanting to give Sarah the chance of being asleep before he retired himself, Jack steadily worked his way through the contents of the whisky decanter. The more he drank, the more sober he felt, aware of his solitude and, at last, of his own reaction to the news. At first, he worried only about Sarah and about how he might find ways to build a bridge across the void between them. In time, though, he came to realise the sadness and regret that was building in him. He hadn't, until it was gone, thought about the child in anything but the most abstract terms and even then mostly in the context of how it related to Sarah.

Now it no longer existed, his lubricated mind tortured him with images of specific children, boys with his hair, his nose, girls with Sarah's dark eyes and cascading hair. The sense of loss that gradually pervaded was all the more intense for being a surprise.

The sound of Rose arriving home some time after one in the morning finally roused him from his contemplation. Stiff and cold, he headed to his dressing room. For a moment, he contemplated sleeping in there on the settle but he feared the effect of his own behaviour reinforcing Sarah's. He had to keep the door open.

It was hard, though, lying next to her in bed, a careful gap maintained between them, her back turned towards him. He knew she was not asleep but she kept her eyes closed and every rigid muscle rejected him. He lay on his back, staring at the ceiling and praying for sleep to come for both of them. In all his life, even lost and damaged in France, he had never felt so alone.

* * * * * * *

He maintained the illusion of normality the following morning. He rose at the usual time, breakfasted with Mr Samuels and departed with him in the car to head to the bank. Sarah did not emerge.

Arriving at the bank, though, he ordered his secretary to cancel his day's appointments and closed the door of his office.

After an interminable amount of time, the exchange finally connected him to the butler at Richmond House. He asked for Rachel.

"I need to find the address where Mrs Westerham has an appointment this morning." Silence at the other end. "Rachel, I need to meet Mrs Westerham after her doctor's appointment this morning but I don't have the details. Can you remember?" A silence at the other end. Not just hesitation but an actual silence, as of one refusing to speak. "It's very important I meet Mrs Westerham today."

A hesitation this time. "Forgive me, Sir, but if Mrs Westerham had wanted you there, wouldn't she have given you the details?"

Jack took a sharp breath. He should – could – have been angry, particularly in his current anxiety, but he had to admire her loyalty. He made a guess. "Rachel, were you with Mrs Westerham when it happened?" An intake of breath at the other end too. "Then you know why it's imperative I see Sarah today." He put just an edge of command in his voice, hoping she was still young enough to be impressed by authority but still leaving the decision in her hands.

"Mrs Westerham," a hesitation and the voice faded slightly as if she had just looked over her shoulder to confirm she wasn't overhead. "Mrs Westerham wants to keep it quiet, Sir."

"I understand," Jack assured her.

"She was so distressed." It sounded as if Rachel was too.

"That's why I need to be there for her," Jack responded quietly. "You and I, we need to help her," he encouraged. "Both of us."

* * * * * * *

The expression on Sarah's face when she found him waiting on the steps of the consultant's offices later that morning almost made him regret following his instinct, had he not also seen the split second of relief that flickered across her eyes before she adopted the outer shell of distance.

"You're supposed to be at the bank," she chided, standing on the bottom step so that their eyes were on a level.

"I couldn't find anything to do that I considered to be more important than being here," he responded, keeping his voice calm and resolutely refusing to mirror the anger in her tone.

"You don't need to be here," she argued. "I'm perfectly well."

"It's not about need," he disagreed. "And while you may be well, I feel far from sanguine myself and decided there was no one I wanted to be with at this time so much as you."

"Who told you where to find me?" confrontation her armour.

"How do you know I didn't just wander up and down Harley Street until I spotted the chauffeur?" he proposed.

That made her look down the street. "And what have you done with him now that you've found me?" she accused.

"I sent him away. I thought we might take a walk."

"I'm not in the mood for games, John."

"Nor I for playing them," at last taking a slightly harsher tone to convey his determination.

Sarah turned away and started to walk at a pace down the street. "What if I hadn't been in a fit state to walk?" she challenged, glancing briefly at him.

"Dawson is only round the corner." He couldn't help raising an eyebrow at her as he pointed to the car parked in the next road. The slightest hint that she was relenting showed in the pursing of her lips but then she raised her chin and, staring ahead, stepped up her pace.

They walked for a good forty minutes in silence, Sarah determinedly not looking at him again. Eventually, she turned into Green Park and sank onto a bench. Jack took the seat beside her. "You're like a damn puppy," she exclaimed, exasperated. "Traipsing after me with those damn soulful eyes of yours."

Anger. Good. He would take that over silence any day of the week. He contemplated her between narrowed eyes.

"It doesn't mean I don't bite," he cautioned.

"Oh, enough, John!" putting her hand to her forehead. "Enough with the damn riddles."

"At least you're talking to me," he observed. "That's more than last night."

"Last night," she snapped, "I spent three hours pretending to my father that all was well with me while he prattled on about Rose's wedding date and how much he's worried about poor Charlotte and shouldn't I be thinking about going out there again, that my sister needs me. And all the while, all I was thinking was where were you and how much longer were you going to be. And I got more and more angry that you weren't there but I couldn't say anything to my father. And by the time you got home, I couldn't say anything to you either." She stopped, her breath coming faster, conscious suddenly of how much she had raised her voice.

He tried to take her hand but she pulled it away. He turned in his seat to face her.

"I'm sorry I wasn't there," he said softly. She turned her face away.

"If you say it's the fault of the hospice keeping us apart..."

"It's no one's fault," he interrupted her. "But I am more sorry than you know that I wasn't there for you." She slightly turned her face towards him and didn't object when he reached out to take her hand, though she only let hers lie limply in his. "And I'm sorry that you had to face it alone."

"I wasn't entirely alone," she corrected. "Rachel helped me."

"Will you tell me?" he suggested gently. Automatically, she shook her head and looked away again. "Then," covering her hand with his, running his thumb over her knuckle, feeling the ridges beneath the smooth leather of her gloves, "I'll tell you. I feel," he sought around for the right words, choosing carefully, "bereft. I feel robbed because I didn't even realise my hope existed until it had gone. I feel grief for a child who never truly existed but who, nonetheless, was a part of you and a part of me and who, whatever

333

happens now, will never exist again." He stopped and realised that she was staring at him and that her cheeks were wet. He brushed his thumbs over each cheek. "I feel," he told her, "that I have failed you by not being there," not allowing her to interrupt and to contradict him. "I know it's not rational. I can rationalise – and say it honestly to you – that there is no blame in this but that doesn't stop me blaming myself. And I wish I could take all your pain on myself because it hurts me to see you suffer so much. I would gladly take on all your pain, tenfold your pain, because it would be so much more tolerable than knowing there's nothing I can do to relieve your hurt."

"I was afraid you would hate me," Sarah admitted. "Then I wanted to make you hate me because I hated myself. I was angry and I wanted to direct all that anger at you, to wound you. You make me ashamed of myself." Her eyes were tight with grief.

"Are you still angry?" She shook her head. "Will you tell me, then?" She looked uncertain. He took her left hand in his and stripped off her glove. He held her hand gently, running his thumb over the plain gold band he had put on her finger. "I made you a promise always to be there for you, no matter what we faced. But for me to be able to do that, you have to let me. Sarah, you have been independent your whole life and everyone else has always relied on you. It's time you let someone else do that for you."

She looked down at his hand and slowly entwined her fingers in his. "You're right," she accepted. "But not here. Let's go home."

* * * * * * *

In the silence of the afternoon, broken only by the intermittent noise of the servants, they sat together on their bed, their own private space, with a shaft of warm afternoon sun slowly working its way across the counterpane. They sat close together, Jack's arm around Sarah's shoulder, tucking her protectively into his side, and they talked.

About how Sarah's discomfort gave way to anxiety at the cramps that caused her to double up in pain in the middle of a meeting with the Major.

About how desperately she prayed for that tiny life, lying on her side in the darkened bedroom, utterly alone, her legs tucked into her stomach in the vain hope that she could prevent what had already started.

About how Rachel had found her, shivering with cold, blood soaked into the bed sheets, her muscles rigid with long-held denial.

About how she had stripped her and cleaned her, as tender as a mother with her child, her own eyes full of tears as an apparently endless flood released just as her locked muscles released and tears streamed down Sarah's face.

About how she cried herself to sleep, vainly attempting to smother the great wracking sobs that consumed her, Rachel sitting by the bed the whole night, still there each time Sarah stirred and the grief flooded over her again, as fresh and potent as the first time.

About waking the following morning to a painfully glorious new day, the bright blue sky and brilliant sun making a mockery of her grief.

About realising she wanted nothing so much as to be with her husband but that this would entail putting on a face for the rest of the households in Cambridge and in London. About starting the process of walling up the grief inside her, her eyes dry and her mind set.

About waiting and waiting for Jack to return from work, each minute walling in her emotions behind another layer and yet another layer. About the anger that grew as she built the defences until she no longer wanted to see her husband and resented that she would need to explain to him something that she had now so thoroughly closed off, knowing that to do so would entail breaking the wall down again and rebuilding it.

About finding herself unable to speak to him, her mouth stoppered by grief and her way of avoiding it overwhelming her.

About how his words to her in the park had torn at her soul, shredding her selfish defences.

About finding relief, not only in the tears that flowed as she relived the experience with him but also in realising she didn't need to rebuild the wall he had caused to crumble because he had become her wall, her shield, her defence against the world.

And they found relief in silence, realising they were neither of them alone in their loss and coming to know the unassailable intimacy of having shared that grief and that, whenever they felt it again in their lives, in those quiet moments when their deepest, hidden emotions resurface, someone else was feeling it too.

* * * * * * *

Eventually, arms entwined around each other, they started to talk about other things. Inevitably, the subject returned to her family.

"What do you want to do about Charlotte?"

She sighed and rested her cheek on his shoulder. "I wish I knew. On the one hand, if Father has noticed and raised his concerns, there must be something quite seriously wrong."

"But?"

"But what if part of the problem is that I've always been there to sort things out for her? I can hardly fix her marriage, if that's the problem, now can I?"

"You think she should learn to stand on her own feet?" Jack concluded.

"Don't you?" His silence corroborated it. "But then I go around in circles and I worry that she might be in real trouble. She's alone over there. How can I abandon her to that?"

Jack wasn't about to give her an answer, knowing there was no right or wrong in this. "Have you spoken to her recently?" She shook her head. "Written to her?" Another shake. "Are you still angry?"

She raised her head and looked at him directly. "I was. But after what we've just been through, how can I be? I felt betrayed. But I also understand how she must have felt I betrayed her. I know it's not rational but she obviously thought I was trying to steal her child. Rational thought has nothing to do with that. I just hope she's not still holding a grudge."

Jack hugged her hard. "You may just be too forgiving for your own good," he cautioned. He rested his cheek on her hair for a moment, keeping away from her gaze. "Will you tell me what the doctor said?" he asked gently. When she didn't respond, he released her slightly so that he could see her face. Her eyes were filled with unshed tears, which broke free and dropped onto her cheeks as she numbly shook her head, biting her lip against voicing the words she wanted to deny. "Oh, Sarah," he despaired, pulling her against his chest and cradling her head. She wept.

Chapter Twelve

New York, summer 1922

Sarah decided against returning to the US too soon, citing the demands of the project and arrangements for Rose's wedding as too demanding of her time. She tentatively re-opened the channels of communication, though it was some months before Charlotte reciprocated the lengthy news-filled letters Sarah determinedly produced. Sarah shared her father's concern, particularly when the news came that Charlotte and Williams would not be returning to London for Rose's wedding. On their side, they cited Charlotte's second pregnancy as the excuse.

On the surface, Sarah seemed to take the news well. After the events of March, they had both accepted that they should minimise their time apart, Jack staying at Richmond House from Thursday night until Monday morning and Sarah, as much as the demands of the project would permit, returning to London with him for the remaining days. He was there, then, when the brief note arrived from Charlotte and read it as soon as Sarah had perused it. She shared the news with Mr Samuels and suggested they telegraph their congratulations and arrange delivery of a bouquet of flowers. She remained as adept as ever at hiding her feelings in front of her family but it was her honesty in sharing those feelings with Jack that was making her all the stronger.

A two-week trip to Paris around Sarah's birthday had cemented the new honesty in their relationship. Sarah admitted what he had long suspected, that an ever-increasing part of her resented the maternal role that had been thrust upon her at an early age, that she spent much of her teenage years trying to live up to her father's cherished memories of her mother, that she still worried that she would never achieve those unparalleled heights and that much of her inclination to do some lasting good in the world stemmed from wanting to build her own place in it too.

In his turn and for the first time in his life, Jack shared stories of his childhood, memories and youthful ambitions, his brief regret for his lost chance at a university education and his one-time jealousy of his brother's content but unstriving existence. The only aspect of his life he still could not bring himself to discuss was the war. He felt guilty that he couldn't let Sarah into that darkest part of his life, that he should feel it necessary to hold anything back from her but she respected his position and showed no resentment of it.

Lying in bed in their hotel on a sultry Paris evening – the night air unseasonably warm, the floor-to-ceiling shutters opened onto their balcony to benefit from any slight breeze and the bed clothes cast in disarray around them, too hot to bear anything but each other's touch on their skin – she finally shared with him the doctor's diagnosis.

A combination of ovarian cysts and twists in her fallopian tubes made conception difficult and carrying to term all but an impossibility. He speculated her miscarriage had likely been the result of the foetus developing in the tube instead of the womb and declared her fortunate to have ejected the unsuitable pregnancy naturally as she would certainly have faced a threat to her own life instead. In hindsight, he speculated some or all of these possibly hereditary problems might have been implicated in the early death of her mother.

Sarah declared the man an insensitive imbecile and promised never to visit him again but she accepted the diagnosis that instinct told her was accurate.

Sarah had spoken to Rachel to reassure her after Jack's phone call. Listening to the other end of the brief conversation, Jack was a little surprised and somewhat encouraged by the level of familiarity that already seemed to subsist between the two women. When they returned to London, he made of point of seeking Rachel out himself to thank her for helping Sarah. He had thought it would feel strange to be joined in such an intimate secret but one look at her face told him all his compassion, sadness and loss was not only understood but shared.

More. That he was no longer alone in his efforts to protect and cherish Sarah.

* * * * * * *

Rose won the prize for the most grand of the three sisters' weddings. But, then, she was marrying the second son of a lord and gaining upon her marriage a title of her own, albeit a minor, archaic and asset-less one, but it did give her seniority in society over her sisters. Sarah furnished Charlotte with a lengthy narrative on the church, the guest list, the fashions and their new brother-in-law's family quirks. She received for her efforts a brief, two-paragraph response, bemoaning the growing summer heat and the inadequacy of their apartments against the state-of-the-art air conditioning now installed in the Upper East Side house and looking forward to the spectacular party planned for Isabella's society wedding.

Two days later, another letter arrived. Jack was reading investment proposals over breakfast, a new habit Sarah frowned upon but the only way he could stay ahead. He was not so absorbed, though, as not to notice the silence that had descended opposite him. He put his papers down and watched her finish reading. Distracted, she automatically started to refold the sheets of paper and return them to the envelope when she caught herself and realised Jack was watching her.

"I need to leave for New York," she stated, steel in her voice. She handed him the letter to read and left the breakfast table. He recognised the writing as Williams'. He scanned the letter in half the time it had taken her and followed her upstairs. She was in their bedroom, her case on the bed and already instructing Rachel on what items to pack.

"You won't try to stop me, John." It was a statement, not a question.

"No," he concurred. "I'll make some calls and see what passage I can book for us." That brought her up short. "I don't think you should go without me," he suggested, coming close and dropping his voice while Rachel was present. Thankfully, she had the discretion quietly to remove herself from the room, heading to the adjoining dressing room to gather more clothes together.

"How can both of us go now?" Sarah seemed to be hoping he might have a solution for what she had already been through in her mind. The project, the bank. They couldn't afford for both of them to be away at this time."

"How can I let you deal with this alone?" he challenged in response.

"Be practical, John," turning her back and continuing with the folding of her clothes.

"I thought we had agreed," he reminded her. "You can't go through this alone."

"I'll manage," she assured him but still not looking at him, he knew, because her face would betray her.

"No, Sarah." He caught both her hands and pulled her round to face him. "This isn't fair on you."

She shook her head. "She's my sister. I have to be there for her. I've always been there for her."

"Then I need to be there for you," he insisted. "I know how strong you are," he acknowledged, softening his voice, "but are you really strong enough for this?"

"Who would understand better than I?" Her eyes were bleak. If she was already this distressed, she was never going to manage. A miscarriage at four-and-a-half months. The child would have been recognisably human. Worse, the doctor suspected the child's heart had stopped beating as much as a week before.

"Understanding isn't what she needs right now, Sarah," he disagreed. "What she will need is someone to molly-coddle her, to make her the centre of their world because you know damn well Williams won't do it for her. She will drain all the strength and soul out of whoever is nearby because that is the only way she will ever feel better about herself after this. Because we both know she will be blaming her past for this. She won't just be upset. She will be bordering on clinical depression and whoever is nearby will get sucked into the vortex of her downward progression. She will curse everyone around her who is stable or content and she will do her utmost to make them more miserable than she."

He was painting a black and cruel picture but none the less true for that.

Sarah's white face told him he had struck home. "I can't leave her to it," she objected.

"And I won't desert you to it either," he pledged.

"The timing couldn't have been worse," Sarah bemoaned. "Another week, ten days…"

"There's nothing here that can't be managed by someone else," Jack returned, trying to convince himself as well as her. In truth, he did need to be here in London for the end stages of negotiations on a new investment in a shipping company and someone from the Board of the hospice, on which both he and Sarah now sat, was supposed to be helping the Major with the final staff interview process ahead of the first stage of the project opening in two weeks' time. Unfortunately, Sarah could read his self-deceit as clearly as he could read hers. She started at him, both at an impasse.

In the silence, they both heard the sound of a drawer closing in the other room and Jack saw Sarah's eyes flicker towards the open adjoining door. She didn't even have to voice the idea. They both reached the conclusion at the same time. If anyone could support Sarah in this other than Jack, it was Rachel.

"Find us two berths, John," she asked, calmer already. "As soon as you can."

* * * * * * *

Instinct drove him to seek out Rachel before they sailed. While Sarah was making calls to cancel her full diary of appointments, he found her completing the packing but, as he stepped into the dressing room, he was suddenly uncertain what to say. He crossed to the window in an effort to force some sort of control on the situation. She stopped folding clothes and watched him, a garment folded over her arm, then, to his surprise, started the conversation for him.

"You're worried how she will cope," she suggested, looking directly at him. It was the most direct she had ever been with him and he found himself responding, meeting that disconcerting gaze.

"She's strong but I don't know if she's strong enough after what she's been through."

"None of us does," she concurred. "It's impossible to know how any of us would react. But what we think is irrelevant. She's not one for putting her own problems ahead of her sister's, is she?"

He frowned and, to ease his awkwardness, perched on the window ledge, bracing his hands against the woodwork. "How is it you know her so well?" It was curiosity, not a challenge.

She turned away and continued folding clothes. He read it for the deflection it was. "We talk," she responded, briefly. Absurdly, he felt excluded.

"You will keep an eye on her while you're away?" he suggested, quietly, trying to avoid a tone of command. There was no response but, somehow, he knew it wasn't because she disagreed but because his suggestion was, for her, a given. He tried again. "Will you let me know how she gets on?"

343

She straightened and looked at him. Her expression was controlled but he saw the internal conflict between her instincts and her position. She shook her head.

Strangely, that amused him and he had to school his expression to hide the fact. "No?" he challenged, softly.

"I must do what is right for her," she defended. "She is my priority. Sir."

He considered her for a moment, hating how her use of the title reminded them both of their positions. He nodded and rose, pushing his hands into his pockets in a way that betrayed how nervous she was making him feel. "That's all I can ask," he acceded and rapidly left the room.

* * * * * * *

By eight o'clock that evening, Sarah and Rachel were berthed on a small liner sailing out of Southampton, their passage bought at considerable cost from a middle-aged couple who were prepared to delay their departure for twenty-four hours in return for a not insubstantial amount of money and an upgrade to the fleet's latest, most luxurious ship. There were advantages to be had from years of helping to fund investment in the transport industries.

Mr Samuels, when informed of his daughter's news, was rather more sanguine than either Jack or Sarah anticipated. Though sympathetic for her loss, he took solace in her youth and health, and the fact that his wife had similarly miscarried twice between Sarah's birth and Charlotte's but they had both believed it would come right in the end. The shock on Sarah's face told Jack that this was news to her as well as to him. He was astounded his father-in-law could be so unfeeling, knowing as he did the ultimate cause of his wife's demise. He thanked God George Samuels knew nothing of Sarah's own grief.

He was, as a result, perplexed by Sarah's decision "to go running off to New York". "You always were over-protective of those girls," he chided indulgently.

Sarah turned away to control her anger.

* * * * * * *

She telegraphed from the ship their safe arrival in New York harbour. It gave him the peace of mind finally to concentrate on completing the negotiations. He had sat through two days of interminable interviews with Dr Alexander and the Major, and was able to rubber-stamp their hiring decisions, but he knew his distractedness had impaired the value of his contribution to the process.

Returning to his office after a lengthy meeting with the lawyers on the final details of the investment agreement, he was surprised to find Miss Richardson, his secretary, hovering anxiously by his door. He took the telegraph from her as he pushed open the door and deposited the paperwork on his desk. By the time he absorbed the instruction and turned back to Miss Richardson, she had stepped forward with all the necessary tickets and paperwork to get him on a train, down to Southampton docks and on the six o'clock sailing to New York.

"Hesketh and James packed a trunk and it's already in a car on the way to Southampton," Miss Richardson informed him, secretly pleased by her own efficiency.

Jack turned over the paper in his hand, perplexed. "Is this all?" he queried, re-reading the staccato words instructing him to depart for New York immediately and detailing the berth that had been booked for him.

Miss Richardson shrugged her thin shoulders and crossed to the desk to gather up his papers. "The car is waiting downstairs to take you to Waterloo station," she informed him.

* * * * * * *

Given the circumstances, he expected the distraction of wondering what was happening New York to make for a most unsettled journey. He soon discovered that the enforced sedentariness of a multi-day sea crossing overcame even the most nagging of distractions. The sheer tedium – exacerbated as it was by his self-imposed isolation from the other passengers – drove him to seek temporary refuge in books he had long since selected to read but for which he had, until now, not found the time. Thankfully, James had had the foresight to pack them. As a result, he arrived in New York unexpectedly refreshed, alert and clear-headed.

Which was just as well because he walked into a maelstrom.

He could hear the yelling from the other side of the solid oak front doors. The maid responded to his knock and let him in. Clearly attired for going out, she ignored him and went back to cowering – there was no other word for it – behind Madison, the butler. Jack had thought him a short man from his previous visit but he now saw him drawn up to his full height and realised the man almost matched him.

"I will not have thieves in my own house!" Charlotte screamed at him.

"Madam, the item has been located," he spoke quietly but with deep authority.

"Of course it has," Charlotte's sarcasm was biting and her gesticulations wild, "because she knew she's been caught out and hoped to cover her theft."

Jack caught sight of Sarah standing some distance behind her sister. She looked tired, he realised, and it pulled at his heart. Jack stepped forward to intervene, taking hold of Charlotte's arm and planting himself between her and the servants. "Hello, sister," he greeted her, kissing her on the cheek. She turned the full force of her malevolence on him.

"Don't call me that!" she spat. "And what are you doing here? If you think you can talk me into taking that cheating bastard back, you can think again." She spun on her heel without another look at the two servants and stalked back upstairs.

Jack turned and extended his hand. "Madison," he acknowledged.

The older man accepted his handshake. "Welcome back, Sir," as polite and as calm as if the scene had never happened.

Jack looked beyond him to the maid. "Annabel, perhaps you would be good enough to bring Mrs Westerham and I some tea in the garden room?" he requested, giving the girl the power of deciding to walk away. He saw mutiny in her eyes, which was unsurprising given her treatment, but she looked to Madison for guidance and he helped her to the right decision. She shed her outdoor coat and scuttled, without speaking, in the direction of the kitchen. Madison took Jack's hat and coat then excused himself.

"I knew it would help to have you here," Sarah remarked drily, her mouth twisting in a wry smile. Unspeaking, Jack opened his arms and she walked into them. He hugged her for a long moment until the sound of a door being slammed upstairs jolted them out of their intimacy.

"Should we go to her?" he nodded towards the upper floors.

"Perhaps I should fill you in first?" she suggested, leading the way to the sun-flooded garden room at the back of the house.

"I wish you would," Jack retorted. "Your summons had me jumping to all manner of conclusions."

"I fear they may none of them be so bad as the reality," Sarah sighed. He noted the effort it cost her not just to collapse into the wickerwork chair as Annabel arrived with the tea.

"How was your journey?" she asked.

"Don't," Jack chided as Annabel departed. "You don't need to do small talk with me. We'll have time for us later. Tell me what's happening here and how you want me to help."

"I should have let you come with me in the first place," covering her eyes with her hand and leaning her head back against the chair. "Thank God Rachel was here."

"I gather Williams isn't here?" Jack surmised.

She rocked her head from side to side in denial, still not lifting her head from the chair. "He's moved into his club. At least, that's what he told me."

"You suspect otherwise?"

Sarah rubbed her forehead, easing the ache. "I know he been seen dining with a woman, an old friend, he says. I don't know if there's anything in it but Charlotte's made up her mind."

"Did she throw him out?"

Sarah raised her head at last to look at him. "No," she replied and her voice was bleak. "She just made life so unbearable that he couldn't stand to be here any longer."

* * * * * * *

Charlotte's descent into chaos had been both rapid and unchecked by those around her. By the time Sarah arrived, barely ten days after Charlotte's miscarriage, the house was in disarray. Half the staff had walked out or been fired, meals were half-hearted efforts and perpetually late, and the place was in dire need of a damn good clean. Charlotte, on the day Sarah arrived, was still in bed at four in the afternoon, having arrived home at three the previous morning when she carried on drinking with the two men and three women – most perfect strangers – she had met in a speakeasy in Harlem. It was a visit from one of her old friends, one of those who had abandoned Charlotte during her first pregnancy, that introduced Charlotte to the oblivion she craved.

At first, it was just dancing and the appeal of the vibrant Harlem jazz scene. Then it was illicit alcohol, just enough to loosen up this stiff-necked English girl and get her into the liberated mood of New

York's bohemian underworld. In no time, though, Charlotte learned the power of alcohol – especially the noxious substitutes, sweetened to mask the undrinkable flavour – to make her forget. Oblivion she sought and oblivion she found, even failing to return home one night and having to call Sam out the following morning to fetch her from someone's filthy back room.

Williams was either not there to notice or so wrapped up in his own hurt and resentment that any brief exchanges between them almost instantly resolved into bitter, malicious arguments. Charlotte's tears, too painful to be sustained beyond the first few fights, were replaced by anger and shame, subsuming her own guilt and self-doubt.

Arriving in the middle of the downward spiral, Sarah found herself in the unusual position of being utterly helpless to arrest Charlotte's descent into darkness.

She took it on herself to do only what she could, taking charge of the household and the child, and being there for Charlotte whenever she surfaced from her self-imposed prison of despair.

Williams had been half out of the door when she arrived. She emotionally blackmailed him into staying but, forty-eight hours later, she let him go. Better, in some ways, to have him out of the house than to see and remember Charlotte this way. Jack couldn't fault her logic but he feared Sarah's arrival had only made it easier for Williams to walk away without guilt.

The one bright spot for Sarah in all this – and the one Jack feared the most – was her niece. Ignored by her distraught mother, abandoned by the nurse who took Sarah's arrival as her opportunity to depart, the child's care fell to Sarah and to Rachel. Jack found it hard to begrudge her that when he saw the peace and joy it brought her in this otherwise distraught household.

He left the house as soon as he reasonably could for the office. He didn't entirely expect Williams to be there based on the reports he had been receiving in London but it made as good a place to start as any.

The place wasn't in disarray but it was clearly a rudderless ship. The sense of pride and commitment he had witnessed on his previous visit had all but disappeared, as had the discipline of strict office hours and regular correspondence with customers. Williams' desk had disappeared under unread paperwork, unsigned contracts. No one had seen him for more than an hour on any day that week.

Calling the managers together, Jack informed them he would be taking charge until Williams returned and asked each of them to prioritise their backlogs to bring the most critical decisions to him first. Then he asked the secretary to being him coffee and shut himself away in Williams' office to go through the papers.

By the time he re-emerged, it was almost nine and the growling in his stomach had turned from a nuisance into a sharp pain. He still had some way to go before he could claim to have broken the back of it but, hopefully, he had at least stemmed the haemorrhaging.

He wanted nothing more than to head back to the house but he ordered Sam to make one stop first.

It is a peculiarity of the very best hosts that they combine all the usual standards of courtesy and discretion with almost photographic memories. The manager of Williams' club was one such. After only one brief meeting almost a year before, he instantly recognised Jack and offered to escort him to where Mr Williams was dining.

Williams didn't look up as Jack approached. He motioned to the waiter to bring another glass and filled it with what even Jack in his limited knowledge recognised as an outrageously expensive Bordeaux. Jack ordered a steak.

"I wondered how long it would be before you were summoned."

"If you were looking to get my attention, you've succeeded." Jack was in no mood to sympathise. "How long do you intend staying here?"

At least Williams looked ashamed. "I should never have left," he admitted. "Stupidly, I thought it would jolt her out of this...mania. But all it did was confirm in her mind that I was having an affair and was desperate to get out of the marriage."

"Are you?" Jack's gaze was unflinching.

"My, you're not pulling your punches tonight, Westerham." Williams looked at him, a little perplexed. "I was beginning to write you off as not tough enough, a bit of a yes man, based on recent experiences. Am I going to have to revise my opinion?"

"I have no interest in your opinion right now, Williams," he told him harshly but calmly. "What I'm interested in is whether you intend honouring your wedding vows or you're just after the easy way out."

Williams, a genuinely good-humoured man, had no interest in picking a quarrel with his friend. He sighed and pushed his hand through his hair. "The irony is that when she could justifiably have accused me, she didn't and now that she suspects me, there are no grounds for it."

"None?" Jack needed to be certain. "What about this old flame?"

"Melissa Johnson?" Williams dismissed. "There's nothing in it. We had dinner once."

"Johnson?" Jack's methodical mind was putting pieces together. "As in Baines Johnson of Chicago?" That odd investment proposal made sense now. The question was only how badly implicated in it was Williams.

Williams visibly blanched. "Damn," he muttered.

"You were thinking I wouldn't spot it?"

"Hoping, maybe. Perhaps in part hoping you would so I could genuinely tell them I tried but couldn't help."

"Them?" Jack was beginning to feel like an interrogator. This was not the conversation he had expected to have.

"It's not really for Melissa," Williams defended. "Her father and brother own the business. They couldn't raise the capital but the business will fold if they don't."

"Then it probably deserves to fold." Sentimentality was out of the window. "What about the business you folded it into?"

"That wasn't me. Her father arranged it then brought it to me."

Jack frowned. "And you expect me to believe there's nothing going on with the daughter when you're prepared to go to such lengths for the father?"

"Honestly, Westerham," angry now, "you can believe what you damn well please. You don't know what it's been like here."

Jack relented. There was difficult news he had yet to break and he needed Williams on side. "Alright. Tell me."

Williams shook his head. "Anything I say now will just sound like whinging at best, self-justification at worst."

"I know about the partying and the alcohol. I know she's been neglecting the child. I know about the miscarriage. What more would you have me know?"

"You say those things as if you understood," Williams argued. "But unless you've lived through it, you don't. If it was just about Charlotte having a good time or trying to distract herself from her grief, I'd understand. Hell, I'd probably even join her." In a flash of pain behind bloodshot eyes, Jack recognised the grief of a father. "But she's punishing herself. Somehow, she sees the miscarriage as her fault. And as part of her punishment, she's punishing me too." He leant heavily on his elbows on the table, holding his head in his hand. "You should have seen her at this speakeasy. I'm no saint and I know what to expect in these places. I don't shock easy but the way she was dancing with some random guy, she shocked me. I dragged her out of there, so drunk she could barely stand. She was like a hellcat, fighting me every step of the way. I've got the scars to prove it." Williams' head came up, his eyes challenging Jack to disbelieve him. Jack waited, sensing there was more to come. "The mood swings seem to be a feature of the hangovers. Maybe it's the hooch. I hope to God it is."

"Meaning?" Jack prompted.

"Meaning," Williams challenged, "I found drugs in her coat packet. I have no idea if she's taken any," holding up his hands, "but given her behaviour, it wouldn't surprise me."

"How did you come to leave?"

"I'm sure Sarah can tell you," defensive. Jack didn't respond and Williams gave in. "She blamed me for bringing Sarah here. We fought – not physically, just arguing – but she was getting more and more wound up. At one point, she started tearing at her hair, ripping it out of her head in handfuls. I tried to restrain her but that only made things worse. So when she ordered me to get out, I thought it was the best thing I could do. And now I don't know how to go back." He sank back in his chair, a man defeated. It was then that Jack noticed the scratches on his neck and the hollow shadows around his eyes.

He leant forward, resting his arms on the table. "I'm sorry about the child," he condoled with his friend, sympathy at last in his voice.

Williams looked at him. "It was a boy," he said bleakly. "Did you know that?" Jack shook his head. "Sarah said it happened to you too?"

Jack nodded. "It was much earlier, though," not wanting to share his pain with Williams. "Not the same."

"Still," Williams observed and Jack knew his friend understood.

"Still," he agreed.

Williams refilled their glasses, draining the bottle. "Do you think it's something hereditary? Given both sisters…" He left the sentence unfinished.

"The mother too," Jack informed him.

"Is that so?" raising his eyebrows.

353

"I think you should come back with me tonight," Jack suggested.

"How do you know it won't make matters worse?"

"I don't," Jack admitted, "but I trust Sarah and she says that's what we should do. You'll have to sleep in the guest room but you should be there. Charlotte's still moody but she's not been out since you left, according to Sarah, and the mood swings seem to be lessening."

"But what if she won't believe me about Melissa?"

Jack tried not to lose his patience. "It's your job to make her believe," he ordered. "And," rationalising, "staying away is hardly helping to change her mind, is it?" He drained his glass. "One more thing. You need to focus on your marriage until we can sort this out so I'm taking over at the bank." He avoided the temptation to try to justify his decision or to try to soften the blow.

"For how long?"

"As long as it takes."

If he had expected an argument, he was surprised to see Williams nod his acquiescence. "To tell the truth, Jack, you've been making all the decisions anyway. We might as well be up front with everyone about it."

* * * * * * *

Williams returned to the house with Jack that night. The household seemed settled and, at least temporarily, calm. The place was in darkness when they arrived, the oak timbers creaking as the heat lessened and the cooler night air stole through the open-windowed rooms, carrying the sweet fragrance of the summer jasmine blooming in the garden room.

Williams left Jack to find Charlotte and start the process of rebuilding their marriage. Jack prayed the peaceful stillness stealing through the house might not be broken. For a long moment, he

354

thought about going in search of Sarah, a part of him craving the chance to share with her the decisions and conversations of the day. A strong instinct overrode him though, that sense that he needed nothing so much as solitude and silence. That sense that, after a day of talking and negotiating at the bank followed by the long conversation with Williams both at the club and in the car on the way home, he had run out of words. Would that Sarah could read his mind. He could, then, fulfil that inherent need to share the day's experiences with her without having to utter another sound.

His instinct made him seek out the small library tucked into the corner of the house, an inadequate room by the standards of most of the house's inmates but perfectly fulfilling Jack's notion of a bolt-hole. It struck him that he had spent much of his life in such confined spaces, escaping into a world beyond the barriers of his present physical environs, whether his childhood bedroom, the study at Lyall Street or the darkest corner of the dugout tucked into the trench wall as a rudimentary shelter-cum-living-space.

The disappointment as he opened the door and discovered his private space had been invaded was intense and his natural politeness almost deserted him. It was only her obvious embarrassment and her natural desire to escape that shattered his more selfish instinct and drove him to reassure and calm her.

"Rachel."

She was moving towards the door where he stood with the evident intent of slipping past him and he had to put out his arm to stop her flight. She came to a rapid halt only a foot or so away from him, her eyes cast down, her fingers picking nervously at the spine of the book she was clutching. He had never appreciated before how very slight of frame she was.

"I didn't mean to intrude." She spoke so low that he instinctively leaned towards her to catch her words. "Mrs Westerham said I might…"

"Please don't rush off on my account," he assured her, his manners and an innate sense of wanting to reassure this slight, quiet creature not only overwhelming his wish to be alone but also making it suddenly seem unreasonably selfish. He wasn't the only one suffering in this place. "You're more than welcome to use the library as well."

"Thank you, Sir," still staring at the floor and every muscle of her being poised for flight, "but I should retire. Good night, Sir," and before he could stop her, she had slipped away.

"Rachel," he called after her, his tone of command forcing her to halt, though she only half-turned back towards him. "Are you well?" he enquired, surprised by the question even as he asked it. A very slight nod was all the response he got. "I must thank you for looking after Mrs Westerham." Without thinking, he took a step towards her. He was glad when she didn't move further away.

She looked at him hesitantly. "I owe you an apology," she noted. "For the way I spoke when I saw you last. It was..." she hunted around for the word, "disrespectful."

That left a bitter taste in the mouth. "It was right," he countered, holding her gaze. "I respect you for having disagreed with me. I should never have asked you to report to me behind her back." A slight nod of acknowledgement. "You're very protective of her," he observed. Another nod. A compulsion made him ask, "Why is it that you feel so strongly towards her?"

Avoiding his gaze now. "Life has been difficult. She gave me another chance." A direct look, so expressive, so pained. "She gave me hope."

He held her eyes for long seconds, neither of them, somehow, able to look away. The strength of the wave of protectiveness that flooded through him caught him completely by surprise, making him intensely aware of her slight, fragile frame, so at odds with the fire he saw in her eyes.

He pulled himself together, seeking refuge in the safe bounds of the master-servant relationship. "Has your mistress retired?"

"No, Sir," now refusing to look at him. "She's tending to little Millie in the nursery."

Jack thought it wise to go in search of his wife.

* * * * * * *

He stood in the open doorway to the nursery, watching the two of them together for some minutes before Sarah realised he was there. He had never before experienced such a sense of contentment and homecoming as watching his wife cuddle and croon over her one-year-old niece. It gave him an utterly unexpected sense of sadness and loss that, for them, this would never be more than a borrowed moment.

When she finally looked up, he could see it took her several seconds to register and recognise him, so intent had she been on the child in her arms. Her slow smile spoke her share of his sense of contentment.

"She was fretful," she explained quietly. "I know I should leave her to work it through and get back to sleep naturally but I can't bear to leave her alone."

Jack smiled his understanding and crouched on his haunches beside the nursing chair, gently running his fingers over the downy hair. The child snuffled in her sleep and turned her head in towards Sarah, cuddling against her.

"She has a look of Williams," he observed quietly, "or, rather, of Isabella, I think."

"She has the Samuels nose, though, and something of our stubbornness too, I fear," Sarah smiled.

"Her father is back," Jack informed her. Sarah nodded and touched her hand to his temple where, he knew, the touches of grey were thickening in his hair. "Tell me tomorrow," she advised. "You look like you need to sleep."

* * * * * * *

Returning the following night after a second long day in the office and satisfied that they were starting to get on top of the issues created by Williams' negligence, he discovered a delegation awaiting him in the drawing room.

"Am I late?" he asked Sarah quietly as she rose to greet him, fairly certain in his own mind that this hadn't been pre-arranged. He couldn't interpret the look she gave him so he decided to co-operate and crossed the room to greet Isabella and Williams' parents.

"Aren't we missing someone?" he asked of Sarah, raising his eyebrows. The mood of the room seemed to be redolent of nothing so much as a war cabinet and it struck him that the subjects for discussion were notable by their absence.

"Freddie and Charlotte have gone out for dinner," Isabella interjected. "We thought it an opportune moment to discuss how we should proceed."

"We've stood by long enough," Mr Williams explained, a determined expression on his face. Jack got the impression he thought the moment to intervene had arrived long since.

"We didn't want to interfere," Mrs Williams justified. "They needed to be allowed to try to sort this out for themselves."

"But it's gone on long enough," Mr Williams overruled. "And with all due respect to Mrs Westerham," he addressed Jack, "her efforts of recent days have come to naught. Now it's damaging to more than themselves." He was looking to Jack to step in and force common sense to rule.

Lined up on the sofas, this was a family closing ranks, if it proved necessary, against Sarah, seated opposite. Jack, standing behind her, moved now to take a seat alongside her.

"What do you propose?" he asked, taking charge of the negotiation.

Mrs Williams looked at her husband for permission, which she received with a brief nod. "Charlotte and Freddie must come and live with us. For a while at least. Life here is obviously not suiting them. Charlotte will benefit from the stability and structure we can give her and Freddie would welcome the help in managing her."

"Managing her?" Sarah echoed.

"We know Charlotte's been through a lot," Isabella acknowledged to Sarah, "but being here is not helping her to recover. You shouldn't have to take this on and we may be better placed to help."

"We?" Sarah echoed again. "Isabella, you won't be living at home soon or won't your husband expect you to be home with him?"

Jack could sense Isabella go rigid. "Sarah, we know you're doing what you can but…"

Sarah's muscles tightened too to hold in the anger he knew was building within her. "Are you suggesting I don't know how to handle my own sister?" Sarah fought to keep her voice level if not stable.

"Mrs Westerham, this is not a criticism of you," Mrs Williams tried to soothe but her tone was aggravating. "We're only suggesting how we might help the young couple through this."

"We are not suggesting," Mr Williams corrected. "I have already spoken to my son who has agreed and he is informing Charlotte tonight. We are here not to discuss but to inform you. Mrs Westerham," raising his hand to stall her objection, "my daughter-in-law is part of this family now and it is our responsibility to bring her back to the right path."

"And Millie?" The question Sarah feared to ask and to which she already knew the answer came out as a whisper.

"We have engaged a wonderful nursemaid to replace the one who left," Mrs Williams smiled kindly, evidently thinking their reassurance would be welcome to Sarah. "Our granddaughter will be very well cared for and when Charlotte is quite well she will be able to see her again."

Shock was visible on Sarah's face. "You mean to keep her from her mother?"

"Only temporarily, Sarah," Isabella soothed. "For the child's sake as much as Charlotte's. None of us could forgive ourselves if anything untoward occurred."

Sarah was now aghast. "Just what do you think has been going on here?" she demanded, sitting forward in her chair.

"We know exactly what has been going on," Mr Williams retorted, in a tone that seemed to suggest he held Sarah as accountable as Charlotte for her sister's actions. "We know about the drinking, the debauchery, the physical violence." His expression showed his distaste.

"You go too far," Sarah accused faintly. "You're exaggerating this out of all proportion."

"Whatever proportion," Mr Williams' voice was cold as Sarah's defence seemed to confirm his attitude, "we do not expect nor will we tolerate such behaviour in our family."

Jack noted that Isabella had the grace to look down, avoiding Sarah's gaze.

"You make her sound debauched," Sarah exclaimed. Mr Williams' expression said he agreed with her analysis. "She's just an intensely unhappy young woman. A young woman, I hasten to add, who could have benefitted from greater understanding and support from her husband!"

"This is not my son's fault," growled Mr Williams, his face flushed. His wife placed a steadying hand on his arm.

"This is not about blame," she insisted. "We are only wanting to help both them and our grandchild."

"It makes sense, Sarah," Isabella cajoled. "After all, you aren't going to be here forever." Jack sincerely wished she had left the argument to her mother. He decided it was time to step in.

"I'm sure," he observed neutrally, "that Charlotte would welcome the support of a loving and understanding family at this emotionally traumatic time. Particularly," he said pointedly, "now her husband has remembered where his obligations lie. And," forestalling Sarah's objection with a gentle look, "she has several times expressed the wish that she lived closer to the friends she met when she first arrived here. I am sure we would all be happy to know she had a strong group of good friends around her." Sarah stayed silent. She couldn't disagree that it would be good to remove Charlotte from her proximity to the group of people who had drawn her into her present lifestyle. "I know you will acknowledge that my wife is at least as concerned as you for her sister's welfare and that of her niece and I am sure you will be most welcoming when she visits to see either of them." His look froze Isabella's building objection in her throat. "We shall not be leaving New York for some time yet," he informed them. "Not at least until my wife is satisfied that she is no longer needed here."

Mr Williams looked angry but his wife smiled her relief at the resolution.

"Mrs Westerham would be most welcome as often as she pleases to visit," she assured Jack, evidently glad the necessary confrontation was over and her husband had got his way.

"I can come over tomorrow to help Charlotte pack her things," Isabella sought to make amends now they had got what they wanted.

"Thank you," Sarah returned coldly, "but I think Rachel and I can adequately manage that task."

Mr Williams rose and his women took their lead from him. "I bid you both good night," he said stiffly.

Jack took the opportunity to walk alongside him down the stairs to the hall.

"I'm glad you can see sense, Westerham," the older man congratulated him. "I feared we might see in Mrs Westerham the kind of hysterics evident in her sister."

Jack was riled but he didn't show it in his voice. "You should know, Mr Williams," he lowered his voice slightly but wanted to be sure that Sarah, just behind him, could still hear, "that I relieved your son of his position at the bank yesterday. Temporarily, of course," he added smoothly. "At least until we are, on both sides, satisfied that he is no longer distracted by his current distressing circumstances and is able to fulfil his duties once more." The other man's red-flushed face confirmed what he had suspected, that the son had not had the courage to break this piece of news to his father. "I know I hardly need remind you that the terms of the agreement entitle Richmond Bank to take this step in extremis."

Mr Williams' colour suggested he was almost apoplectic with either rage or embarrassment. Jack had to respect the way he forced himself to control his reaction. "Has Mr Samuels already sanctioned this move?" he forced himself to ask.

Jack nodded. "I received his confirmation by telegraph this afternoon. I hope, Mr Williams," extending his hand, "we will be able to work well together on this. I can assure you we share a common interest in the continued success of the venture."

Grudgingly, Williams shook his hand but briefly and without another word. He turned and ushered his wife and daughter out into the street ahead of him.

Turning as Annabel closed the door behind their guests, Jack discovered Sarah was already absent. He knew where to find her, though.

There was only a night light in the nursery, casting a soft glow over the woman standing, shoulders hunched, over the crib. Jack came to stand alongside her.

"I thought at one point I was going to slap their smug faces one after the other," she whispered.

"I'm glad you didn't," Jack reflected. "It might have made future family Christmases challenging."

"I did rather enjoy the slap you gave him at the end," she said with slightly shamefaced relish. "There's no risk he could overturn it?"

"It doesn't matter," he assured her. "We will rebuild what we had before. Neither side is stupid enough to throw it away. You know me. It's not about the power. Someone needed to take control or what we've built so far could have come undone. Williams will get involved again as soon as possible. After all, we're not planning to stay, are we?"

She didn't answer and he realised she was distracted by the little girl stretching in her sleep, flexing her small hands.

"You knew it would come to this," he reminded her gently.

She nodded. "At least she won't be far away." Jack knew she was trying to be strong to stop him worrying but she couldn't hide the break in her voice. "I so wish..." she whispered.

"Hush," Jack silenced her. "It hardly matters what we wish so there's no point dwelling on it."

She looked at him. "Wouldn't you want...?" her voice tailed off again. She sounded so full of doubt Jack felt he should reassure her she wasn't alone in her regret.

"More than you know," he admitted softly, then realised his error as shock widened her eyes and her hand flew to cover her mouth.

"Oh, John, I'm so sorry," she mouthed. "I'm so sorry to have taken that away from you." Instinctively, she hugged her arms around her chest in that defensive gesture he so feared.

"Don't," he ordered, more harshly than he had intended. "You haven't taken anything away from me. Sarah," he grabbed the top of her arms, almost shaking her. "How can you even think that? You, who have given me so much." The bleakness in her eyes spoke her disbelief. "Listen to me," raising his voice. "I am who I am because of you. If I could choose again knowing everything I know today, I would still choose you. Don't you understand?" he told her, desperate to break through her self-blame. "You complete me. I would be half the man I am today if I hadn't met you."

At last, her eyes focused and she saw him clearly. He saw the doubt still in her eyes, though, and seeking to drive it out, he pulled her into his arms. Emotionally overwrought, she responded to him with a passion and fervour that, for a split second, took him aback. Then his body, his emotions and his heart took over and he pulled her even tighter against him, cradling her face with one hand the better to kiss her deeper. He felt her tilt her hips in against him in that age-old yearning gesture and eased one arm around her waist, taking her weight on his arms and easing her yet closer.

He didn't hear the footsteps in the hall but Sarah did and she broke away from him, slightly breathless and more than a little flushed. She smoothed down her dress as Rachel came in to check on the child. She hesitated at the entrance until Sarah gave her permission to enter.

"We must make the most of her," Sarah warned her. "Mrs Williams and Millie shall be moving in with Mr Williams' family tomorrow."

The look that passed between Sarah and Rachel brought Jack up short. What he saw was mutual compassion and shared pain. He looked from one to the other but Sarah had moved away and Rachel schooled her features, hiding her emotions. The thought that was starting to form in his mind disappeared as Rachel turned towards the cot and Sarah, slipping her hand into his, led him from the room and down the corridor to their bedroom.

* * * * * * *

He knew he was being fanciful but the house felt empty when he returned home the following night. It was compounded by Annabel's announcement, as she took his hat, that Mrs Westerham had already retired, pleading a headache. He ordered a light supper on a tray and headed towards his sanctuary.

In a way, he was half-expecting, perhaps even half-hoping that he would find Rachel in the library.

"No," he ordered, gesturing that she should return to her seat as soon as she set to flee at his appearance. "You don't need to go," he assured her, reinforcing as she seemed to doubt. "I would welcome the company." Continued hesitation. "Please, Rachel. Stay for a short while."

Reluctantly, she saw down again but, he noticed, now on a chair at a distance from the one she knew he would choose.

"Tell me," he encouraged. "How was Mrs Westerham today?"

The room was not well lit, just a few table lamps, each positioned to cast light on an individual reader's pages, yet Jack could read so much in the expressions of her face, clear, expressive and open. He saw sadness, regret, sympathy, pain and loneliness chase one another across that face, so young and, surely, too painfully knowing for one so short in years.

"It was a difficult day," Rachel informed him. Tell me something I don't know, he thought. He contemplated for a moment that she wasn't going to continue and he might have to draw the details out of her when she observed, a tone of criticism in her voice, "Mrs Williams looked like the cat that got the cream, she was that pleased to be moving into the grand house."

"I expect she is," Jack concurred. "This place never suited her ideas of her station as Williams' wife."

"Strange the things that make people happy," she noted, almost to herself. "And the things they take for granted."

"Millie, you mean," Jack surmised.

"People are complicated creatures. It's always the one thing we want most that is most out of reach."

"Or stop wanting it the moment we have it?"

"I think it's worst," she contemplated, "when you've had what you want the most and then lost it. Better never to have known it than to have had it taken away without any prospect of return." He sensed she not only spoke from experience but that the wound was still open and raw. Nothing would induce him to pry, though.

"Did Mrs Westerham go over to the house to see them settled in?" he changed the subject.

She nodded. "Perhaps it wasn't the best idea," she considered, "but Mrs Westerham seems to care little for her own pain while she's worrying about everyone else."

"What she needs is people who will worry on her behalf," he said quietly.

"Yes," she agreed simply, turning over the book in her hand as a way to avoid looking at him.

"May I ask what you're reading?" he sought a neutral topic but the blush that coloured her cheeks said he had failed again.

"It's the second volume of a history," she admitted. "Of Cromwell's Commonwealth."

She had surprised him. "It's an era that interests you?" he projected.

The way she was turning the book over in her hands told him she feared to answer him truly. "It's politics that interests me," she forced herself to respond, her defensiveness making her tone almost aggressive. "I know most people think it's not appropriate for women…"

"We live in the age of the Pankhursts and Lady Astor," he interrupted. "I would hope we were beginning to move beyond such stereotyping. On either side," he added as a teasing rebuke.

She looked at him then and her clear grey eyes, curious, questioning, captivated him. This strange young woman was starting to intrigue him. Simultaneously defensive and yet vulnerable. Apparently educated or at least intellectually curious.

They were interrupted by Annabel arriving with his tray and Rachel used it as an opportunity to make her escape. As she approached the door, Jack called to her and she hesitated, turned back.

"When you've finished the book", he told her, "I'd be interested to know what you think."

She nodded once and slipped out of the room. Jack rose and, crossing to the bookcases, sought out the first volume in the series.

Chapter Thirteen

New York, summer 1922

*It was a strange time over those next few weeks in that echoing,
empty house. I felt isolated, disconnected almost from everything
that had been real, tangible.*

August hit and so did the heat. A thick, stultifying wall of heat
that made it impossible to move, to converse, even to think.

The others had decamped to the coast a month since along with
the rest of the chattering classes. Unaccustomed to New York
summers and naïvely thinking he could tolerate the heat, Jack had
stayed, unwilling to abandon his workers for whom the only relief
was the freedom to work in shirt sleeves and the inadequate breeze
of distractingly noisy electric fans around the office. By the middle
of August, though, he gave in to the combined sense of loneliness
with Sarah gone and his increasing inability to concentrate in the
humidity. He called ahead to the house and confirmed his travel
plans.

On the train north, he finally allowed himself to think about
Sarah again. If he was honest with himself, he had been avoiding
leaving New York for more than one reason. Work had been a
convenient excuse. Now, though, he had to face a reconciliation with
Sarah and he didn't know what to expect, given how they had parted.

During the late spring, he had grown more and more used to
coming home and finding himself alone in the house.

It didn't help that he was always busy at the office. Their
success was becoming self-fulfilling. The more money they made for
their investors, the more investors were finding their way to their
door, and the more he had to work on finding the right investments
to justify their faith in him and in the company the longer his hours
became.

Williams had returned to full-time work a month after they moved out of the Upper West Side property and handed it over, with Aunt Millie's blessing, to Sarah and Jack. Williams knew how to work a gentleman's hours, though, arriving at ten o'clock and frequently leaving before four in the afternoon or, if he was entertaining clients over lunch, not returning to the office at all. Jack was grateful that he could leave the wining-and-dining of investors to Williams and, though he occasionally resented Williams' more casual lifestyle, he could not bring himself to go against the Protestant work ethic so deeply engrained in his upbringing.

He longed for Sarah's calming company when he returned from these long and often fraught days at work. More often than not, though, she was over at the Williams' house, whether or not Charlotte was there. Her sister, the centre of attention and now living in the luxury to which she had long aspired, was recovering rapidly from her brief excursion on the dark side. Jack and Sarah would normally visit together once a week to dine with the Williamses – often the one opportunity he had to spend any amount of time with Sarah – and Jack noted Charlotte's rapid improvement in health and temperament. In no time, she was back to being the vivacious young woman he had known before her marriage, albeit with just the lightest shadows at the edges of her moods.

In the meantime, Sarah was becoming increasingly drawn and withdrawn. It wasn't a quick change but, watching Rachel help her finish dressing for dinner one night – strange how he felt so much more comfortable talking to Sarah while she was around than with Ellerby – he noticed how her dress hung more loosely and how the softness of her jaw had been lost to reveal the harder bone line beneath. Looking closer at her reflection in the mirror before which she sat, he saw now the shadows of grey beneath her eyes. He looked at Rachel, expecting to find confirmation there but she was focusing on fitting the diamond clip into her mistress' still long but noticeably less lustrous hair.

He felt guilty that he hadn't noticed it before now. Hell, he saw so little of her, surely he should have seen the change?

It made him realise how often he ended up eating at home alone. And how he talked to Rachel more than he did to Sarah.

With Sarah so often absent, it was perhaps inevitable that they should fall back on each other for easy company. The house could be eerily quiet in the evenings, isolated somehow from the noise and life of New York throbbing away not so far from their front door. Rachel was known for keeping to herself, not seeking to build any friendships either with the servants or beyond the walls of the house. Jack, tied up with work, had neither the time nor the energy to build new relationships.

In the dark, comfortable space that was the library, they read in companionable silence, they shared books, they talked while Jack ate his supper. He discovered in her a passionate and instinctive debater, if one who relied more on the strength of her convictions than the articulation of her arguments to carry her point of view.

It had taken a long time for them to get beyond anything but polite conversation. He soon learned that trying to draw her out with questions about her family met only a wall of silence so he chose neutral topics instead. Politics – at home and at both the federal and local level in America. Books – she adored Joyce, laughed out loud at Wodehouse but distrusted Fitzgerald as "too pleased with his own cleverness". Current affairs – she admitted a weakness for the gossip magazines that Annabel left lying around the servants' hall but was also an avaricious consumer of the daily newspapers and missed the press from home. Jack asked the Major to collect together a selection once a week and ship them across to her. From neutral topics and mutual interests, they gradually, eventually shared cautious disclosures about themselves. Before she ever told him about her past, he had identified for himself her educated, if not altogether refined, background.

The night after he noticed Sarah's weight loss, he tackled Rachel about it.

"What do you expect?" she challenged, putting down her book, her expression critical. "She's miserable."

Jack rose to push open the sash window, dispatching his tie as he returned to his seat. Outside, the noise of the city hummed distantly in the background but, inside, the house, as ever, was still, the servants either out – more often than not up at the clubs in Harlem – or hidden away in their basement or attic rooms. Sometimes, it felt to Jack, it was like living in a house of ghosts, almost invisible beings occasionally making their presence felt but, usually, maintaining the smooth running of the house while rarely being seen or heard unless summoned.

"I don't understand," he admitted, sinking wearily into his chair. It was almost ten o'clock but the night air was still thick with the day's residual heat. He was late back from work again, tied up with finalising the terms of another new investment, this time in a company supplying materials to the building industry whose extensive housing estates were mushrooming in the suburbs, now more people had cars to get to and from work in the city. "I thought she wanted to be here. I thought spending time with Charlotte and Millie would make her happy."

"She was happy," she marked the place in her book and put it on the side. "At first."

"Does she talk to you about it?"

"Doesn't she talk to you?"

He shook his head. "It's a difficult subject," he understated. "Help me understand."

She looked away. "I think instead of being a relief, being with Millie is becoming a burden. It reminds her of what she can't have and she's afraid to give Millie the love she would give her own child because of how Charlotte may react. That woman doesn't appreciate what she's got." Her tone, in speaking of Charlotte, was nearly

371

always heavily critical. "According to Sarah, she spends hardly any time with the child and there's no kind of bond between them."

"But Sarah can't be a replacement mother."

"The love she's free to give is a pale of shadow of what she's capable of giving and it isn't enough."

Jack stared out of the window for a long moment. "What do we do about it?" he muttered, half to himself.

She looked away from him so that he couldn't see her expression. She had a strange habit of not answering him when she didn't want to. She was never evasive, would never give him a half-answer, but she would sometimes refuse to answer or even to acknowledge a comment. She also had the most open and expressive face of anyone he had ever met. He could read her thoughts and emotions so clearly. It was why she hid from him now.

"Has Sarah said something?" he probed. "Does she want to leave? Would leaving Millie make it better for her or worse?" Still no answer. He thought he caught a slight shake of her head. "What aren't you telling me?" he demanded.

At that, she rose, collected her book and, ignoring his plea and apology, walked out of the room.

The silence closed in on him as she closed the door behind her. He sank back in his chair and stared out of the window again, turning over and over in his mind what they should do.

* * * * * * *

By the time he heard the front door open, it was past midnight and he was stiff and cold from sitting in the same position for so long. He rose and made his way to the hall where Sarah was shedding her hat and gloves. She didn't just look tired; she looked bone-weary and heart-sore. He should have seen it before now.

The smile she gave him was so weak it barely warranted the name and she made to walk past him without even speaking a word.

He gently put out one arm and she came to him, resting her cheek on his shoulder but with her face turned away from his. He kissed her hair softly.

"Come and sit with me," he encouraged softly.

"I'm so tired, John," he heard her whisper, not even having the energy to return his half-embrace.

"I know," he reassured. "I can see. And we need to talk about what we do about it."

She turned her face towards him and tilted her head up to meet his eyes. Her mouth was so close to his he was almost overwhelmed by the urge to kiss her pain away.

"Has Rachel said something?" a slight frown on her face and, strangely, the slightest sound of hope in her voice.

He shook his head slightly, mirroring her frown. "Nothing," he assured. "Should she have?"

She sought out his hand with hers and twined her fingers into his. "You're right," she asserted and there was suddenly a hint of energy and life in her voice. "We need to talk." Taking his hand, she led the way back to the library and closed the door on the rest of the house.

The air had, at last, turned cool and he crossed to push closed the window. As he did so, Sarah started turning out the lights until just the lamp by Jack's usual chair remained lit, casting it in a pool of light, a haven in the darkness. She motioned to him to sit and pulled one of the chairs slightly closer but still at a slight distance from his. He felt strangely at a disadvantage, his chair at an uncomfortable angle to hers so that he couldn't easily see her face, cast into shadow by the lamplight.

"Sarah," he started but she interrupted him.

"I'm worried about Rachel," she observed, staring at her hands, twisting her wedding ring round and round.

He was taken aback but he caught in her tone a sense that she was deflecting him. "This isn't about Rachel," he cautioned.

373

"But something odd happened today," she persisted. "A man came looking for her, asking after her with the kitchen staff. Thankfully, she was out running errands for me so they sent him away."

"It must be a friend," Jack proposed, wondering why they were talking of this.

Sarah looked at him. "That's just it, she doesn't have any friends."

"Sarah," he wasn't going to let her get them off track, "it's not her I'm worried about. It's you."

He reached out as if to take her hand but she evaded him, drawing her clasped hands back ever so slightly. It could have been a negligent movement as if she had missed his intention but he didn't think so. She had stopped looking at him too. He contemplated her carefully. "Sarah," he said gently, "I know you're not going to like what I have to say but I have to say it. Please remember that I love you and that I want to do what's best for you." He took a breath, trying to watch her face closely but struggling to see her expression in the darkness. "I think you need to spend some time away. From Charlotte...and from Millie."

The slightest nod and, perhaps, even relief on her face. Where was the anger? The denial?

"You're right," she agreed, standing up and walking across to the bookshelf, putting, he felt, distance between them. "I came to the same conclusion myself recently." Jack stood but he didn't move towards her. "Do you think I can't see what this is doing to me, John?" She ran her hand across the spines of the books, distracted. "I can barely sleep at night. I'm so distracted I find it almost impossible to hold an adult conversation." Her words were emotional but her voice was unnervingly calm. When she hugged her arms to herself, Jack suddenly realised how much she was controlling her emotions and reactions. How much had she been hiding this away? And for how long? "I see Charlotte and how happy she is," she

374

observed. "And part of me could hate her for it. She has everything she wants. The one thing I want, she has and it means nothing to her." She stared in silence for a long moment across the room, unseeing. "I never expected to feel this way." It seemed she was speaking as much to herself as to him. "My whole life, I've been independent and capable. When Charlotte and Rose were the flighty, emotional ones, I was always the reliable, logical one. Everything I wanted to do, I attained. I've always worked hard but it's never been a struggle. But this..." She turned her face towards him and he saw the lamplight catch a tear on her cheek. "I have never felt so lost," she told him. "Like I no longer knew who I was."

He started to move towards her but stopped immediately when she fell back a step, one hand extended to ward him off. "Please, John, stay where you are. There's something I need to say and I don't think I'll manage it if you are too close." She looked at him directly, challenging almost, and brushed away the tear, an unwelcome sign of the emotions she was forcing under control. "I've been unhappy for a long time. It was knowing there was no solution, no way out. It's like a permanent ache inside me. A hollow, empty feeling that gets bigger and deeper every day. When I admitted that to myself, being with Millie just became a burden. But how could I walk away? How could I abandon the child to the attentions of a disinterested nanny and a detached mother?" She was voicing the questions to herself.

"Why have you not told me this before?" he pressed, his heart aching for her pain and guilty that she had shouldered this burden alone.

She shrugged and it was a strangely dismissive gesture. "There was no point before. Telling you wouldn't have made any difference to how I was feeling and it would only have made both of us miserable."

"Why, then, are you telling me now?"

She turned away, back towards the bookcases and walked slowly up and down a short stretch of carpet, still hugging her arms to herself. "What made it pointless was knowing there was no solution, no way out. I tried to pretend it didn't matter to me. Or to you," with the slightest nod in his direction. "But there came a point when I couldn't lie to myself any more. It matters more than anything and I know I shall never be happy the ways things are. I know," sensing and forestalling his interruption, "you'll say there's nothing we can do about it. And that's what I thought for the longest time. It was the point at which I gave up that I finally saw a way through." There was such hope in her voice suddenly, such a counterpoint to the emotional dullness of her words before.

"What way, Sarah? Adoption?" Jack proposed, his voice rough. The deep emotions that she was suppressing, that she was hiding from her voice were tearing at his heart. His throat was choked, thick with compassion and shared pain. He had never realised before how much her emotional control was undermining his own, how his instinct to prevent her shutting him out was making him vulnerable. It was through showing his emotions that he broke through her protective walls but it had left him defenceless.

She shook her head, finally looking at him again. "It's not just about any child," she told him. Her voice was so low that he instinctively took a step towards her to catch her words. "I know that from Millie," she attested. "I love her, John, but I'm not allowed to love her properly. I need a child of my own. Our child, John. Your child."

His quick mind was already leaping to what she was thinking but every fibre in his being, every essence of his soul rebelled against it. "I don't understand," he lied. "We can't have a child. We already know that."

"I can't, John," she caveated. "I can't have a child," with just the slightest break in her voice. "But you can." He held her gaze and was shocked to see the brightness that was suddenly lighting up her face. The hope that was breaking down her walls. It was seductive and destructive. He couldn't speak. "You could have a child, John," she urged, taking a step towards him now. "Our child."

"You can't ask this of me," he denied, cold fingers closing around his heart and an empty, sickening feeling in his gut. She took another step closer and he could see the hope turn to triumph in her eyes. "You can't be serious in this," he tried.

She stepped in front of him and placed her hand on his cheek.

Too late, he realised the trick she had played on him. He had thought he was breaking down her emotional walls but she had destroyed his instead and her hidden walls, unscalable, indestructible, were in place around her resolution.

"I won't do it," he challenged, his voice hard. "I won't break my vows to you. I won't sleep with another woman so that we…" his voice caught, "so that you," he emphasised carefully, "can have a child."

"You've slept with other women before," she murmured pointedly.

He brought his face close to hers. "But I wasn't in love with you at the time," he reminded her forcefully.

For a flash of a second, he looked into her eyes and caught sight of the emotions she had walled away, the black despair that had held her in its grip for months – years? – now. He saw how she had pretended for him, for all them. The pain she had hidden behind a mask of normality. The soul-deep anguish she had buried inside her, hoping desperately it would diminish over time yet, all the while, feeding it against her will almost with her desperate, irrepressible desire. This was not something she could control and it had consumed her. He was defenceless in the face of her pain and he knew she could see it in him.

"Don't ask this of me, Sarah," he pleaded, taking her face in his hands. She almost flinched as his skin came into contact with hers and he felt a stab of hope that he might yet break her resolution. "I

377

love you, my darling," kissing her desperately. "I love you. You don't know what you're asking. You can't ask me to do this. I will do anything for you," interspersing his words with kisses, on her mouth, her cheeks, her forehead, her neck, "I will go to the ends of the earth for you. Just don't ask this of me." He looked directly in her eyes, a warning in his. "It will change everything."

Was that doubt? He no longer trusted his instincts but he would push any advantage he might have and when her body betrayed her and reacted to his touch, he pulled her hard against him and fixed his mouth on hers, tormenting her. "Come to bed," he murmured, teasing the corner of her mouth. She nodded her acquiescence, breathing hard, and, taking her hand, he led her from the room.

* * * * * * *

He woke to a new reality and the whole world took on a surreal hue.

They had made love, passionately, desperately almost at first, as if validating that their love was stronger than any test they could throw at it. But it was also the clash of two different wills, both trying to impose on the other, both trying to resist.

Later, they made love slowly, tenderly, almost despairingly on his part. He felt as if the very foundations of his love, his marriage, which he had considered to be built on solid bedrock, had suddenly been found sitting on shifting sands.

One look that morning told him nothing had changed. Her determination was fixed, her decision made. Worse, she was leaving that day with the Williamses for the summer and he sensed the decision would become ever more concrete with each day's separation that passed between them. Dressed for work and unable to stomach breakfast, he readied himself to leave early, trying to find a way to make it a normal farewell.

378

She was in her dressing room, packing the last of her belongings for the extended vacation. She handed a pile of dresses to Rachel as Jack entered, meeting his eyes with a clear, calm look and a gentle smile. Standing there in his formal suit while she was still in her dressing gown made him feel awkward, overly formal.

"I have to go," he informed her, bending to give her a farewell kiss. He brushed the back of his hand over her cheek. "Let me know that you've arrived safely," he asked.

She smiled her agreement. The passion of last night had gone but, somehow, so had the tenderness. Her kiss was automatic, almost, her smile a little distant. "We'll see you in a month or so." It was a dismissal.

He turned but the thought that was tearing at him made him turn back. He looked into her eyes and deliberately held her gaze. "This isn't a thought of the moment," he conjectured and saw the confirmation in her eyes. He nodded. "Then, who?"

Her eyes slid away from his and took in Rachel, carefully folding clothes and packing them in the trunk.

Jack's heart stopped. He looked hard at his wife for a long moment, wishing she could read in his eyes how violently his soul fought against this. She refused to look at him. Without another word, he turned and crossed to the door. As he left the room, his movement caught Rachel's attention and she involuntarily looked across at him. Their eyes met and his heart thumped.

He was lost.

* * * * * * *

The idea tormented him. Not just because he feared what it would do to their marriage, though that was the thought uppermost in his mind, but also, however much he tried to hide the thought from himself, because he had grown close to Rachel in those months and could all too easily imagine himself complying with what Sarah asked of him. Of them.

* * * * * * *

He had never seen anything like it. And, in his view, he had lived well for the last couple of years. The house at Newport, rented for the summer, was an exquisite colonial-style mansion; long, white-painted and multi-windowed, it glittered in the late afternoon sunlight, set against a perfect backdrop of a brilliant blue sky and that crystal-clear light that seems reserved for coastal locations. Everything about this property was exquisitely but extravagantly rendered. From the unnecessarily long approach road that by its very length shouted a denial at anyone but welcome guests, planted all the way with rhododendrons and azaleas that would be spectacular in spring and, in this season, enhanced with an opulent display of sunburst-coloured flowers, most of which Jack had never seen before in his life. To the almost-floor-to-ceiling windows and French doors that adorned the façade of the house; Georgian in style but self-evidently never tortured by the strictures of a window tax, they reflected the light back onto the approaching visitor, a diamond-like display that dazzled the eyes. To the beautifully proportioned colonnaded veranda that banded the lower floor of the house; timber-built but painted the same white as the house, it reflected back the brilliance of the sun to the sky so that the house almost shone in the sparkling light. It welcomed, brightened and promised a better way of life for however short a period a man might enjoy its pleasures.

The property, Jack concluded, of someone who knew something about a life well lived.

As he paid off the taxi and a servant appeared to collect his luggage, Jack could hear the sounds of life from the back of the house, laughter, chatter and the clinking of glassware. He followed the footman into the house to find an interior décor intended to

380

reinforce the impressions gained upon arrival. The glass front doors opened onto a wide, full-height hallway, light ash floorboards, white-painted walls and a crystal chandelier drawing the eye up and up, round the wide circular staircase that bound the walls to a glass rotunda at the apex, white-metalled like a conservatory and exposing the indoors as well to that flawless azure sky.

He followed the sounds of people through a doorway at the back of the hall and into a vast, almost empty room, a well-used ballroom to guess by the scuffed floor and the ranks of chairs pushed back against the walls, single file, disappointingly, beneath portraits of long-dead ancestors, most of whom surely belonged in an English castle, not this pantheon to an American summer.

All along the far wall French doors stood open, billowed about by voile drapes. The warm breeze rose up from the estuary, where two young children were dashing around in the wind, and eased over the long lawns, which must take an army of gardeners to keep them so pristine. It was just strong enough to flap the scalloped edges of the large parasols dotted across the crest of the lawn where it rose up to meet the house. It teased the fine material of the ladies' dresses, defining more clearly their elegant contours where they relaxed in deck chairs or lazed on picnic blankets, propped up on an elbow, the better to look down on the men lying prostrate near them, hands behind their heads, legs comfortably crossed at the ankle. By the time it reached Jack, this zephyr ruffling his hair carried the salt tang of the sea, the sweet smell of roses, the sharp freshness of mint from the cocktails and the underlying pungency of bootleg gin. He breathed deeply and felt some of the tension of the last several weeks ease out of him.

As he stepped out onto the veranda and down the steps to the lawn, he had already noted Sarah's absence among the dozen or so bodies laid out to bask in the soft afternoon sun.

A shout of his name and he saw Williams rise up from one of the blankets, one hand raised in greeting. "Westerham!" holding out his great paw to shake Jack's. "Thank God you've come. Now at last, Peter," addressing one of the crowd, "we'll get a decent conversation! I've discovered," he confided in Jack, "there is such a thing as too much of a good thing when it comes to Hollywood gossip and women's prattle." The fact that he made no effort to lower his voice told Jack this was a running joke among the party.

"Darling," crooned the woman who had been sitting next to Williams on the rug and who was now propping herself up to shade her eyes from the sun and take in the new visitor. "When one is tired of Hollywood, one is tired of life." She was wearing too much make up and was clearly attempting a flirtatious pout at Williams who, thankfully, laughed at her.

"Elise Thoreau," Williams introduced her. "Our resident Hollywood starlet. Apparently every party must have one," he observed drily. "And that," pointing to the opposite end of group where an older man was engaged in intent conversation with a young woman easily half his age, who glanced nervously at him from time to time with shyly adoring eyes, "is her husband, Walter Vickers. The young lady is Daisy, daughter to our neighbours," pointing them out, "Peter and Thelma Heydon. And those are Peter's middle two playing down by the river." The bountiful Thelma also had a young babe in a cradle beside her, gently rocking it. "Peter works for the Bank of Morgan. Next to them, that's Gilbert Parker, Elise's agent, and Lauchlin Troeller and his fiancée Mabel, who are staying with the Heydons. Isabella and Wendell, of course, you know."

Jack acknowledged them all and received some friendly greetings in return. He shook Wendell's hand, sympathising with the man who was looking distinctly uncomfortable in this, to him, louche company, still dressed for New York instead of New York society on vacation.

"Have a drink," Williams encouraged, a broad sweep of his arm taking in the hovering footman. Jack spurned the noxious-looking cocktails on offer but gladly accepted a chilled beer.

382

"Do sit down, Jack," Charlotte ordered proprietorially, raising her arm to shield her eyes from the sun, ostentatiously Jack thought as she was already sitting directly beneath one of the wide parasols and had a wide-brimmed hat casting a shadow over her face. She had obviously concluded that this pose showed her healthy curves to good effect. Because Jack had to admit she was looking extraordinarily well, her skin glowing with a gentle tan, her hair cut short and softly framing her face. She was also, he noted, eschewing the cocktails on offer. "And do take that tie off," she teased. "You can leave that stuffed-shirt look in New York. You're on holiday now."

In the absence of her parents-in-law, she was behaving as if she owned the place, showing off in front of her guests.

"Actually," he declined, "I think I'll go and find Sarah first."

"Sarah?" Charlotte looked around with surprise, evidently not having noted her sister's absence for herself. "Oh, she'll be indoors somewhere," she concluded easily, waving her hand in casual dismissal of the subject. "Millie will be fussing or want feeding or something. They'll be back soon enough."

Jack exchanged a look with Williams who, thankfully, had the consideration to call forward a servant to direct him towards the rooms allocated to Sarah.

Climbing the stairs, he caught the murmur of women's voices and a sudden burst of soft laughter. The door to their rooms was ajar and he stood in the doorway for a moment, watching the two of them together. They were seated on a wide window seat, their backs turned towards the party going on below. Their heads were bent together over a magazine, the clothes Rachel had been folding temporarily discarded, two glasses of what looked like lemonade on the seat beside them, Sarah's shawl discarded on the bed. With their dark hair and their familiar posture betraying how comfortable they were with each other, they looked like sisters, sharing secret amusements, the

383

more so for Sarah's recent weight loss giving her a figure that more closely resembled Rachel's smaller frame.

If he had been concerned about Sarah's health before she left, he was horrified now. Undoubtedly her deterioration was the more marked for its contrast with Charlotte, the picture of health again and, if Jack was reading the signs better this time, surely on the verge of announcing another pregnancy. It had taken an inordinate amount of determination not to leave with Sarah the second the family exodus began. He cursed himself for his obstinacy, fearful that this could now be doing real damage to her long-term health.

The way things had been left – inconclusive but, he suspected, with Sarah firmly grasping the hope she had created for herself – he had expected, wished, that her health might improve. That the idea would have given her enough to hold onto that she might cope with the situation with Charlotte and Millie.

Because he was desperate still to talk her out of the idea and he didn't know how to deny her when she was in this state. In the cold light of day, the idea, against which every part of his heart and soul had revolted, seemed all the more absurd. How she thought she could ask it of him – of her – he didn't know. It was as if everything normal and true had been distorted in her mind, warped out of all proportion by her obsession. How did she even think they could get away with it? Surely she didn't think she would be truthful about it with friends and family? How, then, did she think were they to conceal it? He cut off that train of thought. Every time his methodical mind had turned to the practicalities over the last month, he stopped his thoughts, unable to accept the concept, let alone the implementation. In all its aspects.

Sarah looked up and saw him standing in the doorway. For a second, her face lit up with pleasure but, before he could even greet her, she seemed to shut down, her face becoming a mask of calm neutrality. She turned to Rachel – Jack kept his eyes on Sarah, unable to look Rachel in the face – and muttered a word, at which Rachel rose, collected the clothes and disappeared through a connecting door into another room. Jack heard the door close.

Sarah rose and approached him. He leant forward to kiss her but she turned her head slightly, offering her cheek instead. Stunned, he kissed her cheek, unconsciously holding her shoulder and rubbing his thumb over it. She stepped back from him, not meeting his gaze.

"How was your journey?" She turned her back, collecting together the books and magazines scattered on the window seat and tidying them in a pile.

"Fine, thank you." He couldn't believe he was giving into this false conversation, so unnatural to them, but he was at a loss how to respond, knowing that he wanted to destroy the one hope she was holding onto. "How are you?" He said it with feeling, trying to convey the emotion she seemed unwilling to accept from him.

She gave him a sharp look and, for a moment, he thought he saw a flash of the old Sarah. "As you see," she responded, slightly acerbic.

Some emotion, even negative, was better than none and he took hope from it. "Are you angry with me?" he probed.

"Why?" she asked, not looking at him again, continuing to straighten the already immaculate sitting room. "Do I have reason to be?"

What was this? It was like she was trying to shut him out. From the very beginning, it had felt like they were on the same side, shared opinions, shared values, shared emotions. He had seen Sarah determined, influential, perhaps even manipulative, but he had always been behind her, not on the receiving end.

He tried a different tack. "Charlotte thought you were with Millie."

"She's sleeping."

"And you don't want to be with the rest of the group out in the sunshine?"

She stopped her tidying at that and stared out of the window, folding her arms over the shawl she had picked up from the bed. He caught a change in her expression and, remembering the scene below, thought she was watching the two Heydon children run around the lawn. She had, he sensed, been isolating herself from normality, from everything that would give her back a sense of proportion. Whether to feed her obsession better without the constraint of normal values and emotions, or whether to protect herself against the daily reinforcement of her lack of that which she most desired, he didn't know. Either way, she was probably in the worst place he could have imagined for her.

"Sarah," he crossed the room to stand behind her and slid an arm around her waist, "talk to me."

Her instinct, for a moment, was to give into his touch and he felt her weight briefly against his chest as she leaned into him, but the next second she was in control of herself again, drawing herself upright, hugging the shawl closer to her chest, turning to face him.

"There's only one thing we need to talk about, John," she asserted, her face frighteningly calm. "When you're ready to discuss it, then we can talk. Now, I need to check on Millie before dinner. Your dressing room is through there," with a nod. "Your cases have already been brought up." She left the room.

"Sarah!" Jack felt impotent anger well up inside him. He gritted his teeth hard and closed his eyes, propping himself up with one hand against the window embrasure and resting his forehead against his hand. He fought the anger, breathing hard, until the red rage that threatened to overwhelm him started to subside.

"She's dealing with it the only way she can."

He opened his eyes to see Rachel standing only a few feet from him, the folded shawl draped over her arm in a gesture strangely reminiscent of Sarah's posture only moments before.

"How can you defend her?" he challenged, the residual anger coming out in his voice.

He saw her eyes harden, ready to match his anger with her own. "How can you look at her like this and not want to do everything in your power to change it?" she fought back. "If you really love her, it's such a simple solution."

"You can't be serious?" he argued. "Are you really entertaining this ridiculous notion of hers?" A thought flashed through his mind. "Have you been encouraging her in it?" Unconsciously, he took a step towards her, threatening almost.

She stepped forward to meet his threat. "I owe her everything for what she has done for me. I am alive and well because of her." He saw passion flare in her eyes. "I would die for her."

"Don't you realise that you could?" he fought. "How many women still die in childbirth?"

"Don't try to tell me about childbirth," she disdained. "Believe me, that's one area I know much more about than you." She stopped, her face draining of colour. Evidently, she had disclosed in her anger more than she had intended but she covered quickly and returned on the attack. "But this is about Sarah. Have you looked at her? Really looked at her? If this carries on much longer, I can't bear to think what might happen to her." There was real anguish in her voice and it made the anger drain out of Jack in an instant.

"At least there we're of one accord," his voice calmer. "We both love her, I know," he acknowledged, running his hand through his hair with a sigh. He sank onto the window seat and looked up at her. "And you're good for her, I can see that. You seem to be the only friend she has around her." He saw some of the fight go out of her but she retained her defensive posture, hands on hips. Even with him sitting, her head barely topped his. In her passion and anger, it was so easy to forget what a tiny thing she was. With her hair tied back from her forehead, it emphasised her bone structure, her slim neck and shoulders, her carved cheekbones, the curve of her jawbone. And those disturbing, penetrating, passion-filled eyes. He

387

frowned. "You are seriously considering what she's suggesting?" he asked, bemused.

"No, I'm not considering it," she contradicted. "I've already told her I would do anything that would make her happy." Jack shook his head, unable to keep looking at her. "Perhaps," she challenged, "you should ask yourself why you're not willing to do the same." Then she, too, turned and left.

* * * * * * *

He sat there for a long time just watching the party below, watching Mrs Heydon with her children, seeing how frequently they ran to her for attention before diving back into their game, how the elder daughter looked across to her mother for reassurance, how amusement, exasperation, annoyance, even, crossed the mother's face but always, always, underlined with a total, unquestioning, undemanding love.

He realised how much Sarah had been playing that role for her sisters for years and that, now, that role had been taken away from her, both sisters rejecting her maternal ways, forging their own paths without her. Had that vacuum naturally been filled, none of this would have mattered. Instead, it had become all-consuming.

When he finally heard the sounds of Sarah's return, he crossed to his dressing room to prepare for dinner. It was as he was buttoning the waistcoat of his dinner suit that he realised Sarah wasn't the only one losing weight.

He was waiting for her in the sitting room when she emerged. Even like this, she looked beautiful to him, her hair dressed on top of her head, a pale blue dress, fitted to her new shape, showing off a narrow waist and the flat-chested style of the season. His instinct was to approach her and to take her in his arms but the eyes she lifted to his were still defiant, daring, so he only offered her his arm, which, after a moment's hesitation, she accepted.

"I think we should talk later," he suggested. "After dinner."

She nodded her agreement and they descended the wide circular staircase, their footsteps muffled by the extravagantly impractical thick cream carpet, to find the rest of the party on the terrace. Mr and Mrs Williams had joined them after a day in Newport and were looking as tanned and content as their son and daughter-in-law. Whatever they had once thought of Charlotte, it seemed all had been forgiven.

"Westerham," Mr Williams Senior greeted Jack warmly, shaking his hand and then kissing Sarah's cheek. "We were beginning to think you would miss the entire summer."

"It's a shame you couldn't make it yesterday," his wife supported him. "You missed the ball. The entire neighbourhood came. Even one of the Vanderbilts made a brief appearance."

"You didn't tell me about the ball," Jack intimated to Sarah but she shook her head.

"I wasn't feeling well so I retired early."

"I'm astonished you could rest at all with the amount of noise we were generating," Susanna Williams remarked. "Such a shame you didn't feel up to it. Still, it looks like a bit of rest has put some colour in your cheeks at last," she observed sympathetically, patting Sarah's arm. "Perhaps now Mr Westerham has arrived, you might feel better."

Sarah smiled her thanks for her concern and, slipping her arm out of Jack's, headed towards where Charlotte was sitting, surrounded by a number of her guests. Jack made to follow her but was forestalled by Mr Williams. "As it happens, I'm glad you're here, Westerham. Fred and I have been talking to Mr Heydon and there's an investment opportunity we want to take up. Why don't you come through to the library?"

With a click of his fingers, he attracted his son's attention and, together, they wandered back through the ballroom to as ornate and grandiose a library as Jack had ever seen, towering stacks of shelves ranged all the way around the walls and jutting into the room in places, creating private alcoves still large enough for half-a-dozen people to sit together. A footman appeared as they entered and Williams Senior ordered whiskies for all of them. Jack, who had long since grown beyond his surprise at the freedom with which New York society was able to procure liquor and the comfort with which it was consumed in relatively public spaces, readily accepted a large measure.

Never one to beat about the bush, Williams Senior signalled that they should take a seat in one of the alcoves, perching himself on the edge of the window seat to gain the height advantage, and got to the point.

"Heydon says the Bank of Morgan is about to start investing in Germany again," he opened, taking a large slug of his drink. "He says that since the reparations were reassessed, there's been a boom in the industries supporting the redevelopment and the reparations."

"Such as?"

"Coal, steel, agriculture, as well as house-building and general construction."

"They're looking for investors, Jack," Williams picked up his father's theme. "There's no money in Germany to put into these projects, which is why they've come looking to Wall Street for funding."

"Of course there's no money," Jack observed drily. "The rest of Europe is on its knees and anything the Allies make gets paid back to you guys to pay off the war loans."

"It's a sound investment," the senior Williams continued, ignoring Jack's jibe. "Put money into bricks and mortar, something tangible. Isn't that your usual argument, Westerham?" Jack was happy to concede the point. "So we'll look at putting money in through the joint venture?"

Jack frowned. "If this is such a nice opportunity, why are you even sharing it with us?" he questioned. "Why aren't you investing directly?"

There was a look exchanged between the two men. The older one took the lead. "There's been less new money coming into the bank of late," he admitted. "We don't have the level of reserves we'd like right now but we don't want to miss the opportunity. In part," he defended, "it's because I've been pushing so much of the new money in your direction. We've been generating some good returns through the venture and some customers are more interested in what we can deliver there."

Jack sat back, contemplating the two men. Something about their body language was worrying him, though he couldn't quite say what. "You do see the irony in all this, don't you?" he tested. Father and son gave him identical frowns. "In order for more capital to come into the US, we have to invest capital into Germany so she can pay her reparations, so Britain and France can repay their war loans."

"What's your point?" Freddie challenged him.

"It's hardly the happiest of virtuous circles, is it?" Jack suggested.

"Does it matter as long as we can make money out of it?"

That short-termist view had never had much appeal for Jack. His naturally cautious nature worried about the downside more than the potential for the upside. He knew, instinctively, what so many of his peers were happy to ignore, that with good potential growth came just as much risk of failure. "The same rules apply," he insisted. "Debt first, equity investments only in companies looking to borrow from us and I will vet every investment opportunity as usual."

"Be serious, Jack," Freddie argued. "You can hardly manage the volume of work we currently have coming across our desks. How do you propose to take on even more?"

"He's right, lad." Taking on the elder statesman role, Williams Senior backed up his son. "We'll be short-changing our investors if we're not expanding our capacity as fast as we're taking on their capital. And we wouldn't want to be taking you away from your family," was there a strange inflection in his voice as he said the word? "more than we have done already."

Jack watched Williams for a second or two through narrowed eyes; the older man didn't hold his gaze. That worried him all the more but he recognised the sense of what they were saying.

"I'll hand-pick a small group of researchers to assess the opportunities, then, around an agreed group of criteria," he conceded. "Will that suffice for you?"

Freddie looked about to jump in but his father got there ahead of him. "Fine," he concurred. "But I want Freddie in that group too."

Jack happily gave in on that point. Nothing Freddie assessed would be getting through to approval without him scouring it himself anyway. "I'll need to run it past the partners," he caveated, standing to leave.

"They're meeting next Tuesday, aren't they?" Jack reached out for his glass and downed the remaining whisky, using the action to cover his surprise at Williams' familiarity with the schedule of the Richmond Bank partners. "Perhaps you could get a proposal to them before then?"

Jack met Williams' steady gaze. "Perhaps."

Williams nodded, accepting the progress he had made. "Then let's join the ladies, shall we? They'll be serving dinner shortly."

The two men started to leave the room, walking side by side when they were called back by Williams Junior. "Wait!" he demanded. "We're not done. I wanted to discuss putting some of the bank's money into the stock markets."

Jack shook his head vigorously. "Absolutely not, Freddie," he refused bluntly. "The partners' position on that is clear and immutable."

He sensed Williams Senior tense next to him and almost missed the look of anger that he shot at his son.

"But the partners didn't want to take equity stakes in the lending companies either," Freddie argued, "and you talked them round on that."

"Not on this, Freddie," Jack reiterated.

"Drop it, Fred," Williams Senior ordered his son, freezing his next objection with a glare.

Freddie shrugged off the rejection. "Perhaps Heydon will convince you over dinner," he suggested with conspiratorial grin.

*　*　*　*　*　*　*

With his mind so preoccupied with concerns about Sarah, Jack expected dinner to drag but, in the end, the business debate at his end of the table kept him entertained and even drew Sarah out of her silent introspection for a while.

Charlotte had evidently decided to keep all the entertaining people to herself, convincing Susanna to surround her end of the table with Elise Thoreau, her husband and her agent, together with the young couple staying with the Heydons and Daisy Heydon, who was of an age with the girl, Mabel.

At the far end, presided over by Frederick Williams Senior, sat the unfortunate Thelma Heydon, who spent the entire meal clearly wishing she could join in the gossip and conjecture happening at the other end, together with her husband, Sarah, Jack and Freddie.

As Freddie had intimated, Heydon was a merciless advocate for stock market investments, his own specialism at the bank. To look at him, Jack couldn't have imagined a less likely champion of the level of risk he was proposing for their capital. A more dour and conservative demeanour you were unlikely to find outside a funeral parlour.

Heydon had launched his case at Freddie's invitation even before the first course had been cleared and Jack endured an almost

393

ten-minute diatribe from his neighbour before he could get a single counter-point across.

"The stock market is for those who missed the investment opportunity in the first place," Jack finally countered. "We're making plenty of money out of that so why would we want to change the risk profile now?"

"If you're happy with that 'safe as houses' attitude, that's fine," Heydon criticised, "but where else are you going to make the kind of returns you can make in stocks? The Dow saw an 82% increase in two years after the war."

"Yes," Jack countered, "and it almost halved in the following eighteen months, ending up at a level below where it started in 1918."

"We're already back at 100 points in just the last few months," Heydon insisted, "and it's only going one way in the current economy."

"He's right," Williams pursued. "US industry is booming now we've come out of the recession and there are plenty of opportunities out there that we've already missed. The only way to get on the back of those is to buy their stock."

"I'd hardly describe it as booming," Jack disagreed. "A third of this country is still reliant on agriculture for its income. The bottom has fallen out of the cotton market, commodities are crashing and it looks like it's going to be another bumper harvest this year."

"What does agriculture matter when we've got the consumer?" Williams' enthusiasm was almost infectious. "Everyone wants a radio, a vacuum cleaner, a Ford, their own house. And they're all prepared to borrow to get it."

"Don't tell me," Jack joked, "we're going into private lending next."

"I think you can safely leave that side of things to me," Williams Senior inserted himself smoothly into the debate, which he otherwise seemed happy to let wash around him.

"Oil is where you should be putting your money." Heydon suggested. "They control every aspect now from production to petrol stations. If ever there was a licence to print money."

"You have to admit he has a point there," Sarah's interjection surprised Jack and he looked across at her. She shrugged casually. "I'm not a fan of the stock market either but look at the yields they're generating now. All the manufacturing companies need the oil as well."

"The partners have been very clear on where they want to invest," Jack responded.

"The partners have been known to be wrong in the past," she countered. To Jack, this was a revelation. He had never heard her voice any opinion contrary to her father's before.

"What about Germany?" he tested. "Would the partners go for putting money into the rejuvenation efforts?"

Sarah played with the stem of her glass, considering. Heydon was about to leap in but a slight hand movement from Williams Senior forestalled him. "I'm afraid there your issue is not economics but jingoism," she observed, meeting the gaze of each of them in turn. "There are few who were unaffected, personally, by the war. It will be a test to see who can put the interests of finance above their affections for their family." She deliberately held Jack's gaze.

"We'll have to pick each of them off," Williams proposed. "Work out how to tackle their concerns individually. Collectively, they'll be too naturally negative."

Jack had stopped listening. Was that what she thought? That he was putting the business ahead of her? That was entirely unreasonable. After all, which of them was it who was waiting for the other to return home night after night?

But what if she had been avoiding returning to an empty house? A quiet voice started to undermine his assurance. What if, having left Millie each night, she couldn't face being alone? He had never stopped to think about being there early in the evening for her, had he?

He sat back in his chair, his appetite gone, and watched his wife on the opposite side of the table. Sparked into life by her feeling for the subject, there was colour in her cheeks again and a light in her eyes. She became animated, leaning into the table to be heard more clearly, gesticulating carefully to emphasise a point. She had all three men, and even Mrs Heydon, focusing their attention on her, each talking over the other to counter or to reinforce the point she had made. A sharp witticism, delivered with a flourish of her hand, had both Williams men burst out laughing at a blushing Mr Heydon, whose wife patted his hand consolingly, a secret smile curving one side of her mouth.

Around the table, there was no one to compare with her. He doubted he had ever met another woman who could match him as she did. She was his partner in so many ways, intellectually, in business, in compassion, in love.

He wondered if she even knew, had even contemplated, how that might change if he gave into what she proposed. He hoped so. She was a far-thinking woman, not one to be blinkered by the here and now, but was she thinking as clearly on this?

Heydon, in spite of Sarah's teasing comment, had been warming to his subject. "And property," he insisted. "The Florida market is the place to be. Holiday homes and retirement homes in the sun. Disposable income, that's what it's all about. Meeting the needs of the consumer. Soon, everyone will have more money to spend than they've ever had before. And anyone who can give them the things they want, instead of the things they need, is going to make a packet."

* * * * * * *

396

"It's a while since I heard you show an interest in the business," Jack observed as they slowly climbed the stairs.

"It's a while since you were around long enough to hear what I have to say," she countered, without the slightest hint of amusement or teasing in her voice to alleviate Jack's instinctive concern.

"I was trying to say," forcibly staying calm, "how nice it was to hear you engaged in the debate. It feels as if little has been of interest to you of late other than…" He stopped, unwilling to put into words the thoughts in his head.

She stopped at their door, her hand on the doorknob, and looked up at him. "Other than my obsession?" she finished for him. "Is that the right word, John?" she challenged. He didn't argue. Only inches apart, he suddenly caught the scent of her perfume and memories of intimacy overwhelmed him. She must have seen the passion flare in his eyes because, for a second, he could see an equivalent reaction in her. "There's such a simple solution to all of this, John," she told him, her calm tone belying the fact that her breathing was coming slightly faster. "It would put everything right and we could go back to what we had before." Her gaze flicked from his eyes to his mouth and back again, deliberately teasing him with their closeness but still not reaching out to him.

"Open the door, Sarah," he ordered quietly. This was not a discussion he wanted to have in an open hallway.

In the privacy of their room, he leaned back against the door, hearing it click shut and then locking it. The room was in darkness, the lamps unlit and the doors to the adjoining rooms all closed but the curtains undrawn to benefit from the cool of the evening air. In the clear sky, an almost full moon cast a pale glow over the night.

Sarah stood only a couple of feet away, her face turned towards the window, lit by the moonlight. He pushed himself away from the door and came to stand before her, closing the distance between them but not reaching out to her.

397

"Tell me," she ordered, trying to meet his gaze steadily but betraying her own nervousness with the rapid beat of her pulse in her throat and the shallowness of her breathing.

He so wanted to touch her, to make a physical connection at the same time. He was used to the reassurance of her touch, her embrace in their most intimate and personal conversations. This way, she was making him as vulnerable and defenceless as possible, trying to force his acquiescence. Not that it was needed.

"I'm not saying 'no'," he told her, holding her dark gaze.

Triumph flared in her eyes but wariness too. "But?"

"But," he caveated, his voice gentle but firm, "you are my priority. Being here, like this, is making you ill and I can't stand it any more. Sarah, we have to get you out of here. Only when you're well again will I even contemplate what you suggest."

"That's not enough for me," she appealed to him. "I need to know. I need to be certain. That's what will make me well again."

"I can't, Sarah," he defended. "It's my one condition. I want us to leave here as soon as we reasonably can. I want us to go home, back to England. I want to find our life again there. I want to make our life together the priority, instead of running around looking after everyone else's concerns." Now he reached out to her, sliding his arm around her waist and pulling her gently towards him. "I want to make you the centre of my world again."

She came willingly, splaying one hand on his chest and running the other around his neck, into his hair. Her upturned face, pale in the moon's shimmer, reflected his passion back to him, but still she leant backwards against his arm, looking into his face.

"Tell me 'yes', John," she urged him, "and I will go anywhere with you. Tell me 'yes' and we can both have everything we want. Tell me 'yes' and make me happy again."

She met his kiss eagerly, as compliant and willing as if nothing had ever been at odds between them. Even as he responded to her, part of him worried that she should be so able to turn her emotions on and off like that – or, at least, to suppress them and release them almost at will. While he prided himself on having learned to control his anger that way, he couldn't understand how she might do the same to love. For him, it was the most life-affirming of emotions, the one that, now he had experienced it, he couldn't imagine being without. Certainly he couldn't understand the impulse – let alone the ability – to choose to be without it, even for a moment.

But as she passionately responded to him, he forced himself to cast aside his doubts, giving into his belief in her, his trust, against his own instincts, that this was the right choice for both of them.

Chapter Fourteen

England, autumn 1922

*We came back to England and I held onto the hope that,
being back, she might loosen her grip on the notion that
fixated her.*

It was such a relief to be back in England. It came most
immediately in escaping the heat and humidity that, even in late
September, was inflicting New York. He had never been so grateful
for soothing, healing, soft English rain as when they disembarked at
Southampton docks.

They had stayed on in Newport until the rest of the family was
ready to return at the end of another three weeks. Even in that short
time, he saw a visible improvement in Sarah. With him around, she
had the perfect excuse to spend time away from Millie, beginning
the painful separation process. The pain this time, though, was
evidently mitigated by the prospect of returning home and, in her
mind, at some point in the future getting what she wanted.

Superficially, it was an idyllic time, a precious, decadent
interlude enjoying that peculiarly American outdoor lifestyle born of
a favourable climate and an inherited familiarity with external
activity, whether work or leisure. He learned to sail, he lost,
frequently, to Williams at tennis and took long walks with his wife
around the beautiful Rhode Island coastline. He rediscovered an
appetite for physical activity that had long since disappeared beneath
the weight of his desk-bound responsibilities. Just briefly, he
glimpsed the appeal of Williams' less guilt-ridden approach to work
and envied him his relaxed lifestyle.

Beneath the surface, they were struggling a little to regain the
ease of their relationship that had come so naturally to them in the
first years of their marriage. Everything seemed calmer but such a

sudden return to apparent normality became for Jack a concern of its own. He tried to suppress his overly analytical nature but he knew it was only an illusory escape.

Once the family returned to New York after the Labor Day weekend, it was almost another month before Jack was ready to leave the business in Williams' hands. During that time, Sarah evaded a return to her Millie-centred routine but it left her at a loose end for much of her day and Jack was sure it was only the prospect of their imminent return to England that maintained her newly recovered equilibrium.

The only shadow cast over this time came with the confirmation of Charlotte's pregnancy just before their departure, combined with her anger at her sister's continued insistence on departing.

Thankfully, Mr Samuels was delighted to welcome them home. A trip that had started as a mercy mission in mid-May had, after all, turned into a sojourn of some four months and that shortly after the departure of his youngest daughter to her new marital home in India alongside her attaché husband. In fact, news had arrived just a week before their return that Rose and her husband had been recalled to England, the unexpected death of his older brother suddenly propelling him into the position of heir to the substantial Marshall estates in Warwickshire and Rose to a status beyond her imagination. Rumours abounded that the elder brother had been shot in suspicious circumstances during an expedition in Africa but Rose had learned discretion and was remaining tight-lipped.

In no time, Jack, Sarah and Samuels settled back into their previous rhythm of work at the bank, dinners with the partners, though without Mr Marsh who had sadly passed while they were away, and, for Sarah and her father, entertaining of clients. For the first couple of weeks, Jack insisted on joining the client dinners, keen to keep an eye on Sarah, but she soon insisted that they return to their previous routine of allowing Jack an amount of private time to escape and to rebalance.

He wasn't sure if Sarah knew how often he and Rachel spent those evenings together, continuing their habit of conversing or reading together. There was nothing in it but it did make him uncomfortable that she always made a point of leaving the study as soon as they heard Sarah's car draw up before the house. Yet, Jack couldn't help but wonder if perhaps Sarah had a hand in their spending time together.

In his mind, there was no question of him fulfilling her plan any time soon. Indeed, he admitted to Rachel that he hoped by spending time together again in a better-suited environment Sarah might yet be persuaded to abandon the scheme altogether. The look she gave him suggested he was deluding himself but, for him, that was a preferable reality.

Their first stay at Richmond House brought both of them a deep and lasting satisfaction. In little more than five months, the conversion of the stable block had been completed and a dozen recovering soldiers had moved into their new accommodation. For now, while the new facilities were being built, Richmond House's doors had been opened, at Mr Samuels' behest, to accommodate families visiting their loved ones. The hallways rang with the noise of scampering, laughing children and the once sparsely used morning room was now a mess of newspapers, books, toys and women's magazines. Hesketh claimed to despair, formally delineating for Sarah the many indictable offences made against this treasured home, but his authority was undermined by one young lad of four or five who, escaping from his mother and sidling up to the butler, asked 'Uncle Eric' to 'play trains' with him again.

The greatest transformation, though, and the one that brought Jack the deepest joy, was in the Major. Indeed, when Stephen Thomasson came out to greet them in the hall of Richmond House, Jack barely recognised the man he had met two-and-a-half years before in Paddington. The hollowed-out eyes and unkempt beard were gone and a clean shaven man, easily ten years younger than the one he had first met, greeted them. The way Jack was feeling, he suspected the Major could have passed for younger than he.

Nor was the Major long in reflecting his own observations back to Jack. After proudly showing Jack and Sarah around and introducing them to each resident and whichever family members happened to be present, they stood watching Sarah as she crouched on the floor with one of the young mothers, playing with her three-year-old son as his father sat by.

"I'm beginning to think the two of you could do worse than to check in here for a taste of your own medicine," Stephen commented drily. When Jack shrugged his observation off without a comment, he persisted. "Seriously, man. What have you been doing to each other? I've never seen a woman so changed in such a short period of time."

Jack glanced at Sarah, already more immersed in entertaining the boy than in talking to his mother. He drew the Major out of earshot.

"It's why we've come home," he started and explained Sarah's distress at not being able to have children.

"I'm very sorry for you both," the Major commiserated. "If ever there was a woman born to be a mother."

"It's become an obsession, Major, and, honestly, I don't know what to do for the best." Jack sat down heavily on a bench against the wall. Suddenly he was feeling the weight of the burden he was carrying, now he had the chance to share it with his friend. "She's desperate to be near children, she's drawn to them, but the more time she spends with them, the more it reminds her of what she can't have herself. How is that fair?"

"Come on, lad, since when did fairness have anything to do with it?" The Major was not about to let him slide into unconstructive self-pity. "There's no hope then?"

403

Jack hesitated. While he still wasn't, in his most rational moments, giving real credit to Sarah's scheme, an instinct made him leave the door open. "There's always a remote chance," he hedged, "but it's only the slightest possibility. She has," he hesitated again, "considered other...possibilities."

"Adoption, you mean?" the Major jumped to the logical conclusion. "What's holding you back? Is it her?"

"No," Jack denied swiftly, "it's me. It doesn't...feel right."

The Major gave him the sort of clear-sighted, challenging looks he knew he should have been expecting.

"Then you're more of an idiot than I thought," he condemned. "Most men would give their right hand to have the chance to make that woman happy. Thankfully for you, she's still deeply in love with you or I'd throw over all my gentlemanly values and make a play for her myself." Only a part of him was joking but the look Jack gave him said he wasn't taking him seriously enough. "Have you forgotten what a damned fortunate man you are, Westerham?" The Major's tone was hard now. "You weren't this complacent when I first met you, following her around with your eyes."

"Enough, Major," Jack tried to laugh off the Major's enthusiasm. The raised voices broke into Sarah's consciousness and she lifted her head to look at the two of them with a question in her eyes. As she looked back at Jack, she held his gaze for a long moment and that half-smile of hers played over her mouth.

"What I would give to have a woman like her look at me like that."

Jack held her gaze a moment longer. "What would you give, Major?" he asked quietly.

The Major contemplated the two of them. "For what you two have, there's nothing I wouldn't give. But," pulling himself up and straightening his jacket, "as I see that I still don't have a chance, perhaps I'll go in search of your silver-eyed angel instead. I assume she came back with you?"

"She's arriving this afternoon," Jack confirmed.

The Major started to walk back towards the main house but turned back to call to Jack. "Someone was looking for her, by the way. Did you hear? A man asking questions in the village. Seemed confused about her name but there was no doubting his description of her."

Sarah appeared at Jack's side, slipping her hand into Jack's.

"When was that, Stephen?" she asked.

"Couple of months back." He waved a farewell and disappeared back up the path.

"What is it?" he frowned at the concern on Sarah's face.

"Rachel. There are things I haven't told you about her background."

"What things?"

She shook her head. "It's not my story to tell. But, John, we really need to keep whoever it is away from her. You don't suppose whoever it was also came looking for her in New York?"

"How is that possible?" he questioned.

"You don't know…" she defended. He was surprised to feel her tremble.

"You're shaking." Concerned, Jack covered the hand she had placed in his own.

"I have a dreadful feeling," she whispered, a cloud of doubt and fear settling over her face.

The jolt Jack received at seeing Sarah's fear and thinking of Rachel in danger surprised him and he reacted instinctively.

"We should send her back to London," he concluded. "Mr Dawson could meet her train and drive her back immediately."

Sarah shook her head, trying to dislodge her fear. "I'm sure I'm being foolish, over-reacting. The Major said it was months ago."

"Perhaps I should send the Major over to guard her. Now he's finally given up on making a play for you," he teased, lightening the mood.

405

"Is that what the two of you were arguing about?" she matched his mood as they turned to walk back towards the house.

He smiled. "No, he was telling me what an idiot I am and that it should be my mission in life to make you happy, whatever it takes."

"I always did like the Major," she responded lightly. "And what did you say?"

Jack dropped her hand and slid his arm around her waist. "I know I may not always say it or show it," he confided, "and you'd be forgiven for thinking otherwise, but you are the most important thing in the world to me and I think you have been since the day I met you."

She leaned her head against his shoulder for a second. "You didn't answer my question," she noted, "but I think I prefer it your way."

They walked back to the house, heads close together, more at peace with each other than they had been for a long time.

* * * * * * *

Her recovery was gradual but visible. Surrounded day-to-day by familiar faces, her equilibrium returned and, with it, her previous energies and diverse enthusiasms. Jack came to appreciate how isolated, in fact, had been their lifestyle in New York, a narrow group of friends dominated by the Williams clan. Sarah's usual preoccupations with business, bank relationships, charities and fundraising efforts had been entirely absent during their stay. During October, she quickly picked up some of those most important relationships and activities again and, by November, was organising a Christmas bazaar to raise funds for the Richmond House hospice.

For himself, being back brought him to a better understanding of his innate wish for the comfortable and the familiar, recognising in himself less appetite for change and risk-taking than he might previously have anticipated. He knew his ability to take on new challenges and to cope with different situations but, simultaneously, he became aware of his preference for the world he already knew and that knew him.

It was, for a while, a challenge to rely on others to make decisions for him in New York instead of controlling everything. Having identified a six-man research team from within the existing pool of employees in the New York bank before he left, he was now receiving regular reports of proposed investments. Williams had stepped up, showing evidence of keeping more regular work hours and continuing to put forward proposals himself, the quality of which was much improved. Reports of a couple of investment decisions having been taken by Williams on his behalf concerned Jack briefly, not least because he was alerted to them by one of the team, not by Williams himself. On scrutinising them, though, he was satisfied by the business case and forced himself to accept that they had needed a faster decision than he could reasonably have made from London.

He received a set of accounts unexpectedly in mid-November, though, that could not be rationalised away as easily. For two days, he kept coming back to the report, trying to convince himself he had missed something or was misreading it. On the second day, he had one of the clerks make some discrete enquiries and received his report before the end of the day. Still he didn't act, wanting time to think through the implications overnight.

He took the paperwork home with him, suddenly paranoid about leaving it in the office and still hoping a further review in the peace of the study at Lyall Place might resolve this tangled web.

He was late home and met Sarah and Samuels as they were on their way out to dinner. He was so distracted, he very nearly missed that she was at least as distracted as he. Arriving in the hall to find the two of them donning hats, coats and gloves, he absently kissed Sarah's cheek in greeting, handing his case to Hesketh to put in the study and asking for supper to be served on a tray in the study. Samuels, stopping for a moment, enquired after the closing position of the markets and, for several seconds, Jack struggled to focus his mind enough to dredge up the data. He was absently watching Sarah as he relayed the information, noting how she was picking at her gloves, her face turned away from them in her apparent agitation to be gone. When he enquired after her day, she didn't appear to hear him and, in spite of repeating the question, it wasn't until he touched her shoulder that she spun round to face him, shocked out of whatever she was thinking about.

"Are you well?" he asked in a low voice, positioning himself between her and her father so as not to be heard. The changes in her health had not been remarked upon by his father-in-law and he didn't want to flag the issue to him now.

Her eyes were wide as she glanced up at him but she seemed unable to hold his gaze for more than a second, looking away, over his shoulder, down at her gloves. Anywhere but at him.

"Sarah?" he prompted.

She nodded, briefly. "I'm fine, John. Don't fuss." She turned away and, taking her father's arm, encouraged him out of the door and down the steps to the awaiting car. Jack watched her go.

As he turned, he caught sight of Rachel, in the shadows of the hall, watching them. She turned and disappeared as soon as he noticed her.

Trying to shake off an increasing unease, he went upstairs to change then headed to the study to settle in for the evening. There, though, the papers were waiting for him and the unease started to settle over him again. He deliberately ignored them while he ate, turning the pages of the evening newspaper instead, but he couldn't ignore them for long. Just as he was about to open the briefcase, the door opened.

"I need to show you something." Direct as ever, her voice did, however, betray a certain nervousness. So unlike her, it distracted him from his own worries, focusing his attention on her.

"Come in, then," he invited, surprised when she chose to sit on the footstool next to his chair instead of taking her usual position in the chair across from him. He leant towards her, concerned. "What is it?"

"I'm not sure I should be giving you these," she admitted. Close to, the bundle of paper in her hand had resolved into a number of envelopes, each opened and housing their original letter. He thought for a moment.

"Why are you, then?"

She gave him that direct, challenging look to which he had become so accustomed. "Sarah's trying to avoid the issue but I'm concerned about the effect it's having on her."

Opening all the letters, he arranged them in chronological order. She sat silently by as he read.

The first, neither headed nor signed, was from Charlotte and had been written in anger the day they left New York.

How you can think of leaving me at this time, I don't know. I never had you pegged as selfish, Sarah, but you've put my interests and welfare so far down your agenda I have to revise my opinion. You have abandoned me yet again to people who do not really know me and who will never care for me as well as my own family should. What could be more important than the health of another grandchild? What is there in your life that is so critical that you have to be away from me now? Don't you know how much I rely on you in this? The last time you were here and everything was fine. Then you left me and you know what happened. If something happens this time, it will be on your conscience. Can you take that? Can you?

The second also came from Charlotte, a month later.

The doctor has been. It's a different doctor and a different midwife. Mrs Wilson won't be here. Why is everyone abandoning

409

me? Don't they know how important this is? The sickness is back. I can hardly move from the sofa, certainly can't leave the house. Oh, why does this burden fall on me? I'm so young. I should be out there enjoying my life, going to parties, drinking cocktails, dancing. Instead, where am I? Cooped up in this pokey little room with all the blinds drawn for fear my migraines will start soon, bloated and uncomfortable, and dreading Aunt Millie's daily eleven o'clock visit.

Are you feeling sorry yet, Sarah? Say you will come. I need you here desperately. I can't imagine going through all this without you to keep me sane. Send word of when you will arrive. It must be no later than the first week of December. I won't go through that time again without you.

From about the same time came a rambling missive from Isabella, full of stories about her latest dance or weekend party before she got to the point.

Sister (I will call you such for so you have become to me), I must tell you that I write because Charlotte has asked me to implore you to visit. Was she sick this much that first time? I don't remember but, I am now ashamed to say, I left much of the work to you on that occasion. I wish I had your strength and patience. Charlotte, much as I adore her, can be a challenging friend at the best of times. In sickness, I fear she indulges her selfish, self-pitying side rather more.

She worries me. She is, understandably, fearful that the same thing might happen as last time, but she seems to go beyond fear almost to hysterical paranoia. Could she actually cause what she most fears by obsessing about it? I hope not but her fear is infectious. You were so good with her last time. Might you consider even a brief visit? I'm sure just the thought of your impending arrival would calm Charlotte considerably.

One blessing in all of this for which I thank God: Freddie stands by her. While business ensures he has but little time to spend with her directly, at least being in our parents' house ensures there is no question of him repeating the follies of last time.

In hope of seeing you soon. Your loving sister,
Isabella.

By the end of the month, even Williams had been prevailed upon to add his voice to the chorus, albeit in his typically abrupt style.

Sarah, I fear we are in need of your services again. Charlotte shows signs of relapsing. I know how difficult this is for you. You don't need me to tell you how important you are to helping us through this. If you can, please come.

The final letter, dated a week ago and which, Jack guessed, had arrived that day had been torn in two.

My dearest Mrs Westerham

I am aware my children and your sister have all written appeals to you during the course of the past weeks, to no avail. I am compelled to make this final appeal, a last-ditch attempt to reach out to the humanity I have witnessed in you but which you seem to have buried deeply since your departure.

I appeal to you as a mother. Though not one yourself, I know you share my sensibilities and have experienced some of my parental anguish yourself as the elder sister to two young motherless girls.

I wish I could convey to you my utter anguish and impotent fear in witnessing your sister's current attitude. I fear for her soundness of mind, so distressed is she at your continuing absence. I fear for her physical well-being as she continues to endure the daily sickness. I fear for the health of the child with the distress its mother experiences. My son is dismissive but I have seen expectant mothers in less turmoil than this destroy not only their own health but that of

411

their unborn child too. As a mother and a grandmother, I can no longer sit by and wait for this impending disaster to unfold.

I do not wish to judge but I must ask what it is that keeps you from returning to us? If it is your husband, perhaps Freddie might apply pressure on your behalf? If not, is there any other way I might assist that could expedite your arrival? At the very least, please accept our invitation to join us for Christmas at our home in Chicago. I know you must be aware that Charlotte's fear most particularly revolves around the time in the pregnancy when she lost the last child. Only the hardest of hearts could resist such an appeal. I am sure Mr Samuels could spare you for a short visit and, if he cannot, perhaps he might be prevailed upon to accept our invitation too?

I beg you, Mrs Westerham, to give serious consideration to my appeal. You may think me melodramatic but I fear I am not being so when I say that lives may depend upon you.

We have a duty to my unborn grandchild. I hope, in this, I have discharged mine.

Yours dutifully,
Susanna Williams.

When Jack finally looked up, he found himself staring into those extraordinary grey eyes. Silver, the Major had called them and he wasn't far wrong. He read there a deep compassion, mingled with the same divided allegiance he imagined Sarah must be experiencing.

"Why did she keep these from me?"

"She had already made her decision."

"So why are you showing them to me now?" She dropped her head, staring at her hands clasped in her lap. He half-reached out to her but drew back. He had never touched her and, illogically, he felt aware of that unconscious embargo and could not bring himself to break it. "Tell me," he urged.

412

"Her decision is wrong."

Simple as that. No qualifying, no caveating. "You do know what it could do to her to go back there?"

A clear, hard look. "I was there before."

"And yet you would put her through it again?"

She stood up and walked away from him. She stopped in the middle of the room, her hands at her sides, staring straight ahead of her at the door. She spoke without turning back to face him. "Should anything happen to the child, she will torment herself. That would be much worse than anything she will face, particularly if we are both there to support her."

"Should anything happen, she will hardly be in a position to prevent it."

"But she will have done her duty and none will question her commitment, including her."

"It need not be a long visit," Jack mused. "And," looking at the unopened briefcase beside his chair, "it seems likely that I need to make a trip out there myself now, for the business."

She turned back to face him, relief in her eyes. "You will raise it with her, then?"

"I will," he agreed. "At the earliest opportunity."

* * * * * * *

The opportunity presented itself sooner than he had expected. Sarah and her father's dinner was unusually short and they returned home shortly after ten, at which point Jack came out of the study to meet them and they adjourned to the drawing room for a drink.

To his surprise, his proposal to Samuels that he might need to return to New York to scrutinise the accounts was met with instant agreement and a revelation. "Sarah was only saying tonight," Samuels observed, "that she would like to visit Charlotte for Christmas, having received an invitation from Mrs Williams to join

413

the family. It sounds like you might kill two birds with the proverbial."

Jack's frown in Sarah's direction was lost as she didn't look across at him. "That's fortunate," Jack commented, keeping his tone level. "And it would be pleasant to see them before the next arrival is due to make his or her appearance."

She met his look briefly at that comment and the caginess of her expression confused him.

"I would join you myself but I'm not sure I can face another sea crossing at this point," Samuels demurred. "Is there something of concern in the business that takes you back so soon?"

Jack shook his head. "Just a couple of investment decisions that I'd like to clear up," he deflected. "And what will you do for Christmas as we're away?"

"Ah, Sarah has already arranged that for me," Samuels explained. "I'm spending the whole of the festive season with Rose and her young man in Warwickshire. I'd be surprised if some pleasant news were not forthcoming from that direction in the not-too-distant future as well," he speculated, "so we should make for a jolly party."

Sarah wouldn't meet Jack's intent gaze again. Thankfully, Samuels soon retired for the night and left them together.

"You didn't tell me we had been invited to Christmas," he observed neutrally.

"The invitation is recent," Sarah excused, rising to stoke the fire smouldering in the grate.

"And you're comfortable with the idea of returning?"

She nodded, still standing by the fire and with her face turned away from him. "The last several weeks have been good for me," she analysed. "I feel more like my old self. I'm sure I can manage a short visit and Charlotte has been asking it of me for some time now."

Some honesty, then. "What did you have in mind?" he probed cautiously.

"I thought we might sail around mid-December. We can take the train from New York to Chicago. If you need to be in New York for the business, you could stay there for a few days and then join us in time for Christmas."

"You're not thinking of staying too long, I hope?"

A shake of the head. "We should return in the New Year." Still she wouldn't look at him.

In the end, he rose and went to join her by the fire, taking the poker from her hand and setting it down so that he might take both her hands in his. He faced her and she had to meet his eyes at last. "Is this really what you want?" he challenged. "I fear the effect that even such a short visit might have on you."

Sarah laughed dismissively. "It seems absurd, doesn't it?" she mused. "That I should have allowed myself to become so unwell. From this distance, I find it hard to believe it had such an effect on me. You were right, John. All I needed was some time away from them. I feel like myself again," she reiterated.

He held her gaze, somehow unconvinced but unable to say why he should question her sincerity. "My only concern is your welfare," he caveated.

She smiled and leaned forward to kiss him briefly. "Then what could go wrong?"

As she left the room, an unwelcome thought flashed through his mind: he felt like he had been played. His mind revolted against the idea but every instinct told him he was right. Though, for the life of him, he couldn't understand why.

PART III – GRACE

FRIDAY

The phone clatters as he drops the earpiece back onto the cradle. In the silence of the hall, the noise echoes back, emphasising the emptiness of the place.

He is alone.

He looks at his luggage, standing in the hall, ready for the arrival of the taxi cab. He calls to cancel.

For the first time in he can't remember how long, he is truly alone. In this vast brownstone house, he is the only one left. Not even the servants who, being informed they were not required for Christmas, have scattered to far corners, unexpectedly released to spend the festive season with friends and loved ones.

For a moment, the emptiness almost overwhelms him. Ironic. This solitary, slightly distant man has finally grown used to other people and the weight of their absence is oppressive.

He is being absurd. The snow storm might last no more than a day. Tomorrow, he might be on a train to Chicago, looking forward to Christmas with family and time with his wife again after a couple of weeks' separation. Thank God for the telephone. Being able to speak to her every day has helped mitigate if not alleviate his anxiety about being back in America.

He should have listened to the warnings about the snow. Preoccupied with the problem at work and naïve to the challenges of American weather, he – they – have underestimated the issue. If only he had left yesterday. He might even now be sitting before a blazing fire with her beside him again at last.

At least he has been able to conduct the investigation discretely without Williams present. He doesn't like what he has found and will have to disclose it soon but that is a problem for another day.

For now, his problem is fending for himself. Starting with supper. Where is the kitchen in this echoing house?

Rummaging around in the basement rooms, it is a relief, if something of a surprise, to find both the larder and the refrigerator relatively well stocked. Not what he expects of a household that has wound down towards an absence of some days for all its inhabitants. Still, he is grateful for it now. It is fortunate he retains some of his makeshift cooking skills, certainly enough to produce for himself a plate of chicken and potatoes. Not great cuisine but adequate nourishment.

Dining alone in the vast dining room seems absurd. It is logical, then, to retreat to the study as usual. The fire, laid but not lit, is easily dealt with and soon takes off the chill in the air.

Through the one curtain he has left open, the better to watch the predicted blizzard arrive, the first few flakes of snow are now visible. They look pretty, benign. It is hard to imagine the fall that has closed the roads and train lines between the east coast and Chicago. Turn off the one light in the room, the better to watch the world outside. Only the fire to throw a dim light into the darkness, casting long shadows. He has always loved snow. Even in the bitter cold of a trench winter, hands, feet, face frozen, boots and greatcoat perpetually sodden, a detached part of him had still appreciated the beauty of it, smothering the devastation they had wrought on man and land alike in the short, futile space between them and the German men, the husbands, brothers, sons they had to remind themselves daily were the enemy.

The stillness is allowing long-controlled memories to creep back in. Keen to suppress them, at least temporarily, he goes in search of his favourite Jura whisky, soft, peaty, warm. The first slug swallowed in one gulp, the glass filled again en route back to the study.

How is Sarah getting on, he wonders. Strange how she had seemed almost eager to get to Chicago. Only one night with him in New York then on the first train she could. With luck, it means she is stronger now, strong enough to cope with not only her sister but also her niece.

He remembers how, even surrounded by family, they had yet managed a private celebration of their second wedding anniversary while in Newport, spending the evening together at a restaurant, the better to avoid the rest of the family. They made slow, tender love that night, their bodies slick with sweat in the heat of the evening. She fell asleep in his arms.

He loves his wife, deeply. She is a remarkable woman and he is blessed to have the right to love her. The more so when he looks at couples around him and realises how rare it is to have a partnership in their marriage, to share an interest in both work and other areas, to find security and reassurance in one another's love, to find passion in one another's arms. Life could have been so different. Had Mr Samuels not taken him under his wing. Had he not allowed Alfie to talk him into applying for jobs at the bank. Had it been him that day, not Billy. He is a lucky man. What if his luck runs out?

Pouring another shot of whisky, he acknowledges he is getting maudlin. He needs to distract himself. Perhaps a book? He forces himself out of the chair and, lighting the lamp next to his seat, casually trawls the shelves, trying to find something to distract himself. Not that he needs to look really. He knows every book in that room, has read a substantial number already. What he needs is something to challenge his mood. Indeed, he might be needing several to occupy him over the coming days.

Another shot of whisky. A third of the bottle gone. No wonder he is feeling drowsy. The book unopened on his knee, he leans his head back, watching the flames make the shadows dance.

* * * * * * *

He must have slept. Something has stirred him – is it a noise in his dream or in the house? – and he eases his neck, stretching the crick out of it. The fire still burns but has dampened down somewhat and chill fingers are reaching back towards him from the darkened room now the fire no longer keeps them at bay. He should bank it down shortly and go to bed. Rubbing his eyes, he leans down to retrieve the book from where it has fallen to the floor, still unread.

As he sits up again, he catches from the corner of his eye the slow opening of the door. Beyond is darkness and the weak light in the room casts the figure only in a paler grey without illuminating but there was no mistaking that slight frame.

"What are you doing here?"

No answer. She steps into the room and closes the door behind her, slowly. He waits, his breath stilled, as she crosses the short space between them. As she nears, gradually more light falls onto her face but he still can't read her expression clearly. Determination? Uncertainty? Anxiety? All of them are there. He looks into the bewitching silver eyes and reads what he both fears and, in a deeply buried part of him, desires.

Holding his gaze, she stands in front of him and, slowly, sinks down, kneeling up before him and bringing her hands to rest on his legs. Her touch – her first ever touch – sends shock waves through him and his breath comes shallowly now, anticipation shooting adrenaline through him until he feels light-limbed, his pulse beating fast.

She leans into him, lightly, running her hands down his thighs as she leans forward, putting her weight against him through her arms. Her action is provocative but her face, just inches from his, looking up into his eyes, is so innocent, fragile, luminescent in the feeble light, her eyes shining.

"It's time, Jack," she whispers, bringing her mouth temptingly close to his. Still he hasn't touched her.

He searches her eyes for a long moment, trying to understand how willingly she comes to this. Those deep, penetrating eyes draw him in, commanding him, and he feels his will dissolve beneath hers.

"Oh, Christ." His voice, low, rough, betrays him and she lifts her chin, her eyes flicking now to his mouth, unconsciously inviting. Torn, he lifts one hand and brushes the back of his fingers against her mouth. Her lips part and he feels her breath caress him. Slowly, mimicking her careful drawing out of her movements, he lowers his head and brushes his lips against hers.

It is like a shock of energy passes between them in that most tentative of touches. He draws back slightly, seeking and finding confirmation in her eyes that she has felt it too. He can see the fear behind it. She has expected to be in control. Now she isn't so certain.

He can't help himself. He seeks her lips again, one hand hesitantly stroking across her cheek, running down her neck and, as she opens her mouth to him, sliding round her nape and sinking his fingers into her hair, lifting her towards him, kissing her deeply.

By the time they break apart, his fast and shallow breathing matched by hers, she is sitting in his lap, one arm around her as he traces her face, from temple to jawline, with gentle fingers. Her hand, entwined in the hair at the top of his neck, clenches as she reacts to his touch and commands an equivalent reaction in him.

He holds her gaze, doubt, bewilderment, guilt flooding his brain, even as his body reacts to her light touch as she draws her thumb across his mouth, rubbing his sensitive bottom lip.

"Are you sure…" he starts, barely a whisper. Her eyes stop him and she gives the slightest shake of her head, forbidding speech. She rises and, standing before him, holds out her hand, asking him. Without her touch, her closeness, he starts to doubt, to question. He takes her hand as he rises but he needs more to keep denial at bay. Holding her gaze, he slides one arm around her slender waist.

Anticipating him, she follows his movements, running her arm across his shoulders as he bends and lifts her into his arms, cradling her, so slight, against his chest. She bends her arm in order to run her hand into his hair again, resting the other lightly on his chest, toying absently with the open collar of his shirt, teasingly brushing her fingertips against the bare skin of his neck. His skin betrays his arousal, goose-bumps rising down the hair on his arms. He claims her mouth, kissing her hard, though she reciprocates with as much passion. As he carries her from the room, she sinks her head against his shoulder, her hair soft, silky almost, against his cheek.

Turning on the electric lights brings a harsher reality than either is ready for. He can see the shock in her eyes, soon replaced with doubt and nervousness. He kisses her forehead, holding her tight against him but feeling the desire that had overwhelmed them both begin to wane as nerves take over.

As he stops at his bedroom door, she suddenly shakes her head, mute still but her eyes communicative. He seeks one of the other rooms down the corridor, a guest room, neutral territory. Setting her down, he turns the handle, still holding her hand. Unused, the air is chill but at least the bed is made. He leaves the light off, only the light from the hallway through the slightly ajar door alleviating the darkness.

He sits down on the foot of the bed, conscious how his height might intimidate her. She stands before him, awkward now, both her hands held lightly in his. She wears a dress he had never seen before. It is strange to see her out of uniform, to see her thick, dark hair cascade around her shoulders, framing her slight face, almost hiding her stunning eyes. It is like seeing her as a woman for the first time. She is beautiful and it makes him catch his breath.

"You don't have to do this." He seeks to reassure her but catches a flash of anger in those eyes, the shade of mercury in this dim light. She has made up her mind and she doesn't want him undermining her decision. "My God but you're beautiful," he

424

breathes and is rewarded with the slightest uplift at the corner of her mouth. He transfers his hands to her waist, hers naturally coming to rest on his shoulders, and eases her closer to him until she is standing between his knees. He can feel her tiny frame through the thin fabric of her satin dress, a cool, fluid material that just begs to be stroked. He slides his hands carefully over her, running across her back to the buttons of her dress. As he cautiously releases each one, she turns her trembling fingers to the buttons of his shirt but fumbles in her nervousness. He slides both the dress and her slip from her shoulders and she lets them slide to the floor. Her skin gleams in the dim light but her stance speaks her nervousness, the awkwardness that has overwhelmed her. He finishes for her the task of unbuttoning his shirt and sheds it. Tentatively, she rests her hand on his shoulder again, bare this time, testing the feel of his naked skin against her fingertips. Cautiously, he draws her down on the bed next to him and, tentatively, runs the palm of his hand over her cheek, lifting the curtain of hair away from her face. As he leans in towards her, she shifts slightly and he feels a wave of relief as her skin touches his and the spark leaps between them again.

* * * * * * *

He tries. They both do. But with the initial spark of passion cooled by nervousness, it is fumbling, peremptory and soulless. For a long time after, they lie side by side in the darkness, unspeaking, untouching, unable to bridge the divide, the gulf, that has opened up in the space lying between them.

He is overwhelmed with guilt. He feels as if he has betrayed not only his vows but also her trust. This is an impossible situation for both of them and she has trusted him to make it bearable. He feels he has rushed, has relied on a physical connection between them. One that he knows now he has long denied and which he would have continued to deny had they not been placed in this situation. It isn't enough, though. He admires this woman, enjoys her company and her quick brain. He has tried to diminish the friendship that has already grown between them, to supplant it with a purely physical interaction. But it isn't right. He knows enough of himself to know he could take one without the other. But not with this woman. Somehow, this needs an emotional dimension for it to work for them.

He hears her breath catch and she suddenly turns on her side, her back towards him. He can see the slight tremble of her shoulders as she suppresses her tears. For a moment he hesitates but his compassion takes over. Gently, he tucks the blanket around her, careful to create a barrier between their bodies, then he too turns on his side and tucks in behind her, one arm cradling her head and the other slipping over her waist to draw her back against him, holding her as she cries.

* * * * * * *

Slowly, her sobs gentle and ease until she is lying quietly in his arms. He lets her make the first move, giving her time. Eventually, she shifts, turning over to face him, drawing the blanket against her chest, protecting her nakedness.

"I can't do this," she whispers, her eyes reflecting her despair.

He raises the hand that had been cradling her head and brushes her hair away from her face. "Neither can I," he admits. "Not like this."

Her despair turns to distress. "But we have to," she insists unhappily. "I promised myself I would do whatever I can for her. She deserves to be happy."

"Did she send you?" finally asking the question that has been on his lips since she arrived. The look in her eyes gives him the answer to his question. "What was the plan, then?" Seeing the fear creep back into her eyes, he seeks to reassure her. "I'm not angry. I just want to understand," slowly stroking the skin at her temple.

"It was an opportunity. We had no idea if it would work or even if I would make it to New York before the snow set in. I'm supposed to be visiting a distant relative who lives just outside Chicago, so that no one will suspect. It seemed too good a chance to pass up, with the house being empty."

"So we would have some privacy at least?" A nod. "For how long?" A frown of confusion. "How much time do we have together?"

A shrug. "The weather in Chicago isn't expected to clear for two or three days and then they will have to clear the tracks. She will come home after that."

Maybe three days, maybe four. "If this is going to work," he reflects slowly, still turning the thoughts in his mind and picking his words with care, "we have to make this about just you and I. I know why you're doing this. I know why I am too. But it can't be about her." He takes a deep breath. "You were my friend before you were my lover," he observes, pleased to see her skin flush at his words. "If we carry on like this, it will destroy what we had before. I don't want that."

She looks at him, clear-eyed and calm now. "What do you suggest?"

"Three days, three nights," he proposes. "For this time, it's our world, our time. There's no one but the two of us." He holds he gaze, intent. "But I want all of you in that time. Not just physically. I want to know you, to talk with you. No secrets, no embarrassment, no hiding. Two free souls together, unencumbered, open and honest with each other."

She seems to turn his words over, assessing his proposition. He can see the moment the decision is made. "And what happens then?" she whispers. "At the end?" Even as she speaks, she is reaching for him, loosening the blanket barrier between them and bringing her mouth close to his.

"Then, it stops," he promises her hoarsely. "We both love her too well to do anything else."

* * * * * * *

They make love so slowly, an exquisite, drawn out torture, exploring each other, teasing, pleasing.

They meet each other as equals, passion meeting passion and flaring like a bright flame between them. He loves the feeling of running his hands into her long hair, cradling her head in his hands, holding her from him so he can watch her silver eyes darken as the passion overwhelms her, even as she arches her body against his, demanding, begging, tormenting.

It is like nothing he has ever experienced, suddenly freed from societal constraints, from any sense of obligation, honour or guilt.

And he can tell from the combined bewilderment and joy in her eyes that it is the same for her.

* * * * * * *

They rapidly lose any sense of time that night, drifting in and out of sleep, holding each other, unwilling to break the bond that now ties them together. When one moves, the other responds and the spark ignites again, instinctively making them reach for each other.

Sometime in the middle of the night, her stomach growls loudly and he laughs softly, tucking her against him and sinking his lips into the hollow between her collar bone and her shoulder even as he runs his hand down over her gently curving stomach. "It seems you're enough for me but you need rather more than I can supply," he teases.

She arcs against him, catching her bottom lip between her teeth at the sensations his hand is setting off in her skin. She turns her head round towards him and pulls down his head to meet hers, kissing him hard. "I think you'd be more worried about keeping up my energy levels," she advises, sliding her hand down between them and causing his stomach muscles to contract in reaction. He evades her and slips out of the bed to pull on his trousers.

At a loss knowing what to serve, he resorts to what is easiest. He is spreading butter onto the toast as she appears in the kitchen doorway, her slender body wrapped in a dark satin robe. Shyly, she takes a seat at the kitchen table, watching him with evident amusement as he boils water and makes a pot of tea.

"You're more domesticated than I would have assumed."

He smiles and places a plate of buttered toast in front of her, taking the seat opposite, a decent distance away across the wide table. "I think even I can manage tea and toast," he responds. "My mother would be most disappointed if I couldn't."

"Is she still alive?" He nods and explains about his family in Devon. "It sounds idyllic." Her voice is wistful. Distracted, she doesn't realise the melted butter from the uneaten toast in her hand has run down her thumb and onto her palm. She drops the toast as he reaches out and catches her wrist, bringing her hand to his mouth, licking the butter off, deliberately sucking at the fleshy skin of her palm, watching her face as her eyes close in pleasure, her head tipping back slightly, biting her lip against the unfamiliar sensation. He laughs, a deep, dark sound and her eyes fly open, her pupils contracting in reaction. For a moment, anger registers in her face but then she smiles, a slow secretive smile.

"What just happened?" Jack catches the sudden change in mood. "Were you angry with me?"

"For laughing," she admits. "I don't like people laughing at me. But I suddenly saw in your eyes what doing that," she nods towards where he still holds her hand in his, "is doing to you and it didn't matter any more. I like that I can do that to you," she concludes shyly.

He brings her hand to his mouth again, burying a kiss in the palm. "I rather like that you can do it to me, too," he teases. "And I

429

wasn't laughing at you. It's just that the look on your face was giving me pleasure. But I promise I won't laugh at you."

"Don't," she denies. "I don't want you to change yourself for me. I only react that way because of the past. I'd sooner learn a new way than to know that I've made you a different person."

He frowns. "Will you tell me about it?" he requests.

She shakes her head. "Not now. Perhaps. If we have time."

"I feel I know so little about you. When we've talked before, it's always been about politics or history, never about who you are or where you've come from or what's happened in your life. Tell me something about yourself," he encourages. "Tell me about your family or about where you grew up."

Almost instantly she grows solemn. "It's not a particularly edifying story," she caveats.

"That's not important. I want to know you."

She draws her hand back from him, as if she needs to retreat into herself to be able to give something of herself to him. She laces her fingers together, the better to stop herself betraying her discomfort through her movements, it seems. "I'm the second of two children, my brother some years older. My parents were devout Methodists," she starts, hesitantly. "After I was born, I think my mother decided she had done her duty by her husband and by her church. She didn't let him touch her again, ever, as far as I'm aware. My father was a teacher and he turned his energies into trying to drill a love of learning into his pupils. At first," she reaches for her mug of tea and wraps her hands around it to warm them, "he provided private education for the sons of middle class families and we were comfortably off. His religious convictions overtook him, though. He felt he had a mission," the word carries notable disdain, "to bring learning to those who could least afford it. He worked in church schools, mostly in the East End. It meant we had next to no money and ended up as poor as the families of his pupils. Only, it was worse because we had known comfort before and now we were without.

430

They gave me an education wholly unsuited to my prospects, which only served to make me discontented with my lot. I've spent my life striving for something more or seeking a way to escape. Ironically, the one thing they left me with of any value is my love of learning."

"When did you lose them?" Jack asks sympathetically.

"They're not dead," she admits. "Though they are dead to me."

She doesn't explain and he doesn't probe. "And your brother?"

Suddenly choked with unhealed grief. "Dead. In the war." She won't look at him.

She shivers suddenly and he realises how cold it must be for her in the kitchen. He seeks to change the subject. "Has your stomach stopped growling? I only ask as I don't think I'll be able to sleep above the noise."

She rises and walks round the table, forcing a smile to her lips, to take his hand. "Enough to keep me going for tonight," she promises, standing right up on her toes to touch her lips to his. He holds her there with one hand, keeping her body against his.

"You're a remarkable woman," he says softly. "I'm glad of the chance to get to know you, Rachel."

She freezes then pushes away from him, dropping his hand and walking almost blindly towards the door.

For a second, shocked into immobility, he fails to react but then he recovers and rapidly steps forward, catching her wrist to stop her leaving. "What?" he demands. "What did I say?" She shakes her head in denial and looks away. He feels sick to his stomach at her rejection and his body cries out a denial. He comes to stand in front of her. "You promised," he insists, trying to keep his voice soft but failing to keep from it the uncertainty that has suddenly swept through him. "You promised honesty," he reminds her hoarsely. "Please, don't hide from me."

She looks up and there is a glimmer of tears in her eyes. "It's just," she starts falteringly, "that's not my name. For almost two years now I've lived as someone she created. I know it was done with the intention of protecting me but do you know how hard it is to live as a different person?" Her expression is so bleak it tears at him. "I wish," she whispers, despairingly, "I wish you could know me as me. Even if it's just for now."

He cups her face in his hand. "For this time," he commits, "you are who you are. If we aren't honest in this, it will be impossible for either of us to face what we're doing. Afterwards. We don't have time," he reflects, "so we will give each other something else instead. You will know me, for these short days, as not even she does. I will tell you anything you want to know about me. I will share with you things I can't bring myself to talk about with anyone else. Even if it is difficult, I will be entirely truthful with you. And I want to know you. As no one has ever known you before. So tell me," he encourages. "Let me know you."

She reads the emotion in his eyes for a long moment, finally covering his hand with hers and leaning her cheek into his caress. "Grace," she whispers, her eyes holding his. "My name is Grace."

He runs his hand into her hair, gently easing her head back, casting light onto her face and seeing the depth of emotion and grief concealed there. "Grace," he repeats in a whisper. He holds her eyes for a long moment. "I can't imagine a more perfect name for you," he murmurs bringing his mouth down to hers.

SATURDAY

Dawn blends slowly into the winter skyline, easing fingers of light between the New York skyscrapers, casting long shadows across the snow-dusted streets. As the world outside the partially curtained window gradually lightens, he lies awake. He hadn't slept much, even when she has, but he feels no tiredness, enjoying the warmth of her body against his, the soft, soothing sound of her relaxed breathing. She lies tucked into his side, her head on his shoulder, her long hair splayed out on the white cotton pillow and as a gentle caress against his skin, one leg bent and resting across his thigh.

He has expected to wake with doubts and qualms. Part of him worries that he didn't. The other part is enthralled. Such freedom, such liberation he has never known in his life before. The prospect of freely opening himself up to this woman, to share his soul-deep cares, his fears, his hopes, his emotions, without judgment, condemnation, criticism or guilt, to replace a lifetime of growing and sharing with a fragment, a moment of utter honesty, is exhilarating.

His one fear, quickly suppressed, is that he might allow himself to feel too much.

Knowing the awkwardness that will exist between them in the cold light of day, he draws her closer, seeking to avoid it. She stirs slightly but doesn't wake, unconsciously easing closer to him, burying her face in his shoulder, her warm breath tickling his skin. He feels his body react and automatically reaches out to tease an equivalent reaction out of her, lightly drawing his hand down her arm, falling onto the curve of her waist and tracing the line over her hip. She murmurs in her sleep and falls backwards slightly, her arm falling back above her head, the better to give him room to trace his hand back up over her stomach, the muscles contracting, along the line of her breastbone and over her neck. As he eases her onto her back, gently bearing her back with his own weight, her eyes flicker open. The long, slow smile and the softest moan she lets out on an aroused sigh take his breath away. She closes her eyes and stretches languorously beneath him, which inadvertently brushes her breast against him and she sighs again.

"If you're a dream," she murmurs, "don't wake me."

He runs his thumb across her cheekbone, watching the play of emotions across her face, then lowers his mouth to hers, feathering the faintest touch over first her top lip and then the bottom one.

Another sigh and the slightest sound of pleasure in the back of her throat, and her lips part. Tempted, he kisses her deeply, teasing her with his tongue, feeling her hand wind into his hair as she arches her back and mutely implores his body, held now at a controlled distance from hers, to sink his weight onto hers.

Still holding himself at a distance, he waits until her eyes slowly open again, smoky with desire. She raises her knee, rubbing her leg against his hip, even as she covers his cheek with her hand, bruising his bottom lip with the brush of her thumb, following her action with her eyes. "Thank God," she whispers, looking back into his eyes and meeting his gaze steadily. "I was afraid you weren't real."

With a growl in his throat that elicits a throaty laugh in hers, he pins her arm above her head and bears her back into the soft mattress.

* * * * * * *

She wants to explore his body in the light of day, like she is committing him to memory with her eyes, mouth and hands. He submits, uneasily at first but then, by forcing himself to shed his inhibitions and allow her the freedom, with an increasing sense of how it binds them together. She frowns over his scars, her eyes reflecting back to him his pain, like a mirrored memory, then tenderly kisses the healed but permanently marked flesh. She runs her fingers over the muscles of his back, shoulders and arms, learning his strength, his control. She finds how her touch discovers hidden sensitive areas, the arch of his feet, the backs of his knees, the hollow behind his collar bone. Until he can submit no longer and teaches her the cost of her freedom, revealing to her the same sensitivities of her own body, teasing and coaxing them until she cries out for relief.

* * * * * * *

He can't get enough of those eyes. Lying face to face on the pillows, silent, still. Staring into those brilliant grey eyes, finding how they darken at the edges and again at the centre, ranging from gun metal grey to clear, sharp silver, flecked with dark blue, almost indigo. Seeing the pupils contract in response to him.

* * * * * * *

Talking. Their bodies entwined, satiated, for now. Arms in loose embrace of the other. Legs intertwined, still now but close enough that the slightest movement might change the temporary balance. Fingers threading through her hair. Fingers splaying against his chest, sensing the steady pulse of his heart.

"Tell me about the scar on your back." A challenge. Pushing at the boundaries of what she feels comfortable disclosing.

"Tell me about the scar on your hip." A response. Testing his willingness to give as well as receive. He tells her.

A faint straying of the eyes away from his, remembering. Then back again. "He beat me. Once with a belt."

"Your father?"

The slightest shake. "My husband." Almost uncontrollable rage sweeps through him.

* * * * * * *

"We should eat."

"It's too late for breakfast."

"I don't care what the time is. Our rules. We can eat what we want when we want. And I'm hungry."

He dresses her, the tenderness of serving her, wrapping the dressing gown around her shoulders then tying the belt at her waist, loosely so that it drapes open slightly and he can still glimpse her

435

nakedness beneath. He puts on his trousers but she objects when he goes to pull on his shirt.

"You are beautiful," she tells him simply. "Don't hide from me." She reflects his words to her back to him and he compromises, pulling on his shirt but not buttoning it.

Sitting at the kitchen table while she collects together the ingredients she wants. The satin dressing gown – where did she get such a thing from? – is like fluid against her skin as she moves, clinging to the curves of her body, sensuous. She blends a batter to make pancakes, sure, competent movements that speak of one at ease in this task.

"You're used to running a kitchen," he surmises, drinking the coffee she has put in front of him.

"I ran my own home for almost four years. We might have starved if I hadn't worked out what to do."

"Your husband?"

She pauses and looks at him, her expression saying there is something she needs to reveal.

"And my son."

He absorbs the information, seeing how sensitive she is and how she doesn't want him to probe now. She will tell him when she's ready. Even in the short time they have together, they know there will come the right moment.

"How did you meet your husband?" This at least seems an acceptable subject.

She talks as she makes the pancakes, allowing her to keep her eyes on her work instead of on him. "I went into service when I was fifteen. The master of the house was a philanthropist who supported some of the work my father was doing in the East End. I was young and desperate to escape my parents' house. But my education had given me ambitions beyond my reach. I knew too much of the world not to want to see it for myself. So I became just as desperate to escape service. He was a route out. A friend of the under-gardener.

He was charming and attentive and, like a naïve fool, I assumed the man I saw when we went out for dinner or to the pictures was the man he was in reality.

"I almost didn't marry him," she remembers. "The lady's maid was getting married and she was searching for a replacement she could train up to the lady's peculiarities, of which there were many. My education stood me apart from the rest of the servants. I was polite and well-spoken, and she decided I might do. For almost six months, she trained me. During that time, we travelled to Scotland, to Dublin. I saw a way for me to get the life I wanted without having to marry him."

Watching her closely, he catches the slight shake of her head, as if she is shaking off a bad memory or an uncomfortable thought. He follows her train of thoughts and knows what happened. "You fell pregnant," he guesses.

A rueful smile tells him he is right. She pushes a plate of food across the table to him and takes the seat at the head of the table, at a right-angle to him. Silence stretches between them for some moments. She is remembering.

"I had never thought of myself as maternal," she muses, pushing at her food. "I was seventeen. I don't suppose I really thought of myself as that grown up. Then, suddenly, it didn't matter what I thought because my body was doing what it needed to without any intervention from me." He wonders how to react to what she has told him then starts to realise he doesn't have to; in this relationship, he has only to ask, to listen, to share. "When he was born, my husband was out drinking. They put him in my arms and I swear the world stood still. He'd given me so much trouble. He weighed almost eight pounds, being almost two weeks late, and I could barely stand towards the end. But I looked into those eyes and I promised him it was us against the world."

"What's his name?"

A smile, resting her chin on her hand, an unclouded memory showing on her face. "Thomas. Tom."

She pushes the memory away and rises to fetch the coffee pot, topping up his cup.

"Do you know how much your face gives you away?" holding her hand, threading his fingers into hers. "I think you have the most expressive face I have ever seen."

She smiles and brushes their joined hands tenderly against his cheek. "Don't you realise you're the only one who reads me that well?"

That startles him. He assumes everyone sees what he sees. "That can't be true," he disagrees, bemused.

"Would I lie to you?" she challenges. "After we promised?"

There is pride in the acceptance of what she says but it also unsettles him. Suddenly, he has to question whether there is more to this than he has allowed himself to think – to feel – before.

She releases his hand and turns away, hiding her face from him, and he realises this isn't one way. She reads him too.

He stands and comes up behind her, sliding his arms around her waist, pulling her back against him. He is almost overwhelmed by an impulse to declare himself but he knows it's the one thing he has to hold back. For the sake of both of them. She reaches behind and curves her arm around his head. He sinks his teeth into the flesh above her collar bone and she leans back against him, her eyes closing with pleasure.

* * * * * * *

Retreating to the study. They seem, mutually, to seek places in the house that can be their own and to avoid those that either are already imprinted with memories of other people or that they can't risk forever associating with the other hereafter.

Somehow, the study is acceptable. His own intensely private space, the one he has only ever shared with her.

They keep the blinds closed, both of them fearful of random chance working against them, of being spotted through the ground-floor window by someone they know. Pulling the sofa in front of the fire so they can sit together, neither wanting to be physically separated from the other. He sits at one end, a book in his left hand, and she settles back against him, her feet up. They read in silence for a while, she a new novel by James Joyce, he an anthology of war poems. It's her anthology. She bought it in a bookshop recently, part of her wanting, needing to understand, she says, what her brother went through. He surprises himself by wanting to read it and steals it from her. He has avoided so many routes back into his war memories in the past but, here, with her, somehow he feels safe.

The fire warms them through their insubstantial clothing and he enjoys the decadence, the rebellion almost, of their having thrown off society's uniforms. But it makes for a distraction too, especially the curve of her breast, hugged by the satin. He reads the same poem four times before he accepts he doesn't need to pretend.

For a while, she pretends to ignore the gentle but determined movements of his hand across her body, first through the fabric, then beneath it. He massages her skin, feeling the heat as she flushes involuntarily, then trails his fingers so lightly over the same area that her breath suddenly becomes ragged. Still she ignores him, making a show of turning the page in her book, and he laughs at her challenge. He turns his attention to her sensitive areas, toying around the edges, the inside of her elbow, the hollow at the base of her throat, the area behind her ear, the curve of her waist. Drawing the fabric so slowly away from her legs, he teases his fingers across the back of her knees, then slowly, slowly draws the tip of one finger down the inside of her thigh. He hears her frustration as he starts the trail back up the line of her other thigh, hearing her start to lose control. He repeats the movement in the opposite direction, hovering over her inside thigh this time, tracing absorbing patterns in her skin with the lightest of touches. Her book falls to the floor and, knowing he has her attention this time, he starts again with the inside of her elbow, the base of her throat. Impatient, she tries to take control, scrambling from her lying position onto his lap, straddling his thighs, inexpertly trying to force the pleasure he has withheld from her. She tries to adjust their positions so that she is lying beneath him but he prevents her. Frustrated at first that he is holding out, she comes to realise what he intends and the shock registers in her face. He sees her struggle with it, to cast off the shackles of her narrow upbringing. When she finally succeeds, he takes her face in his hands and brings it down to his, kissing her hard. She relaxes into him, trusting, until her impatience overtakes and she finally takes control. He is absorbed by her face, watching her take her pleasure, the shock, the revelation, before losing himself in her.

* * * * * * *

"Have you slept with many women?"

Sitting in his lap, face to face, watching him.

"Are you sure you want to know the answer to that?"

"I wouldn't have asked if I wasn't ready to know."

He accepts her comment. "I was nineteen the first time. We had our date for shipping to France and a friend decided we couldn't go to war without having had our first experience with a woman. He took us to Soho and bought us fifteen minutes each with a couple of young girls in a club. Though I don't think they were as young as I thought then; the poor lighting hid a myriad of flaws. It was as grim as you might expect but he was right: it freed us."

"So you didn't have to face dying a virgin."

"Worse. We thought we were more likely to die for being such."

He catches a hint of a smile at that.

440

"After that, it was easy in France. Whenever we had leave or were stationed away from the front for a while, there was an opportunity. Girls in every town. We had to find something to do with our time and we didn't always have the money to get drunk."

"How many?"

"Maybe half-a-dozen. To be honest, it palled for me after the first year. It's like a new reality sets in when you've lasted that long. You realise you can't keep behaving as if you're going to die tomorrow. Even if it's likely that you will."

"Is that where you learned...?"

He holds her chin in his hand. "Do you want more?" he offers. "I've tried to be careful. I don't want to embarrass you or make you uncomfortable."

She blushes but her eyes still hold his. "I want you," she replies simply. Her face shows more than he expected. Trust, embarrassment, defiance, excitement.

"Do you think we might go out?" she proposes. "I'd like the chance to be...normal...with you."

He smiles. "That would entail getting dressed," he caveats.

A wicked gleam in her returning smile. "Only for a while," she promises.

* * * * * * *

"The snow is so beautiful, isn't it?"

She stands at the window of her bedroom on the top floor of the house, a dormer window in the roof giving her a view over the rooftops of the city and to the park beyond. A couple of inches of snow have stifled the city so that, at this height, there's hardly a sound from below.

He stands beside her, his arm around her waist but only lightly touching her. It feels strange to be in here with her. Where she sleeps, she dresses, she escapes. Unlike most of the other servants, she

441

doesn't share a room and that pleases him, though he finds the lack of comforts in the room depressing.

She has already helped him to dress, selecting for herself the clothes she wants him to wear. Not his best suits, not his most expensive shirts. She chooses a worn pair of trousers, the kind he keeps for comfort when travelling, and a plain white shirt, good quality but simple. She lets him button the waistband of his trousers but insists on managing his shirt, choosing a pair of cufflinks to fasten the cuff. He strokes her long hair as she fastens the shirt buttons. She looks so young when he tucks her hair behind one ear.

There is both pride and some small embarrassment when she opens her wardrobe to his scrutiny. She has left her uniforms in Chicago so what she shows him is her private wardrobe. Its sparsity is a wake-up call, an unwelcome reminder of the disparity in their fortunes, but her pride in each and every garment soon dismisses the thought. She has made each item for herself over the years, not quite the latest fashions carved out of old-style dresses or end-cuts of luxurious fabric, velvet, satin, silk. The colours are exquisite, jewel-like, a brilliant turquoise, sumptuous purple and rich burgundy. She has an eye for what suits her colouring and for styles that will emphasise her slight stature. In these, she would not only fit easily into any society gathering, she would also outshine them all. He touches the fabrics lightly, marvelling at the intricacy and quality of the work, trying to avoid the sadness rising up in him that she should have no opportunity to wear these extraordinary pieces.

"This is who I am," she tells him, like him running her hand over the material. "This is what I want to wear for you."

He fights the closing of his throat. "Any less and I might have been tempted to keep you barefoot and naked," he responds lightly, "but these clothes deserve to be worn."

He chooses the turquoise for her, imagining that he would prefer to see her in richer colours later, in the dark of the evening, before a blazing fire. She sheds her robe with less embarrassment than previously though she keeps her back towards him a little self-consciously. She finds her underwear and refuses to let him near her one good pair of silk stockings for fear he will tear them. She sits on the side of her bed to put them on and he kneels before her, holding the dress over her head and gradually pulling it over her arms, sliding the silk down. She stands briefly to shimmy the skirt over her hips then sits again to let him slip on her shoes. His care overwhelms her and he finds unshed tears in her eyes when he looks up. She brushes them away, forcing down her emotion with a smile. Until now, there has been passion, there has been tenderness. Now there is caring, a deep, sweet emotion that seems to bind them more closely. He leans forward and she leans into his embrace, a gentle hug without strain, without expectation.

* * * * * * *

The street outside the house is almost abandoned, people driven indoors not by the snow fall so much as by the bitter cold of the wind, which howls through some of the back streets. They head into the city and, by the time they walk down Columbus to 57th, the streets are heaving, mostly with last-minute shoppers.

They walk side by side, not touching, barely talking. He has rapidly concluded this is a mistake or, at least, this is not the place they want to be together. They are losing their closeness with every moment, crowded out by the volumes of people. He wonders how to improve this for her, to make it bearable. He stops at the corner of Fifth Avenue. She stands by, is jostled against him by people pushing past. She is angry.

"Let's head towards the park," he suggests and she nods, relieved. As they turn, he spots one of his team from the office, hurrying as much as he can through the crowds, burdened with parcels, presents. He glances at her, concerned. Somehow, without him saying anything, she reads the situation and slips away from him, walking down the street as if they weren't together.

"Mr Westerham," the younger man greets him, shuffling his parcels to free one hand to shake his. "I thought you would have left for Chicago by now."

"Not yet," he evades.

"I'm doing the final present run," indicating his bundles. "The wife's at home with the two little ones and the rest of the family arrive tomorrow so time is short."

"Merry Christmas, Hapworth." He moves away.

"Merry Christmas, Sir. And to your lovely wife."

Something akin to panic sets in when he can't spot her in the crowd but she finds him, slipping her hand into the pocket of his coat and twining her fingers into his. Silently but with what pace they can manage in the crowds, they make their escape. Soon, the volumes of people diminish and, conscious again, she releases his hand and buries hers in her own pocket. He misses the contact.

As they reach the corner of 87th and Columbus, they both look towards Central Park but, as one, they turn back towards the house. In the almost empty street, he draws her arm through his, covering her hand with his to keep her warm. She doesn't smile but she does rub her thumb against his skin.

* * * * * * *

The telephone is ringing as they open the door. His instinct is, of course, to answer but as he looks at her he sees the constraints she has thrown off start to crowd in. She, like he, hates this second intrusion of the outside world into their private reality. He knows he should answer it. He knows it's probably Sarah. But speaking to her would shatter the small world they have created for themselves here and it's already fragile enough. She leaves the decision to him, as he knows she must, but he knows how the decision will affect her and this is what decides him. He helps her out of her coat while the incessant ringing continues, hanging it along with his in the hidden

444

closet, and, taking her hand, walks past the telephone, leaving it ringing. To their relief, it stops as they start to climb the stairs. The last sound reverberates around the hall for a second. He halts, returns to the hall and pulls the cable out of the socket, then leads her upstairs.

* * * * * * *

In the security of their room, hidden from the world, they lie on the bed, still clothed, on their sides but facing each other. Their hands are entwined between them but their heads are a distance apart on the pillows, the better to read each other's faces.

"Just us," she asserts, a tear slipping from her eye and across the bridge of her nose. He wipes it away.

"Just us," he agrees.

"Are we being naïve?" she questions after a while. "Out there, this somehow seemed so absurd."

"Out there, it would," he reassures, having been through this thought process himself while they walked back. "No one will ever understand this but you and I. As long as it works for us, does it matter what it seems like out there?"

"You didn't doubt?" she fears.

"Did you?" fearing now. She refuses to answer, needing his response first. "No, I didn't doubt. It felt odd, thinking how this might look to someone else but nothing felt so right as the moment we turned out backs on all that and came home."

"The one thing I don't doubt in all this is us." She frowns. "Why is that?"

"There's something right in what we have here," he tries to find his way, not knowing how to explain. "Ever since I left Devon for the war, I've never known a place I would call home. But when I said the word now, it felt right. Not because of the bricks and mortar but because coming home means being here with you."

"I haven't had a home since leaving the place I grew up in. Perhaps not even then. It was such a cold, unemotional place. My parents barely talked to each other, certainly never touched each other. Michael couldn't wait to get away either."

"Where did he die?" The brother and sister, in spite of the years between them, had been very close. He was devastated by her marriage to the wrong man, she more so by his death.

"At Loos. September 1915. He's buried out there. One day I will visit."

He could so easily promise to take her there. He has to remind himself he doesn't have that right. He knows, though, that she reads the wish in his eyes and, somehow, that is almost enough. "I was there," he tells her, knowing even as he does so what it will open up.

"Will you tell me about it?" she asks. "I need to understand what it was like for him out there."

"I will," he promises. "Later. Will you tell me something?"

"Anything." Unhesitating in her promise.

"You said you didn't doubt us."

The clear gaze clouds over. "You're wondering what it is I do doubt." He holds her gaze, seeing the doubts take form as tears. "I doubt," she whispers, "that this will work, that we can actually give her what she wants. I doubt that I could ever do this again should it not succeed this time." She draws a deep breath but it doesn't prevent the crack in her voice. "Most of all, I doubt my ability to walk away when I must."

He closes the gap between them before she even finishes speaking, taking her in his arms, cradling her head on his shoulder. He feels his throat thicken in response, knowing the truth of what she says, and buries his face in her shoulder too, breathing deeply the scent of her hair, her skin, desperate suddenly to have memories to hold against the long, bleak times to come.

* * * * * * *

446

The days are short and the light soon leaches out of the afternoon. For a while, they sleep, compensating for the lack of sleep the night before and drained by their emotions. When they stir, they naturally reach for each other, adjusting their positions for comfort but staying as close as comfort will allow. When they wake, they wake to a rekindling of their desire, reassured to find it matched in the other, yearning to impose a small part of themselves onto the soul of the other. Hurried now, desperate even, their clothes are discarded in a pile on the floor. Until he remembers and, retrieving her dress, drapes it over the back of a chair to protect it before returning to her arms.

* * * * * * *

He tries to cook for her that night but her impatience at his inadequate skills soon turns to laughing frustration. She doesn't take over but she works alongside him to produce something recognisable as steak pie.

They eat in the study. He sits in his usual chair, she on the floor at his feet. He tries to prevent it at first, feeling it is an unwelcome reminder of their positions until she tells him her memories of sitting before the fire at her maternal grandmother's cottage, toasting muffins in the open flames, a rare, happy, uncomplicated childhood picture. He doesn't argue after that.

He pours them both a whisky afterwards, laughing as she shudders against the unfamiliar taste and the burn in her throat, and again when she asks for a refill. She stays sitting on the floor, her head pillowed on her arms resting on his lap. He strokes her head, her hair so soft beneath his fingers. While they're like this, the silence is a joy, muffling them against the world, protecting them. Only when they are not touching does it become alien, oppressive almost, as if it too was conspiring to part them.

He reads to her from the anthology of war poems. Owen taps uncomfortably at the closed door of his soul. Graves elicits acknowledgement but no empathy. Sassoon makes him angry, feeling the betrayal of what they had stood for.

"He should know better," barely controlled anger resonant in his voice. "It was never about the politics or the incompetence of the command. It was never about the rightness or otherwise of the cause. Not for us."

She hugs her knees to her chest but still resting her weight against his legs. "What was it about?"

He is glad she is nearby. He knows he will expose parts of his soul in this that he has so carefully kept contained and controlled. It is his promise to himself and to her that he will share this with her and her alone.

"It was only ever about the men. By the time we arrived, the reason was no longer relevant and, to me, that perpetual harping about the injustice of the cause is the beating of a hollow drum. It was our officers who taught us that. By the time we got there, the first wave had already been wiped out. The pride of Harrow and Eton slaughtered on a bloody French field. But, my God, they showed us the way. Seventeen and eighteen years old, our age – younger by the time we were done – who arrived knowing their average lifespan was six weeks, three months if they were lucky, and, still, they put all of us first. They made us coffee in the trenches, shared out their cigarettes, arranged letters home. They encouraged the ones who held, punished the ones who failed. I saw so many of them come and go. I have never known better men. That's what it was about." He looked down as her, her chin resting on her hands, looking up at him with that clear, uncompromising gaze. He lifts her hair from her temple with a gentle finger. "You want to know what it was like for your brother?" he questions. "Are you sure you do?"

She nods, a slight movement with some fear in the eyes but more determination. "He kept his letters so neutral I could never understand. We've always been so close I find it difficult not knowing about that side of his life. Just describe it to me. Help me see it."

He leans his head back against the chair, the back of his hand resting against her head. He closes his eyes briefly but the darkness threatens to overwhelm him and he stares at the ceiling instead.

"I met a man in Italy once who told me what it was like in Ypres. He said the ground was always wet because the water table is high so most of their trenches were only partly dug, partly built up with sandbags. I think we were more fortunate in some ways in Loos. We could dig deeper and we had extra protection from the slag heaps in the coal mining district.

"By the time I arrived, there were yards and yards of barbed wire set up at the front of our trench and in front of theirs. Wire netting, too, to keep grenades out of your trench. We would go out under cover of darkness to repair it. We had dugouts in the side of the trench wall, just big enough to shelter three or four of us or as a telephone position for a signaller. They always stank of mud, sweat or stale food and the air was so clammy. We had duckboards in the base of the trench when it rained. It froze in the winter and then the trench foot gave way to frost bite.

"You don't spend that much time at the front line, although it could seem interminable when you were there. Otherwise we were training, running supply lines or resting. We worked as a group of ten of us, four days in the front, four in close reserve and then four days off. During the night, four of us were posted, one during the day. We'd either be in the trench or out in the saps, the trenches going into No-Man's Land. We'd have a couple of us in there, listening for activity. The strain was terrible, not only your hearing but also your muscles, frozen in position for hours at a time, afraid to miss the slightest noise, afraid also to be heard on the other side. The lack of sleep made us all go a little mad. If you were caught sleeping on guard, you could be court-martialled and shot. At dawn and again at

449

dusk, we'd all have to stand to, manning the trench in case of enemy attack. In between, we took sentry duty and we repaired the trench and maintained our equipment and uniforms. The boredom was intolerable.

"Rations were always brought up by night. If we were lucky, we could cook ourselves a breakfast over the braziers." He laughs, remembering suddenly. "The latrine was just a deep hole in the ground, with a plank to sit on. I went in one day and there was a bloody great rat sitting there, cleaning his whiskers. God knows how he could stand the smell. It didn't help that sometimes we couldn't change or even wash for days or weeks at a time.

"The rats were everywhere and the lice and the maggots and the flies. Anywhere there was a decomposing corpse, whether human or animal. They were always in the food, the scraps we discarded, the empty tins.

"Winters were bad. It seemed to rain almost the whole winter and when it didn't rain it blew, straight into our faces when on sentry. Water ran down the trenches in rivers. We slept in soaking clothes with our boots full of water. Whole sections of the trench collapsed into a chaos of slime and ooze.

"Then the spring came. We dreaded the spring. There were frogs and slugs everywhere. The smell was always much worse in the spring. In the winter, the corpses and body parts froze or were covered with snow. When the thaw came, the stench returned. Cats took to nesting in the corpses, waiting for the rats to appear. But we dreaded it most because the offensive would start again. During the winter, you couldn't attack so we all hunkered down. Spring meant we started again.

"Sometimes they targeted the trenches beforehand to destroy the barbed wire and the gun positions. I don't know which was worse: the fighting or the waiting. The noise of the bombardment was terrible and it went on for days. You couldn't sleep. Your nerves were shattered before you even faced the enemy. But the silence meant we were ready to attack. That hour of silence before we went over the top.

"There was no bombardment before Loos. We had broken through in one area on the first day but we had no support. The infantry were stationed too far back and by the time they arrived the Germans had regrouped. They still sent us in. Hundreds of cheering men moving forward as fast as they could. Until a hundred yards from the wire when the guns were let loose on them. Right along the line men started to stumble and to fall. The firing seemed to go on for hours. The German machine guns were protected behind barbed wire, in some places 30 feet thick. We walked straight into the guns. Their work had never been so easy.

"We made it to one section of the German trench. When we came out again, we couldn't stand to look. The whole slope was one mass of prone figures, some lying on top of one another. So many were dead. The wounded were trying to help each other. It was terrible to hear their cries, men lying wounded and dying on the slope. We couldn't help most of them. Even if the Germans had allowed us, we had no stretchers.

"The fighting went on for weeks but I'd been invalided out by then. When I came back, I didn't recognise half the men there. We'd lost so many of the men we'd started out with. I was just grateful to be back with Alfie and Billy. I could so easily have been assigned to a different regiment. After that, it felt like the three of us were meant to stick together, to help all of us get through the war.

"We fought in the Somme in '16 and Ypres in '17 then they sent us to Italy. The Italians had had a disaster in the November and the Austrians were being bolstered by German units. They ripped through the Italian front line. When we got there, the men we met we so disillusioned. Half of it was tiredness and lack of food but the other half was the brutality of their commanders. When we arrived, you wouldn't believe the crowds that greeted us, like when the first British troops went into France.

"Most of the men had never seen anything like it. After years of staring at the mud in France, it was like another world, so lush and beautiful, the snow-capped mountains behind the river. We didn't really know what we were facing. All we knew was that the Russians had pulled out of the eastern front so we were facing bigger numbers of Austrians and more Germans than ever before. They were so much more afraid of the Germans than the Austrians. But there were rumours all around the towns how the Slavs and the Czechs wanted independence and were disrupting everything. By the October, we were ready to fight.

"The bombardment on the first day destroyed their barbed wire and their trenches. The noise of the shelling was tremendous and the smoke was so thick we couldn't see even as we pushed across the river and up into the mountains so we climbed close together up the steep slopes.

"We hunkered down in one of the small villages on the mountainside. There was nothing left but rubble from years of shelling by one side or the other but the walls provided enough shelter for us to rest our backs against. It hid us too from the searchlights as they swept the hillside.

"We were exhilarated. It had been hand-to-hand fighting. Desperate, bloody and brutal. None of this walking into organised machine guns. The men were scattered across the village. I sat there with Alfie and Billy, eating bread and cheese they had scrounged from God knows where and smoking. Rain began to fall and it was turning bitterly cold but we had nowhere to shelter.

"I could see Billy getting more and more agitated, more tense. I think he sensed victory, or at least hoped for it. He was seventeen when he enlisted. Four years later, he was starting to believe he might go home soon.

"Alfie has stolen a bottle of whisky from somewhere. It took the chill off so we just kept drinking, though I think Billy was getting more than his share. He started talking about home. About some girl

452

he had met up with the last time he had been on leave, some lass he'd known from his school days. I tried to shut him up so that we could get some sleep but he just kept talking and talking. About her blue eyes and her blond hair and her tiny waist and her curvy figure.

"Suddenly, he got up and started walking around, throwing out his arms and challenging the Austrians to come and get him because he'd had enough and he was going to finish this war here and now. One of the other soldiers nearby rugby tackled him and brought him crashing down to the ground and the captain came over and demanded what all the fuss was about.

"I promised to keep Billy quiet and practically sat on him to stop him getting up again. The captain went away and we all settled down again. Billy crawled a little distance away and lay down with his back towards me.

"The rain stopped and the skies started to clear. I lay there looking at the stars, unable to sleep, though I could hear Alfie snoring. I must have slept because I was woken by the sudden bark of a dog, quite nearby, and saw that the sky was starting to lighten in the east. I was a little dazed but it only took a moment to figure out that Alfie was still there but there was no sign of Billy. I lay still for almost a minute before I heard someone crashing about in the undergrowth on the edge of the village. I crawled across the floor, trying to stay hidden by the ruined buildings, until I got to the dark perimeter. I heard the noise again and followed it.

"It took some minutes but, eventually, I caught up with him. He was crawling forward on his stomach, like we used to on scouting missions in No-Man's Land. He was edging up the mountainside in the direction of the Austrian army. But he was too drunk to be careful and he was crashing around like God knows what.

"As soon as I was in reach of him, I grabbed at his ankle to yank him backwards. He yelped so loudly. He obviously hadn't worked out I was behind him and leapt to his feet to run before I could stop him.

"In that moment, the search lights swung in our direction. I could see him stop and he just stood there, staring at the light, blinded. I leapt forward to drag him back to the ground but he was already hit before I got there. It was the easiest target a sniper ever had.

"He seemed to fall in slow motion. The bullet spun him round so that suddenly he was facing me and he had such a look of surprise on his face. Then his knees gave out beneath him and he sank to the ground. He put one hand to his chest. I could already see the blackness spreading across his jacket and he looked in disbelief at his hand when it came away covered in blood.

"I caught him as he fell forwards. The bullet had gone clean through him but it had hit his stomach, not his heart. It's the worst of all wounds because it takes so long to die. I dragged the two of us across the ground until we were in the shelter of the mountainside and I leaned back against the rock face and pulled him back against me. His face was so white in the moonlight as his blood seeped onto the ground. He looked so young. I'd forgotten. After four years together, I'd forgotten how young he was. He hadn't even yet come of age. But I saw it now in his face. In the fear that overwhelmed him and the regret. He knew he was dying and it terrified him. The loss of all those years before him. No wife or children to mourn him. Only his mother and father and brother to remember him, to regret for him.

"It took such a long time. I can't remember what I said to him but I know he talked. Such nonsense, he talked. About going to Rome once the war was over and from there to Singapore and onto New Zealand. How he was going to bring his girl out there and build a home with her. How they would have half-a-dozen children and his parents would come out to live with them in clean air and open countryside, leaving behind the smog and dirt of home. How proud his parents were of him. And how afraid his mother was the last time he took leave. Bidding him farewell with tears in her eyes.

454

"He looked me in the face as he felt his life leaving him and there were tears streaming down his cheeks. He begged me to see his mother once the war was over and to tell her what kind of soldier he had been. I could feel him growing cold in my arms and I pulled him closer. He didn't even grimace at the pain. And I knew it was because he couldn't feel anything any more. And in a few moments, he had gone."

He stops. He hasn't noticed until now the tears that have soaked his cheeks, kept talking through. He notices, though, the terrible anger that has built and built inside his chest. "Three weeks. Three fucking weeks and the whole thing was over. If only he'd waited three more weeks."

His breathing is choked inside his windpipe and his vision starts to darken at the edges with the anger. The stupidity of it all. The absolute, fucking stupidity. So many lives wasted, so many more destroyed, even more left empty and unfulfilled. What the fuck for?

He pushes roughly to his feet, blind to her as the rage, so long suppressed, threatens to overwhelm him. He must get back in control or he knows he risks losing himself, as so many of those other souls have sought oblivion, insanity, death even, to avoid living with the reality. Whisky to take the edge off. A bottle on the table in the corner. His hands shake so much he spills quantities of it as he pours a glass. The first large measure disappears down his throat and he welcomes the harsh burn, whether for the pain or as a reminder that he's alive, he doesn't know or care. Pouring the second glass empties the bottle. He stares at it in disbelief. What a bloody idiot. What a damn fool. They had been so near the end. To have taken such a risk. To have left them to deal with the mess. What kind of friend did that? What kind of fucking friend? Before he knows what has happened, the bottle smashes against the opposite wall.

Any other woman would have stayed well clear. He stares at her in disbelief too. Her face has been dried but her skin in ashen and the lashes of her eyes betray her hidden tears. She stands before him, this tiny woman, barely coming up to his chin. He sees her pain and it seems to amplify his and then it subdues him, pushing out the anger which instantly drains away, leaving him shaking, staggering. He falls against the wall, crumpling to the floor. She goes with him, holding him as his body shudders with huge sobs, the release of years of suppressed pain. She holds his head, stroking his hair, his cheeks. He fights to get her closer, pulling her onto his lap, cradling her as she cradles him, holding onto each other in the blackness that could consume them both.

She pulls him back from the brink. Soft kisses of tenderness and reassurance against his temple, his cheek, his jaw wake him to a remembrance of himself. His grasp on her gradually weakens, relaxes. He rests his head back against the wall, closes his eyes, steadies his breathing. Still she plants gentle, reassuring kisses on him, taking his two hands in hers and burying her face in them, kissing his fingertips, his palms. He realises how cold he is when he notices the warmth of her breath and lips. Slowly, she stirs his soul and he finally meets her eyes. She shies away at that and he brings his hand up to hold her face so that he can stare into those compassionate, reassuring, rejuvenating eyes and find himself again.

She holds his gaze for as long as she can bear. He can feel her heart pounding in her chest and the warmth starts to flood back into his limbs. Nervously, almost, he lifts his chin to bring his mouth closer to hers, still holding her gaze, needing the reassurance of her permission. For a fraction of a second, she holds herself at a distance then it is she who closes the gap and claims his mouth in a hard, desperate kiss.

Instantly, he is lost. All the pent-up anger, controlled again, manifests in his desire for her and reacts to the passion she ignites as if he is on fire, pulling her against his body, rolling her onto the floor, pinning her there with his weight. He takes her there, hard, just on the passionate side of brutality. She responds in kind, a life-affirming, purging passion that, threatening to consume them both, leaves them clinging to each other for safety. His iron-clad walls are suddenly as fragile as glass in the face of the emotional and physical onslaught from this woman, her sobs as ecstasy takes her turning to silent, streaming tears as she trembles in his arms. Knowing she weeps as much for him as for her brother, and for all those like them, shatters his defences. He buries his face in her shoulder and silently weeps.

SUNDAY

He sleeps like he hasn't slept in years, only once disturbed by a confusion of memories and dreams. She is there for him throughout, she holding him tonight. At some point, he reaches for her and she responds willingly but he is exhausted and slides back into the sheltering darkness.

By the time he finally wakes, dawn has come and gone. The morning light floods the room, reaching into the farthest corners. She is watching him, her head propped up on her hand, the other warm on his chest. Thankfully, her eyes are clear and there is even a slight smile playing around her lips.

He closes his eyes for a moment, ashamed at how he has used her. He has noticed the bruise on her shoulder where he has held her too roughly.

"Are you alright?" Her soft voice makes him open his eyes again.

"I was about to ask you the same thing."

The smile deepens. "A little sore, maybe, but nothing I can't handle."

"I'm sorry," he murmurs.

"I'm not," she reassures.

"I have never told anyone the things I told you last night."

She nods, "I know," and, winding her fingers into his, brings his hand to her lips.

He shifts and turns on his side, the better to face her, strokes her cheek with the back of his fingers.

"You will always carry a piece of me with you now," he warns. "For the rest of your life. Please, be gentle with me."

The shimmer in her eyes is caught by the sun breaking through and it sparkles.

"Whether you know it or not," she tells him, softly, calmly, holding his jaw in her splayed hand, "you have had a part of me since the day we met."

He feels his heart catch and the bottom seems to fall out of his stomach. He runs his hand into her hair, drawing her closer. "I may be slower on the uptake," he whispers, transfixed by the emotion in her silver gaze, "but I feel the same."

He touches his lips to hers, so gently. All tenderness, caring and gentleness, their lovemaking is slow and careful, an affirmation one to the other of their joint survival.

* * * * * *

"Will you tell me about these scars?"

She is sitting up in bed and he lightly traces the white lines on her back. Her response is to shake out her long hair to cover them and to reach for her dressing gown, pulling it around her shoulders as she leaves the room.

"Grace!" he calls after her, grabbing his clothes and running to follow. She has already vanished by the time he gets to the corridor. Her room is empty, as is the study. Eventually, he finds her in the kitchen, standing at the stove with her back to him. She hears him enter but doesn't turn around. He takes a seat at the table and waits. For some minutes, she continues to ignore him as she cooks breakfast and he allows her the distraction, the time to marshal her thoughts.

458

She prepares only one plate of food and puts it in front of him, taking the seat opposite.

"Eat," she orders.

Sick to his stomach by how she has shut him down, he has little appetite but he does as he is bid. She stays silent for some moments longer. When she speaks at last, he finds her head is raised, defiantly almost, but she is not looking at him, rather beyond him, staring at the far wall.

"From when he beat me." Her tone is controlled and clinical. Only her distant tone is keeping the flash of anger from controlling him. Perhaps that is why she speaks that way, although he rather suspects it has more to do with her wanting to stay in control of herself. "He beat me often but normally left only bruises. This is the one time he left a lasting reminder."

He pushes away his half-finished breakfast, doing it with enough emphasis that she is finally forced to look at him. He doesn't say anything but he deliberately folds his arms on the table and looks at her, showing her they are going nowhere until she has been honest with him.

"Oh, Christ," she swears, pushing her hair away from her face. "I didn't want to do this." He has already worked that out for himself. "I was seventeen when I fell pregnant with Tom and I was just over four months gone when we married. At first, it was fine. I mean, we had hardly any money because I wasn't working and shared a two up, two down with another family, but I was young and, I thought, I was free. His work was always sporadic. It turns out that was because he drank to excess and frequently didn't get up in time for work so jobs came and went.

"I tried to make do with what we had but it was never enough for him. The first time he hit me, it was because there weren't enough potatoes for his dinner. He was drunk, of course. I ran next door to a friend but her husband sent me straight back again. He told me it was a man's right to treat his wife as he saw fit and no one should ever

459

get involved. The other wives in the street, they all had their own stories but most of them could hide their bruises. He didn't care where he hit me or who saw. In some ways, there was more honesty in it but more brutality as well.

"Then, one night when Tom was barely ten months old, he came home late from the pub. He stank. Of booze, of sweat, of vomit. I almost retched myself at the smell of him. He clattered around the room, staggering into furniture. The woman upstairs screamed at him to be quiet and that, of course, woke Tom. He went off swearing and yelling, just making everything worse, and he took a swipe at the baby. He didn't connect, he was far too drunk for that. In fact, he caught himself off balance and collapsed on the floor. He was too drunk to stand so I left him where he fell.

"I was shaking so much I could hardly fasten my clothes. I had nothing to put Tom's things in but the laundry bag so I stuffed it with what little I had, grabbed him and I ran. Thank God it was summertime or the poor lamb might have frozen to death in the time it took me to walk across town that night.

"I hadn't seen my parents since I told them about the pregnancy. They threw me out. Not that I cared because, as far as I was concerned, I was escaping anyway. But I thought they would help me for the sake of their grandson. I couldn't have been more wrong. How I had misjudged them. Their pride meant more to them than forgiveness. They couldn't face the embarrassment of a fatherless child in their house. They wouldn't even let me in. I sat on the doorstep for I don't know how long, wondering what to do. My father came out eventually. I had made my bed, he said, and he was going to make me lie in it. He dragged us onto a bus and he rode all the way back with us. He walked right up to the door of the house and he watched me go back in with his grandson before he turned his back and walked away.

"The drunken sot hadn't even noticed we had gone. He was still lying exactly where I had left him. I sat in the corner of that room

460

with Tom in my arms and I cried for hours. I cried until Tom couldn't take it any more and he started crying too, which woke his father, of course.

"After that, everything was about protecting Tom. It didn't matter what he did to me as long as he left my boy alone. He only took his belt to me once, though. I took it off him the next time he was too drunk to wake up and I burned it in the range. The smell of burnt leather pervaded the house for weeks."

She almost smiles to herself at the memory, though with her head now bent over her hands, it's hard to tell.

"Where is he now?" he probes.

She shakes her head, denying an answer.

"And where's Tom, Grace?"

This time, she gets up from the table and turns her back, making a show of collecting the cooking utensils together for cleaning. The sound of him pushing back his chair is loud in the silence. He crosses to stand in front of her, raising her chin with the side of his index finger. She is dry-eyed but she keeps her eyes cast down, veiled. Accepting her decision not to tell him, he lightly kisses her forehead. Relieved, she leans against him and his arms naturally come around her, rocking her gently.

"Thank you," she whispers, slipping her arms around his waist.

He nods and holds her close.

* * * * * * *

It's snowing again. They have been indoors too long and both stare jealously at the outside world, watching the large flakes drift slowly down and settle on the previous fall.

"Can't we?" she asks hesitatingly. The look of longing is too much to resist, particularly when it melds with his own will.

The temperature has dropped even further so he finds her one of Sarah's cloaks to wear, one with a hood to shelter her. The street is deserted. She stands for a moment letting the flakes fall on her face. Such an innocent pleasure. He smiles, pulls the hood up for her and they walk away from the city down the empty back streets, enjoying the muffling effect of the snow and the quiet of the city. It is Sunday, Christmas Eve, and they can hear distantly the bells of the churches ringing their congregations forth.

Apart from his wedding day, he has had nothing to do with the church in years, since before the war, but she shyly tells him she would like to go and he finds he can't deny her.

They follow the sounds and find one not far from the house. A slow straggle of people are arriving and they are able to slip into the back row without much notice. He's not a fan of much of the church architecture here, which lacks the centuries-long mellowing of churches in England, and this one, in carved greyish granite, is cold and forbidding.

Inside, though, he finds the building warm, welcoming and strangely intimate and comfortable. Used to the austerity of Anglican chapels, the high level of decoration here surprises him. The blue painted ceiling reflects stars back at him, like the church roof is open to the heavens. The paired octagonal or cylindrical columns supporting multiple arches on either side of the nave are likewise painted in blue and in striking red and gold bands. Stained glass, even in this weak winter light, casts glowing colours over the congregation, pictures of angels and archangels flanking Christ at the far end of the church, less elaborate but no less beautiful two and three panelled geometric designs above the arches to left and right, each with a cross intricately picked out in blues, yellows, oranges, purples, greens. Gold shines and warms with the light of the multitude of candles, reflecting off the canopied enclosure above the high altar, the elaborate filigree work of the three-tiered lights in the body of the church, the Christ crucified in one of the side chapels. Each alcove hosts a saint's shrine, marble statues and altars enclosed behind matching carved pillars and gates: Agnes, Mary, Patrick,

Ann. He realises how this faith – unlike his mother's – is peopled with reminders of those who have lived well and what they have stood for, and with the vivid depiction of Christ to his right, a visible and vivid reminder of his suffering.

She is silent beside him. She follows the words of the liturgy and stands for the hymns but she is not here to join in either. She sits close beside him, her arm a slight pressure against his, but she will not otherwise touch him. Her grey eyes are solemn and dark in the poor light and she keeps her cloak on against the chill of the unheated air. It gives her an otherworldly air and he can't help but feel she is distant from him. She prays while others go up for communion, kneeling on a hassock, her hands clasped before her on the back of the pew in front. When he sees a single tear escape from her closed eyes, his heart goes out to her. He does not know what is preying on her mind but he hopes she finds comfort here if not from him.

They leave before the blessing, she taking the lead, seeking his hand and leaving hers in his as they pass through the door and down the steps. He wonders if her renewed comfort with his proximity means she has found answers in there.

The snow has stopped while they were inside and patches of blue sky bring a lighter feel to the day, though more snow seems to hover in low grey clouds on the horizon. The sun appears intermittently, cheering for all that it lacks warmth. She is quiet, lost in her thoughts, as they walk down Amsterdam Avenue, slowly, wanting the walk more than the destination.

She shivers suddenly and he knows it is as of someone walking over her grave, which disturbs him more than he thinks reasonable. It causes him to draw her hand through his arm, bringing her closer, within the shelter of his proximity. She is wary, pulling away slightly until he resists.

"We shouldn't," she whispers uneasily. "What if we see someone you know."

He knows he should care, that he should worry, but he doesn't and he tells her as such, bending to murmur his response in her ear, deliberately touching his lips against the tip of her ear as he speaks and again against her hair as he straightens. He is discrete in the movement but his discretion is for her sake, not because of those around them.

Being closer together enables quiet conversation as they walk. He wants to ask what she was praying for but if feels too much of an intrusion in this public space, though he wouldn't have hesitated in their private bolthole. Instead, he asks about her views on art, on books, on movies.

Less hesitant than he, perhaps, she tolerates this for a while before redirecting the tenor of the conversation by asking what it was at work that brought him back to New York earlier in the month. He looks at her for a long moment, surprised at her question, and she starts to withdraw it, shyness overcoming her, as if she fears she has gone too far.

"I know it's none of my business…"

"That's not why I hesitate," he informs her. "I'm just startled. My work is one of the few subjects we've never broached. I guess I assumed you weren't interested."

"I am," she defends. "I'm interested," she hesitates then allows the admission, "I'm interested in what you do. Besides," a flash of amused defiance to cover her vulnerability, "you should know better than to assume anything about me."

He accepts the rebuke with a smile.

"I've been investigating some discrepancies," he explains. "Specifically, some decisions that appear to contravene what has previously been agreed."

Even as he speaks, he finds himself strangely hesitant. She misreads the silence that elapses for a few moments.

"If it's not appropriate for you to tell me…"

"It's not that," he denies, stopping suddenly. "Yes, I'm aware of the sensitivity," he continues, "but I trust you and I know…" He stops as if to double-check the accuracy of what he is about to say. "Instinctively," he reaffirms, "I know you wouldn't betray that trust. It's more that," he searches for a way to explain what he is suddenly feeling, "by talking about Williams, I feel it will allow that other life to invade. It will infiltrate what we have here and now. Every instinct in me rebels against that. I want to keep that other world at bay. For as long as we possibly can," he urges her. She nods her understanding. He automatically leans into her, drawing her arm closer to his chest and wrapping his gloved hand into hers. "I find it hard to believe we've had so little time together – and yet I've felt so much. For almost two days now, I've lived with you…" he stops and shakes his head, his eyes narrowing as he again seeks the right words. "No, I was going to say, as with a wife, but that's not right. There's been so much more between us than that. I don't know have the words to describe it," he falters.

"It's like," she picks up the thread, her grey eyes crystal clear in the harsh winter light and staring directly into his, "being with one's own true self. It's as if I have become more myself for being with you. As if, what I am to everyone else is somehow a reflection back to them of what they want or need or expect me to be. But with you…"

Her voice fails as he pulls off his gloves and cups her face with his hands, his eyes alive with shock, understanding, disbelief.

"…you see me for who I am," he finishes, his voice tense and intense. "You see through me and into me. You know me and I feel you understand me. You accept me and yet you make me want to challenge myself to be more than I am." His eyes question. "How is that even possible?"

"When we know so little about each other? When we've spent so little time together?" She looks at him clearly, unflinchingly, sadly. "When you're in love with someone else?"

465

"But I'm not." His denial is neither strained nor emphatic. It is a simple statement of fact. "The person I am to her, isn't the person I am with you. I know," he interrupts, seeing the impatience in her eyes. "It sounds trite. But that makes it no less true. I feel as if I've just discovered the person I truly am in these hours and minutes with you."

The sadness in her eyes is growing, tinged at the edges with shades of anger. "And in the next twenty-four hours, forty-eight at the most, it will all become utterly irrelevant," she condemned. "For both of us."

It makes him feel sick to his stomach and he tries to deny it to himself but he can't lie to her. She speaks the truth that neither of them can do anything about and it opens a chasm before them. He tries to speak but the words won't come. He tries to hide the despair from his eyes but she has already seen it and it is mirrored now in her own eyes.

"Don't," he denies, pulling her close and burying his face in her neck. "Oh my love, please don't."

She shakes her head, choking back her tears, and forces his head away from her, putting even a slight distance between them, holding her hands at his temple to force him to look into her eyes.

"What use are tears to us now?" she fights back, anger her weapon. "Should we waste what time we have like this? Or will we take these moments of time while they are ours and make of them a lifetime?"

He meets her anger with resolution, crushing her to him again, his hands rough on her body beneath her cloak and his mouth pinioning hers, demanding, desperate. She meets him halfway until she finally breaks free, breathless and laughing. She smooths his bewilderment away with quick kisses against his mouth, his cheek, under his jaw, until she provokes a reaction and, with a growl, he holds her from him.

"Are you trying to create a scene?" he demands, a disbelieving laugh breaking free. "I thought you were wanting to be discrete?"

"Hang the discretion," she whispers hoarsely, "Take me home. Now."

* * * * * * *

"I wish we could go dancing."

She is padding around their bedroom, draped in her dressing gown, twisting her long hair in her hands, pushing it, unpinned, into a loose chignon, then shaking it out with her hands as it tumbles about her shoulders again. There is a nervous energy about her.

The room is dark, the curtains pulled against the remaining early evening light, with only pools of illumination in opposite corners where she has lit a couple of lamps. It casts a warm glow over her skin and darkens those luminescent eyes. Lying on the bed with the sheets around his waist, his eyes don't leave her.

"When is your birthday?"

A direct look but a shy smile. "The same day as yours."

"I don't believe you," he disagrees and receives a warning flash of anger from those mercurial eyes.

"Don't ever…" she warns and he holds up his hands in apology.

"I didn't know," he defends.

"Something to carry with you," she promises with a whispered smile. He's been playing this game for the last half-an-hour. It's as if he wants every part of her he can, to hold onto from this day forward.

"What about Tom?" he says the name tentatively, hoping she won't reject his trespass onto her protected memories. "When was he born?"

The smile falters slightly but she still gives him the answer. "On the 24th of October, 1916. Around three in the morning. After thirteen excruciating hours of labour. I wouldn't recommend it," she smiles to cover her discomfort.

"Why 'Tom'?"

"Ah," teasingly as if drifting into an old, pleasant memory, "Tom was my first love."

"Who was he?" No jealousy, no rancour. There is no doubt in this world.

"One of my father's pupils, the son of the local match factory steward."

"Was it love at first sight?"

"Enough, Jack!" she kneels on the bed beside him, bracing herself with an arm on either side of his hips. "Enough with the questions!" She stops suddenly, a question on her own face.

"What is it?"

She frowns. "Why does she call you John? I've never heard her call you Jack but everyone else does."

He shrugs it off. "I don't know."

She kneels back and folds her arms, still frowning. It is an arresting image, her hair falling forward over her face and he struggles to concentrate. "You're hiding from me. Don't," she urges.

"Why does she call you Rachel?" he responds.

"To protect me. To hide me."

"Is it?" he challenges, softly. "Or is it about control?"

"What do you mean?"

He thinks for a moment before speaking. "She has her own view of the world," he observes carefully, "and she's very adept at shaping the world to fit that view."

She accepts his analysis, in part, he suspects, to move off the subject as quickly as possible. It's not an edifying subject for either of them.

"Did you hear what I said before?" she deflects.

"About dancing? Yes."

She shifts her position, easing closer to him, resting across his lap, her face close to his. "I want to dance with you," she breathes, threading the fingers of one hand into his. "Imagine it," she breathes. "Feel the rhythm, the heat of the dance hall crushed with too many bodies, couples fighting for space to be alone together in the midst of the throng. You hold me so close, so safe in your arms as we move to that rhythm, two bodies moving as one. I want," her eyes shining, "to be seen with you where anyone who sees us can recognise we are part of one another. Where we can defy society's constraints. Where we are free to be nothing but what we are to each other."

The picture she paints for him is incredibly seductive and, as she leans forward, he pulls her across his body and onto the pillow beside him, smothering her beneath his upper body as he pinions her arms above her head, holding her wrists together with one hand, the better to free his other hand to trail teasing devastation against her skin. She curves upwards to capture his mouth with hers but she can't hold herself there while her hands are still pinned and falls back against the bed, frustrated. He succumbs to her unspoken demand and leans down to tease open her mouth, feeling his temporary control slip as she willingly returns his kiss and draws him in. The second he frees her wrists, her hands claim him, the one grasping his neck then clawing at his head the better to increase the pressure in their kiss, the other hand between his shoulder blades, forcing his torso against hers, pinning them both deeper into the mattress even as her body rises to demand release.

* * * * * * *

She is half-lying across him, one leg resting between his, her cheek against his, one hand clasped in his as he cradles her to him with his left arm. He has never felt so languid, so satiated, repeatedly drawing his hand through her long hair from crown to tip, feeling the heavy hair slide through his fingers like satin.

469

"It's Christmas Eve," he points out, too comfortable and drowsy now to give real thought to her request. He closes his eyes. "Where are we going to find a dance hall open on Christmas Eve?"

He barely feels her shift her head but senses the closeness of her mouth to his ear as her lips and breath brush his skin. "Harlem." The word is barely a breath.

He slowly opens his eyes to find her propping her chin against her hand, flat against his chest.

He doesn't know how but, somehow, she knows the magic and the temptation that resonates in that word for him.

* * * * * * *

There is no denying the illicit appeal, the sense of somehow encroaching upon, discovering even, this subculture that not only stands apart from the mainstream, from the familiar puritanical mores of his upbringing, but actively undermines them. Perhaps it is unsurprising it should have appeal for both of them at this point, driven into an alien world where the normal and accepted is subverted and they are forced to set their own rules and standards, born of consideration and humanity, not buried beneath layers of long custom and other people's expectations.

They stand at a crossroads, the junction of the old and familiar, trusted world and the undiscovered, tempting, threatening new one. Outside, the world is dark, still, cold and calm, dusted with starlight above and snow at their feet. Inside, the darkness is punctured and punctuated with pockets of light, brilliant, dazzling pools that serve to emphasise the appealing darkness beyond, and it is hot, crowded and heaving. The thumping pulse of the drum beat reaches them before they can discern the strains of the music or the words of the gossip, a throbbing, incessant beat that seems to rise up through the bare treads of the descending staircase and vibrate into the soles of their feet and from there out to their tissues, muscles and bones. It grips them from their first step on the stair, driving them undeniably downwards into the darkness.

A pungent smell greets them, a heady concoction of perfume, alcohol, smoke and sweat. The cigarette trails, rising to the low ceiling, have nowhere to go and drift around like wispy entrails until they meet and merge, blending into a grey cloud handing inches above their heads. The intermittent lighting drains areas of colour then punctuates them with startling brilliance, highlighting the iridescent peacocks, dressed in aquamarine, fuchsia and yellow, satins and silks, whose brilliant plumage dazzles against the formal black and white foil of their partners' dinner suits.

Down here, the Italian men who man the door upstairs are replaced by black staff, exquisitely attired in elegant tuxedos, the women as well as the men. The heat is stifling and a sheen is evident on the skin of the man who guides them – surely more by instinct or habit than by sight as it's far too dark to discern anything beyond the vicinity of the pools of light – to a table in the far corner against the wall, slightly more privacy bought with the quick exchange of a note between the men. Jack keeps his hand protectively on the small of her back as they cross the floor. Most of the clientele are too absorbed in their own selves, partners or drinks to pay them any heed but Jack notices one man almost do a double-take as he passes them en route to his own table, large and over-populated, in the centre of the room. He feels the man's eyes follow them across the floor.

Their table, a small, round one, set against a semi-circular seat, faces the stage. The room must hold thirty, maybe even forty, tables, most for groups of four or six. There is an anonymity in being on a smaller one, on the periphery of the room, but, now they are here, it also feels as if they are skirting around this alien world, not embracing it like most others who are here.

The table at the middle of the room is the power centre. The attitude of those seated around the table, particularly the women, speaks a superiority, of people who live more brilliantly, shine more brightly, are part of some inner crowd. Like moths to a flame, others from around the room are tempted into the circle of light, using the slimmest acquaintance with anyone at the table to become part of the group, even for a moment, standing over their friend, a hand on the back of the chair or, more daringly, leaning across them to interject into the conversation. At least half-a-dozen conversations are happening around the table to judge by the various attitudes of the men and women, turned in their seats or leaning across the tables, and those gathered around them.

Only two men are not engaged in the febrile chatter and gossip. One, the man who looked at Grace earlier. His eyes, never still, dart around the room but never fall on those at the table. He is seated to the left of the other. A short but wide man, thinning hair slicked back, dressed in a double-breasted lounge suit instead of the obligatory dinner suit and smoking a fat cigar; he is the flame. He neither joins in any of the conversations nor, to judge by the lack of eye contact with anyone around him, shares any interest in them. His eyes, indeed, hardly move yet there is a sense he is taking in everything that is happening, not just at his table but around the room.

From their small stable in the edge, they have a good view of everything in the room, the constant flow of yet more people arriving and swelling the already-packed room, the incessant comings and goings of the dozens of waiting staff squeezing between the overcrowded tables with their trays laden with drinks, and, across the heads of a dozen other tables, the band that is thumping out the vibrating rhythm.

Twenty musicians, all black, all dressed the same way as the waiting staff. This is Harlem putting on a show for the whites who have dared to stray beyond the normal limits of their safe lives. He has seen a full orchestra before, attended classical concerts at the Albert Hall, but there are instruments he doesn't even recognise and the tunes he has heard on the gramophone are a pale reproduction, an inadequate facsimile of this.

The music is loud and fast, the kind of up-tempo numbers this generation wants to dance to, risky, rebellious, liberating. Yet, somehow, still there is depth and there is complexity to their playing and they seem almost to be in a world of their own, oblivious to the bodies on the dance floor, to the ripples of applause that break out at moments around the room or to the sudden shouts of an argument in the darkness at the back of the room. He is as absorbed by watching them as they seem to be by their playing. Their attention is only on their instruments and on each other, a flow of music between them like a living thing. An extraordinary unspoken understanding moves the music around them, the rest falling back into a background rhythm as two of them briefly take the lead, standing out from the rest, the background supported and co-ordinated, kept together, making room for those who take centre stage and paint the foreground subject, the music flowing from one to the other like a conversation, the pleasure, laughter even, reflected on each other's faces. It is mesmerising. A revelation.

The triumphant conclusion of the tune, with the musicians applauding each other even as the audience applaud them, brings him back to an awareness of himself. Their drinks have arrived; she has ordered a cocktail for herself, whisky for him. He looks at her, embarrassed that he has lost all awareness, even for a short time, but she seems to take pleasure in it.

"I was watching you," she tells him, laughing. "It was extraordinary. Like you were somewhere else altogether."

"I'm sorry," he apologises, taking her hand.

"Don't be," she assures him, sliding across the seat to be closer to him. "I was enjoying your enjoyment."

He brings her hand to his mouth and kisses the palm, enjoying seeing the reaction flare in her eyes. "Have I told you how beautiful you look tonight?"

She laughs, a soft, sensuous sound this time. He has, three times already. When she rises from the bath he has drawn for her and steps

473

into the towel he holds out for her before slowly rubbing her dry. When she sits in front of the dressing room mirror, her dressing gown loosely tied at her waist, and he brushes her long, dark hair until it gleams. When she stands before him, barefoot, in her claret red dress, her hair loose around her shoulders, the calf-length satin, fragile and fluid, moulding itself to her shape, emphasising the curves and lines he knows so well but, somehow, is seeing anew.

He almost tells her a fourth time. The moment the world stops. When she stands with him before a mirror to show them both together. Dimly aware how they must look together – he tall, slim, a dark foil in his black dinner jacket, white shirt, black waistcoat, she slender, tiny and vibrant – he is unable either to take his eyes off her or to speak his emotions. It is an image that will stay with him for the rest of his life.

"Have I told you the same?" she returns the compliment in a whisper against his mouth. The band strikes up again, a slow, throaty number, the brass muted, the drums brushed, the bass throbbing the persistent beat. She looks at the dance floor, which the bright, young things are abandoning to the couples. "Dance with me," she urges breathily. He doesn't need to be invited twice.

He takes her hand to lead her out to the dance floor but she slides her arm around his waist instead, under the cover of his jacket, and tucks underneath his shoulder. This time, they head into the midst of the crowd, disappearing among the dozens of other bodies in the dark, avoiding the pools of light on the periphery. He formally offers her his hand and his skin tingles as she eases hers into his, instinctively closing around it and turning inwards so that he brings their joined hands back against his chest. She splays her fingers against him, feeling the soft fabric and his muscle beneath. She slides her other hand under the lapel of his jacket up to his shoulder and he can feel the heat of her skin through the heavy cotton of his shirt. She is so slight his arm at her waist reaches all the way around her back so that his formal dance posture is almost an embrace. He lowers his head until his forehead almost touches hers and she tilts her head up towards him, face to face. It matters little that the dance floor is so crowded that they can hardly move. The tempo is all they need and, as they slowly move together, their eyes lock. Now, there is no strain, no desperation. For a moment out of time, beginnings and endings cease and the prospect of loss disappears. In the midst of this heaving, uncomfortably hot, noisy, violent room, the world falls away and they are all that exists for the other.

* * * * * * *

"When you were a child, what did you expect from your life?"

Back at their table, more drinks delivered, heads close together, hands entwined. There is privacy amid so much noise, even with the next table just inches away. He considers. "When I was very young, I expect I thought I was going to be like my parents. Running the farm, probably with my brother, working with the boys who were my friends at school."

"And when you were older?"

"Then I just wanted to escape. To be anything but that. I dreamed of fleeing to a foreign land, of labouring on a farm in Australia or South Africa."

"Still labouring?"

"I didn't see how I would qualify for anything else."

Now she considers for a moment. "No dream of a wife? A family?"

He shakes his head. "I think I couldn't imagine being that to anyone else until I had found what I was meant to do with my life."

She holds his gaze. "And now?" she questions softly.

He brushes her cheek. "I think that is what I'm meant to do with my life," he responds. "In whatever form it takes."

Tears glisten in her eyes. "I wish I could be part of it." Her voice is low and achingly sad.

A hollowness forms at the core of him, an emptiness locked around by the grief he knows is already forming but is determinedly being held at bay. "You are," he disagrees. "You always will be." But they both know it's not what she means.

"What about you?" he tries to distract her. "What did you plan to be when you grew up?"

Her smile is faint. "I wanted to teach. I wanted to be everything I felt my parents had originally planned to be but had lost along the way. A passionate, enthusiastic teacher. A caring mentor. A warm and loving mother."

"You could be yet," he encourages, though the thought fills him with despair. "You're so young, your whole life is ahead of you still."

The sadness returns to those expressive eyes. "Then why is it I feel so old?"

He feels his heart ache with sadness for her, for everything she's already been through in her short life. He corrects that: for everything they've both been through in their short lives. He wishes he could reassure her, that he could give her the platitudes the situation demands. But he can't lie to her. He can't tell her that everything will be alright because he doesn't know himself that it will be. They are pawns in someone else's game and he has no idea if he will ever feel in control of his life again. So all he can do is control the here and now, the world they have created between the two of them. And for that reason, he can't lie to her.

He brings their joined hands to his mouth and deliberately kisses the third finger of her left hand, the finger he so desperately wishes he could put his mark of ownership on, to know that she will never walk away from him, nor he from her. The thought that it is impossible is becoming a scar on his soul.

* * * * * * *

"What happens from here?" he asks. It is the first time he has thought of the future in these two days and nights. He fears why that should be the case now. "How is this supposed to work?"

"We will go away, she and I." She is looking at their joined hands now, avoiding showing him her face. Her voice shakes with unshed tears bitten back. "We will tell people that she is going for specialist care, to minimise the risk of a miscarriage. It will be natural for me to go with her."

"And where is it you will actually go?"

"There is a woman who will help us. Mrs Wilson. She was the midwife when Charlotte gave birth, I think? When her husband died, she moved back to her home town to live with her sister. It's a small place, miles from anywhere. No one will know us."

"For how long?"

"We can't risk anyone suspecting. So, as soon as I'm sure. Certainly before I show any signs. For six months, maybe more."

"What will you tell Mrs Wilson?"

"I think we will tell her the truth, or a version of it. But as far as everyone else in the town is concerned, the story is that I have recently lost my husband and my sister and I are staying with Mrs Wilson to help me cope with my grief."

"What happens after?"

She takes his hand in both hers and bends her head over it, kissing it. "That's the bit we can't plan for." Her hands tremble. "I don't know how I will react. How I will feel. When Tom was born, what I felt for him was overwhelming. The second I saw him, before I even held him in my arms, it felt as if the whole of my world shifted. Nothing was about me any more. It was all about this tiny creature who now depended on me for his entire existence." Suddenly she looks up and there is such bleak emptiness in her eyes that he instinctively catches her to him, crushing her in his embrace, desperate to take away that pain. Inevitably, the tears break, her control shattered by his mirroring of her pain. She rests her chin on

477

his shoulder, her head turned in towards his neck. "If I feel that again," she whispers, "I don't know how I will live with it. I don't know how to face losing another child."

* * * * * * *

At last, he sees and understands what she is giving up to make this happen and the knowledge devastates him. Anger threatens to overwhelm him and he knows he can't stay here any longer. Blindly, he throws a stack of bills on the table to cover the cost of their drinks and, taking her hand as gently as he can force himself to be, he flees the room, snatching their coats from attendant in his impatience.

He pushes forcefully through the crowd of people who are queuing to get into the club and starts to walk rapidly down the street, looking to left and to right for somewhere – anywhere – for them to be alone together. Unexpectedly, he comes across a garden square, railed like those at home, dark and silent. He pushes the gate open and closes it behind them both. He drops her hand and walks into the centre of the space, enclosed around with dark trees and shrubs, dusted white with the snow.

"This has to stop," he orders, pushing his hand into his hair. "Here and now. I won't continue with this charade." She stands where he has left her, her hands pushed into the pockets of her long winter coat, her hair spread out over her shoulders. His anger has temporarily stoppered her grief, her emotions controlled in the face of his breaking down.

"We can't stop," she contradicts. "And it's probably too late anyway."

"This is so wrong. She's playing with people's lives and she has no right."

"She has every right to ask," she tells him, her voice steady. "And I have every right to choose."

He stares at her, keeping his distance for fear of his own anger. "But why?" he demands. "Why would you do this for her? Why would you put yourself through this? Does she even know how you feel?"

She nods. "She knows everything about me."

He takes a step closer at that, bewildered. "More than I do?"

She holds his gaze. "In some ways, yes."

He hates knowing that. He has shared so much with this woman, the thought that his wife knows more about her than he makes him feel absurdly jealous. It brings him another step closer. "What about me?" he provokes, trying to counter the conflicting emotions raging through him. "Does she know how you feel about me?"

"I've never said anything to her but I know she suspects."

"My God! How can she do this to you, knowing all this? How can she inflict so much pain?"

"She's in pain herself," she states simply and he hates the empathy he hears in her voice. He fears the way it ties and constrains her. "She hurts so much and the only way she knows is to fight it. When you fight like that, you can't worry about who else gets hurt in the process."

"Then," coming to stand in front of her, feeling the adrenaline flow though the anger is ebbing away, "I won't let her," raising his hands to hold her face. "I won't be part of inflicting this hurt on you."

"It's no longer your choice," she challenges weakly, her control ebbing as fast as his anger.

"It is if I refuse to carry on this way. I won't do it," he argues, "I can't bear the thought of going back to living how I was before, without you."

"Don't," she denies, anger flashing in her eyes as she tries vainly to push him away. "I don't accept it. And you have no right to say it."

"I can't go back," he refuses, bringing her face closer to his. "We can't go back. How can we even contemplate it when we've lived – when we've loved – like this?"

"Don't," she denies again, but her voice is a weak whisper now. "Please."

He claims her mouth in a hard, deep kiss, gathering her to him, a wave of triumph flooding through him as he feels her give in and sink against him, her arms going round him, desperately trying to pull him closer and closer. When he breaks the kiss, his breath coming fast, she grabs the back of his head and pulls him down to her again, rising onto tiptoes the better to hold her body against him, her eyes open and holding his, challenging his. He bends her backwards, his arm around her waist pressing her lower body hard against him.

"No!" Her sudden refusal stuns him and, catching him unawares, she succeeds in breaking free, using her hands against his arms to push herself away. She staggers backwards, putting several feet between the two of them. "No, Jack." Holding her hands out to fend him off as he starts towards her. "This is wrong. This is so wrong."

He stops, catching his breath, not believing her denial. "How can this be wrong?" he asks. "How can you expect me to believe this is wrong when nothing in my life has ever felt so right? When no one has ever known me as you know me?"

She straightens, hardening her eyes. "But you don't know me," she denies flatly. "I'm not the person you think I am, Jack. There's so much you don't know about me."

"Like what?" he demands.

"Like how she tried to kill her husband."

* * * * * * *

The voice that interrupts them is rough, male and clearly from London's East End. In the darkness, he is an indistinct form until he levers himself away from the gatepost he has been leaning against and comes into the open area of the garden. As the moonlight falls onto his face, Jack hears her gasp and sees her take a step back, her hands instinctively clutching at the skirts of her dress as if gathering herself to run.

"Hello, Gracie."

In a second, Jack crosses the space and plants himself between Grace and the man he saw watching her at the club. She hesitates behind him, her hand on his arm, perhaps to reassure herself, perhaps to restrain him.

"That's no way to greet an old friend, Gracie," the man continues to address himself to her, ignoring Jack. "Particularly one who brings good news."

"What do you want?" Jack demands, his pulse pounding loudly in his ears but the calmness he knows from battle starting to settle over him. He sizes the man up. He is short but also broad and the outline of his jacket suggests muscle not fat. There is also a poorly concealed distortion in the area of the left breast pocket.

The man's eyes lazily slide from Grace to Jack but there is nothing lazy about the brutality or the threat that lies therein. He looks back at Grace again.

"Don't you want to know how Dougie is doing?" The man is relishing the power he wields. "I imagine you must have been so worried about him. I was worried myself for a while. Never seen so much blood. And, believe me," his eyes returning to Jack's for a moment, "I've seen plenty of blood in my time." Back to Grace again. "Just as well I found him when I did else the doctor reckons he would have bled out in another ten minutes. It was touch and go for a long time in the hospital even then. But you know Doug. He's a strong man. To my mind, he seemed determined to live too, like he had something he needed to finish." He takes a step closer and Jack feels Grace shrink away in response.

"There's a lot of people have been looking for you, sweetheart. There's some coppers may have thought you was doing them a favour but that doesn't stop them wanting to ask you what happened that night. I'm sure they'll be delighted to know you're still alive. The way you disappeared, some suspected you'd been done in. But I never doubted, Gracie," he persists, a threat behind the smile in his voice. "And I always had a hunch I'd be coming across you again some day.

"I've got myself a sweet gig, Gracie." The almost conversational tone is somehow even more threatening. "The brother of some Italian from Chicago. Looking to extend the family business here in New York. It's a great place to come when you're in a spot of bother at home, ain't it, sweetheart? There I was looking to protect myself and I discover there's money to be made in protecting others instead. Couldn't think of a job that would suit me better."

He takes another step closer. "You may be needing some protection yourself, love. If you do, I'll know where to find you." He takes one more look at Jack then back to her with a smile. "I'll be seeing you, Gracie."

* * * * * * *

For a long moment after he has disappeared and the gate has shut behind him, she stands rigidly still, unable to move, then she staggers over towards the dark edges of the garden and retches. As the heaving subsides, she is unable to control her terror any longer and collapses onto her knees, huge sobs shaking her body. Instantly, Jack gathers her up in his arms and carries her to a nearby bench, holding her to him as she huddles up as small as she can. He wraps the two sides of his coat front around her for extra warmth and folds her into his arms, holding her head against his shoulder.

482

It is a lack of breath rather than the draining of the emotion that finally stops the tears. Her chest heaves as she struggles for air and she presses her hand to there to calm herself. He finds his handkerchief and tenderly wipes her face, brushing her hair back where it has stuck to her damp face.

"Oh God," she mouths the despair rather than speaks it, then suddenly struggles to her feet, pulling her coat closer against the cold in the absence of his warmth. "I can't stay here," she pleads. "Jack, I can't stay here. Get me out of here. Please, God, get me out of here."

He is on his feet in an instant and, holding her against him again to fight the shaking of shock and cold that he can see in her hands, he walks them rapidly out of the garden and in the opposite direction from the club.

The further they walk, the emptier the streets become, the more silent the world is around them. It calms them both gradually but they have walked a long way before she feels secure enough and steady enough to speak. He lets her talk without saying a word himself.

"He's

He's my husband's best friend. They grew up together. He always did scare me, right from the beginning but my husband didn't care what I thought. He was around a lot, always dragging him down to the pub or getting him into God knows what kind of messes. If there was something going on in our neighbourhood, he was always behind it somehow but the police never caught up with him.

"He would look at me sometimes, when he was sure Doug wouldn't see. It gave me the creeps. It wasn't that I thought he found me attractive. I'm not even sure he likes women. It was like he wanted to control me or maybe to prove to me that Doug would always choose him over me.

"He's the opposite of Doug in so many ways. His violence is very controlled. He wouldn't ever lash out in anger but he has no qualms about inflicting pain to achieve his own ends. And he liked to see Doug hit me. I swear, there's something not quite right in his head.

"It was maybe three years after my father had taken me back to my husband. Tom was due to start school in the autumn. He was so looking forward to it. I'd been reading with him since he was small, books that I got from the Sunday School. Doug hated it. He said I was making the boy soft. He wanted a strong boy, a fighter, but Tom was never that. He never joined in the games the other kids played in the street. Doug blamed me.

"One day, he decided he's going to teach Tom a lesson in being a man, teach him to fight. Like he believed the boy just needs the confidence to know he can beat anyone in order to change him into the kind of son he wants. He took him out in the yard, strapped up his hands and started tapping away at him, catching Tom's face with his fingers to show how he's getting through his guard. He tried his best but Tom was never that co-ordinated or strong and he couldn't do what Doug wanted. So Doug got angrier and angrier, and his hand-taps were turning into fists, not hard but more and more aggressive. I was stood in the kitchen, watching this, hating myself for not interfering, knowing where it's headed. He caught the boy on his cheek, harder than he intended, I know, but the boy cried out and I couldn't take it any longer. I rushed to the back door and shouted Doug's name, ready to put myself between him and my boy if I needed to. It distracted Doug for a split second and, in that moment, Tom showed he had a flare of his father's temperament in him and, furious, went to slam his little fist into Doug's stomach. But he's so short and he missed his target by some inches lower. Doug went down, howling in pain, clutching his groin and swearing. Tom realised what he'd done and tried to flee, dodging past his father, but he was too quick for the boy. He grabbed him by the neck and started choking him, one-handed. It's like I was rooted to the spot. I stood there watching my child's face turn red and then start to turn purple, his tongue hanging out and his little eyes staring. He wasn't even trying to struggle, he was just letting it happen. And then I saw red. Literally. It was like a red-coloured mist came over my eyes and there was a buzzing sound in my head, fit to burst.

"The next thing I knew, Doug had fallen forward and Tom had collapsed on the floor, his hands scrabbling at his throat as he fought to get air back into his lungs. And the kitchen knife I'd had in my hands was now buried in the side of Doug's neck and there was blood everywhere. I took one look at Doug as he collapsed onto his side. His eyes were staring at me in disbelief and he was trying to claw at the knife to pull it out. I waited long enough to see the life drain out of him, to see him sink down onto the floor and let his life ebb away.

"Then I grabbed Tom, I threw on my coat and I ran. I had no idea where I was going, I just had to get as far away as fast as I could.

"I had nothing with me, no clothes, no money, not even a coat for Tom. My right hand was covered in blood and Tom was rigid with fear. I could feel him turning colder by the second. I wiped my hand on a clump of weeds, hiding behind the factory wall because I knew no one would be there on a Sunday. I didn't know if Doug was alive or dead, I just knew I was never going back. If he was alive, he would kill me. If he was dead, the police would have me instead. Of the two, the latter was infinitely preferable but I had to get my boy somewhere safe first. I couldn't have them putting him into an orphanage or the workhouse. Of course, no one on the street would know he had grandparents to take care of him because I'd seen nothing of my parents since that day three years before so it was up to me to get him safe.

"With no money, I had no way to get us on the bus and I was petrified my crime had been discovered already. So I walked, carrying Tom all the way. It took me hours and I nearly cried with the exhaustion.

"I didn't even know what kind of reaction I could expect but I had no other hope and nowhere else to turn.

"By the time I got to my parents' street, Tom was practically unconscious. Thankfully, it was pretty much dark by then so I didn't have to worry about the neighbours seeing.

"It felt like it took them forever to answer the door when I knocked. I tried to set Tom down but I discovered my muscles had frozen in place and it hurt unbearably to try to move them so I stayed where I was, carrying him against my chest, his little head against my shoulder.

"My heart sank at the look on my father's face. We neither of us said anything, just stood there dumbly staring at each other. I could hear my mother calling from the kitchen to ask who it was and then heard her footsteps as she came to the front door. She took one look at me and started to shut the door but then something stopped her. She was staring at Tom, lying in my arms. I'd never seen such emotion on her face before but it was like the floodgates that had held back years of emotion suddenly broke. It was like her face crumpled in on itself. She whispered "Michael" through the hands covering her face and then she reached out and she took him from me. I almost collapsed from the relief of having that weight taken off me. I certainly stumbled and stepped backwards, off the doorstep.

"She had disappeared back into the house with my son. I could hear her but I couldn't see her. I looked at my father. Then he slowly and very deliberately closed the door in my face.

"I don't remember what happened for some time after that. I know when I came too I was sitting against the wall of the house and I was freezing cold, as if I'd been there for hours. I could barely stand my muscles hurt so much. The house was in total darkness. For a long time, it felt as if I couldn't get my brain to function because I couldn't work out what I should do next. The only thing I could recognise is that I needed to get away from that house. I couldn't risk anyone knowing that was where I had taken my son. His safety, his future, depended on my not existing as his mother.

"So I started walking again, back towards the centre of London. I wasn't running. I honestly didn't care if the police caught up with me. A part of me hoped they would. What could be worse than the life I had been living so far, after all?

"But no one stopped me, no one even seemed to take a second look at me. It feels so unreal. To know that you have committed that kind of crime and to think that no one can see it on you. I felt as if people would only have to look at me to know it. Because as far as I was concerned he was dead. And the world was better off for him being so.

"I don't know how many days I was like that. I found food in Christian shelters but I didn't stay in any of them. I just kept walking, waiting for the police to catch up with me. In the end, I was so exhausted I fell asleep sitting at the table in one of the shelters.

"They put me to bed and, of course, I fell ill. I had no mental or physical reserves left. They told me afterwards I was delirious for days, which only made me fear what I had told them in my delirium. They were incredibly kind but I shut myself off from them, terrified that I would inadvertently give Tom away.

"When I got stronger, I was more accepting of their kindness and I set to work to pay off the debt I owed them. At first, it was unpaid char work at the shelter. Then I started looking for paid work so I could give them back some of what it had cost them to care for me. That's when I met Sarah.

"She had been doing fundraising work for the charity and visited the shelter one day to meet with the manager. He brought her out to meet with some of the workers and introduced her to me.

"I think I surprised her. There weren't many there with either my accent or my manners, and she was intrigued to know more. She came back after that visit and sat with me while I worked, talking to me about my life. When she said she could find me some work, I felt I had to be honest with her. I told her about my husband and said I had left him because he beat me. I didn't tell her about Tom or about how I came to leave. Not then.

"She seemed to sympathise, whether or not she could understand, and she offered me the chance to get away, out of London. For the first time in months, she gave me hope. I didn't expect or want to get away with what I'd done but I thought I might find a way to make enough money to send some to my parents as well as to pay back the shelter. That's how I came to Richmond House.

"I kept to myself for a long time, not knowing who among the servants I might trust. But Ellerby got through my defences. She saw herself as something apart from the servants and decided she saw the same in me on the basis of my upbringing. She took me under her wing. I thought at the time she was being kind but now I know she was serving her own purposes as well. She wanted to give up her job and go and live with some woman in Bournemouth. She said she was her sister but that's just a cover. I think they had been close for some years but Ellerby had always resisted leaving Sarah, until this woman fell ill and almost died. After that, I think Ellerby was always looking for a way to leave Sarah with the minimum of fuss. In identifying me as her replacement, she saw a way out.

"And then no one was there for her when she miscarried. She was utterly distraught and I saw a side of her she'd never shown me before. She was so vulnerable. She cried in my arms when it was over, so in need of human warmth, someone to be there for her.

"Afterwards, she was afraid to sleep, as if she felt she had to keep a vigil for the child she had lost. We talked through the night, telling each other things neither of us had ever admitted to another human being. It was inevitable that I would tell her the truth about Doug and about Tom. She told me how desperately she wanted to be a mother.

"Sometime around dawn, it was like she started to shut down. She stopped talking so much and her responses to me were becoming more and more clinical. She said she had decided to go to London, to see you but also to see that specialist.

"I was adamant she couldn't travel alone, not in her condition, but she overruled me. I think she was afraid she couldn't control herself if I was there to remind her. During the course of the morning, I could see her becoming more and more withdrawn, until she shut herself away in the morning room and ordered that she shouldn't be disturbed. I packed a bag for her and the chauffeur collected it. She didn't come to say goodbye.

"I was so angry with you for not being there for her. I blamed you for putting her through this. And then you called the following day to ask about her doctor's appointment and I could hear the distress in your voice too. I hadn't expected that. I'd already put you in the same camp as my husband, only probably worse for being richer. I wasn't expecting you to be upset too.

"And then when I saw you, you surprised me again by being kind to me, by showing me consideration. I had grown used to Sarah's kindness but I knew from my experiences before that the relationship I had with her was very unusual. It was like she treated me as more of a friend than a servant. But I didn't expect the same from you.

"And I started to listen more when Sarah talked about you, told me about things you had said or done. I felt like a fraud because I was getting to know you so much more intimately that you knew me. It made me feel awkward when you were around and so shy. But you persisted and when we came to New York and Sarah was spending more and more time with Charlotte at the other house, I could see how lonely you were. As was I. Sarah was spending so much time away but I didn't fit in with the other servants in that house. They seemed to view me with so much suspicion and would always stop talking when I entered the room. I started seeking solace in your study. I told myself it was just that I wanted the books and that I liked that room. But it wasn't. I was hoping each night that you would be back early and that you would want some company. At first, I dreaded those nights when you were so tired you couldn't talk any more but then I found I enjoyed those all the more, just sitting and reading in the same room with you, surreptitiously watching the emotions play across your face in reaction to what you were reading.

"I didn't think Sarah saw, she was so wrapped up in how she was feeling, in caring for her niece. If I hadn't been so wrapped up myself, I might have seen sooner what it was doing to her. As it was, I didn't really notice at first but as the summer went on and we were preparing for the trip to Newport I started to notice how her clothes no longer fitted properly. I took them in and then had to take them in again only a few weeks later.

"But she had seen. All it took was one stray look one morning when you were readying for work. I caught her looking at me a couple of times, almost speculatively. She didn't wait long to test the idea on me.

"I was appalled. I couldn't believe she was expecting such a thing, of either of us. Or that she could live with the thought. But I started to understand how she compartmentalises things in her head. The things she is prepared to accept and the things she puts away where she doesn't have to deal with them. The ends justify the means.

"And she's so persuasive. Even if I didn't feel I owed my life to her, I think she could have talked me into it. But, as it was, how could I refuse anything to the woman who had not only saved me but had given me a new life.

"I tried not to think about you, to think how you would feel about it. But when she came to me on Friday morning and said there was a chance the upcoming snow storm could hit Chicago and close the roads and the rail, and I should get across to New York as quickly as possible, my defences suddenly came down. She'd never told me how you felt about it. Whether you had even agreed to it. She just

490

said this was our chance and we needed to take it. She was so excited she overcame my fears, while I was with her.

"As soon as I was on the train, though, my fears swept in. It's a long train journey from Chicago to New York and yet I thought about you the whole way here. By the time I arrived, I was a mass of nerves and I was petrified that you would reject me. I couldn't take that. Not only for her sake. I couldn't stand the thought that you might not want me.

"Then I saw the look in your eyes when you realised it was me and why I had come. And suddenly it was an entirely other fear that gripped me, that whatever I was feeling for you already was only a pale imitation of what I could actually feel. I was already way out of my depth, unable to control my emotions or reactions. I felt like such an idiot, trying to seduce you. I was so embarrassed. But when you picked me up in your arms, for a moment I felt so safe. It was like coming home. Then the discomfort overwhelmed me again, so conscious that I was trying to seduce you in her house. It didn't matter that she had asked this of us, that she had engineered it. It felt like betrayal because I knew what I felt for you.

"Afterwards, I was ready to walk away from this altogether but the thought of failing her was unbearable. I was turning it over and over in my mind, trying to find a way through. But you found a way for us. The one way I could never suggest to you because of how I already felt.

"I never expected it to be like this. I've felt passion before, I've even believed myself to be in love. But I've never felt like this. And I want nothing so much as to carry and bear your child because I know that will bind me to you forever. I can't have you. I have no right to love you. But whether I'm there or not, that child will mean I will always be a part of your life. And that wherever I am, however far apart we are, at some point you will look at that child and you will think of me."

She stops, both talking and walking. He has no idea where they are. The street is deserted, the darkness alleviated only by the weak light of the moon, only half-visible behind a bank of cloud.

He takes her face in his hands, gently. His heart is so full he hasn't the words. So he uses the only ones that will convey even a fraction of what he is thinking and feeling. "I love you, Grace," he tells her, losing himself in those silver eyes. "No," he denies as she tries to prevent him, "for here and for now, while it is only the two of us and while this world is still just ours, I love you. And for the rest of my life, my soul shall carry you with me."

She closes her eyes in despair and he kisses her then, so gently, so tenderly. And he doesn't know whether the tears he feels on his hands are hers or his.

* * * * * * *

There is silence between them as they find their way again and haltingly turn their feet towards home. Emotionally and physically drained, their progress is slow, their arms around each other, supporting but also reassuring, their need for physical closeness something that is accepted without question by both of them.

As they reach the Upper West Side, a church clock starts to strike the hour, long, low, sonorous chimes, minor notes to remind of the inherent sadness in the passing of time. He counts then pulls out his pocket watch to check. "Midnight," he remarks. "Merry Christmas, Grace."

She takes the watch from his hand to see for herself then turns her face up to his. "Merry Christmas, Jack." He kisses her, lightly. "It's a beautiful watch."

"My father's," he agrees, turning it over to show the inscription on the back. "My mother gave it to him on their wedding day. She gave it to me when he passed earlier this year." He unfastens the chain from his waistcoat and drops it in her hand. "I wish I had something more considered to give you," he tells her, "but I can't think of anything more personal. Something of me for you to keep."

She shakes her head, carefully covering it with her other hand. "I can't accept this, Jack," she tells him. "This is part of your heritage, part of your family. You should pass this onto your son. You can't give it to me."

He runs his hands into her hair, lifting her face towards the moonlight so he can see her better. "That's why I want you to have it." It is a spur-of-the-moment decision but he wouldn't have thought of any better gift if he had spent days considering it. "You are part of me, now. Part of who I am. We are a family, you and I. Not conventionally, I know, but it feels no less true for that. Please, I want to know that, whatever happens after this, you have something of mine with you, wherever you are."

She reaches up to hug him, burying her face in his shoulder. "I'll hold it for you, for now," she pledges. "And if things work out and when the time is right, I will return it to your family. To your son or daughter."

As she pulls away, she catches an expression in his eyes that makes her laugh. "That pleases you, doesn't it? The thought of a child? Your child?"

He draws her hand through his arm and they start to walk down the street again. "More than you can know," he admits.

She's intrigued. "What is it about that thought that pleases you?" she teases. "Are you as Neanderthal as other men underneath and just proud to have living proof of your virility?"

He laughs at that and moves his arm around her shoulder to bring her closer as they walk. "If you really believe that, I'll start thinking you've learned nothing about me."

"Well, enlighten me, then. What do you like about the idea of being a father?" He walks on for some moments in silence, considering his answer until she playfully smacks his arm. "Stop

493

thinking and tell me!" she demands. "I don't want a fully formed answer, I want to know what's going through your mind. So tell me."

"So many unformed ideas," he defends. "Pride, I guess, that my life won't end with me but carry on, in some form, in another human being. Doubt, that I can be the kind of father I would want to be. Fear, that I will unthinkingly pass on the worst aspects of my own father, and that I won't remember to pass on those things that made me love him. Responsibility, that I should have such an influence on shaping a life that can have an effect on the world. And joy," he admits, looking at her directly, "that there might be a life created out of how you and I have loved."

She is deeply moved, he can see it in her eyes, and it stirs her passion again, which he sees in the slight upturn of her mouth on one corner. "You'd better hope we've succeeded then," she teases to cover the depth of her emotion.

"What if we haven't?" he teases her too but the thought is there in both their minds.

"I can think of worse things to do than to keep trying with you," she laughs.

"I'm serious." He sobers suddenly and they stop again, the better to read the reaction of the other in their faces. "You said before you couldn't do this again."

She nods. "We've been through so much," she reflects. "I never thought it would be this intense and I don't know if I can face the idea of keeping up a pretence in front of others. We're so lucky, having this time together. I couldn't contemplate sneaking around behind other people's backs, grabbing a hidden moment here or there. I can't demean what we feel for each other that way."

"I knew from the beginning that it would never be a purely physical thing with you," he agrees. "The thought of diminishing what we have here and now is intolerable."

"So if it doesn't work...?"

"We'll find a way," he assures her and his heart quickens at the thought of legitimately continuing this relationship with her. "But," teasing again, brushing his thumb over her bottom lip, "perhaps we shouldn't waste any more time?"

She smiles, that slow, playful smile that makes his pulse beat faster. She pulls his head down and kisses him, her mouth opening beneath his. When she breaks away, she puts her hand in his and quickens her step, picking up her skirts so they can walk faster down the road. He stops her at the corner of West 87th Street and pulls her back into his arms, propping up her against the wall of the end house, the better to press his body into hers. She gives a throaty laugh and bites at his earlobe, running her hands into his hair, as he runs kisses down her jawline and onto her throat. She pushes him away again and re-starts their rapid progress down the street, almost running now along the sidewalk where the snow has thawed and swathes of pavement are now visible.

He starts to overtake her as they near the house because she has suddenly slowed her pace, her footsteps hesitant. As they reach the bottom step of the brownstone, he realises why. Lights are ablaze in the house, coming from both the drawing room and the dining room on the first floor. They had left it in darkness.

She looks at him, fear and uncertainty in her silver eyes, so bright against the cold-tinted redness of her cheeks. Her hair has been blown awry as they ran and falls around her face in waves, framing her beautiful face. He meets her eyes again and knows what she reads there. He tries to hide the despair, the regret, the grief but he sees it mirrored in hers. He takes her in his arms one last time, a quick, hard kiss, his hands framing her face, holding her to him.

Then he breaks away, looks at her as if he is trying to engrave her image on his memory, then, alone, walks up the cold stone steps and lets himself into the house.

PART IV – AMERICA

Chapter Fifteen

New York, Christmas Day 19??

Sarah got her way, as she always did. She engineered for us to be together, forcing her plan through. And then she returned to pick up the pieces.

She had fallen asleep, curled up in the corner of the sofa. On the table in front of her were the remains of a plate of food, the paraphernalia for tea, an empty Scotch glass and newly opened bottle, the accumulation of a couple of weeks' unopened correspondence and, on the seat next to her, a book propped open against its spine. She appeared to have been there for some time.

He readily admitted to himself he was glad she hadn't arrived in time to forestall their outing to Harlem. Not only because he was sure she wouldn't have understood what drove them both to it. More importantly, because he wouldn't have missed what he had just shared with Grace for the world.

He wondered what frame of mind she would be in. She had created this situation but could she really be so emotionally detached from it? In her shoes, would it have played on his mind to think of her in the arms of someone else, however much the ends justified the means? He rapidly abandoned that train of thought. He couldn't understand how her mind worked on this situation; he could only trust that it was what she wanted and accept that, by playing his part, he could make her happy.

How did he feel about her now? He tried to believe he could delineate one situation from the other with as much clarity as she but he doubted it. He could only rely on his will and his honour to respect the lines he and Grace had drawn for themselves in this. He did believe he could trust her as much as he could trust himself.

The room had grown cold, unused during the last few days. She had lit the fire, left ready by the servants, but it had dampened down while she slept. It was better to damp it down properly and he crossed the room to complete the task. As he crouched before the fire, tidying the coals and then setting the guard in place, she stirred. He settled back on his haunches and waited for her to wake properly. She opened her eyes slowly, gave him a slight smile and closed them again.

"Hello, John," she murmured.

"Welcome back, Sarah." He tried to keep his tone neutral but he feared he allowed rather too much of his suppressed emotions – confusion, judgment, resignation – to permeate because she opened her eyes properly this time and looked directly at him, stretching out her limbs.

"Where have you been?"

He refused to answer that question on the basis that he felt she had no right to ask. "What are you doing here, Sarah?" Her faced showed confusion. "It's Christmas Eve," he explained. "Actually," pointing at the clock, "it's now Christmas Day. I thought you were stuck in Chicago?"

She seemed to come to at that, with the remembrance of what had occurred. "Mr Williams is dead," she reported bluntly. "Freddie's father. He had a stroke yesterday morning in Chicago. He died in hospital a few hours later, never having regained consciousness."

That set him back. He rose and crossed to take a seat. Only for a moment did he hesitate before sitting next to her on the sofa. "I'm sorry to hear that," he commiserated. "More sorry than I can say."

She nodded. "It's a tragedy for his wife, still so young."

"Why aren't you still in Chicago, then? Won't the funeral be held there?"

"It's Charlotte," she explained. Of course it was. Why hadn't he thought of that for himself? "She became hysterical, said she couldn't stay in a house of death for fear of what it would do to the baby. She wouldn't stay there a moment longer than she had to. It was awful. Susanna and Isabella were distraught anyway and Freddie was trying to calm all three of them. In the end, I said I would bring Charlotte home so that they could focus on dealing with the funeral arrangements."

His sympathy started to break through. "I'm sorry you've borne the brunt of it again," he sympathised. She shrugged off his concern. "Where is Charlotte now?"

"At the house. I took her there when we arrived. The doctor came and gave her a mild sedative. Her maid is with her. The snow wasn't as bad as we had originally feared." Her admission was made without making eye contact. "We were able to take the train and I had the chauffeur pick us up. I haven't ordered the servants home. We will have to go to the Upper East Side house tomorrow anyway so we don't need them back before Boxing Day."

He rose to collect a glass from the tray then poured himself a whisky. She declined another.

"John, why was the telephone unplugged?" He frowned his failure to follow her train of thought. "I've been trying to call you since yesterday – Saturday – morning when Mr Williams had his stroke. The exchange said the line was fine so I couldn't understand why I couldn't get through. When I came home, I found the telephone disconnected from the line."

He stayed standing. "I didn't want to speak to anyone."

"Not even to me?" Her eyes held a challenge but also concern. He didn't reply. "What happened here, John?" she questioned, her voice quiet but authoritative.

"You sent her here, Sarah." His tone of voice matched hers. "What were you expecting to happen?"

"You're angry with me." Her voice betrayed her hurt and it tugged at his conscience.

"No," he denied, sighing. "I'm not angry."

She frowned. "What aren't you saying? What aren't you telling me? Tell me, John," she demanded.

He looked at her clearly then, seeing the root cause of her frustration less in fear than in lack of control. "You're going to have to accept that not all of this is in your command, Sarah. You made a choice. So did I." Some element of shock or surprise registered in her face. "I'm going to have to live with my choices, Sarah, but you are also going to have to live with yours." He returned to the sofa and sat down, the better to prove to her that there was no animosity behind the words he spoke now. "You will not know what has happened here. You never will." It was neither a threat nor punishment. It was, to him, a simple statement of fact and one that he needed her to understand sooner rather than later. "We are all paying a price in this. That will be yours."

"You are angry," she reinforced.

"No," he refuted. "Honestly, I'm not. I am trying to make the best of a difficult situation."

"You're different," she accused. "You've changed."

"Yes, I am different," he accepted. "If we are the sum of our experiences, then I was always going to be different. How that affects us from this point on is up to you and I. It will be strange and it will be strained until we find a new reality for ourselves. It's not the same as before. You changed that and you're going to have to live with the consequences as well as I."

Her face paled in the dim light but he could see she was starting to accept his words. She drew a deep breath and folded her hands in her lap. "I have to go back to the house in the morning to be with Charlotte. I think you should come with me."

He nodded. "I think that would be wise."

She rose. "Then I should go to bed." She crossed the floor but turned back before she got to the door. "I accept what you say," she observed. "It is difficult for me when I feel I am the same as I was when I saw you last but I accept what you say. Still, you are my

502

husband and I know we will find a way through." She waited to see him nod his agreement. "Will you be up shortly?"

He thought for a moment, weighing the options, then shook his head. "Not tonight, I think," he refused but softened it with a look of reassurance. "Sleep well, Sarah."

She stayed for a moment longer, doubt in her eyes, then left.

* * * * * * *

He sat for a long time in the dark of the study, no fire, no light, only the light cast from the open doorway to the hall outside. The house settled to silence once Sarah had retired and the world was still outside.

He thought for a long time about these two extraordinary women. About their strength, their compassion, their self-sacrifice. About obsession and loss and redemption. About how he could fall in love with two such different women and yet find in both that which made him whole. About how he must close one door in order that they might open another.

* * * * * * *

He knows it is her the second she is silhouetted against the light from the hall. "She's sleeping." He nods but can't bring himself to speak. She hesitates before taking one step into the room. She opens her mouth to speak but the words won't come.

"I know," he acknowledges. "I don't know what to say either."

He sees the tears glisten in her eyes, catching the light as a shimmering reflection, holding, not falling.

"We've already said so much," she whispers.

He rises slowly and crosses the floor, stopping still some feet away and folding his arms to stop himself reaching out to her. "With more truth than I have ever spoken in my life," he affirms.

She half steps towards him. Stops. "I wish…"

"I know."

Silence.

"I hold you forever in my heart," she pledges, a break in her voice as the tears silently, finally fall onto her cheeks.

"I carry you with me in my soul," he whispers in return.

She turns and walks away. And his soul fractures.

Chapter Sixteen

Chicago, December 1922

I went to Chicago for the funeral. In some ways, it was a blessed escape, giving us a little time and distance to settle into that new reality.

"Scotch?"

Jack gladly accepted the glass Williams held out to him. "To your father," he tipped his glass towards Williams in a toast, which he acknowledged slightly before throwing back his glass and then refilling both of theirs.

"At least it was a decent turnout," he observed. "I knew the old man knew a lot of people but the number today was a surprise. It helps Ma."

"It's a shame Charlotte couldn't be here."

That elicited a non-committal grunt from Williams. "I'm just glad your wife is there to handle mine. You must be missing her. You can't have seen much of her in the last few weeks."

Jack was astute enough not to give a non-committal grunt of his own, however appropriate a response it would have been. He had been in the same city as Sarah for four days after her return to New York and he hadn't been entirely ungrateful to be shipped off to Chicago shortly thereafter to represent their side of the family at Williams Senior's funeral.

He had to believe they would eventually settle down again but, at this stage, he and Sarah were both overly sensitive to the other, reading too much into meaningless words or glances. It was hardly helped by Charlotte, whose intermittent vomiting, hysterics, migraines and self-pity would be intolerable for one without Sarah's fortitude or patience.

They were sitting in Williams' father's study in their extensive Chicago property, built at the turn of the century on a wide expanse of land on the outskirts of the city. The room was everything Jack would expect of banking money: richly furnished but old-fashioned, dark and heavy, styled like an old bank board room in mahogany furniture, oak panelling and green leather. Williams, for all that he was not even thirty himself, was already looking at home in it.

Of the couple of hundred mourners who had packed the church, at least that number had attended the house for the wake, yet they had been comfortably accommodated in the expansive ground floor areas of that substantial building. Susanna Williams was in her element, suppressing her grief to host her guests, graciously accepting their condolences and ensuring the staff were keeping their glasses topped up and their plates filled. The external caterers were clearly glad of the substantial sums of money offered them to manage such a large event at late notice just before the New Year.

It was a dignified and impressive send-off for a man who commanded affection from friends, family and clients alike. It was a motley congregation who gathered, from ancient and long-standing clients, some old enough to regale Jack with stories of the Civil War, to affluent neighbours from this exclusive suburb, to the local padre, whose eulogy at the church had painted a more charitable and God-fearing man than had been Jack's experience. Aunt Millie was at her most maudlin, warning anyone who would listen of the dangers of taking any time on this earth for granted. She was particularly taken by a small group of young men, sharply dressed but little inclined to socialise with the wider group. They seemed, Jack suspected, better acquainted with Williams Junior than with his deceased namesake.

It was now almost midnight and the women had retired after the last of the guests had finally departed a little over an hour before, much the worse for the alcohol that had been blatantly passed around, under the nose of the local police chief himself at one point.

"We need to talk about the business."

Jack's hackles rose. He was, himself, far from sober and wary about discussing work with Williams in such a state. From early on he had recognised in Williams a capable if lazy businessman but was fully aware that their approaches could easily diverge. Moreover, for all that he trusted Williams as a friend, his instinct told him to apply a different standard of assessment when it came to the business.

"Can't it wait?"

Williams ignored him. "I'm taking over the business here, immediately. The old man had neglected things, too busy either in New York or indulging himself."

"You might think that's a good thing given how things turned out for him," Jack remarked pointedly.

"He was getting soft," Williams condemned, "and I won't waste any more time before turning things around. It means I'm going to be on the ground here most of the time so I'm going to move the family back here for the time being. And I want you to move to New York permanently to run the operation there."

Jack felt as if he was being treated as an employee. While he might be one, he had never considered himself in the employ of the Williams family. "Permanently?" he challenged.

"For the next couple of years, at least. That business is only going to get more important to me and I need someone I trust at the helm." He bit back his tempted retort at Williams' high-handed tone and his convenient forgetfulness that it was Jack who had stepped in when Williams was mishandling the operation. "But we need to resolve the issue of your investigation first." Jack's surprise must have been evident on his face because Williams smiled, a superior smile of one who has the upper hand. "Did you really think I didn't know what you were doing in New York for the last month, Westerham? Or that Adams wouldn't keep me informed?"

Jack stood his ground. "I was doing what I considered necessary to protect the interests of Richmond Bank."

"Hey, don't get defensive," throwing up his hands. "I'm not criticising, Jack. But I'm not going to let you undermine what I've been doing either." The words had steel behind them. It was something of which Jack had long suspected Williams was capable but he had seen little evidence to-date. "I know you're only doing what you consider to be in line with the remit you have been handed by Richmond. So, I propose to change the remit."

"What do you suggest?"

"Submit your report. Tell them I've been putting some of their capital into equity as well as debt. Then I will provide a supplementary report, showing them the level of returns I've been able to achieve from those investments, even in the last few months. Chicago First will be proposing that the venture extend its remit to include equity investment and Richmond will have evidence for itself of the value of what I propose."

"Why are you so set on building equities into the portfolio?"

"Why are you so set against them?"

Jack accepted another refill of his glass as he considered. "It's about risk appetite. While I see lower risk opportunities that can deliver a decent return, I don't feel the need to be exposing our clients' capital to higher risk on the off-chance of a higher return."

"That's exactly why I want to include them: a higher return. Debt is too safe for me. The opportunities in equities are more diverse and we can mitigate the risk with a sufficiently diverse portfolio."

Jack wasn't convinced. "There's more to it than that," he challenged.

Williams' laugh was a little off key. "That's what I like about you, Westerham. Your in-built bullshit detector." He looked at Jack for a long moment. "Alright," leaning forward and resting his elbows on his knees, his hands before him. "I have some investors who want us to manage their money. Serious money. But they want it in equities. It was their initial investment that I put through the bank's

508

books in August. They gave me a small amount to play with and they wanted to see what I could achieve with it. They were pretty satisfied with the returns so they're ready to put in more."

"Why can't they do it through Chicago First? Why does it need to go through the bank?"

Williams' discomfort was transparent on his face. "It's local money but they've got enough investments here already," he displaced. "They want this invested outside the state."

"Is that supposed to make me any more comfortable with what you're proposing?"

Williams sat back and gave him a hard stare. "Understand this, Jack. We're friends and we're family. But when it comes to business I will treat you like any other man working for the business. You are an employee of Richmond Bank but you will become an employee of this bank and, when you are, you will recognise that you do not have the right to question my decisions. If I decide I want to take on this client, that is my decision, not yours."

"Actually," Jack disputed, "under the terms of the venture, all decisions about clientele as well as about investment approaches have to be agreed by both partners. Equally."

Williams laughed. "Then there's no problem, is there? I'll clear it with Samuels and then we can set that brain of yours to proper work, making all of us seriously wealthy."

There was little that appealed to Jack the way Williams described it but he recognised the limits of his authority. "I will speak to Sarah in the morning about moving to New York," he caveated.

"No need," Williams dismissed, pushing himself to his feet and heading for the door. "I mentioned it to her before she left Chicago. She's already agreed."

* * * * * * *

He had drafted the report to Richmond Bank before he even returned to New York and had it typed up as soon as the office reopened on the second of January. He knew he was treading a fine line. He still strongly advocated Richmond's previous investment policy but there was no denying the level of returns being generated on the stock investments. He could also hardly accuse the owner of their venture partner of dubious dealings, though there was no question in his mind that Williams had not only invested in stocks but had also gone ahead with the investment in Baines Johnson that Melissa Johnson had asked him to make more than six months before. To him, the fact that this particular investment was proving successful was a moot point. So he carefully laid out for the Richmond Bank partners the news of the unauthorised investments but balanced it with an update on the performance of the portfolio overall. Suddenly, he was discovering he was living in a more political world than that to which he had originally signed up.

He did not challenge Sarah on her silence about Williams' proposal. He understood full well how staying in the US would better suit her scheme, should it come to fruition, and now they were on that path it seemed futile to question it.

During January, for a while he developed a new routine of leaving for work before Sarah rose and returning late in the evening, late enough for her usually to have retired already. He wasn't avoiding Sarah. He was avoiding Grace. Thus far, they had succeeded in not seeing each other for several days at a stretch, and then only passing in the corridor or the dressing room, her head down and he studiously avoiding eye contact.

It wasn't that he was afraid of either himself or her. It was just easier on both of them this way and they seemed to be complicit in the conspiracy without having discussed it.

* * * * * * *

After the monthly partners' meeting in the third week of January, the answer came back promptly: after due consideration, the partners were amenable to Chicago First's proposed change to the investment policy and sanctioned investment of up to one third of the bank's capital in equities. What surprised Jack was the news that some of Richmond's own clientele were intending to invest through the bank as well to take advantage of this new opportunity.

"There is much that appeals in our proposition," Mr Samuels wrote to Jack. "As a British bank based in New York, we are trusted to apply the same standards there as we have become known for here and there are plenty who see greater appeal in America's growth rates than in what we might generate domestically."

Mr Samuels was not a reliable correspondent, being too infrequent a letter writer, so Jack turned to the Major both for news from home and as an independent confidant. To a point.

"I share your scepticism," the Major replied to his explanation of the shifting sands within the bank. "In my limited experience, that which looks too good to be true usually is. And, if I continue down the theme of my father's favourite homilies, there's no such thing as a free lunch. But, my friend, one can hardly deny the returns now to be made by those 'speculating' on the stock market. The news of some spectacular gains permeates even this charming backwater on occasion. Given your naturally cautious attitude, are you not best placed to make these investments, with a clear eye and a calm head?"

The Major also continued to be a good source of information from home, still furnishing Jack with regular copies of the London papers, though Jack was no longer passing these along to their previously intended recipient. From time to time, however, he noticed the latest ones were missing from his study and deliberately left them out for her after that.

For all his entertainingly phlegmatic views on the idiots running the country, the Major made an inadequate substitute for

Jack's previous conversational companion. The hours he spent at work, in part, filled the gap at home.

They marked his birthday quietly at the end of January, not least in respect for the Williams family's mourning, just with dinner for Sarah and Jack at a local restaurant. Gradually during the course of the evening, they moved from stilted and forced conversation to something that more closely resembled how they used to be together and when Sarah laughed at one point and reached across the table to cover his hand it almost felt natural. Only for a moment did he allow himself to reflect that it was not only his birthday that day.

Thereafter, as January drifted into February, they both made more of an effort, Jack coming home earlier at least a couple of times a week to dine with Sarah. And when, one night, a nightmare woke her and she reached for him for comfort, it was instinctive to hold and console her, and he almost did not wonder whether her fear was genuine.

During this time, though he saw Grace but rarely, and then never to speak to, he couldn't help but witness the change in her, even the slightest changes somehow magnified to his over-observant eyes. Outwardly, she was the healthiest he had seen her. Her porcelain-like skin glowed with health and her hair shone. But, in her unguarded moments when he could look into her eyes before she realised he was watching her and veiled her expression, he also saw how withdrawn she looked, a wariness in her eyes.

By the end of February, just a glance at her left no doubt in his mind. She was pregnant.

It made him wonder, what must it feel like to nurture a life? To know that it is entirely reliant on you for its health and well-being? Worse, to know that you are entirely responsible for it for nine months but that, thereafter, you will surrender all claims, all rights to love and cherish that child? To be asked to live in the moment, knowing that their future is not yours?

What did Sarah intend after the child was born? Did she expect Grace to continue to be part of their lives, always present but forever on the periphery of her child's world, with no rights and no status? Or was she supposed to disappear, to leave this gift with them and vanish from their lives? Selfishly, that thought appalled him even more, for all that he recognised it might be the better solution all round.

In his darker moments, alone in the silent study when he forced himself to confront that thought, he wondered if he was deluding himself. Could he really spend the rest of his life living this existence, maintaining this outward image with Sarah while shutting himself off from the void at his core, that other person he had become? Would it, like a bereavement, improve with time, a gradual lessening of these raw emotions? Did he even want that? Where was the honesty in that for any of them?

He slammed the door shut on that thought. He had made promises and commitments, to both of them, and he would honour them whether it was what he wanted or not.

* * * * * * *

He waited for Sarah to start the conversation, for her to confirm to him the conclusion he had already drawn and to discuss with him their next steps. He was startled, then, by the manner of her disclosure.

Williams, Charlotte and his mother had arrived back in New York for a few days in mid-March, primarily to attend a charity dinner being held to honour Williams Senior by the Bankers' Association.

It might have made for quite a solemn event but that Williams was determined to avoid it being so and strained to be his most charming and entertaining all evening. From champagne at the club before the event, through his speech before 150 industry dignitaries and their wives to the journey back to the Upper East Side house, he was full of anecdotes about his father, whether remembered or passed on by colleagues and friends. It probably helped that Charlotte, too heavy now to face a long evening out, had stayed at home, though this equally served to put a dampener on things as soon as they walked back through the door. It probably didn't help that Williams delivered the punchline to an anecdote at that moment and the collective audience – Susanna, Isabella, Wendell, Sarah and Jack, all predisposed to amusement by their unspoken determination not to allow too much solemnity and, Sarah aside, with an indecent amount of alcohol inside them – all burst out laughing as they walked through the door.

Charlotte, indulging her natural talent for drama, was standing in the doorway to the drawing room, a scowl on her face, one hand meaningfully placed in the small of her back both to ease and to emphasise her discomfort, the other resting on the top of the curve of her belly. Jack couldn't help but draw a mental contrast between this pregnant woman, sullen, discontented, whey-faced, damp-haired and bloated, with the other example in his life.

"If you're all drunk, I suggest you go to bed or leave as soon as possible," Charlotte threw at them. Sarah, seeing Williams about to respond and wanting to avoid a scene, rapidly crossed the hall and, kissing her sister in greeting, put her arm around her shoulder and steered her back into the drawing room.

"It wasn't the same without you," she assured, "but we did our best to give Mr Williams the send-off he deserved."

"It's been miserable here," Charlotte complained. "Aunt Millie went off to bed hours ago and I've been left here alone to wait for you all."

"It was kind of you to wait up," Sarah soothed. "We would have understood had you decided to retire too."

"It's a shame you didn't see Freddie, Charlie," Isabella intervened clumsily. "He did us proud."

"Well some of us need to take care of the next generation," she retorted, "while you've off living it high." Isabella blanched in anger. The lack of child yet was already a bone of contention with the Dexter White family. Charlotte was playing dirty.

"Drink, Westerham? Dex?" Williams sought to deflect the situation.

"Actually," Sarah intervened, "Jack and I should be heading home. We just wanted to share our news first, as you're heading back to Chicago tomorrow." She left her seat next to Charlotte and came to stand next to Jack, threading her arm through his. For a long moment, she let her words hang in the air, waiting, it seemed, for her audience to put two and two together. Jack looked at her just as did everyone else in the room. He wondered if she was expecting him to say something. Thankfully, Mrs Williams seemed faster on the uptake than the rest as she suddenly raised her hands to her mouth and exclaimed in a soft tone, "Oh, my dears!".

Charlotte stared at her mother-in-law, bemused, as she closed the short space to Sarah and gave her a quick, slightly embarrassed hug. "I'm so pleased for you," she pronounced, holding one hand out to Jack as well. "For both of you. I was afraid it was never going to happen for you."

Charlotte, slowly reaching the same conclusion, showed horror on her face and seemed unable to move as Williams, Isabella and Wendell belatedly joined the celebration.

"Well, that certainly calls for a drink," Williams insisted, pouring a large one each for the three men and clinking their glasses with his. "You'll be next, Dex. Mark by words," he reassured, soothing over his wife's earlier malice.

"You can't be." The flat-toned denial came from Charlotte, still seated on the sofa and separate from the party. "You said it was impossible."

Sarah looked hard at her sister. "I said," she corrected calmly, "that it was unlikely. That doesn't make it impossible."

"But is it risky?" Isabella's genuine concern for her sister-in-law only underlined Charlotte's uncharitable attitude further.

"It could be," Sarah admitted. "I will have to be careful and the doctor wants me to be closely monitored. In fact, he's recommended a centre he wants me to go to for as much of the pregnancy as possible. They have the best facilities and a good success rate with women who have miscarried," there was just enough hesitation and emotion in her voice to be convincing, "in the past."

"That sounds very wise, my dear," Susanna Williams counselled. "I'm sure you wouldn't want to take any risks. It's such a miracle," clasping her hands together as if in prayer.

"I don't like to be away from Jack, though," Sarah reflected with a sideways glance at him.

"Don't worry," Williams chided, slapping Jack between the shoulders. "I'll keep him so busy he won't have time to notice you're not around."

"Just don't make me do any client dinners," Jack warned with a grimace. "Not if you want to keep your clients."

"Where is the centre, Sarah?" Wendell's obvious interest in a solution to something only he and his family yet considered to be a problem earned him a disdainful look from his wife. Jack had suspected for a while that this issue had more to do with Isabella's unwillingness to conceive just yet than with any inability to do so, and the look confirmed it for him.

"I don't think we need concern ourselves with that just yet, Dex," Isabella directed quietly and her husband lapsed back into his usual silent, supine role.

"It's in Iowa," Sarah answered the question anyway. "In Plymouth county."

"You aren't leaving before my baby arrives, of course." Charlotte commanded their attention again from her throne.

"Actually, Charlotte," Sarah started but she wasn't allowed to finish.

"No!" Charlotte denied. "There's no reason for you to go yet. Look at you," a dismissive gesture inviting everyone to scrutinise Sarah's form, "you hardly look pregnant at all. It's less than two months for me now. Surely you can manage 'til then."

Her high-pitched tone spoke of building hysteria but, since she never saw fit to check her own temper, Jack had little patience with her fear.

"Charlotte, you have to understand my point of view…" Sarah defended.

"Why?" Charlotte rose to her feet now, deliberately emphasising the awkwardness of her condition as she confronted her sister. "Why does it always have to be me who understands? Why do I always have to make allowances and sacrifices for everyone else? When will someone make allowances for me?" Her selfishness was breath-taking and Jack knew he wasn't the only one feeling that way. "I'm the one who is seven-and-a-half months gone. You're showing no signs whatsoever. You can't be more than two months along. How do you even know for certain?"

Her face was as flushed as her sister's was drained of colour. "I'm just short of three months," Sarah whispered, her voice as ghostly as her face.

"There!" Charlotte denounced triumphantly. "Any manner of thing may happen in the next few weeks. It would be pointless to go running off for nothing when I need you here."

"Enough!" Jack's refusal came out more angrily than he had intended. He forced himself to take a breath before speaking again, putting his arm around his wife's shoulder and drawing her to him at the same time. He felt the tremor run through her and, for the first time in weeks, he felt his protective instinct surface. "Sarah has spent years putting you before herself, Charlotte," he stated, outwardly calm. "For once in her life, she needs to put herself first, for the one thing that would mean more to her than anything else. You must understand that."

She mistook his controlled tone for a less-than-iron will.

"But, Sarah…" she appealed, deliberately ignoring him and brushing past him to grasp her sister's forearm in an attempt to drag her away from Jack.

"Charlotte, your mother died giving birth to Rose." Jack allowed the anger to resonate in his voice now and he was pleased to see some of the colour drain from Charlotte's cheeks as she finally looked him in the face and recognised the strength of her adversary. "Sarah and I will do everything in our power to protect her and to protect our unborn child. And, for me, that starts with getting her as far away as possible from you." He turned towards his hosts. "Susanna, Williams, forgive me. Thank you for involving us in tonight's event, it was a pleasure. But if you will excuse us, I shall take my wife home."

He steered Sarah out of the room, knowing he left a stunned Charlotte behind. Susanna, Williams, Isabella and Wendell all came back out to the entrance hall to see them off and there was much warmth and congratulation in their albeit muted farewells. With promises of regular correspondence on the part of the women and more jovial back-slapping from Williams, they made their escape, leaving Charlotte, still and silent but with her back now turned towards them, in the dark drawing room.

* * * * * *

They were silent in the car home, both acutely conscious of the chauffeur, but they sat close together on the back seat of the car, their hands wound together and Jack's thumb gently caressing the back of Sarah's hand. As they drew up at the steps to the brownstone, he helped Sarah out of the car as tenderly and considerately as if she had been carrying his child.

518

As of one accord, they headed to the drawing room on the first floor and Sarah bent to stoke the subdued fire in the grate as Jack poured them both a drink.

"It will have to be a discrete one," he warned as they sank onto the sofa together. "Once the servants know, you will be expected to be abstemious, I'm sure." He put out his arm and she eased under his shoulder, her arm around his waist.

"Thank you for defending me."

"But I went too far," he finished for her. Her silence confirmed it. "You will always allow her to get away with too much and, unfortunately, Williams is no better at checking her failings. She will never think for herself how much you sacrifice for her. It's no bad thing if she is finally forced to consider the implications for once. I'm sure it won't weigh on her mind for too long anyway." He leant his head back against the sofa, suddenly tired.

"I hope I will warrant a good send-off myself one day," Sarah mused.

"I hope that day is a long way off," Jack murmured in response, his eyes closed.

"Don't you think about it? What sort of legacy you will leave behind? Or, at least, what impression people will be left with of you or your life or how you've lived?"

He opened one eye and closed it again. "You're very philosophical all of a sudden," he teased. "It must be the pregnancy."

"Don't," she warned with a plea. "Not when it's just us."

He raised his head and looked at her. "What is it?"

"It doesn't come naturally to me," she defended. "The lying."

He nodded. "I know."

"Do you?" she challenged and he realised just how defensive she was being.

"What is it?" he asked again. "What's concerning you?"

She closed her eyes and shook her head. "I don't know," she muttered. "I used to be able to read you so well but now..."

"Read what? What is it that you want to know?"

"Everything. I have no idea how you actually feel about all this. I feel as if I'm entirely alone in all of it."

"Is that why you announced it tonight in front of everybody? Why you didn't feel the need to tell me first?"

"Ah. You're angry."

"I'm not angry, Sarah," he disagreed calmly.

"Well, I wish you were!" she retorted. "You so rarely get angry and it's hugely frustrating. At least if you were angry I'd know you cared!"

He removed his arm from her shoulder and turned in his seat so that he could face her. "Is that what you think?" he demanded. "That I don't care? Do you really think I wouldn't want to know about our child," he could easily have said 'my child' but, even now, he was thinking clearly enough to know the difference, "before the rest of the world does?"

"That's my point, John," she defended. "I don't know any more. When I came back, it was like you shut me out. Everything we'd had before disappeared. Our closeness, our honesty. All we've talked about is your work. There's so little in my life over here and you took away the foundation I was relying upon."

"I think you're overstating things."

"Of course I'm overstating things!" She almost growled with anger and frustration. "But only to make the point. Are you even listening to what I'm telling you?" She started to rise from her seat but he put his hand on her arm and stilled her.

"Don't walk away," he told her and she sank back down. "You're right," he conceded. "I did shut you out. I had no choice. It was the only way I knew to deal with everything. And I know it's taken a while to get past that but I thought we were. I thought things had been returning to normal in the past few weeks."

"Maybe," she sighed, "it's knowing you've shut me out that's making me hold back. I know things have been better. But I can't deal with not knowing."

He took her hand. "Sarah, you are going to have to deal with it. I don't do it to spite you or to hurt you. I do it because, now it's done, I need to shut that part of me away, from both of us. If I don't, it will destroy our marriage. And, believe me, I don't want that to happen."

She looked at him. "Do you still love me?" Her voice was steady.

"How can you even need to ask that?" he demanded.

"Just tell me, John. I need to know." Less steady now.

"Yes, Sarah, I do." He put his hand to her cheek. "You are my wife and I love you." She let go an uneven breath, as if she had been holding it all this time, and he saw her mouth tremble. "My God, Sarah. Did you really believe I didn't?"

She gave a slight lift of her shoulders. "I haven't known what to believe."

With a sound of frustration, he pulled her to him and kissed her, hard at first then more tenderly. When they broke apart, her eyes were shining. "Please," she asked. "Make love to me." Neither of them had ever had to ask before. That realisation shook him.

He rose and held out his hand, slipping his arm around her shoulder when she came to him. Arms around each other, they made their way upstairs.

* * * * * * *

Later, in the darkness, their arms still around each other, they talked.

"I've never seen you that uncertain before," Jack reflected. "I'm sorry to have been the cause of that."

She shook her head. "I was seeing shadows that aren't there."

"There are shadows, Sarah," he contradicted, "ones that didn't exist before. But know that I shall keep them at bay, for both of us."

"It's hard for me to have to rely on someone else like that."

"I know," he acknowledged. "And it's good for you too."

"I know," she returned with a smile. "Will you tell me, though, how do you feel about it? About being a father? Is there any part of you that wants this for yourself or are you just doing it for me?"

"I don't think anyone's motives are ever that selfless," he observed. "Least of all mine."

"You're deflecting," she admonished.

"Maybe," he accepted. "Perhaps because I don't know exactly how I feel. I'm excited, yes, but I'm daunted too. Concerned that we may not get away with it and worried what implications that would have for our families. I don't think people would understand."

"Do you? Understand?"

He considered then answered honestly. "I don't think it's possible for me to understand your need or what drives you. Nor, though, do I think it's necessary. I accept that's what you need and I trust that it's the right thing for you."

"You're putting a lot of faith in me."

"Is there any reason why I shouldn't?"

She smiled a denial. "You are excited then?"

"Yes," he reassured her. "If you'd told me a year ago we'd be planning like this, I wouldn't have believed you. Is she right, though?" concerned suddenly. "When Charlotte said it's still early and anything could happen."

"It's almost three months. We visited a doctor, one out in the suburbs who wouldn't know us or see us again. He confirmed it and checked her over and, so far, so good."

"What happens from here, then?"

"She and I will leave next week. I can't risk any sign of her showing and raising suspicions. I don't want the staff knowing anything yet either. We'll travel to Des Moines and then we'll let it be known here it's because I'm staying near a medical centre during the pregnancy. It's natural that she would stay with me."

"Six months?"

"I know," she shrugged. "It won't be easy to be away that long but it's the only way."

"What's the arrangement with Mrs Wilson?"

She didn't reply immediately and he realised it was because she knew his question meant he had talked with Grace about this. He waited, unwilling to cover his mistake. It was for Sarah to accept and move on. She did eventually, with a single, brief nod of her head as if she had come to a decision. "Mrs Wilson will know the truth. At this point, she just knows that I'm coming to stay with her and I'm bringing someone with me. When her husband died, she moved in with her sister but she's continued with her midwifery to give herself an income. It's a big house and there's space for both of us. As far as everyone else is concerned, we're sisters and she lost her husband a few weeks ago. We're staying there because she's too grief-stricken to be at home."

"Am I allowed to visit?"

She considered. "I don't think that's wise. She has already said she doesn't want anyone else to be there for the birth." He had no right but the rejection stung. "I was hoping, though," Sarah continued, "that you would travel with us next week. Do you think you can manage a day or two away from the office?" He hesitated. It would be the first time all three of them had been thrown together for any amount of time. How would they manage it? "I know," she acknowledged. "I've also been wondering if it would just be too awkward."

He tensed at that. A gut instinct told him she was testing him.

"It's not that," he denied. "I was just thinking how to rearrange my schedule." It sounded lame, even to his ears. "Of course I will travel with you. I wouldn't be comfortable thinking you were travelling all that way alone."

The way she relaxed at that told him he was right. He may have told her she had to accept the situation but it wasn't going to stop her testing his loyalty every step of the way.

* * * * * * *

It was even more difficult than he had feared.

From the moment they departed in the car for the train station, he and Sarah in the back, she travelling up front with the chauffeur, he didn't know whether he was expected to treat her as a servant or not. He didn't even know what to call her or how to think of her. To him, she was Grace, the woman who had changed his life. To the world, she was Rachel but he could neither think of her that way nor bring himself to use that name, knowing that, to her, it was like a prison.

It seemed, also, that Sarah never wanted to leave the two of them alone together so there was no opportunity to establish new ground rules between them. It was like being in limbo: too changed from before to fall back into old behaviours, too uncertain about how they should behave now. Sarah wasn't so unsubtle as to emphasise her ownership but, whenever she took the seat next to him, he couldn't help but wonder if she was being proprietorial or whether it was the natural thing for her to do.

Part of him was thankful that Sarah had booked them all into the first class carriage. Nothing could have been more embarrassing than to think of her sitting alone in a different carriage from them. Another part was dreading the prospect of a long train journey together, uncomfortable silences of words that couldn't be spoken.

Though there was also one part of him, he had to admit to himself, that was deeply satisfied to be in her company again. However uncomfortable the circumstances, however little he was able to converse with her, however much he was having to guard against giving Sarah any sign that she might misconstrue, to be able to look on her again and, in the silence of his own mind, remember, was a pleasure.

After suffering long silences broken occasionally by stilted conversation for almost half the train journey, he elected to stop pretending when they broke their journey and bought himself the first semi-interesting book he could find in the inadequately stocked station store. As a second thought, he also bought a range of newspapers and magazines that he knew would appeal to her.

Sarah was already seated in the carriage. He deliberately took the seat diagonally opposite her, stretching his long legs out alongside her as an excuse for his chosen position, and opening his book. She narrowed her eyes at him but there was at least a hint of a smile there too. The book became the escape he sought and the second half of the journey passed much more agreeably than the first.

By the time they stepped down at the local station, the train was almost empty, as was the platform. He sought the large trunks and cases they had piled into the baggage car and whistled for a porter to ship them to the nearest taxi.

The last few days of March were holding onto the winter chill for all they were worth, ignoring the imminence of Easter that coming weekend, and the glowering, rain-filled skies brought dusk early.

Somewhere between New York and here, there had been a shift in their roles and he felt it as he helped the ladies into the taxi. It was an odd awareness, as if her servant position had been shed like a coat and a new position status taken on. From this point forward, she was – as far as anyone in this town was concerned – his sister-in-law. It was strangely liberating.

* * * * * * *

What they drove through was everything Jack anticipated from a small mid-western town. The main street was a hotch-potch of new and old buildings, general merchandise stores, specialist stores, the barber, the baker, the butcher, a quaint coffee house, the one town hotel, a scatter of small restaurants, the police house. Cars were parked randomly down the sides of the wide main boulevard, cherry trees not yet in flower creating an avenue along the walkways, flags snapping in the breeze on diagonal poles jutting out from several of the shop fronts. Those shops that weren't shut already were in the process of closing and the pedestrians were either hurrying to their cars, their shopping in paper-wrapped parcels in their arms, or congregating in their usual haunts, the coffee house for the women, the bar – dry, of course – for the men. It took barely two minutes to drive through and he couldn't help but wonder how Sarah, used to the varied entertainments of London and New York, would feel during her extended sojourn here.

They kept heading out of town, past the white clapboard church, the local hospital and the small, one-storey library, until they finally turned off the main road onto what appeared to be little more than a dirt track. A hundred yards or so ahead, they could see the lights of a house, sheltered by a spreading old apple tree to the east and backed by a few spindly birches to the north but otherwise quite exposed to the sweeping fields surrounding it. The weatherboards of the house itself seemed to have borne the brunt of the wind sweeping across the plains, the paint flaking visibly. It was a good size house but not at all what Sarah was used to. There appeared to be some attic rooms but the majority were clearly spread across two floors. A porch provided a small outdoor seating area, facing towards the road. It was small, practical and homely.

As they drew up, a thin, middle-aged woman that Jack vaguely recognised as Mrs Wilson pushed open the screen door, wiping her hands with a cloth. She greeted Sarah warmly as they all climbed out of the car but her welcome for the two of them was noticeably muted. She instructed the taxi driver to carry the larger bags into the living room, leading Sarah through and leaving them behind.

* * * * * * *

Jack pays the driver, who rapidly takes his leave, then, turning towards the house, he sees that he isn't alone. It is the first time they had been alone together since Christmas Day.

He keeps his distance and is careful not to look at her too directly in case they are being watched from the house, though he still takes in how she looks and notes that, like him, she is hesitant, uncertain of what to say but clearly wanting to use the opportunity.

"Are you well, Grace?" he asks her quietly, making a show of collecting the rest of the bags together, ready to take inside.

He sees how she blanches and then flushes at the sound of her name, spoken softly but warmly.

"I am, thank you." Too formal for his liking but he can understand that.

"You look well," he observes, deliberately turning away from her at that moment, pushing his hands into his pockets and appearing to take in the sweep of the landscape around him.

"We're both healthy," she murmurs softly, reading his mind. She mirrors his movements in looking out at the surrounding land, greying now in the diminishing light, but still stands a few feet away from him. "And she's very happy."

He gives the slightest nod. "And that's what we both wanted."

"Yes," she affirms, with only the slightest waver in her voice.

"I hope you will be comfortable here," he suggests, hating how formal and distant the words, though well intentioned, sound once spoken. He is glad she doesn't respond to them.

"Are you heading straight back to New York?"

How strange to have endured several hours' journey with her and yet for them to be so distant with each other. "Tomorrow," he confirms. "There's an early train so I shall leave before breakfast."

527

He senses rather than hears her intake of breath at that. "What is it?" tempted to look at her to understand what has just shocked her.

She drops her head so that words came out very softly. "Then I may never see you again after tonight."

At that, he cannot avoid but look at her, a strange fear running through him at the words. "Why do you say that?"

"Sarah said you wouldn't be here for the birth, that you wouldn't be able to get away from New York. And I don't know if I shall be returning to the household."

"Because of how you might feel?"

"In part. And in part because of how it might make Sarah feel."

"I don't accept that, Grace," he denies. "I can't accept the thought that I shall never see you again."

"Don't," she denies him. "We both knew it could – would – come at some point," she reasons, though the tremor in her voice undermines her.

"No," he refuses.

She draws a breath, appearing to draw courage for something. "Then," hesitant. "Perhaps you would be here? For the birth?"

He looks away. "Sarah told me you didn't want me here." Her silence makes him look back again. "She lied?" he questions. Her lack of a denial confirms it for him. He glances towards the house and notices a silhouette in the doorway. His sense of fairness rebels and overrides his caution. "I'll be here," he promises. "For as long as I can."

* * * * * * *

He had never known such loneliness in his life. Everyone he knew well was now distant from him: Sarah and Grace in Iowa; Williams, Charlotte and Susanna in Chicago; the Major in Cambridgeshire; Mr Samuels in London; his family in Devon; even Alfie, of whom he had heard nothing since his departure just before his wedding, two-and-a-half years ago. He dined with Isabella and Wendell from time to time and occasionally joined a wider group of the Dexter White family members for nights at the theatre but he knew he was increasingly poor company and the invitations came less and less frequently.

Not that it didn't, in some ways, suit him. He had never read so much in his life, having worked through a significant proportion of the house's library and expanded it for himself, and his productivity at work, with little else to distract him, was unsurpassed. Which was just as well because Williams was keeping him incredibly busy. The size of investments they were now handling were, by his standards, mind-blowing. He knew that, in the context of both Richmond Bank and Chicago First, the bank was handling only a fraction of what they did but the responsibility he felt was considerable and he found himself unable to do other than take it personally. They continued to expand the operation, moving into a new building in the financial district in June. More than a dozen analysts were now working to identify new investment opportunities but they were still unable to keep up with the demand.

The evenings, though, could be long and silent and time occasionally weighed heavily on his hands.

Letters from the Major kept him going. They had taken to playing postal chess, which was a good incentive for both of them to maintain a regular correspondence, although the Major, busy with the operation at Richmond House, sometimes lapsed into two line notes with little more than his next move and a reassurance that all was well.

Those from Sarah seemed only to emphasise how distant he was from them, not just physically but in contrast with those very personal letters the two of them had exchanged during the first prolonged separation of their marriage.

He wished he could write to Grace and even took up his pen a couple of times. The draft letters still sat in the drawer of his desk.

He knew he could not send them. He hoped, vainly, that Sarah might share his letters with her, imagining them sitting on that porch of an evening, reading together, talking. Sisters. How easily might they maintain that illusion for the local populace.

The emptiness of the house bothered him. He became acutely aware of every noise, aware of the comings and goings of the servants, doors slamming in the basement or the back stairs creaking or footsteps on the floorboards in the attic rooms.

It wasn't just the emptiness. It was the empty rooms that haunted him, taunting him with memories. All too frequently, he found himself outside the door of the guest bedroom, the one he had shared with Grace. Once, he turned the handle and stood on the threshold for a long moment, seeking in the darkness any sign of what they had shared. The room was dark and still, the bed made up, the air a little stale with undisturbed dust. Not even a hint of her. He wasn't altogether sure he wasn't going a little mad.

At one point, he wrote a letter to Sarah to suggest that they consider buying a different house, a place where they could put their own stamp on the bricks and mortar. The unfinished draft lay, unsent, in the same drawer as those to Grace. He knew he couldn't leave this place, tied and bound as he was to what he had experienced there, knowing also that, at some point, that might be all that was left to him.

In June, Williams' application to make him a member of his club was approved by the membership committee and he found company of sorts among the other men who were variously escaping their homes, whether avoiding their wives and families or seeking like-minded companions and friends. The library likewise held some appeal, not only for its extensive and varied contents but also for its policy of enforced silence, enabling him to enjoy the presence of others around him while he read without having to pretend an interest in engaging with them. In no time, it became his regular routine to dine at the club after work and to retire to the library or the smoking room thereafter, occasionally even making use of the guest bedrooms to stay for the night when he couldn't face returning to the isolation of the house.

He knew all he was doing was existing. Outwardly he appeared to be progressing, particularly to anyone who saw him at work, but inwardly he was marking time.

Time that started to drag even more slowly as summer arrived and New York was first flooded with tourists in June and July, and then drained of inhabitants in August as the summer exodus began. Sarah's letters were coming ever more infrequently and, when they did arrive, were frustratingly short on information. Through the intolerable New York summer heat, he became intolerable himself, short-tempered with anyone failing to come up to his exacting standards, impatient of the slightest faults. His attention wavered and he grew angry with himself, driving through an ever-more-demanding work schedule to compensate for his inability to focus for any period of time.

The Labor Day weekend came and went. And then he couldn't stand it any more.

Chapter Seventeen

Iowa, September 1923

I don't know what I expected to feel when I got there. The months of separation had served only to blur my thoughts and emotions even further.

Standing in the shade of the apple tree, he has lost track of how long he has been watching her. His bags are forgotten on the ground beside him, the soreness of his feet after the long walk from the station a distant memory.

He has not expected this. While he has been away he has missed the company, the conversation. He has remembered their closeness. He has, in unguarded moments, recalled their passion, their intimacy. All that has left him unprepared for this overwhelming surge of protectiveness.

Her back bothers her. Twice now while he has been watching, she has leant backwards as she dead-heads the flowers and eased the curve of her spine, her hand rubbing at the ache.

Her hair has grown. She has loosely tied it back with a ribbon to keep it out of her eyes but strands keep coming loose. There is a pleasant breeze alleviating the heat of the day and it teases at the strands, blowing them across her damp face. Her light cotton dress ripples against the curve of her belly and she runs a hand slowly over the bump, the slightest smile teasing one side of her mouth.

His heart is in his mouth as she brushes the hair from her forehead with the back of her hand. She has never looked more beautiful.

If she only looks to her left, she will see him. He half wants her to, half hopes she won't so he can continue to watch, unnoticed.

But he was not unnoticed. He caught a movement from the corner of his eye, the screen door opening. Sarah stepped out onto the porch. How long she had been watching him, he could not know. The moment had passed and reality had rushed back in.

Picking up his bag, he crossed the parched grass and climbed the two steps onto the porch. His movement had caught Grace's attention and he was aware of her turning towards them. He put his hand on Sarah's waist and leaned in to kiss her cheek. He could see she both did and did not want him there.

"Hello, Sarah."

"John. It's a pleasure to see you. A surprise, but a pleasure."

"I'm glad to see you too."

"Are you staying long?" taking in the bags he dropped at his feet.

He held her gaze. "As long as it takes."

"You didn't write." An accusation.

"Nor did you." A retaliation. "She's due sometime in the next two weeks, isn't she?" A nod. "I thought you might have suggested I be here."

"I didn't think you would be able to take the time away from work," she defended. "Besides, most men would prefer not to be around."

"Sarah," he softened his tone, not wanting to argue with her on this but determined to make her understand, "how could I not want to be here for the birth of our child? Besides," lightening the tone, "you married me because I'm not 'most men'," he reminded her with a smile.

She returned the smile though she still kept her hands on her hips. "Then you had better come into the house and say 'hello' to Mrs Wilson."

"I will be there in a moment." He looked at her steadily, conveying both his intent and his determination. This time was too important to be worrying overly about whether she might

533

misinterpret his behaviour. He trusted his own loyalty and she would have to trust him.

She pursed her lips for a second but she also gave a slight nod of her head as she turned towards the house and disappeared inside.

Turning slowly, he finds her still standing where she was and knows she has been watching them, even if she's too distant to have heard their exchange. She turns her head away as Sarah leaves but otherwise she doesn't move. For a second, he steels himself. He has already indulged himself too much and needs to remind himself that this is not about him. He slowly descends to the lawn and crosses the short distance to where she is standing.

"You came." Her voice is heavy with emotion and it can't help but tug at him.

"I promised." He keeps his voice low and is careful to stand in a way that anyone looking on might interpret this as a casual conversation. All the intensity is in their voices and their words.

"I'm glad." He hears more than that in her voice. He hears relief and not a little fear. "You will stay?"

"I'm here for you, Grace," he interprets for her. "For you…" the slight hesitation gives additional emphasis, "…and for our child."

Her breath catches. "I shall be glad of the company."

That surprises him and he looks up at the house. The windows, reflecting the low late afternoon sun, are blind to him. "I will go and make my proper greetings," he suggests, casual still, "and sort my things. Then I will come and find you."

"There are chairs at the back of the house," she responds. "I'll be there." He turns to leave until he hears his name spoken on a slight whisper. "Jack. Thank you."

In spite of himself, his heart reacts.

* * * * * * *

534

"We were about to have tea. Will you join us?" Mrs Wilson was polite but there was no mistaking the ice beneath her words.

He took a cup with thanks but refused the offered cake and remained standing, his back to the window. The sun warmed his shoulders. The sitting room was small, stuffy and heavily decorated in florals and chintz. The three ladies – Mrs Wilson, her sister Mrs Michaels and Sarah – were seated together on the sofas facing across a small mahogany coffee table.

"How have you been keeping?" He didn't direct the question to any of the woman in particular, allowing them to pick it up as they chose.

"We're well, thank you, Mr Westerham," without so much as a glance at Sarah for verification. "We're all well."

"You must have been keeping busy," he notes, pointedly but without rancour. "Your letters have been less frequent of late."

"Mrs Westerham has become a valuable member of the community during the last six months." Mrs Wilson seemed determined to hold the conversation. "It's been a pleasure to have her here."

"You know how I like to keep busy," Sarah remarked. "The ladies of the church have been kind enough to involve me in their fundraising efforts while I'm here. We've had some little success, too."

Jack nodded. "I'm glad to know you've found ways to occupy your time. I was fearing it might be quite tedious for you. And I know how much you missed your charity and community work while we were living in New York."

She didn't respond but let the comment fall.

"I hope you will understand, then," Mrs Wilson seemed unaware of the tension building between him and Sarah, "why we won't be here this evening for supper. We all," taking in the three of them in the room, "have a prior engagement at the church hall to

535

discuss the weekend's Harvest Fair. I'm afraid your unexpected arrival has quite caught us out."

"It's been a long journey. I'm sure I shall be glad of a quiet evening." He drained his cup and returned it to the tray. "Perhaps I might go and settle in? I would be pleased to change out of my travelling clothes."

Sarah rose, as he had intended, and led him out to the hall to collect his bags.

"It's a small room," she caveated, opening the door to a room at the back of the house. "I hope you will find it adequate."

"I'm sure I shall," he demurred. So used to the smaller scale of the Manor compared with the opulence of Richmond House and Lyall Street, it was unlikely that he, of the two of them, would have an issue with the accommodation.

This was clearly a female-dominated household, with the décor of the sitting room flowing through to the bedrooms, a preponderance of pink and yet more florals and flounces on the counterpane and around the windows. Jack wondered whether it had always been thus or whether it had been redecorated after the demise of Mr Michaels. He hoped, for that man's sake, it was the latter. He could not imagine himself tolerating such an oppressive décor for more than a matter of days.

He deliberately sat down on the end of the bed, trying to inject a greater sense of ease into the stilted atmosphere that existed between them and encouraging Sarah to stay for a moment.

"I'm pleased to see you," he told her, resting his hands on his knees. "But it strikes me that you are less than pleased to see me, Sarah."

She carefully closed the door so that the latch barely clicked. "You caught me by surprise, that's all," she defended, leaning back against the door.

He contemplated her for a second, how she wouldn't quite meet his gaze. "I've missed you," he tested, acknowledging to himself the

536

truth of what he said. When she didn't reply, he pushed again. "You haven't written much of late."

"As Mrs Wilson said, we've been busy."

"Did you think I wouldn't want to know about how things are here?"

"Oh, John," exasperated, "I can't be worrying about you as well as about everyone else." With a sigh, she pushed away from the door and crossed to the window, looking down over the lawn at the rear of the house. He waited. "It's been hard," she admitted, her arms folded around her waist. "I hadn't thought how hard it would be, watching our child grow but seeing another woman nurture him."

"Him?"

She kept her back turned and her face carefully turned away. "I don't know but I think of it as a he. Mrs Wilson thinks so too." She stared out of the window for a while and Jack suspected she was watching her. "When we came here, I thought it would be a time of closeness for us, like sisters. But, instead, we've grown further apart the longer it has gone on. She's become so withdrawn from me. We barely say a civil word to each other from one end of the day to the other now."

"Why is that?"

"Honestly, John," annoyed again and finally turning back to look at him, "I couldn't tell you." Her face was in shade, the light of the window behind her, so he couldn't tell if she was lying. He nodded once, accepting her outburst. She calmed and automatically straightened her dress. "We will be leaving in fifteen minutes so I will say goodbye now as I'm sure we will depart before you come down again."

She hesitated only a moment longer before disappearing from the room and back down the stairs.

* * * * * * *

He deliberately waited until he heard the taxi draw up at the front of the house, then the slam of the car doors as the three ladies embarked and the noise of the engine pulling away again.

After a few minutes of silence, he headed in the direction of the kitchen and, finding a young maid there, the general help for the house, requested tea in the back garden for the two of them.

* * * * * * *

She is slowly walking round the garden, her hand in the small of her back to ease where the baby is distorting her spine. She dead-heads flowers as she goes, her hands filled with blown roses and pinks. Now she is not working, she has removed the ribbon and shaken her hair loose. It falls almost to her waist, heavy waves of dark hair, tinted in places to a shining auburn where the rays of the early evening sun catch and enflame it.

"Shouldn't you be sitting?" he suggests, shrugging on his blazer as he crosses the lawn. The warmth of the sun is slowly seeping out of the day. He bends down to pick up her shawl, folded over the arm of one of the chairs, and holds it out for her. She turns her back to accept it, holding up her hands to take it from his as he slips it over her shoulders but careful not to make contact.

She indicates the two chairs at a slight angle to one another, facing down across the lawn. "It's difficult for me to get into them unaided now," she explains with a wry smile.

He offers his hand to help lower her into the chair and, after a long moment's hesitation, she takes it. The shock that runs through them both, though, makes them release as soon as she is settled. Whatever has been between them before, it is still there. Neither of them can afford to spark it off again.

The maid arrives and sets a tray of tea, cake and sandwiches on the table between them. She smiles politely at him but he can't help but notice how he's the only one she acknowledges.

538

"You didn't take tea with the others," he observed, "and I thought you might be hungry after your work in the garden."

"Your kindness will not be approved of in the house," she counters, "but I thank you for it."

He takes the other seat and stretches his legs out, easing his stiff muscles after the long journey. "It's a beautiful garden," he acknowledges. "I don't remember this from when we arrived."

"It was here but mostly buried under weeds. I think it must have been Mr Michaels' garden because his widow doesn't show much interest in it."

"You've done all the work?"

She nods. "I've always wanted a garden. We had a poor excuse for one when we were young but never the money to buy seeds. It's kept me busy while we've been here too."

"I expected to find a harmonious household," he muses, hoping she will enlighten him. He is struggling to comprehend the undercurrents he can see. "I took no hint from Sarah's letters that it was anything other."

She looks away from him, turning slightly so her face is in profile and it is harder for him to read her. "It has been difficult for Sarah," she condones. "I don't think she expected it to be. At the beginning, she was so excited about the baby, but it's hard to maintain that excitement for months at a time. As it dissipated, I think other emotions took over."

"What emotions?" She hesitates to respond to him. "Is she jealous?"

She looks down at her hands. "Resentful, maybe."

"Why?"

She shakes her head and it causes her hair to fall forward, curtaining her face from him. "The longer this has gone on, the more, in her mind, she has thought of the baby as hers. It has made it hard for her to accept that she and the child must rely on someone else. I think…" She hesitates and he waits. "I think I have stopped mattering to her. Now, I am only an encumbrance." She draws her shawl a little tighter over her dress.

"Are you cold?" he worries.

She shakes her head. "Only a little down, maybe." She looks at him at last. And he quickly looks away. He could so easily lose himself in those eyes.

He distracts her with tea. "Will the others be gone long?" he asks.

She nods. "Usually the committee meetings last most of the evening. I'm sure the business is transacted quickly but they like to take their time."

"You aren't involved?"

She shakes her head. "It would be difficult for me to be seen much in the town."

He frowns. "Why?"

"I'm sure Mrs Wilson and Mrs Michaels are glad to do their Christian duty, but they wouldn't want to impose a fallen woman on their neighbours more than is absolutely necessary." She makes it sound so reasonable.

"A fallen woman? What are you talking about?"

She frowns at him in turn. "Isn't that what they were told? That I had got myself in trouble and that you and Sarah were kind enough to help me out?"

"No," he denies, appalled. "As far as I'm concerned, the story was that you had lost your husband and needed to come somewhere safe to wait for the birth."

"That's the story that they've told in the town, yes, but…"

"But Mrs Wilson was to know the truth," he argues. "Or at least part of it."

"I thought so too," she agrees.

"Did Sarah lie to her?"

There is a ghost of a smile on her lips. "We're all lying, Jack," she points out. "It's only a case of which lie."

540

He stands up and walks away, pushing his hands into his pockets. He quickly returns, though, and sits sideways on the chair so that he is facing towards her. "How has it been for you?" he asks, his voice low. His hands are only inches from hers and he notices she folds her defensively.

"It's been fine," she denies, trying and failing to hold his gaze.

He resists the temptation to touch her, though he knows it would be the most effective way to the truth. "Don't lie to me," he appeals, leaning forward ever so slightly and keeping his voice gentle.

She flaps her hand as if she is trying to ward him off. "Let's just say I've had a lot of time to myself and leave it at that," she counters.

He's not about to. "Have you left the house much?"

She closes her eyes. "Church twice a week and visits to the hospital to check on my condition," she admits.

"Do they even talk to you?" he challenges.

She tries to push herself to her feet, keen to put some distance between them. It is impossible, though, and she has to accept his intervention, his hand under her elbow to help her rise, but she shakes him off as soon as she is on her feet. He stands too but stays where he is as she walks a slight distance away.

"You have to understand," she orders, keeping her back to him. "This isn't about me. It never has been."

"And I suppose you'll just walk away," he challenges, fear putting anger into his voice, "after he's born."

"Oh, don't you start doing that too!" She rounds on him and there is real anger visible in her eyes, even at this distance. "What if it's not a boy?" Her voice is raised and almost alarmed. "What then? Is everyone going to be disappointed?"

He crosses the short distance to where she is standing and, without thinking, takes her arm. "Our child could never be a disappointment," he assures her, his face close to hers.

541

He sees the anger drain from her eyes, affected as much by his proximity as by his words. "Not to you, maybe," she accepts in a low voice.

He drops his hold on her. "Sarah will love this child whatever happens," he promises.

"I hope so," she acknowledges. "Sometimes when I hear her talking, planning, I'm afraid."

He can understand that fear, knowing how much Sarah wants to be mother to the grandson that will inherit the family business. The irony of that is not lost on him.

She turns away and starts to walk the perimeter of the garden. He naturally falls into step with her.

"I'm sorry it's been this way for you," he apologises.

"You weren't to know," she dismisses.

"No," he agrees. "But, still."

She nods her acceptance of his apology. "There were moments," she admits, "when I worried I wasn't going a little mad." She laughs it off but there is a hollow ring to it and he hears in the echo some of the doubt that has affected her.

"Is it much different for you?" he asks carefully. "From last time."

She considers for a moment, running her fingers over a rose as she does so. "It's been easier, I think," she reflects. "No sickness this time and I'm less tired. Only..." She stops. Her embarrassment intrigues him.

"Only?" he urges and enjoys seeing her cheeks flush pink.

"There have been moments, times when I have felt very..." she stops, unable to find the word. She closes her eyes and laughs at herself. "It's given me the most peculiar dreams. Very vivid." Unconsciously, she moistens her lips with the tip of her tongue and, caught off guard, his body automatically reacts. "Although, maybe not dreams," she frowns and suddenly opens her eyes, staring directly into his. "More, memories."

His eyes are drawn back to her lips as she moistens them again. She is not doing it deliberately but she is tormenting him. He takes a step back, distancing himself, and reads regret then almost embarrassment in her eyes as she realises what has happened. "I'm sorry," she whispers, dropping her head and hiding her eyes from him behind her hand. She turns and walks slowly down the slope of the lawn towards the far end of the garden.

"Don't be," he catches her up and stops her with his hand. "Please. You know the effect you have on me."

"I know it's irrelevant," she enforces, shaking off his hand, though he catches the trace of bitterness beneath her words. "What either of us wishes is irrelevant. Because neither of us is ever going to betray her and because, from now on, the only thing that matters," running a protective hand over her belly, "is this child."

"Our child," he corrects.

"Why are we even talking this way?" she challenges. "We agreed long ago how it was going to be. Nothing has changed here."

"I don't like how you have been treated," he argues. "Mistreated."

She shakes her head. "If this is mistreatment, Jack, I'll take it any day of the week over what I had with my husband. Let's not make more of this than it is."

She winces suddenly and her hand goes to her side. "She's got strong legs this one," she jokes, winded by the sudden kick and leaning forward slightly to ease the pain.

He has automatically put his hand on her back as she leant forward, protective and concerned. "Are you alright?" She nods her head, then rests her hand on his arm to help her straighten up. "She?" he questions, smiling almost in spite of himself.

She rolls her eyes. "Don't read too much into it," she warns him. "I may just be counteracting the rest of you."

"May?" he teases.

She exhales on a sigh. "I'm carrying differently from last time," she admits. "It may be nothing but it's what my instinct is telling me."

"She." He absorbs the idea of a daughter, somehow so much more concrete than the idea of a son. A wave of protectiveness and pride floods through him, stronger even than that which he feels for Grace. "With your eyes."

She frowns at him. "You had better hope not," she warns. "Otherwise people will talk. Much better," she softens, "if she has your eyes. Such kind eyes."

"Are they?" She has taken him aback.

She looks at him steadily. "Do you know," she murmurs, "nothing has haunted me these past months so much as the image of your eyes. So expressive, so concerned, so intense." He stares at her, unable to take in her words. "No one's ever told you that?" He shakes his head. "It was the first thing I noticed about you. I found it almost impossible to look away. I kept avoiding your gaze for fear of embarrassing myself." She laughs. "Like I am now."

"I didn't know," he tells her, bemused.

She turns away and starts to walk through the garden again. The light is failing now, a rose-tinted sunset visible on the expansive western horizon. The scents of the garden have become more intense in the still evening air, the honeyed sweetness of the ripening apples on the tree, the muskiness of the roses, the heady perfume of sweet peas. The sky is brilliantly clear and the evening star has appeared alongside the pock-marked moon. The air is broken intermittently with birdsong but is, otherwise, beautifully still.

She glances at him as they walk, wondering. "What else don't you know, Jack?" she asks quietly. "What else don't you realise about yourself?" He is uncomfortable with this scrutiny but, coming from her, it also intrigues him and he lets her muse. She picks a fading rose head from a bush and slowly pulls apart the petals as they walk. "Do you know, for instance, that you are probably the best

544

listener I have ever met?" His frown answers her question. "It's not just that you listen, though that is rare enough. It's the intensity of how you listen. It's something Sarah remarked to me once and I've seen you do it since. She said you had an odd habit of tilting your chin down and to the right, like you were trying to block out the other noises around you."

He smiles a grimace at that. "It's because the hearing is impaired in my right ear," he explains. "A shell went off too close by and it's never been the same since."

She laughs, a sudden, free sound. "Well, that will teach me not to romanticise," she chides herself.

"Sorry to disappoint you," he regrets.

She shakes her head. "Never," she counters with a smile. Suddenly she sobers, though, and glances back at the house. "I should go in," she proposes. "It gets chill here in the evenings now."

Something has changed and he doesn't know what. Unable to argue, he walks her back to the porch and watches as, slightly awkwardly, she climbs the steps. She notes his hesitation. "You're staying out here?"

He nods. "For a while, maybe. It's been a long journey today and I would enjoy the peace to clear my head."

She acknowledges his words. "Goodnight, then, Jack," her voice soft.

* * * * * * *

He waited in the garden for as long as he could, not enchanted with the idea of being surrounded by all that feminine décor for longer than was absolutely necessary, but she was right about the chill in the air and it soon drove him indoors. He settled himself in an armchair to await their return.

It was approaching eleven before he finally heard the sound of a car drawing up at the front of the house and the sound of slamming doors and chattering voices as they made their way up to the house. He rose and awaited their arrival. Sarah led the way, half-turning back to the older women with a suggestion when she noticed Jack standing there. It was as if she had forgotten him.

"John, I trust you enjoyed a relaxing evening?" Still angry with him then.

"Thank you, yes." He kept his tone polite though his anger had been simmering for some hours by now.

"Well, I shall retire," Sarah addressed herself as much to the ladies as to him. "Goodnight, Mrs Wilson, Mrs Michaels. John, I assume you will be up shortly?" He nodded an acknowledgement.

He waited in the hallway after she climbed the stairs, seeking his chance to speak. As he called Mrs Wilson's attention to him, her sister glanced at him, then her, then made her way up the stairs.

"Mrs Wilson, I fear there has been some confusion about the circumstances here."

She frowned at him. "What is there to be confused about?" she contradicted. "A child conceived out of wedlock…"

"I am afraid you are labouring under a misapprehension, Mrs Wilson," a tone of deliberate concern in his voice at her mistake. "There is a husband."

She looked shocked but quickly recovered her equanimity. "Then that woman's place is with her husband," she condemned.

"It was because he beat her and threatened the life of her child that she is where she is now," Jack argued.

"That may be what she says," she disputed. "But how are we ever to know the circumstances inside a marriage."

Jack controlled his anger. "That, Mrs Wilson, is for Mrs Westerham and I to judge and we have decided to support her," he stated clearly. "I don't know from where the confusion was derived but I'm sure it hardly matters. In your Christian charity, I know you will have treated her well regardless of her circumstances." He enjoyed seeing the older woman's face drain of colour and look uncertainly up the stairs. "I'm sure my wife will be willing to corroborate this in the morning," he encouraged. "Clearly there's been some misunderstanding."

"It hardly matters, as you say," she stammered. "She has been made a welcome guest in this house, for Mrs Westerham's sake at least."

He nodded. "As I suspected. You have been a kind and considerate host, and I know both ladies rely heavily on you for your expertise. I'm sure we shall all be very grateful to you when this is over." It seemed he had learned to play politics after all.

She flushed with apparent pride. "I was always most happy to assist my husband. It is satisfying to know my skills aren't going to waste now he is no longer with us. Goodnight, Mr Westerham."

He waited until the rest of the house had settled before he climbed the stairs himself and sought out his and Sarah's room.

She had left a light burning for him but was feigning sleep when he entered. He sat down heavily in the chair in the corner, leaning forward to rest his hands between his knees. It took some minutes but she finally discarded the pretence and sat up in bed, pulling the sheets around her.

"If we're going to argue, couldn't we leave it until the morning?" she suggested.

"If there are things to be said," he countered, "isn't it better that we both say them now and get them out in the open?"

Sarah folded her arms across her chest. "What things?" she challenged.

He cut to the chase. "How did Mrs Wilson come to believe this pregnancy was the result of improper behaviour?"

At least she had the decency to look a little shame-faced. "She drew her own conclusions."

"Of which you didn't see fit to disillusion her?"

"I admit," jutting her chin in defence, "I found it easier to allow her to continue down that road. I was uncomfortable lying to her."

"Never mind that she," nodding in the direction of the bedroom she now occupied, "has borne the brunt of that decision."

"How?" she demanded. "How is she suffering in this? She's had a comfortable home throughout, she's well-fed and she has not been required to work a day in the last six weeks. How has she been bearing the brunt of this?"

"I don't believe you don't know, Sarah, so I must conclude you're just not prepared to admit it to yourself."

"You haven't been here, John," she condemned. "You don't know how it's been. You don't understand."

That fired his anger, though he still kept his voice low and controlled. "Don't you realise how much that woman is giving up so that you can realise your dream?"

"Don't defend her to me!" Sarah smacked the bed with the flat of her hand. "I won't tolerate my husband taking sides against me in this."

He stared at her in disbelief. "Can you hear yourself?" he queried. "What's happened to you?"

Her shoulders sagged, suddenly, the anger draining out of her in the face of the grief she had been suppressing. He saw and his heart went out to her. He rose from his chair and came to sit on the side of the bed alongside her.

"You don't know," she repeated, her voice breaking.

He took her hands. "Then tell me," he urged.

"I can't," she disagreed. "I brought this on myself. I can't blame you for it now."

He frowned. "You're jealous." He said it, half-disbelieving, until she raised her face and he saw the truth of it in her eyes. But not of what he and Grace had shared. He saw that too. "You're jealous of the bond between her and the child."

"It doesn't matter what happens when he's born," she despaired. "I can never be to that child what she is to him now."

He didn't know how to respond to that. It didn't matter that she would have known that from the very beginning. He rose from the chair and went to sit on the edge of the bed next to her. "Sarah, this will be our child and you will be its mother. Nothing has changed. This was what you wanted. Surely, it is still?"

"To be a mother? I know you don't even need to ask that. But I see how she is, when she thinks I'm not looking. She's so protective, so careful of him. What if something goes wrong? What if she decides she won't give him up?"

"We both know that isn't going to happen. Sarah, this isn't like you. You're such a determined woman. Why are you doubting like this?"

She raised her knees suddenly and hugged them to her. There was such vulnerability in the gesture. "It's not been easy here," she admitted. "I think I lost my way, trying to be accepted by Mrs Wilson. I know what we're doing would be frowned upon by others. I've doubted so many things recently. Whether I can be a good mother to this child. Whether I have the right to try."

"Why didn't you tell me any of this? We used to be so open with each other, when we wrote before. Why not now?"

"You shut me out, John." Her answer came back so quickly he knew she had been turning it over in her mind.

"You're punishing me?"

"No." Her rejection was vehement.

"Then what? You don't trust me?"

"I don't know." The admission showed as doubt and fear in her eyes. "You shut me out and I don't know how to deal with it." He didn't answer because the answer to that was hers and hers alone. There was nothing he would do that could change that for her. She looked away. "I'm tired, John," she deflected. "I want to sleep."

He rose from the bed and she turned out the light. With Sarah turned on her side to face away from him, the silence settled around them.

"For what my opinion is worth, Sarah," he reflected, "this child will be fortunate to have you for a mother." He thought she gave a slight nod but, in the darkness, he couldn't be sure.

* * * * * * *

By the third day of rising late and floating wraithlike from room to room, unable to settle to anything, not even reading, and with little to occupy him, he was suffering from both cabin fever and a surfeit of judgmental, narrow-minded, parochial females. By the time he had been lectured by both Mrs Wilson and Mrs Michaels on the perils of alcohol, particularly to the working classes, he had never been so much in need of a drink himself. Sadly, the town appeared to be the only truly dry one in Prohibition-era America. He had at least managed to evade being forced to make up a four for bridge by the timely arrival of Miss Klein, the librarian, who, heroically insisted on living up to the archetype of her role and, to his mind, had been delegated the responsibility of gleaning as much as she could about the latest arrival at Mrs Wilson's increasingly crowded house, but the pressure to attend church with them had been considerable and his flat refusal to do so had created further tension with Sarah.

It was hardly a comfortable situation for the three of them and, since his discussion with Sarah, they seemed to have made little progress. Sarah, keen to maintain appearances and conscious of keeping Mrs Wilson on side, was adamant he should attend church with them on the Sunday morning, having already used the excuse of the previous day's travel to avoid the Thursday morning service. Nothing, though, would induce him to step inside that church with those women, not even Mrs Michaels' unsubtle aside about the appropriateness of him being left alone in the house with 'that woman'.

As a compromise, and to find himself something with which to keep occupied during his stay, he volunteered to undertake some of the desperately needed maintenance work on the exterior of the house. The glance that passed between Mrs Wilson and Mrs Michaels said they could hardly afford to refuse his offer. Once he committed to it on the Saturday night, he found himself waking with a sense of purpose and a much improved mood on the Sunday morning and was out on the porch, in his oldest travelling clothes which was all he had with him suited to the task, before the women had even sat down for breakfast.

It was set fair for another beautiful day, the skies clear and the sun already warm on his back. A quick rummage around in the late Mr Michaels neglected tool store had elicited enough sandpaper, varnish and paint to make a start on the task of refurbishing the porch, veranda and window frames, though Mrs Wilson or her sister would need to visit the hardware store to supply the rest.

Just before nine, the three women appeared in their Sunday best and, with a brief farewell that, on Sarah's part at least, spoke her continuing anger, they departed for church.

After the buzz of New York, he enjoyed the remarkable silence as he worked, broken only by the occasional car on the dusty road, the chirping of the birds and, as the sun warmed, the background hum of the crickets. He tried not to wonder where Grace was, assuming she was in the back garden while he worked at the front.

By ten o'clock, the heat of the sun had intensified so far that he was forced to strip down to his shirt sleeves, rolling them up over his forearms. The sweat ran down his spine and his hands were covered in sanding dust from rubbing down the existing paintwork. As he climbed down the ladder, the prickling of the hairs at the back of his neck suddenly gave him the sense that he was being watched and, turning, he found he was not alone.

* * * * * * *

She looks embarrassed at being caught watching him and her skin flushes red. Her loose dress clings damply to her, emphasising her curves, and tendrils of her hair, otherwise tied back, have escaped and cling to her forehead.

Knowing she won't approach him now, he picks up a rag to wipe down his hands and crosses to where she was standing at the corner of the veranda. She holds out the glass she has brought for him, deliberately keeping her distance. Her eyes are wide and dark; he realises she wants him and he feels his automatic response to her desire, his heartbeat picking up its pace.

"Thank you," he responds, instantly regretting having spoken because his voice betrays him.

"I dreamed..." she whispers and he sees confusion in her eyes as she fights against herself. It is like she is still partly in a dream state.

In spite of himself, he takes half a step nearer but it succeeds only in breaking through her confusion. Her eyes clear and she takes a step away.

"It's good of you to do this work for them," she comments, distancing herself and reminding both of them of their surroundings.

"It's not altogether altruistic," he deflects. "I fear I shall go crazy without anything constructive to do."

She looks away. "Sarah apologised to me," she tells him. "For the confusion with Mrs Wilson."

He is surprised and finds himself proud of his wife for showing some generosity of spirit. "I'm pleased."

She looks at him again. "It wasn't necessary," she asserts.

"It was to me," he contradicts.

She watches him for a moment. "I think she's very unhappy," she informs him, quietly. "I don't want her to be that way."

"You think that's my fault?" he frowns.

"There's no question of fault in any of this. We're all just trying to find our way. All I know is that the two of you had a strong marriage before and I want it to be that way again " The rejection hurts more than he likes, certainly more than he should allow. "She is sore and distrustful. I don't know what happened between you but it is making it harder for all of us," she asserts, her voice stronger now "There's not much further to go in this. Please," she appeals, "it would help me to know that everything is well between you before we finish this. Make an effort with her. Please."

He knows the rightness of what she enforces and the wrongness of his regret. He nods his acceptance and, slowly, she walks away.

* * * * * * *

Sarah was surprised by his suggestion that they dine out together the following evening but there was also pleasure behind the surprise and she seemed more conciliatory the rest of Sunday and through Monday.

To say their options for a restaurant were limited was an understatement, which was how they found themselves at a corner table of the down-at-heel steakhouse on the far end of Main Street. Thankfully, on a Monday night the rest of town's inhabitants seemed to prefer home cooking so there was only one other couple in the restaurant all night. The downside was the over-attentiveness of the waiting staff, though whether from consideration for their customers or curiosity about these outsiders was unclear.

They were awkward with each other at first, overly formal in their conversation, both at least trying not to take offence or to make comments that would give it. If felt, though, as if they were skirting around the issue and Jack was frustrated, uncertain how to break through the barrier of politeness.

"You will be glad to get back to New York, I think?" he suggested, watching her carefully for signs of a negative reaction.

She eased the back of her neck with one hand, as if it ached from strain. "I will," she admitted, tiredness showing around her eyes. "I shall certainly be glad of rather more diverse company and entertainment."

"I'm sorry I'm not sufficiently entertaining company for you," he attempted to tease her, trying to bring some levity to the atmosphere.

She raised a smile, albeit slightly forced. "You know I don't mean you," she corrected. "Mrs Wilson and Mrs Michaels have helped us admirably in the circumstances but more narrow company you would not hope to meet."

"I've gained an appreciation of how it's been for you in the past few days," he acknowledged.

"I keep reminding myself it will all be worthwhile in the end."

He observed her for a moment, hoping he saw a spark of her original excitement, which seemed much dampened by the circumstances. "Have you thought about how it will be for us when we return to New York?" he asked, thinking to encourage her enthusiasm.

She rubbed her forehead as though it too ached. "I did, in the beginning, but I've found it difficult to focus of late."

"Tell me what you were thinking originally, then." She narrowed her eyes in that questioning way she had. "Sarah, we've not talked at all about how this child will be cared for or what changes we might need to make," he pointed out. "I know you. You will have thought about this."

"I didn't think you would be interested."

"Try me," he suggested.

"I've engaged a nursemaid who will have moved in by the time we return to New York and Madison has arranged for one of the servants' rooms on the top floor to be given over to a nursery, which will suffice for the child and the maid for now. The nursemaid has been charged with arranging the supply of clothes and other

554

materials." She was more prepared than he had given her credit for. "I have also engaged Mr Frost of James, Frost and James to search for an alternative property for us in Manhattan, somewhere with sufficient space for a full staff. Charlotte was right. That house is not conducive to raising a family and maintaining the kind of household we will require."

He covered his surprise. "You expect us to be spending some time in New York, then?" he observed.

She looked directly at him. "Freddie made it clear to me he would not be in a position to pay much heed to the bank following the death of his father. It is rational that we should stay in New York for now so that you might continue to lead that business." When he didn't respond, she drew a breath, as if she were building up to something. "I have also engaged a new lady's maid. She will be finishing her existing role in a fortnight and joining the household."

He met her gaze. "A temporary position?"

"No," she denied. "It is a permanent appointment."

Was she testing him, challenging where his loyalties lay? If so, he did not respond well to the idea, resenting the sense that she was pushing his boundaries to assert her authority over him. He let the silence hang between them for some seconds before continuing with the question he knew he had to ask. "What's going to happen to her?"

Her eyes hardened. "She will not be part of our household after this." She only confirmed what he had already determined for himself. He waited it out, knowing he need not ask the question again, challenging her with his silence to show some humanity in this. "She herself proposed that she should not return with us after the boy is born." Again, she expected him to leap to the defence but he waited, watching. "I can hardly be expected to keep her position open for six months while she detaches herself emotionally from my child."

"Sarah." His voice was low, a warning but also an appeal.

"I have arranged for her to stay with Mrs Wilson for a month after the birth. Thereafter, the choice will be hers. I will either arrange an alternative position for her here in America or I will pay for her passage back to England and arrange a position for her there." Her expression still challenged him to argue.

So, she was to be discarded, having served her purpose.

He knew from the heat of his skin that his face was flushed with anger and he had to look away to avoid Sarah reading it in his eyes. He longed to lash out, to condemn her for her ingratitude, her callousness, her selfishness. How could she treat her this way? Didn't she know how much she had already given up for her? How painful it was for her to lose a second child? How would she face her future knowing she was never to see her child again? He closed his eyes as he imagined her pain, her desolation.

But, in all honesty, what had he expected? That the three of them could return to a cosy domestic life, raising their child in a world of lies and suspicion while pretending everything was normal? It wasn't what he wanted for this child.

He was honest enough with himself to acknowledge that, selfishly, the thought of living with her in such close proximity was also impossible and he knew already his marriage would hardly return to normal while they all continued to be so on edge.

And if he was selfless enough for moment, he knew she had already intimated this could be the best outcome for her. A clean break. Without hope to keep the flame alive.

He should have known either Sarah or Grace would engineer this outcome. Perhaps they both intended to, only Sarah was the one honest enough – strong enough? – to tell him.

But the thought that he would walk away and never see her again created such an emptiness at the heart of him, such a sickness in his stomach that he finally realised this was the sacrifice he was being called on to make. Sarah had given up her husband. Grace would give up her child. He, it seemed, would lose too.

Getting back under control took all the will and determination he had ever learnt. As he came to an awareness of himself, he realised not only that she was watching him closely but also that there was something akin to fear in her eyes. Of his anger? Or of the path he might choose? She had played her hand and she knew it was now up to him to decide the future of their marriage.

When he considered it in those terms, looked at it from her perspective, it gave him clarity. There was never any question of him walking away from her.

In her uncertainty, shielded by her determination, he saw again the woman he respected and loved. The woman who was intensely loyal to those she loved. Who had stood by Charlotte when everyone around her walked away. Who had been strong enough to suppress the pain of her own miscarriage to carry her sister through hers. The woman, too, who knew to let her go when the time came. It was time for him to show where his allegiance lay.

"A new life," he reflected. "A new start. For all of us."

The relief he saw in her eyes was so intense that he felt almost a physical reaction to her pain. He had created that pain. His behaviour had generated that uncertainty. While it may have been initiated by her, he had made the situation worse and he was continuing to do so every time he allowed himself to react to Grace. He had thought himself capable of enforcing the separation of the two worlds he had allowed himself to live but he saw now how one was infiltrating and impacting upon the other. It had to stop.

"A new home?" Her voice revealed her hesitation, her doubt.

"We will be needing more space," he conceded, pushing aside the traitorous stab at the thought of divorcing himself physically from the places they had shared.

"A schoolroom for him as well as a nursery," she suggested. It rang a warning bell.

"Sarah," he started. The alarm in her eyes as the warning note in his voice made him reach across the table and take her hand in his.

"I know you don't want to think of this but I think you must. What if it's not a boy?"

It was as if there was no doubt in her mind. "It is a boy," she insisted. "It has to be. It will be."

"Sarah…"

"No, John," she interrupted. "This is our only child. It must be a boy. Someone has to inherit the business. Charlotte seems only to be producing girls and Rose's children, whenever she has them, will be the heir to the estate so the bank will hardly be of interest. No, our child must be the one to inherit and you will take over from my father when he retires and will run the bank until our son is old enough to take over from you."

Her determination was bordering on obsession. "Sarah, you must consider the possibility," he insisted. "I would hate for this child to be a disappointment to you, after everything we have gone through."

"A girl?" She seemed to be testing the idea as if for the first time.

"Our daughter," he pushed.

"That's so difficult for me," she admitted.

"Why?"

He saw her fight herself and blink away the first prickle of tears. "Because I could always think about a boy in terms of you. How am I supposed to think about a girl?"

He brought their joined hands up to his mouth and kissed her fingers. "This is our child," he enforced, low and determined. "This child will be as much yours as mine. More, in many ways, as you will have their education and development in your hands." She seemed satisfied. "Sarah, there's one thing I must ask." She raised her eyebrows in question. "You have been happier here for being active, involved in projects as you were in London. I think you must start to do the same in New York."

She nodded. "That I can do," she agreed. "Once things have settled down."

He looked at their joined hands and rubbed the back of her hand with his thumb. "It won't be long now?" he mused.

"It's hard to say," she judged. "Mrs Wilson remarked that first children are often late."

He looked up, bemused. "It's not though, is it," he observed. "Her first."

A cloud passed over her eyes. "I didn't know of how much you were aware," she justified.

"Don't do that, Sarah," he warned, his eyes serious. "Don't go probing."

"I can't accept that," she retaliated and he saw pain in her eyes.

"What's done is done," he insisted. "This needs to be a fresh start for us."

"You ask a lot of me," she challenged.

He leant forward. "As did you of me," he retaliated, quiet and insistent, and, at last, he saw understanding in her face.

* * * * * * *

The work on the house has been strangely satisfying, leaving his muscles aching but giving him time to clear his mind and to get his thoughts back under control. He has made good progress, finishing the porch and veranda by mid-week and moving onto the window frames.

There is a new peace between himself and Sarah, more comfortable and easy than of late. For the first time in months, they have even talked about his work as, during the evenings, he has reviewed investment proposals, sitting in the corner of the sitting room while Sarah and the two sisters play at cards.

By unspoken mutual consent, he and Grace have avoided each other and he has been careful not to be left alone in the house with her. Now, though, it is Thursday morning and the ladies are heading to church as usual. Not for anything would he break his tenet and join them, so he returns to his work on the house and hopes that Grace, who seems to have recognised the change in mood since he and Sarah returned from dinner, will continue to respect their silent accord.

There is a prickly heat in the air, the residue of an overnight thunderstorm that failed to disperse the thick atmosphere. In the distance, far on the horizon, dark clouds hold promise of more disturbance. It is yet some way off, though, and he continues his labours with a weather eye on the coming tempest.

"Jack."

The air is oddly still, perhaps presaging the storm, and her voice carries to him from some distance away. He turns but he can't see her at first glance and, after a moment, returns to the paintwork.

"Oh, God. Jack, please!"

The strain in her voice makes him drop everything this time. He breaks into a run, heading towards the back of the house.

She is standing, propping herself up with one hand on the back of the chair and the other supporting the baby's weight, but she is half leaning forward, as far as the bump will allow her to. She is gritting her teeth so hard a sweat has broken out on her forehead.

"Grace."

Automatically he calls her name, unthinking. She puts her hand out and he takes her arm, supporting her and easing her back.

"How long?" he asks, noting as he does so how little he really knows about this process and whether he would even be able to understand her answer.

She holds her breath to wait for the pain to pass before answering. "It started a couple of hours ago but it's getting more frequent now."

"I should fetch Mrs Wilson," he proposes and almost drops her arm in his haste to depart.

"No!" She grabs his arm and tries to compose herself having betrayed her anxiety in her instinctive reaction. "Just get me indoors, up to my room. Then you can send the maid for Mrs Wilson."

"I would likely be faster," he suggests, gently.

She straightens, as much as possible, and, resting her weight on his arm, looks him in the face. "This will be the last time we have together and, forgive me, but I want every last second with you that I can get."

Her grey eyes warn him, implore him, and he cannot resist.

She leans heavily on him as they negotiate the narrow stairs of the house, his arm around her, her hand in his to support her.

He has not, of course, visited her room in the time he has been here, and he thinks it's just as well. The narrow, single bed, pushed up against the far wall, takes up most of the room and the faded old curtains and bedspread belong to a bygone era. Where the rest of the house is stuffed with adornment, her room is bare of all but a crucifix over the bed and a printed prayer in a plain wooden frame. She is comfortable but they have made no effort to make her welcome.

She eases onto the bed, dispensing with all pretence at elegance in preference to her comfort. He fetches pillows from his room to support her back, enabling her to sit upright, and fetches a chair so he can sit next to her bed. Only once she is settled does he propose finding the maid; she nods her permission.

With the maid on her way down the dusty road to the church, he hesitates at the bottom of the stairs, longer than he knows he should. It is that moment of hesitation he has known before, in the trenches before a night-time foray or pushing over the top, when he examines his own conscience, faces his fears and decides how to deal with both.

He checks his watch – more habit than necessity – and runs up the stairs, two at a time.

Another contraction has taken her while he was downstairs and she is gripping the counterpane with both hands, her eyes closed and

561

her jaw locked, riding out the pain. As it ebbs and she tentatively releases her locked muscles, he slowly takes the seat beside her and reaches out to take one of her hands in both his, rubbing where the knuckles have turned white with the strain.

"We haven't much time," she notes, turning her hand over in his and threading her fingers through his. "After this, we shan't see each other again."

"No," he acknowledges.

"When they arrive, you will have to leave the room. They won't let you stay. After, as soon as I can be safely moved, I am going to a guest house to recover. They won't let me see the baby. You and Sarah can stay here with the child for a few days before you travel back to New York. I believe Mrs Wilson will be travelling back with you to help the handover to the nursemaid."

"You know more about this than I," he observes, wryly.

"Sarah has been very kind," she continues, reassuring him. "She will help me find a job and she's promised I can take as long as I need to recover before looking for work."

"Will you go back to England?"

She hesitates before answering. "You don't need to know, Jack. What happens to me after this is my concern only." She is being harsh but he can hear the weakness behind her tone, the fragility of her determination.

He drops his gaze, worried his own determination is as fragile as hers.

"I've been planning this for so long," she is reflective suddenly, "but now that we're here, I don't know what to say to you."

He stares at her hand between his, the long, slender fingers, unadorned. He runs his fingers between hers, feeling the rub of their skin against each other. "It's all been said," he reflects, sadly, curving her hand between his and bending to rest his forehead against their joined hands.

562

"Not even close," she whispers and he feels her hand on his hair, fingertips brushing against his temple. "I have a lifetime of things to say to you. But I have no right to say them " Without even looking at her, he knows her cheeks are wet with tears. "So, instead, I must release you, Jack, and wish you a happy and fulfilled life."

"Would that it was in your gift to give, Grace," his tone regretful. He raises his head and looks at her. "I will try, though, and with all my heart I wish the same for you. If you ever need me..."

"You shall be the last person I come to." She attempts resignation at the impending separation and brushes the tears from her face, but the pain catches in her chest and her breath comes raggedly. "I can't do this," she denies. "Be strong for me, Jack, because I can't be right now. This is our last moment and I'm going to be selfish, just once, and you're going to have to take it and carry that burden for me because I can't be that strong." She breaks her hand from his to be able to rest her palm against his cheek. "I love you, Jack, with all my soul. You are the most caring, the most passionate, the most intelligent man I have ever known. You have always treated me as your equal. You never once looked down on me nor condemned me and you are the only person in my life not to. Even your dark side, your anger and your control, I love. I hate her for having you and I love you for loving her. I could wish you were a less honourable man and could walk away from her but that I would love you the less for it." She takes his hand and rests it on her stomach. "Cherish our child, Jack. I'm leaving her in your care and it's killing me to do it." The tears are running freely now. "If I didn't love Sarah so well, I would beg you to take both of us away from here." They can both hear the sound of a car coming down the road, the engine loud in the silence. Her eyes stray to the window and panic almost takes her but, suddenly, she draws a long breath, closes her eyes and lets her anguish go on a long sigh. "But I made my choice long ago and now I have to live with it." She opens her eyes and meets his. "We both do. Time to go, Jack," she orders.

But he stays where he is, staring into her silver eyes. He can't speak, knowing that in doing so he would lose control. She touches his cheek again, so softly, just her fingertips. "Goodbye, Jack," she whispers.

He stands, takes one last look, then walks away without looking back.

* * * * * * *

Their daughter was born just over three hours later at the stroke of one in the afternoon. From his fixed position sitting on the step of the front porch, he heard the chimes of the sitting room clock, then the sudden cry of a child.

By then, it had been raining hard for more than an hour, the storm having broken directly over them. The rain lashed at him, driven into his face, whipped up by the wind. He felt numb. As if, by suppressing what he wants to feel, he has stopped feeling altogether. His hair and face were soaked, his clothes sticking to his body. His muscles had seized a while back from sitting too long in the same position, his arms resting on his thighs, his hands joined, his head bowed. Only his fingers moved, tensing and untensing, tensing and untensing.

The cry galvanised him, though, and he forced himself to his feet, ignoring the scream of agony from his frozen muscles. For the last hour, he had been listening to other screams, letting them pierce his heart to punish him – or to stop it beating.

He hesitated at the porch door for more than a minute, uncertain of his role but knowing he needed to see his child. When he reached the top of the stairs, the door facing him at the far end of the short corridor was still shut so he waited, one hand on the bannister as if he needed something to ground him. The weariness and despair had left him with that one cry and his heart thumped, nervous.

A long time later – or perhaps only a matter of seconds – the door opened, just wide enough to let Sarah through. Had he looked, he would not have been able to see beyond her into the room. As it was, he couldn't see beyond the small bundle of white cloth in her arms. His pulse slowed as he held his breath.

"Come and meet Rebecca." She approached him and his eyes were inextricably drawn down to where the tiny face emerged from the folds of cotton. Huge eyes, wide open, stared back at him, unfixed but strangely transfixing. Brilliant, deep blue eyes. His eyes.

He looked up into Sarah's face and, suddenly, it was as if everything they had gone through fell away. The rest of the world didn't matter. Nothing mattered now as much as his responsibility for this tiny new life and the woman who was her mother. Sarah had never looked so radiant, so alive, so at peace. She had found her world.

"Can I hold her?" She hesitated, clearly reluctant. "Just for a moment, Sarah." Cautiously, she transferred her to his arms, easing the fragile head back against the crook of his arm. He looked down into that innocent face for a long moment. What was it Grace had told him? "They put him in my arms and I swear the world stood still." Now, he understood.

PART V - NEW YORK

Chapter Eighteen

New York, November 1928

Life has a way of getting away from you. Buried in work and with Sarah absorbed by Rebecca, time passed without me noticing. Five years went in a flash. In the five years of war, lifetimes were lived and ended, lost or changed forever. In these five years, Lindberg had flown the Atlantic and President Coolidge had brought stability to America. In England, Prime Ministers had come and gone and the general strike had rocked the ruling classes to their core. Henry Ford had sold millions of cars. Alexander Fleming has discovered penicillin. Talkies had arrived in cinemas and the television was starting its road to domination.

Five years. Five years, yet it might just have been yesterday.

His mind is spinning. So much time but how little has changed. The same house, the same job, the same city. So much is the same. And, yet, so much has changed. Major changes and small ones, some so gradual he hasn't noticed them. But from this distant vantage point, looking back to that time before, he recognises how different the world is now. How different he is now.

They returned with such promise, such hope when they brought her back to New York. A quiet, contented baby, picking up on and reflecting back the deep contentment in her mother. Seeing the bond between them, no one doubted Sarah was her mother. She adored her daughter, couldn't bear to be parted from her for more than a moment. How jealous Charlotte was of that closeness. Once she had finally plucked up the courage to visit, so long after everyone else had come and admired.

They were all so happy for them. The miracle had happened and they were a family. What everyone had wanted for them. What everyone knew Sarah had wanted so desperately. But his heart was frozen. Try as he might, he struggled to recover that close connection he had with Sarah before, those intimate ties born of shared pain and hope, of knowing so much about the other person, of trusting because they know so much about you. He tried for Rebecca's sake, his instant love for her compelling him to try to create the home he wanted for her.

Rebecca. Strange how she has grown into such a thoughtful, serious child. Cautious and considered in her speech and her actions, as if she has carried from an early age an innate awareness of the consequences of her life.

She might have thawed his frozen emotions, had he been given the opportunity to be a part of her life, but, from the first, Sarah shut him out. He was sure she didn't do it intentionally but her obsession made her blind to those around her, blind to everything but her daughter. She didn't notice his pain, rejected anything that might cast a shadow over her perfect world.

It was easy to allow work to take over. There was more than enough to occupy his time and little enough reason to return early to the house at night. Even less reason when family commitments started taking Sarah back to England so often, of course taking Rebecca with her. The house was too empty without them. He missed them, missed the noise and the chatter when they were in the house, however little that chatter tended to involve him. It was the background noise of a comfortable – if empty – life.

So the business prospered. Inevitably, given the hours he was putting in, just to give his existence some purpose, some meaning. They expanded and moved offices, twice.

But they never sold the house. Somewhere along the way, that intention got forgotten. And by the time it was raised as a question again, Sarah was happily settled with Rebecca and he – he was losing himself in memories of the past. The guilty indulgence he turned to in his lowest moments, just to remind himself that his heart still beat, somewhere deep in his empty chest.

And what is he now? His mind stops. He's almost entirely grey, like his grandfather whose hair turned silver before his fortieth birthday. The limp is more pronounced too. That damned ice. And that damned hospital. And that damned war. He's thirty-two years old and he fears he looks like an old man.

* * * * * * *

Because he could not face going home to an empty house again. Because the prospect of dining alone, reading alone, falling asleep in the chair was, today, anathema to him. Because the alternative was just as unpalatable; dinner at the club with men a generation older than he, reading in silence in the library or disputing some long-irrelevant point of history with over-enthusiastic scholastic types or re-treading over long trodden political or commercial debates with dogmatic, close-minded old men.

He is at a loss. Normally, both options would have appealed but he is restless, discontented, unsettled. He left the office, unable to concentrate, and deliberately walked in the opposition direction from the house, heading down routes he had never walked, streets he had never known. How narrow a life he has lived in New York, rarely straying beyond his confined Upper West Side existence. It is not easy to get lost in Manhattan but he wanted at least to lose track of where he was.

It is dark outside and the cold and slight drizzle were driving normal people home with all possible haste. They pushed past him, parcel-laden in preparation for Christmas, keen to get past this dawdling pedestrian wandering while they rushed. The street lighting here is not what it should be but disappearing into the anonymous darkness and crowds was a relief. Residential areas, not impoverished but not rich either. He didn't know what he was seeking or even if he was seeking anything at all, until he strayed onto this local neighbourhood group of shops, part of, the heart of, their local community. The launderette, the grocer's, the bakery and, at the far end on the corner unit, a double-fronted café adjoining a bookshop.

The smell as he entered was so redolent of England that it almost overwhelmed him, the musty, dusty smell of Donaldson & Sons on Charing Cross Road, of books loved but long undisturbed. He wandered among the stacks, lost in overheight bookshelves, renewing acquaintances with long forgotten friends, discovering new treasures, remembering old ones. He selected three and was tempted to cross into the café area by the mouth-watering smell of home cooking.

The café extends back some way, back into increasing darkness, the far end offering the promise of appealing isolation, a comfortable and easy escape from this world.

He ordered his food and started to make his way cautiously through the closely placed tables.

* * * * * * *

His brain denies what his eyes register but he stops regardless. The muscles of his limbs are frozen but his heart starts to race, an uncomfortable pace, long forgotten, long out of use. Her head is bent over but he knows her without seeing her face, her eyes. There is no thought of turning around and walking away. In the most feared, least acknowledged depths of his mind, he has dreamed this. There is a book on the table but she's not reading, staring distantly at the table, her eyes downcast. Somehow, though, she senses she is watched and looks up.

The shock on seeing him isn't the same as his. She is surprised but it is the surprise of a moment, not the bone-deep shock that shakes him.

Five years. Five years yet it might have been yesterday.

He finds he can't say her name, so long out of use, so long forbidden to him. But he can't take his eyes off hers, the shimmering silver shining almost cat-like in the subdued light. He doesn't even notice his movements as he walks the distance to her table and takes the seat opposite her, the move entirely without volition

"Hello, Jack." Such a simple, mundane greeting. As if they saw each other only days ago. He's in shock and he doesn't know how to respond. He sees the confusion in her eyes but also some little amusement. "Jack…" She leans forward and covers his hand with hers, concerned.

The jolt that goes through him jars him out of his confusion and he pulls back, suddenly, harshly, pushing his chair back to distance himself. He can see the rejection in her eyes but he is at a loss how to respond to her.

"What are you doing here?"

She sits back in her seat, closes her book and folds her hands in her lap. "I live here, Jack. Or," indicating somewhere east of them with a nod of her head, "nearby."

"When? For how long?" He knows he is being rude but his mind is racing and it won't settle to normal politeness. Not yet a while.

"Four years. A little more." She scrutinises him and he wonders how he seems to her. Older, certainly. Thinner, he suspects. He fears he has made a fool of himself with his instinctive reaction against her touch. There is a slight smile in the corner of her mouth. "It's good to see you, Jack."

He finds he is holding his breath, as if he has forgotten how to breathe, how to behave normally. "Grace."

Her name comes out on a sigh that, did she but know it, speaks all the despair, all the loneliness, all the guilt, all the yearning he has known and suppressed over the last five years. His breath is ragged. He can't stop himself. He leans forward and, after the slightest

573

hesitation, takes her hand in both his. He needs to convince himself she is real. "I never thought to see you again."

He sees guilt flash through her eyes and, thinking it is because of Sarah, drops her hand. She catches him, though, before he can pull back and draws both his hands into both hers, bringing them closer together. "Don't," she encourages, her voice barely a whisper. The slight smile is back as she looks at him and he sees the uncertainty, the disbelief he is feeling, mirrored in her eyes. "Remember how we needed to be touching, before? Connected."

"Where have you been all this time?" He has so many questions flying around his head he hardly knows where to start.

"Right here," she admits, with some chagrin. "I couldn't think where else to go."

His heart thumps. "I wish I'd known."

She holds his gaze. "Why, Jack?" Her voice is a gentle challenge, not really a question. "What would you have done?" There is only the slightest trace of despair in her voice, well-concealed.

She's right. He wouldn't have been able to see her. Knowing could have made it a lot harder. He can hardly cope with seeing her now.

"What are you doing with your life?"

"Small talk, Jack? Is that the best we can do?" She is teasing him but he can tell it is also to cover her nerves.

"I don't know what to say to you," he admits.

"I've spent five years thinking about what I'd say to you. Don't tell me you haven't."

Of course he has. So many times in his head he has run through this conversation, told her how she has tortured his memory, his dreams. How he willed himself to put all thoughts of her aside but she proved too strong for him. How he has sought the comfort of those memories in his despair. How she changed him, irrevocably.

574

"I was in such a daze when you left." In his mind, it is as if that long ago day was but yesterday, the pain is so sharp, so fresh. "We stayed almost another week. All I could do was keep working on the house. It was the only thing I could find that would blank out my mind." He holds her gaze, the compulsion to speak the truth to her overwhelming him, even as he feared his own honesty. "It felt like I was grieving for you."

She catches her breath and her face reflects his fear. It reassures him. "I felt the same," she admits with a whisper. "Like the world was unreal suddenly. Or I was dislocated from it, somehow." She drops her eyes and shakes her head as if trying to shake off the memory. "I sat in the room in that guest house, staring at the wall, knowing I should be overwhelmed but feeling nothing. I went numb. My mind wouldn't function. I couldn't concentrate on anything, couldn't focus for more than a minute together."

"That time is like a distant dream," he reinforces and she lifts her eyes to his. "So unreal. And then," he hesitates, frowning slightly as he looks into those silver eyes, "there are moments when it seems the time now is the dream and if I could only wake I would be back where I belong." He tears his eyes away and runs his hand through his hair, an expression almost of disgust on his face.

Her eyes show the pain in her own heart. "I thought your life was full..." she intimates. "I hoped you were happy. Both of you."

He looks at her for a long moment. Her eyes are so expressive. He has nowhere to hide from her. Or from himself. "We tried. We convinced everyone around us. For a long time, we convinced ourselves. Then I was content because she was content and that was enough." She doesn't speak. He can see she wants to understand but they both fear the admission between them. "She has rebuilt her life. Rebecca fills her heart, the charities fill her time when she's here, her family when she's in England. I don't begrudge her," he caveats. "She's given so much to people her whole life. She deserves her happiness." Her eyes are sad. They speak the sympathy she won't

575

say. He hesitates before admitting to her: "Sarah fell pregnant a little more than two years ago. She miscarried in the third month." He drops his face, stares at his hands, uneasy. "There were complications after that. We had to be…careful. She couldn't risk getting pregnant again."

He hears in her voice rather than sees the ghost of a smile. "Ellerby got her way in the end."

"Yes." He keeps his face turned away, feeling the tension shoot through him at the admission, wondering how she will read it.

"But she still loves you." He wonders how she knows that but he doesn't disagree. She ducks her head slightly to catch his eyes, causing him to raise his. "And you still love her," she recognises, seeing the rejection that has stunted their relationship.

"I suspect I always shall," he acknowledges. "We've been through so much. It's just different now." Something changes in her face. He can see her withdraw, trying to shutter her expression to him. She picks up her book and coat, leaves cash on the table for their uneaten meal.

"I should go." She is out of her chair and across the café before he can even react. Stunned, he stays where he is for long moments. His mind is a whirl of confusion. Anxiety at opening himself up again to the unhealed wounds. Guilt at the thoughts running through his head, the unsteady thumping of his heart. Fear of the long, empty life that stretches out ahead of him.

He propels himself out of his chair, grabbing his stick, coat and hat.

* * * * * * *

"You can't just walk away," he demands, using his cane to propel himself as fast as possible down the street after her.

"What are we doing? This is a mistake," she counters, keeping her head down against the drizzle, pulling her coat tighter against herself. He grabs her arm to force her to stop, knowing he can't now keep pace with her.

576

"Don't say that," he denies, harshly. "I won't let you walk away like this." She pulls away and starts to walk again. Struggling, he forces himself to walk alongside her. Pride makes him try to hide the limp, knowing all the while he is being absurd. But she slows her step to match his pace.

* * * * * * *

She slows again as they near a large, anonymous apartment block on one of the side streets. He has no idea where they are now and can't see a street sign to remind him.

"Time to go, Jack," she informs him, increasing the distance between them as she burrows in her bag for her keys.

"Can I see you again?" So clichéd but he feels the situation slipping away from him and he can't let go.

She stops. "That wouldn't be wise," she denies him. With her head down and her eyes hidden, it is the tremor in her voice that betrays her. She moves away from him towards the steps of the apartment block.

She turns as she stands on the lower step and it brings her closer to his height, though he still looks down into those mercury-coloured eyes. She is closer than either of them has intended but in that moment neither can bring themselves to step away.

The scent of her, close to, is so familiar it sends a rush of blood through him and he instinctively breathes in, intoxicated. Her hair is damp from the rain, escaping from its ribbon, as it always did. All thought is suspended, all doubt, all contradiction as he raises his hand and brushes her hair back from her face. Her eyes seek out his, seeking reassurance, belief. Her silver eyes shimmer with emotion, long held back, so long denied. And five years melt away as he lowers his head and brushes his lips against hers.

The fire instantly ignites, just as it did so long before, and his careful control explodes as she yields to him with a murmur, sinking against him as his arm comes around her shoulders, the better to cradle her against him and kiss her, long and deeply.

"No!" She whispers the denial with such despair as she pushes her hands against his chest to break their hold. Her eyes speak her torment and her hands come up to cover her mouth, shock at her own actions, fear of his. "Don't. Jack, we can't."

But her eyes betray her. She has yearned for him as he has yearned for her and the five years of loss, of emptiness stretch cavernously between them. He breathes hard, watching her, reading her face, knowing she is as little able to prevent this as he. He is defenceless in the face of his own need and hers.

He cups her cheek with the palm of his hand and, against all her beliefs, she gives in to her instinct and leans into him. He holds her gaze, seeking her permission, whether she wills it or not, and runs his thumb over her bottom lip. She shudders in response, her breathing matching his. And then she takes his face in both her hands and brings her mouth back to meet his.

When they break apart, there is no longer any doubt, any questioning. He finds her hand and winds his fingers between hers, a silent binding, an unspoken commitment. She turns and takes him with her, letting them both into the hallway and then, down the corridor to the back of the building, into her ground floor apartment.

There's no time to take in anything more than the narrowness and sparsity of the hallway before he closes the door behind him and, leaning back against it, pulls her into his arms again. She tastes so sweet, the reality so much better than the shadowy memory he has lived with all these years.

Her heavy coat deflects

him. His hands shake as, still kissing her, he fumbles with the buttons then eases it over her shoulders, the better to relearn her slight frame, her slender shape.

He runs his hand up her neck, under her jawline, lifting her towards him, her mouth opening willingly beneath his. She runs her hands into his hair and over his head, pulling him down, curving her body into him, teasing him, begging him. She slides her hands under his jacket, over his shoulders and down his arms as she sheds his coat and jacket, discarding them on the floor. His skin burns at her touch through his shirt and he eases her backwards, blindly reaching out for the hall wall as he keeps kissing her, pinning her body between him and the wall. She murmurs against his mouth, her hands scrabbling between them to unbutton first his waistcoat and then his shirt.

At the sudden touch of her hands against his naked skin, shock makes him open his eyes and he eases back from her, the better to look into her face.

Her eyes are dark with passion, her pale skin flushed, her breathing shallow. "My God, I want you, Grace," he breathes, seeing his passion reflected in her eyes. "If you want to stop this, you have to stop it now. Because, God help me, I can't."

She rests her hands back against the wall to steady herself and breathes hard. "I have watched you from a distance," she tells him, her voice husky with desire, "for more than four years. I have dreamed about you so often, thought about you so much more than I should. Don't ask me to be the one who stops this. I don't have it in me."

He looks at her as he allows his breathing to slow. There is no justification for this, no permission. This time he is breaking his vows and there is nowhere to hide from that truth. He is what he has always hated, a dishonest man. But faced with the black-and-white truth, suddenly the world is all manner of shades of grey. And silver.

He runs his hand into her hair, resting his forehead gently against hers, their mouths almost touching. He holds her gaze. "Then I think we are both lost," he murmurs.

She holds his face again and brushes her lips against his, the lightest, feather-like caress that sends shivers through his body. She smiles, that slow, serious, enticing smile that he so loves, threads her fingers through his and, turning, leads him into the room at the far end of the corridor.

* * * * * * *

"Will you stay? Now that you're back in my life again." Naked beneath the sheet, lying on her side, turned away from him. He leans over her to trace the back of his fingers over her cheek.

"Not like this," she denies. "She's done so much for me. I still can't betray her."

"I think it's too late for that," he murmurs, running his lips down her shoulder, enjoying her shiver of pleasure.

She turns over into his arms. "There's a big difference between what's happened tonight and planning to lie and cheat," she rationalises.

That makes him pause. "What has happened tonight?"

Her breathing is ragged and there's a shimmer of tears in her eyes, but she holds his gaze. "My soul despaired and yours found me."

His heart is in his mouth as slides his fingers through her long, dark hair and, lowering his mouth to hers, bears her backwards.

* * * * * * *

Through the undrawn curtains, he can see how the moon casts a silvery glow over the small walled garden outside the French doors. The world is still and silent, as if that one has fallen away again and only their world exists.

Her head rests on his shoulder, her arm across his chest, her fingers tracing the lines of his muscles. "Talk to me about Rebecca," she whispers. "Tell me how it was, after I left."

She reaches for his hand and winds her fingers through his, such a familiar touch.

"Sarah loved her from the beginning," he starts tentatively. "I should never have worried how she would be with a daughter. I think

580

the maternal instinct in her is so strong she was always going to love that child. For weeks, she wouldn't let her go, just wandered around the house with Rebecca in her arms. She couldn't bear visitors because she had to put her down or hand her over. It was like the separation was a physical pain."

"And you?"

She looks up and he finds a powerful curiosity in her eyes. "I adore her," he states simply. "After she arrived, nothing else mattered but that I should live up to what I wanted to be for her."

She frowns. "But you can't?"

He stares up at the ceiling, sighs. "It's difficult. Sarah can't bear to be parted from her but she has needed to be away so frequently and I work such long hours now. We lost one nursemaid after another because they couldn't manage Sarah's intense interest in Rebecca's upbringing and her constant presence in the child's life."

"Were you ever happy?" It's pained curiosity, not prying.

His regret throws up a memory, long lost. "There was one perfect Christmas, Rebecca's second one. George dared a visit, forcing himself to overcome his sea-sickness to make the trip. Rose came with her husband and their first son. Charlotte and Williams too, though Charlotte was in the early stages of their third at that point. They all stayed at Williams' house but they came to us for Christmas Day and we saw in the New Year with a ball at Wendell's parents' house. It seems as if that was the last time things were right."

"With the family?"

"With all of us. With Sarah. She was the happiest I have ever known her then, surrounded by the family she had helped to raise and the one she had created. After that... First, Rose almost died after giving birth to her second son. Then her father was diagnosed with heart and liver disease. He had a series of attacks over a period of years. It was a drawn out illness, very painful for Sarah. She's spent most of the last three years over in England. Naturally, Rebecca has travelled with her. But Sarah wouldn't condone my travelling too. She didn't need me there," he observes.

She doesn't probe, though she could. Instead, she tries a different tack. "You stayed in the same house?"

"We planned for a long time to leave but somehow never found the right property. When Aunt Millie died, it was easier just to buy the property from Williams. Part of me is glad. I didn't want to leave that house," avoiding her gaze. "So many memories I couldn't walk away from."

"So many memories to haunt you," she observes, acutely. He meets her eyes and his intense gaze tells her the truth, that she has never been far from his mind during that last five years. She changes the subject again. "Sarah seems very content now she's part of New York society. I hear her name lauded so often for the works she's done for the local community, for the veterans." She drops this reflection in almost casually, a simple aside but laden with meaning.

"I was worried she would just transfer one obsession to another," he comments, a covering response as his mind turns, "but she was true to her word and started getting involved in projects and charities in Rebecca's second year." He frowns and looks down at her. "But you already knew that."

He feels bereft as she pulls away and, reaching for her robe, leaves the bed, wrapping the satin around her slim frame. She ties the knot at her waist as she goes to stand by the French doors, looking out at the garden. The moon catches her silhouette, framing her in silver light, her long, heavy hair cascading down her back. She runs her hand down the curtain, holding it as if to ground herself. "Sarah got me a job helping at a school and I trained as a teacher."

He stares at her. "Sarah has known where you were all this while?" He feels sick.

"More than that," she admits, still not looking at him. "I've seen Rebecca every day since the new school year. I've been here from six months after Rebecca was born." Her head is tilted downwards, as if she is ashamed. "I couldn't stay away," she confesses, a break in her voice, "but I didn't want to cause trouble. I certainly didn't expect anything. But Sarah has allowed me to be near, always at an appropriate distance and never singled out. Rebecca would never have cause to suspect."

He struggles to take it in. She has put distance between them and it is making it, somehow, harder to accept what she is telling him. He rises from the bed, pulls on his trousers and sits down at the foot of the bed. "What do you think of her?" he deflects, not looking at her.

"Rebecca?" He feels her turn towards him but can't bring himself to meet her gaze. "Oh, Jack, she's beautiful. And so considerate of those around her, as if she's worried she's responsible for looking after all of them. She's quiet but she's such a bright girl. So like you."

He meets her eyes now. "That was a relief to Sarah."

"That she couldn't see me in Rebecca?" She can see the confirmation in his eyes. "She's been very kind. She forgave me the second Rebecca was born. I could see it in her face when she held her."

"You weren't allowed to hold her." He feels her pain.

"Couldn't," she corrected, suppressing it anew.

He is silent for a moment. "I heard you leave that morning," he admits, experiencing again the guilt behind his confession. "I was lying awake when the car arrived. I wanted to go to you."

"You couldn't either."

The memory of the pain is almost overwhelming and, instinctively, he crosses the room, drawing her into his arms, exorcising the pain of loss with the reassurance of her closeness now, burying his face in her hair. She cradles him to her and he hears the unlatching of her own pain.

583

"I can't stand to let you walk away from me again." He hears her sob of agreement and feels her clutch him closer, her arms around his neck, her face buried in his shoulder.

The next moment, though, she releases him and pushes him back, putting distance between them. "Then it stops here and now." Her voice is serious, harsh, and she wraps her arms across her chest as if to ward him off.

"I can't lose you again," he disputes.

He can see the fight in her eyes, knows she is fighting herself as much as he. "Friends only, Jack," she insists. "That's all we have to offer each other." But she isn't strong enough to fight her own emotions. "After tonight," she concedes with a whisper.

"After tonight," he reflects, reading the emotions chasing across her face. "You don't want me to leave?"

Her breath is uneven as she allows him to close the gap between them. "Our world always was the darkness and the night," she murmurs. "But sanity will prevail with the dawn."

Desperate now, he pulls her hard against him, claiming her mouth again with his, running his fingers into her hair as if he would tie her to him, and she sinks against him with a sigh of surrender.

* * * * * * *

"Have you been back to England much?" Lying across his chest, her chin resting on her hands, her face only inches from his. Watching him.

"I'm starting to fear doing so," he admits. "It feels as if I only return for funerals now."

"Who have you lost?"

"Gramma went first. But, then, she was never the same after my father died. I think she stopped wanting to live. Then George Samuels last year. I miss him so much. The last time I saw him, I couldn't believe how much he'd changed. He lost so much weight so quickly, it was like he became a shadow of his former self. I'm missing him so much right now. I could do with his support, as well as his counsel. I feel like I'm trying to carry on his legacy but I don't have his sway with the partners." The strains of recent months start to impinge, that feeling of being simultaneously overwhelmed and yet unable to act threatening from the edges of his mind. He looks away, not wanting to show this side of him to her, not wanting to admit the weakness. He's a fool to think he can hide from her, though.

"Problems with Williams?"

He looks up, surprised at her intuition. It isn't, though. Somehow she sees more than he knows. It gives him the strangest feeling. To know that she's been that close all this time. As if the last five years have been a monumental waste of time.

"He's a manipulative man, more than I gave him credit for. Certainly more than I am prepared to be. After George made me a partner, I thought I would have more say in the direction of the business but after his first seizure he couldn't contribute any more to the Board's decisions and I didn't have the time to build the status I needed with the other partners. It's the saddest thing," he reflects, sober suddenly. "To see a vital and determined man like George Samuels immobilised physically but still active in his own mind. I think it was the despair that killed him in the end."

"You feel his loss."

"In so many ways. He was my mentor as well as my father-in-law. He was also the only thing holding that disparate group of self-serving bankers together. Without him, it's fallen apart. Which, of course, gave Williams exactly what he needed to get his way, and when he saw I might be a block to him, he flattered me into a six-month secondment at Chicago First to work on a project there. Naïvely, I went. Which, of course, gave him all the room he needed to reshape the venture into just the business he wanted." He shakes his head at himself. "George saw all of it coming. He was so worried about where Williams was taking the business. If the other partners would only look beyond the results, they would see it too."

"Sarah's in England." It's a statement, not a question.

"And Rebecca with her. Hopefully she can finalise the estate now. It's taken more than a year already."

"What about the rest of your family? Your mother?"

"She's in her element, filling the matriarchal role now Gramma has gone. Ed's youngest will be two next week. Their third. And I wouldn't be surprised if a fourth followed."

"What about Charlotte? Sarah never speaks of her now."

"It's the one thing Williams didn't get his way in. Three daughters. Even he had to concede defeat after that, though I can hardly blame him for wanting to avoid further intimacies with Charlotte."

She frowns. "You speak of him with such distaste now. Of both of them. That's changed."

"A more selfish and self-centred being than Charlotte you would hope never to meet," he condemns. "Mercifully, Chicago seems to have more attractions for her than New York these days. A bigger fish in a smaller pond, I guess. Still, whatever she is, it's difficult to condone Williams keeping a mistress, however discrete he might be about it." She absorbs that knowledge without commenting but the irony of their position hangs in the air between them. "At least Rose and Isabella both produced eventually," he reflects to cover the silence. "The Marshal and Dexter White lines secured for another generation."

"And what happened to you?" she asks. She means the limp and the cane.

"An old wound." He tries to avoid explaining but he can't evade her insightful eyes. "I slipped on a sheet of ice last winter. When they took me into the hospital, they found the piece of shrapnel still embedded in my thigh and decided they should remove it. The operation was fine but the wound got infected afterwards, down to the bone. It aggravated the old injury. They should have left well alone."

"You manage alright?"

"When I can cope with the humiliation."

He hears the smile in her voice. "That sounds like the old Jack."

He gives a wry smile in return. "Old is the word," he accepts, running his hand through his grey hair.

"If you're fishing for compliments," she warns him, "I'm fresh out."

He holds her face in his hand. "You're as beautiful as the day I met you," he retaliates. "More. Like you've grown into your beauty."

She gives him a heavy-lidded glance. She is pleased but she doesn't know how to react. "You never noticed me when we first met," she dismisses.

"I noticed more than you realise," he disagrees, serious suddenly. "You mesmerised me, bewitched me with your eyes." She wants to deny it, he can see, but she knows him too well to disbelieve him. He gives her an escape route. "And you? Have you been back to England?" She shakes her head and he remembers the old wounds, the long separations. "That man. Your husband's friend. Did you ever see him again?"

Another shake. "Why do you ask?" Anxious.

"He came looking for you once." He sees the alarm on her face, however much she tries to hide it from him. It seems he can still read her, after all this time. "He was just looking for money. Tried to blackmail me by threatening to tell Sarah about you and I." He laughs, mirthlessly.

"You never saw him again?" Her skin is ashen and he feels that surge of protectiveness again, so familiar, so long unused.

"I shouldn't have mentioned it," he blames himself. "If I had thought it meant anything, I would never have raised it. He hasn't been a problem for you, has he?"

She shakes her head and the moonlight catches the stray grey hairs at her temple. It is the only thing about her that tells him any time has passed. He looks at her and time falls away. But her face can't hide the trace of fear that remains.

"Grace, I will never let anyone hurt you," he promises, cupping her face again.

Her eyes are sorrowful. "It's too late for that," she reminds him. "I think we hurt each other."

* * * * * * *

They can't sleep, either of them, fearful of losing time, so they drift through the darkness, reaching for each other just as they did before, holding onto each other through long moments of passion and even longer moments of fear and denial, desperate to keep the world at bay.

But they can't and they both watch, curled against each other as the sky shows the tell-tale lightening, betraying their night.

"I can't be without you," he insists, his head resting against hers, her body tucked backwards against his as they stare through the window at the grey shapes taking form in the garden.

"I won't be your mistress," she refuses, as honest as ever.

"Then be my friend," he suggests, winding their hands together and holding them against her heart.

He feels her slight shake of the head. "How would that even be possible?" she denies.

"If that's all I can have, it's what I'll take, not to be without you again."

"We're deceiving ourselves if we think we can live with only that."

"We both know it can't be more than that," he acknowledges. "But I cannot live with less. I cannot live without you in my life. I've lived in that world. I can't do it again."

She draws their joined hands up to her lips and kisses his hand. "It will be the hardest thing I've ever done," she reflects. "But I can't live without you either. I tried for almost a year but it was like you were drawing me back to you, even though you didn't know I was here."

He eases backwards to give her room to turn onto her back, enabling him to look into her eyes. "I can't believe I didn't know. I always thought I would be able to sense if you were nearby."

She smiles but it is a smile tinged with sadness, regret. "I always shall be nearby," she promises. "For as long as we both shall live."

* * * * * * *

He must leave early, before the street is much astir, before his presence can be noted. It is difficult to bring an end to their time, though, and he leaves it later than he knows he should, drawing out their meagre time. He turns again at the door, pulling her into his arms, one last time.

"We'll meet at the café," he suggests. "Somewhere public but not too obvious. Come whenever you can and I will too."

He can see she thinks she should disagree but is relieved to know she is unable. "One day at a time," she counters. "If we ever get close to this again, we have to walk away from one another."

He knows she's right, trusts that they can keep each other honest.

"I feel more alive now than I have in the last five years," he tells her, holding her face between both hands. He kisses her, one last time. "Don't take that away from me."

* * * * * * *

He knows he should be discrete, cautious, that if he were wise he would stay away for a few days at least, but she is on his mind all day so it is inevitable he should find his way back to the café again. That way, he makes it her choice whether or not to see him again so soon.

* * * * * * *

She is there, waiting for him, her eyes unable to hide her joy at seeing him again. As if, like him, she has doubted the reality of the previous night.

They are careful to keep their distance, both reassuring the other that they can maintain their agreement, both fearful of the black void awaiting them should either weaken.

They eat together, for all the world like old friends, and talk long into the evening, until the staff start to stack the chairs on the tables and they realise the place has emptied.

After that, and for as long as Sarah is away, they meet every night, to eat, to talk, to read together. He brings her books and the newspapers and magazines from home that the Major still sends him. Then Sarah and Rebecca return and they meet less frequently, which only makes their meetings more sweet, while the memories – which have tormented before – now make the time apart more tolerable.

* * * * * * *

Mid-January. Sarah is at the Morgans' for a fundraising meeting for the veterans hospice she is now planning with Elsa Morgan, an expanded version of the one at Richmond House. Knowing she will be out, he has been looking forward to his evening all day, which makes him increasingly distracted during the afternoon.

At last, it is a decent hour for him to leave. He waits with increasing impatience as he struggles to hail a cab at this busy hour.

She is there before him and his pulse starts to race, as it always does when he sees her.

But even before he sits down, there is a sick feeling in his stomach. Her face betrays so many emotions: anxiety, fear, determination, guilt. And, deep down, an intense, suppressed joy.

He doesn't touch her. They have been careful not to make physical contact since that night, knowing the effect it can have on them both. Tonight, though, the temptation is great, the need to reach out to reassure her.

She doesn't speak, only looks at him. And he doesn't need to ask. He has wondered, has even watched her for the same signs as before. He's been wondering for weeks now.

"You're certain?" She nods. He breathes hard. "It's still early, isn't it? We need to be sure. Before we act."

"We also can't leave it too late," she caveats.

He frowns. "Too late for what."

She looks away from him, down at her hands. "We need to talk about the options."

"Options?" He stares at her, disbelieving. "You can't be suggesting what I think you are?"

She looks appalled. "God, no. I could never get rid of it."

He leans forward but still doesn't touch her. "I'll take care of you," he promises. "Of both of you. You know that, don't you?" She looks at him sadly and he realises with a jolt she has been thinking this through for some time already. He feels like he's behind the curve. "Grace, talk to me," he urges. "Tell me what you're thinking."

"I can't keep this child and stay here, near you, Jack."

"I don't understand."

She looks away again. She's hiding her face from him. "If I stayed, we couldn't risk Sarah finding out about the child." He follows her train of thought now and he doesn't like what he fears is coming. "So either I must leave, with the child, or I have to give it up."

Neither option is tenable. "There must be a way," he disagrees, sitting back, distancing himself from her to try to think clearly. "I could buy you a house away from here. Somewhere near enough for me to visit but where Sarah won't find out." Even as he says it, he knows it is absurd. "I won't let you give up another child, Grace," he defends. "I know what that would do to you."

The bleakness in her eyes confirms it for him. "Then I have to leave. To move as far away as possible." The pain that stabs through him is mirrored in her eyes. "I know, Jack, but we have to put our child first."

"Our child…" It's been a vague notion until now, a fear more than anything. Suddenly, the idea solidifies and a wave of protectiveness sweeps through him. "Our son or daughter." His voice is thick, choked with emotion. "Grace, what if I left…?"

She holds up her hands to stop him. "Don't, Jack. Don't even think it. That's not an option for either of us. We would end up hating each other."

"But either I lose you or I lose the child or I lose both of you." Despair is making him angry now. "How is any one of those a solution?"

Her expression is hard. "They're all solutions, Jack. It doesn't mean we have to like them."

His anger is met with hers and, for the first time, they stand for a moment on opposite sides, their anger dividing them.

Only for an instant, though, as she suddenly leans forward and places her hand on his. In his anger, his reaction to her touch is even more violent than usual and he grasps her hand in both his, closing one hand around her wrist.

"We broke the rules, Jack. Now we have to pay the price." Her voice is frighteningly calm.

"I won't lose you," he denies. "Either of you."

Her eyes are intensely sad now. "Then there is only one other route available to us. We need to tell Sarah."

* * * * * * *

He had never been more anxious in his life than standing in the hall, waiting for Sarah to return. He knew he was not thinking straight; the result of a night without sleep, turning the options over and over in his mind, trying to find a different way.

When he left Grace the evening before, having walked her to her door as usual, he wandered the streets for another hour, trying to clear his head. It didn't help. Nor did the hours of pretending to work in the office, all the while turning the problem over in his mind.

His child. Their child. It was so different from what had happened with Rebecca. Even while Grace was carrying, he had half-thought of her as Sarah's child. His daughter was born of Sarah's desperate need for a child. But this child. This child was the creation of their desperate need for each other.

He already loved it, unconditionally and unequivocally. But there was nothing unequivocal about the other emotions running through him. Guilt that he had broken his vows. Embarrassment that his actions had brought them all to this. Shame that he had failed his wife. Humiliation that they should have to turn to Sarah for the answer. Anxiety for their unknown future. Fear of losing what he most loved, trapped into living a life he could no longer tolerate.

* * * * * * *

They had arranged to meet at the house, to speak to Sarah when she returned with Rebecca from their visits. He had left work early and was waiting for Grace when she arrived. A hood shielded her face from prying eyes. He let her into the house and led the way to the study, then took up his vigil in the hall, determined to catch Sarah without any of the servants interfering.

He waited almost an hour, feeling the tension build in his muscles and his head. The light outside ebbed away and the maid passed through the house, lighting the lamps.

Eventually, he heard the key in the lock and the door opened to allow Sarah to usher Rebecca in ahead of her. She glanced at Jack but otherwise ignored him, helping Rebecca out of her coat and straightening her dress. The nanny appeared on the stairs having heard their arrival.

"Rebecca, go to Nanny Jones now," she instructed. "She will give you your supper in the nursery. I'll be up in a while." She nodded to the nanny and gave Rebecca a small shove in her direction but stayed standing at the far end of the hall from Jack, Rebecca's coat folded over her arm.

He watched as his daughter obediently passed him and headed towards the stairs, with only a quick glance at his face. At the foot of the stairs, she stopped, though, and turned back, coming to stand beside him. Easing his damaged leg, he crouched down at her instruction and she put her arms around his neck and kissed his cheek. He smiled as she let him go.

"What was that for, sweetheart?"

She gave him a look of quiet contemplation and his heart thumped as he recognised Grace in that expression. "You look lonely," she observed, her voice as soft as her mother's. "You used to look that way before."

He stayed where he was for a long moment as she turned away and ran up the stairs to her nanny. They both waited in silence until they heard the nursery door on the top floor open and close. He stood up again.

"Why is she here, John?" Her voice was low but he heard the strain in it already. She must have seen Grace through the study window onto the street.

"We should go through to the study," he suggested, keeping his voice low too. "We need to talk."

She looked at him, her face impassive as she walked past and led the way to the study. As they entered, Grace rose from her chair at the far end of the room.

"Close the door, John." There was quiet authority in Sarah's voice and he did as she instructed, locking it to avoid interruption. Then he crossed to close the curtains, shutting out the world outside. Sarah turned her back on him and faced Grace. "What are you doing here? Rachel." There was heavy emphasis in her use of the servant name she had given her. He wanted to correct her, to tell her to use Grace's real name, but they couldn't afford to be confrontational.

Grace held Sarah's direct gaze, forcing down the shame and embarrassment that Jack saw cross her face. "I'm pregnant, Sarah." She could be as direct as she. "It's Jack's child."

Even in the dimmed light, he saw her blanch. All the colour drained from her skin but her eyes didn't so much as flicker. She stared at Grace.

"When?"

"Last November. One night only. Never since."

"Then how do you even know it's his? Why should I believe you?"

Grace flinched. "I deserve many things, Sarah, but I don't deserve that."

"And I don't deserve this." Her voice was as harsh as he had ever heard it.

Grace held her ground. "No, Sarah, you don't. And I know it's a shock…"

"A shock?" Sarah broke their locked gaze and turned towards Jack. "This isn't a shock. It's betrayal."

"Sarah…" he tried to placate her.

"How did you even know she was in the city?" she demanded, her gesture behind her towards Grace so disdainful.

"By accident," he defended.

595

She looked back towards Grace. "You expect me to believe that?" she cajoled. "That you didn't engineer this somehow?"

Now Grace's face lost its colour. "I made you a promise," she reminded her. "I never made contact with him. Do you think I would risk losing what little contact I have with Rebecca?"

"I can promise you, you will never see her again after this."

Their voices, so full of anger, were frighteningly controlled.

"Sarah, I know you're angry but you need to listen. We need to resolve this." Grace's tone was carefully conciliatory but not pleading. She was meeting her on equal ground at last.

"There's only one way to resolve it," Sarah spat. "Get rid of it."

Jack intervened. "I will not let that happen," he insisted, his anger also controlled.

She swung round to face him, redirecting her disdain, her humiliation onto him. "You can't expect this bastard to live."

He had never seen her this way before. Her anger and hurt were brutal, ugly. "Sarah, one way or another, my child will be born and will grow up, with all the benefits of whatever resources I can make available."

"You had better not be thinking about leaving me, John," she warned, her voice frighteningly controlled. "Because I will destroy you. I made you and I can take it all away again. Then where will your whore be?"

"Sarah." Grace's voice had a tone of command he had never heard from her before. "You need to hear me out. Before you say any more and destroy everything."

Sarah turned back to her but her hands at her sides were clenched fists now. "Talk," she ordered. "Before I have you thrown onto the street."

Grace took a step towards her, schooling her features. "I'm here to make a proposal. That we do the same as before. That we go away, you and I, and when the child is born you bring it back here and raise it as your own."

596

Jack felt sick to his stomach. He couldn't quite believe he was condoning this but he had no other solution.

"And why," Sarah scorned, "would I want to raise your bastard as my child?"

Grace raised her chin and looked her directly in the eye. "Because Rebecca is this child's sister." Her voice was forceful, steady.

Sarah's face, coloured in anger, turned white again. She had long since convinced herself that Rebecca was her daughter. She couldn't stand to be reminded. "You will leave my house," she hissed. "Now," turning towards the door.

"Think about it, Sarah." Grace kept her voice steady. "Your son." Sarah stopped walking but her back, turned towards them, was rigid. She was bluffing. There was no way she could know if she carried a boy or a girl but it had the effect of making Sarah turn back again. Grace deliberately placed her hand over her still-flat stomach. "Your son and heir, Sarah."

Silence fell in the room. He watched them both, Sarah's stance shouting her anger and hurt, Grace so determined, so controlled.

"How far gone are you?"

"Eight weeks."

"Thank God you had the foresight to tell me before you started showing," Sarah retorted bitterly. She threw a disdainful look at Jack. "It's just as well I came home when I did last November or our cover story would have been shot to pieces."

He could see the relief in Grace's face and it sickened him. "You'll do it?" she pushed.

Sarah's face betrayed her disgust, her disdain. She held them both in suspense for long moments as she walked back to the door, stopping with her hand on the handle.

"I have one condition," she caveated, looking directly at Grace. "Afterwards, you will never see my husband or my children again. I will pay for your journey home, I will pay to create a new name for you, I will find you a place in service. And if you ever come near my family again, I will destroy you. Do you understand?"

"Yes."

"No!" Jack's denial was loud, instinctive and raw. "That's not what we agreed," he challenged Grace.

Sarah turned her disdain on him. "You don't seriously think you can carry on seeing her, John? Not after this. Do I need to remove her from your life as I removed that idiot, Alfie?"

The shock clearly registered on Jack's face because he saw the slightest tremor in Sarah's before she reasserted her righteous anger. "It's not me," he argued, suppressing his reaction. "She needs to see her children."

"They're not her children, John. They're mine," Sarah warned him, her expression frighteningly blank.

"Grace…" he appealed.

"No," Sarah denied, not giving her the chance to reply. "Those are my terms. That is how it will be." She held open the door and looked back at her. "Now get out of my house."

Grace crossed the floor, not looking at Jack as she passed him. She paused only for a moment to look into Sarah's face then passed through the door. The sound of the front door closing echoed in the silence. Sarah looked at him then and, at last, he saw the pain he had inflicted.

"Sarah…" he started to apologise but she looked away, walked out of the room and, so quietly, so controlled, closed the door behind her.

* * * * * * *

They had left within weeks, before Grace could show. The school was sad to see her leave but understood why Sarah would want her with her again for this second pregnancy, apparently further complicated by Sarah's age on top of her previous issues.

He had, of course, tried to see Grace before they departed, visiting the café several times and waiting long hours alone. She never came. He wrote to her, visited her apartment. No response.

It was painful to witness Sarah's departure, the tears, forcibly held back so as not to upset Rebecca. She hated him for being the cause of her first ever parting from her child. Thankfully, Rebecca didn't feel the same. He saw her bewilderment as her mother departed, unable to understand the need for the parting or to comprehend the scope of several months' separation, but she was otherwise calm and measured. For him, it was the one shining light in this dark episode: the opportunity to spend time with his daughter.

She was shy with him at first, a little intimidated by this apparently austere man who had had so little impact on her life thus far. When she discovered their shared passion for books, though, she slowly let him in and it became their pleasure to read together before her bedtime, books of his childhood as well as hers. She delighted to sit with him in his library, a grown-up environment, an escape from her childish nursery.

He would read Sarah's letters to her – the kind of long, personal letters they had once shared between the two of them and that she now wrote to her daughter instead – and became her scribe for letters back to her mother, finding a new role as their intermediary and, through that insight, a sense of repairing his and Sarah's relationship, bridging the chasm they had both created between them.

Seven months is a long time to get used to an idea. He witnessed with relief the transformation in Sarah as she began to write letters to him directly as well and these became increasingly regular. She seemed to transition from simmering anger through distant calm to slow acceptance and, finally, hesitant anticipation. She had, as before, successfully segregated in her mind that which she wished to accept and that which she couldn't.

He worried how little interest Rebecca showed in childish things until he discovered her one day reading to her collected group of toys. He watched her in silence for several minutes from the doorway, as still as he could be to avoid interrupting her lesson; she had, it seemed, inherited her mother's talent for teaching. When she saw him, though, she abandoned her class and ran to him, throwing her arms around his neck as he bent down to greet her, ignoring the pain shooting through his leg.

On days when the nanny had her afternoon off, he would collect her from school himself and take her to the office for a couple of hours where she entertained herself with copies of the old ledgers, running her hands down the long columns of numbers, deciphering the entries, or making them up where she couldn't read the looping script.

She was quiet but had such an intense nature underneath, insightful, capable of deep caring and consideration. Sometimes, though, it felt as if she still held herself slightly at a distance, capable of giving love but wary of receiving it. During the summer, when the heat grew too intense for her, he took her to stay with her aunt and cousins at Newport, in a house even more grand than the one he had stayed in before. When he could get away at the weekends, he would watch her at play with her cousins and wonder if she wasn't a little intimidated by Charlotte's rowdy, boisterous, indulged and ill-disciplined children. It made it hard for him to leave her, come Sunday evening, but if his departure distressed her, she never showed it to him.

Normally, he would have taken the excuse of the weather to take a break during August, however tedious staying with Charlotte – and the often-absent Williams – might have been. This year, though, there was no question of anyone leaving the office. They sweated their way through July and into August, inadequate air conditioning supplemented with so many desk fans the papers were constantly being blown around the room.

600

The demand for their services – and everyone else's – had reached a fever pitch. Money was flowing like water around the city, debt the tap that turned it on and off.

For all his activity, he felt paralysed by indecision. The more he pushed back against Williams, the more he found himself isolated on the venture board, unable to counter the tidal wave of demand for ever increasing returns. For three years now, they had been lending to individuals as well as to companies and for two years they had been offering unsecured loans almost to anyone who wanted them. The risks appalled him. Debts were spiralling, personal and corporate, and the city was high on easy money, people borrowing to buy stocks and selling them weeks or even days later for an absurd level of profit. His anxiety was intense; he knew it was only his time with Rebecca that was keeping him sane.

Had he not been responsible for Rebecca, he would have returned to London months since and argued with every member of the Richmond Bank Board until they saw sense. As it was, they were blinded by their successes and deafened to his arguments by Williams' eloquent reassurances. He had made his arguments so many times, he was starting to lose credibility with the other partners, his Cassandra-like predictions failing in the face of ever greater success. By the summer, he had lost all will to argue, his energy sapped by the unimaginably long hours and the absence of support.

Williams, by contrast, had never been more ebullient. He visited New York at least once a month now for a week at a time, staying with his new mistress who had replaced the previous one in the Diamond District apartment within a week of removing her from it. His swaggering confidence served only to make Jack even more nervous as he arrived, each time, carrying inordinate amounts of cash from his clients in Chicago, depositing it with the bank to invest.

It came to a head for him one weekend in Newport. August had arrived with its usual blistering heat. He continued to write regularly to Sarah but from the end of July, her letters became increasingly infrequent.

His sense of paralysis seemed to be infiltrating all aspects of his life now, keyed up as he was with anticipation of news from Sarah while anxious about work. Having worked much of Saturday to keep up with the volume of paperwork generated during the week, he had arrived too late to see his daughter, leaving him resentful of the work that distracted him and irritated by the prospect of an unfeasibly large dinner party hosted by Williams and Charlotte for their Newport neighbours. Enforced socialising over dinner with people for whom he had little time and less respect only worsened his mood, leaving him in no frame of mind to cope with Williams' gloating over drinks and cigars in the library after dinner. His bad mood deepened when Williams started telling tall tales of the investments their clients had made and the returns they had achieved, all with money borrowed from them to fund their stock exchange gambling. Not that any of them saw it as such. These were the times of the sure-fire winner when no one could lose. He lost all patience at the point at which Williams boasted of having ordered a junior to turn down a request for investment funds from one of their longest-standing corporate clients in favour of ploughing ever more money into the highly profitable loans to naïve private investors looking to make a quick buck, just like so many around them.

He couldn't allow it to continue unchecked any more. Returning to the office on Monday morning, he called in his two most trusted lieutenants and, throughout the day, they worked through all their accounts to identify ways of rebalancing the portfolio without too many people noticing. Calling in certain overdue private loans. Declining to roll forward others. At last, money would be released again to put into funding good quality businesses, the kind that put investments into something more tangible than someone else's paper. Between the three of them, they identified ways to redirect a quarter of the capital by the year end.

602

He went home that night more fulfilled and less anxious than he had been in a long time. Until, that is, he collected the post from the hall table when he got back to the Upper West Side and, counting back, suddenly realised they hadn't heard from Sarah in more than a week.

By then, it was late August. Since the beginning of the month, he had been waiting for, half-expecting, news. Now, the month had almost passed and not only was there no news, there was also an absence of any correspondence.

Unwilling to let anything sour his good mood, he pushed the thought aside temporarily and, loosening his collar, went in search of his daughter.

For six months, it had been just the two of them and they relied on each other to fill the vacancies created by those who had left. As he became parent and confidant to this small human being, he had started to appreciate how close her relationship was with her mother and just how much he had been shut out of her life previously. Whatever happened when Sarah returned, he would ensure that, at least, would not revert.

At this time of day, she liked to read in the garden room, hidden behind the plants with a favourite book. It took him a moment to find her as his eyes adjusted to the brilliant light filtering through the glass ceiling, but a slight movement gave her away and she emerged, her shy smile in place, when he called her name. Picking her up, he hugged her tightly and carried her over to their favourite sofa in the corner.

An hour later, when the nanny came to find them, Rebecca's eyes were dropping and his stomach was starting to demand supper.

It was as they were crossing the hall, Rebecca's hand in his, that the bell sounded at the front door. He continued their way across the hall, leaving the maid to answer the summons, but something made Rebecca stop still, her eyes seeming to take on a strange anticipation, a quiet hopefulness.

He was stunned to see Sarah step past the maid into the hall. Stunned even more by her appearance.

She looked radiant. In five years, he had never seen her this happy. Yes, she was tired, the lines around her eyes deeper than he remembered, but her dark eyes were alight with a deep inner contentment.

He fully expected his daughter to fly from him and into her arms, and was intensely touched when she looked from her mother to him and deliberately, calmly, led him across the hall, holding onto his hand and only dropping it as Sarah bent down and she put her arms around her mother's neck. Jack's heart contracted as Sarah's eyes closed, just for a moment, at the pleasure of holding her child again, the pain of their enforced absence banished in a quick, hard hug.

As she stood again, she made way for the nursemaid who had entered behind her, a bassinet in her arms, which she deposited on the hall cupboard.

"Rebecca," she drew her close, "I want you to meet your brother. This is Daniel."

Jack's breath caught as the little girl stood on tiptoe to lean over the edge of the basket, reaching in with one hand. It was a solemn expression she adopted as she looked from her brother to her mother.

"Will you be happy now, Mama?" she asked. "Now you have a boy as well as me."

Sarah hid her pain behind a smile. "Rebecca, why don't you show Nurse May the nursery? I'll be up shortly with Daniel."

Ever obedient, Rebecca automatically kissed her mother goodnight, just as if she had never been away. To his relief, though, she also turned to him and held out her arms for her usual hug. As he knelt down and put his arms around her, she whispered in his ear, "I'm glad my family is back now." He hugged her harder for a moment, then released her to her nanny.

Alone in the hall, they looked at one another, both at a loss. "She's grown," Sarah remarked.

"She's wonderful," he told her, as if they had never discussed their daughter before. "And, Sarah, you look beautiful." The honesty came so naturally, like it used to.

A slight smile was his reward. "Don't you want to see your son, John?" she asked, eventually, holding his gaze though her voice was not altogether steady.

"Daniel?" he asked gently, trying to avoid any sense of judgment.

"My grandfather."

He nodded. "I like it."

"I thought," she conceded, "we might give him Albert as a middle name."

As he approached the bassinet, he saw one small fist emerge as the little lad stretched his arm. He put out a hand and, tentatively, touched the tiny fingers, which flexed and closed again in reaction. His eyes were wide open and a fuzz of blond hair showed on the top of his head.

Automatically, instinctively, he reached for Sarah as he looked down at the boy and, surprisingly, she came to him, sliding her arm around his waist as he rested his across her shoulders and they stood together, looking down at their son.

"When was he born?"

"Ten days ago. The nineteenth of August at three twenty-two in the morning. He arrived in a flash, so impatient to be born. We hardly had time to fetch Mrs Wilson."

"No problems?" He didn't know how to ask about Grace without mentioning her by name.

"None."

They watched in silence as Daniel stretched and yawned, Sarah tucking his blanket around him with one hand.

"I'm sorry you had to be parted from Rebecca," he conceded. "But I shan't ever be sorry for having had that time with her, just the two of us."

"It's one of the hardest things I've ever had to do," she acknowledged. "But it was worth it. I have never been as elated in my life as the moment the nurse put him in my arms. I felt the connection the second he looked at me, such beautiful blue eyes."

They say love is blind. Perhaps it was just as well. For his son was looking up at them with the clearest grey eyes Jack had ever seen.

Chapter Nineteen

New York, autumn 1929

Even today, I look at you and I see her. It's not just your eyes. I don't know how but you have her expressions too, and her mannerisms. I had to search for her, even set a man to the task, but events overtook us that autumn. We had all lived the high life that decade and we were about the pay the price for it.

Sarah had been true to her word. Grace was gone. She told him she had allowed her a week but then she arranged for Grace's passage back to England and a position in a household; she wouldn't say where.

In the weakest, most cowardly part of him, it was a relief. The decision wasn't his to make, he only need bear the pain.

In the part of him that he kept hidden, from Sarah but also, when he could, from himself, he was hurting and he was alone in his pain. She may have expected him to accept Grace had left their lives but he couldn't. Every time he looked at his son, he saw her and he felt responsible for her.

He had expected to see her again after the birth. Whether he had thought Sarah would relent and allow her to be part of the children's lives or whether she would have returned to New York to close out her life there before starting elsewhere. Either way, the one outcome he hadn't anticipated was not to see her. He felt as if he were in limbo, unable to close the past, unable to contemplate the future.

With neither the time nor the freedom to pursue it for himself, he hired a private detective to search for her. He didn't allow himself to think so far ahead as to consider what he would do when he found her; he only knew that he must.

* * * * * * *

In the meantime, he had more work than he could manage to keep him occupied. Long hours in the office got longer. They kept hiring but they still couldn't keep up with the demand, and yet more money flowed in for them to invest and more people found their way to their door to borrow.

The downward spiral started on 3 October. Jack read about the comments by Chancellor of the Exchequer Philip Snowden in both the Wall Street Journal and the New York Times the following morning on his way into the office. The US Treasury Secretary Andrew Mellon had weighed in too, as had the Times' editor. It seemed he wasn't the only one worrying about speculation on Wall Street. By then, the utility stocks had already been hit.

After that, there was a steady and ever-increasing flow of people coming to the office, wanting to offload their stocks, interspersed with brief respites as the market seemed to rally, only to start plunging again, compounded by the margin sellers and the short sellers. Unprecedented volumes of shares were changing hands every day. The Journal was reporting nine million individual investors had jumped onto the bandwagon during the summer, fuelled by self-styled expert tipsters in the newspapers and fed by credit from the banks.

The last to jump on the bandwagon were also the last to see the end coming. While institutional investors had been quietly dumping shares throughout September, it was October before most of the private investors cottoned on and started turning up at the office. There were queues of people waiting for the office to open every morning and another queue that had to be turned away at the end of the day. Jack found himself with a steadily swelling group of people wanting to see him to plead their special situations. Longstanding clients who had speculated and, losing more and more value every day, were desperate to stop the haemorrhaging. More recent clients who had been buying shares on margin and now found themselves

608

without the capital to meet the short-term loans they had taken. Even corporate clients, more than one of whom had diverted funds loaned to them in order to buy shares.

The pressure of the heart-breaking stories was immense. The relationships he had been so careful to garner with some key clients over the last several years were now strained to breaking point, desperate men pleading with him for more time to meet their commitments, for leniency, for clemency.

By the end of October, millions of dollars had been wiped off the value of shares. More than a fifth of their clients had given them instructions to sell their entire stock portfolio.

At noon on the Thursday, Williams arrived. He pushed past the crowds of people waiting outside Jack's office, his face as white as a sheet, and slammed the door shut then sat down heavily in the chair opposite Jack's.

"Get me a drink, Westerham." Jack dug out a bottle from the cabinet and poured him a large measure, which disappeared in one gulp. He thought twice but he did also pour one for himself. His head was thumping, he hadn't eaten all day and the client appeals, from begging to blackmail, were leaving him emotionally drained. "I've never seen anything like it, Jack. The market was down eleven per cent. at the opening bell. There's panic selling everywhere. They're saying there could be 15 million shares traded before the close of business today."

Jack stayed silent. The situation was too grave to debate; they were into coping strategies now.

Williams pushed to his feet and went to stand by the window, open in a vain attempt to counter the stifling heat of the office but, as a result, letting in the noise of the city as well. The fan on Jack's desk whirred ineffectually, barely stirring the thick air.

"Morgan and some others are trying to force a halt. Whitney's buying blocks of US Steel and other stocks on their behalf. They think they can repeat what happened in 1907." Williams was staring

609

blankly out the window, distracted. When Jack rose and poured him another drink, he stirred himself. "We have to protect the Chicago money." His voice betrayed his anxiety. "Stop selling anyone else's stock until they've been covered."

"You know that's almost a third of what we have invested," Jack caveated. "We will struggle to sell that alone."

"I know but we have to be seen to try."

"We don't have to sell. We could sit on the shares and wait this out. It may take years but the value will come back, eventually."

Williams knew the logic of what he proposed but he shook his head. "I've had my instructions," he negated. All the fight and confidence had gone out of him. He looked like a shell of himself, a broken man. "We need to start pulling in the private debts too. Get the call loans in. And anything that's secured."

"We can't do that," Jack disagreed. "Anyone who has lost the value of their shares won't have any cash to pay us back."

"Then we'll take their businesses and their houses." Williams' tone was blunt. "Jack, they are demanding their cash back and we have to liquidate whatever we can to return as much as we can."

"Then you have to explain it to them. They will lose so much more money doing it this way. Even on this scale, the value will come back again if they're patient enough."

Williams was scornful. "Patience is not a virtue they hold in much regard. I'm not giving you a choice in this."

"This isn't only Chicago First assets you're playing with here," Jack reminded him.

Williams rested his arm against the window pane and leaned his head against it. "We both know I've been making the decisions here ever since Samuels died. We haven't got time to consult Richmond's Board. We need to act and we need to act now." For all his words were forceful, his tone was defeated.

Jack sat back down, rested his head against the back of his chair. He was exhausted. For the last weeks, he had been working at least fourteen-hour days, whether in the office or taking work back to the house with him. He couldn't remember the last time he hadn't worked through the weekend. He hadn't seen Daniel for more than twenty minutes at a time since they had arrived home two months ago and he was desperately missing his time with his daughter. At least things with Sarah were more settled, more comfortable than before, even if he doubted they would ever be as close as they had been at the beginning of their marriage. He felt old.

The noises of a scuffle broke out on the other side of his office door, a man's shouts counteracted first by his assistant's female tones and then overwhelmed by the sound of two or three other male voices, disputing, arguing.

Wearily, Jack rose and crossed to the door. Williams moved to leave. "You understand your instructions, Westerham?" he checked.

Jack gave him a hard look but it was difficult not to feel sympathy for the state of his brother-in-law, for all that he had been the root cause of their problems. "I'll do everything I can to achieve what you want," he responded cautiously.

Williams seemed to accept his non-committal response or, perhaps, was finally accepting that, while he might demand, it was only Jack who could now get him out of this hole.

"Lives depend on it," he muttered prophetically.

As he opened the door, two men who were physically confronting each other turned towards them. "Westerham," the one demanded, "I insist you deal with me before you see this man."

"Mr Westerham," the other was in pleading mode, "I've been waiting hours. You have to help me. I beg of you."

Jack gave Williams a final glance and shook his hand before he left, then stood back to allow both men to enter his office.

* * * * * * *

They were already calling it Black Thursday. Almost 13 million shares traded and only the intervention by Morgan and a bankers' consortium stopping the price of shares collapsing completely. At ten o'clock, Jack finally accepted that his brain was so overwhelmed he couldn't achieve anything more, however long he sat there. He called down to the garage to warn the chauffeur he was on his way, then wandered through the office, eerie now, standing silent and empty in the darkness.

When he reached the Upper West Side house, he was surprised to see from the street that lights were on in the study. He let himself into the house quietly and stood for a moment, listening. He was so drained he couldn't face having to be polite to anyone tonight. His headache had worsened throughout the day, compounded by a lack of food and listening to gut-wrenching stories of desperation but still having to turn a deaf ear to their pleas.

The voices were too low for him to distinguish. He could just make out it was a man and a woman. Drawing a deep breath, he forced himself to walk through from the hall.

Sarah was in his chair by the fireplace, sitting upright, her back rigid, her hands folded in her lap. Her expression as she looked up at him was quickly suppressed but he had caught sight of what he would only have described as fury before she hid it from him. Williams was standing in front of the fire, his back turned towards her, leaning his weight against the mantel. It was as if the weight he was now carrying was so great that he could no longer bear it himself. In this light, where he had been white earlier he was grey now, a sickening pallor born of fear and the kind of desperation Jack had been facing across his desk all day. There was also a drink in his hand, again.

"You're late." Sarah's tone was as carefully controlled as her face.

He ignored the comment, though he was sorely tempted to ask when he had last been home early. Instead, he went to pour himself a drink, downing one and instantly refilling it.

"You saw how the market closed?" He decided to try conversation before getting into why Williams was here, talking to his wife.

Williams held his glass out and Jack, reluctantly, crossed the room to refill his too. "I went to the exchange after I saw you. Jack, you've never seen anything like it. It was like they'd all gone crazy. I saw Rogerson and Mitchell clawing at each other's throats like they were animals. Baldwin collapsed on the floor when Auburn fell again." He threw back the whisky and took the decanter from Jack to top up the glass himself.

"John, we have to do what Frederick suggests. We need to claw back all the money we can to save the business."

He stared at Sarah. In all the time they had been in New York, she had rarely shown an interest in the joint venture. Now, suddenly, she was expert enough to tell him how to be running their business? He turned it on Williams. "What have you been saying?" he challenged.

Williams looked shamefaced but he was going to brazen it out. "Only what I told you to do earlier."

"Have you, John?" Sarah rose and took a step towards him. "Have you been doing as Frederick instructed today? How much of the stock have you liquidated? Have you started calling in the debts?"

"Sarah, I know what the business means to you," he responded, holding back his anger, "but you're not close enough to it now to know what is the right thing to do."

"I don't care about the right thing," she retorted. "I care about saving Richmond Bank and our families," a sweep of the arm bringing Williams into the equation too.

"We're both agreed," Williams tried to explain. "We've talked it through tonight. There's nothing else for it but to take as much as we can and to walk away."

Jack turned on him, control of his anger making his voice cold now. "If you want it done that way," he suggested, "perhaps you should be the one sitting in that office all day and listening to people begging us to treat them well. People who have made us wealthy over the last several years, who have welcomed us into their homes. What you're asking," turning his gaze back to Sarah, "what you're telling me to do is to pull the rug from under them for a group of investors I've never seen, never spoken to and who do God knows what to generate the sort of money you've been bringing in from Chicago month after month."

"It's the right thing to do," Sarah justified.

"No," he retorted. "It's exactly the wrong thing to do. We should be standing behind these people – those we should have been supporting in the first place – not walking away from them when they need us most."

"John, you're a dreamer. You've got to be a realist," Sarah enforced. "It's everyone for themselves now. It's time to put your family first."

"The talk at the club is that Morgan and the others can't hold back the tide," Williams tried to interject some rational debate into the argument. "The agreement was forced through but no one has any confidence it will hold after the weekend."

He had found time to go to the club, then. Resentment flared in Jack.

"What did you expect?" he condemned. "The Dow has doubled in a year. How was that ever going to be sustainable?"

"John, 'I told you so' isn't going to help anyone now." Sarah didn't look at him and, somehow, that made him angrier.

"So no one wanted to listen to me before and still no one wants to listen to me now," he commented, forcibly steadying his tone.

614

"I'll listen," she retorted, suddenly raising her head and letting him see her anger simmering not far below the surface, "when you've got something constructive to say about how you're going to save my father's business."

"Sarah..." Something about Williams' low warning tone made Jack realise this was what they had been discussing before he returned to the house. He looked from one to the other.

"You think this is my fault?" he challenged, bewildered. "You think there was something I should have done?"

"No, Jack..." Williams tried to calm the rising tension. "I know you tried to make us listen."

Sarah rose and walked away from them towards the far end of the room, her arms wrapped around her chest. That old defensive gesture. She was afraid. He watched her movements, waiting for her to speak.

Williams made to leave. "I should go..." he started. Jack held up his hand to silence him, still watching his wife.

"Sarah," he prompted, "if there's something you want to say, I think you should say it." He saw her jaw clench, her face still partially turned away from him. "Sarah," he demanded.

She spun round, her face contorted with fear and anger. "How could you let it come to this, John?" she demanded. "My father's business. My son's legacy. All of it is at threat because you didn't act."

"Sarah, that's hardly fair..." Williams attempted to interject but she turned her fury on him and her expression silenced him.

"I don't care about fair," she denounced. "I care about the bank. I care about whether our baby son will have anything to inherit when he grows up. I care about whether John did everything in his power to stop this happening to us."

He looked at her, a strange sense of calm stealing over him. The calm of war. "Sarah, I did everything I could to convince the joint

615

venture board that we were taking on too much risk. There isn't a step that I was in a position to take that I didn't take."

"Really?" Her tone changed. It became menacing, somehow. "Really, Jack?" She spat his name, using it as she never did. As she had heard Grace use it. "Are you telling me there was nothing distracting you from your work? Nothing that you were putting above your obligations to this family? To this business?"

He felt his face grow cold, like it was draining of colour, not because there was any justification in her accusation but because he had never expected her to use it against him. And because it told him he had hurt her more than he had dreamed possible. "Don't…" he warned, his voice low, conscious of Williams' eyes on him.

"Why not?" she demanded. "Isn't it about time?"

"No," he refuted, crossing the floor, closing the gap between them in a matter of seconds. He stood over her, forcing his breathing to slow, his expression to stay neutral. "Our children are upstairs," he reminded her, staring into her eyes, praying she would read his thoughts and bring herself out of this rage before she did irreparable damage. "Our children," he emphasised quietly, keeping his voice at a level he hoped Williams wouldn't hear.

He couldn't break through. Her anger was dominant, clouding her judgment. She wanted to punish him. For hurting her. For betraying her. For, in her mind, letting her down. She saw her world crumbling around her and she was fighting for its survival.

"Get away from me, John," she whispered, staring hard at him. "I can't stand to be in the same room with you right now."

He took a step back and allowed her to walk past him. As she reached the door, though, it opened suddenly and the maid appeared, carrying a sheet of paper. Sensing the tension and realising she had interrupted something, she rapidly handed the note to Sarah and backed out of the room.

It was a telegram. Even at this distance, it was distinct and recognisable. She unfolded the paper and scanned it. Twice.

616

The room had gone silent. Waiting. She stood at an angle to him, side on so that he saw her bend her head, pause, consider. She looked again at the paper. Refolded it. Reopened it. Eventually, she looked up at him, glancing across her shoulder, and, for a reason he couldn't begin to analyse, his blood ran cold. She held the paper between two fingers, extended her arm. She held that position, waiting for him to cross the room to her.

He almost couldn't move. It was dread that held him back but the fear of not knowing that propelled him forward. He knew Williams was there somewhere but it was as if the periphery of his vision had disappeared. His whole being was focused on that small piece of paper.

Impatient now, she moved her arm, raised it briefly and brought it back to the same position. A gesture of demand. She wanted this over with.

He took the paper from her, watching her as she released it. A shiver of distaste ran through her.

BODY PULLED FROM THAMES STOP IDENTIFIED AS GA BY MOTHER STOP CAUSE OF DEATH STRANGULATION STOP

He read it three times though he could no longer form the words after the first time. He felt sick, nausea welling up inside his gut, threatening to overwhelm him.

"GA?" He already knew but he had to have it confirmed.

"Addison." Her tone was filled with vitriol. "Grace Addison." She looked him directly in the face, watching his reaction as his world shattered. "Perhaps now you will stop behaving like such a damn fool."

617

PART VI: JACK

Chapter Twenty

New York, October 1929

The blood is singing in his ears. Like he is about to pass out.

Any attempt at control is impossible. He knows she is watching him. Distantly, he knows his reaction is hurting her. But, in that moment, he can't help her. Every defence he has ever learned, every control he has ever asserted is useless. He is overwhelmed.

He covers his face with his hand, instinctively trying to hide his expression, trying to find privacy for his private torture. He can't. He knows it is all there for her to see. And Williams too. His distress. His bewilderment. The death of hope.

He has to get out. He has to get away from them, to be alone in this. No one can be allowed to see what this is doing to him.

He sees Sarah's anger drain from her face as he stumbles from the room, staggering against the door jamb as if he were drunk, hearing Williams call his name but having to ignore him. He gets himself across the hall only by propping himself up with one hand, propelling himself along. How he gets the door open, God only knows.

The fresh air he craves only makes it worse. It is like a rush of reality, slammed into his face. He staggers again and leans over the railings, vomits. His gut wrenches. The whisky burns his throat.

As he straightens up, he can feel the sweat on his face and body, a cold chill stealing over his skin. He still has his suit on but it is freezing outside now and he needs the coat he has left on the hall table. He stares at the open front door, knowing how he needs to act but seemingly incapable of putting the simple steps into effect. He can still hear voices in the study. God knows what she's going to tell Williams. How much will she explain to him? Will she paint it as an affair? The thought sickens him but he knows she won't put her children at risk.

He has to move before either of them emerges. He can't see them. He can't see anyone. His whole being revolts at the thought of having to speak to anyone, letting them see how everything has fallen apart. It is like his very soul is exposed to the world and he needs to escape to find a way to protect himself. It propels him at last and he runs up the steps, as much as his weak leg will allow him to do, grabs his coat and turns his back on the house.

Instinctively, he heads west towards the river. The streets are mercifully dark and empty. The weak moon lights the Hudson, a shining reflection lightening the world around. It is colder here, though, cold, damp air drifting off the water. He turns up his collar and pulls his coat tighter, folding his arms across his chest.

He feels numb. He can't think, certainly doesn't know where he is going. The path takes him south but he can't think beyond that. He just walks.

* * * * * * *

He has no concept of time though he knows he has walked for hours. He has left the houses behind and is near the docks now, great warehouses looming ahead of him. He walks until his bad leg aches and forces him to slow his pace but he keeps moving. As if to stop would be to let everything in. Instinctively, he fears that moment, like he has never feared anything in his life before. He feels it hovering on the edge of his existence, a gathering storm, threatening and powerful. He can sense it building, even as he tries to ignore and deny it, knowing he will never be able to suppress or to control it. He takes solace in the respite before the storm, the numbness that weighs on his mind and stops him thinking or feeling. Abstractedly, he is aware of his surroundings, the shapes in the darkness of ships on the river, warehouses on the wharves ahead, serried ranks of still and silent houses lined up against him to the left, the life on the river even as the houses sleep. It is as if he is outside himself, looking in, seeing the grief that waits to claim him, seeing him struggle to keep it at bay.

Slowly, inevitably, in spite of the cold autumn air, his body warms with the effort of walking and it brings him to an awareness of himself. Of the dull, throbbing pain in his leg. Of the ache in the muscles of his arms from having held them too long in the same position. Of his fingers, frozen in place where, unaware, they have gripped his coat, the knuckles now screaming in pain as he releases them.

He shoves his hands in the pockets of his coat to warm them, to ease them. And his right hand encounters a scrap of paper.

Suddenly, instantly, he stops. His eyes are blank, unseeing. He knows what it is. He hadn't realised he had put it there. He must have done it without thinking when he left the house.

It brings rushing in the reality of everything he has denied while he walked. But it's not possible. There has to be some mistake. A misidentification. A different interpretation. Something. Anything. His hand clamps involuntarily around the telegram, such a fragile thing against his skin. He must keep it at a distance a little longer. Just walk to the next pier. Then to the next. And then to the next. He forces his legs to move, focusing on the physical effort, the pain of the movement, distracting him from thinking about anything else, from letting it in.

Keep walking. Focus on the ships, the first stirrings on the cargo vessels as they prepare for the dawn. Keep walking. Watch the gulls wheeling overhead at the prospect of the fishing boats returning with their overnight catch. Keep walking.

But he's lying to himself. He can feel it in how his throat is thickening and his head is throbbing. His breath is coming faster as he tries to suppress the tension he can feel growing inside him, knowing it will soon demand release. He needs privacy. He has to find somewhere he can be alone.

He wanders past the warehouses by the piers, moving ever southward, away from any signs of activity. His chest is closing and he grasps his coat collar with one hand, pulling the sides together against the chill that now strikes him, pressing his hand against his chest to hold back the pain a little longer. Breathing hard, choked.

He finds a warehouse door slightly ajar, distant from any moorings. Sliding it just enough to let himself in, he stops to let his eyes adjust. The huge, echoing space is empty except for a few pallet loads of filled hessian sacks maybe ten yards ahead of him. He gropes blindly for the brick wall behind him, feeling the rough surface drag against his hand. He feels his way to the corner of the building, still too dark to make out anything more than rough shapes. Only when he reaches the corner does he stop. His legs give out and he falls to the floor, scraping his hands as he tries to support himself. The pain is a brief relief, distracting him long enough to get into a sitting position, his back braced where the two walls join. But the pain in his lungs rapidly reasserts, causing him to bring his knees up against his chest to try to suppress it. Too late. The respite is at an end and what limited control he has exerted is exhausted. He stares into the blackness of his despair and it consumes him.

* * * * * * *

He comes to an awareness of himself only gradually. Sounds first. The noise of voices further up the quay. Shouts from dockside to deck. The screams of gulls behind a trawler. An engine, coughing as it starts in the cold. Smells next. The salt tang of the sea drifting up the river. The warm, musty smell of whatever crop is in the bags in the warehouse. The dampness of the wet cobbles outside. The dry dust of the brick wall.

His body aches. The soles of his feet, his ankle ligaments, long unused now to exercise. The old leg wound that throbs in complaint.

His arm muscles, braced too long across his chest. His lower back, cramped in the same position for hours.

The grief has ebbed but it is not gone. It waits on the edges. Waits to strike again.

There is a shaft of sunlight filtering through where he has left the warehouse door ajar. Weak, winter light. The air from his lungs freezes as he exhales. A clear night, a chilled morning. The night is over.

He can't stay here, though he has no thought of where he could go and, aching, doesn't relish the prospect of shambling around the city. Knows, too, that he can't afford to see anyone he knows, that he needs to stay clear of the financial district and the Upper West and Upper East sides. He is trapped on this island and he needs somewhere to hide.

He stumbles out of the warehouse into the daylight, struggling on his blistered feet. He has no idea where he is, beyond being on the western edge of Manhattan, and he starts to walk northwards again.

Physical pain is giving him respite from his emotional torment but he knows it to be temporary. The hollow, empty feeling at the heart of him is controlled for now but he must find somewhere private before he must face it again. And somewhere that can make her real for him again. As if she is already leaving him and he can't let go. He tries to imagine her face and it scares him that he can't bring her to mind, can't see anything beyond those silver eyes, burned into his memory.

It is instinct, not thought, that leads him in the direction of the restaurant where they met again, a natural call back to where he had rediscovered his life. He is relieved to find it open, serving late breakfasts and early lunches to the working trade that passes their door. Relieved not because he can face food but because, for a while, he can sit and remember.

One of the waiters seems to recognise him from before but the rest give him uncertain glances, his dishevelled appearance at odds

625

with his tailored suit. He guesses they're wondering if he has lost his money on the stock market so pays for his coffee when it arrives at his table, allowing the waiter to see he has plenty of cash on him. Only for a moment does he wonder about the state of the market today. It couldn't have become more meaningless to him.

From his retreat at the back of the café, he watches the staff, the other diners and the world passing the large-paned window, noticing the world around him as a helpful distraction from his inner thoughts. He sits in his usual seat, the one he would choose when arriving first and watching for her to arrive, seeking out that distinct figure in the crowds of people flowing past the window. As if, at any moment, he will catch sight of her again and she will appear, silhouetted in the doorway, then approach him, that slow, gentle smile curving her mouth.

But she's not here. And he can't sense her in this overcrowded, noisy place.

Where can he find her? How can he bring her back to him? He needs to be where she has been, desperately seeking echoes of her in the spaces she has inhabited. The ones they inhabited together. But he can't contemplate going back to the house. He's not ready to face his own existence, to confront reality. He must find her elsewhere.

His coffee, forgotten, goes cold as his mind drifts. Eventually, the waiter, wanting to seat a couple seeking a meal, forces him to make a decision. He declines the offer of food and leaves.

* * * * * * *

There is no sense to it. It is months since she left. Someone will have dealt with it, cleared it and sent her things onto her. Always assuming she didn't come back briefly to do it for herself.

But very little makes sense today so why should this be any different? Besides which, he is exhausted and he can think of nowhere else to go.

He watches from the other side of the street for almost an hour before approaching, watching other residents come and go. As he sees one returning with a bag of shopping, he takes his chance and approaches the building entrance just as they walk up the stairs and let themselves in through the shared front door. He nods briefly, as if he is one of her neighbours, and she holds the door to let him in, only the slightest frown at his appearance.

What now? He hovers in the entrance hall, glancing at her door, inextricably drawn to it even as he knows he should be looking for the supervisor's office. He is in luck, though, as the door to the left opens suddenly and an old woman, emerges, tutting to herself.

"I'm here about the woman who lived in that flat," he announces, his sense of dislocation, of desperation, making him awkward, clumsy. He had planned it so carefully in his head.

The woman looks him up and down, weighing the quality of his clothing. "Friend of hers?" she challenges.

"Yes."

"Good. Then perhaps you'll pay the bill. She owes for the last month already."

His heart thumps. "I'll pay if you let me in," he bargains. "And give me a key," as an after-thought.

Another assessing look. "How do I know she'd want you to have one?"

She's dead, you stupid woman, his head shouts. It doesn't damn well matter. Instead, he takes out his pocketbook and ensures she can see the colour of his money. "How much did you say is owed?" She reaches across and helps herself to two notes. He holds out a third. "The key," he emphasises carefully.

With another tut, she turns back into her office and reappears seconds later. "If she's not coming back, someone needs to clear her stuff," she orders. "I can let that place in a matter of days."

"No." He knows it makes no sense but he can't bear the thought of anyone else being in there. "I'll pay the bills. Just leave it alone."

627

She shrugs, hands him the key and disappears up the stairs.

Now he has achieved his goal, all the fight has gone out of him and he sags against the wall by her door. This is what he wanted but now he's here part of him is afraid he won't be able to cope. He rests his head back against the wall, closes his eyes and breathes deeply.

And, somehow, catches the faintest trace of her perfume.

He opens his eyes and breathes again, his heart thumping. The trace has gone but it is enough to overcome his fear, the inexorable draw of that lost memory of her. He forces the key into the lock and pushes open the door.

Instantly, memories flood in. He leans back against the door to close it and, closing his eyes, lets the emotions flow. Remembering the spark between them as he pulled her into his arms. The passion with which she met his need. The touch of her fingers against his skin.

Then he opens his eyes and the memory vanishes, leaving only the hollowness in his gut and silence of the hall.

He stumbles forward, desperate to catch another of those echoes. Straight through to the bedroom at the end of the hall. The scent is more powerful in here. Stale from long disuse but still recognisable. And so memorable. He pulls open the wardrobe, half expecting to find it emptied, though he can see the rest of her things are still here, on her dressing table, on her bedside cabinet. Her dresses are here, the ones she made for herself. He can't believe she would have left them here of her own volition but he is so grateful she did. He pulls the burgundy one from its hanger, the velvet draping softly in his hands. It holds her scent and, as he buries his face in the cloth, the pain floods over him again. He sinks onto the bed, cradling the material in his arms, and gives himself up to it.

* * * * * * *

It is only when he wakes that he realises he has slept, physically exhausted, emotionally drained. He has no comprehension of how long he has slept but, beyond the undrawn curtains, the world is dark again. His mouth is dry and his eyes feel gritty but he stays where he is, lying on her bed, his head on her pillow, her dress in his arms.

Now he can see again the images that eluded him earlier. Her teasing smile as she danced with him. Her solemn glance as she told him about her son, sitting at the kitchen table. Her passion-filled eyes as she gave herself up to him. Her compassion as she held him when his anger broke. Her tears as she told him she was setting him free. Her internal conflict as they both lost themselves to their need for one another.

He stared at the ceiling, the questions coming now. What had she been doing in London? Surely she hadn't gone back to find her son? What was her frame of mind? If only he had seen her, just once, after Daniel was born. Had she despaired? Had she been so depressed at the thought of never seeing Rebecca and Daniel again that it had driven her back to her son, to Tom?

It wouldn't have been safe. She wouldn't have felt safe. Even after all this time, the police could still have been looking for her. What would her husband have done if he had found her?

He stops again, his breathing choked as the cold hand of realisation clamps over his heart. It makes him aware how much the shock has affected his brain, that it has taken him this long to understand. Strangulation. Her husband.

Oh, Christ. Oh, Grace. How afraid she must have been. How much would she have fought? How much would she have felt she had to live for? Was that how he had found her? Had he been watching the parents' place, waiting for her to return someday? Or had he already taken his son away from them? Had she had to go to him just to be with one of her children again?

He sits up on the bed, his head throbbing. He can't take the pain any more tonight. He has to find alcohol to take the edge off, to anaesthetise the pain.

* * * * * * *

Perhaps it was inevitable that he would end up here. Sitting here, now, he felt it was somehow fated. He could have chosen a hundred different speakeasies, any one of them keen to part him from his money. Why should he be surprised that his dysfunctional mind has drawn him back here?

The place is heaving, more than before if that were possible. While much of the city is holding its breath, praying that Wall Street can keep its nerve, there are plenty who choose instead to live every minute life sends them and most of them seem to be crammed into the dark corners of this club.

No chance of him getting the same table he sat at with Grace. He's lucky they let him in at all, given the state of him. So he sits at the bar, downing one shot after another with rapid regularity, frighteningly sober for the amount he has consumed. He loses his mind in the raucous sounds of New York City's pleasures, the men's shouts and arguments louder, the women's clothing brighter and their laughter more piercing than ever before, the music fighting to drown them all out. The alcohol numbs not only his pain but also every memory, just as the volume of noise makes it impossible to think.

He blocks out the other noise by focusing on the band, trying to distinguish the jazz amid the buzz and interference of the people celebrating around him. Defiance as the world they know teeters on the brink of extinction.

He sees the moment the man enters. Her husband's friend. He walks a step behind the big man, the wide Italian, sharply dressed, surrounded by his entourage, fawned over by drunken revellers as the rest make a path for him to cross to his usual table in the middle of the room.

He must have sensed Jack's eyes on him because he looks around suddenly, scanning the room until he finds what he has guessed. A word in the big man's ear and he is heading in this direction.

"On your own tonight?" He stands with his back to the bar, his elbows propped on the counter, casually surveying the room.

Jack didn't think he had come here to pick a fight but he's starting to doubt the reliability of his own mind now.

"I'm just here for the drink," he defends, emptying one glass and catching the bartender's eye for a refill.

"If you're looking for some company, I'm sure we can find you a nice piece of ass here somewhere."

"I said," through gritted teeth, "I'm just…"

"Yeah, yeah." Fake familiarity with a clap on the shoulder. "You're just here for the drink. What's wrong? She leave you high and dry?"

A wave of relief floods through him as he recognises the flare of his anger, raw and uncontrollable. Perhaps this was what he was looking for after all. "No, you piece of shit," he grinds, standing now and looming over the smaller man. "She's dead." There is a bitter sense of release in saying the words aloud, admitting them to himself.

The jovial camaraderie is dropped instantly, his face taking on a steely control. "Watch what you're saying," he warns, coldly.

Jack throws back another drink. "What does it matter?" he bites. "There's nothing left now anyway."

"Ain't no woman worth getting that hung up about," the smaller man chides, a leering smile stealing over his mouth. "And in that particular case, I'm sure she got what was coming to her."

The anger has hold of his heart now, his pulse racing, his vision darkening at the edges. "Say that again," he challenges.

The man levers himself away from the bar, confronting Jack though he only comes up to his shoulder. "That bitch is a two-bit whore who always thought she was above the rest of us," he spits. "If she's dead, the world is a better place without her in it."

His self-control is gone and his eyes mist over with rage, all his grief channelled into his anger. He knows from the pain in his fist that his first blow has connected but he has no time to get in a second. Too late, he realises their raised voices have attracted attention and there are three other men behind him. Two grab his arms as he lashes out, pinioning them behind his back, the third flashes a blade, discretely, just enough for Jack to see and to demand his co-operation.

Together, they march him up the stairs, through the door and out to the alleyway round the side of the club.

As the punishment begins, Jack welcomes it, not even trying to shield his face from the blows and the kicks, relishing the sound of a rib breaking beneath one well-aimed boot. His anger has drained, unleashed in that single blow then lost to him. His will to fight has gone.

The man hails a cab from up the street and they throw him into the back seat. At a nod from him, the other three men disappear back down the stairs to the club. He rummages around in Jack's breast pocket and pulls out his pocketbook. He removes half the cash for himself then throws what's left at the taxi driver. "Take him away," he orders, spitting in the road as they pull away.

The taxi driver takes him four blocks then dumps him on the sidewalk, heading out with the remainder of Jack's money.

* * * * * * *

He wakes with a sense of disgust as well as the despair that is now his familiar companion. At least that means he no longer feels so alone. Something he can rely upon.

He lies still for a moment, testing the various aches in his body, before staggering to the bathroom. He throws up before collapsing on the floor, finding some temporary relief in the coolness of the wall tiles against which he rests his head.

Eventually, he forces himself to his feet and to confront his reflection in the bathroom mirror. The blood on his face has long since dried and it takes minutes to wash it away. Beneath, there is a black swelling on his cheekbone and a gash on his forehead. His chest hurts as he inhales and he feels for the rib he knows is broken. He strips off his shirt and washes himself as best he can in the sink, washing his hair, rinsing his mouth.

He has been wearing the same clothes now for almost three days. He needs a bath, a shave and a clean set of clothes. But that would entail going home and, while his mind now accepts what he has doubted before, that he will return, he can't yet.

He has one more place to go.

* * * * * * *

Mass is underway as he slips through the doors at the back. He stands for a moment, letting the gentle rhythm of the words flow over him, the stillness of the air calm him. The church is well attended, even on a Saturday morning, and he feels that same sense of welcome that drew him in before.

The seat where they sat is vacant and he makes his way slowly, keen to avoid attracting attention. He sits throughout, not participating in the service and yet feeling he is not altogether apart from it. As it ends and the congregation slowly disperses, he stays where he is until the church has emptied. Then he leans forward, places one hand over the other on the pew in front and rests his forehead on his hands. He closes his eyes.

* * * * * * *

"It's a peaceful place, is it not?"

He feels the pew give beneath the weight of someone sitting down beside him and looks up. He knows his eyes are red with crying. With his bruises and gashes, he must look a sight.

The elderly priest glances at his face only a moment before looking ahead of him, turning his eyes instead towards the golden crucifix at the far end of the nave.

"Forgive me, I don't mean to interrupt your prayers."

"I wasn't praying. Father."

He nods. "Sometimes I find my most effective prayers are those when I'm not doing the talking, but just allow God to be with me."

"I can't find God in this," he retorts, bitterly.

"And yet you are here," the priest rejoins softly. "And He has a habit of being here whether He is looked for or not."

The grief overwhelms Jack again and he returns to his previous position, his head turned down, his tears falling straight onto the tiled floor below.

"I've lost her, Father." He can barely form the words through his despair.

"Someone you love."

He moves his head in a slight nod then feels the weight of a hand on his shoulder as he sobs, and is relieved to know he is no longer alone.

* * * * * * *

"I came here with her once, years ago." Calmer now. Sitting, talking. Finding he needs to tell someone about her. "We sat here, just here, and she prayed. I wish I knew for what."

The priest looks at him kindly. "Did you ever think she might be praying for you?"

He half smiles, half grimaces at that. "I didn't but I rather hope now she was. I need her strength to get through this."

"You have others who can help you?"

"My family," he admits. "Two wonderful children."

"You have been blessed, then."

He grimaces again. "I'm sure I shall come to believe that, Father, but not just yet."

* * * * * * *

When he finally leaves, he finds a sense of calm has stolen over him. Not peace. That would be too much to ask. Nor strength, and he doubts his ability to maintain this state for long. And yet, though the fire within him hasn't yet burned itself out, it is dampened down, at least for now.

He wanders the streets again until the dusk closes in and night finally brings silence. He retraces their footsteps from before, remembering. He is saying goodbye.

* * * * * * *

The church clocks are chiming the eleventh hour as he turns the corner into 87th Street. Most of the houses are shrouded, heavy curtains drawn against the chill autumn night. There is a light burning in the window of their house, a lamp set by the uncurtained window of his study, though the rest of the house is in darkness.

Quietly, waiting to identify sounds of movement in the house, relieved to hear none. He crosses to the study, stands on the threshold briefly as an unbidden memory rises. But now is not the moment, however tempting it is to succumb, and he keeps it at bay. Instead, he draws the curtain and switches off the light.

He climbs the stairs carefully, though his tread, with his tired limbs, is inevitably heavy. Exhausted though he is, he keeps climbing, up to the top floor.

All the doors along the corridor are closed but the one he seeks. A nightlight from the nursery casts a soft glow into the hallway, guiding him. Standing in the doorway, resting his tired body against the door jamb, he can hear their breathing, soft snuffles from the cradle, the more rhythmic, gentle pattern from the single bed by the wall.

As he approaches, his weight creaks a floorboard and he sees his son's eyes open. His heart is in his mouth as he leans over the cradle and those silver eyes gaze up at him, so trusting. He was wrong. How could he say goodbye when she yet lives in this tiny child? He brushes his hand over his son's downy hair and the eyes close again.

His rib protests as he eases onto his knees by his daughter's bed. She is lying on her back, one arm thrown above her head, her dark hair splayed across the white pillow. He brushes her hair back from her forehead and she murmurs at the light touch. He leans forward and kisses her forehead, then painfully forces himself back to his feet.

Sarah is standing in the doorway, watching him, a dressing gown thrown over her nightdress. He pauses as he approaches, wary, but there is no sign of her anger, her jealousy or her fear in her face. Only deep sadness and concern.

"I'm so sorry," she whispers, and he can see her regret reflected in her face.

He knows he must heal this rift if they are to move forward, if they are to give their children the kind of childhood he would wish for them. She half holds a hand out to him, uncertain.

He holds out his arms to her and she comes to him, rests her head on his shoulder as his arms go around her. He leans his head against hers, staring blindly at the far wall. "It is done," he asserts, his voice quiet and steady. "It's over."

EPILOGUE

He stops talking and the room falls silent, just the tick, tick, tick of the clock breaking up the stillness. In the time they have been here, the light of the day has gone and streets lights are casting a strange orange glow over the room. He goes around the room, switching on lamps and re-drawing the curtains.

They are sitting in silence, Daniel leaning forward, his hands hanging between his knees, his head down, considering. He looks so like Jack in that moment. Rebecca is sat back on the sofa, arms folded, head turned away. She doesn't want to look at him. So like Sarah.

"After that," he continues, shifting his chair so that it is now turned towards them, "the New York business all but collapsed. The Wall Street Crash came the following Tuesday. I worked through that and then I walked away from it. Your uncle insisted on taking charge. He foreclosed on hundreds of businesses. To salvage what he could, he destroyed lives. People lost everything, banks closed, America went into the Depression. Chicago First's assets were stripped to pay back your uncle's obligations and it became one of the first to go. Your grandfather had protected Richmond Bank more than we had given him credit for but, even so, it took a beating because of the New York venture failing. It was always weaker after that and the partners seemed to lose heart, embarrassed by how they had failed their clients. We struggled on for years but it made sense to sell it when the opportunity came after the war. Particularly after your mother died.

"When she was dying, she made me promise never to tell you about Grace. It made no difference to me as I had no intention of doing so, there seemed little point, so I promised and it seemed to give her some ease.

"A few days later, I think she sensed she had little time left. I was sitting in the chair beside her bed, reading to her, when she put her hand on mine to stop me. She told me she had something she needed to tell me before she died, not so much to seek my forgiveness, as she didn't think I would forgive her, as to leave with a clear conscience. I told her I couldn't imagine she needed forgiving as much as I did, to which she replied she had forgiven long ago, forgiven herself too.

"Then she told me she had lied. That she had arranged the telegram. That she had sent Grace back to England and set her up with a new life but that she hadn't kept track of her after that. She hadn't wanted to know what happened to her. She told me she had known about the detective I hired in New York and that she had had to find a way to stop me looking for Grace. All she could think of was to make me believe Grace was dead."

"Did you forgive her?" Rebecca. Her tone condemnatory already.

"She was dying. I would have said anything to make her passing easier."

"Have you forgiven her now?" Daniel this time, a more gentle tone. He looks at his son and senses understanding. It is more than he has hoped for.

"Not for a long time," he admits, wanting to be truthful with them now. "I was so angry, not least that she had left me with this at the very end, with no right to turn that anger on her. But I also understood why she did what she did." He looks at them both, trying to speak from the heart. "I know how much you both loved your mother. So did I."

"But you loved Grace too?" Daniel suggested.

"Sarah was the heart of me," he confesses. "Grace was my soul."

639

Rebecca stands with a sound of disgust in her throat and turns away. He is grateful she hasn't walked out of the room. The questions fall to her brother.

"Dad, if you made a promise to Mum, why are you telling us this now?"

He looks directly at his son, speaks directly to him. It makes it easier, somehow. "When your mother died, I mourned her for a long time. I had to get past the anger first but, once that was gone, I missed her terribly and, eventually, it meant I forgave her. It was only then that I allowed myself to think about Grace. Not with any real hope because I knew nothing of the life that Sarah had set up for her, but I paid an agency to find out what had happened to her."

Daniel follows his train of thought, just like Grace always did. "They found her."

He nods and all the emotion of the last few days thickens his throat, threatening to choke him. "Six years of searching and he found her three weeks ago fewer than ten miles away."

It takes Daniel a moment to absorb this information and the implications it has for him too. Eventually he asks, "You've seen her?"

A pause. Remembering. The power of emotions so long suppressed but never forgotten. The anxiety of hope. The fear, the anticipation. And, at long last, the sheer joy. He nods. "I married her yesterday."

Rebecca turns on him, her disgust apparent on her face now. "Well, don't think that I will meet her," she condemns. "You betrayed our mother. You cheated and you lied." There are tears in her eyes, tears of anger as she stabs at the air with one finger. She draws breath now she has given way to the anger. "Were you ever a good husband to her, Dad?"

He looks at her sadly. "I hope I was a better husband to her than I was a father to the two of you."

His confession brings her up short and the fight goes out of her as the sadness of his words shocks her. She shakes her head and, unable to speak, covers her mouth. Her eyes speak her own sadness and she takes one look at Daniel then leaves the room. They hear the front door open and close again.

Daniel rises too now, knowing he needs to go to her. "She'll come around," he promises. "Eventually. She's stubborn like Mum." He hesitates, looks across at him. "I wish I'd known before. There always was something about you," he observes quietly. "Like an emptiness at the heart of you. I'm sorry you've lived with that, Dad." He moves towards the door but, on an impulse, turns back. "I have the watch, you know. Your father's? It came to me when I turned eighteen. Just arrived in the post. No note, no postmark." He glances to his left, back towards the hallway. "I'd like to think she was watching." He glances back towards his father, nods and quietly leaves the house.

* * * * * * *

Now it is done, the emotion overwhelms him. He turns his head towards the ceiling, breathing hard, and the tears slide silently down his cheeks.

He hears her light footsteps crossing from the other side of the hall and looks for her as her silhouette appears in the doorway, not trying to hide his hurt from her. She sees how things are and, as he opens his arms to her, she comes to him. His body shakes with the release of such long suppressed emotions and she cradles him to her, her eyes shining with tears too.

She holds him for a long time until the emotion subsides, then she leans back in his arms, far enough to be able to see his face, and pulls his head down until his mouth meets hers. The same spark of passion ignites between them as it always has and he cradles her head in his hands, kissing her deeply as she curves her body into his. Still slender, still tiny, though more curved now, the body of a three times mother. He runs his hands into her still long, though greying, hair and breaks the kiss so he can lose himself again in those mesmerising eyes.

"You heard?" he asks, needing to know she understands.

"So much of that I didn't know," she admits. "I'm so sorry for what you've been through."

"What we've all been through," he extends. He looks at her curiously, remembering what Daniel said. "You sent him my father's watch?"

She smiles, slightly apologetically. "I said it wasn't mine to keep."

He needs to understand the implications, though. "You've known all this time where we were? You've stayed close?"

"I promised you once that I would always been nearby, for as long as we both lived."

"You didn't know I thought you were dead?" A shake of the head. "Would it have changed anything if you had?"

She considers for a moment and he kisses her again, lightly, brushing her hair back from her face with his hands. Her arms around his waist keep them close. "Not while she was alive," she concludes. "I owed her that. But, perhaps, afterwards." She looks at him sadly. "So much wasted time, Jack."

"No more," he promises. "No more sadness after this, either. We've both had enough of that for a lifetime."

"What about the children?" she dares to ask.

"Daniel's right, Rebecca will come around, sooner or later. She's always had the stubborn streak of her mother's."

She smiles. "Which mother?"

He laughs. "Both, I dare say," kissing her again. Now they're together again, that old habit of always needing to be touching has resurfaced.

"And Daniel?"

He reflects. "Of the two, Daniel has always been the one who reminded me more of you. It's not just the eyes. Though, God knows, those eyes have haunted me the last twenty-three years."

"I'm sorry you were always reminded," she teases.

"I'm not," he denies, pulling her close again. "Sometimes, in those early days, it was the only thing that kept me going. Knowing I still had a part of you in them. Though," he admits, "it has made it a difficult relationship between Daniel and I, at times."

"You said 'it's not just the eyes'," she prompts, looking into his face again.

"He has your insight, too. The way you have always been able to read me. He has that. Not just with me but with so many other people around him. I think it makes him over-sensitive, sometimes, and he seems to keep people at a distance to protect himself. Other than Sarah and Rebecca."

"Do you think he will want to meet me?" He can hear the tentative hope in her voice. She has watched her children from a distance for almost thirty years and the fear that they will reject her is considerable.

He strokes her face with the back of his fingers. "He'll be back before the day is out," he predicts. "And when he gets to know you, he will love you. Almost as much as I have always loved you."

She smiles, that slow, deep smile that tears at his heart, but hides the depth of her reaction behind teasing. "Do you love me, then, Mr Westerham?"

He holds her face in his hands, the better to tilt her mouth towards his. "With all my heart and soul." And he loses himself in the shining depths of those brilliant silver eyes.

* * * * * * *

Printed in Poland
by Amazon Fulfillment
Poland Sp. z o.o., Wrocław

54320366R00363